Such Is This World@sars.com*e*

Library of Congress Control Number: 2011920005

ISBN-13: 978-0-9816989-1-5

http://www.raggedbanner.com

Printed in the United States of America on alkaline paper

Such Is This World@sars.com*e*

a novel by

Hu Fayun

Translated from the Chinese by A. E. Clark

Ragged Banner Press
Dobbs Ferry, New York

CONTENTS

PREFACE

In China, this novel by Hu Fayun was hailed for its sympathetic depiction of the inner life of a middle-aged woman, for its treatment of historical episodes about which the State inhibits discussion, and for a prose style that marshals a careful, often elegant diction into the rhythms of colloquial speech. The Western reader may be struck by how the story reckons the costs of authoritarian information control, dramatizes the empowering but ambiguous effect of the Internet, and challenges the conscience of intellectuals.

These latter themes were thrown into relief by the history of the book itself. Initial plans for publication were shelved after two politically daring works were banned, and their publishers penalized, in 2004.[1] In the summer of 2005, friends of the author posted his manuscript to the website *Reform and Reconstruction*, which had been founded by a respected economist after completing a long prison term; within weeks, the entire website had been permanently shut down without explanation. In January 2006, a new editor at the literary magazine *Jiang Nan* published a slightly abridged version of the novel in her first issue. That issue went through several printings without repercussions; in the autumn, a Beijing publisher was emboldened to bring out the work in paperback. The Beijing edition bowdlerized most of the politically sensitive passages[2], but the tenor remained unmistakable. Then it was reported that at a closed-door meeting with publishers in January 2007, a senior official from the General Administration of Press and Publications had singled out eight recent books (including this one) for censure, declaring that they should never have been published and warning of future consequences. When a fierce protest was raised by one of the authors who had been thus stigmatized, the banning of these eight works was widely denounced in China and deplored in the West. After some delay, a spokesman for GAPP said it had all been a misunderstanding: no books had been banned. Technically—if retroactively—this was true. However, this ban which was not a ban was not without impact. Mr. Hu's publisher and booksellers discontinued their advertising, and on the mainland there were no further printings of *Ru Yan@sars.come*.[3] And the impact was far-reaching. A year later it came to light that a planned American translation had been abandoned on account of the Chinese government's hostility to this book.[4] The reason for such caution is known: the careers of many China experts depend on continued access to China. In recent years, the selective termination of that access to about a dozen Western academics after they published work displeasing to Beijing has conveyed a quiet message. Self-censorship does the rest.[5]

In societies as in psyches, what is repressed is revelatory. In Chapter 29, the guests at Night Owl's banquet voice a shocking insecurity about the health of their nation. Teacher Wei and Damo trace this insecurity to what the former calls a systemic problem, and his discourses on fear, cynicism, and the cultural ravages of Maoism offer a framework for understanding the contradictions of the present as well as the horrors of the past. The author goes beyond diagnosis to suggest a remedy: woven throughout is the yearning for a morality founded on truth. His may be a minority view; there are thousands on the Internet who will be glad to tell you, perhaps for a small fee, that their country is in the best of hands and shall go from strength to strength. Even in the symbolic final scene of this book, no prediction is ventured. Hu Fayun is content to show, with the deep feeling of one who is both a son of China and a humanist, what is at stake.

Such Is This World@sars.come avoids a failing typical of politically charged fiction. Especially in modern China, at least since Mao's talks at Yan'an on the mission of writers, there has been a tradition of using art to caricature one's political adversaries. By contrast, this work is remarkable for the dignity it grants to characters whom the reader will ultimately recognize as antagonistic. There are no straw men here, and no monsters or demons.

The central character, who meets us as life's delicate child, stumbles into greatness. Fate offers her a happiness she does not think she wants, and only after two conflicts have played out concurrently (between her fear and her desire, and between her natural honesty and the mendacity ruling her world) does she begin really to live her own life. This is a universal theme, but Ru Yan's world is China, and the spirit within her that gets hammered on its anvil is a Chinese spirit; the tale therefore holds particular interest at the dawn of what many have hoped or feared will be China's century.

The story takes leave of Ru Yan abruptly and we can only guess at her future. In this respect it is reminiscent of *The Magic Mountain*, where we last see Hans Castorp running into battle in the First World War: neurosis surmounted, the protagonist comes fully alive but is soon lost from sight amid the rough brushwork of vast historical forces. In the mid-1920s Mann's readers probably thought they had survived those forces (which by then seemed spent), even if Hans Castorp had not. They were in for a surprise. In our day we are perhaps more conscious of uncertainty and recognize an unresolved historical tension in our heroine's unknown fate.

The author has made a point of associating her with Plato, however, and in the penultimate chapter she seems to turn from this world of generation and decay toward that realm where time takes no toll, and where she herself can stand as an archetype. The last words of Teacher Wei hint at Ru Yan's significance. When a thing is, she has insisted on saying that it is; and when it is not, she has said that it is not. She has met without flinching the question which officers of more than one empire have asked in jest, and would not stay for an answer.

A. E. Clark
December 10, 2010
Dobbs Ferry

ACKNOWLEDGMENTS

Two consultants, L. and A., helped me read a text that far exceeded my Chinese-language abilities, and they answered thousands of questions about the novel's cultural background and allusions. It would be hard to overstate their contribution. They wish to remain anonymous.

In response to inquiries, Hu Fayun graciously explained many points.

Zemin Zhang watched *Song at Midnight* with me, cleared up more than a few mysteries, and recounted pertinent experiences of his own from the Cultural Revolution. Han-ping Chin offered detailed corrections to the advanced reading copy, which Margaret Sweeney also checked.

Stacy Mosher, John O. McGinnis, Howard Goldblatt, Yang Shengming, and Melissa Frazier all provided corrections and helpful observations. Professor Frazier and her colleague Natalia Dizenko located most of the Russian lyrics and explained an ambiguous Russian name.

Su Xiaokang recommended this book and spent an afternoon discussing it with me.

Jin Zhong acted as a literary ambassador and later explained difficult passages.

Liu Hongbin shared insights into some of the classical poems quoted in the text.

Alison Armstrong of the New York Public Library tracked down a reference with few clues.

Errors that remain are my fault alone; readers who report them to me will be thanked on the errata page at the Ragged Banner website.

Ellen Hurley Clark and Johanna Clark supported, endured, and loved.

ABOUT THE TRANSLATION

This edition is more heavily annotated than is customary with works of contemporary fiction, and with reason. The text abounds in literary and historical allusions, and I expect much of the literature and history alluded to will be as unfamiliar to other English-speaking readers as it was to me. Furthermore, the dialogue includes a plethora of quotations from songs, films, and speeches of the Mao era. Some of these might prove obscure even for young Chinese readers, since they constitute an ironic vocabulary peculiar to the generation that came of age during the Cultural Revolution of 1966-76. The foreign reader undeterred by these challenges will be rewarded. It is possible to enjoy the story without reading the notes, but in this oratorio of voices and verbal memories, many nuances will become clearer with their aid.

Some choices made in the translation are best explained up front:

- In Chinese, the term Cultural Revolution (*wenhua [da] geming*) is often abbreviated as *wenge*. I have sometimes rendered this as "C.R." to avoid the ponderous effect of the English term in dialogue.

- Though I have converted most measurements of weight and distance into units familiar to Americans, I have left sums of money in the Chinese yuan or RMB. The informal *kuai* may be rendered as "bucks," large sums may be counted in "grand," and the subunit *fen* may be rendered by "cent"; but the reader should not take these for U.S. dollar amounts. It may not be easy for a foreigner to get a feel for the values. The conversion rate at which the yuan is pegged to the dollar has changed over time, from as high a value as 1.5 to the dollar (at the start of the Eighties) to as low as 8.6 to the dollar (in the mid-Nineties). But the rate has never reflected the purchasing power of the two currencies in their own lands. At present, the yuan can be exchanged for about 15 U.S. cents, but its purchasing power is at least twice that. Sometimes the notes, or the text itself, report the average urban worker's monthly wage at a certain point in time. When the historical context lies farther back than the 1980s, the reader should bear in mind that the levels of both wages and prices were very low.

- Chinese regularly attach an age descriptor to a surname in order to acknowledge a relationship of seniority, respect, or familiarity. I have usually left these forms untranslated:

  Xiao and *Lao*. Colleagues and acquaintances can put Lao [Old] or Xiao [Little] before someone's surname to informally acknowledge (or claim) seniority. A man or woman surnamed Wang, for example, might be addressed as "Lao Wang," Old Wang, by people who considered themselves junior to him or her, and as "Xiao Wang," Little Wang, by people who considered themselves senior. (Xiao, by the way, is pronounced approximately 'shyow' to rhyme with 'now.') This is not the same as putting "Lao" *after* the surname (Wang Lao); it is then strongly honorific and generally applicable only to fairly old people.

  Shushu and *Yi*. People who belong to the generation of the speaker's parents are likely to be addressed informally, but respectfully, as "Uncle" (*Shushu*) or "Auntie" (*Yi*). Teacher Wei's wife is known to his younger friends as Zhao Yi. We do not learn her given name.

- An important office of the Chinese government (at Central, Provincial, and local levels) is tasked with *xuanchuan*. This used to be translated "propaganda"; the government has for some time now preferred to translate it into English as "publicity." The word "propaganda" reproduces a Soviet term and suggests the religious zeal which gave birth to this word in seventeenth-century Rome; in the Mao era it was not inappropriate. But in English today, "propaganda" is overtly pejorative, and it would be misleading to impute it to Chinese speakers who intend no such judgment. I have chosen one or the other translation according to the context.

- The Nationalist government which the Communists overthrew in the Civil War (and which then took over Taiwan) is usually referred to in the translation as the KMT. The pinyin abbreviation would be GMD for Guo Min Dang, but the Wade-Giles transliteration of Kuomintang is so well-established in English writing that I have retained it.

Such Is This World@sars.come

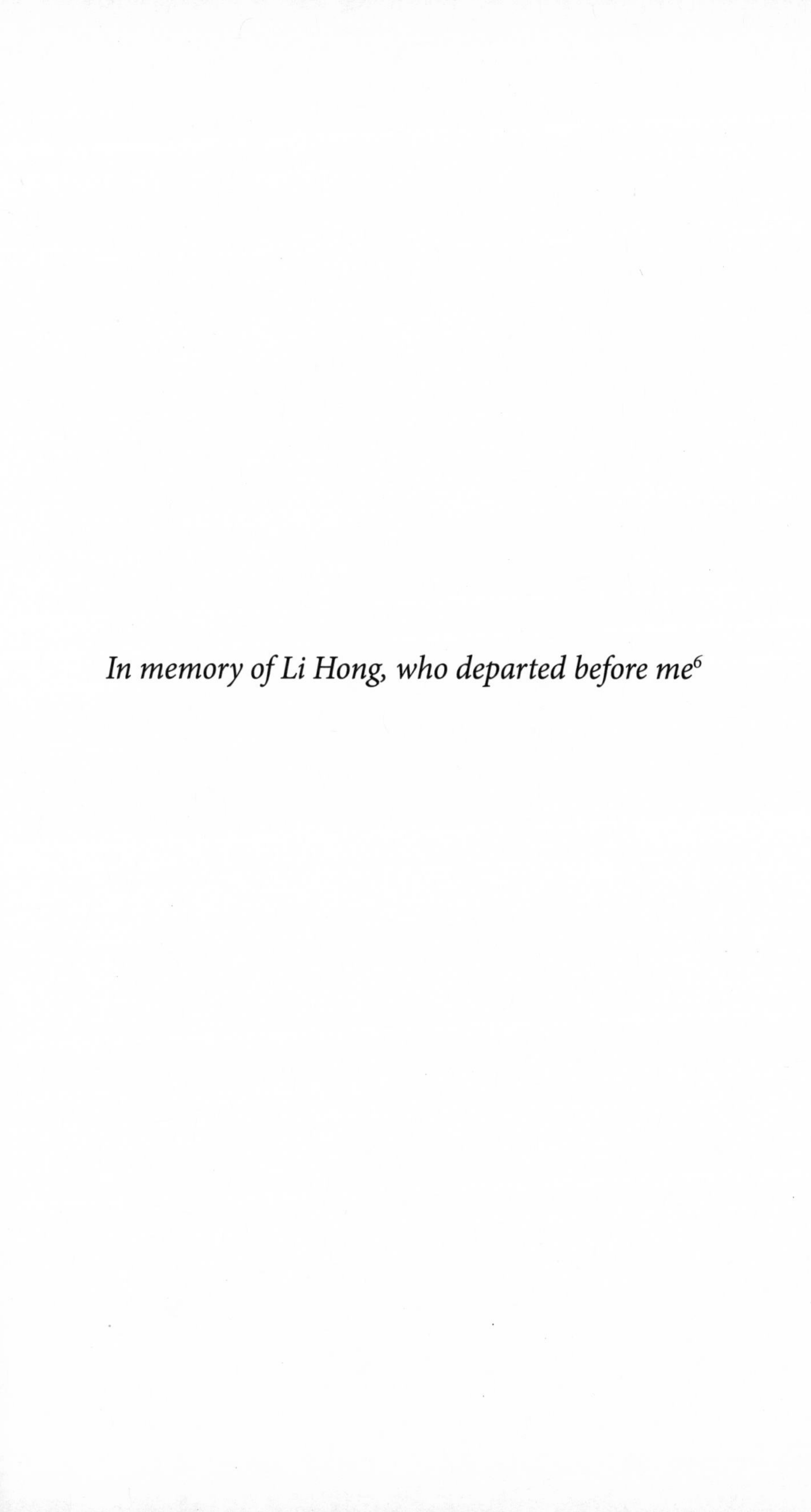

In memory of Li Hong, who departed before me[6]

1

When her son went abroad, he left two things behind for Ru Yan: a puppy and a computer.

He had found that puppy and taken it in. One night when she phoned him long-distance, he had said in a rascally voice, "Mom, I've got a girlfriend."

He was a senior in college; she had always expected to hear these words someday. But now that it was happening, she felt edgy and at a loss. She tried to ask breezily, "OK, your Mom was waiting for this. Where's she from?"

"Our college."

"She a classmate of yours?"

"Roommate, too."

Ru Yan's heart gave a thump. She was aware that it had long since become normal for college students to live together, and some made no bones about renting an apartment off-campus and moving in as a couple. But when she opened her mouth, what came out was the same old conventional response, though uttered without conviction: "It's too early for you two . . . this is such a crucial year, and for God's sake, don't do anything to get yourself into an awkward position."

Her son had said, "No way! I wouldn't do that, not even to save my life."

"In that case," Ru Yan suggested, "it's better if she goes back to her dorm."

"She's got no place to live," her son said. "Somebody threw her out."

"What are you saying?" Ru Yan cried out.

At the other end of the line her son gave a great belly laugh, and she heard a bunch of young men in the background laughing mischievously with him.

"Mom," he said, "she's a dog, a little lady-dog."

Ru Yan asked, "What? What's this about a dog?"

"She's just a little dog," he said, and then used the English word, "DOG! DOG!—the kind with four legs and a tail."

"Good Heavens," Ru Yan said, "You can't even take proper care of yourself. How are you going to take care of a dog?"

Her son said, "A few of us are taking care of her together."

"Is this any time to be thinking about a dog?"

"It can't be helped: she's grown attached to me."

Ru Yan knew that force never worked in these situations: the more you said No, the more he would dig in his heels. It was the same way with affairs of the heart. Her marrying her husband had been half due to her mother's opposition. What's more, Heaven is high and the Emperor is far away: the boy can raise a colony of mice and what are you going to do? Later she had realized that her mother was mostly right, though it had taken time for that to become clear. It was one of the fruits of life experience: no point giving lectures about it. She asked her mother, so why don't you think he's good enough? Her mother said, it's not that I don't think he's good enough: *you* don't think he's good enough. Here, too, her mother had spoken the truth. Her mother had been born into an upper-class family, and though she married a revolutionary cadre[7] it didn't change who she was in her bones. Or maybe it was *because* she had married the kind of man who could protect her and give her privileges that she managed to preserve her old outlook. Ru Yan had seen some of her mother's relatives and classmates of more or less the same social background, who had married men who for the most part would have been considered a good match. But in the end they, along with their husbands, were broken by life. They spoke meekly about petty and vexing things and they'd all lost the haughty air which her mother still had. But this was another one of those truths that can be grasped only with life experience; it's not as though a few words would make it all clear.

Keeping calm, Ru Yan told him to give it a good bath and guard against disease.

"There's nothing wrong with it," he said, "It's spunky. And I'm an old pro, right? Didn't I have a dog when I was five?" The last remark had been for the benefit of those classmates of his.

"Were *you* the one who took care of it," she asked, "the feeding and walking and cleaning part? You still don't really know how to do this for yourself."

He explained how it had happened. One evening, he was just walking along after leaving the library when he ran into this dog. He stopped and took a good look at it. It stopped and took a good look at him. He squatted down and petted it; the creature wagged its tail shyly. When he had been little, her son had had a dog, a gift from his father. His father was often away on business and out of guilt he had bought a puppy to be the child's companion. They'd had that dog till the boy was in third grade, and then one day it had gone out and been struck dead by a car. Her son had been sad for a long time.

Now *this* dog, her son was saying, was dirty and scrawny but it was well-bred: you could tell by the gleam in its eye. It was innocent, a wimp that would never hurt anybody, not like the wild dogs who've long roamed the wide world and whose watchful faces say, "I'm a wild dog, you don't want to mess with me." Her son fished a sausage out of his bookbag, peeled the skin, broke off and offered a piece; the dog's tongue rolled out and made that piece of sausage disappear. He broke off another piece: repeat performance. A few more times and the whole sausage was gone. He showed the dog his empty hands: "No more." That puppy was real hungry, her son explained, it had never learned to eat the garbage other people threw away. He rummaged through his bookbag and found a piece of salted bread. The dog ate that, too. Her son said bye and went to his dorm. First thing in the morning, when one of his roommates opened the door to go to the bathroom, he encountered that dog just sitting there. Hearing something, her son sat up and had to roll out of bed and invite the creature in. At lunchtime, he brought it to the cafeteria: "From now on, you stay here. You stay here and you won't be hungry." But early the next day, the dog was waiting on its haunches at the door of his room.

So it stayed. His roommates all liked it and together with him they took responsibility for its meals. When they had free time they played with it, and it brought much merriment into the lonely lives of these bachelors in their senior year. But none of them had the patience to take it outside at the right times to relieve itself, so their dorm room reeked of urine and the fumes got stronger over time, which fortunately didn't bother these kids much, as they were pretty dirty themselves.

The roommates named the puppy after her son: Yang Yanping.

2

His father had named him. "Yan" reflected her son's position in the family tree; supposedly you could tell from these first two characters that he was a descendant of the martial Yang clan of the Northern Song,[8] and "Ping" was the name of his grandfather's native town, Ping Village.

For several generations, now, most of the Yangs hadn't bothered to name their children according to the traditional genealogical scheme. But for some reason, when their son was born her husband had been filled with deep thoughts about his heritage and pored over the old family book until he came up with a name that was just right. Whenever his father called the boy, it was always the full name: Yang Yanping. She on the other hand would call him Yanping, Ping'r, Pingzi, Ping'rzi: when she addressed him as Yang Yanping it invariably meant the kid was being called on the carpet. These days, when Ru Yan went all over the house shouting for a dog named Yang Yanping, that dog had become connected to herself, and to this family, by many a tie that tugged at her heart. The first time she shouted the dog's name after her son had gone, the tears ran down like rain.

As for the computer, it had been purchased when her son

was preparing for his sophomore year. He had come home for summer vacation and had at first given no indication what was on his mind as he undertook household chores with unwonted diligence. Then after a few days he said, timidly, that he would like to have a computer. He was studying architectural design and he needed his own computer. At first she didn't agree; she was afraid it would interfere with his schoolwork, that he'd play games, or worse . . . for there were unhealthy things out there. Ru Yan was a traditionalist. She liked to keep a skeptical distance from new things until they weren't new anymore, and then she would start to like them. She was this way especially in her style of dress and makeup. Fads of colloquial speech she resisted even more staunchly. The phrase "Bye-bye" had been around for more than twenty years, but she just couldn't bring herself to say it: when someone said "Bye-bye" to her, she'd always say *zai-jian.*[9] As for 'Cool,' 'Foxy,' 'Wow', and 'Get real' . . . these phrases assaulted her ear like a shard of pottery being scraped on glass. When eventually she went online, she felt practically illiterate.

His father, on the other hand, had been receptive. He said we'll have to buy it sooner or later, and the sooner we buy it the sooner he'll stop pestering us. Father and son immersed themselves for a couple of days at the computer mall and put together a state-of-the-art PC. Her husband said, "Computers have a short upgrade cycle. You bring one home and it starts getting obsolete the first day. If you're a little ahead of the game now, you can hang onto it a bit longer. What's more, the boy's going to need a good machine for drafting." Her son looked up to his Dad for thinking this way: "Pop really keeps up with the times."

When the summer vacation drew to a close, the father packed the computer carefully in a box and took his son to the train. "Call home often," he told the boy, "Don't let the computer make you forget your mother."

A month later on a business trip the husband was killed in a car crash.

When that dog had been run over by a car, Ru Yan had had a premonition because her husband, year-round, was always on the road. In nightmares she saw him in an accident, and she always wanted to talk to him about this but never found the courage. Now she would never have the chance.

After graduation, her son brought the computer home. It was in the original box with his father's handwriting on top, where he had written such-and-such University, such-and-such Department, and the boy's name, as well as VALUABLE EQUIPMENT—HANDLE WITH CARE. It still had the baggage tag with the date they had seen him off at the train station.

Her son's academic program was jointly operated with a French school of design. Upon finishing their undergraduate studies in China, students who had done well in all subjects were eligible for graduate school over there. If their marks were outstanding, the foreign partner had considerable funds set aside for scholarships. With thrift and a part-time job one could manage the living expenses. After her husband's death, the son had said that whether he went to work or stayed in school, he was going to pay his own way. Actually his father had, long before, set aside a sum to pay for his going abroad, but when Ru Yan heard the boy declare his resolve to be self-sufficient it made her heart ache. She really didn't think much of kids who took money their parents had earned with sweat and blood and squandered it abroad in profligacy, and she had even less respect for playboys whose decadent life overseas, complete with trophy cars and a mansion, was funded by Mom and Dad's graft or fraud. But when her son said he wouldn't let her support him, it gave her an empty feeling. Then she realized she'd spend that money on him eventually as his father had wished, when he got married and began raising his own children: it made no difference.

In *Tale of the Red Lantern*[10] there's a good song about how the children of the poor learn at an early age how to manage a household. After her husband died, her son knew straightway the right thing to do. Two years before he would go abroad, he got a job in the business office of an architectural firm and earned enough to pay for his travel to France. As he saw it, the computer had been a good buy, because it had paid for itself ten times over. When he came home for the last time before going abroad, he gave the computer an overhaul, adding memory and a bigger hard drive, installing the newest version of XP, providing a webcam and headset, installing broadband—all of which he insisted on paying for. Consider this my gift to you, he told Ru Yan; someday you'll realize it's a good thing.

But for her part, Ru Yan had never imagined she would have anything to do with computers and the Internet. In her view, these things—like disco, drag racing, McDonald's, video games, and animated cartoons—exemplified the mindless and life-stealing self-indulgence of a commercialized era. When the Internet appeared in the news, it was usually in connection with truancy, arson, confidence schemes and swindles, or crimes of passion. She was past the age when people take an interest in such matters. At her work unit[11] a few years earlier, for some crazy reason they had sent all the people in mid-level positions or higher for computer training. It lasted a couple of weeks. They went without a clue and came back without a clue. Never mind learning to actually do something, DOS itself baffled them. They muddled through to get their certificates and clean forgot the whole thing. Ever after, the sight of that machine would make them uneasy. Her son always said she was behind the times. She thought, if I'm behind the times then that's just who I am. There were so many things she'd fallen behind of in this life that even if you gave her another lifetime to catch up, it wouldn't be enough. For the ancients had it not been exquisite, and more than enough, to pass one's life with a book and a blackened lamp? But when she saw her son do all this so earnestly, spending his hard-earned money, she had to accept it as a gift of his love. When the setup was complete he tested everything. He had made it all idiot-proof; you had only to press the On button and then it would all be laid out for you. He had even compiled a User's Manual and placed it on the Desktop, so that if she should encounter any problem she need only open the manual and take a look. When all was done he said, Mom, I'll take a couple of days to give you a crash course.

For those two days, her son was like a wise matron, teaching systematically and patiently. He didn't mind taking the trouble to show her, step by step, how to do things of which she had known nothing. Whenever Ru Yan was intimidated by difficulties, her son would say, "You're going to have to learn this sooner or later; it's the 21st century, anyone who can't do this is practically a Neanderthal. Later you will realize this is a thing like sunlight and air and water. Moreover"—at that moment her son was testing the webcam, and there appeared on the monitor an image of them both looking busy in front of the computer—"It's convenient and cheap. Later we'll make intercontinental videophone calls for free, you can talk for as long as you like. I'll be able to see home, and you'll be able to see my place."

Ru Yan saw herself and her son talking on the screen like characters in a TV show; it was new and strange. She said, "When you go to France, will I still be able to see you from here?"

He said, "As long as you've got an internet connection, you could see me even if I went to the moon." Her son picked up the little webcam as if it were a video camera and panned around the study. "You can also take pictures," he was saying, and when he clicked somewhere, the monitor froze with a picture of Ru Yan in the study. "It can double as surveillance equipment: when you're not going to be at home, turn it on, it will keep recording activity in the room, like if a petty thief—"

Ru Yan exclaimed, "Don't frighten me! I'd rather let him steal from me than watch and be terrified."

So she'd be able to see her son in far-off France. Ru Yan thought that even if this were all the computer could do, it would be enough. And with that same eagerness with which she had once pounded on the college door, armed with only a middle school education (it was right after the entrance exam was reinstated), she now tackled each new concept and each new operation, and kept learning computer skills till she was dizzy.

He was, after all, her son; he knew how to make his mother understand. Once he started to teach, he was a hundred times better than that exorbitant training class. He didn't give you any terminology or theory or processes. He made it like going shopping at the supermarket: pick out what you want, it's comprehensible at a glance. What's more, this XP system he'd installed was a lot quicker and easier than the stuff she had previously tried to learn; it seemed designed for computer dummies like herself.

Her son set up an e-mail account for her and installed both MSN and QQ.[12] QQ was neat, he chuckled, it was like a dog's leash: "At any time, just give it a tug and I'll know. And when I give it a tug, you'll know." Ru Yan smiled and thought, this kid has a way with words: on his leash, there's a dog at both ends.

He had her choose a screen name for herself, so she could register for discussion groups and QQ. After a moment's thought, she suggested *Ru Yan*, "Like Smoke." But someone was already using this screen name. "Add two characters," her son said, "The Past is Like Smoke." They tried it, but somebody had claimed that one too. "Now you know," he said. "If you don't get online now, pretty soon even the crappiest names will all have been taken."

Ru Yan didn't believe it. He said, "Let's try a few, off the top of your head." 'Stinking Fish,' Ru Yan suggested. As he predicted, it was taken. 'Dirty Cat': taken. 'Second-Class Loser,' also taken. Even 'I Am A Scoundrel And I Fear No Man'[13] was in use. Ru Yan couldn't stop laughing: this online world seemed a gallery of freaks and horrors. In the end, her son tweaked her first choice into *Ru Yan*, 'Such Is This World'. [14] This time the registration went through without a hitch.

It was her mother who had named Ru Yan. You could tell from the name that on some level her mother had identified with the refined women of the Imperial era. Ru Yan's older sister and younger brother had also been named by their mother. She had not let their father name them. Fathers of that generation tended to express their enthusiasm in the names they gave their children: Jianguo, Xinhua, Kangmei, Yuanchao, Jianshe, Xiansheng, Yuejin . . . and later there came Siqing, Weidong, Weiqing, Weibiao, Jiuda.[15] With this fashion in names, a family of seven or eight children could serve as a concise history of modern China.

Forty-odd years later, Ru Yan had her own screen name, a name that her son had given her: Such Is This World. She liked it, oddly enough: she felt it was more down-to-earth than her original name, and imperturbable, in the style of a saint or a sage.

3

A few days later, Ru Yan was en route to the capital to see her son off at the airport. She had insisted on doing this. She knew why he didn't want her to come.

At the security gate, her son bent down to hug her. Only then did she realize how tall he had grown, with a masculine smell of sweat as well as a certain scent that had once been familiar . . . a legacy from his father, a scent that would never go away. Could this be the little meatball to which she had given birth out of her own body? The little thing that made you mindful of all its needs, major or minor, for twenty-four hours a day? The tiny person you didn't want to scrub too hard in the bath, for fear its little bones might break?

When the boy had been very young, six or seven, he had become averse to physical contact with her. Sometimes on a crowded bus she would hold him in her arms, and he would look embarrassed and become rigid, and then struggle to make her put him down because he preferred to stand beside her and hold on to the railing. It was not like before, when he had stuck to her like a magnet and caressed her neck and her cheeks with his soft hand.

After his father died, for a long time the son became taciturn and extremely reserved toward her, choosing his words carefully to avoid touching any sore spots, whether hers or his own. He almost never mentioned his father.

When he hugged her at the airport he squeezed her tight, and she felt that if he had straightened up he would have easily lifted her into the air like a baby.

A few seconds, perhaps longer, then he released her with a smile: "See you online."

"See you online," she laughed. Her voice in that moment had become tender and vulnerable, like a little girl's voice.

It was her son's rite of passage.

He'd been smiling for so long it had become a fixed smile. They couldn't keep this up. When he had come home, they had never talked about his going away. The day before his departure, he said he wanted to go to the cemetery to see his Dad. Don't go, Ru Yan said. Keep your father in your heart, that's all that matters.

The final boarding call was sounding. *Better get moving*, she said; *Take good care of yourself.* Then she gave a big smile and waved and turned to leave. She was afraid that at the last moment she would break down. After a dozen paces, barely holding back tears, she turned her head and saw he had reached the far end of the line and she said in her heart, *Don't look back, Son.*

When he disappeared round the corner of the security corridor, she felt like a yellow leaf falling from a wintry bough, floating and spinning; who can tell where it will fall. Never had she felt so hollow and helpless as now. The strength of her son's hug had been searing, like a fiery brand across her shoulders. In that invisible embrace she was a fragile shell, and whatever might once have been inside that shell had been extracted at the moment her son parted from her. From that point on, she could have been sleepwalking; how she got on the train, how she returned home... it was all a fog.

She retrieved the puppy from the downstairs neighbor. When it saw her, the dog whipped its tail back and forth and waggled its little rear end like a toy rattle. Ru Yan thanked the neighbor and called, "Yang Yanping! Come home!" and the tears she'd bottled up for days gushed forth in a stream.

The puppy pranced around her all the way upstairs. It recognized only its full name, Yang Yanping: if you called it Ping'r or Ping Girl, it would look confused as if asking, "Huh? What did you say?"

When she got home it was 9 A.M. If the flight had gone smoothly her son would already have arrived. Ru Yan figured the time difference: over there it must be 2 A.M. for him. She realized that he could not possibly have gone online yet but she turned on the computer anyway. Surprisingly, the avatar of a dog's head, which represented her son, was bouncing perkily in the lower right corner of the screen. Her hands shaking with excitement, she gripped the mouse and tried to stay calm. *For God's sake, don't screw up*. She mentally rehearsed the steps, then ever so carefully clicked on the cute little dog. A QQ webpage opened up, with messages from her son on top. His screen name was Droopy, an intelligent cartoon dog of sober mien. As a child he had loved this character.[16]

Droopy: Mom, arrived safe, everything went fine. Temporarily staying at the apartment of a fellow-alum. I'm using his computer to get online. After this it may get hectic for a week or so, the main thing is to find a place to live. The University here doesn't provide lodging, not even for big-name professors. (*a face sticking out its tongue*)

Droopy: This is really a good place to study architectural design. Paris itself is a museum of architecture. Someday I'll bring you here so you can have a good look.

Droopy: After 5 P.M. (that's midnight your time) I may come back online to check messages. Don't wait up for me. If you have something to say you can leave it on QQ.

Droopy: I found an apartment. I'll get a phone and an internet connection installed right away, then it will be a lot more convenient. Practice your typing first so you won't make me antsy. (*a blushing face*)

Droopy: I'm going to go to sleep, my biological clock is out of whack. They say you're all right after a few days.

Droopy: 8888888888888 (*a rose*)[17]

This was Ru Yan's first experience of the Internet. It gave her a kind of vertigo. Your son, thousands of miles away in another land, was alive and kicking in front of your eyes as he spoke, made faces, and even presented a red rose.

Ru Yan launched Smart Pinyin[18] and plucked out, one by one, the characters she wanted, and one by one composed the words. She was a person for whom the writing would just flow from the tip of the pen with a rustling sound, without need for thought; now it felt that she had returned to the time in her childhood when she was just learning to write, and whenever the desired character or word appeared, she would feel the thrill of finding a treasure.

But these characters were tapped out on the keyboard, and when you tap one out, you can't see any strokes, it just appears on this small box in front of your eyes, and snakes its way through the slender phone line, across oceans and seas, to an apartment in a building in Paris, to emerge in front of your son.

Such Is This World: Ping'rzi, I saw your messages, I'm very happy

—a line of characters hopped into the Send edit box, and with a press of the Return key it joined the list of messages left for her son. For the first time in her life, Ru Yan had sent a message over the Internet.

Such Is This World: Your Mom misses you. You'll never really know how a mother worries. When I got 'Yang Yanping' back from the neighbors, I suddenly felt you had left a part of yourself with me. You know, whenever I'm home it gives me a reason to call my son...

Thus did Ru Yan keep writing, character by character, word

by word, sentence by sentence, as if in thrall to some compulsion: she couldn't stop.

In the evening, when there were still a few hours before her son had said he'd be online, Ru Yan started QQ and loaded MSN. The figure representing her son—it looked like a Chinese Checkers piece—was still a reddish-brown color and he had explained that if it was green that meant he was online.[19] She waited for it to turn green. Ru Yan put on her headset, testing it the way he had taught her, and heard her own voice in the earphones: *Hello, hello, hello Droopy, hello my son, hello Ru Yan*...She turned on the webcam, and a video window displayed her upper body. She tilted her head this way and that, and the Ru Yan inside the window did the same. She took a searching look at herself and noted a faint expression of childlike mirth as if this were a prank. Remembering how her son had taught her to take pictures, she clicked the "shutter" and a photo of her popped up at the side. She turned her head slightly to change the way the light fell on her face and took another picture. She wanted a picture good enough to send to her son. There was also Yang Yanping and she wanted a few pictures of it, too, to send to him. She called Yang Yanping and held the dog in her arms. Whenever she held it that way, it brought back the times she had held her infant son in her arms, so soft and supple and sweet to the touch. Until now, Ru Yan had not liked animals with fur; actually, she hadn't really liked any animals. She could watch creatures such as sparrows and goldfish from a distance but was quite unwilling to touch them, as if she had some kind of phobia about germs. With regard to contact between the sexes, she was not comfortable with anything beyond the conventional: even shaking hands with men (especially strangers) felt distasteful, and dancing of course even more so. Back when she had been in college, dancing had been all the rage, and her female classmates dragged her along, but she would always stay on the sidelines, watching her friends' coats and pouring the tea. The women in her class judged her to be the elegant type, and attractive. But Ru Yan's attractiveness was not the provocative kind: it had to be savored slowly, for with closer examination over time it revealed an exquisite quality. She was not like some women, who at a glance may be strikingly pretty, but as you continue to study them their mediocrity comes to the fore. The difference between the two types is like the difference between tea and sugar water. Now, wallflowers generally fall short in temperament and looks. They are always looking forward to the start of the next song, hoping that a male student or teacher will step before them and extend his hand. Ru Yan was exactly the opposite. Every time someone came up to her, she got flustered and stammered, "I can't, I really can't, I only came along to look after their things." Her husband once said this was the influence of classical literature: Plato had ruined her.

When she had completed her preparations, she started to leave her son a message on QQ. She was eager now to do some typing on the keyboard, like a child who's gotten a box of crayons and can't wait to draw something with them. She told her son about the first time she had used the computer by herself; about the dog who shared his name; and about how she'd learned to take pictures with the webcam. . . Ru Yan was an intelligent person and had a natural penchant for writing. The keyboard and the method of entering text had quickly become familiar, and as her fingers leaped across the keyboard like ten little persons, she soon got the hang of it. She liked this intricate dance. She even liked the sound she made on the keyboard, rather like the sound of tap-dancing. She decided to wait for her son no matter how late he showed up. It was barely after midnight, though, when QQ began to chirp like a cricket and the little icon of Droopy began slyly blinking.

She hurried to open the Received Messages box and saw her son had written a line:

Droopy: Wow! Mom, you're a pro! You typed all these characters? I'll take my time to read them. (*one thumb up*)

Such Is This World: I type slow. You'll have to be patient. (*a red face*)

```
Droopy: Let's go on MSN.

Such Is This World:  OK.
```

On MSN, her son's avatar turned green. Ru Yan clicked to open the window for two-way communication.

```
Droopy: Mom, let's try using the A/V, nice
and slow, don't get nervous. First I invite
you, then you click "Accept" and we're on.
```

The video gradually appeared and Ru Yan saw her son. The few days since they'd parted seemed like a hundred years. He was wearing a white long-sleeved T-shirt and smiling energetically at her. After a bit, his voice came over the headphones: Hey, can you hear me, Mom?

Ru Yan said, "I can hear you, very clearly. Didn't you say you wouldn't be able to make it before one o'clock?"

"This afternoon I finished what I had to do a little early. After supper I still have to go out."

"It's going well?"

"Yeah, it's OK. Tomorrow I go to school and then someone's taking me to see an apartment. These days are going to be a little crazy; I won't have time to go online."

"You know what you have to do, and that comes first," Ru Yan said. "I've seen you, and I'm not worried now."

"How's Yang Yanping?"

"At my feet."

"Hold her up so I can see."

Ru Yan lifted up Yang Yanping: "See?"

Her son called, "Yang Yanping!"

Ru Yan took off her headset and held it to Yang Yanping's ears. The little dog couldn't make out the miniaturized two-dimensional image, but on hearing her son's voice in the headphones, it looked around with some agitation. When it couldn't find anyone it began a loud and anxious yapping.

Her son said, "There's a lot of dogs in France. The streets are full of 'em, all kinds."

"Don't tell me," Ru Yan said, "You just got there and you're looking to get a dog?"

"Yeah, I'd like to get one."

As they chatted on, Ru Yan saw a Chinese woman walk up behind her son and nudge him. He turned his head. The woman mimed eating. He nodded.

"Mom, I've got to go eat."

"Please, go eat." She thought hard for a moment, but then went ahead and asked: "Who is she?"

"A woman student," he said.

"That 'fellow-alum' you mentioned?"

"He's busy; he usually doesn't come home for dinner."

"I hope you'll thank those people for me," Ru Yan said.

"OK," he said, "I'll log off; you should turn in early and get some rest."

'Turn in early and get some rest' had always been her son's way of signing off before hanging up the phone.

"There's a website you should check out," he added, "I'll paste the URL for you, just click on it to go there."

"What website?" Ru Yan asked.

"It's for middle-aged people, an online community with a regular column called 'Children studying overseas.' It's got news about studying abroad; on our college's website there was a link to it. There's also a forum called 'The Empty Nest' that's popular with parents of overseas students. Go take a look and you'll understand."

In the video frame he waved to Ru Yan, and then the window closed. His voice, too, disappeared in the darkness. Ru Yan thought of fairy tales she had read as a child, with their mirrors and crystal balls and genies' lamps haloed in light, where supernatural beings appeared and disappeared without a trace.

This was the first time Ru Yan had seen France in some way connected to herself, because her son was there—even though this France was only an ordinary room, and in a rather Sinicized house at that. In her mental life, Russian literature and French literature occupied a large place. It was the France of Dumas *père* and Dumas *fils*; of Zola, Hugo, and Mallarmé; it was the France of Romain Rolland and Balzac. A lovely, haunting, and melancholy metropolis; a countryside of villages that were mysterious and Romantic and licentious; the Court, full of luxury and deceit; garrets where humane warmth met the chill of poverty, and cobblestoned lanes along the Seine leading to Esmeralda's Notre Dame. All through Ru Yan's youth, these dreamlike scenes had enveloped her and made it possible, whenever she put down the Little Red Book and the long-handled hoe, to enter in an instant into another and wholly different world.

Ru Yan knew that the France of today had long ceased to be the France depicted by those classic authors, but whenever she thought of France, it was their version. This couldn't be helped: that was the France that had taken root in her heart. So the first time she saw that French apartment where her son had lodged, it felt unreal.

4

Ru Yan went to the website to which her son had referred her, "Midlife." It contained quite a few forums, much as a gated community contains many buildings:

Forty and Bewildered[20]
Exercise for Health
The Emotions of Middle Age
Helping Your Children be Successful
Cultural Hobbies
Use Poetry to Meet Friends
Our Years in the Countryside[21]

as well as the two her son had mentioned, "Children Studying Overseas" and "The Empty Nest."

Ru Yan went to "Children Studying Overseas" first. Here

there was information about studying abroad, country by country: career counseling, shopping guides, travel advice, telecom services.

She looked up the section on France and the colleges there that took students from China, specifically her son's school. There were pictures. The campus was lovely, like a country estate with classic architecture: gardens, ponds, tree-lined paths, all sorts of fine sculptures, a computer room, a reading room, an exhibition of students' work. There was a student orchestra, too, and when you opened the program you could listen to them performing. Their standard was pretty high, not far below that of a mid-level professional orchestra in our country. The exhibition of students' architectural work was quite diverse, including offbeat and unusual styles. One model showed a house that was, in fact, a recumbent pig: the pig's snout was the front door, and the pig's tail was a spiral stair by which you could climb onto the pig's back, a vaulted glass chamber. Ru Yan hoped her son wouldn't adopt this style.

He had said that a basic principle to keep in mind whenever you had the browser open was, "Wherever it points, that's where we click."[22] In other words, as soon as you see a hand with the index finger extended, go ahead and click on it. Following this rule, Ru Yan was like someone who's bought a ticket to Disneyland and wanders about in a pleasant daze, entirely forgetting the way back. A web page had links, and the links had links. It was as Lao Tzu says: The Way gives rise to One, One gives rise to Two, Two gives rise to Three; and Three gives rise to the Ten Thousand Things.[23] As her son had taught her, she bookmarked the sites and pages that interested her until her list of bookmarks overflowed into multiple columns.

And now she came to the forum called The Empty Nest.

When she opened that page, there appeared on her screen a bird's nest from which a little bird flew out and then flapped away out of sight. Two dejected old faces looked out from the nest, an old man and an old woman, and then the two faces morphed into two Chinese characters: Empty Nest.

The moderator went by the name of Lonely Goose. In his or

her introduction, Lonely Goose said,

> Our little chicks have all flown away and only a couple of old birds are left in the deserted nest, maybe just one old bird. But we must still pass our days in wistful thoughts, with hopes and fears and joys, sending money, sending parcels, transmitting documents, or waiting for our little bird's return. As for our little birds' affections, we are doomed to a long spell of unrequited love. They have their own lives, they want to sail ahead; we can only watch their silhouettes recede into the distance,[24] until that day when they'll slip from our view. Let us old birds support one another here, chatting about our children and about ourselves. You, too, are welcome.

Ru Yan was moved as she read this. She recalled the days of her son's college entrance exam and the throng of parents who waited anxiously under the fierce sun outside the locked doors of the examination hall. In that brief interval, these middle-aged men and women who had been complete strangers to each other developed an extraordinary intimacy, a feeling of being comrades in hard times.

There were many posts in the forum—about the weather where their children were, about discounts on flight tickets, about how one college had gone bankrupt and left its foreign students high and dry . . . and there were many posts reporting events of the parents' daily routine, how they missed the kids, how lonely they were, sometimes recounting their children's entire lives. There were posts about how to adjust and get over it, posts about fitness, beauty treatments, travel opportunities, calligraphy lessons, dancing, the pleasures of keeping a cat or a dog. In these posts one could sense the glow of a second youth.

And some told tales of other people, of what it was like to be the spouse of an overseas student and struggle to make money there; some expatiated on the hardships or consolations that the older generation had known in their youth. Many snapshots had been uploaded, ranging from landscapes to portraits of cats and dogs and group pictures taken as souvenirs on trips abroad to visit the children. Ru Yan read page after page, utterly delighted. Of varying lengths, these posts were not organized in any way. Most had replies appended to them, expressing emotion, admiration, a different viewpoint; or providing further information. The discussions were lively and everyone seemed to be talking at once. It was like what you find in a corner of a park where a relaxed group has gathered, people who may or may not know each other but chat and listen in the friendliest way.

After reading all this, Ru Yan had an impulse to say something, the same way she had struck up conversation with those parents outside the site of the college entrance exam. In truth, Ru Yan was a person of considerable reserve, unaccustomed to speak before strangers, and she was diffident even in front of people she knew, if they were in large numbers. But she decided that this was not, after all, a public setting, and she drafted a few sentences and pressed Enter, whereupon there appeared for the very first time on an internet bulletin board a message from a newbie named Such Is This World: `I'm new here. My son just went to France. I read everybody's articles and looked at the pictures: it's really nice. I'd like to talk more with you all later and learn more from you all.`

She read this over a couple of times and found no typos. Looking up, she saw it was two in the morning and suddenly felt very tired. She closed the computer, washed up, and went to sleep. Thus began Ru Yan's life on the Internet.

5

Ru Yan worked in a leisurely research institute. Their field was botany, and it was a low-stress environment. Job security there was still iron-clad, and though the money was not great and you couldn't make anything on the side, the wages and bonuses were dependable. Not many young people worked there; for quite a few years the Institute hadn't recruited any college graduates. Most of her colleagues and managers had been in their positions for a long time. The Institute was housed in a 1950s Soviet-style office building that was spacious, sturdy, no-nonsense. In its antiquated frame one could sense what passed for luxury in an earlier day. The work unit comprised more than a hundred people divided into two groups: one handled the scientific research and the other did administration. The research division was pretty quiet because those people were often in the field, which gave it the appearance of having a small staff. Administration was bustling, in comparison, with figures and voices always filling the corridors. People said that during the Fifties, the research group had been 'in', for it boasted many experts of national reputation who had studied overseas, and they were rather snooty toward Administration, and enjoyed top wages and benefits. With the Cultural Revolution, it was Administration's turn to be 'in'; for now the drivers, bookkeepers, HR staff, and cafeteria cooks formed the Revolutionary Committee, and when they said "jump" the research scientists said "how high?" When the Cultural Revolution was over, things settled down and everyone was about on the same level. Ru Yan had joined in the Eighties and had heard these tales about the old days.

On the third floor of the east wing was the Resource Room, where you could always find a few people who had little to do, gathered for some idle chat. The men talked about food and drink and mahjong and poker.[25] The women talked about children and husbands and clothes and housing. In mixed company, they enjoyed slightly off-color stories and teasing in moderation. They were all people of much experience who had worked together for many years and knew each other thoroughly, so they knew how far they could go without offense, how to laugh off a joke and move on.

Though it was in a big city, the atmosphere at the Institute was like that of a small county town: calm, self-sufficient, satisfied with the way things were. There was perhaps a certain Philistinism, the small-mindedness of a residential compound.[26] Her colleagues' children had not done very well academically, so the fact that her son had made it into such a good university on merit and then gone abroad to graduate school—with a scholarship, even! (unlike some kids, for whom money has been the key that opened all doors)—drew much praise, and more than a little envy. Everyone said Ru Yan was rather gentle and quiet, and that her husband had picked a terrible time to die, but that to have raised such a son was better than coming into a pile of money.

There was a computer in the Resource Room. It was generally used for typing up documents; she hadn't heard that it had any other use.

When she went to work the next day, Ru Yan showed her face in her office, talked a little about her son, and then hurried to the Resource Room.

The Resource Room was a place everyone liked to go, a place to flip through magazines, browse the newspaper, send a fax, photocopy an ID card or a child's homework. A reason could always be found to tap someone to contribute to the kitty from which candy and melon seeds were purchased and left out for everybody. One advantage of the Resource Room was that if by chance some diligent boss should wander in, everyone could instantly pretend to be searching for reference materials or reading reports. Ru Yan often came here to listen to the gossip and find a good magazine article. But today she had come for the computer.

She saw it was free, and asked Xiao Li[27], the typist, if she had any work to do.

Xiao Li said, "I've got a few things, but no rush, I'll type them later."

Ru Yan said, "I've got some free time, can I do some typing for you?"

Xiao Li grinned. "You trying to steal my job?"

"The Department Head's daughter-in-law? Who's going to steal *her* job? Even our boss has to watch his step with you."

Xiao Li snorted. "You intellectuals! Even if I let you do it, you'd consider it beneath you." But as she spoke she picked up a sheet of draft paper[28] and handed it to Ru Yan: "Let me guess: you want to practice typing!"

"You're a sharp one, you saw right through me. Hey, can we go online with this computer?"

"Yeah," Xiao Li said, "It's dial-up, you plug in the phone line. It's just really slow. You can send e-mails, but for chat or video it'll kill you. I'm used to broadband at home, so I don't bother to go online here."

She was plugging the power cord and the phone line into the "cat",[29] and after a spell of caterwauling it made the connection.

Upon hearing that Xiao Li, too, liked to go online, Ru Yan warmed to her and started chatting about the Internet.

Xiao Li listened for a while and then her face lit up with a crafty smile. "Ru Yan my pal, are you into the online dating scene? People who do that can't afford to type slow. If you're slow you can let a good man get away. I tell you: the key is speed, not beauty. A fast typist can carry on affairs with three guys at the same time."

Blushing, Ru Yan answered this cute young girl, "How's a wrinkled old lady like me going to carry on affairs over the Internet?"

Xiao Li said, "You don't get it; online dating was *invented* for wrinkled old ladies! Nobody can see anyone else. You say you're eighteen, how're they gonna to catch you out?"

Some women who had been discussing home renovation at the far side of the room caught wind of this juicy topic and they now crowded around. One said she went online only to check stocks. Another said she liked to play cards and there was a regular group, now, and when even a single day went by without a game she missed it terribly. When something made her late, QQ would start chirping, her cell phone would start ringing, it was like a hand was reaching out from the screen to pull you in. Someone else mentioned you could watch movies online, films from Hong Kong and Taiwan, films from Europe and America, adult films. Ru Yan asked what adult films were. A few of the women snickered and explained these were films that had the things you do with your husband. After mentioning Ru Yan's husband, they all realized they had put their foot in it and, with grins hastily removed, tried to steer the conversation toward Ru Yan's personal situation. Her husband was gone three years, they said, and she'd sent her son overseas: she should take the opportunity before she was too old, find a suitable guy, get married, join as partners. Some of them then expounded on the hardships of single women and added that attitudes had eased, nowadays: if you found someone who seemed more or less OK you could live with him first, and if your personalities clicked you could take care of the formalities later. Another said, Hey, these days, married or unmarried, it's no big deal. After listening to a few minutes of this, Ru Yan said with a thin smile, "Did you girls come here to hold a mass rally?" An older woman said, "If you're interested, there are still a few to choose from." Since they meant well, Ru Yan didn't want to rebuff them, so she said her son had just left, her head wasn't clear yet, and she was in no condition to choose the right man.

Xiao Li said, "Who can claim these days to be able with one look to choose the right man? If it doesn't work out, you try another one. You've got nothing to lose."

It was obvious that the conversation was going to become more outrageous the longer it went on, and Ru Yan couldn't keep fending them off. She said, "Do you mind if I tell you you're a little scary? If I help with your work will that shut you up?" Whereupon she propped up the short document which Xiao Li had given her and began to type.

6

Ru Yan was of a studious nature and was particularly fond of writing. The enthusiasm with which she had just learned how to type was much like that of a little boy learning to ride a bicycle. So she just tap-tapped away on the keyboard, starting the work and paying no attention to the babel of sopranos that surrounded her. The document was not long and when she finished, the women had dispersed and Xiao Li had gone off somewhere. Ru Yan started up QQ, but her son's icon didn't budge; over there it was still the middle of the night. Then she returned to the Empty Nest and was surprised to find five or six responses to the short post she had uploaded the night before.

The first was from Maple Leaves Are Red, who greeted her with a subject line of "`Welcome! Welcome! A heartfelt welcome!`" It was a zero-character message, i.e., there was nothing in the body of it. The second person with a message for her was Spring River Flows,[30] with the subject line "`Hello, please come in`" and the message read, "`My daughter is also in France, she went two years ago, she's studying fashion design. We'll be in touch.`"

The third was from Lonely Goose, the moderator, who also extended a hand in welcome. "`I'm a bit late, please excuse my poor hospitality. Well, the ranks of us old birds have been increased by one! Are you an older man? An older woman? A young man, a young woman?`[31] `I hope you will find friendship here, and kindly affection, and sympathy, and love—don't get nervous, all I mean is the friendly affection of us old birds. If you go and register with the forum, that will be more convenient: you'll be able to join the chat room. We respectfully await you.`"

Like many another unwitting and unwary internet newbie, Ru Yan completed her registration very honestly. She accurately filled in her age, sex, province, profession, level of education, e-mail address, QQ number—everything except marital status. Later this would cause her no small measure of trouble. She thought it was like a file that would be submitted to the Party apparatus, and that it was necessary to give concrete particulars.[32]

And there were a few follow-up messages that all extended a warm welcome.

Reading them, Ru Yan felt a spring breeze pass through her heart, a sensation of softness and warmth that brought a peculiar happiness. For many years, in her real life, she had been guarded with strangers, even to the point that she would stay out of the conversations that sprang up among passengers in a crowded train compartment. Even with people she knew, she was not accustomed to personal exchanges. Now that she was facing these invisible people, she was surprised by an urge to enter into dialogue. After each of the welcoming messages she wrote, `Thank you. Please bear with me`. To the moderator, Lonely Goose, she wrote, `I am a novice, I'll be asking you lots of questions.`

When she realized she had idled away two hours on this—and just then, Xiao Li returned from wherever she had gone—Ru Yan turned off the computer and went back to her office.

7

That night there was still no word from her son, and Ru Yan felt somewhat forlorn. She told herself that he had just got there and was awfully busy, with no time (and, for that matter, no place) to go online, so it was perfectly understandable. She'd heard stories of children who didn't get in touch with their families for half a year after they left, it was like they had dropped off the face of the earth. She tried to comfort herself this way. She came back to the Empty Nest, read through all the postings a few times. And then she had the impulse to write something.

On that lonely evening Ru Yan wrote her first essay for the

Internet, and it was the piece that made her reputation: "A Son's Rite of Passage." She wrote about how her son had come home for summer vacation, how he taught her to go online, how they had parted at the airport. By writing about them, she let go of many things that had become like a blockage in her heart, and felt tremendous relief in doing so. She didn't write about the boy's father; she didn't want to talk about that. She didn't realize that this was leaving a lot to people's imagination.

When she finished writing, she hesitated for a moment and then posted it to the forum. Then she took a stroll through some of the other discussion groups on the site. There was one called "Our Years in the Countryside", clearly for people who had been inserted into the work teams during those years.[33] Ru Yan had come at the tail end of those sent down to the countryside; this massive, decade-long torment would end, rather abruptly, less than a year later. When Ru Yan was sent down, the experience had already become a kind of game, just like the "Learn from Workers! Learn from Farmers!" lessons she had had in school. There was no longer anything of the tragic nobility of the first wave who had put down roots in the countryside, resolved to change the world. With more than a hundred other kids she had come to a farming district associated with her mother's System,[34] lived in a communal dorm, dined in a communal mess, and each month she got a dozen yuan in wages. When it was time to go to work, more than a hundred young men and women scattered giggling into the broad fields; they had no fixed quota of work, nor was a particular harvest expected. When they got off work they ate supper, sang songs, played the fiddle, played cards, and got into fights; and the bold ones had figured out how to carry on surreptitious romances. Every now and then, people from their System would come and screen a couple of movies in the open air. For all these reasons Ru Yan and her generation, the youngest of the educated youth, never felt the earnestness or endured the trials of the earlier cohorts; compared with their older brothers and sisters, they didn't think so much about those years or have such deep feeling for them.

Several posts on the "Our Years in the Countryside" forum

were devoted to a debate: regrets, or no regrets? This topic had been inspired by the memoir of an educated youth published some years before: *No Regrets About Youth*,[35] and the dispute was still going strong, as men and women graying into their fifties waged a war of words with the same passion they had shown back when they were young militants. Ru Yan skimmed some articles and, except for a few whose language was over the top, they all seemed fairly reasonable. She herself had never reflected on whether she had regrets, but she thought that should be a matter of personal feelings, and other people had no way to change those feelings and no need to sit in judgment on them. Just as she was pondering this, she came upon a posting that said pretty much what she had been thinking, but in a clear and logical way, quite beautifully; the writing was forceful but measured. It was signed "Damo."[36] She smiled. It was no surprise that "Damo" had cultivated such mental discipline after facing a wall for ten years.

She read for a while and then checked out the links to some personal web pages, like a little girl fooling around at the mall after school. In "Use Poetry to Meet Friends" she found collections of writings, both long and short, by many of her new Net friends including Lonely Goose and Maple Leaves Are Red. She plunged into them with great interest, and like a young lady with a new dress who unobtrusively takes note of what others are wearing, she couldn't help comparing their work with her own. Then she studied some of Damo's pieces. She was hooked after a few sentences. Ru Yan was finely attuned to good writing, much as a connoisseur of feminine beauty picks out in an instant the most beautiful woman in a crowd. She had this knack in much higher degree than many a prominent critic or professor, the kind who has lived off literature all his life; sometimes she'd read a book one of those types had praised and find she couldn't get through more than a few paragraphs without muttering, "How can you call this stuff *good*?"

She came back to the home page of the Empty Nest, and... Wow! (That was a favorite interjection in the forum.) Her article, "A Son's Rite of Passage," had garnered a slew of laudatory comments. *So beautiful*, and *Such a talented woman!*, and *Lovely writing!*, and *It made my eyes brim with tears, I've bookmarked it and sent it on to other websites*. It made Ru Yan a bit giddy. Among the reactions there was a comment from that Damo, which moved her deeply though it was only eight characters long: *Fine woman's literary grace; tender mother's hearfelt emotion.*

Just then, QQ sounded. Ru Yan thought it must be her son and hurried to bring up the screen, and then saw it was Spring River Flows, the person whose daughter was in France.

`Spring River Flows: Hello, Such Is This World. Am I bothering you? I got your QQ number from your registration data and am taking the liberty to contact you. I just read your article and wanted to talk with you. You really know how to write! You put into words much that's been in my heart.`

`Such Is This World: Mothers feel alike.` (*smiley face*)

`Spring River Flows: I am a father.`

`Such Is This World:` (*very red face*) `I didn't expect a father, too, would have such tender feelings.`

`Spring River Flows: Since she was ten, I've been both dad and mom to her; that's why my feelings for my child are out of the ordinary.`

Ru Yan had not guessed he was a man, much less a single man, and she wasn't sure how to respond. A moment's thought, and then she typed:

`Your situation is not an easy one.`

Spring River Flows: That's all water under the bridge now. (*smiley face*)

Such Is This World: Right, even the toughest times will pass.

Spring River Flows: In the few years my daughter's been gone, she's come to know her way around, and her mother's over there for a long time. If your son runs into difficulties and needs assistance, don't hesitate to tell me.

Such Is This World: If there's any problem I'll let you know.

Ru Yan suddenly wanted to know a little about his daughter's circumstances, even what she looked like. But on second thought she decided it would be presumptuous to ask, and rebuked herself.

The two continued talking for a while about their children. Then Ru Yan mentioned Damo, and asked who was this Damo?

Spring River Flows: Damo's an old bird at our place, he knows more than all the rest of us! He was one of the founders of this Midlife website, but later he started a forum devoted to philosophy and politics[37] and let somebody else take care of this one.

Such Is This World: Do you have the URL for that other forum?

Spring River Flows: I used to, but it's often been shut down these last two years and been moved around, so I couldn't tell you where it is now. You could look for it on Google.

Such Is This World: I'll do that now. We'll be in touch.

They exchanged their children's QQ numbers and e-mail addresses and said goodbye.

8

Damo lived in the same city as Ru Yan. On the Internet, however, it made no difference whether someone was on the other side of the wall or on the other side of the Pacific Ocean. Had they not met by chance through the Empty Nest, it's unlikely they ever would have run into each other on the street, and even if they had, they would not have known each other.

Ru Yan had come late to the Internet and had no idea that Damo was already a hero in the online world, especially on sites devoted to politics and culture where he was recognized as a master for his trenchant essays. Many a time his postings had been deleted and the ISP had banned him, and many a time the forums he organized had been either shut down for good or suspended due to technical difficulties. His milder essays frequently appeared in the press under a different pen name. Curious Net friends often guessed he must be some university professor or a scholar at a research institute, and some claimed he lived abroad, and swore he was none other than So-and-so. You couldn't really tell what his field was. Sometimes he wrote about Western religions, sometimes about the unofficial histories of the Ming and Qing; sometimes it was the Cultural Revolution, or the war against Japan; at times it was politics, at other times economics; sometimes he wrote about literature, film, and TV. His range of interests was exceedingly broad; politics, economics, literature, history, and philosophy were all grist to his mill. Some people hailed him as a unique genius, others called him eclectic, and there were some who said he was nothing more than an academic dabbler. He had very few close friends who knew who he really was.

At the start of the Eighties, Damo was still a worker at a

State-owned enterprise. That S.O.E. had its own adult-education college, and in the spirit of keeping up with the times[38] the college wanted to teach the "Three Theories" which were then in vogue, namely cybernetics, information theory, and systems theory. The college did not have anyone who could teach these and invited an instructor from outside. Unexpectedly, after the first few classes this gentleman stopped showing up. They inquired of his work unit, and his work unit said, "We're looking for him, too; rumor has it he went South." The college didn't succeed in hiring a replacement. One of the students said there was a guy on the factory floor who lectured a lot better than this teacher had done. The people at the education office thought he must be joking. "If you don't believe me," said the student, "have him come and give some lectures." They didn't want to just drop the course, so the college dispatched someone to find Damo's work group in the factory, where the foreman said, "Yeah, we've got that one, on the electricians' team. He's smart enough, but ideologically not so good." When they asked in what way was he not so good, the foreman said he was not of one mind with the Party. "When I realized his talent, I assigned him to help with the workers' blackboard newspaper, on things like mass criticism sessions, but he said he didn't go in for that kind of nonsense." The men from the college asked when this had happened. The foreman said Damo had been like this for many years.

The foreman sounded old-fashioned, and all the men from the college could do was smile.

They arranged a private interview with Damo to evaluate him. In a roundabout way they brought up the Three Theories.

"I know a little about that," Damo said.

It's very new, they said.

"You can call it new, but it's not, really; it depends on your frame of reference."

"What do you mean?"

"Domestically, of course it's something new. But among foreigners the research is already several decades old."

This startled them. Again they asked him what he meant.

Damo said, "During the second world war the Americans

used the principles of cybernetics to shoot down German aircraft. Basically, you'd input in a bunch of factors such as speed, course, weather conditions, course corrections, and angle of deflection and the process would output the best solution."

The college staff were flabbergasted and asked Damo where he had learned this.

"Oh, books I guess, magazines, the Reference News[39] . . . you just haven't been paying attention. When Qian Xuesen was in America he was researching cybernetics; how else could he have built the A-bomb after he came home?"[40]

The college decided to bring Damo in to teach a few classes. They could get a better idea of what he knew and meanwhile continue the search for a replacement. They told him to come for a few days the following week and act as a tutor, informally talking with some students about cybernetics. They didn't dare say they were making him an instructor.

Well, when Damo showed up, none of the students said anything. He began presenting in a measured way, not rushing but not wasting any time either, and explained the most abstruse ideas in simple terms. They had never heard anyone speak to them that way and two periods went by very quickly. The college had put an observer at the back of the room. The students all said, He teaches so much better than that wimp from Shanghai! A few more classes were ventured, and the reviews got even better. In those days, people didn't yet set much store by academic credentials and the college was, after all, an in-house affair at the S.O.E., so the rules were not strict. The students all spoke well of him and if they could pass their exams, who was going to complain? At the end of the term, Damo was transferred to the college with the opaque job title of "tutor." He was pleased. He didn't have to work regular hours, he would get winter and summer vacations, and he could shoot his mouth off in the classroom.

That year Damo turned thirty and was well-established.[41] Before that, he had been an educated youth for five years[42] and a worker for eight. He had spent more than ten years reading all kinds of books: books for amusement, 'yellow books', and 'black books.'[43] He had a ninth-grade education and was a Class 3 electrician. [44]

Later his friend Maozi (who landed a position at the Academy of Social Sciences[45]) would privately ask him, "When the hell did you learn cybernetics?"

Damo grinned. "Who said I ever learned it properly? Only a smattering. Quick turnaround,[46] you know."

That student from his work team, who had enjoyed hearing him shoot the bull on the factory floor and had casually recommended him to the college, let him know right away about it. Damo was getting tired of life in the factory and figured the adult education institute must be a comfortable place. So he pulled himself together, gathered a stack of materials, and studied like mad for several days. When he muddled successfully through the first couple of classes he began to feel confident. You could say he was actually learning the basics of the Three Theories along with his students.

Someone said to him, "You're such a brain, how come you didn't take the college entrance exam when you first had a chance? If you had done that, you wouldn't need to put up with these aggravations now." Damo said he had been afraid studying for the test might make him stupid. When the exam was reinstated,[47] Damo didn't have the slightest interest in taking it. He was a proud, perhaps an arrogant man, and he felt no need to devote any time now to the crap that passed for liberal arts at the universities, because the scope of what he'd already read went far beyond the ken of any liberal arts graduate. He just didn't foresee, then, how important that diploma would later become, nor did he imagine that the company where he had a dependable, indeed enviable, job would go bust one day. There was also a practical reason: his wife was going to have a baby.

After he had taught the Three Theories for a couple of years, the college began offering liberal arts. They added World History to his course list, and later History of Literature, and Logic. The college grew accustomed to assigning to Damo any course for which they couldn't recruit a professor; it was OK as long as the students said he was fun to listen to. And Damo now had figured out how to keep one step ahead: each time he started a new course he would sit down with the students and study with them. They would progress together, and when he finished teaching the subject he had also finished studying it. Again and again he found that this worked. Later, he wrote a pseudonymous essay about this way of teaching by learning. In it he said this novel approach let the teacher retain a sense of discovery, of freshness, and of urgency as he explored the subject along with his students. The teacher was the leader of a small study group, that was all. The conventional approach of dully feeding to students knowledge that one had chewed over for decades and could regurgitate—the teacher showing no passion and the student no interest—deprived the student of his right to learn. The essay drew strong reactions when it came out. People who had long relied on regurgitated knowledge took Damo to task. But the controversy ultimately faded without being resolved. In private, Damo said, "When I'm rich someday and start my own college, there won't be a single regurgitator on the faculty!"

Good times don't last, and soon the college was struggling as its enrollment dried up, and in the end it closed its doors altogether. That was the year all the people became businessmen[48] and even the officious crones of the neighborhood committees were keen for "information."[49] Damo had taught the Three Theories for a number of years, and now there was one word which elicited hushed respect throughout society: *information*. When people saw each other, their first question was "Got any information?" More simply: "What does the last player have? What does the next player want?"[50]

A few teachers transferred to other schools. Others retired, and still others found a different kind of job with the same company. The college became an empty shell, and they needed a few people to stay behind and take care of the property. Damo became one of the caretakers. The job paid a few hundred a month and there wasn't much that had to be done: looking after the library and office equipment, managing the leasing of classrooms, reimbursing the expenses of people still connected with the college ... these latter duties offered a chance to make a little extra money. But Damo, without hesitation, chose to work as a watchman.

The library had a few computers. Years before, he had sat right here in front of the only 386 they had, and he had completed his basic computer training course on that machine.[51] In the Nineties, when China began encouraging Internet training, it was here again that Damo went through one of the first training courses when Net access was still dial-up. He would always remember the thrill of going online for the first time. After a bit of fiddling, he got the modem to warble and a web page started to appear in the browser. The Web was slow, then, and he watched the page load incrementally from top to bottom, just the way a baby emerges from the birth canal: the hair, the head, the arms, the body . . . at last the whole page opened up with pictures and text. The Internet was not yet tightly supervised at that time; there were all kinds of news and a wide range of opinion. Compared with traditional media, it was both bold and fresh. Just like when the automobile was new and there were no traffic laws yet.

Those old machines were still here, gathering dust in a corner of the library. In the online world, such machines were called fossils, and so were the people who used them. Subsequent development was fairly swift, and a machine with a hard drive smaller than a gigabyte would soon inspire the same feelings as the sight of a steam locomotive from the 1800s.

Notwithstanding his self-effacing manner, Damo thought rather highly of himself. He felt little need for self-improvement. These leisurely days went on for two or three years, and they were for Damo a time of wonder and enchantment. He would go to work, complete his rounds, and then make a beeline for the library, where he would read books, go online, drink tea, and type essays. But alas, good times never last, and one day the factory was sold off in its entirety. Along with more than a thousand other people, he got twenty or thirty grand in severance pay and said goodbye to that company forever. This happened when his daughter was in high school and his wife needed an operation. He watched the money dwindle to nothing and realized that reading books and going online could not put food on the table. He eked out a living with a succession of temporary jobs, always on the lookout for the next.

9

In that city Damo's family belonged to the part of the population which could most truly be called "the common people." His father had sold tea all his life. Before Liberation,[52] he had sold tea for a capitalist; after Liberation he sold it for the Communist Party. He was then assigned an official class status of "sales clerk," which was almost as good as being counted among the laborers.

The tea shop where his father worked was more than a hundred years old and working conditions were not bad; he really had not had a rough time in the old society. In the new society, they had more children and it was harder to make ends meet, so the mother now had to work outside the home.

In this tea shop Damo learned to love reading.

For years, except for the high-grade varieties (which were sold in tins), all tea had been packaged at the shop in paper bags. At the time of the three years' famine,[53] paper came to be in short supply and the shop couldn't get paper bags. Even Damo's schoolbooks and workbooks started being printed on recycled paper that was dark and coarse. When you tried to write on such paper the strokes of the characters would run because the penpoint got stuck in places, and the resulting inkblots looked like a landscape painting. The paper also carried traces of old characters which imperfect recycling had not removed, as well as palpable little bumps that were like Braille. In class, Damo would run his fingers over the pages and they didn't feel right, so he'd dig the bumps out with his fingernail, and sometimes he found part of a blade of grass or a wad of cotton fiber, and one bump turned out to be a small dead beetle. As a result of his digging these things out, the pages of his schoolbooks had many little holes, making a pitiable impression. Although he knew he was ruining them, Damo couldn't stop, he simply couldn't stop. In the end they were all riddled with holes. Later he read some psychology and learned this was called a compulsive disorder.

So the tea shop began purchasing scrap paper—newspapers, books, any kind of printed matter—and gluing it into paper bags with which to wrap the tea. A page of 16mo could wrap two ounces of tea, a page of 32mo would be sufficient to pack one ounce, and for more than a pound they would use better-quality magazine paper, or folio-sized newspaper.[54]

From early childhood, therefore, Damo came into daily contact with tea and with paper that had writing on it: two of the finer things in life. Thus was this true-born child of the common people contaminated with an air of scholarly refinement. The boy liked to go into his father's shop and smell the aroma of the tea, and with glimmers of understanding he would read the stacks of printed matter that had not yet been cut up to make bags. In the Sixties there could still be found in his father's shop many books and periodicals that were no longer to be seen in the world outside. You would frequently catch a glimpse of various people who had long since disappeared, along with their writings, from the fifties or even from the thirties and forties. As far as the tea shop was concerned, it was all just packing material. But to Damo it was 'illegal information' that he would never get his hands on in school. Once he discovered an old textbook of 'national language' from before Liberation—such courses were later called 'language arts'[55]—and found this collection of writings so interesting that he wanted to take it home. His father said, "Each piece of paper here is like the tea: don't even think of taking it." His father was such a rigorously honest shop clerk that, because he worked in this trade, he never drank tea in his life and no one in his family would drink it either. (Even now, Damo was OK with cigarettes and alcohol but he could hardly bring himself to drink tea, and when he did, he couldn't taste any flavor.) So the boy took that book of 'national language' and sat down to read, and kept reading until it was time for his father to quit work.

When his father noticed how much Damo was attached to the book, he relented and reached an understanding with the head clerk. For any materials Damo coveted, his father would pay double the cost. The scales in the tea shop were small; they could weigh a few ounces or fractions of an ounce. In those days, when common folk bought tea it was usually an ounce or two at a time. The shop had a product, which Damo long remembered, designed for people who liked tea but couldn't afford to drink it. It was a mixture of the stems and the little broken tips which had been sifted out of the saleable tea leaves. This stuff was quite inexpensive and if you steeped it a little, it tasted like tea. Actually, the little broken tips yielded their flavor faster than full tea leaves did. Decades later, the bags of quick-brew tea that would find use in big hotels were really nothing but those broken tips of the leaves.

Little by little, Damo amassed his book collection. The earliest batch mostly had notations of weight scrawled on the front covers, such as "3.7 oz." or "1/2 lb" or "1 lb. 1 oz." and even five, six, seven, or eight pounds—that would be the total weight of a stack of periodicals. It was a mix of all kinds of literature, the good and the not so good, and in time there was more than a hundred pounds of it. His father said, "A hundred pounds for you means two hundred pounds for me, and at sixteen cents a pound, I'm out thirty-two bucks! That's a month's wages for your mother."[56] When the Cultural Revolution came, book collectors who had thousands upon thousands of volumes started burning them, but Damo went right on tirelessly collecting. There were times when it was an advantage to be one of the common people. Who would even notice what books a kid like this owned? Later Damo would remark that in that first batch of his books there had been works which only senior officials got to read, books with yellow jackets and gray jackets, such as *Trotsky's Memoirs*, and *The New Class: an analysis of the communist system*,[57] and Hayek's *Road to Serfdom*. Some of the books were incomprehensible to him, but he read about as many as he didn't read.

He had no inkling that this Hayek, who was little known, would later win the Nobel Prize.[58] Decades later he would become the intellectual godfather of a group of Chinese theorists. Alas, in the meanwhile Damo had once loaned the book out and never got it back, or else he could have used that fine edition (which happened to have "6.5 oz." written on the dust jacket) to pass himself off as a Chinese authority on Hayek, a role for which he was better qualified than the experts who became famous as Hayek scholars in the Eighties.

An incidental benefit was that Damo learned how to read books printed in columns of complex characters. It was a struggle, since no one taught him and he often had to guess. But he figured out the conversion to simplified characters and gained the knack of reading from top to bottom in columns that proceeded from right to left. In that era when the principal way to acquire information was through books, this one skill enabled Damo to find out a great many things that other boys could not.

10

Recounting Damo's young life as a reader, it is impossible to avoid mentioning a certain person.

The tea shop where Damo's father worked was called the Chamber of Enchantment and had an antique air, being more than a hundred years old. At the front door, a classical couplet was carved in wood, green characters on a brown background. On one side: *My only close friend, the tune 'Clearwater' played on the qin* and on the other: *And for long-time companion I have tea from Mt. Meng.*[59] It was said that both this couplet and the shop's name came from a poem by the great Tang poet Bai Juyi. His father said it was exquisite. He never explained why it was exquisite. The calligraphy was the work of some literary personage of the Qing[60] and there was a caption on the inscription mentioning the umpteenth year of Daoguang.[61]

One day at the start of the Cultural Revolution[62], word reached the shop that Red Guards were coming in that direction, making a sweep, and you could already hear from afar a crackling sound, the noise of things being hammered and broken, and dense smoke swirled up over the far end of the street. A few old employees who had been with the shop for decades made a desperate rush to obtain some big sheets of festive red paper, wrote a couplet, and pressed the paper tightly over the carved work on the doors that was more than a century old.

Four oceans surge, clouds rage,
Five continents shake with wind and thunder. [63]

Likewise, they papered over the shop's old signboard with a new banner: "LONG LIVE CHAIRMAN MAO!" They even brought a big barrel of fine tea out into the street and put a placard beside it: "You must be tired, young militants of the revolution! Please have a cup of revolutionary tea!" All the employees stood in the doorway, wearing big smiles as they welcomed and bade farewell to the Red Guards who came and left. The shop escaped looting. Late that night, some of the old employees sneaked by and ever so carefully took down the carved couplet and the old signboard, wrapping them in oilpaper and putting them on a rack in the warehouse where they looked like shelves and would stay more than ten years, practically forgotten. With the new era of Reform and Opening[64], it was decreed that shops should have their traditional names restored, and only then was this clever rescue recalled. By then, unfortunately, of the few men involved in that affair the only one still alive was Damo's father. He had been retired for some years. A reporter tracked him to his home and interviewed him for a moving article about how the masses in those years had resisted the retrograde Gang of Four. When the piece came out, Damo's father brushed away tears as he read it with great excitement. The article included a photo of Damo's father standing in front of the old woodcarving, which had been hung anew, and pointing out what the couplet said. He was well into his seventies, but it was the first time he had ever been in the paper. Damo took him off guard by chuckling, "Dad, you're not thinking. How could there have been a Gang of Four back then? At that time Wang Hongwen was still working as a two-bit security guard in Shanghai!" This remark spoiled the old man's happiness. He murmured, "What do I care? Gang of four, gang of five . . . We saved this thing, wasn't that a good deed?"[65]

The main room at the Chamber of Enchantment was quite large. Upon entering, you faced a bar that was chest-high: the countertop was black marble, always polished as clean and bright as a mirror, inlaid with pieces of white marble about as broad as a teabowl, and it was supposed to be for patrons to inspect samples of loose tea. On either side was a big old square table from which you could see out into the street through a wooden lattice. Behind a screen on each side were side-tables and chairs. The seats outside the screen were for ordinary customers to sit down and quench their thirst. There had long been tea available for free here, and once brewed it would be poured into an enamelware pot plaited with palm-fronds and left on a table next to a tray of porcelain cups. A sign on the wall said: COMPLIMENTARY TEA PROVIDED AS A SERVICE TO THE PEOPLE. Behind the screens sat long-time customers, and also the professional purchasers from hotels, restaurants, and government agencies who found their seats in this inner sanctum and sampled a bit of everything, and after they had done their sipping and chatting they would purchase some of everything. When no one was around, Damo would often sit reading behind the screen, and if he was thirsty he could drink the complimentary tea.

Damo's father was glad his son was studying hard and learning well, but he felt that if this went on it might cause some annoyance in the shop, so he often had the boy help with chores such as moving furniture and gluing paper bags. There were many old-time employees at the shop, and since the tea business is marked by an air of gentle refinement, they were all fond of this boy.

Before Liberation, the Chamber of Enchantment had been one of those three-in-one establishments with the store in front, a work area in back, and residences upstairs.

The rear courtyard had several workshops where newly-arrived shipments of tea could be processed, for there were secret techniques known only to the master craftsmen. The building had four stories and was one of the more imposing edifices on that street. Offices were on the second floor, the families of the owner and the accountant lived on the third, and the fourth was home to a few of the most senior employees, Damo's family among them. After the company was turned into a cooperative, the people who lived in the building had to use the back door in order to distinguish their living arrangements from the business of the shop. But this was no problem for Damo. He'd leave by the back door and come round the block to the front: it only took a few minutes.

11

Two years before the Cultural Revolution,[66] one day Damo was ensconced in a corner of the shop reading an old magazine. A tall, gaunt gentleman came in, a man in his forties or fifties with a thin bespectacled face on which time had written its lines. He was wearing a gray four-pocket cadre's suit that hung loosely on him, the kind you wash often but never quite get clean. Damo knew he was a frequent customer familiar to all the staff. They called him Teacher Wei[67] and said he came from a neighboring high school. It was a very ordinary high school that wasn't called "No. 1" or "No. 2" but was just named after the street it was on.[68] Damo understood this kind of high school to be of low caliber, solely for students with poor grades or a very bad family background.[69] So he had never paid much attention to this man. He had only heard people say he was somewhat eccentric, in that he drank nothing but Premium Jasmine. Jasmine tea was divided into six grades, and Premium Jasmine cost more than two bucks an ounce; for that money you could buy a pound, or more, of No. 5. In those days most people made only 35 yuan a month;

even if you managed to go without food or drink, you could barely buy two pounds of this most expensive tea.

Everybody knew what kind of people came in to buy Premium Jasmine, apart from the purchasing agents who've already been mentioned. Any private citizens who bought the stuff were either rich people who'd managed to hold on to some of their property from the old days, or major intellectuals, or famous actors, ranking cadres, or individuals who bought small amounts occasionally when they were expecting guests. This Teacher Wei did not seem like a rich man, not from the way he dressed, nor from the way he bought only one or two ounces at a time; most of all, it seemed he was not rich because on those occasions when he bought more than a couple of ounces, he would not show his face again for months. But he only wanted Premium Jasmine. More than once the staff had urged him, "You know, the Premium and the No. 1 are practically the same, the jasmine flowers are only slightly more fine, but the No. 1 is half the price." Teacher Wei would crack a gentle smile and sigh, "Ah, the difference between Heaven and Earth!" He refused to lower his standards even when he was broke. Damo's father said that once this Teacher Wei had had only a single yuan on him, but he had insisted on Premium Jasmine, so they measured out a half-ounce for him on the scale. Before they knew who he was, unable to guess what manner of man this odd fellow might be, the staff had referred to him among themselves as "Premium Jasmine." Then one day a former student of his ran into him in the shop, and from the two men's conversation they learned he was a high school teacher. That school was many blocks away from the Chamber of Enchantment; a number of tea shops would have been closer. Nobody knew why he came such a distance to buy tea. Later someone asked him, but he only smiled.

The magazine Damo was reading that day, *High-Schoolers*, dated from the Republican era.[70] It had line drawings and old-fashioned ads for skin cream, cod-liver oil, soaps, matches, etc., and the ads featured modern girls with perms and lipstick, wearing cheongsams that showed their thighs. Such rarities had long vanished from the mainland Chinese press, and Damo was studying this magazine with great curiosity. Teacher Wei had bought his tea and was about to head out the door when he stopped, as if by some intuition, and came over to Damo and plucked that copy of *High-Schoolers* from his hand. His eyes lit up.

After leafing through it, he asked, "Where did this come from?"

Flustered, Damo said he'd borrowed it.

The man pressed him: Where did you borrow it?

Damo couldn't think of a good fib on the spur of the moment so he said he'd borrowed it from the shop.

"Here?"

Damo nodded. Teacher Wei returned the magazine with a smile and said, "Strange . . . passing strange. Who would have guessed I'd see this here." He took it back and looked at it more carefully, murmuring, "So many years, gone in a flash." Then he pointed out a few names at the top of the table of contents and asked Damo who were these people, did he know?

Damo said he knew Bing Xin and Ye Shengtao.[71]

"Not bad, not bad at all: you could say who two of them were. I'm afraid the students at my school couldn't do that. I tell you, this man at the top, here, he was a great writer, more famous than you could believe. Even in college we studied his work."

Teacher Wei had become quite animated. He pulled up a chair and began giving Damo a thumbnail sketch of each of the authors and scholars and famous people in that magazine, including the artist Feng Zikai.[72] Damo said he didn't like that man's drawings. Teacher Wei was taken aback. "Come on, he's a *great* artist. You're still young, you don't know how to appreciate what you see. A versatile mind: poetry, music . . . he mastered it all."

Teacher Wei had a good talk with Damo. The boy's father, along with the other clerks in the shop, was astounded that this strange man who had never said much, but only smiled a little, was now chatting away so affably with a kid who was barely into his teens. Teacher Wei then asked a favor: could he borrow the magazine? He promised he'd bring it back the next day, without fail. Damo said, "This is, um. . . this belongs to the shop."

Teacher Wei then went up to the clerk who'd just sold him some tea and asked, "Is it all right if I borrow it? I'll tell you what: I'll leave my tea here with you and I'll pick it up tomorrow when I return the magazine."

But the clerk said, "I wouldn't think of it, Sir; you are one of our long-time customers; just take it and read it, along with your tea." Damo's father came over and said, "Please, Sir, take anything you'd like to read. Tomorrow I can accept anything as a replacement. For wrapping tea, any printed matter will do."

Teacher Wei quickly agreed: "Then tomorrow I'll bring you a few magazines with better-quality paper." Damo's father said, "You don't need to make the trip; tell me your address and I'll send my son to get it."

The next day after classes, Damo found his way to the teacher's house. It was in an alley near his school, and when he came to the gate of a residential compound he saw Teacher Wei standing at the entrance waiting for him. "I was afraid you might have trouble finding it," he said graciously, and Damo said he knew the place because some of his classmates lived on the same street. Teacher Wei led him in. A dozen households occupied the compound, which presented a chaotic scene. His apartment was in a corner of the rear courtyard. Damo stepped in and wondered, how could you call this a home? A single dingy room, partitioned. In front was a small area that served as a kitchen, with a coal stove that had an unwashed iron pot on it. There was also a low table with one broken leg propped up on bricks against the wall. A bowl with chopsticks, and containers for oil and salt, stood in disarray upon the table. Down on the floor were a few turnips that had already turned black. The rear half of the room was even darker and Teacher Wei lit a lamp there. One look brought to mind the saying, "home but four walls."[73] There was a plank cot supported on two long benches and the rear wall had a small high window. A narrow table was ranged under the window with a square stool. The only other item was a wicker bookcase with a few books and magazines and a pile of homework. There was a big trunk on the floor, the sort that looks like a packing crate made of coarsely hewn boards; and on top of the trunk lay a leather suitcase of the finest workmanship, the kind you see in the movies when a rich person is boarding an ocean liner. Here it was incongruous.

Teacher Wei invited Damo to take the square stool while he sat on the edge of the bed. He picked up a few issues of *Red Flag*[74] and handed them over, expressing the hope they'd be a good replacement because the paper was newer. Damo accepted the copies of *Red Flag* and prepared to leave.

Abruptly, Teacher Wei asked, "Do you know why I wanted this magazine?"

The boy shook his head.

With a gleam in his eye, the teacher said, somewhat mysteriously, "My maiden *opus* is in here. " With that, he flipped to a dog-eared page and pointed out the author's name: "That's me."

Damo leaned over and saw it was someone called "This Wei."

Teacher Wei continued, "Yes, 'This Wei' is me. I was seventeen and had just started my freshman year in college. Ye Shengtao personally helped me with this essay and made corrections to it." Then he added, "Don't mention that to anyone . . . let's keep it a secret."

Teacher Wei asked Damo what books he had read. Damo mentioned a few. "Good, very good," the teacher said as he listened. "To have read so much at such a young age, excellent." But he told him not to bother reading So-and-so's work, and named a few books that were not worth his time.

Why not, Damo wanted to know. Teacher Wei said, "They're just no good, there's nothing there; it's a dead end for a young person." Then he gave his recommendations, exactly what and who Damo ought to read. "Unfortunately I don't have any of them, or I'd lend them to you."

Those books and authors which Teacher Wei had recommended, or at least some of them, stayed in Damo's memory. In the second year of the Cultural Revolution, when anarchy reigned and students were looting the libraries, some of those names came back to Damo amid the frenzy and he managed to steal some books of extremely high quality. Thus did the teacher's guidance have a beneficial effect on his later education.

Thereafter, whenever Teacher Wei came to the Chamber of Enchantment, if Damo was there the two of them would have a good talk, the old man and the boy. Wei was not like the teachers at Damo's school. Everything he said was novel and fresh, and Damo would listen spellbound. Occasionally Damo would come across a book he thought Teacher Wei would like, and he'd give it to him to read.

12

Soon it was the summer of 1966, just a few days after the old employees had taken action to save the carved inscriptions when the Red Guards were coming down the street to sweep away the Four Olds. Schools had stopped holding classes so that students could carry on the revolution with undivided attention. Damo was in seventh grade and was a nobody at school: he hadn't even been appointed a group leader, but was left to his own devices with no responsibilities. So he strolled about, observing the excitement everywhere.

One day, on one of the main thoroughfares of the city, he saw an enormous crowd marching his way. They were lined up in ranks with big red flags and colored bunting and banners with quotations,[75] carrying portraits of the Leader, shouting slogans and warlike songs while the rat-a-tat-tat of their drums beat a tattoo. The sight could be described with a phrase that was commonplace in those days: a river of five colors. As he waited for the parade to draw near, he noticed that squeezed within the main body of marchers was a bizarre contingent of individuals daubed with blackface, wearing conical hats on their shaven heads, with placards hung round their necks. The placards said all kinds of things:

FEUDAL BOSS
FUGITIVE LANDLORD
SOCIAL BUTTERFLY
CAPITALIST
C.C. SPY[76]
WHORE
HOOLIGAN
BAD ELEMENT

They carried on their persons ornaments that accorded with their various identifications. The capitalist had dozens of rumpled neckties tied round his neck. The social butterfly wore high-heeled shoes, and had additional pairs hanging on her chest and back. The fugitive landlord had rolls of papers stuffed under his arms, labeled: "Keeping accounts in hope of a comeback." The C.C. spy looked like a spy from the movies, with dark glasses and a fedora worn at a slant. Each carried some kind of percussion instrument, a cymbal or a gong—in some cases it was a basin or a spittoon—and each time they struck it they would utter a cry:

"I am Zhang So-and-so, I am a criminal profiteer!"

"I am Wang So-and-so, I am a member of the Yiguandao!"[77]

Each howled his name and his status, and the throng on either side would then shout "Down with them!" The voices rose and fell like a wave.

Damo had beheld such scenes only in the movies, movies about the great revolutionary era of the 1920s; he had never dreamed you could see such things these days, in the flesh. As the marching throng kept flowing past, Damo caught sight of Teacher Wei. He was in the middle group. The inscription on his placard was long and unusual:

WEI LIWEN,
MEMBER OF THE REACTIONARY CORE OF THE
COUNTERREVOLUTIONARY HU FENG CLIQUE [78]

The three characters that spelled his name, Wei Liwen, were writ large and each was crossed out with a red X. Damo knew hardly anything about the Hu Feng clique; he faintly remembered caricatures of a balding man with a dogskin plaster[79] at his temples like Chiang Kai-shek, and a pistol hanging off his butt as he clutched in his hand an enormous pen that dripped blood. He was supposed to be some sort of spy, evil and cunning, skilled at both words and war. Who could have guessed that this urbane and gracious, almost pedantic Teacher Wei would turn out to be that kind of a person, and a core member at that? Damo felt a chill even under the blazing August sun. He took another look at the ashen-faced man, who was staring dazed through his spectacles at the tip of his nose, holding a piece of firewood in one hand and an iron pot in the other. It was the same pot Damo had seen in his kitchen. In time to the march, he beat the bottom of the pot, which had become dented and made a clattering sound.

After that, Teacher Wei came no more to the Chamber of Enchantment to buy Premium Jasmine.

13

Five or six years later, Damo saw Teacher Wei again. The boy had wandered the land for three or four years, experiencing all that was to be experienced in the grime of the countryside, and had grown into a weather-beaten lad acquainted with hardship. The one thing that had not changed was his fondness for reading, which had become habitual, and he had made friends with a few others who had a literary bent. One was in a commune, another lived in a different district, and a few others lived in town. He had finished enough pages in the book of mankind that he no longer saw everything as beautiful, the way it is in fairy tales. But if in his boyhood he had been driven by simple curiosity, now he felt a pressing need for answers to life's questions. He and his new friends tried to make connections between the ideas they garnered from their reading and the social reality around them. They debated; they challenged assumptions; they wavered, and they sighed with regret. Sometimes they'd write long letters to each other, exploring some question; but when they learned that others had gotten into big trouble this way, they stopped writing letters.

That year Damo went home to visit his family for the New Year's holiday. A few friends got together, including Maozi, who would later become a Marxian theoretician.

"I'm going to take you guys to meet someone," Maozi announced.

Damo asked who it was. Maozi said it was an eminent man. "You'll know when you see him. He's mentioned in the Selected Works of Mao Zedong."

They asked why he was mentioned there. Maozi did not answer directly.

"Who do you think there are more of in the Selected Works: good people or bad people?"

They had all read the book, more or less, and went back and forth about it and came to the somewhat surprising conclusion that its pages contained many more villains than heroes. As for the heroes, well, there were Marx, Engels, Lenin, and Stalin; there was Henry Norman Bethune,[80] and Zhang Side,[81] and Old Man Yu Gong.[82] There was also Li Diming,[83] even though he was really only an enlightened gentleman . . . when you add them all up, there aren't that many. But the list of bad guys goes on and on: from antiquity and the present, both Chinese and foreigners, from the ranks of the Party, the Government, and the Army: all kinds of people. From Chiang Kai-shek, Enemy of the People, to Leighton Stuart, the American Ambassador[84]; from the grafters Liu Qingshan and Zhang Zishan[85] to the Rightists Zhang Bojun and Luo Longji[86], from the Nationalist general, Du Yuming, to the Communist Marshal Peng Dehuai[87] . . . After taking stock, the group more or less had an idea what kind of person Maozi was talking about. Years of experience had taught them all that there are things which it is best not to express too clearly. Should there ever be an investigation, you can say that you misspoke, that you didn't know. Anyway, in this group the bloom was off their youthful idealism. During years of upheaval in the Cultural Revolution it had become clear that the worst elements in society were rising to the top. No certainties were left intact, for plenty of dirty linen had been aired in high places. The truly unpardonable scoundrels did not turn out to be people who *looked* like monsters; no, and even the 'monsters & demons', the secret societies of traitors and capitalist-roaders, no longer looked as wicked as they once had seemed. So since this group was young and impetuous, they got together and went to see Maozi's mystery man.

They followed him into a residential compound and Damo thought, wasn't this the place where Teacher Wei, that is, Wei Liwen, had lived? Sure enough, Maozi knocked at that door in the corner and the person who came out was Teacher Wei. The man looked uneasy at the sight of four or five men come to see him, and Maozi said, "These are all close friends. I've mentioned some of them to you." Teacher Wei then let them come into his room, where nothing seemed to have changed except there were now a lot of folding chairs which made it seem there were frequent meetings here.

When everyone had sat down, Teacher Wei still had not recognized Damo. Indeed, the swarthy and stocky fellow in front of him was a different person from the gentle, shy boy he had known. After he and Maozi had exchanged pleasantries, Damo asked him, "Teacher Wei, do you recognize me?"

He took a good look at the young man. "Your face is familiar..."

Damo said, "Premium Jasmine."

Teacher Wei gave a cry of astonishment and delight. "The kid from the Chamber of Enchantment?"

Damo smiled.

"Let me tell you something," Teacher Wei said, "I don't have that copy of *High-Schoolers* anymore. They took it when they searched my home. It was considered very incriminating."

Maozi and the others were quite surprised to hear Damo and Teacher Wei chatting on such familiar terms about that earlier time when they had known each other. "I didn't realize..." Maozi said.

"Back then I didn't understand anything," Damo said, "I didn't even know who Teacher Wei was." He came close to mentioning what had happened on the day of the huge march, but could not find words for that.

They had a long talk that day, and much of it was about politics. One phrase stuck in Damo's memory: concerning China's prospects and destiny, Teacher Wei said, "It's a systemic problem." This expression would gradually enter widespread use and become fashionable, but only twenty years later. What surprised Damo was how Teacher Wei, whom he remembered as a mild-mannered gentleman with a tendency to mumble, was now quite forceful and provocative in his speech, even though between then and now he had undergone the ordeal of that march.

"You've changed a lot," he said. Teacher Wei smiled and said back then he had still harbored illusions, even believing himself guilty; but not anymore.

On the way home, Damo asked Maozi what was the story with Teacher Wei. "You mean you don't know?" Maozi blurted. "He was a famous theoretician in our province; for a while he held high office in the Party and served as the deputy chief of the Propaganda Department. He went to Yan'an. He went down South.[88] You take a look in the library at newspapers and magazines from the early Fifties: many of the articles are by him, a great many. You must have missed a lot during those years you knew him!"

After a pause, Damo asked, "It was 'cause of the Hu Feng affair?"

Yes and no, Maozi said. He actually never knew Hu Feng. Before Liberation, he had submitted manuscripts to a journal of which Hu Feng was the editor. Then in a few essays he said things which tended to support Hu Feng's position from the standpoint of aesthetic theory, with no inkling what trouble this was going to cause him.

Later Damo and Maozi made a number of visits by themselves. The more they talked, the better Damo hit it off with Teacher Wei, and he felt a pang of regret that he had really come to know this man only now.

He mentioned Teacher Wei to his father, who said, "Now I see why he hasn't been back to buy tea." Once when Damo was making a visit with Maozi, his father had him take along two ounces of Premium Jasmine as a gift.

After thanking him, Teacher Wei said, "I don't drink tea."

"Then how come you used to buy Premium Jasmine?" Damo asked.

For a long time he gave no answer, and there passed over his face a shadow of grief. Damo didn't know why this was a sensitive question but he felt embarrassed and was about to change the subject when Teacher Wei finally began to speak.

In '55 they had arrested him and put him in solitary confinement. They'd made him confess to being in league with Hu Feng and working against the Party. On searching his home they had found drafts of some letters to Hu Feng. These had all been written years before Liberation, in fact during the war against the Japanese, when Hu Feng had managed a journal in Guilin. The letters contained submissions for the journal; he couldn't remember exactly what they had been about, but this was conclusive evidence and in combination with a few other issues it meant he was doomed. While he was in prison, his wife divorced him and moved far away with the two kids: she didn't even tell him where she was going. Teacher Wei said that before this happened, when he had been a successful young man, not only did his wife love him but a crowd of young female admirers were always swooning over him. So this was quite a blow. Often he felt it would be good to die, and he knew of others who had taken that route. The only problem was that in prison he remained under strict guard and could never find an opportunity, nor were the necessary implements at hand. He had been locked up for more than a year when he learned they were sending him to an outlying district for labor under supervision.[89] He thought this would give him an opportunity to cut himself off from the people and from the Party.[90]

But before he was sent away, his work unit held a criticism session[91] for him as a going-away present. Most of those in attendance had been his subordinates and there were also many people from the arts and culture work units over which he had had administrative responsibility. Many of these had worshipped him. Whenever he gave a speech, they all used to listen with shining eyes and applaud wildly. But now they were all filled with indignation as if they were struggling against Huang Shiren.[92] The slogans rose and fell. They shouted themselves hoarse. Wei Liwen smiled sardonically, as in his mind he settled on an elegiac couplet for himself: *From this moment I can take my leave, / There is nothing that still ties me to this world.*

But something happened as he was leaving the meeting hall. A pretty young woman blocked his way and said calmly, "I am So-and-so, art designer for the drama group."

He peered at her. The face was familiar, but he couldn't remember ever having any dealings with her.

"I only learned about the meeting this morning," she continued. "On my way here I bought you a little tea." And with that she handed him a canister of fine tea, turned, and left.

Teacher Wei said that in that moment he was struck dumb. He stood rooted to the spot; he couldn't even utter a word of thanks, but just gaped and watched her stride away. His guards snatched the can of tea and immediately opened it, emptied it onto a newspaper, and carefully picked through it. There was only tea, there was nothing else in it. They conferred among themselves and then handed it back to him.

Thus it was that Teacher Wei took that can of tea with him to a lonely, dreary corner of the countryside.

That evening, by the light of a single lantern in the chill night when all around him the world was hushed, he felt enveloped in a desolation more terrible than what he had known in prison. In prison you could at least hear the harsh voice and heavy footfall of the jailer. He began considering ways to die. Then he remembered the young woman's gift of tea. He had never been a tea-drinker, but out of respect for her intense emotion he felt he had to sample it. When he opened the can, a sublime fragrance wafted out into the air. It was a heavenly blend of the aromas of tea and flowers and a woman's heart. He breathed deep to take them all in, holding nothing back, propelled into a kind of intoxication. In that moment, he said, he quit thinking about ways to "cut himself off."

As for the can of loose leaf tea, he never drank it. In the bleakest hours he would open it and take a sniff. Years later when they brought him back to the city as a geography teacher in an ordinary high school, he still had never touched a single leaf of that tea, but it had gradually lost its ineffable aroma. On the can was printed:

Exquisite . . .
PREMIUM JASMINE
The Chamber of Enchantment

"So later," he explained, "I looked up the Chamber of Enchantment and started going there to buy Premium Jasmine, which I kept in my room. The aroma made me feel I was with her. I never drink it. When did you fellows ever see me drink tea?"

Damo and Maozi were curious about the woman and asked if there was any more to the story.

"She heard when I got back," Teacher Wei answered, "and came to see me. At this point she had been labeled a Rightist and was working in a neighborhood garment factory.[93] She said, 'Before I was labeled a Rightist I had thought if I waited for you to come back I might live with you. But now, we'll just have to leave things as they are.' I understood her meaning and answered, 'I have already lived with you. It was only the scent of you that let me fall asleep each night.' I brought out the can of tea and showed it to her, still full, just a little faded. She wept. 'That's nice,' she said, 'Real nice. It makes me happy.'"

Teacher Wei said that after that, she never came to see him again. He looked for her but didn't know where she was living and never found her.

One evening at the start of the Cultural Revolution—the very day he was forced to march in that parade—he overheard the Arts & Letters Militants[94] guarding him say that the drama group had a pretty woman Rightist, a painter, who had defied them when they tried to cut off her hair. She had rushed into the street and been hit by a truck . . . gravely wounded . . . was in the E.R. at the hospital. Instinctively, he knew it was she. When night fell, the Red Guards brought him home and left after one more tongue-lashing. Exhausted and distraught, unable to eat or drink, he found the hospital and said he was a member of a wounded person's family. "Oh, that one's in the morgue," they said. Teacher Wei found his way to the morgue, where several corpses had been dumped casually on the floor. She was among them. Her body had been covered with a few sheets of newspaper, from under which a single long strand of hair, crow-black, reached out as if floating on air, as if she were flaunting it, *This is my hair, I didn't let you cut it off.* Gently he lifted a corner of the paper. Her face was changed: the side turned to the ground had been wrecked, but the other half of her face was bizarrely smiling, *See, I didn't let them cut off my hair.*

Teacher Wei said that when he got home that night he put the can of tea in his leather suitcase and never bought any more Premium Jasmine.

Thereafter whenever Damo was in town he often visited Teacher Wei. Neither of them could have guessed that this rather frail man, blasted by life's storms, would survive into the next century where, in advanced age, he would become a forceful and creative warrior in the world of ideas. It often occurred to Damo that Teacher Wei's penchant for outrageous unconventionality was a sign of inconsolable pain, and once indeed he saw him hang a couplet in his humble room:

> *Walking beside the stream, I recite 'Asking Heaven';*
> *Lifting up mine eyes, I sing the Song of Guangling.*[95]

It bore the title *'This Wei' congratulates himself on his fiftieth birthday.*

Damo studied it for a long time in silence, for it made him realize sadly that Teacher Wei's experience was that of a long-serving honest official, like Master Qu, who had been forced to rethink his position and ultimately had made a clean break, even though that might mean he would someday like Ji Kang go cheerfully to his death. Forcing a smile, he joked, "Teacher Wei, if they see this they're going to send you to Hell." Teacher Wei matched his smile: "I'm already in Hell. We are all in Hell."

Each time he went away to the countryside, Damo had a premonition and wondered whether he'd be able to see his friend the next time he returned. But the way of this world is ever-turning; once the mid-seventies were past, those people didn't worry about Wei any more. He told the group that visited him, "They've got their own problems . . . what's the world coming to?"

Later Damo often asked himself how it came to be that a man who had grown up under the mighty apparatus of the State with its omnipresent propaganda, who had been personally upright and from a blameless family, had had his life so easily ruined by a malefactor who hid in seclusion like a rat in its lair. This question, when later he raised it more formally on the Internet, would stir fierce controversy.

14

That evening, Ru Yan heeded the suggestion of Spring River Flows and searched Google and Baidu for "Damo." When she entered "Damo" and pressed the Return key, Good Heavens! There were about forty thousand citations. On closer inspection, many of them had nothing to do with Damo but were about Bodhidharma: "Shaolin Damo," "monk's staff of Damo," "Damo founder of Zen" . . . Ru Yan didn't know what she had done wrong, so she sent a QQ message to Spring River Flows. He replied, "You've got to add some related terms after 'Damo,' like 'Cultural Revolution,' 'educated youth,' 'political thought,' 'Yugoslavia,' '9/11,' so as to do a more specific search." Ru Yan followed this prescription and got back the Damo who wrote articles on these subjects, page after page of listings. The earliest items were four or five years old. Back then, the Internet in China had been no more than a few rivulets in the desert.

Most of Damo's articles were about social philosophy, arts and letters, political debate, and current events, but there were also a few literary works and informal essays. His style was laconic and understated, but taut and clean, and it breathed the aloofness of one who enjoyed a transcendent vantage point. All the same, you could feel an intense emotion at the core of his rational disquisitions. Ru Yan wasn't very fond of analytical writing but in these articles of Damo's the reasoning was wrapped in a poetry that covered the hardness within. She located and read a few more of his articles; those she didn't have time to read, she saved. Gradually she accumulated a compendium of his works.

She found herself wondering what kind of man this Damo could be. Forthright, yet often leaving things unsaid; rich in ideas, but lean in expression: he must be an extraordinary man, broad-minded, temperate, and classy.

In writing courses during her first two years in college, she had written essays on assigned topics. She had never written anything on her own after that. She only read. She was very particular in her tastes, but never assessed her own writing; just as, when she was growing up, she never took stock of her own figure and looks until when she had matured she heard people praising her to her mother. They'd say, "My oh my, your Ru Yan just keeps getting prettier! So gentle and refined and intelligent! I wonder what family's going be so lucky. . ." This insinuating talk made her realize that a person's beauty was connected with other things and had consequences. It pleased her, but it was also vaguely disquieting. (In that era, girls knew remarkably little about relations between the sexes.) What was happening now, the praise showered on those articles she had written, was similarly unexpected. She felt that in much the same way as her good looks had grown, unguessed and unannounced, even so the excellence of her writing had appeared on its own, naturally. Now she was hearing people praise her writing, just as once she had heard them say she was beautiful; now, as then, the experience made her happy. But she was always quick to reply with thanks in a self-deprecating tone. And her Net friends would follow up saying how eagerly they looked forward to Ru Yan's next article.

So now that she had started, she couldn't stop. She wrote many pieces about her son, about his birth and schooling, about the times he was naughty, about him and his dog, about his college entrance exam, and about how, later, he had left home. It was an insane burst of creativity such as she had never known before. The ideas came as soon as she began to write.

Thus began Ru Yan's honeymoon with the online community of the Empty Nest. To a great extent it made up for the loneliness she felt after her son left the country.

A few other websites, especially those catering to the middle-aged, began to run articles by someone named Such Is This World. Some of these pieces were re-posted multiple times on different sites, so that the Empty Nest gained wider influence, especially since many of the repostings contained links back to the Empty Nest. In response, the Empty Nest provided fraternal links to the other sites. In a short while, Ru Yan had become a heavy hitter at the forum. Every night when she came home and turned on her computer, there was always a pile of messages in her mailbox and awaiting her on QQ. The empty nest of her real life was quickly filled.

15

At her work unit, what that gang of women had said turned out not to be a joke. A scheme must have been in the works for some time, awaiting only her son's departure to be put into action.

One day, not long after she reached the office, Xiao Li came into her lab and beckoned with a mysterious smile, "Ru Yan my dear, come this way."

Ru Yan thought it was probably something about typing or connecting to the Internet. Lately (it was around National Day[96]) there had been a flurry of documents to handle and Ru Yan had given Xiao Li a lot of help. Xiao Li had even expressed her thanks with a gift of expensive skin creams.

When she reached the Resource Room, Jiang Xiaoli was already there, sitting in a side office. Jiang Xiaoli was the Chief Administrator. She and Ru Yan had started at the Institute around the same time, almost twenty years before. One had transferred from the military, while the other had come straight from college; one worked in administration, while the other had stayed in her scientific field. Although they were not close, they knew each other quite well and in fact their fathers had been acquainted.

The inner room where Jiang Xiaoli was seated served as an archive for scientific records, and ordinarily no one was allowed in it. After Xiao Li led Ru Yan in, she quietly withdrew, closing the door on her way out. A tray of bananas and a bowl of pistachios had been neatly set out on a small coffee table. Upon seeing that Ru Yan had come in, Jiang Xiaoli went straight to the point: "Today I am acting as your matchmaker."

"You can't be serious."

"Why shouldn't I be serious? You think we're all going to sit back and watch a charming, beautiful woman get older and lonelier by the day?"

Caught off guard, Ru Yan didn't know what to say.

Jiang Xiaoli studied her and smiled. "Look at yourself. Just look at yourself! You're not a teenager anymore, yet you blush to discuss this? You're like someone from the old society.[97]"

Ru Yan tried to cover her embarrassment with a laugh. "Have your say. I'm listening."

Jiang Xiaoli began. "A certain person has asked me to help him find a true love."

Ru Yan emitted a groan.

Jiang Xiaoli continued. "This person has laid down guidelines which are somewhat idiosyncratic. Old maids: no, thanks.

Young unmarried girls: no, thanks. It's a question of temperament: the former are quirky, the latter are bratty. Old maids have lived alone so long they're inflexible in many ways. With a young one there would be too wide a gap, wouldn't work out. Divorcées: no, thanks. Doesn't want a childless widow either, or one with a young kid still in school. High educational level: no, thanks: doctorates, post-doc, forget about it. But educational level too low, doesn't want that either. Best is a B.A. or a vocational degree, something like that, but—"

Ru Yan burst out laughing. "What planet did you find this man on? All he can say is 'No, thanks!'"

"He's a little cocky," Jiang Xiaoli conceded, "but he's got reason to be. Divorce, well, there's always some fault on both sides. Childless, well, that always gives a woman a sense of incompleteness, and if she decides she wants a kid late in the game . . . big headache. A young child in the picture, her affections will be divided."

Ru Yan sighed, "If he wants to be particular, that's his prerogative. But has he thought about whether anyone wants *him*?"

"A fair question for an ordinary man. But not for him. You have no idea how many would like to have him, from cute twenty-somethings to beautiful professionals in their forties and fifties. They all want him."

"Let me guess," Ru Yan said. "It's Vladimir Putin." (She had heard a song online, 'The ladies all want to marry a man like Putin,' and had read that the women of Russia, both old and young, were head-over-heels in love with Putin.[98])

Jiang Xiaoli laughed. "I'll give you a hint: as far as our city is concerned, you could say that he *is* a Putin."

"Who?"

Jiang Xiaoli advised, "For now, don't ask. Let me give you some information. First, he's a leader at the municipal level, graduate of an elite university; handsome, tall, and well-spoken. He knows the arts, loves to read, and has a disciplined lifestyle. Few men of his class have gone so many years without a sex scandal. His wife died a couple years ago, after an illness. Two years for a man like that can't have been easy. For others there would have been a new woman in the house the next month. His age is about right for you. As for housing, finances, etc., I don't need to go into that: I'm sure it wouldn't make any difference to you."

Jiang Xiaoli stopped at this point, like someone proffering a rare and precious gift with both hands, waiting for Ru Yan's eyes to light up.

Ru Yan gave the same thin smile as before, peeled a banana, and observed, "This kind of man, what they call a gem of a bachelor . . . who's going to aim so high?"

Jiang Xiaoli had not anticipated Ru Yan's indifference, and she wondered *Is this how you play hard-to-get?* But she did not want to show herself so quickly disconcerted, and grinned suggestively. "What if someone is aiming high at you?"

Ru Yan scoffed. "This person is *way up there*, how's he going to know about a little woman named Ru Yan?"

"To tell you the truth, one could almost say he knows you like the back of his hand."

"You must be wildly exaggerating."

"He has seen you," Jiang Xiaoli said. "I'll tell you something else. He has read your articles on the Internet."

At these words, Ru Yan felt a chill run the length of her spine. "Have you been getting information from State Security?"

"I'm telling you," Jiang Xiaoli answered, "this is no joke, it's for real. The gentleman is quite serious. It's uncommon for men of today to act this way. It's been going on for half a year."

"You've been discussing behind my back how to sell me?"

"To this kind of man . . ." Jiang Xiaoli answered, "I wish I could sell myself. You ought to know this: there are women Ph.D.s, women officials, women millionaires, actresses, who would all fling themselves, in a heartbeat, sobbing into his arms. One person even said that if anybody could set her up with him, she'd express her thanks with a snappy new Buick."

"This makes me even less inclined to step into the limelight. Once I got there, wouldn't all those women rip me to pieces? Besides, how am I going to come up with a snappy new Buick? And hey, if he turns out to be a corrupt official and gets tossed in the slammer, I'll spend years bringing him food in jail."

Jiang Xiaoli was beginning to look annoyed. "I don't get it. Ordinarily you're a reasonable person. What's got into you today? You must stop this and take a proper stand. I'm telling you, he's the last man on earth . . . if *he's* corrupt, they'll *all* have to be executed."

Ru Yan realized that she was acting a little odd today. From the very beginning of this conversation she had felt somewhat at sea. After her husband's death, Ru Yan had thought that the second half of her life would illustrate the proverb about the three great misfortunes that can befall a woman, one of which is to mourn in midlife for her mate. And she had always been a pessimist, so much so that she didn't even want to think about this. All in all, in the limited circle of men with whom she had any contact—married or not—none had ever moved her heart. Looking even farther afield to include singers, movie stars, athletes, celebrities, scholars, and magnates, there had never been one whom she considered a lover to dream about. She suspected she was simply a person of cool passions and emotions, somewhat otherworldly. It's true that when she read tear-jerking novels or watched stormy disks[99], she was moved with romantic feelings and often couldn't contain herself. Maybe it was as her husband had said: literature had ruined her. What Jiang Xiaoli had revealed today was not something Ru Yan took lightly, but it was only an introduction conveyed by a third party and could not stir the same feelings as a flesh-and-blood encounter.

Somewhat chastened, Ru Yan said, "You gave me strong medicine; I haven't had time to digest it. You all have been operating in secret and now you've put me on the spot, though I still can't see what's going on. What do you expect me to say?"

"On Sunday," Jiang Xiaoli said, "a Russian troupe will perform at the city's new Ballet Theater. You are invited to accompany him to the performance."

Ordinarily Ru Yan would have leapt at the chance to see a Russian ballet troupe, but the thought of going with such a prominent person and being exposed to public scrutiny made her queasy. "For the first meeting, that would be so public. . . If I didn't measure up, wouldn't it set tongues wagging?"

Jiang Xiaoli saw that Ru Yan was finally being serious. "If he's not worried, why should you be? You're both unattached, it's not like this is an illicit affair!"

But Ru Yan persisted timidly, "Yes, but for the first meeting, something quieter would be better, otherwise . . . I might make a fool of myself."

Jiang Xiaoli pondered. "Let's do it like this. The first time, I'll invite you both for a visit at my house; it's no big deal, I happen to know you both. OK?"

Ru Yan still felt uneasy, but it wouldn't do to withdraw her suggestion now. "I leave it up to you. But when we're at your place, you've got to stay with us the whole time!"

Jiang Xiaoli snorted. "We're all going to be at my place, how could I not stay with you? You think I'm going to slip you the key and steal away? Do I look like a pimp? My dear Ru Yan, you've been quite unreasonable today; is it just insecurity? What you've heard should have made you ecstatic. You're not usually like this."

Seeing that Ru Yan was at last turning compliant, Jiang Xiaoli was giving free rein to the irritation she had held in check until now. Throughout the work unit she was famous for her sharp tongue. The rebuke made Ru Yan even more uncomfortable; she herself didn't know what was wrong with her today. Did she really want what was being offered her, but was afraid to face it squarely? Or did she not want it in her heart, and was only intrigued by this man's superficial attractions? Feebly she said, "I didn't expect I'd ever have to think about this again. I had no idea you people would bring this up . . ." The tears burst forth, making her feel foolish and good-for-nothing.

Jiang Xiaoli recovered her customary off-hand manner. "You're a piece of work. If you found a silver coin on the sidewalk, you wouldn't pick it up? I'm telling you, some people have all the luck; they dream in color, and even the roaches in their house have double eyelids.[100]"

16

Ru Yan's home was a little more than ten minutes' drive from her workplace. When her son had lived in the house she would rush home each midday to fix him a good meal. When she began living alone, she often ate lunch in the cafeteria and would then repair to the Resource Room to do some reading or take a nap or otherwise pass the time for a couple of hours. Now that she had the dog it was as if she had a small child again: when work let out, she had to hurry home.

Yang Yanping was a Pekingese, though by no means a purebred. Her fur was a light brown, while the ears, forehead, and tail were a darker brown; when washed, she had a charm and beauty which pure-white Pekes don't have. As a breed, the Pekingese is a very feminine dog with big, bedroom eyes that are moist with a lovely sadness; add in that fine coat of fur and it was no wonder her son had found the creature irresistible and had taken it in.

But during its sojourn in the dormitory Yang Yanping had acquired some bad habits, such as using any accessible place as a toilet. Ru Yan was by nature fastidious. Even her baby's poop had made her gorge rise, never mind dog excrement. Fortunately his father didn't mind and took care of those things when he was around. She got used to these things slowly, over time. Then her son grew older and her fastidiousness returned. In the first few years that he had a dog, what he feared most was that she would get rid of it if it couldn't stay housebroken. When he came home from school his first item of business—more pressing than homework or TV—was to take the dog out for a walk, three times a day. It developed his sense of responsibility and his will-power, so Ru Yan found that owning a dog had unexpected advantages. Now that her son wasn't around, this chore fell to her. Her feelings for the puppy were complicated. It was as if she had gone back to when she first started raising her son. When she watched this little creature jump up and down, without a care in the world yet dependent on her for everything, it always inspired a tender affection. At times she felt that she had taken over her son's role and must fulfill the responsibility he had entrusted to her. When he came back some day, she would show him: "Look, you gave us a mission, and we never faltered."

At her son's college the dog's diet had been a mess. Leftovers, steamed buns, sausages, pickled eggs, fruit and sweets: it ate anything available. Ru Yan herself favored a bland and simple diet, so she had few such things to give it and began buying dog food, which at first it spurned but later would eat nothing else. Consequently she had to go shopping for it at the supermarket. Yang Yanping's pooping and peeing then became more regular. Until Ru Yan came home, the creature would hold it in heroically with an expression that seemed to say, "When you don't come back, I just have to hold it; are you sorry?" So now Ru Yan raced home just as her son had used to do, and the first item of business was to take the dog downstairs, after which it would dash under the hedge to the soil of the flowerbed. There, with rump pinched tight, it would pee for a long, long time before rambling around as it deliberated, until, circling faster, it picked the spot and—not caring whether anyone was standing there watching—began to poop with its tail held high, its rear end in mid-air, the rest of its body hunched tight, and a very curious expression on its face. When it finished, Ru Yan would always lean over the hedge to inspect: was it dry or watery? Were there worms? Anyway, this little dog had a transforming effect on Ru Yan. The obsession with cleanliness which her husband had found neurotic was largely cured.

Though Ru Yan had never really noticed, there were quite a few families in her housing development that had dogs. When out walking her own, she'd often run into a couple of animals, even four or five of them, white or black or patchwork-colored—there were all kinds. At a first encounter the dogs, just like humans, would check each other out appraisingly. Some would cower, some would be blasé; some would turn aggressive and leap at each other barking and snapping. Others would have no guts at all and when they glimpsed another dog their tail would get tucked under their belly. For the first time, Ru Yan understood why the song says, "Imperialism runs away with its tail between its legs."[101]

But these dogs were all pets, so most of them were gentle. On repeated encounters they would reveal a yearning for friendship, rather like today's kids who are kept cooped up inside: after sniffing each other, they would start wagging their tails and chasing each other with good-natured rowdiness, and their movements would become agile and exaggerated, like lovers in the movies who pursue each other with overwrought passion. Naturally, between dog and dog there was favoritism. Yang Yanping, for instance, showed a marked affection for certain dogs but would give others the cold shoulder. She was especially smitten with a white curly-haired beagle[102] and when she caught sight of him from afar she would pull her leash as taut as a tug-of-war, snorting uncontainably, and the white curly-haired beagle would strain against *his* leash and make it clear that Yang Yanping's ardor was not unrequited. If the dogs didn't get enough of each other, their owners would have to haul them away to their homes as if dragging sacks of garbage. When the animals began frolicking with each other, though, the owners had little choice but to strike up a conversation, initially about the dogs, but after a few encounters the talk would turn to other things. The weather. Where they lived. The cost of living. Local crimes. National news and neighborhood gossip. These small animals, so frank and unaffected, supplied a motive for conversation to many of the residents who otherwise would have passed each other by without the slightest acknowledgment.

One day when Yang Yanping caught sight of the white frizzy beagle and the two had inspected and sniffed each other at both ends, Yang Yanping began leaping up and down and then climbed on the beagle's back without a by-your-leave. Once there she began making odd rhythmic motions, which Ru Yan instinctively sensed were indecent. Reddening, she scolded her dog, quickly attached the leash, and yanked her away. The beagle's owner was a young married woman about thirty years old, and she laughed, "That girl of yours is going to lead our innocent little boy astray; he doesn't know the ways of the world." This embarrassed Ru Yan even more, and she quickly answered that hers was just a little dog too, and picked up Yang Yanping in her arms. On seeing her take hold of his girlfriend, the beagle erupted into angry yapping. The other woman tightened the leash and stepped in front of Ru Yan to take a close look and pointed out some bloodstained fur on the dog's backside. "Your dog's in heat, see? She's having her period." Ru Yan stammered, "Dogs get periods too?" and the woman laughed, "How could they not? They're like people, you know."

"Good heavens," Ru Yan cried, "She's so little!"

"This kind of small breed is mature by seven or eight months," the woman said. "We had a dog that was a mama at ten months." As they spoke, Yang Yanping squirmed and whined in Ru Yan's arms, eager to jump down to where her diminutive sweetheart stood. Her eyes glowed with longing. "Unh-uh, no way," Ru Yan said. "I can't handle even one; if she presents me with a litter, I'm sunk." And with that she carried the crazy lover home.

Once home, Yang Yanping would neither eat nor drink but ran to the door and stood there whimpering. "You're still young," Ru Yan said, "I can't let you do whatever you want." Yang Yanping ignored the sermon and just looked up at the door, and then looked up at her. It was exasperating and touching.

For days afterward, before walking the dog Ru Yan would check whether that bewitched beagle was outside. Once she heard barking downstairs and glanced out the window to see that the beagle had somehow got away by itself and was sitting at the front door of her building, howling. When later she ran into that young married woman, her neighbor gave her a strained smile: "That girl of yours will be the death of me. Our little guy has been carrying on for more than a week; he almost ran away."

Yang Yanping also carried on for about a week, by turns fidgety or depressed, and looked as though she'd lost weight; she was light as a feather in your hand. Fortunately, canine love-affairs have a fixed term. When it was over, it was over, as if nothing had happened. Not like with human beings.

Chatting with her son one day on MSN, she mentioned, "Yang Yanping wants to fall in love."

"So soon?" her son said. "*I* haven't even done that yet."

"Those who should fall in love, don't; and those who shouldn't, do."

But her son answered, "Why the should and shouldn't? Let it happen naturally."

Within two weeks of going to France her son had settled in. He was renting an apartment with two other young men and they had installed a phone and an internet connection. They took turns with the cooking and the laundry. It was a furnished apartment and had come with a washing machine, an electric stove, and kitchen utensils. Each man used his own computer. Her son had taken a laptop with him, one he'd bought second-hand with his earnings in college, and every two or three days he'd send Ru Yan a QQ message or an e-mail. Occasionally they'd turn on the video with MSN and exchange a few words.

When classes started, his schoolwork became pressing. Moreover, he had applied for a part-time job and was helping clean the library every night. (The college used these jobs to assist students in straitened circumstances. When her son filled out the form and mentioned that his father was deceased, his application was quickly approved.) So Ru Yan didn't have the heart to take up his time, and now she often found herself using the expression he had used for so long: "It's late, Son, you'd better turn in and get some rest." Her son would always laugh. "Mom, I haven't had dinner yet." She could never remember the time difference. So they stopped using QQ and MSN. But the paragraphs that went back and forth from time to time reassured her that she had not lost contact.

The Empty Nest remained a place where Ru Yan spent much time each day. The moderator, Lonely Goose, had set up an anthology of Ru Yan's articles and called it "The Past which is Like

Smoke."[103] Lonely Goose had re-done the layout and added pictures and music clips to make a beautiful ebook. It gave Ru Yan a tremendous sense of achievement to re-read her own works and discover, with a little vanity, that she did have literary talent after all. Some of her Net friends said, *Ru Yan, if you keep writing like this, those famous authors won't be able to compete with you!* Others said, *Keep writing! This is a great book.* It was exciting to have come suddenly into the spotlight. She fell in love with writing as a young girl would fall in love. Having spent so many years becoming familiar with the written word, she was now using it to give shape to the decades she had lived, and there was something intoxicating about that. The number of websites carrying her articles grew steadily, and some invited her to write more for them. So when she posted an article to the Empty Nest, she often cross-posted it to several related sites.

17

Jiang Xiaoli phoned her on Saturday morning. "I hope you haven't forgotten what we arranged for tonight?"

How could she have forgotten? She had been nervous and ill-at-ease about this matter ever since. She couldn't quite say what it was she was feeling. Anticipation? Elation? Fear? Ambivalence? She just felt it was one more thing to worry about and wished it weren't happening.

Jiang Xiaoli was telling her what to do. "Go to Forest Beauty for an aromatherapy treatment and then to Exuberance to get your hair done. Comb it yourself when you get up from the couch, it looks more natural. Pick something to wear that's poised, tasteful, of good material and pretty new but not brand new—"

Ru Yan broke in, "Um, what exactly are you talking about? Give me a hint."

Jiang Xiaoli realized that Ru Yan didn't know what aromatherapy was, or what a permanent was, and didn't even know that Forest Beauty and Exuberance were the names, respectively, of a tony salon and a hairstylist's shop. "What kind of a woman are you?" she cried, and then explained it all step-by-step.

Hearing this made Ru Yan even more agitated. "Didn't you say he'd already seen me without my knowledge? I don't want to scare him away by suddenly changing into a fox fairy[104]!"

"That was from a distance," Jiang Xiaoli said, "he couldn't see the little lines in your face. This will be up close. . . OK, what you do or don't do is up to you, but when I come to pick you up I'll look you over and if you pass, we go."

"At this critical moment," Ru Yan said, "Don't you think you should tell me who he is?"

"When you meet him you'll recognize him. Play the part of a bride in the old society, where they lifted the crimson veil just before they entered the bridal chamber. You think I'm going to stick you with a blind man? A cripple? A guy whose face is all pockmarked?"

At dusk, Ru Yan heard the downstairs bell ring and saw from the window that Jiang Xiaoli had come by car. As soon as she breezed in, she took off all the clothing Ru Yan had on and started flipping through everything in her wardrobe, passing her dresses and skirts and pants to try on. She kept trying things on until they were both too muddled to tell what was good or bad. "I didn't realize you had so little," Jiang Xiaoli said; "If I had known earlier, I would have taken you to Metropolis this afternoon to buy a suit."

Ru Yan muttered, "It's not like you haven't seen me before. How many years have I got by with these few outfits! Oh, forget it. I'll wear the same clothes I usually wear, otherwise I'd make a fool of myself."

Jiang Xiaoli's parents lived in the municipal compound, like the man she was to meet. After they cleared the guardhouse and drove onto the grounds, they passed a long line of tall trees in whose shade brownstones were scattered. As they went by one town home, Jiang Xiaoli said "That's his house. If you get married we'll be neighbors."

The Jiang residence was the same kind of town home with units side-by-side. Each unit was two and a half stories, for the top story was smaller in order to make room for a rooftop garden. These were two-family houses: that was the standard enjoyed by deputy mayors and above, and that was the rank at which Jiang Xiaoli's father had retired. At present the old couple had gone South to visit their son's family, so there was only a young maid at home and it was very quiet.

Jiang Xiaoli had Ru Yan sit down in the parlor and brought her tea and fruit. Then she stepped quickly into her own room and emerged in an elegant, soft, and close-fitting silk dress. It was a light tan, with a bit of simple embroidery in front. And in just those brief moments she had also managed to apply some alluring makeup. Ru Yan did a double-take. "Jiang Xiaoli, this evening it is you who must be the leading lady."

Embarrassment flickered in Jiang Xiaoli's eyes, quickly concealed with a laugh and a jest: "You mean you're the only one who's allowed to be pretty? I guess I'm supposed to make you look good. I'll go change right now."

"Don't you even say 'thanks' when someone compliments you on your looks?" Ru Yan shot back.

"Hey, aren't I doing this for you, to act as your bridesmaid? Because this night means so much for you, I canceled an important meeting."

Jiang Xiaoli was two or three years younger than Ru Yan, but the tone with which she always spoke to her was that of an older sister. When she sat down, Ru Yan noticed what she had on her feet: sandals with narrow velvet straps across the instep, revealing the five smooth, roseate, and perfectly proportioned toes on each foot, which thereby gained several degrees of loveliness. Only a very confident person would choose such simple footwear. Without thinking too hard about it, Ru Yan had always considered a person's hands and feet important. At times she thought that these two parts of the body mattered more than a person's face. This was probably the influence of her mother, who had come from a privileged family. As a child she had often heard her mother appraise someone's hands and feet: *She has such pretty hands* or *I'll grant you that one is pretty, but the feet leave a lot to be desired. With such feet it would have been better not to wear those shoes. More's the pity! If the feet aren't right, you can't be perfect.* At the time, she had been surprised and wondered how her mother could see people's feet through their shoes. Her mother often maintained that to gauge a person's upbringing it was enough to examine the hands and feet. *Faces can lie, but hands and feet never lie.* Such remarks made her sound like a wandering fortune-teller, but she was often proved right. There was one time when a haggard woman, coarsely dressed, had come to their house looking for Ru Yan's father; they said she was a menial employee at his work unit come to recount some incident to the leader. On these occasions Ru Yan's mother would usually tell the person to go to the office. But that day she had this humble worker sit down at the house to wait, and poured her a cup of tea.

Later, Ru Yan's father said, "Don't look down on that one. She was at the top of her class in Western Languages at Catholic University.[105] Her father was the KMT's banker and fled to Taiwan." Ru Yan's mother made it clear this came as no surprise to *her*. "As soon as she walked in the door I could see it. A humble worker, right! Where did she get those hands? Worn a little rough, maybe, but you couldn't miss the fine shape of them. And when I looked at her feet, it made no difference that she was wearing cheap cloth shoes, her feet were beautiful."

Her mother liked to say that from a woman's hands and feet you could tell her past and her future. Her father scoffed, "You with your hands and your feet! A petty capitalist, you've never changed your tune! If I hadn't married you, you'd have been cut down to size long ago." She riposted, "You don't live the way you talk, you hypocrite!" When her father noticed the young Ru Yan watching, he grinned sheepishly and offered no rebuttal. When she grew up, Ru Yan gradually came to understand her mother's innuendo and her father's embarrassed smile. She came to value her own hands and feet, knowing that men would value them.

Jiang Xiaoli was a strong, buxom woman, quite attractive, with chiseled features but very feminine—type-cast to be a female official. It was surprising that she had such gentle and graceful feet: at the first glimpse, Ru Yan blurted "Xiaoli, your feet are really lovely, and in those shoes they're stunning."

With feigned bafflement Jiang Xiaoli answered, "You mean it? Wow, praise from Ru Yan is praise indeed!" She looked down and studied her feet for a bit. "I look like my Dad, but my hands and feet are like my Mom's. People say that's practically a guarantee of great good fortune. Not for me; I sure never had much luck."

Ru Yan inquired about Jiang Xiaoli's mother.

"If you went back fifty years," she answered, "and asked around in the city of Rongcheng, Shandong, you wouldn't find anybody who didn't know the second daughter of the Sun family. I'll show you some pictures of her when she was young. There weren't many Shanghai starlets who outclassed her."

It figures, Ru Yan thought. But she still marveled that her mother's superstitious way of thinking had been proved right again.

As they were speaking, the downstairs doorbell rang.

Jiang Xiaoli gave a sly smile. "He came right on time. I like men who are on time."

She went downstairs to let him in. Ru Yan could hear her saying, a bit too loudly and emphatically, "Well! Such a rare treat! You're so busy, what wind has blown you here?"

Ru Yan strained to catch the visitor's reply to Jiang Xiaoli's clumsy line. What she heard was in a natural, easy voice: "And the lady? The person to whom I have come to pay my respects?"

Seeing that he was not interested in joking around with her, Jiang Xiaoli answered, "She got here a long time ago. If your Lordship would come upstairs—"

Ru Yan stood up and went to the doorway of the parlor. A man of medium height appeared, casually dressed in slacks and a tan sweater. At first glance you could not tell his age. His walk was quite vigorous; he stood straight and trim. This was noteworthy, because for some reason today's officials all have water-bucket waists and are even stouter than foreign heads of state. On their way over, Ru Yan had pressed Jiang Xiaoli to tell her how old this man was. "One cycle[106] older than you. When a woman reaches our age, to get a man only twelve years older is a good deal." Ru Yan calculated that he must be fifty-six or fifty-seven, and had prepared herself to meet a youngish old man. If that's what he is, she thought, then that's what he is; nowadays even really old men dare to marry young girls. Anyway, Ru Yan wasn't taking this meeting too seriously.

He walked up to her and put out his hand. "Ru Yan?"

"Yes," she said.

"Jiang Xiaoli has talked a lot about you."

Ru Yan remarked drily, "I understand you have not relied solely on hearsay."

He burst into peals of laughter, finally gasping, "Oh, Jiang Xiaoli, you're a double-agent! I'll have to open a direct line to Ru Yan and go underground.[107]"

"I don't like the sound of that," Jiang Xiaoli objected. "Double-agents always come to a bad end. Go ahead and go underground, I can't wait. You can make yourselves a nice burrow this evening."

Jiang Xiaoli was like that, sharp-tongued: she could shut people up with a one-liner.

But he only laughed, "Jiang Xiaoli, the way you talk! They ought to make you press secretary for the city government. You could handle any problem."

The three sat down. Ru Yan's first impression of the man had not been bad. He was frank and poised, and he had a sense of humor.

"Actually, we *should* keep your meeting a secret and I haven't blabbed at all," Jiang Xiaoli said. "On the way here, Ru Yan was still asking me who you were. I told her, 'Just go and you'll know him.'"

She turned to Ru Yan. "Now you see the true face of Mt. Lu[108], don't you?"

Ru Yan stared at him awkwardly, perplexed.

Jiang Xiaoli was astonished. "You mean you don't recognize him? Isn't he familiar from TV?"

"I don't watch TV much," Ru Yan said with embarrassment,

"and the local channels hardly at all."

She took a closer look. He stood upright and seemed in good repair, his hair basically still black except for a few strands of white at the temples, which proved it wasn't dyed. Maybe it was the fact that he was not wearing one of those dark formal suits, but was in a private setting and had an animated face and a genuine laugh, which made him look different from those rigidly smiling 'friends of the people.' But she had no recollection of him. Ru Yan didn't know much about officialdom, couldn't even have named all the top figures in the Central Government. When her husband was alive he had cared a lot about affairs of state and was fascinated by reports of conferences, public notices, lists of names and rankings. Ru Yan would look over his shoulder and ask who it was about. He'd guffaw and say she could spend a few days with the Chairman and not recognize him. He could rattle off names, positions, assignments within the Party, where someone had been promoted from. Ru Yan would listen to all this but she still wouldn't recognize anyone.

The gentleman said, "Well, look at that. I must have overrated myself; I clearly need more exposure." Again he put out his hand: "Liang Jinsheng."

Jiang Xiaoli shrieked. "Unbelievable! In real life, a person from the Peach-Blossom Spring![109] She doesn't recognize the renowned deputy mayor! Our research sector is under his oversight, you know."

"The name rings a bell," Ru Yan said. "I must have seen it in the paper."

"That's right," he said impishly. "Intellectuals don't watch TV, they only read books and papers. TV is for the uncultured."

"Who says I'm an intellectual?" Ru Yan said. "I just muddle along in my little job."

"At my slightly more advanced age," Liang Jinsheng reflected, "I am credited with muddling along in a big job. Not much difference. I've got a few years to retirement, and then there will be no difference at all."

So it was that this arranged meeting, which Ru Yan had supposed would be quite awkward, started off on a humorous note.

Liang Jinsheng's portfolio consisted of Science, Education, and Public Health. Ru Yan's institute fell under the rubric of "Science," children's schooling constituted "Education," and the medical needs that come with middle age were part of "Public Health." The topics of conversation flowed along, each connected to the next, and the conversation never faltered. Concerning Ru Yan's field of botany, Liang Jinsheng said this was a very suitable field for women to specialize in, because women themselves have the nature of plants.

Jiang Xiaoli said provocatively, "That explains why, when we're talking about men, we say they touch the flowers and vex the grass[110], and when we're talking about women we say they summon the bees and attract butterflies.[111]"

Liang Jinsheng demurred. "How is it that, no matter how serious the topic, once you start in, it goes off the rails? What I mean is, in primitive times the women gathered vegetables while the men hunted. We study according to our nature. Plants are gentle and quiet; animals are violent; the plants get eaten by animals—"

"You're going to scare Ru Yan with this kind of talk," Jiang Xiaoli broke in, "for fear she'll get eaten by you someday."

"I'll tell you something, Xiaoli," he said, "in this world of today, who will get eaten by whom is hard to predict."

On the subject of education they talked about their own children. When he heard which university Ru Yan's son had graduated from, Liang Jinsheng was pleased. "What a coincidence! Then the two of us are alumni of the same school. Only in those years I wasn't much of a student. I had no sooner enrolled than I had to go to the countryside for the Four Cleanups[112], and when I got back, then it was the Cultural Revolution, so I never had a chance to really learn anything in my field. I learned by heart a lot of quotations from Chairman Mao, and to this day they're likely to come out whenever I open my mouth. Maybe I should be considered just a high-school graduate; I certainly can't be compared with your young fellow. He's gone abroad for grad school now, and when he comes home I won't be able to hold a candle to him."

Jiang Xiaoli then started a contest with him to see who could recite, or better still, sing, the most quotations from Mao, complete with the gestures that went with the songs. They all rocked with laughter.

When it came to public health, Jiang Xiaoli and Ru Yan fired a volley of complaints. The hospitals were corrupt; medicines cost too much; even getting to see a doctor was an ordeal. Liang Jinsheng could only smile as he heard the two women—one gentle and mild, the other fierce and hard—cite one example after another of how services were being delivered under his authority. In the end he said he would invite them both to the next meeting of the Public Health Department to address the staff, and he would arrange a speaker's fee.

At no time in this first encounter did they discuss the actual business at hand, yet with all the talking it had grown late. Ru Yan said she had to get back, her son might be trying to reach her online. "Plus," she said, "I've got a dog at home who hasn't been walked since noon." This led to a discussion about dogs. Liang Jinsheng said he liked dogs, too, but unfortunately didn't have time to take care of one. "That's good," Jiang Xiaoli said, "once a certain matter is concluded, you'll get a dog as part of the deal."

He ignored the comment, and looking straight at Ru Yan offered her a ride home. Ru Yan said there was no need for that, it would be easy for her to call a cab. "Oh come on," Jiang Xiaoli said, "It can't be beneath you to have a mayor act as your chauffeur. Oh, well. Starting tonight, I'm getting out of the double-agent business for good."

On the way home, Ru Yan asked whether it was true that he had read her articles on the Internet. "Yes," he said. "The writings were like the person who wrote them. The person is as good as her writings."

"How were you able to see our website?" she wanted to know.

Liang Jinsheng chuckled. "If I wanted to see it, what would stop me? It's not a private place. You know, people tend to think the Internet consists of lots of little rooms behind closed doors, but actually it's just a lot of windows that let you see everything."

"You go online too?" she asked.

"You think you young girls are the only ones who go online?"

"Oh," mused Ru Yan, "I've become a little girl? When I registered for the forum, I didn't have the nerve to fill in my age."

"It's like that with me, too," Liang Jinsheng said. "I usually put in just about anything as a date of birth—1973 maybe, or 1968. But there's a limit to how young I can claim to be."

"Do you ever post articles or comments?"

"No, just a lurker—don't have time to post."

"How did you come across my website?" Ru Yan wanted to know.

"Ah," Liang Jinsheng said, "Let that be a secret for now. Someday I'll tell you."

Ru Yan had another question. "How did you know I was the one who wrote those pieces?"

"You go by the name Such Is This World, right? Isn't that Ru Yan minus the grass top and the woman lateral[113]? And from your articles I learned who you are: the son, the dog, Paris."

They had driven fast through the night, and while they were still speaking he pulled up at her house. Liang Jinsheng got out first and opened the car door for her like a gentleman. "Aren't you going to invite me up for a visit?"

She laughed awkwardly. "Oh, no, I left in such a hurry, the house is a mess . . . and I haven't arranged proper security for you. I'd hate to be responsible if anything were to happen to a mayor." After a pause she added, "I will make a formal invitation once I've got the place in order."

"Very good, I will look forward to it," he said. "If you happen to speak online with that young fellow-alumnus of mine, tell him an old grad (who never really finished school) says hello."

"Should I tell him who the old graduate is?" Ru Yan asked.

"That would be within your rights," he said. "My name is not a State secret." He reached into the car and picked up two tickets, separated them at the perforation, and handed one to Ru Yan. She had noticed the tickets while riding in the car and had been debating whether she should go. Now that he had finally brought it up, she suddenly felt shy.

"I'd really like to," she said, "but I'm afraid in that kind of setting..."

"I understand," he said after a moment's thought. "What if I don't go either? I have many opportunities to see these shows ... sometimes I don't feel like it but I have to go anyway."

She was touched. "No, don't miss it, that wouldn't be right. Perhaps some day there will be more opportunities for me, too."

He was seated in the car, now, and offered his hand in farewell. "This evening was very pleasant."

Ru Yan was moved, and stammered a goodbye. Then she hurried inside.

She had not met privately with a man for many years, had not even experienced a handshake with such personal feeling. Occasionally there had been staged encounters with high-level leaders who would shake hands woodenly and mechanically. But the few times she had shaken Liang Jinsheng's hand today, a curious sensation had lingered afterward in her palm, as if the touch had transmitted its own spark into flesh from which all fire had departed long ago.

18

Her son didn't show up and when she figured the time difference she realized that for him it was still 3:00 or 4:00 in the afternoon. She left a note for him on QQ. For a while now, Ru Yan had made a point of writing him a few words every day. Sometimes it was a longer message, sometimes a shorter one; sometimes it was about him, sometimes it was only about her own mundane affairs of daily life, whatever was on her mind, so that these messages had become a kind of diary. In this exchange or outpouring, she found her relationship to her son was quietly changing. Since that parting at the airport, it was becoming less natural to regard him as her son than as a friend.

She wrote a little about Yang Yanping. Then she mentioned that in another week it would be the Mid-Autumn Festival and wondered whether the holiday would remind Chinese kids in France of their loved ones far away. Then she added one more thought: *an old fellow-alumnus of yours asked me to relay his greetings*. After typing this she realized it sounded abrupt and seemed to come out of nowhere. She considered deleting it but as she hesitated, her finger bumped the Return key and the message got sent, hopping into her son's Received Messages box. There it was, and she couldn't do anything about it.

She closed QQ with a wry smile. Next time he replied, she wondered whether he'd ask about this old fellow-alumnus. It was past midnight, but she wasn't even drowsy. A sudden breeze lifted the curtain at her window and she heard a fine rain pattering on the awning outside. She had always been fond of this sound, which seemed to her the closest that denizens of a modern metropolis can get to the sound of raindrops on ancient eaves. She started a new document, something hazy in which the ideas flowed from her fingers without being thought out: "Recalling rainy nights on Ba Mountain." It was a piece that had lots of mood but not much of a plot, and no characters either, just a dawning awareness. It was like a poem. She wrote three or four hundred characters without a pause.

I love the rain. It always feels mysterious. It brings Heaven and mankind together, yet cuts off my humble home from the dust of this world.

I love the rain. Amid the patter of raindrops and the dripping eaves, you can almost hear faint whispering voices, ever so many. They prompt you to take chances, to let your imagination lead you, to try new things. Your tender feelings, like the fine rain, flow unceasing.

I love the rain. Especially the night rain that comes down in darkness to wash the dust from our air, so when people awaken they see everything moist and fresh.

I love the rain. Whether it is the spring rain that falls thick and fast, or the soft rain of autumn, or a summer downpour, or the drizzle of winter, it makes people warm or sad or calm or cozy. A world without rain would be dreary and bleak.

In the still night, if the raindrops come drumming on your roof, if the rivulets wind down your windowpanes and puddles overflow the lanes, it shall reflect your lamplight and make your darkness fresh and alive.

The rain drenches with tenderness. It gives life and harmony.

I like rain, and I like Li Shangyin's poem:

You ask the date of my return; no date as yet.
Night rains on Ba Mountain cause the autumn
ponds to rise.
When shall we two tend the candle in the
west window,
Remembering rainy nights on Ba Mountain?[114]

She looked it over once; it didn't seem to need any changes, so she posted it to the Empty Nest. She was like a little girl collecting candy-wrappers, who inserts one after another of the brightly colored papers into her schoolbooks, filled with a dreamy delight, and hoping the collection will grow.

In third or fourth grade Ru Yan had been in love with writing. She had just received her composition book and felt that it was a wonderful thing to use recently-learned characters to express ideas, paint scenes, and even formulate morals to stories. The teacher often read her compositions and excerpts from her weekly journal aloud to the class. But soon afterward[115] the teacher stopped reading her work and her grades started going down. On her homework the teacher would write comments like *I hope you will intensify your study of the writings of Chairman Mao* and *You should quote more from Chairman Mao's sayings*. From that point her written work, compositions and journal entries alike, got all messed up. But she did not follow the teacher's guidance, and that proved fortunate.

In writing, some people are like lotuses that poke their sharp tips above the water early but after a long period of growth turn out to be quite ordinary. Ru Yan was more like a narcissus, for which long ago a tiny seed was planted and which takes forever to grow, fostering its bulb without fuss until an accidental rainshower comes its way and it thrusts out green leaves, and soon blooms into a water-sprite that is lithe and graceful and fragrant.

19

The forum moderator, Lonely Goose, announced that she would soon be traveling to visit her daughter. Since it might not be easy for her to get online over there, she wanted to appoint a Net friend to take her place for a while. She was convinced the best choice was Ru Yan. Below this post were several concurring replies. Ru Yan quickly thanked the moderator for her great kindness and thanked all the others for their goodwill, but explained she hadn't even attained the competence of a "newbie" yet, so how could she have the effrontery to assume the responsibilities of a moderator? She added that she would be happy to pitch in and help with the grunt work under the leadership of a more qualified candidate, who, she hoped, would step forward.

Rising early the next day, she washed her face and straightened the apartment while her computer was booting. Since entering the online world, she'd discovered that the computer is like an importunate suitor, a fellow who demands your attention day and night. After taking Yang Yanping for a walk, Ru Yan fixed herself a quick breakfast and sat down with the insistent fellow and began going through a series of tasks. First she opened QQ and found a reply from her son. His message summarized his recent activities and then asked who was that old fellow-alumnus of his? He said there were a few graduates who were two years ahead of him and had helped him a lot. But he had not stayed in contact with them since his own graduation... could it have been one of them?

Ru Yan replied, Um, not just two years ahead of you . . . I'm afraid more than ten times that far ahead of you!

Her second task was to browse the Midlife website and open the collection of her own writings. Her article of the previous evening, "Recalling rainy nights on Ba Mountain," already had a few comments. One of them, signed 'Fanyi' [116], abruptly said, "Yan my dear[117], are you dating someone now?" It startled her and left her uneasy. As a rule, Ru Yan made a point of replying to the comments her posts received—not to acknowledge them seemed discourteous—and if there was nothing to say, she would leave a smiley-face. But to this unidentified and insinuating 'Fanyi' she couldn't think of the proper response.

The third thing she did was to visit the Empty Nest. The moderator's proposal had now been seconded by almost twenty messages of enthusiastic approval. One person said that if Ru Yan needed any technical assistance, he (or she) would gladly serve as her aide-de-camp and take care of the little things. Lonely Goose said that if Ru Yan agreed, the basic techniques for moderating the forum could readily be taught to her: it's simple; if you can write such great articles, you can do this with half your brain. Others expressed a similar view, As a bamboo fence needs three stakes, an able person needs three helpers, and Ru Yan, you light the fire, and we'll gather the wood.

In this online society, apart from Lonely Goose and a few others, Ru Yan did not know the gender of any of these people.

Everybody addressed Lonely Goose as Older Sister Lonely or Madam Lonely. When Such Is This World had first appeared online, the name gave no indication whether the writer was male or female, but once she started writing, her sex could be inferred from her style, so she started being called Older (or Younger) Sister Such Is This World. In most cases, the age was not clear either. As they say on the Net, "If I call you Older Sister, I may be a lot older than you; if I call you younger sister, I could be a little girl. Whatever you do, don't take anything at face value."

That night Lonely Goose contacted her by QQ and went over the basic tasks of a moderator. She had Ru Yan enter the forum and walked her through how to edit and correct, how to delete, how to block an IP. Lonely Goose gave her the administrator's password, explaining it was like a housekeeper's key. "If you can get online at your office, when work is slow you can take a stroll around the forum, and if there are any inappropriate posts you can deal with them. Being a moderator is really just like being the hostess in a salon. You welcome family and friends and guests from all over. I'll bet you know the song Madame A Qing, of the Spring Is Coming Teahouse, sings in *Battle of Wits*. It's just like that.[118]"

And that's how Ru Yan moved into the role of moderator.

For years, Ru Yan's life had been as placid as still waters. But now one wave after another had roiled it: the Internet, the puppy, and that old alumnus of her son's college who had appeared out of nowhere . . . as well as the many discussions which those developments were inspiring at her office.

20

When Ru Yan came to work on Monday morning, she wasn't sure whether she was just feeling high-strung or her female colleagues had got wind of something. They all seemed to be wearing a sly smirk. She had barely sat down to a cup of tea when Jiang Xiaoli phoned from downstairs. “Ru Yan, you are one tough operator!”

“What?!”

“The Mayor, no less, personally asks you to a show, and you’ve got the nerve to turn him down.”

Ru Yan looked around: fortunately, at that moment there was no one else in the office.

“Celebrities, high society: how the heck was I going to walk into that? Afterward, I thanked my lucky stars I didn’t go: there would have been TV cameras, *Who’s that woman sitting next to Mayor Liang?* and by now I wouldn’t dare venture outside my house.”

“There you go again,” Jiang Xiaoli said, “I can’t tell whether you’re pretending to be too clever or pretending to be confused. Nowadays what woman *wouldn’t* want to be in front of a camera like that? They all want it but they can’t have it. I’m going to tell you something, something big, and I’m wondering how you can thank me.”

“What is it this time?”

“When I give this kind of assistance,” Jiang Xiaoli declared, “my judgment is always sound. That night, when he came back from your place, I phoned him and asked how it went. He said he told you.”

“Told me?” Ru Yan said. “Told me what?”

“Oh come off it,” Jiang Xiaoli said, “this is getting to be a bit much.”

Ru Yan made an effort to think back but couldn’t recall that he had declared himself in any way. “Don’t keep me in suspense.”

“How soon the great forget,” Jiang Xiaoli bantered. “Didn’t he tell you, ‘The writings are like the person who wrote them, and the person is as good as her writings’?” Gee, what do you think that meant? . . . *You unna-stand?*[119]”

Seeing that this had, for the moment, rendered Ru Yan speechless, Jiang Xiaoli went on, “Aw, forget it; in a few more days I’ll be in no position to talk to you like this. Maybe you won't even take my calls."

Jiang Xiaoli's semi-serious upbraiding gave Ru Yan conflicting feelings. She wasn't sure what to say and only muttered, "Don't let your imagination run away with you, Jiang Xiaoli; even I am not clear how things stand in all this, and in the meanwhile don't say anything that would prove embarrassing for him and embarrassing for me."

"Don't be so nervous, he's already thanked me. Would it kill you to utter a gracious word? Very soon—wait for it!—there will be another event."

Sure enough, the event she had mentioned was not long in coming. The next day, Liang Jinsheng phoned her to say, "Have you made any plans for the Mid-Autumn Festival[120]?"

"No, I haven't."

"Would you like to go out and enjoy the moon?" he asked.

Now this was a fine "event." For many years, Ru Yan had usually observed the occasion at her window, trying to catch sight of a dull yellow moon rising amid the forest of skyscrapers. She didn't know how one might still catch a glimpse of that bright orb which lights up the sky in the literature of the ancients. She asked him whether there was still a moon that could be enjoyed.

"Always, as long as your heart is true. But I'm sorry I'll be a little late that evening. Up till nine o'clock I have to be at a holiday party in the newly-completed Central Square. Or wait—maybe you'd like to join the party?"

"You'll be there in an official capacity," Ru Yan said, "If I went, where would I stand?"

"OK," he said, "then when the ceremonies are over, I'll come pick you up and take you someplace nice."

"Where?"

He chuckled. "Well, it will be a place where you can see the moon."

"What if it rains?" she asked.

"The weather service puts the probability of rain at ten percent. Hey, if it rains, it'll be a mid-autumn rain: *Parasol trees and the soft fine rain.*[121]

Liang Jinsheng was alluding to Ru Yan's most recent article.

She thought, *this fellow certainly knows how to please people.*

It would be their first date.

After some hesitation, Ru Yan told Jiang Xiaoli, who said, "Whoever would have thought this bigshot of a mayor would tumble so easily into the snares of love! It shows our Ru Yan is a force to be reckoned with. The soft overcomes the hard. You have any idea how many people try to get a meeting with this man, invite him to dinner, use all their wiles . . . and still get nowhere?"

Jiang Xiaoli was moved that Ru Yan had shared this with her, so she gave her some information she had never mentioned before. Liang Jinsheng, she said, had been married twice. The first time had been to a college classmate. Subsequently her father had been implicated in the Lin Biao affair[122], and the two had eventually broken up. The second marriage had been to someone he met while he was working as a technician in a factory; a couple of years ago she had died of heart disease. From what people said, both marriages had been pretty good in terms of love and affection, though both had been cut short: one by politics, and the other by illness. By each marriage he had had a daughter, and both of them were now living abroad. The younger was married; the older was still single. But both of Liang's daughters had made it overseas by their own efforts, not because he had shelled out the money to send them; among their kind of people this was an extraordinary achievement. He also had an aged mother, well into her eighties, living in Beijing with his younger brother. He supported her, visited a few times a year, and was considered a filial son. "I expect he's told you these things."

Ru Yan said she had never asked about them.

She recognized that it was odd that she had had no interest in digging up his background. She didn't know whether it was because from the beginning she hadn't treated this thing seriously, or because she wanted to be able to believe whatever she would see. But she made a joke of it: "Who would dare inquire into the private life of a leading cadre? It might be classified!"

21

On the night of the Mid-Autumn Festival, visibility was unusually good; it was one of the clearest, brightest nights they had had in years. From the moment when the round moon began to ascend from behind a line of high-rises, Ru Yan watched it steadily. It had neither jade rabbit nor Chang'e nor sweet-scented osmanthus.[123] The moon—which is naturally associated with thin clouds, scattered stars, the shade of trees and shrubbery, gleaming lakes and glowing mountains, and babbling brooks under small bridges—now was set among stiff skyscrapers like a construction spotlight. She reflected that it was a good thing the ancients had left so many odes to the moon, because if they hadn't, what would there be to savor in this festival?

When the moon was high in the sky, the phone rang. He said, "I'm downstairs."

Only then did Ru Yan realize she had been sitting idly, awaiting this moment, ever since night fell.

In the car, she remarked at once, "They say it's hard for an ordinary person to get to see you."

Liang Jinsheng pulled slowly away from the curb and answered soberly, "That's true. It's even hard for me to get to see myself."

Seeing that she didn't understand, he explained, "In what sense do they want to see me? They want to see a deputy mayor. If they want to see *this* deputy mayor, it is only because there is some advantage to them in doing so. So tell me: since what I see all day is likewise this role, isn't it hard for me to see myself?"

Ru Yan laughed heartily. "You guys are such good talkers. How is it that the speeches in the papers and on TV are all so boring?"

"You don't think much of us," he sighed. "But you know what is the first requirement for becoming a Party cadre? You've got to be able to give speeches. Go over the classic documents down through the years[124], how many were speeches? Even at the lowest level, say, the director of a neighborhood office: when he gives a speech it will always be a good spiel, and he has no trouble going non-stop for a couple of hours. Now some of these men may not understand logic or have any literary style, but when you first hear them they sound so coherent, so reasonable."

This made her laugh even harder, but she said, "Your generation is different from my father's generation."

He grunted quizzically.

"If they said one thing in public," Ru Yan elaborated, "they would say the same thing when they went home."

Liang Jinsheng commented, "Well, we've made some progress, then."

"Progress?" Ru Yan was confused. "Saying completely different things in public and in private, that's progress?"

"Someday," Liang Jinsheng said with a knowing smile, "I'll explain this to you. It's a tricky subject, but it's not as bad as you make it out to be."

The small car was heading into the outskirts of the city. They drove and drove until Ru Yan had lost her bearings. This was a new road, lined on both sides with newly-constructed buildings that were all big and modern and luxurious, really very fine, whether in Western or Chinese style—and there were even some in a Middle Eastern style. Many were set back behind landscaped areas. There were no other cars on the road and no pedestrians on the sidewalks; the place was spacious and empty to the point of being surreal. As far as the eye could see, it was like a fairy-tale kingdom in the moonlight.

"Where are we?" Ru Yan asked.

"You don't know this place?" Liang Jinsheng said. "Then my P.R. work has been unsuccessful. This is the famous new quarter of our city! It will be a hub for high-tech, education, culture: it's going to be the ritziest part of town."

At a traffic island nicely planted with greenery, the car turned right and entered an estate filled with villas. From time to time they passed a four- or five-story apartment building in the Western style. Some of these had soft yellow or pale blue light raying out through arched windows and French doors, creating an air of mystery. As they continued on, a shimmering expanse of silver light appeared in front of them: a lake! A paved track led to the water, and when they had almost reached it they had to stop at a cast-iron gate whose bars were wrought with floral designs. A watchman in a guardhouse studied Liang Jinsheng's license plate and opened the gate.

"They know your car?" Ru Yan asked.

He shrugged. "Probably."

Ru Yan realized that being a mayor brought its own peculiar lack of freedom. Anywhere you went, people would recognize you. She wondered what they'd be saying tomorrow: "Last night Mayor Liang brought a woman to the lakeside." It made her feel queasy.

He must have guessed her thoughts, for he chuckled, "You're worried people will recognize me? Can't a mayor lead his own life? I guess I'm going to have to buy my own car."

She smiled but didn't say anything. "He's a sharp one," she thought.

Liang Jinsheng drove for a while along the lakeside track and parked in an out-of-the-way spot by a big rock near the beach. Ru Yan stepped out and stared up at the moon suspended in heaven, huge and bright and round. At a glance you could make out the osmanthus and the jade rabbit; it was all there. She gave a squeal of delight, like a little girl: "We have this kind of moon here, too?" Liang Jinsheng had opened the trunk and was taking things out. She went on, "Everyone says the moon is more full in America than in China, and now I see some basis for that: here in this wealthy place the moon is more full than back where I live."

"The air's a little better here," he said, "sightlines are less obstructed and there are fewer objects near the horizon that you can compare the moon to, so it looks a little bigger and rounder; it's that simple. If the mid-autumn party had been held here, it would have been a lot more interesting."

The items he was removing from the trunk of the car were a plastic ground cloth and a cardboard box. He spread the cloth on the sand, then opened the box and drew out his provisions: two fine small mooncakes, a few bananas, two apples, and a few bags of snacks. He also drew out two paper cups and a bottle of dry red wine. He put things on plates and filled each of the cups less than half full with wine. While Liang Jinsheng was preparing the picnic, Ru Yan walked eagerly to where the lake waters lapped gently on the sand and the faint breeze brought the wavelets, line after line of them sparkling in the moonlight. It lifted the heart. She squatted down and swished her hand in the water and was surprised when a feeling welled up that she had not felt since she was a little girl.

Liang Jinsheng had finished setting up the picnic and now he too came over to the water, bending down to scoop up a handful of sand, which he fingered like a farmer sifting grains from his fields. "It's beautiful, isn't it?"

"I didn't know such fine places still existed," Ru Yan said. There started going through her mind a Taiwan campus song[125] she'd heard in college: *Sunshine, sand, the ocean waves, cactus, and an old sea-captain*[126]—

Liang Jinsheng remarked, "This beach is man-made."

"Man-made?" she cried in astonishment. "A beach this big is man-made?"

"When did you ever see a beach in our part of the country?" he said. "Our lakes are all silted with mud. This sand was transported in dozens of freight cars from the coast, more than a thousand kilometers."

"Practically a world-class beach!" Ru Yan said.

"That's exactly what people call it. And it's one of the few unpolluted lakes we've got left. In the summer I'll bring you here to swim; it's even better than Beidaihe[127]."

They both sat down on the plastic sheet. Liang Jinsheng raised his paper cup: "A happy Mid-Autumn to you; may flowers bloom and the moon be full[128]."

Ru Yan smiled and lightly bumped her paper cup against his. "Thank you for introducing me to such a fine lake and such a fine moon. I can't remember the last time I ever saw them like this."

"You know," he said, "They're there every day."

She sensed the implication but chose not to pursue that line of talk and changed the subject. "Would people expect you to spend the holiday this way?"

He shook his head. "No. The norm is song and dance and playing mahjong, or bowling, or hitting the sauna. That sums up the ordinary night-life of officials nowadays."

"For you, too?"

"Often."

"Even playing mahjong?" Ru Yan asked.[129]

"Sometimes, when a social occasion requires it. Not too many people actually enjoy that sort of thing."

She persisted: "Do *you*?"

He parried: "If I liked those things, would I come here? Bringing my own provisions to eat and drink, opening and pouring my own bottle of wine?"

"You don't like doing things for yourself?"

"In those kinds of places," he grinned, "it's impossible to do anything for yourself. If you do, the hostesses will get chewed out by their boss, maybe even lose their jobs. So I should be thanking you for enabling me this once to live like an ordinary person."

Spontaneously, Ru Yan now asked, "In the past, when this holiday came around, did you and your wife use to have such romantic nights?" As soon as the question was out of her mouth she regretted it; it sounded presumptuous. She added quickly, "I'm sorry—"

But Liang Jinsheng answered very mildly and easily, "Nope, never did. It's not that I didn't love her. And I'm not going to say I was always too busy to break away from work. It's that I wasn't aware a day would come when I'd no longer have the chance to do this."

His words touched a sore spot and changed her mood. She said vaguely, "It's true."

"It's not wrong for me to talk about my former wife, is it?" he asked.

She felt she wanted to cry, and could only mumble, "I asked you about it."

"After she died," he explained, "for a long time my state of mind was not good. It made me understand many things."

"Me, too," she said.

For a while, neither of them spoke. They listened to the nearby lapping of the water on the shore.

From time to time, the moon hid itself in wispy clouds, then slowly drifted out again. Ru Yan found herself remembering that fine, melancholy song,

> *The moon sweeps through cottony clouds,*
> *Wafted on the evening breeze there comes a happy tune.*[130]

When she had sung this song in her youth it had always been with a feeling of anxiety and gloom. Now she began to hum it out loud. After a few phrases, she felt embarrassed and stopped.

"Go ahead, sing it," Liang Jinsheng said, "I was just remembering that song myself."

"I haven't sung for years," she said. "I liked to sing when I was little, but only when no one was around, and even then I'd only hum. I can't sing in front of people."

The land stretched wide under the vault of the sky. A sobering chill came into the air by the lakeside. Somehow, this evening of moon-viewing beside the waters had taken on a note of pathos. Ru Yan knew that Mid-Autumn was a holiday that could easily make people maudlin. The Lantern Festival[131] on the other hand, with its colored lights and fireworks, its village theatricals and temple processions, always felt like the start of the year. Winter was departing, spring was coming, everything looked fresh and new; there was reason to celebrate. Or the Dragon-boat Festival[132], when everything was coming back to life in a riot of lush growth and the year's first wheat crop was ripe for harvest: then, too, there was reason to celebrate. But Mid-Autumn, when the fall would soon be half over, and the cold was intensifying as winter drew nigh . . . and it deepened the melancholy to associate these developments with the course of a human life. The poetry with which the ancients hymned the autumn was for the most part sad, and they expressed that kind of sadness very well.

How long have you been here, bright moon?
With wine in hand, I question the dark sky.
I wonder, in the Celestial Palace
What year is it tonight?[133]

Somewhere to the northwest lies my home.
Here in the southeast, oft have I watched the moon grow full.[134]

This life, as brief and lovely as this night;
Where shall we view next year's moon?[135]

The bright moon rises o'er the sea,
Seen from far ends of the earth;
All through the night we lovers complain,
The sunless hours brood with yearning.[136]

And the indomitable Qiu Jin[137], more valiant than any man, once wrote on the occasion of the Mid-Autumn Festival such melancholy lines as "In this vast and dusty world, where can one find a soulmate? My dark dress: drenched with tears."

In a calm voice, Ru Yan told Liang Jinsheng these thoughts.

He was startled. "I had no idea you were so well-versed in classical literature."

"Well-versed?" she scoffed. "I just remember a few lines, that's all. Early on, when you fellows were waging your factional wars[138], I was too young and it wasn't my business. I just stayed home and read this petty bourgeois literature. Whether I understood it or not, I could feel the cadences and the rhythm. I slowly came to understood some of the emotions after I grew up. My mom was very funny. Once she said, "I'm going to burn all our books so no one gets in trouble." Not long after, she said,

"Oh, these poems of the Tang and lyrics of the Song, nobody's going to even remember them." It might sound callous, but she said it with a sigh; she thought I couldn't hear. She had snatched a book from my hand and I thought she was going to hide it somewhere, but later I saw her just sitting there, transfixed as she turned the pages."

"Why didn't you enroll back then as a liberal arts student?" Liang Jinsheng asked. "In those days, wasn't liberal arts pretty popular?"

"At that time," Ru Yan said, "It was easier to get in if you had picked botany as your major."

She said it nonchalantly. But as far as she was concerned, liberal arts, or more precisely literature, had been too sacred; she lacked the confidence—perhaps the courage—to draw near for fear the subject would do damage to her, a kind of damage she knew she could scarce endure: so she was content to love literature from afar. Much the same thing had happened, also in her college days, with that male student . . . she wouldn't let herself think about him seriously and didn't dare follow her impulses. The whole time until graduation, she never looked into her own heart to see the affections that were buried there.

The moon had slid into the western sky as they watched. This time it was Liang Jinsheng who broke the silence. "Got to go back."

"It was a lovely moonlit night," Ru Yan said.

"It was," he agreed. "You know, we can come again next month if you'd like."

"I'd hate to put you to the trouble," she said.

"What if I like being put to the trouble?"

She smiled but didn't say anything.

"Next time," he said, "We'll have to have a talk about that."

They got up and as Liang Jinsheng began to gather the things he had spread on the ground he couldn't help chuckling, "Breakfast for a week."

"You mean even *you* worry about where your next meal is coming from?"

"Sure I do," he said. "And on the subject of eating, you know eight meals a day is a tough regimen, you want to try it with me sometime?"

"I don't want to get the 'Three Highs.'[139]" Ru Yan said.

They didn't talk much on the ride home. When they parted at her front door, he said, "If it weren't so late I would ask to be invited upstairs for a cup of tea."

"Next time," she said.

Before he started up the car, Liang Jinsheng suddenly said, "I suppose there will be another article coming out, titled 'May we live long, and unite under the same moon from afar.'[140] I'm looking forward to it."

"You're assigning me a topic?" she teased.

"All the same," he said with good humor, "for the time being, there's no need to introduce the other protagonist."

"I won't," she assured him.

Once home, her first priority was to walk the dog, and she had a long talk with Yang Yanping. It occurred to her that without this creature she would be awfully quiet. On the Internet she had read that women have a natural need to talk, and it's bad for their health if they don't speak at least 5000 words a day. She suspected that when her son had gone to such lengths to bring this dog all the way home from college, he had had motives. One was to leave a part of himself with her. Another was to give her a reason to talk.

Her second task was to turn on the computer and check whether there were any messages from her son or anyone else. On Ru Yan's QQ page there were by now quite a few icons representing her correspondents. Some of these were her friends from the Empty Nest, while others offered feedback, or wanted her to write for their websites, or just needed to chat. Her address book grew bigger every day.

These days Ru Yan was often distracted when she checked the Internet. She was pondering her two encounters with Liang Jinsheng. They had not been boring or embarrassing, as she had expected they would be; but neither had she experienced a head-over-heels falling in love. Some commentator had written online that once a middle-aged woman begins to fall in love, she is more passionate and reckless than a young woman because she senses that this may be, for her, the last battle. Ru Yan did not think she felt that way. But the relationship was slowly seeping into her heart like tea being steeped: however slowly, the leaves expand and the aroma gets stronger. A 'Soundlessly the fine rain moistens all things'[141] kind of phenomenon. But after you drink the first cup of tea and pour more water onto the leaves, the flavor of the second cup is irresistible.

She knew she liked him. She didn't know whether this liking was connected with his power, position, wealth, and competence. These attributes are often fascinating and beautiful if decorously combined with other appealing traits. When a man who wields authority enjoys intellectual distinction, his talent shines with greater luster than an ordinary man's, as long as he keeps things understated and doesn't get carried away and make a fool of himself. Ru Yan knew, for example, that many whose station in life was fairly humble were blessed with a great sense of humor, but for the most part people would say *that one's a jolly fellow, he's got a quick wit*. But if we're talking about a leader, a diplomat perhaps, then people will hail him as a comic genius, a master of the spoken word, and the ceaseless encomiums will please not only the great man but his flatterers as well.

She also knew that he liked her. Ru Yan was not burdened by the inferiority complex that marks so many middle-aged women; for all her meekness, she had a pride of which she herself was perhaps unaware. When all the successful men find it easy to win women's hearts, except for one woman's heart, then attention must be paid to that woman: by not being so easily moved, she reveals a kind of superiority, a self-sufficiency. Nevertheless this man had somehow become a part of Ru Yan's thoughts, and that fact alone was something that troubled her.

A few days later, Liang Jinsheng called to say he'd got word he would be going to Beijing at once to take part in an important conference which would last until the very day he had arranged to set out on a fact-finding tour of Europe and America. He said it would probably be more than a month before he'd be able to do any moon-viewing with her.

"By then," she said, "we'll have to wear coats."

To her surprise she felt a little disappointed. A man you've only seen a couple of times, a relationship that's nothing to speak of . . . whether he goes far away or just disappears, what's it to you? She felt she was being ridiculous.

Liang Jinsheng said, "I may have a chance to visit with my older daughter. Would you mind if I mention to her that I'm seeing someone?"

"That's up to you," Ru Yan said. "Anyway, what you choose to talk about so far away, what could I do about it?"

"Would you give me your cell phone number?" he asked.

"I don't have a cell phone."

"I didn't think such people still existed," he said. "I'll have somebody drop one off for you. It's a spare I don't use much."

"No, don't do that," Ru Yan said quickly. "I'll take care of it, and then I'll give you the number."

22

At the start of the Seventies, there were three or four young dissidents who studied political thought along with Damo. In addition to Maozi, the group consisted of He Qiye and Liu Su, as well as the only woman among them, Xiao Yong. They could be called 'dissidents' only in the political context of that time. If any of today's right-wing internet youths were to read their letters, hear their private talks, or read the notes they jotted about the books they studied, the modern observer would laugh out loud and say these people were more left-wing than the cadres (newly inducted into the Party) who lead student associations today!

They could not understand how an extremely orthodox Marxist-Leninist regime which billed itself as the center of world revolution could be so uncomfortable with Marx himself, its ideological patriarch. The regime did not want people to really understand the fellow with the big beard, and still less did those in power want anyone to use him to question *their* legitimacy. The only Marx they let people believe in was the packaged version. Marx himself would be held in many respects to have deviated from the right path. The first time Damo and his friends read some of the works of Marx and Engels which had not been officially released, such as the letters between them and the young Marx's *Economic-Philosophic Manuscripts of 1844*[142], they were astounded. These texts contained many statements about freedom of the press, the liberation of man, morality, love and marriage that were, well, reactionary . . . but well-written and persuasive.

Damo and the others gave their little group a code name: QM, a pinyin abbreviation of "The Young Marx."[143] In conversation they would just say *Qing Ma*[144]. This was exciting and gave them a feeling of intimacy.

The early Seventies: a few short years that plunged Chinese society into ambiguity, turmoil, and controversy. Many dramatic changes occurred, such as only a great Romantic author could have thought up, and observers were often left stupefied by the course of events.[145] Thanks to his good background and his youth and the fact that he hadn't done anything during the C.R. that could be held against him, Damo got recruited quite early for factory work: he became an electrician. Maozi and Xiao Yong came back to the city separately. Maozi was assigned to a service industry, more precisely a bathhouse, where his job was to scrape the dirt off people's backs, and later he would joke that in those years he had scraped off enough sweaty gunk to make a statue of the Leader. Xiao Yong also found her way into a service industry: she worked as a waitress in a noodle shop. When Damo and his friends showed up at her place for the Triple Tasty Noodles[146], instead of going to the inside window through which the plates were passed, Xiao Yong would walk right into the kitchen, take the chef's ladle and heap on the sauce. When Damo and company came to eat, more than half the bowl was sauce, with just a few noodles. One bowl would fill you up.

Of this group, only Damo was a bona-fide member of the proletariat. What's more, he made radios—transistor radios, and that was high tech. Once Damo bought (at the insiders' price, less than 20 yuan apiece) a dual-band radio for every member of the *Qing Ma*. You could pick up enemy stations. He said, "If you get caught and they give you the third degree, you'd better not rat me out." He gave a set to Teacher Wei, too.

After settling in the city again, Damo went to see Teacher Wei quite often.

At one point, Teacher Wei's health was very bad owing to the irregular life he had lived, indigent and alone. All the major organs were compromised but especially his stomach, which seemed completely shot. After losing a lot of blood he was taken to the emergency room by a neighbor with a bicycle. They cut out two-thirds of his stomach and he almost died. The night before the surgery, Teacher Wei asked the neighbor to find Damo. This was the first time Teacher Wei ever took the initiative in contacting the young man. When Damo got to the hospital, he found Teacher Wei looking as thin and pale as a sheet of paper, and the quilt that covered him in the hospital bed was spread flat, as if he had no body. The patient smiled wryly and said he would never have guessed he had so much blood in him; he had spat up more than half a basinful. Damo shook his hand, which was as hard and cold as a stone, and said that blood was one of those things you could always produce more of.

As Damo started to leave, Teacher Wei said, "There are a couple of favors I'd like to ask you." The first was that in the corner of the south wall of his room, behind the wooden crate, one brick was loose and if you pulled it out you'd find a plastic bag in the hole. These were some pieces he'd written in the last few years. If he didn't make it out of the hospital this time, he wanted Damo to take those papers. The second favor: in a side pocket of the leather suitcase were two photographs of him with children. More than twenty years had gone by without his ever hearing anything about those two kids; they must be all grown up by now. When his ex-wife had taken them away, one had been three years old and the other just one year old. They could not have any memory of him as a father. If Damo could find them, Teacher Wei wanted him to give them the pictures. After explaining these two requests, he added that when he was cremated, he wanted that canister of tea to go with him into the fire.

Damo answered earnestly, "Sir, you will have an opportunity to polish the articles in that bag and make them public someday. As for the photographs, it will be for you to give them to your children in person. If you don't believe me, shall we make a bet?"

Teacher Wei smiled. "That's a bet I would prefer to lose."

As it turned out, he lost the bet.

After the operation, Teacher Wei was frail and shaky for a long time, but he slowly mended. He just couldn't go to work any more. He hadn't taught school since that parade in '66. At first he had been lodged in a cowshed[147] and employed to sweep drill grounds and clean toilets; later he was told to look after classroom articles and sports equipment. When he was cleaning the latrines, male students would often cluster round in small groups to urinate on him. When he was handling sports equipment, the kids would snatch a basketball from his arms and knock him down with it before they ran off, giggling, to the basketball courts. Once he wondered aloud to Damo what kind of power was it that could take innocent children and, with the right education, make them more callous than Nazis? And all these children would grow up with this unfeeling temperament: it would mark them all their lives. This was the most terrifying thing that had ever happened anywhere in the world.

Since Teacher Wei did not return to work, Damo and his friends came to see him more often. They would help a little with the housework and occasionally bring him something to eat. Then they would have a leisurely conversation.

From those visits, Damo came to understand an aspect of the history of revolution about which movies, novels, and schoolbooks had never told him. After the Cultural Revolution, and especially after the death of Lin Biao, Teacher Wei gained deep insight into the world, rather like an advanced monk attaining enlightenment. On many questions his commentary struck Damo as a revelation, opening up new and startling vistas. Much of what he said then was still not being said by many people twenty or thirty years later.

In October of '76 word spread from Beijing that the three men and one woman had been arrested.[148] As soon as Damo heard, he eagerly arranged with Maozi and the others to go to Teacher Wei's house where, practically trembling with excitement, they announced this astonishing development. Teacher Wei listened, and then made a few points. "No. 1: I believe this is true. No. 2: This may mark the end of a phase in the decade of political infighting we have witnessed, but how things may change henceforth is not yet clear. It's important to watch how they're going to treat the man who stood behind the Gang of Four and the system which produced those people. No. 3: Regardless of the actual consequences of this event, it was carried out by extraordinary means: you could call it a palace coup. The messy details will be for history to sort out, but it shows how far we still have to go before China will enjoy democracy and a system of laws."

The official announcement, which followed immediately, prompted nationwide jubilation. There were parades with cheering crowds; people drank toasts and served dishes of three male crabs with one female . . . Damo and the group joined in the excitement and came to Teacher Wei's home bearing food and liquor to celebrate. They told of the scenes they'd witnessed on the broad avenues of the city. Teacher Wei said, "Don't be too quick to believe what you see on the streets. Don't be too quick to believe in the mood of the masses. Back when the friendship between China and the Soviet Union was strong, all those people marched and rallied for it. When the call came to resist Soviet Revisionism, they marched and rallied then, too. When the Cultural Revolution came, they really marched and rallied, from one end of the country to the other; and when the Great Ninth came, when Liu Shaoqi was irrevocably expelled from the Party, they held the same marches, the same rallies. So on this occasion," he said, "let us temper our rejoicing."

Maozi said, "Sir, you have more reason to celebrate than any of us."

"How so?"

"Weren't you tortured by people like them," Maozi asked, "and isn't that what brought you to this state?"

Teacher Wei smiled. "Who were the people who tortured me, and many people like me, as well as many people not like me? Yes, it was the Gang of Four, but it was also people who opposed the Gang of Four. In some respects, they and their adversaries were much the same."

Statements like that seemed too polemical, too acerbic, even for the dissidents of the *Qing Ma*. On another occasion, when they had debated some issue for hours, Maozi asked Teacher Wei if his way of thinking wasn't influenced by what had happened to him. The master grinned like a fox. "I know what you mean: you're asking whether I'm bringing my personal feelings into this. I'll tell you something. Unless you're a robot, you can't help bringing personal feelings into your thinking. But when personal feelings and personal experience have general significance, they can help you get past stumbling blocks and see into the depths of a situation. What's more, all these things I've been saying have been said by others before me."

After the early Seventies, the *Qing Ma* was subject to vicissitudes from within and without—nothing dramatic—and its members finally managed to get over the past. When a new era dawned, this informal association dissolved of itself. In later years they learned what had been the fate of several unofficial groups like their own—some were harshly dealt with even under the Sagacious Leader[149]—and only then did they realize, with a shiver, the risks they had run.

23

In any case, Teacher Wei's life steadily improved. Over the next two or three years, a number of developments occurred. First, for reasons unknown he was sent to recuperate in a sanatorium. Then he was assigned to the Provincial Social Science Scholars' Association, which had been recently re-established, and there he was told to await further instructions. Finally he was completely rehabilitated—even before the head of that alleged clique was rehabilitated.[150] It's not quite accurate to say he was rehabilitated, though. When they reviewed his file, they discovered there had never been a formal judgment against him. It had been a judicial screw-up that had lasted for twenty-five years. Consequently, there was no way to formally reverse this, the worst miscarriage of justice that the Provincial Committee had known, so they just held a welcoming ceremony, as though he had gone abroad for a while and was now returning to a hero's reception. Afterwards they restored his rank and perquisites and made partial restitution of the back pay owed him. He became a deputy director of the Social Science Scholars' Association and got a three-bedroom apartment with central heating.

Teacher Wei turned 60 that year; he had passed through a full cycle of the zodiac.[151] There wasn't yet mandatory retirement at 60, so there were many old cadres and specialists who had just resumed their posts after rehabilitation. For them, this was a second youth, and they prepared to start working hard for another ten or twenty years, resolved to give it their all and to die in harness.

With some of the old friends, Damo went to celebrate at Teacher Wei's new home. He discovered that all the stuff which had been in the old gentleman's hovel in the residential compound had been moved and placed in the same configuration, incongruously, in one of the spacious rooms of his practically empty new apartment. The only difference was that the partition which had separated the kitchen from the bedroom was now missing. "In this room," Teacher Wei explained, "I can think more clearly."

With his back pay he had bought furniture. The bed was a double bed. The old gang laughed at this. "Teacher Wei, is this side of the bed reserved for the new Missus?" The relationship had become free and easy after so many years, like that between a father and his sons, or between friends, or even partners in crime.

"I do have a companion," Teacher Wei said.

Now they noticed something leaning against the headboard: it was the old can of loose tea. With the passage of time, some of its paint had flaked off and it was spotted with rust.

This bedroom was also his study. The other room served as a guest room with two twin beds, to provide temporary accommodation to Damo & friends, as well as other intellectually-inclined vagabonds. At times they were many, and they'd find places to sleep on the sofa, on the floor . . . they'd even spill into the room that recreated his old home like a museum at the birthplace of a great man. Once, at the conclusion of a seminar in unofficial ideology, a dozen young friends who'd come from all over to see him stayed up late talking and finally bedded down, squeezing into available spaces until the apartment looked like a cheap motel. Only Teacher Wei's room was off-limits, and before going to sleep he closed the door as if it were the bedroom of a married couple.

The early Eighties were a flourishing time. Everyone had a carefree intensity, like a young man who has just walked free after a decade behind bars. Many experienced a dramatic reversal of fortune and felt like the sun at eight or nine in the morning.[152] But Teacher Wei never exulted as others did. When everybody was full of high hopes, he would often dash cold water on them. He kept repeating, like a verbal tic, "I'm waiting to see whether it lasts ten years."

Indeed, in less than ten years, Damo and his set would be plunged into despair more deeply than Teacher Wei.

Teacher Wei had started his career as a literary theorist, but later as his interests turned mainly to culture and ideology he began once again to write under the pen name he had used as a young man: "This Wei." He wrote many articles which had an influence both at home and abroad. Damo knew that much of this material had come from the sheaf of manuscripts which had once been stashed in that hole in the wall. When the campaign against Spiritual Pollution came along, and later the Anti-Liberalization movement[153], Teacher Wei became a heretic again.

Before He Qiye went abroad, a few members of the *Qing Ma* gathered at Teacher Wei's place, where they discussed the current political situation. He Qiye maintained, "Anyway, this country is still moving forward. You can see, Sir: I am able to leave the country, and you are able to say what you want to say without anything happening to you."

"If *we* are satisfied with that," Teacher Wei answered, "*they* will have no incentive to keep up the progress. They have only given back what originally belonged to us anyway, and they haven't fully paid it back: does this call for gratitude? Some of these developments seem to have been good for me, but they were even better for them."

'An obstinate old man,' the others sighed.

Teacher Wei remarked on a number of occasions to Damo and his friends, "The thing about young people (especially young intellectuals) is that when their idealism burns out, what comes next is philistinism and cynicism. For young people, the temptations of material gain are even harder to resist. When spiritual and moral satisfactions are no longer to be had, the satisfactions of property and power are the best substitute." These words were borne out, alas, in the era that followed.

24

In time, the members of the *Qing Ma* underwent major transformations. He Qiye, who had vowed to struggle all his life for the cause of democracy in China, and Liu Su, who had long nurtured a plan to found a journal called *Notes of the Fatherland*[154], left for America one after the other in the 1980s. Xiao Yong, who had had such a warm place in her heart for the *Qing Ma*, became an attorney. This vibrant girl, whom they all called "our Sofia,"[155] was now flying around the world almost continuously; for her, planes had become taxis. Sometimes she took two flights in one day. Astute and unflappable, she worked tirelessly on her clients' cases and gained a great reputation and a vast personal fortune. At one reunion, she said when she retired she'd write something about the *Qing Ma* of the old days.

The only one to realize his original ambition was Maozi. He became a Fellow of the Marxian Philosophy Institute at the Academy of Social Sciences, where Chinese Marxism, Western Marxism, classical Marxism, and neo-Marxism were all to be found. At that time it was a bit risky to conduct critical analysis in this field, a field which has since become laughable. Later he developed a particular interest in sociology. That year when he had read *Economic and Philosophic Manuscripts of 1844* he proposed that the ideas therein were connected to both aesthetics and sociology. At the time, people were puzzled that Maozi claimed to find deep meaning in writings that seemed full of gobbledegook. Damo once expressed his skepticism, whereupon Maozi picked a couple of passages and explained as he read them how their implications tied in with aesthetics and sociology. He was only a couple of years older than the others, but his mastery of the scholarly literature and the history of ideas gave him the air of an instructor. Consequently when the Academy of Social Sciences began admitting Master's-level students, he was able to skip college and get admitted with only a high-school background. Everybody thought this was to be expected. Among this group of people, Damo was the only one to stay at the bottom of society. He lived at the economic level of the lower classes and knew the joys and sorrows of the intellectual aristocracy.

The members of the *Qing Ma* stayed in touch by phone over the years, and at irregular intervals they would find a way to meet in person. A pretty well-attended reunion occurred in the last year of the twentieth century when He Qiye and Liu Su had arranged to come home. It was just when the American economy was hitting bottom[156], while the rest of Asia and Europe were also in a slump; but, miraculously, the mainland was booming, and that brought people home in droves seeking opportunities. At that time Xiao Yong was also abroad, but (thinking nothing of the distance) she made a special trip to hurry back for this gathering. The two Chinese-Americans played host. They picked a top-notch hotel, booked an elegant room, and urged everyone to come early so they could all have a good, uninhibited conversation. The first topic when they saw each other invariably concerned the material aspect of existence. The job or career; the wife and kids; house and income, health and diet. He Qiye had gone to inherit the estate of a maiden aunt and with those funds he had opened a Chinese restaurant, and thus practiced an exceedingly dull and unimaginative profession. But it had been dependable: in a little more than ten years he had multiplied his net worth several times. Liu Su had also gone to the U.S. on account of family connections. He had managed to finish his degree in fits and starts and found a job preparing customs documents for an electronics firm managed by overseas Chinese. Both men had basically done all right, nothing like that Wang So-and-so in *A Beijinger in New York* who went over to wash dishes.[157] They were both middle-class, with a house and a car and no worries about life's necessities. They even had more children than other people. But among them all, the one who had really made the big time was Xiao Yong. Maozi once asked her what she was worth. "Oh, seven or eight figures, I guess." He Qiye and Liu Su inquired about the circumstances of everyone who had remained in China. Maozi and Xiao Yong had both turned out as expected; Damo was the only surprise. He Qiye said, "Back then, you know, my impression was that Maozi really knew his stuff, we called him the *Encyclopedia Britannica*. Xiao Yong had tremendous willpower. We called her the female Rakhmetov[158]; she bathed in cold water in winter. Damo was the most gifted, and a literary light as well: I once told someone the most talented of the lot had to be Damo . . . He Qiye's voice trailed off and no one said anything. But Damo laughed it off. "A smidgen of writing ability in the early years, never amounted to much: what could you do with that today? Hey, I've got enough to eat, and a roof over my head; I can read a little when I feel like it: I am content."

Maozi was the one who understood Damo best. He burst out, "He Qiye, you're being superficial. Our Damo is sublime, like some reclusive genius of old times. Even if he never finds the brass ring, he will have outclassed me."

Conversation turned to reminiscences. Nostalgia had become fashionable, especially for a past marked by hardship and tinged with the poetic sadness of unsophisticated honesty, as the *Qing Ma* had been. As they talked, Maozi excitedly announced he had just had an idea: *In Quest of the Missing Persons of Political Philosophy*! Damo said somebody had already written about that.[159]

"I know," Maozi said, "but he was just spouting off. We'll do some real digging, track down the people who played a role back then, see how they're faring now, and as a matter of sociology and the study of civilization try to understand their spiritual evolution. It would be interesting, for sure."

"No way!" said He Qiye and Liu Su, "We'd both be meat on your chopping block."

Maozi said, "Wouldn't I find myself on the block, too?"

"This is not some scandal that must be hidden," said Xiao Yong. "Haven't you noticed how all those cultural luminaries have made their self-denunciations into books?"

When men gather, they always wind up talking politics: for them, it's the main course. If a group were to gather without this course being served, stomachs would rumble and there would be an empty feeling. Especially when it's people who once formed a group such as the *Qing Ma*. The discussion passed from Sino-American relations to the Taiwan Strait, from the Middle East to Southwest Asia, from Yugoslavia to North Korea, and covered the challenges of the domestic economy, the corruption of local officials, the environmental crisis, the conflict between haves and have-nots, the dismal state of health care and education, and the way artists had sold their souls... They talked and they talked, reaching many an amicable disagreement. It was notable that Brother He and Brother Liu, the two who had lived abroad for years and taken U.S. citizenship, spoke quite negatively about America and stood out as patriots, whereas those who had stayed on the mainland and continued getting the Party's education had a great many barbed remarks to make about the state of their country. Of these, the most vehement was Damo.

"They always say," he smiled, "that if you go to America you'll get brainwashed. But with you two gents, the washing has had a reddening effect."

He Qiye retorted, "Not being in America, you've never experienced it personally. All you know is generalities. From the first day we set foot on American soil we felt differently about everything."

Maozi nodded, "Things always look good from a distance."

"I'm afraid so," Liu Su said. "When I first left China, I remember thinking, *I'm finally clear of a sea of troubles: from this hour, I can say whatever I want, I can criticize whatever I want.* Before a few days had gone by, I was too busy to say or criticize anything, but I missed home. You can't help it: that's what people are like."

"Yeah," said Damo, "you missed home; that's human nature. But homesickness is one thing; the kind of patriotism which 'loves the Party' is something else. In recent years the earliest cohort of sent-down youth have also been feeling nostalgic for their place of rural exile, nostalgic to the point of heartbreak. Back in the day, they swore by Heaven that for the rest of their lives they would not even piss in that direction. But eventually they broke down: they called some old friends, started going back in groups to see the hovels where they once lived and the peasants who were once their neighbors. This is nothing but a sentimental attachment to a part of our life that is over. There's no love for the 'sent-down' experience itself: don't you agree? If truth be told, your feelings are like that too. The way people look at a thing is distorted when they are personally removed from the reality of it."

Damo spoke politely but firmly. Xiao Yong overheard and said, "Those who've left their homeland and stayed away for a long time are deeply affected by it in their hearts. Anyone who hasn't experienced this probably can't understand."

He Qiye said, "Overseas, we were better informed than you guys about corruption in China. But the transformation of the Motherland these last few years is so obvious! You need only remember how we used to meet in the old days. When we were still in the countryside, it was in earthen huts and thatched sheds; in town, we met in garrets over back alleys. It all had to be secret, like we were in the underground Party. We've come a long way: here we are in a first-class hotel, and we can speak openly."

Damo smiled. "When I was little, I read a tale of Afanti.[160] The King asked Afanti, 'Here is Gold; here is Truth. Which do you want?' Afanti said, 'I want Gold.' The King said, 'I would choose Truth.' Afanti said, 'Right. Each man wants what he doesn't have.' You guys live overseas where there is lots of nostalgia, so you want to be patriotic. We live here, where there is lots of oppression, so we want to be free."

The two Chinese-Americans laughed and Liu Su said, "You're giving us a hard time, Damo."

Between friends who've not seen each other for years, there are bound to be disagreements; when they couldn't resolve these, they quit being serious. They drank and drank, and smoked and smoked; they told off-color stories and political jokes and the laughter came in waves. It was an ebullient gathering, in the course of which they all decided to visit Teacher Wei as a group two days later. By now, most people called Teacher Wei by the honorific Wei Lao. The alumni of the *Qing Ma* couldn't make that change. They felt it was more intimate to call him Teacher Wei and that was their privilege, for it brought back an unforgettable time, and an unlucky man who had lived in that compound shabbily clad and unsure of his next meal. They did some figuring and were startled to realize that his eightieth birthday was one month away. Judging that the *Qing Ma* could take this liberty, they decided to move up the observance.

Teacher Wei had remarried. His wife had been a professor at a northern university, more than ten years his junior, and it was her first marriage. They had met at a conference near the end of the Eighties. She had been smitten with Teacher Wei in the manner of a young woman. At the instigation of many friends, it eventually blossomed into love in the twilight of life. By all accounts, once married, the two had nothing but tenderness for each other. They were prodigal with the affections each had accumulated over a lifetime, and their strong and extravagant love made the young feel something was missing from their own lives.

Teacher Wei was thrilled when they called to say some of the *Qing Ma* were going to visit him. He Qiye said, "When we come to see you, Sir, we also have a little observance planned for your eightieth birthday."

Teacher Wei was surprised. "I'm eighty now? I'm that old?"

25

On the appointed day, Xiao Yong took a call from a client that turned out to be urgent and she hurried off to Beijing. The rest of them rode in Maozi's car to Teacher Wei's home. At the gate, they saw him waiting outside with his wife. From a distance they looked like a pair of flames. Each was wearing a red satin top with the Golden Cloud pattern and a Mandarin collar. Teacher Wei wore crisply ironed dark stovepipe trousers, and the lady was wearing a long skirt of the same color, windblown.

What was visually striking was that each had a silver head of hair, so they looked like snow-capped mountains on fire. The visitors warmly applauded the old couple's sense of style. Teacher Wei said they'd had the matching outfits tailored for them.

As a gift, the group had all pitched in to buy a stereo system with some classical CDs and they carried it in, all wrapped in red paper, like a wedding procession carrying a sedan chair with the dowry.

"You really know how to hurt a fellow," Teacher Wei said. "I thought I was still only sixty-something." When they were all seated inside, he said, "Looking at you, I realize I must have grown old. When I lived in the compound you were all barely twenty, isn't that right?"

His wife's surname was Zhao so they called her Zhao Yi. The two Chinese-Americans were meeting her for the first time: Teacher Wei introduced them one at a time.

"Please sit down," Zhao Yi said, "It makes me dizzy to see you all standing around." Her appearance and bearing were quite youthful.

With a housewife finally on the scene, the apartment had a new look. The living room sported a sofa, a coffee table and sideboard, and a TV cabinet: the wood had a fine dark stain. On the wall hung scrolls of calligraphy and paintings by well-known masters. The visitors insisted on touring the home before they sat down. The bedroom was now the typical bedroom of a married couple: the study furniture had been moved into the "Historic Dwelling" museum-style room. Only the can of tea remained, still resting on the cabinet at the head of the bed. The ratty old furniture was all gone from the Historic Dwelling room, which had become a study with two desks, on one of which there was even a computer. A few years previously, when Teacher Wei had been unable to get a couple of articles published, Damo had posted them for him, as well as getting some of his published work re-issued online. Other things as well drew Teacher Wei to the Internet: commentaries of all kinds, e-mails from people inside and outside China, and drafts of articles being sent back and forth. Thus had Teacher Wei and his wife, elderly and white-haired, been dragged into the online world. He liked to say he was the oldest Net newbie in China, and he gave himself the screen name Centipede because centipedes don't get stiff when they die. But he hadn't used it much. He'd said, it's a great name, let's register it before someone else takes it.

As the conversation proceeded volubly, He Qiye adroitly finished putting the stereo system together. The first disk he slipped into the CD player was Shostakovich's Seventh Symphony. But before he played it, He Qiye asked, "Teacher Wei, do you still remember Shostakovich?"

Teacher Wei was taken aback, because he didn't know why He Qiye had suddenly brought this up. "I remember: the great Soviet composer. Checking whether I'm senile?"

"Do you remember his Seventh Symphony?" He Qiye pressed.

"I remember," Teacher Wei said. "When I went to the Soviet Union in '54, I heard it performed by their national philharmonic."

He Qiye kept on: "Do you remember how one year you had a discussion with us about Shostakovich?"

Teacher Wei laughed. "I talked a lot in those days. I don't recall that conversation."

"A few of us were at your place," He Qiye explained, " talking about the Model Works[161], and you said *The Red Detachment of Women* was the best of the lot, artistically. It showed extensive knowledge of Western (especially Russian) music. Many passages echoed melodic patterns from *Swan Lake*. You compared one of the scenes with the female soldiers to the Dance of the Cygnets."

Now Damo remembered. In those years, he had lacked an ear for music and about such things as symphonies he had been a complete ignoramus. So Teacher Wei's comments had been unintelligible to him. Of their group, He Qiye had been the one most at home in music.

Unsure what He Qiye might have up his sleeve, Teacher Wei smiled warily, and the younger man continued: "You said it was a pity that the knowledge of Western music which underlay *The*

Red Detachment was so superficial. The melodies, the orchestration, and the performance were all lovely; but inside, there was no soul. The anguish and joy of the artist, the struggle, the pondering . . . these things just weren't there. It was hollow."

At this point Teacher Wei became animated and stammered, "I said these things back then? That wasn't bad, not bad at all."

The others chimed in. Damo recalled how Teacher Wei had said whether it was the Russia of the Tsars or the Soviet Union under Stalin, in that land there had always been a solid contingent of writers and artists who for the sake of art and truth, even if threatened with imprisonment or death, would not compromise beyond a certain point: and their conduct exemplified the nobility, the intrinsic worth, of mankind. Though Pushkin was an aristocrat in Tsarist Russia, he dared to write poems aimed at the tyrannical Tsar, such as "To Chaadaev" and "*Exegi Monumentum.*"[162] It was similar with Shostakovich: there was Hitler's war without, and Stalin's oppression within; yet he still composed such heartfelt and immortal works as the Seventh Symphony. But look at us, Teacher Wei had said: an army routed, a mass surrender. When the orders come down, not a single individual speaks up. We live like pigs, like dogs. We have no tragedies, only terror; no courage, only frenzy; no dignity, only arrogance; for life itself, no reverence, but we're obsequious to power. In his most dreadful hours he had clung to the memory of the writers and artists of the Soviet Union, and they had been a light in his darkness.

"Sir," He Qiye persisted, "on that occasion you said you weren't sure whether you would ever again listen to the Seventh Symphony."

"When I was in the USSR in those days, I heard from some friends that Shostakovich's *Seventh Symphony* had originally been called *Leningrad* because it was about the cruelty of war. But even more, it recorded the cruelty that reigned inside the country in Stalin's time. I bought a record of a performance by the Leningrad Philharmonic and brought it home, but later it was confiscated."

"Would you like to listen to it now?" asked He Qiye and

pressed a button on the remote control. From four speakers resounded that heavy melody full of terror and gloom and anxiety. A martial drumming boomed out, like jackboots trampling the heart. Teacher Wei suddenly cried out, "Turn it off! Turn it off! I'll listen to it by myself, later."

They were all somewhat shocked. He Qiye turned it off.

Teacher Wei shrugged sheepishly. "*Ai*, old age brings frailty. I'll listen to that melody another time, and before I do, I'll take some medicine. It's hard for us all to get together. We should talk about happy things."

They all asked him about his health. "Ah, my health . . . well, you can see what kind of shape I'm in. Internally, I'm told there are no major problems. Around twenty years ago, I didn't think I had many days to live. Never expected I'd last this long. I got a new lease on life after Zhao Yi, as you call her, showed up. It's as somebody said: Love makes people young. Works better than any tonic."

They all laughed. He continued, "Zhao Yi is my third pouring of tea." Maozi asked what this meant.

"At the first pouring," he answered, "it hadn't steeped long enough for the flavor to come out. With the second pouring, I enjoyed only a whiff of the aroma, never got to drink it. Only with this third pouring has the genuine article revealed its fragrance and strength."

Zhao Yi colored with embarrassment as she listened, and then remonstrated with Damo and the others: "This Teacher Wei of yours, as he goes on living he's changing from a grouchy old man into a naughty boy who will say anything."

"It's true," he conceded, "in my youth the work of the Revolution left me no time to talk. Then I became a counter-revolutionary and had no right to speak. Now's my only chance."

Overseas, He Qiye and Liu Su had sometimes picked up bits of news about Teacher Wei from the foreign press. They asked what the situation was like for him now.

He reflected before he answered. "There's no comparison between now and '55. There are people who don't like me, but they can't make me go to jail again. Mostly, they're content just to harass me a little. Too many people paid the price, you see, and after all, the world is different now. In that era they passed for the incarnation of Truth, of Morality: they claimed to embody in their persons the vast masses of the People. Even I believed it then. But today, though they may talk the same talk, it is with much less conviction; and these days I'm a little more confident than they. Everyone knows the history. If they want to discuss the truth, they're not likely to get the better of me, so the best they can do is turn a blind eye and pretend not to hear. Anyway, they know I can't outlive them."

"Some things," He Qiye said, "outlast a life."

"Yes," he said, "Truth is like that. But time takes its toll. Chinese have always been forgetful."

The conversation was beginning to turn gloomy.

"After these hundred years of turmoil," He Qiye said, "the common people aren't asking for much. Stability. Food to eat. Clothes to wear. That's all; that's enough."

Teacher Wei said, "It's understandable that the common people would feel that way. For intellectuals to feel that way is inexcusable."

This was a heavy topic, and no one wanted to pursue it. He Qiye, who had fallen quiet, now changed the subject and pointed out the piano. Damo had noticed as soon as he came in that the biggest change to the living room was the addition of a piano.

"We bought it last year," Teacher Wei said, "It was a birthday present for my lady."

"He says he gave it to me," Zhao Yi countered, "but the truth is it was so I could play for him."

"Only after we were married did I find out she was an accomplished pianist in her youth. But given that fact . . . why shouldn't a pavilion so close to the water get the moonlight first? What's more, at this age, to exercise your fingers on the piano makes you live longer!"

Naturally, they all asked Zhao Yi to play. She played a few short pieces. It was extraordinarily moving to hear such beautiful melodies flow from the fingers of a woman approaching her seventies. Everyone applauded wildly. She became embarrassed and said her fingers hadn't really got their feeling back yet. If they'd all like to sing, she would accompany them. "Actually," she said, "the reason we bought the piano was to provide accompaniment for this fellow you call Teacher Wei. When he wants something, I play it; I'm even more obedient than a Karaoke machine."

Though they'd been his friends for many years, none had ever heard that Teacher Wei could sing. They roared that he must sing something for them.

"Sure I'll sing," he said. "I've always sung. In the years when I was locked up, I sang those songs one after another in my mind. If I hadn't, I would have been dead long ago. When I emerged into a loneliness that was harder to bear than when I was locked up, I never stopped singing in my mind, for then too I would have died without it. Very well, I'll sing for you all a Russian tune, "On the Prairies by Lake Baikal." I'm not sure whether these eighty-year-old lungs can do it justice."

Zhao Yi played the introduction. Teacher Wei entered precisely on the beat, with good pitch and tempo and overall a good feel for the music. His voice was somewhat raspy, which matched the desolate mood of the song.

Across wild steppes beyond Baikal,
Where gold lies hid in the hills,
A wanderer trudged beneath his pack
And cursed life's cruel ills.

His tattered smock and convict's cap
Told whence he'd fled by night.
Much had he suffered, this weary man,
Suffered for truth and right.

Lifting his eyes he saw the lake
Spread out—he felt so frail!
And at the shore a fishing boat
About to hoist its sail.

He boarded soft, and sat alone,
His voice was sad and low.
He sang a song of his Motherland,
A ballad full of woe.

A wind now whispered at the prow,
"In vain you flee, in vain;
You have no hope, you have no friends,
Your destiny is pain."

There met him on the farther shore
His aged mother dear;
"Hail, mother! Of our family tell:
Do they live free from fear?"

"Your father sleeps beneath the ground,
Your brother's banished far,
And iron shackles hold him fast,
Deep in Siberia."[163]

The song could have been written for Teacher Wei. Through the many stanzas he sang it steadily without stumbling. One could imagine how, years before, he had sung it over and over. The long, solemn notes were a strain on his eighty-year-old lungs, however, and near the end He Qiye and the others tried to help by humming (they were a bit vague on the words). When he saw people joining him, Teacher Wei rallied and sang with growing force.

When the song was done, even Zhao Yi was moved to applause.

He gave a long sigh. "To sing relieves the woeful heart."

Song is like wildfire. Once it starts, it gathers strength and there's no way to put it out. Zhao Yi didn't need Teacher Wei to tell her what to play next: she knew. As the night went on, sometimes she would jump to the next number after only a verse or two and for the most part they all knew the songs. It wasn't clear whether they actually felt a desire to sing or just wanted to help

Teacher Wei, but in any event, by the end, every song rang out in chorus though sometimes they would let him take a couple of lines solo. And when the notes were very high or called for great strength, He Qiye sang them alone. The atmosphere had gradually become charged with warm emotion and they all got caught up in it. The tunes that Zhao Yi played and Teacher Wei sang were mostly from Soviet Russia, along with a few Western folk songs and early Chinese leftist anthems such as *Song at Midnight*[164], *Song of Meiniang*[165], *Ode to the Yellow River*[166], and that anthem of progressive youth in the old days when they had such admiration, even adulation, for the Party: *You are the Beacon*[167].

They sang for a long time, with gusto. Suddenly Zhao Yi stopped, saying, "Can't sing anymore; your Teacher Wei won't be able to sleep tonight." Everyone then noticed he was slightly flushed and fine beads of sweat had covered his forehead, and his eyes had a faraway look. So they all returned to their seats. After drinking some tea, they began to chat.

Damo said, "There's a question I've always wanted to ask you, Sir, but I felt that in your case such a question might be somewhat cruel."

Teacher Wei was slowly coming out of the trance-like state which the singing had induced, and in a surprised tone he said only, "Huh?"

"After more than half a century," Damo plunged in, "how do you now see the quest and the struggle of your youth?"

Teacher Wei smiled thoughtfully. "You're right, that is a very cruel question, but an unavoidable one. When a few of us old fellows get together we ask ourselves the same question, and there are many different ways to answer it. Some are quite rational, others have an emotional tinge; some speak after long reflection, while others, lacking any self-knowledge, can offer nothing but the clichés that have been planted in their brains all these years. Let's put it this way: first of all, for the historical context, I think instead of saying that I chose the Revolution it would be better to say that the Revolution chose me, just as a seed that falls from a tree at any given time will be blown to a particular place by whatever wind is blowing then. And that patch of soil, along with the sunlight and the wind and rain, will make it grow. The seed itself has not chosen all this. You think it's been your choice but it's been History's choice, the time in which you live. You'd have to say this about all of us who were the youth of that time. From May 4th[168] on, new schools of political thought and a new culture flourished all across the country. In the dire conditions after Japan invaded the North, it was natural for young people to doubt the authorities and rebel against them. And—this is an extremely important point—the ideas of socialism were remarkably in harmony with the ideological trend of May 4. At that time the principled stance and political agenda of the Communist Party were reasonable and realistic. You need only glance through the Communist newspapers and literature of that time to understand why so many talented and honorable young men and women could give up their careers, forsake a comfortable life and even the love of a family in order to devote themselves to such a cause. That song I was just singing, "Ardor," came from a left-wing film of the 1930s, *Song at Midnight*.

Who wants to be a slave? Who wants to be exploited?
The flames of war have engulfed all Europe;
We take our stand for universal love, equality, and freedom...

I would say that the cries of the Left at that time and the slogans of the Communist Party were almost identical to the slogans that would be chanted in 1989 on Tiananmen Square: against corruption, against dictatorship; for democracy, for liberty; they sought a society marked by equality and justice, they sought to save the nation[169] and make China prosper . . . In those days young people were more naive than today, and more ardent; in addition to the influence of May 4 there was the moral feeling and spirit of sacrifice that came from our cultural traditions, according to which the scholar bears responsibility for the nation. Therefore in such times as those, it was entirely normal for a young man of promise to dedicate himself to revolution and social progress, especially a young intellectual from a well-off family who never had to worry where his next meal was coming from. On this point, note how we are all prone to be stirred by our own emotions when they are of this type, as, for example, the young college students on the Square were moved by their own dedication. This is always a beautiful thing. But we were too young. We had too little experience of political life. We had had essentially no opportunity to recognize and reflect on the profound influence which the authoritarian culture of feudalism would exert on our great revolution. Still less had we seen and pondered the real facts of the Soviet dictatorship and its fatal flaws. Because our party was then still out of power and was subject to persecution and repression, it had to be scrupulous about standing on the side of the masses, on the side of historical progress, in order to appeal to people's sense of morality and justice. The pity is that until the very founding of the new nation, we never had occasion to properly reflect on the problems of our revolution in a theoretical and systematic way. Our victory was too sudden, too smooth. During the time at Yan'an, a few people had already recognized the first symptoms of the problem, but thanks to the Japanese and the KMT no one could pay much attention to it. I remember once in the late Seventies I watched the film *Visitor on Ice Mountain*[170] again. There was a throwaway line that brought tears to my eyes. The soldier who's disguised himself as one of the hill people in order to penetrate the bandits' lair, but who finally gets ambushed and killed: just before he dies, he says to the real Gulandanmu[171], "We were too young." The tragedy of the young causes the deepest grief, though it is inescapable. It was only much later that we had time to ponder the revolution, and the anti-Rightist campaign, and the Great Leap Forward, and the reform of land ownership, and the suppression of counterrevolutionaries[172], and the Three Antis and the Five Antis[173], and let us not forget a campaign of particular concern to myself, the campaign against Hu Feng; and, yes, the Yan'an Rectification of Styles[174]. Finally, let us reflect on something that happened in the early years of the Red Army, the campaign against the Anti-Bolshevik league.[175] Many of these were undertakings in which I personally took part. And with what spirit I took part in them! Such exaltation, such feelings of self-sacrifice. . . it is excruciating to remember this now. You people who came later can look at these events coolly, objectively, with detachment. But for a man who once devoted all his passion and loyalty and integrity to this cause, there is a painful embarrassment such as none of you have ever known. It is a harrowing pain, and the embarrassment is like being stripped naked in public. That's why many of us from that generation prefer to close our eyes and not look back, so we can muddle through what remains of our life without being honest with ourselves or others. To be sure, there are also some extremely practical considerations. We're all old, now; none of us can still support ourselves and take care of ourselves, but it's not yet time to die. We've got nothing left but a little prestige from long ago. In a country where all resource allocation depends on State power, you're like a helpless baby: your housing belongs to someone else; your wages depend on someone else choosing to give them to you. The mere occasion of needing to see a doctor makes many submissive. You want to go to the hospital? You want a room in the cadres' infirmary instead of squeezing into the filthy bedlam of the commoners' ward? You want good care, imported medicine? Want to be operated on by a well-known specialist? Then you'd better not give us any trouble. When they've had to choose between life and honor, Chinese have always chosen the former. Consequently, I have told my wife that if some day I get sick and need a treatment that is beyond our means, let it take its course, don't ask for any favors. I'm repeating this for the benefit of you fellows: if that situation arises, please don't embarrass me by interceding on my behalf."

Teacher Wei stopped for a moment and took a sip of water as if still thinking. "I remember I used to tell you that during my arrest and imprisonment I kept believing in this regime, sincerely believing in the theory on which it was based; so I believed, sincerely, that I myself was guilty. Even though I had been wronged and felt dread and despaired of life, I still didn't reach the depths where I could harbor any doubts. Still less did I suspect that there were any aspects of what I considered the revolutionary program, things that I myself had done, which might require reassessment. I remember in the statement that served as my confession, I mercilessly dissected my offense but also tried to defend myself, pointing out how I had been a progressive at college, how I had made efforts to study Marxism-Leninism and the writings of Mao Zedong, how (after the founding of the new nation) I had taken part in a series of programs to remold my thinking and criticize the work of others. I listed each of the articles I had written in those days, thereby to prove that I had never taken a stand opposing the Party and the People."

Damo said, "Sir, these articles you mentioned, I once read a few of them in the library. I remember a long piece criticizing *The Life of Wu Xun*[176].

"Yes," Teacher Wei said, "I still remember that one. The title was 'From *Franz von Sickingen*[177] to *The Life of Wu Xun*.' The theoretical basis for the criticism came directly from the criticisms which Marx and Engels directed at Lassalle's play, *Franz von Sickingen*. This approach was very common at that time, among us intellectuals, and we were adept at it: we would cloak a crude dogmatism in an air of refinement and rationality, dropping names in order to sound high-minded as we railroaded our victim. When, later, I myself was taken down, it was by this method. Years afterward, I read newspaper articles criticizing me and recognized they were modeled on articles just like the ones I had written. The articles you mentioned, Damo, constitute an extremely sore point for all the intellectuals of my generation. They left a stain which none of us can bear to look back on, even decades later: they're like the muddy footprints that keep following you even after you get out of the swamp. I used to wonder, if it hadn't been for 1955—if I had kept going with the wind at my back, successful and satisfied—what would I have become?"

He looked around at everyone gathered there, as if seeking to read an answer in their faces. They smiled with understanding. "I think the best I could have turned out would have been along the lines of Zhou Yang[178], and if I still had any conscience, time would hang heavy on me now. I am therefore thankful for 1955. By accident, it saved a cowardly and ignorant man of culture and set him, unsteadily, on a path from which there was no turning back. That for him to make what should have been a natural choice it was necessary to immolate several decades of his life is an absurdity for which there is no precedent since ancient times. I think others were in my position and took decades to choose a path that was very different from mine, but from which likewise there was no turning back. Even if by now they know better in their hearts, they don't have the strength to change, and in this way their lot is more tragic than mine, for I am certain that when I die I will rest in peace. The fear must gnaw at them that someday someone will come along and flog their corpse.[179] I, too, know there is still much in my own mind and heart that needs to be set right. I don't know whether Heaven will grant me enough time. I do worry about that."

Again he looked around as if for confirmation. Everyone was quite moved and grave. What had started off as a merry celebration of an old man's birthday had turned into something different: a soul had been weighed in the balance. Damo felt bad that he had asked such a question at such a time. Teacher Wei, however, seemed pleased and he asked whether Damo had any more questions. "I won't say another word," Damo laughed, "talking about these things spoils the happiness of the occasion."

"On the contrary," Teacher Wei said, "my happiness lies in thrice-daily self-examination.[180] That I can correct myself even in old age is a great joy. What's more, there are some problems which can only be worked out through cross-examination. Go ahead."

"It only occurred to me now," Damo said. "All these years I've heard you criticize the impact of ultra-Left ideology on art. But that's exactly the stuff you were singing tonight."

Everyone laughed. Teacher Wei laughed, too. "You're a tough one; you hit where it hurts. After the breakup of the Soviet Union, I went back to visit again. It had been forty years. My feelings were rather complicated. I felt glad they were finally on a path they themselves had chosen, a path of liberty and democracy. But I felt sentimental for the persons who had wholly dedicated themselves during the course of almost a hundred years to something that had collapsed like a sand-castle. I was familiar with many of their writers and artists and could rattle off the names—indeed, some of them I had even met. Many of these have now been forgotten, even spurned, by history; some committed suicide or just died of grief and shame. This kind of sorrow is hard for outsiders to grasp. But we had so much in common with them . . . you know, those with the same illness feel for each other. Especially our generation, which to a great degree was nourished on their ways of thought, their culture. Red Square was still Red Square, and the Winter Palace was still the Winter Palace; the Neva River was the same as it had always been, with that illustrious warship the *Aurora* still moored amid its waves.[181] But the Soviet Union, that colossus, was nowhere to be seen. The people who had dedicated themselves to it with such fanaticism had also vanished. Objectively speaking, many of them were extremely talented and in any normal society, or even in Tsarist Russia, they would have been a source of national pride. Nowadays we still admire, as always, the names from Tsarist times which glitter with eternal fame: their novels, their paintings, their symphonies and plays remain a treasure for Russia and all mankind. But the geniuses of the Soviet era are gone; hardly anyone remembers who they were, and when they are remembered it's most often with contempt or hatred. Out on the streets, young men and women stride along, vigorous and attractive and alive; and elderly people with cultivation and gentleness written on the faces under their fur hats, everything in the finest taste, as if nothing had ever happened in their world. Of course there are paupers too, and drunks, and tourists from all over the globe. Once I saw a lovely Russian girl on a boulevard; you know, Russian women are truly beautiful, with a high-born and elegant beauty. She was wearing a fur coat and a fur hat and when she walked past I stopped and stared, without thinking what I must look like; I just gaped at her, you know? It was like catching sight of Anna Karenina. More than a century had rolled by; Stalin had come and gone, and Beria and Brezhnev, and even Mayakovsky who attained the zenith of fame: they had vanished without a trace, every one of them;

but the beauty of Anna Karenina was still there, more durable in its tender fragility than all the arrogance of power. Almost all the buildings I had seen forty years before were still standing, but most of the people who welcomed me then had died. Some had disappeared without a trace. At a party, I suddenly felt like singing some Russian songs. After I had sung a few, I discovered none of the people there (most of them were fairly young) had any idea what I was singing. *Little Road*, *Lamplight*, *The Lenin Hills*[182]—they said they'd never heard any of these. Rock and roll, on the other hand, and jazz, and modern pop music: they sang all those, styles that had nothing in common with the Russian songs I knew. Afterward an old writer told me that he knew all the stuff I had sung but he didn't want to hear it. I asked why not. He said it reminded him of extremely unhappy things, a painful and humiliating time. Only then did I understand that the feelings which I had for this music were completely different from the feelings they had for it. What we sing is only the love, the struggle, and the beautiful melody; we are singing the songs of a Soviet Union that belongs only to us. Do you still remember, from the years when we listened to enemy radio stations, the signature theme of Radio Moscow?[183]"

He Qiye said of course he remembered, and began to hum the tune. "I think they still use it."

"It's a few bars from a famous song," Teacher Wei said. "A song with a couple of lines that go like this:

> *We have never seen another country*
> *Where one can breathe so free...*[184]

To us this is a vision filled with yearning for a heroic world. But to them, what lies behind this melody is a dreary and terrifying ordeal. It's just like what happens when Westerners watch the Model Operas today and think they are experiencing an ancient Oriental art form, while for us the gongs and drums and arias bring back harrowing details of the time of the Cultural Revolution. Yet for people who grew up to that music, the instrumentals and vocals and standardized gestures record scenes from their childhood, and the memories may be happy and sweet. So it is with my generation: for all our sharp and sober repudiation of Stalin's cruel dictatorship and the long and blighting shadow which the politics and culture of Soviet Russia cast upon China, the music of the Soviets—of the Reds—still casts a subtle emotional spell. So I think for any given person with a particular upbringing, this kind of music (even if it's only on tape) holds a part of your life within it. Here in our country there is a twofold tragedy. Even our private emotional memories have been alloyed with a quicksilver ideological culture that pervades everything. We don't have an untainted cultural vehicle with which to record our own lives; we don't have it, not even the least bit... not at all. Other countries have it. Even the poorest and most backward countries have it; even totalitarian countries like the former Soviet Union had it, for in almost every era there were writers and artists who made their voices heard, leaving works that gleam with everlasting splendor, whether in poetry, music, fiction, sculpture, or drama: Akhmatova, Pasternak, Solzhenitsyn. And Shostakovich, whom we were just talking about. Years later, the Russians don't have to be like us: they are not stuck with the embarrassment, the bittersweet ambiguity, of finding all their memories embedded in the kind of art you alluded to. The terror did not stop *them* from creating great art to enshrine their memories. Once, when I myself was in dire straits, I wondered why I couldn't write a ballad like the song of Lake Baikal, one that I could sing in after years? We had so many writers and artists, but who among them ever wrote down in song what he suffered during those hard years, what the people suffered, so that by singing it now we might authentically remember the history of our suffering and not so easily forget? To lack such art is a more bitter affliction than the suffering itself. The Russians dipped their pens in their own blood and wrote their memories upon the earth. But we let others write our memories and they used knives to write them, and the only record is our wounds.

"In a few decades, we lost the ability to express pain and grief. We lost the ability to express love. What we got instead was something paltry and preposterous. Once I found myself humming a tune that must have accorded with my mood of the moment, and I realized with a start it was a song from the epic film *The East is Red*:

> *When I look up and see the Big Dipper,*
> *In my heart I pine for Mao Zedong. . .*

We are talking about the people with the largest population and the longest history on earth: you have to admit, there is something horrifying about this. Even today we have not fully grasped the effect which such a phenomenon must have on the cultural psychology of a people."

Teacher Wei's face had become wan. "What Damo brought up might seem like a small matter of tunes to hum and songs to sing, but it's actually a big problem. This is why the authorities prefer to let third-rate crooners from Hong Kong and Taiwan dominate the market rather than letting songs be heard which might express in an authentic way the sufferings and aspirations of individuals and the masses. Today, when we can't help recycling the cultural resources of an earlier era, we are unwittingly bolstering the legitimacy of a certain ideology from that era and likewise the legitimacy of today's Establishment. That is exactly what some people want."

He Qiye responded with a nervous laugh. "Yep, our generation is even more pathetic. When we get together overseas we wax nostalgic, and though we talk about a lot of things that were unbearable and crazy in the old days, as soon as we start to sing, there's nothing but adulation for Chairman Mao, 'the sun of our hearts'; there's nothing but the Red Guards saluting the Chairman across the grasslands: 'Mountains and waters acclaim you, songs and melodies sound your praise.' When you're singing you feel stirred but also listless, and once the song is over it feels ridiculous. But come on, when we were young, that's all there was to sing."

Teacher Wei answered, "When you're singing, in other words, you have separated what is denoted from what denotes it: or as the proverb says, use another's wine cup to drown your sorrows. Partly it's what you're feeling; partly it's the opposite. I can remember, a little more than ten years ago when the Army was engaged in a large-scale operation[185], on TV they showed a company of young soldiers artlessly singing "In Unity There is Strength."[186] I listened for a while, then yelled at the TV, "*What* are you singing?!" The song has the words, "Open fire on the fascists, let the whole undemocratic system be wiped out." It was incredible. All those years of singing these songs over and over again, and it was as if they were in a foreign language that people knew how to pronounce but that had no meaning. I can remember how we sang that song in the late '40s when we were fighting Chiang Kai-shek. We'd sing it at rallies; we'd sing it on the march; we'd sing it in jail.

Facing the sun,
Moving toward freedom and a New China,
Glory to the ends of the earth!

This song came from our hearts, so for it to be sung now by that kind of people at such a moment . . . it makes you want to laugh, and it makes you want to cry.

"One more thing. For an individual to sing these songs on account of his emotional needs and a particular history, that's his personal right; but it's a different matter for the organs of the State to disseminate these songs among the masses for their own purposes.

"There's another question," Teacher Wei finally said, "which is connected with the matters we've been discussing. You doubtless remember how we talked about "systemic problems" after the death of Lin Biao, though at that time my language was still fairly restrained and I think I used the term "structural." To tell the truth, it only occurred to me to raise this point after I had been made to pay such a high price. In other words, if they hadn't driven me into a corner I wouldn't have thought about questioning the system. It was just like something that transpired later: when Liu Shaoqi[187] had been arrested by the Red Guards and they were having a struggle session against him, he took out a copy of the Constitution and said, 'I am the President: I am protected under the Constitution.' He, too, had to reach the end of his rope for the systemic question to occur to him. From our youth, all we got in our education was romanticism, revolution, violence, anarchy, Communism. There wasn't much rationality; there wasn't much talk of rules and there was no emphasis on the design of the system. Our spiritual resources were drawn from the French Revolution and the October Revolution. This was the spirit we were all steeped in, like those songs you and I were just singing: boundless enthusiasm without law or morality. It was all about criticizing, smashing, and crushing the old world in order to build a new one, and having a good time while we were at it. I wrote hymns of praise to the Leader; I took part in the earliest mass criticism sessions of the New China; I wrote the first new textbooks for language arts. You could say that the marching students who dragged me through the streets a little more than ten years later, the kids who beat and reviled me, were the products of the education I had crafted. When the revolution came full circle and hit me in the head; when I was cast down so low, with almost no hope of ever being rehabilitated, only then did certain questions occur to me. But by then the cataract of revolution was unstoppable, and thousands upon thousands of intellectuals who had rhapsodized it with devotion, and even revolutionaries of the older generation, were engulfed in the flood and washed away. In recent years my reflections have been painful ones. In '55 and '66 my fellow-men repudiated me convincingly. Lately I have come close to experiencing that again; but this time it is I myself who repudiate myself, and for a completely different reason.

"The things we've talked about today could make a great essay, but I'm afraid I don't have the strength to write it; all I could manage would be a few personal reminiscences. I wonder if any of you fellows have the time to give it a try?"

There was a long silence.

Before they took their leave, the members of the *Qing Ma* asked for a tour of his apartment. Damo recognized two familiar things: one was the can of tea, still resting by the headboard of the bed. The other was the couplet, which had been put into two picture frames and now hung on the wall of his study:

Walking beside the stream, I recite 'Asking Heaven';
Lifting up mine eyes, I sing the Song of Guangling.

The *Qing Ma* gang called that birthday of Teacher Wei's a seminar on political thought and culture, as well as a personal spiritual reappraisal.

26

The Internet is like an unending supermarket. No one can claim to have explored it fully and found its farthest limits. Some who go online are like those strong-willed shoppers who have a definite purpose and hurry to a particular aisle to pick up the towel or soap, or toothbrush or toothpaste, that they came to get; then they turn around and leave. When such people go online, it's just to send an e-mail or look something up, and in five minutes they turn off the machine. But there are others who meander through the merchandise, forgetting to turn back, going farther and farther until their shopping cart is full. The difference is, on the Net you don't have to hand over any money on your way out; if you've ordered monthly broadband service, the motto of this kind of shopping is "to each according to his needs." It's the realization in the here-and-now of that great world hypothesized by Communism.

When Ru Yan first started going online, her ability to imagine this world was quite limited. She supposed there must be a few hundred websites, maybe as many as a thousand. In about the same numbers as newspapers and magazines, she thought, there were news sites comparable to what TV and the papers offered, with bulletins and celebrity gossip. Then she added mailboxes like the QQ and MSN accounts which her son had set up for her, and she thought this was all there was to the Net. Later she was dumbfounded to hear estimates that there were already between a million and ten million websites. It was like looking up into the starry sky, vast and boundless. It seemed this little box could handle everything: in addition to all the content carried in the print media, there were movies, TV, streaming radio, archived video discs of all formats, Karaoke, pictures, photos, Flash, 3-D animations . . . As a child she had treasured her copies of *Three Hundred Tang Poems* and *Selected Lyrics of the Song*[188], but on the Internet you could pick them up, like nickels, anywhere. It took only a few seconds to find anything you wanted to read. As for vocal music, you could listen to old phonograph records from the Thirties and Forties, honky-tonk with tinny acoustics and lots of static; you could also hear the latest pop stars and deafening heavy-metal bands. Ru Yan whiled away many an evening listening to the children's songs that had been current in her infancy; she had never expected to encounter them again. Without the Internet, she could never have recalled them; yet as soon as she heard them online, she discovered they had been engraved indelibly in her mind. Her biggest shock was reading a great many works that had never made it into print. These writings had a point of view, with respect to their theoretical foundations, political doctrine, and conceptual framework, which at first was somewhat troubling to her. Ru Yan was the kind of person who had never concerned herself with political theory, and her indifference implied a certain skepticism and disapproval. But these articles, novel and incisive, with their recklessly bold way of appraising things, mesmerized her even as they frightened her. They also gave her access to raw facts—the true facts of historical events that had been neglected or buried or repackaged, so that this history now began to reveal a disconcerting face. Ru Yan had no way to verify the authenticity of what was presented as fact. But she had intuition. It was the little details that convinced her, more than the overarching narrative. She knew that many things could be faked, but details could not be faked. In a well-attested village in the hills, in living memory[189], a named family of villagers had all eaten a poisonous wild plant that resembled a carrot. Based on what the writer said, Ru Yan could easily identify the plant as *Lao gong yin*[190]. The whole family had put on their best clothes before dinner. Soon after they finished eating, each found a place to lie down and the poison acted quickly. Seven died rolling about on the ground, all but the ten-year-old boy, whose mother had told him before her end that he alone had eaten real carrots and that there were a few more in the woodshed. She wanted him to take them and go out and find some way to stay alive. The writer of the article was none other than that boy, who had luckily managed to survive. At the end he gave his address and phone number. As far as Ru Yan was concerned, other people could argue about whether ten, twenty, or thirty million had died or whether in fact anyone at all had starved to death. For her, the death of this one family was proof enough. Ru Yan had not gone hungry in those days. Her father was still in the armed forces. She had just started nursery school and took her rice and white steamed buns for granted. A toddler has no idea what's going on in the outside world. But as she read the story now, more than forty years later, she felt a pang of hunger.

Ru Yan was starting to feel uneasy about something. It was the same disquiet many had felt in 1966, in 1976, and in 1989, but in each case the feelings had quickly subsided. It was the same indignation her father had felt in 1937 and her mother in 1948, and in their case, too, the turmoil had been tamed. In many areas of life Ru Yan was out-of-step, behind the beat. She was like her beloved late-blooming osmanthus. Other osmanthus trees would have bloomed in season, long ago, and been praised for their scent by people who lingered in their shade; the bees would have gathered their nectar and their flowers would have been already brewed into osmanthus wine: but her osmanthus, calm and silent, would only be starting to bloom. As she read these disquieting posts now, she often couldn't restrain herself from posting a few words in comment: a sigh, or a probing question, an appraisal, an endorsement, sometimes a stern talking-to. Critical reasoning was not Ru Yan's forte; these reactions of hers sprang rather from her emotions, just as she was easily touched by the plot twists when she watched a play or a film. She gave more credence to the nitty-gritty, the concrete human details, than to pretentious verbiage.

Thus did Ru Yan's sphere of activity on the Internet gradually broaden. Like a peasant woman tending her garden she managed the forum of the Empty Nest, but at the same time she enthusiastically set out to explore the online world, like a youth from the countryside newly arrived in the capital. "Such Is This World," that suggestive name of a person with literary language and emotional reactions, was cropping up on several websites and forums.

The Empty Nest had its own chat room. Online friends would occasionally gather there to shoot the breeze, sing, or have private conversations using a duplex exclusive channel. When two people had opened an exclusive channel, the phone icon beside each one's name would turn from green to black, which gave rise to the expression "making a black phone call." This was convenient for talkative people who had no pressing business. On weekends and holidays, the chat room was quite lively.

For some time now the forum had been growing in popularity, and visitors to the chat room had multiplied. There were evenings with twenty, thirty, even forty or fifty people there. Some of them had a child overseas and others didn't; some were getting ready to send their child abroad. Some of the parents in the chatroom were at home, while others were themselves abroad. It was like a noisy, packed room, with people shaking hands, asking after one another, presenting bouquets, pouring tea, and sitting cosily on a bench. For some it was their daytime, for others it was late at night; some had not yet eaten dinner while others had just arrived at their office at the crack of dawn. It's been said that the Internet transcends space and time, and you could feel that in this chat room.

When the forum regulars came to the chat room, some kept using the same screen name, others gave themselves a different one, and still others played it by ear, unpredictably. The person whose screen name was "Black Flag" became Bad Bug[191] in the chat room. "Northern Wolf" came to chat as Blunderbuss; and "d" turned into "b," which was potentially confusing, since someone else was named "db." They would carry on, making jokes and playing tricks on one another. The fooling-around went on until they got tired or caught on or lost their tempers, and then they would resume their usual screen names. Not many ever worked out each other's real identities. If you knew that this was Mr. or Ms. So-and-so, the joking around and haranguing were finished. It was like a masquerade. Not at all like what came later, when the faces behind the masks would prove no longer good-humored and light-hearted, but rather hostile, grim, and scornful.

After the Mid-Autumn Festival, the holidays that mark the turn of the year came thick and fast. National Day, the Double Ninth, and then many would mark an anniversary of being sent to the countryside; then there would be Christmas, Mao's Birthday, New Year's Day, and the Spring Festival.[192] A joyous atmosphere prevailed throughout the forum and the chat room. Over time, personal details gradually emerged: birthdays, wedding anniversaries, the Nth anniversary of being sent down to the countryside, the marriage of a son or a daughter; for those who were older or had started their families earlier, there were grandsons and granddaughters being born. Those wishing to stir things up would solicit articles on these themes. There were song contests and parties. In the kindly, intimate fashion of a village, they called each other Elder Brother and Elder Sister, and the interactions meant gaiety and solace to these old birds with empty nests and brought the warmth of spring to many a cold and lonely night.

Ru Yan did not like public speaking, and *a fortiori* was not about to sing in front of an audience. When she came to the chat room she tended to hide on the sidelines and observe. If she recognized any of those present, she might exchange a few words, sometimes on the Q.T. so that only the other party could see what she 'said.' She was like a little girl who quietly curls up in a corner near the fire on a *kang* where people are conversing volubly.[193] She had posted many articles, then become the moderator, and she even came to the chat room: it seemed she had never gotten a break. Constantly there were calls for the Colon[194] or the Boss, who sometimes couldn't keep up with all the greetings she had to make. Instigators would call on the Manager to give a speech or invite the Moderator to sing.

On one such occasion, the person serving as Webmaster forced the "mike" on Ru Yan. Under this good-natured pressure, Ru Yan started to speak into the mike. Someone immediately typed, "`After a thousand years the sago palm has spread her leaves`" and then someone else typed "`The deaf-mute has opened her mouth to speak.`" Then—give 'em an inch and they'll take a mile—they clamored for Ru Yan to sing. It was somebody's birthday; Ru Yan couldn't dissuade them, and she didn't want to spoil the celebration with an awkward silence. So she gathered her courage and began singing an Argentine song, "A Little Gift."[195] As a teenager she had heard her older sister sing it and she had always loved it. Ru Yan could actually sing quite a few songs, but she always sang quietly for only herself to hear; it was almost a secret, and even her husband, in all those years of intimacy, had not known this about her. When she sang now into the microphone without accompaniment, either because the song itself was deeply moving or because she sang it with such charm and grace, she won rave reviews: `a new star!` and the chat room's page filled up with flower icons as they all showered her with bouquets.

Because of the Internet, Ru Yan had made it through the lonely months after her son's departure. Because of the Internet, Ru Yan heard her own voice after years of silence. Because of the Internet, she had written all those articles which even she herself found touching, and which had made her discover a talent she had never acknowledged. A few newspapers and magazines had contacted her about publishing some of her pieces and had asked her to write expressly for them. Because of the Internet, she had had a chance to look into her heart and her past life, seeing many things that she had never understood before.

27

When the conference opened in Beijing it was as if Liang Jinsheng had dropped off the face of the earth. There was no word from him, none at all. After a while Ru Yan couldn't stand it any more, and she found a work-related excuse to drop by Jiang Xiaoli's office. Jiang Xiaoli asked about him.

"He went to Beijing for a conference, don't you know? You're next-door neighbors!"

"You two have crossed the river. I was the bridge. There's no reason for either of you to speak to me now. Any phone calls?"

"No," Ru Yan said.

"Perfectly normal. Think about what time of year this is. Up and down the line, everybody's under pressure."[196]

Ru Yan asked, "So much pressure they don't have time to make a phone call?"

"You must have gone through this with your Dad; how come you don't understand this Communist Party stuff? At the time of the Great Ninth, my old man went missing and we didn't hear a peep from him for months. We were climbing the walls, thought he might have been jailed. We asked around, but nobody knew. Then at the close of the Congress he phoned us in tremendous excitement and the first thing he said was: he had seen Chairman Mao! The old worthy was the picture of health, it would be a cinch for him to live to a hundred. He said he had also seen Vice-Chairman Lin Biao, and Vice-Chairman Lin Biao was also in great health, did we know he was Chairman Mao's successor? It was all in the Party regulations, he said . . . You think this bothered us? When men enter the world of officialdom, their family means nothing to them. You need to be mentally prepared for this."

When Liang Jinsheng phoned Ru Yan it was almost a month later, and he was in America. To be so suddenly distanced in time and space made that moonlit night in mid-autumn now seem not entirely real. He was saying that he wouldn't be able to come back for another two weeks, so it looked as though they really would need their overcoats to go moon-viewing again. Ru Yan's tone was rather cool—it's not that she was trying to avoid seeming excited, she just felt a little neglected. He heard this in her voice and said with a chuckle, "I just got here; this is the very first phone call I've made back to China. Tell me your cell phone number. That will be better. You know our day and night are reversed."

Only then did Ru Yan remember she had forgotten to buy herself a cell phone.

"I'll have one delivered to you at once," he said.

Ru Yan was embarrassed and thought to herself, *The guy's so busy, and you're not anything to him yet; what are you unhappy about?* On reflection, she saw the humor in the situation. "I'll go buy one very soon," she hurried to say, "there are a few of those shops on our street. Please don't let everyone in the world know that the mayor bought somebody a phone."

Before he hung up, he asked whether she wanted anything from America.

She answered, "A box of hot-dogs, fresh out of the oven."

That same day, after getting the call from Liang Jinsheng, she went out and bought a cell phone. When he called again a few days later, she gave him the number. He hung up immediately and called back on her cell phone to verify it. For a long time afterward, Liang Jinsheng was the only person who ever called her on her cell phone.

He came back in the middle of November and hurried to Ru Yan's house the same evening his plane landed, and phoned from the lobby downstairs. Her heart began to pound with a nervous energy she had never felt before: it was not fear, nor was it a pleasant excitement; it was confusing. Her husband had been dead for three years, and besides her son no other man had come to her home, and certainly no man with whom she'd developed such a charged relationship. She quickly glanced round her apartment; fortunately, it wasn't too bad. She was habitually tidy, so everything was presentable. She opened the door when he rang. He was standing there wheezing and panting but grinning from ear to ear and holding a big cardboard box in his arms. When he said he wanted to change his shoes, she realized she had no men's slippers in the house, and told him not to worry about it because she had nothing he could wear. He took off his shoes anyway and entered in his stocking feet. He put the big box on her table and said, "Here's what you wanted."

"What?" she asked.

"The hot dogs," he said. "When I bought them, they were fresh out of the oven." He made a show of touching the box and remarked that by now they were probably no longer hot.

The box had been prettily wrapped with a big bow on top, as if it contained an expensive gift. "You want to open it and see?" he suggested. "When Westerners receive a present, they open it in front of you; it's considered discourteous not to."[197]

Ru Yan was sure it would prove to be something else; how could he make her a present of hot dogs? But Yang Yanping had caught the scent and was yapping and straining to get at the box. She opened it and took a look: it really was hot dogs, individually wrapped in paper. She burst out laughing. "You must be the only person in all China who has brought something like this back from America."

Liang Jinsheng said, "During the C.R. there was a common saying, do you remember? 'Whatever Chairman Mao says, that's what we'll do.'" He, too, laughed, and after unwrapping one of the hot dogs he took a bite. "Still OK, haven't gone bad . . . you've got enough here for half a month if you put them in the refrigerator."

"Just what I always wanted," she said wryly.

"I guess I bought the right gift," he said, pleased.

Watching Liang Jinsheng already eating, Yang Yanping became even more excited, standing on her hind legs and begging with her front paws. Ru Yan muttered, "Yang Yanping, you're disgraceful." Liang Jinsheng removed one of the franks from its roll and gave it to the dog. At that moment Ru Yan felt an urge to throw herself into this man's arms and let her tears flow.

But what she did was to gesture to the sofa and invite him to sit down. She sat across from him, the coffee table between them.

"Were you ever this romantic before?" she asked.

"No," he said.

"Who taught you to be like this?"

"I just came to understand, pretty late in life, that none of us really has much time."

"Especially someone like you," she said, "you still have to give a lot of time to official business."

"It's true," he nodded. "But that will soon be over, two or three more years. There's still a chance, isn't there?"

"Sure," she said, "Another twenty years for living life to the full."

"Can I have a cup of tea?" he asked.

Ru Yan leaped up, mortified: "I made you ask!"

When she had poured the tea, he stood up and asked if he could have a tour of her home. She told him to feel free to look around.

She had a two-bedroom apartment of eighty or ninety square meters in one of those sturdy, no-nonsense residential buildings that had been constructed a little more than a decade before. Ru Yan had furnished it very plainly, so that it now had a pleasing, understated look; not like others who had gone overboard with bar counters, dadoes, crystal chandeliers, and all kinds of moldings with a cumulative effect that now looked simply crass. Simplicity always stands the test of time.

The living room was not big. There was a coffee table and a TV cabinet, both of hardwood, and light yellow curtains with a faint pattern. Maybe it only proved the proverb, 'When you love someone, you find even the crows on his roof magnificent,' but Liang Jinsheng thought this casual frugality showed the confidence of a person who wasn't trying to impress anyone.

The apartment was indeed furnished simply. The study had a bookcase on one side, and against the window stood a desk with Ru Yan's computer. Cotton cushions in a plain flower pattern were lined up on a wicker loveseat against the other wall, on which hung two scrolls of calligraphy. One had been a wedding present; the other was a lyric by Xin Qiji, painted by Ru Yan's mother.[198] Liang Jinsheng didn't know much about calligraphy but he thought these characters were very handsome. Then there was her son's small bedroom with a desk and bookcase and chest of drawers, all rather small, and a single bed. The walls bore signs that the boy had studied hard: a timeline of history, an English vocabulary list, a periodic table of the elements and a study schedule. There was a hutch with toys her son must have played with at different times: Transformers, a battery-operated car, a Rubik's Cube, and an architectural model. It could have been an exhibit documenting the boy's growth to maturity.

A few pictures hung on the wall of Ru Yan's bedroom. One was a family portrait apparently taken when the boy was just heading off to college, for a railroad platform was in the background and they must have been seeing him off at the station. Another was of Ru Yan's elderly parents at the seashore, and you could see a lot of Ru Yan in the old lady's face. Another was of a middle-aged man, also at the seashore, and the ocean was that limpid blue which one finds in the South. His features were regular, his frame broad and sturdy, and he wore a white short-sleeved shirt tucked into gray trousers; altogether a proper figure.

Liang Jinsheng made the circuit of the apartment and then asked, "Is that picture of your husband?"

"Yes," Ru Yan said.

"So young!"

"It was quite a few years ago," she said.

Ru Yan had fixed a cup of green tea for herself, too, and the two resumed their seats.

"That night of moon-viewing," Liang Jinsheng began, "I said next time we would discuss another topic."

"Is it necessary?" she said.

He gave her a puzzled look.

"Haven't we been speaking of it all along?" she explained.

"Right," he said. "That's it, then. In six months I'll marry you."

Ru Yan realized how much she had longed to hear these almost masterful words, and her face reddened; she quickly concealed her emotions with a smile: "Why six months?"

"It can be tomorrow, if you agree."

Rattled, she hurried to explain, "What I meant was, why not a year?"

"Does it take a whole year, at our age, to judge a person?"

"I'm not that astute," she said mischievously. "I need a year."

In the manner of a strong negotiator, Liang Jinsheng insisted, "Let's keep it at six months. It's settled, then: next May." Then he bantered, "How does that song go? *Next year the flowers will bloom and the butterflies will dance, Elder Brother is set on returning.*"[199]

Ru Yan smiled too, and was struck by this fellow's knack for smoothing over awkward moments with humor. She sang the answering line from the duet, *You seek Jinhua at the foot of Mount Cang; I am Jinhua.*

Liang Jinsheng said emphatically, "Yes! That's just what I mean."

They chatted for a while. Ru Yan noticed that the sun had set and offered to warm up the hot dogs and cook some oatmeal.[200] But he stood up and said he had to go; he still had work to do that evening. "If I'm free this weekend, I'll take you up on your offer, and we'll just add some *zhacai* to that menu."[201]

He had gone to the door and was putting his shoes on. "Oh," he smiled, "there was something else I brought with me, thinking I'd present it to you along with the hot dogs. But now it looks as though it will have to wait six months."

Ru Yan could guess what he was talking about and colored slightly as she stammered, "So mysterious!"

"Shall I give it to you now?" he asked.

"No," she managed to say, "Let's keep things as you said: six months."

28

Like a summer breeze, the news that Ru Yan and Liang Jinsheng were in love spread quietly through all the offices of the Institute. In such a place, where the usual level of excitement was on the order of watching plants grow, the event unleashed a swirl of eager and mysterious whispers. After all, it involved a top official who just happened to have jurisdiction over the Institute's research field. People chose their words carefully.

Ru Yan had not used to draw much attention when she went to the office. She would arrive quietly and leave quietly, and she could go for years at a time without ever meeting most of her colleagues (with the exception of the few women who congregated in the Resource Room). People could practically forget about one another there. But now it seemed there were steadily more people to be encountered on the courtyard pathways and in the corridors, and more and more of them wanted to exchange a few words with her. The bosses of the wetlands group, the pharmaceutical group, the plant chemistry group, and especially the genetics group where she worked: they all started dropping in to Ru Yan's office. The topics they came to discuss with her were baffling. "Xiao Ru," they would say, "you're part of our group's next generation of leadership; you should have more input into what we're doing." She would think, *When exactly did I get picked to be in the next generation of leadership? The deputy heads are all in their thirties; who's going to take over from whom?*

"Xiao Ru, that journal article you published last year was quite good, you should apply for a principal fellowship this year. You're perfectly qualified, based just on that work: it was quite original." *Huh?* she would think, *'published last year'? It was several years ago.*

"Xiao Ru, our department is applying for a research grant, it's going to be vital for the city's long-term development; we've heard the municipal leaders are interested in this, so in a few days we'll run a summary by you for your comments." All she could think was, *What the hell? These are the big guns of the Institute; it's usually difficult to get even a minute with them face-to-face.*

Then one day the Director of the Institute casually walked into her office with his cup of tea, pulled up a chair, and struck up a conversation. "Ru Yan, I'd like to see you get more involved in the future of our Institute, going forward. You know you're something of an elder statesman around here, almost twenty years of service: you and I both have a lot of feeling for this place."

It was all Liang Jinsheng's fault, and she didn't know whether to laugh or cry.

The other women's teasing began to get rather pointed. Sometimes a group of them would invade her office cooing, "We had to come see our dear Ru Yan one last time, soon it won't be easy to get an interview with the mayor's wife." It was even worse in the Resource Room. "Look! What a wonderful complexion our Ru Yan has, lately. Well, of course: *the rain and the dew water the seedlings and make them strong.*[202] Jiang Xiaoli, you're not fair! You don't do any favors for *us*!" At these times Jiang Xiaoli would often come to Ru Yan's defense: "You're out of line, girls, knock it off or I'll have the Director straighten you out." These experiences were frequent enough to make Ru Yan reluctant to venture into the Resource Room at all. Sometimes she would quietly note when few were present and scurry in to go online for a while and attend to some internet business. At such times Xiao Li would be exceptionally solicitous. "What kind of an Institute makes such a high-level research unit depend on dialup access to the Internet? If people found out, we'd be a laughingstock. Tell you what: tomorrow I'll make a formal suggestion we upgrade to broadband. They ought to set up a LAN, and put each department on it."

29

One of the forum's participants, known as Night Owl, made an announcement: `I'm coming to City X and I've already contacted Master Damo to ask if he'll deign to see me on Saturday. Does the Empty Nest have any other birds from City X? I'd like to see 'em all!`

Many of the old birds of the Empty Nest knew one another quite well, and the new arrivals also tended to grow familiar with one another over time, so these offline gatherings had become increasingly frequent. It was ironic: once, these people had deplored and mocked the younger generation's fad of holding parties that brought Net friends together, but now that was all forgotten.

Most of the Empty Nesters were just getting by. But some were rich, some were at leisure, some had achieved positions of power; and some fell under two of these headings, or all three. Consequently the ambiance of their get-togethers was considerably finer than it ever was for the younger generation. They not only got together but held dinners, arranged group portraits and videos, and even organized travel tours: and mementos of these activities were always posted online, where they became the most popular items in the forum. Everybody was eager to meet the others in real life and got a kick out of seeing the true face of Mount Lu. It was often startling: Spring River Flows, for example, whose delicate sensibilities were so tender, turned out to be a worthy old man whose height was 5' 11". Seen It All turned out to be a girl who was studying abroad. Had no one gone there and taken her picture, the older participants would have had a hard time believing it: for half a year they'd been calling her "Elder Brother." On the other hand, many participants turned out to be much as people had imagined, perhaps a little more handsome, or a little older in appearance. Since they were all fairly well on in years, none of them cared much about these things.

When Ru Yan saw this posting, Maple Leaves Are Red had already responded: `Hey! Our moderator, Such Is This World, is in City X! Better come pay your respects, armed with a suitable gift.` Papa Fox chimed in to say he, too, lived in City X and would give his phone number. He mentioned So-and-so and a few others who were also locals, and Ru Yan discovered that quite a few of the people in this disembodied virtual forum were actually living in the same place she was living, some of them just a block away.

Eventually Night Owl notified the forum that there would be a gathering in the lobby of a certain hotel at 6:30 PM that weekend. On entering the lobby, members should call his cell phone. The challenge would be, "What bird is in the forest?" The response: "Night Owl."[203]

This kind of gathering made Ru Yan nervous; it had been years since she had joined in such a lively event. A while back, she had stayed away from a 20th college reunion and endured the reproaches of her classmates. But now she was the moderator, with people coming long distances to visit her part of the country, and someone had blown her cover. She had no choice but to grit her teeth, screw up her courage, and attend the banquet. There was also another aspect to it, an important one: she wanted to meet this Master Damo.

The party was being held at the hotel where Night Owl was staying. She learned later that Night Owl was a mid-level official in a powerful agency of the Central Government: when he swam out to the provinces, he was a big fish. The local government organization which was hosting him would, naturally, pick up the tab for the drinking party he had arranged at a five-star hotel.

Ru Yan rushed home after work, walked Yang Yanping, then changed the dog's water and added some food to her bowl before hurrying out. In the lobby of the hotel she phoned in the password and the voice on the other end said, "We've been waiting for you, but we didn't know your cell phone number. We've gone into the restaurant." Then he told her the number of their banquet room. When she entered, eight people were already seated, evenly divided between men and women. From the looks of them and their age, she judged this must be the right room. On seeing her, one of them asked in an odd tone:[204] "What bird is in the forest?" Somewhat rattled, Ru Yan answered, "The Night Owl." Whereupon they all stood up and cried in unison, "All hail the Moderator!"

Surveying a row of unfamiliar faces and already flustered, she didn't know what to say. So she mumbled, "But you should all tell me who you are."

"No," a slender middle-aged woman answered, "You have to guess. If you can't guess at least half of us, then you must down a drink." The others all seconded this proposal.

Ru Yan was the kind of person who, if you told her your name, would invariably have forgotten it the next time she saw you. "I'll take some guesses, but I'm not drinking." At the head of the table[205] sat a finely-dressed, clean-shaven gentleman, at whom she pointed a finger: "Night-Owl!"

They all cheered. "The Moderator has a good eye!"

The slender woman sniffed, "That was easy. Who but a man on official business would dress so formally? Besides, he sat in the center as if he were the one picking up the tab."

Night Owl protested that they had all insisted he sit there.

As for the others, she guessed almost all of them wrong. Five were locals, one had come from a nearby city, and one was a personal friend of Night Owl, a woman classmate from college days. There were two whom she reversed: Ru Yan guessed that a dignified and gentle character was Maple Leaves Are Red, but actually she was the other one, thin and elegantly dressed. The most surprising one was Master Damo, who was not very tall and looked rather undistinguished in a threadbare jacket. Standing next to that pompous and garrulous Papa Fox, Damo looked as though he might be the other man's chauffeur. When Maple Leaves Are Red introduced Ru Yan to Damo, he only smiled and said that the style reveals the spirit. But Ru Yan exclaimed, "Master Damo . . . oh my!" She had almost said, "Except for being so thin, you don't look like Bodhidharma!" It was on the tip of her tongue, but it seemed impertinent and she said only "How have you managed to look so proletarian?" He smiled again and said, "Indeed. I am an authentic proletarian."

Night Owl remarked, "Those with true greatness don't reveal themselves. How many would like to see this man's true face, but never will? He has honored me tonight."

Maple Leaves Are Red agreed: "All these years on the forum, and I didn't realize that Master Damo was so close by."

With voluble laughter, this gathering of old birds from the Empty Nest now got underway in earnest.

Most of those who can send a child overseas are pretty well-off. In conversation it became clear that the people at this banquet were either white-collar professionals or officials, or in some cases academics, or the managers of State-owned enterprises. The only exception was Maple Leaves Are Red: she had once held a pretty good government job, but after her husband went into business, she stayed at home as one of the Ladies Who Lunch. In such a group, the first topic was naturally the children who were abroad. Ru Yan's son stood out: he had made it on the strength of his high exam scores, he was in graduate school, he had a scholarship, and they had even provided him with a part-time job. The others could only envy such success, exclaiming that the possession and cultivation of talent was worth more than vast sums of money. Then one after another they gave vent to their frustrations: how much it cost each year, how much money it cost to get that degree; and how they couldn't be sure whether the kids would then be able to stay overseas or ever manage to recoup the cost of their education; and if they did, it wasn't clear that the parents would gain anything by it. If they *did* share in the rewards, how much longer would they live to enjoy them? Looking at it this way was quite disheartening. Someone said, "Let's stop talking about this. Any way you slice it, it wasn't worth it. For all that money, we could have kept the kid at home and supported him for life; but as it is, we've signed over both our money and our children to the Imperialists." Papa Fox was a high-level manager in a State-owned enterprise and he said, "There's no expectation that your son will care for you in life and give you honorable burial when you die. I just want him to be safe, to live in peace, even if he has to go on welfare over there. Back here, there's no telling when all hell may break loose and by then there may be no way to escape." These words had a chilling effect on the whole company. They realized that this was everyone's little plan, but this guy was the only one who dared say it openly. Noticing they'd all fallen silent, Papa Fox added, "Everybody knows this without talking about it, right? Otherwise why have the V.I.P.s at every level sent their sons and daughters abroad?"

People are now much freer to speak out over a drink than in the old days, even if they've just come from a meeting full of official claptrap. Touch the winecup and the tune will change. That's why everyone would rather go to a bar than a conference hall. And when they do go to the conference hall, once the meeting breaks up they find their way to a bar, so they won't get sick from keeping their feelings bottled up.

Ru Yan said that, for her part, she hoped her son would come home after his studies. When he went abroad, she said, it was because his field was well taught there, and she hadn't focused on the going abroad *per se*. And you know, she added, one person can leave, a family can leave, but how are a billion people going to leave?

Maple Leaves Are Red answered, "Hey, Moderator, you have the right spirit. People like us are selfish: it's 'Get out while the going's good.' We're hedging our bets, but we hope our socialist motherland will be OK and then in the future it will be convenient to have a foothold in both countries."

Papa Fox observed that Ru Yan was embarrassed and he hurried to say, "Sure, we hope the country will be at peace, too. But sometimes those laid-off workers have a look in their eyes that makes you think if the Great Cultural Revolution happened again, they would beat you into a pulp. People who used to be pretty mellow now want to eat you alive. A few of our managers have moved far from the factory and tell no one their address. It's like working in the underground."

The conversation turned to a certain person who was murdered with his whole family, and that other one who got killed in a bombing[206], and another person who was kidnapped and never heard from again. The talk grew extremely animated, running from one topic to another, as the gathering broke into a few small groups each carrying on a different discussion though they were all sitting at that sumptuous round table. From time to time someone would think of a toast and they'd all raise their glasses. But Master Damo (whom Night Owl had singled out for particular respect on this visit) sat quietly throughout, occasionally smiling and murmuring a few words to the people seated on either side of him. One of them was Night Owl, and the other was a woman who knew Damo through the Internet—apparently quite well—and had come some distance to join this gathering. Ru Yan wanted to talk with Damo: she wanted to ask him for advice about her writing. But she was seated several places away and wasn't going to raise her voice to make him hear her. She thought she might ask for his phone number at the end of the evening and contact him the next day.

Her cell phone rang amid the din. She was still unfamiliar with her phone's ringtone, so it went on for some time, until someone asked whose phone that was and she realized it was hers. In fumbling with the buttons, she had the frustration of accidentally hanging up on the call. Insistently, it rang again.

It was Liang Jinsheng, and he asked where she was.

"I'm having dinner with my internet buddies."

"Having dinner with your internet buddies?" he repeated, incredulous. "What internet buddies?"

Ru Yan was not used to carrying on a phone conversation in this kind of situation, so she started toward the door as she answered. "It's just people from that forum of ours."

He broke out laughing. "So you're starting to see your internet buddies in person, too? Last time didn't we talk about going out to see the winter moon?"

"Wait," she said, "You never said when that would be, did you?"

"I've been so busy lately I haven't dared make appointments in advance. Where are you? I'll come pick you up."

"I just got here," she said, "The party's only starting. Can you give me an hour?" And she told him the address.

"The internet community has come up in the world," Liang Jinsheng remarked, "if they hold their parties at that kind of hotel."

Ru Yan returned to the banquet table and noticed a gleam of amusement in the eyes of Maple Leaves Are Red. When she sat down, Maple Leaves Are Red said in an intentionally loud voice, "Are you going to leave early? We've just made a rule that tonight nobody's allowed to slink away."

"You should have told me that before," Ru Yan said. "I just promised someone."

Maple Leaves Are Red smiled meaningfully. "Don't worry about it. I know it wouldn't have made any difference even if I had told you before."

Night Owl, who was by now slightly tipsy, overheard them and declared, "No matter how important your date is, you must cancel it; or if you really can't, then invite your friend here, I've already booked the karaoke room."

Maple Leaves Are Red smiled dismissively. "You don't even ask our Moderator who her friend might be. Are you sure you have the standing to invite *him*?

Night Owl riposted: "Who is it? The President? The General Secretary?[207] Even if that's who it is, why wouldn't I invite them here?"

Ru Yan realized that Maple Leaves Are Red was playing a deep game and chose not to respond lest it be obvious she was concealing something. So she pretended she hadn't understood, and smiled vaguely. To her surprise, Maple Leaves Are Red nudged her under the table and said quietly, "I guessed right, didn't I?"

Tensing up, and still feigning incomprehension, Ru Yan said, "Guessed what right?"

"The person who just called," Maple Leaves Are Red.

"You know who it was?" asked Ru Yan.

"It's between us girls, no need to hide. I'll tell you a secret: your matchmaker and I grew up in the same compound. She's a generous one, that Jiang Xiaoli: the man she's given you is one she wanted for herself."

Ru Yan's face grew warm. "What are you talking about?" she whispered. "She's got a family."

"You don't keep up with the news," Maple Leaves Are Red said. "She got divorced more than two years ago."

"Why on earth did she give him up for me?"

"Bad luck. It should have been a match made in heaven, but I guess they just weren't destined for each other. For her this was a bitter disappointment, painful for a long time. But for God's sake don't let on that you know . . . she couldn't bear it."

They were interrupted when a few people saw the two women whispering and clamored, "That's not allowed! No black phones!"

30

Liang Jinsheng phoned an hour later. Ru Yan stepped outside the banquet room as she took the call and then seized the opportunity to slip away. Once in the car, she phoned Night Owl and said an urgent matter had required her to leave early; she hadn't wanted to disturb anyone; and if she had the chance in the next few days she hoped to apologize to him in person.

As she finished the call, she noticed Liang Jinsheng suppressing a grin.

"Is this sort of gathering a completely new experience for you?" he asked.

"Yes, it was a little weird."

"I guess it's not so strange that teenage boys and girls steal money from their families in order to travel long distances and meet people they've gotten to know online. You old ladies are playing the same game."

"Well," she laughed, "the old ladies don't need to steal any money. But you have a point: there were people who came long distances today."

Ru Yan glanced out the window and noticed the night sky thick with clouds that dully reflected the lights of the big city. "How are we going to see the moon?" she asked.

"Stick with me," he said, "and you'll see the moon."

To her surprise he drove to his residence. The Armed Policeman on duty saluted his car and waved them through the gate. Liang Jinsheng's town house was not far from Jiang Xiaoli's, and was of a slightly newer design. It had three full stories.

As he opened the front door, he said, "An old widower's home. I don't have a housekeeper: it's a bit messy."

For some reason Ru Yan was a little nervous, the way a young girl is nervous. He asked if she would take off her shoes and offered her a pair of plush slippers from the shoe rack, light tan and finely made. "Just bought them," he said, "don't know whether they'll fit."

Changing her shoes gave her an elusive sensation. When you come to a place, putting on someone else's slippers is of course different from wearing your own leather shoes; but putting on slippers someone has expressly prepared for you is something else again, and Ru Yan felt that feet have a private quality, so that changing into these slippers had a certain significance. The slippers did indeed fit her and were quite soft. It was like walking on a carpet of fallen leaves in the forest, and it made her begin to feel relaxed and at home in this unfamiliar setting. She remembered the things Maple Leaves Are Red had told her and felt a touch of sadness as the relationship between her and Liang Jinsheng took on new shades of meaning.

To mask the mood she had slipped into, she asked jokingly, "Now about that moon of yours?"

"I'll have it for you right away." He invited her, with a gesture, to go upstairs.

Ru Yan had heard Jiang Xiaoli say that on this estate of officials' residences there were four kinds of reception a visitor might enjoy. The first was to be received in the small parlor downstairs. The second was to be received in the small parlor upstairs. The third, in the study. At this point Jiang Xiaoli had stopped. "And the fourth?" Ru Yan asked.

"The bedroom. Actually, there's also a fifth: the coat closet."

Ru Yan didn't understand.

Jiang Xiaoli gave a shriek of laughter. "If the lady of the house suddenly comes home, the visitor hustles into the closet. I made that part up."

These rooms in Liang Jinsheng's house were laid out differently than they had been at the Jiangs'. At the top of the first flight of stairs was a small corridor, and you had to turn right in order to find the small parlor, which consequently had an air of greater privacy. At the Jiangs', everything had been in plain view once you got upstairs. Three interior rooms adjoined that parlor: a study, a bathroom, and a single bedroom where the master of the house could take a brief rest after dealing with official business in the study or the parlor. Presumably the master bedroom was up a further flight of stairs, to the right. Ru Yan tried to estimate the square meters but lost count, there were so many rooms upstairs and downstairs, and for one person to be living here alone gave her the creeps. Somehow it brought to mind the de Winter mansion in that American movie, *Rebecca*.[208] Liang Jinsheng pointed to a water dispenser and, next to it, a drinks cabinet, urging her to help herself. Then he went into a room and brought out a miniaturized camcorder which he plugged into the TV. After he had fiddled with it for a while, the moon appeared on the TV screen.

"The moon in America. This is in New York, and the moon in New York is pretty dim and small. *This* is the moon in Atlanta, you can see the difference, can't you? . . . And *this* is in Alaska. Here the moon is very fine. It almost looks fake, like a stage backdrop. If you ever get the chance to see this with your own eyes, it's wonderful. A sky as clear as crystal."

"You took these pictures?" she asked.

"I took them for you."

"When will we be able to see this kind of a moon back here?" Ru Yan wondered.

He shrugged. "In fifty years?"

She laughed. "I won't manage to see it, then."

"Give it a try," he said. "We're all living longer."

The central heating was rather strong and Ru Yan felt perspiration on her back and chest. There was even a little drop of sweat glimmering on the tip of her nose. "The heat's pretty fierce here, don't you have to pay for it?"

"Feeling warm?" he said. "Take off your jacket."

"Can we open a window a little?"

He slid a window open a crack, and said, "You still have the hardiness of youth; you aren't afraid of the cold."

The parlor was furnished with a profusion of antiques and handicrafts. Some were real, some were fake; some were in very fine taste while others were a bit garish, but even these looked to have been quite pricey.

"How much money do you make?" Ru Yan asked him.

Liang Jinsheng was visibly taken aback by the baldness of her question. He shrugged, "Not much. A few thousand a month."

"You're given this apartment by the State," she pressed, "so we won't count that, but is your salary by itself enough to buy all these other things?"

He laughed. "Oh, Ru Yan, you're a force to be reckoned with. I tell you, not even the CDI[209] would ask these questions. I have some income on the side that would not be considered too shady . . . someday I'll make a full confession to you. One thing I want you to know is that, comparatively speaking, I am a very honest man, and sometimes people have hated me for it."

Ru Yan was somewhat embarrassed by this answer. "I was only curious. I really don't know what the life of an official is like, now. My father had retired by the mid-Eighties."

"I know about him," Liang Jinsheng said.

"You've done a background check on me?"

He smiled mysteriously, and suddenly said, "I've always wanted to tell you something..."

"What?" she asked.

"You're a lot like my late wife."

Ru Yan flushed. Hadn't they agreed they'd wait before discussing that again? He said, "What I mean is, your face is like my wife's."

"Is that all?"

"Of course not. Come." He brought her into the study, where his wife was smiling in a picture frame on his desk. Ru Yan picked it up and studied the picture closely. She had been a dignified and beautiful woman, and seemed to have a pleasant temperament, but Ru Yan felt she did not greatly resemble her. If you had to find a point of similarity, it would be the eyes. There was the same faint air of melancholy.

"The first time I caught a glimpse of you from a distance," Liang Jinsheng said, "I noticed the resemblance."

"So was that the only reason for what followed?"

"Of course not. But it did make me happy."

Ru Yan remarked, "I seem to stir your memories."

Liang Jinsheng said, "Why are you so hard on me?"

That night he told her a lot about his wife. As Ru Yan listened, she thought there was something remarkable about this fellow. Most men in that situation would try to avoid this topic, but he seemed to make a point of talking about it.

He said his first wife had been his classmate in college. She came from an Air Force family.[210] She was an optimistic and self-confident girl, and quite attractive. They had been married less than two years when the Lin Biao affair occurred, and her father was arrested and imprisoned. She underwent an abrupt change as if she had become a different person. For months she stopped speaking. No matter how he tried to comfort and reassure her, she wouldn't open her mouth. One day she announced, "We should get divorced. We should do it now, while we still have many happy memories." At that time their daughter was not yet a year old, and he couldn't believe she was talking this way. "I'm really sorry," she said, "I've got to leave the child for you to bring up; if she comes with me I'm afraid she'll suffer." Not long after they parted, he heard that she, too, had been arrested and sent to prison. She was said to be one of several children of military officers who'd formed a cabal against Mao, and they all received heavy sentences. They weren't let out till the early Eighties. He didn't know what happened to her then. Some said she had left the country.

On account of his former father-in-law, he was soon demoted and assigned to a factory on the Third Line[211], and that was where he met his second wife. At that time she worked as a broadcaster in the factory.[212] They soon got married. She made him send for the baby, who had been living with his parents. She said a child wants to grow up with her mother and father. When the baby arrived, she raised her as if she had given birth to her. (That older daughter believed into her teens that the second wife was her biological mother.) Soon after the first child's arrival, the second daughter was born. Liang Jinsheng talked about the ups and downs of those years and said for various reasons their marriage had gone through crises, and described the sacrifices she had made for the two girls. A few times his eyes grew moist.

When he finished, he was quiet for a long time, and so was she. A life washed by the waves of history had been transmuted into something detached and unconnected to their present situation. Realizing he had grown sentimental, Liang Jinsheng poked fun at himself. "I guess I really have grown old. I didn't use to get so easily worked up. . . Look at that, I asked you to come see the moon, and it got me talking about all those things."

Ru Yan, too, had become sentimental as he talked about his wife, and she found herself thinking about another person, her husband. "I've never liked people who put down one woman in order to please another. You have to be careful with that kind of person, because they'll do it to you, too."[213]

Liang Jinsheng came over to stand beside her, and put his hands on Ru Yan's shoulders to caress her. This was the greatest intimacy he had demonstrated since they had met. But he went no further. "If some day we live together, I hope she won't disappear from our life, but rather become a close friend who will help us understand each other."

"Yes," Ru Yan said, and her eyes smarted.

As they continued talking, Ru Yan remembered the Five Wants and Five Rejects[214] that Jiang Xiaoli had reported to her. She decided to ask him, "I've heard you were very selective, that you even had a list of requirements and deal-breakers."

He was puzzled. "What's this about requirements and deal-breakers?"

She told him.

When he finished hearing about it he started to laugh. "Oh, that girl! How did these become *my* Five Wants and Five Rejects? These are the standards, ever so precise, which *she* applied for my sake!"

There were a few times when Ru Yan wanted to steer the conversation toward Jiang Xiaoli, maybe even ask him point-blank, but in the end she held back.

31

Whenever the members of the online community had an actual get-together, it was customary to provide a detailed report in the forum, sometimes extending over several days: the community insisted on it. If photos weren't included, someone would be considered to have failed in his duty. There would always be an illustrated account roasting the participants. As forum moderator, Ru Yan also had to be ready to submit a report. When she went to the forum, she saw that Night Owl had already posted a long report, with pictures, at the top of the page. Before the group photo there were several shots taken in the main lobby of the hotel before Ru Yan arrived, scenes of members recognizing each other through passwords and secret handshakes. A caption explained: *One by one, the old birds fly in; Moderator Such Is This World has not yet shown her face.* In the first photo showing Ru Yan, the scene was already the banquet room, and it was the instant when Ru Yan had just made her appearance looking rather alarmed and confused, with a crimson face. The caption read: *Moderator Such Is This World, panicked, finally rushes in. Take a look at her expression. She looks as if she's just been doing some-*

thing unmentionable. Next was an enlarged close-up of Ru Yan. *The gifted, brilliant Moderator Such turns out to be as bashful as a young girl, and—even more surprising—she's a knock-out beauty!* Then there were pictures of people clinking glasses, laughing, and urging one another to drink. The next shot showed Ru Yan getting up to take a phone call. *Just when the old birds are growing lively with wine, a mysterious call comes in to the cell phone of Moderator Such. From this moment, it seems the thoughts of Moderator Such are no longer on This World. She gives irrelevant answers when anyone speaks to her.* The last picture showed the empty chair in which Ru Yan had been sitting, surrounded by a circle of indignant forum members. *After a second phone call, Moderator Such disappears, without even an "88"! Immediately we all feel like orphans, lost, sorrowful, and lonely . . .*

This kind of post, blending pictures and text to tell tales about the insiders, always stimulated a deluge of comments and replies. Ru Yan didn't have time to read them all. Some praised her beauty and doubted her age. Some urged her to make a full confession about whatever had been going on that night, promising clemency if she made a clean breast of things.

When she had skimmed through the pictures and captions, her reaction was like that of a commenter whose words doubtless masked some *Schadenfreude*: `Night Owl, you're a naughty old bird! Putting our Moderator Such Is This World on your chopping block, are you? We'll never forgive you!`

Ru Yan had not realized she was being photographed. She vaguely remembered that someone or other was holding up a camera the whole time, but until she saw the pictures, that had seemed like no more than a gesture. She had seen this kind of rapid post-mortem online before, marked by the same humor, raillery, and pranks; it had been good for a laugh and had never made much impression on her. Now that she was the target, it gave her decidedly mixed feelings. The people had meant no harm, she thought, and most were very kindly disposed; you joined in these pranks before, so it's not sportsmanlike to take offense now. Besides, as a moderator you'd better be able to cut people some slack. She replied to Night Owl's post with a non-committal smiley-face and made no comment. In the online jargon, she was playing possum.

In the following days, a gang of the old birds kept at it unmercifully, and their comments spilled over onto multiple pages. Like some martyr of the Revolution, Ru Yan held her peace. One person on the forum said, `I know the names and addresses of both higher-ups and underlings. But I'm not telling!`[215]

That slinking character named "Fanyi" reappeared to yelp: `Stop torturing her! I'm telling you, though it's top secret, she's a V.I.P.! If you turn her against us by giving her a hard time, we're all going to have a hard time!`

Liang Jinsheng phoned her and remarked that lately it had been pretty lively at the Empty Nest. "You troublemaker," she shot back, "I'll bet you're enjoying the show!"

"Can you handle it?" he asked. "Do you want me to ride to the rescue?"

"Ha!" she snorted. "Ride to the rescue. Help them push me into the pit is more like it."

"Then you'll just have to bear it for now," he sighed. "But come May, we'll treat them to some candy."[216]

32

Using the Internet is like driving. When you've just learned how, you are extremely cautious, conscientious to a fault. When it comes more naturally, you start to get complacent and that's when accidents happen. One day Ru Yan received an e-mail with an attachment. In the past, she would have been very careful, looking to see who it was from and checking the addresses in the header, and if these were unfamiliar she would have just deleted it. But since becoming a moderator she had grown used to receiving attachments, whether articles or photos. So she just clicked on it, and her screen went black, and nothing would get her computer working again.

Before going overseas, her son had left her the phone number of a classmate she could call if she ran into any computer trouble. She located the number and placed a call. Someone at his home said he was away on business and would be back in ten days.

Only now did she realize how attached she had become to this plaything of a computer. With a wry smile, she said to herself, "Well, I guess it's for the best, I'll take a break for a few days." At these words a bleak, empty feeling stole over her. All evening she roamed her apartment, fidgeting with things for want of something to do and feeling distinctly ill-at-ease. She glowered wordlessly at the machine on her desk. Finally—and unusually—she made an international call to her son to tell him the computer wasn't working. He said she'd been hit with an e-mail virus and would need an expert to clean it up. But it wasn't a serious problem; she just had to wait for his classmate to come home.

When she hung up the phone, she washed up and went to bed early, taking a book to read. Usually when she finished her work online and went to bed she always wanted to read. She liked the feeling of lying propped on a pillow with a book in her hand and thought it was one pleasure which the Internet would never replace. But this evening, she couldn't get into the book. She then lay down but was unsettled, tossing and turning, and did not sleep soundly that night.

The next day as soon as she reached the office she headed for Xiao Li's workstation to go online. She wrote a post to the Empty Nest about how she had taken a hit and might be offline for ten days or more. Would everyone please keep things orderly in the forum and not hold it against her when she didn't respond to QQ or e-mail messages? Then before she left work that day she went online again and found a message from Maple Leaves Are

Red: `Why haven't you tried Master Damo? He's not just a great writer but a computer wizard, too; to him, your kind of problem would be child's play.` Ru Yan noticed that Maple Leaves Are Red was online at that moment and started QQ in order to ask how she could get in touch with Damo. Maple Leaves Are Red gave her his cell phone number.

Ru Yan thanked her and, feeling restless, dialed the number. Damo sounded hesitant, so she pleaded with him. He said, "I'll come tonight, but it could be on the late side."

Feeling guilty that she was dragging the Master out late, Ru Yan asked him to name a place and a time that she could pick him up. No need, he said, he would come to her place. She told him the address.

He arrived a little after 9:00 on a motorcycle, which surprised her. In her experience, people who rode motorcycles were either of limited means, or they were young people trying to look cool, or they were men with small businesses whose occupation kept them buzzing back and forth around town.

Damo put down his motorcycle helmet and took out a wallet of software CDs. He declined a cigarette, refused a cup of tea, and went straight to work like a professional repairman. A half-hour later everything was fixed and Ru Yan heaved a sigh of relief. She thanked him effusively. Damo told her a few things about her computer that she needed to take care of, and then prepared to leave.

"You've worked without a break," she exclaimed, "wouldn't you like to sit down for a while? When I heard you were coming to that party, I really wanted to meet you and chat with you. I never thought it would be a computer crash that would bring you to my house."

"What do you want to talk about?" Damo asked.

Ru Yan was stumped. After some thought, she asked him to give an opinion of her writing.

"Didn't I do that already?" he chuckled.

"You posted just a few characters . . . there must be more you can say! Or are your pearls of wisdom that precious? And I've written other pieces since then."

He smiled. "Everything I have to say was in those few characters."

"I get it," she said. "This is like a Zen *koan*."

This time he burst into laughter. "But why are you so eager for someone else's opinion? This is how associates in the Youth League used to talk!"[217]

Ru Yan was embarrassed. Seeing that she really wanted to have a talk with him, Damo relented. "OK, serve me a bowl of noodles."

Ru Yan was aghast. "You haven't had supper?"

Damo said, "In our line of work, sometimes it's slow, and sometimes it's very busy."

Ru Yan hurried into the kitchen and put a pot of water on the stove. In the refrigerator she found nothing but leftovers: there was nothing nice to serve him. Distressed, she called from the kitchen, "I wish you had told me sooner. Look, what can I give you?"

"Plain noodles will be fine," Damo said, "Just put a little chili sauce on them." His work now done, he sat back down at the computer and began browsing the Internet.

Ru Yan cooked half a box of noodles, enough for three of *her* meals, and broke a few eggs and plopped them in—also enough for three of her meals—and when it was ready, carefully brought in a big bowl filled to the brim. Damo was hungry. One after another, he seized big clumps of food with his chopsticks and brought them to his mouth, pausing in his speech to slurp them down. "I like your writing. It's not easy to write well. To make up a good story is not hard, to tell the truth isn't too hard, but to make it come together in a good piece of writing . . . that's hard. It's a gift. Like singing. To strike a pleasant tone is not hard, to carry a tune is not too hard, but to sing it out with feeling, making the cadences and the emphasis sound natural . . . that's hard."

She was struck by his words, and felt that he was an extraordinary man. He looked like a simple repairman, bringing to mind the adage that a person of high caliber never flaunts his excellence. The veneration in which he was held on the Internet was not undeserved.

He went on, "When it comes to writing essays, the art of composition can be learned, rhetoric can be learned; knowledge, especially of a theoretical nature, can be learned. But a feel for the writing cannot be learned, not really; it can only be discovered by intuition. That's why I can't tell you which part of a piece is good and which part isn't good. If I pick out a technique and tell you it's good, and you try it in a different context, it may not be good anymore."

She watched him wolfing down the food and felt sad, for it had been years since she had seen anyone eat like that. She said, "We can talk about this, nice and easy, when you finish eating. Please enjoy your meal; no one's going to snatch it from you. What you've been saying is something I've always felt, but wasn't able to put into words. Sometimes reading a fine piece of writing makes me as happy as if I'd found a jewel. But there are works considered masterpieces which I can't make myself finish. Everyone else says how fine they are, how very fine. But if you don't like something, what can you do?"

Ru Yan had exacting standards when it came to prose. If writing wasn't good, she didn't merely feel it was imperfect: she found it repellent. It was like her mother's attitude toward hands and feet, but even more extreme.

Ru Yan broached the topic of the Internet. She said going online had brought her all kinds of new experiences.

"When you've just started going online," Damo said, "everything is fresh and new, as for a child who has just started school: the place is colorful and exciting, and there's a crowd of different children with a range of temperaments. He's eager to meld into this new collective. But with time, problems crop up. What happens in life also happens on the Internet."

"But no one sees you on the Internet," Ru Yan laughed. "Can't you get away from any problems by turning off your computer?"

"It's not that simple," he said, "and I should know. There are people whom the Internet has driven insane."

"You must be exaggerating."

"The Internet is like a performance stage," he explained.

"But experience is more concentrated on that stage than it is in real life. Things get blown out of proportion, and there's a lot of theatrics. People get stirred up, they get addicted; you can't say, 'Turn it off and you're done.'"

Ru Yan said the news on the Internet had been a breath of fresh air. Online, she had read about many things that she could never even have imagined.

"This is specifically a characteristic of China's Internet," Damo said. "In other countries, the Internet is just one among many channels of information and is not a privileged medium of expression. It is distinguished only by the technology it uses. Like if you were going to Beijing, you could take a train, or you could fly on a plane, or you could drive in a car. But in China, there is lots of news which the traditional media are not allowed to report and many things which they are not allowed to say. Yet on the Internet, these things can be reported and expressed. Therefore what makes the Internet stand out is no longer the technology it uses. Herein lies the Internet's strong suit, but also its Achilles' heel, for anything taken beyond normal limits can have unintended consequences. This is an endemic problem in countries that restrict open discussion."

Ru Yan had not been acquainted with the Internet for long, and what Damo was saying did not make much impression on her. But later, when she encountered all kinds of trouble, she would remember his words.

He had polished off the big bowl of noodles as they spoke. A sheen of perspiration covered his forehead and his eyes had lost their look of intense concentration. He was relaxed now, as if slightly tipsy.

"I admire your appetite," Ru Yan said.

"My daughter says it's scary to watch me eat." He thought for a moment and smiled. "More than fifty years of a varied life, but when I start to eat, I still act like a peasant."

She asked him about his daughter.

"She's married and works as a cashier in a supermarket."

Ru Yan was surprised. "Your child didn't study overseas?" She would have expected the child of someone like Damo to make good.

He shrugged. "No. We never considered it. Besides, she didn't like school and squeaked by in a community college. Then she went to work. But you know, her educational background is a little stronger than mine."

"What are you talking about?" Ru Yan scoffed. "You didn't go to college?"

"At the factory, I managed to get an Employees' College diploma. Today it's not worth the paper it's printed on."

Seeing that Ru Yan had never heard of Employees' colleges, Damo explained that they were colleges which State-owned enterprises had maintained for their own workers. Their predecessor was the 721 college.

"What's a 721 college?" she asked.

"You never even heard of that? During the C.R., Chairman Mao issued a high-level directive, it was called the 721 directive."[218]

Ru Yan had never been one to worry about politics. What, she asked, was a 721 college? So Damo had to recite that directive for Ru Yan, and he recounted how painstakingly they had studied such documents in those days, and the way he told the story made them both laugh. And so began an informal conversation. Ru Yan discovered that she was quite at ease with Damo. She didn't feel awed by his status as a "Master," nor did she feel any tension about being with him because he was a man; he might have been her elder brother, or a long-time neighbor. This evening she felt a need to talk, and skipped from one topic to another: reading, computers, tales from childhood, various social issues of the present day. And as she spoke about these things, she felt no constraint or need to choose her words with care, but spoke as casually as if she were at the vegetable market. As for Damo, most of the time he just listened, sometimes with a trace of a smile, sometimes with a grunt of acknowledgment, like a smart person who knows how to pay attention.

Remembering all the online speculation about Damo's background, Ru Yan finally asked him what kind of work he did.

He was a little taken aback by the question, but then he

grinned craftily and asked, "What do you think?"

Suddenly, she had to laugh. You invite a man about your age into your home, he fixes your computer and you have a long talk about literature, but you don't even know who he is or what he does! She had to be nuts!

She made a show of sizing him up, but nothing in her experience helped her classify him. With his manners and appearance—the work clothes, the motorcycle—you could hardly say he was an academic. But placing him as an ordinary fellow, one of the common people, wouldn't wash either because his discourse outshone that of most serious scholars. So she said, in some perplexity, "I see you as a spiritual pilgrim."[219]

"That's about right," Damo said.

"This Damo of yours, is that the Damo who sat facing the wall?"

"Used to be," he said. "Not any more."

"Hmm?"

Damo: "The era of my facing the wall is over. And the time I spent facing the wall was a lot longer than ten years."

Ru Yan: "So now—"

Damo: "Now? You've got to add four letters."[220]

Ru Yan: "What four letters?"

Damo: "C-L-E-S."

Ru Yan of course knew who Damocles was, and she found this answer ominous. But she returned to her first question: "Aren't you going to tell me your profession?"

"I repair electric appliances."

"You expect me to believe that?"

"You think I'm kidding? I fix color TVs, refrigerators, air-conditioners, and now computers and CD-players and stereos ... oh, and I fix cell phones, too." He smiled cagily.

When she heard this she began to think back to when he had been fixing her computer, how his hand with its big knuckles and coarse skin had looked clumsy grasping the mouse, and how there had been some oilstains in the lines of his hand and his fingers had looked rather stubby as if worn down, not fine and tapering as they should have been. Yet these were the hands that had so often moved with the same strange clumsy agility across just such a mouse and keyboard, with such dazzling results. Ru Yan was moved with a confusing emotion that combined admiration with pity and consternation. "How can you be so good with computers?"

"It's my trade," Damo said. "I started off in a radio factory. All these things have a lot in common, you just need a certain knack. Air-conditioners and refrigerators may look intimidating, but they're very simple inside, like toys really." And, matter-of-factly, he recounted for her his employment history.

"Do you run your own shop, now," she asked, "or do you drum up business by circulating through town?" In Ru Yan's district, the cries of such itinerant repairmen could often be heard in the streets below her apartment.

"Both," Damo answered. "I handle service contracts for a number of electric appliance companies. When they get a complaint from a customer, I go to work. Sometimes I also pick up a little business on my own. It's not regimented: how much work I do is largely up to me."

"Why didn't you make a career in your field?" she asked.

"But this is my field!" he said.

"I mean writing and scholarship," she said.

"I'm an outsider," he smiled. "I don't even have a proper diploma. No one will seat me in a place of honor."

"But your influence on the Internet is so great, your essays are written so beautifully, how can you *not* take a place of honor?"

"Making it on the Internet doesn't count," he explained. "You're taken seriously only if you publish in the inner circle of respected journals, or put out a multi-volume monograph. As far as those people are concerned, the Internet is a sideshow. For now, anyway. It's just like blue jeans and bat-wing blouses[221], which at first were worn only by raffish people on the fringe but eventually entered the mainstream."

It occurred to Ru Yan, with some amusement, that she herself was like that, a late-adopter. She asked, "Ever write for those journals?"

"Yes, I have," he said. "But they don't offer the freedom you get online, where you can write whatever you think. After that, writing for the standard periodicals is like putting a halter on a wild horse."

"They pay, though," she pointed out.

"I can make as much, and a lot faster, by repairing a fridge. And a fridge is not subject to editorial deletions."

As if trying to encourage him, she said, "But things of worth are always of value; it doesn't matter where they are found."

Damo now asked what her field was, and she told him.

"That's a good field of study. The world of plants may seem dull and uneventful, but in truth it's miraculous. You take just a little soil, add light and air and water, and a life comes into being and grows before your eyes. And you could say that vegetation is the source of life for all life."

Ru Yan felt that Damo, in his plain-spoken way, had expressed the essential spirit of botany. "Yes," she said, "it's magnificent. From the biggest farm-animals to the tiniest worms—not to mention humans—they all depend on vegetation. It's the first link in the food chain, and the first link in the chain of living things."

"It's worthy of a religion," he exclaimed, "an everlasting religion based on Nature. It should inspire reverence. It's strange that many peoples have worshiped animals—you know, serpents and oxen, the tiger, the monkey—but very few have worshiped plants. Perhaps you botanists know whether anyone has written a paper on this?"

She smiled and said, "What you're talking about is the province of literary people like yourself. What we scientists consider a fit subject for research is which plants are edible or have medicinal properties; which ones prevent desertification and soil erosion, or can serve as raw material for industry . . ."

"With that attitude," Damo said, "With no cherishing of life, no feeling of gratitude or reverence, it's only a matter of time before humans wipe out all vegetation from the earth."

This stunned Ru Yan and for a long time she couldn't say anything.

"It's late," Damo said, "I'd better get going."

Ever since he had told her his trade, she had been thinking that when someone makes a living this way it's only right to pay him for his work. So she said, rather gingerly, "I should give you some money."

"What for?" he asked.

"For fixing the computer."

"Ah, I see. Well, my rates are quite high."

"Even if they're high, I still have to pay; this is how you make your living."

"For a typical housecall," he said thoughtfully, "if the repair is successful, it's 500."

It hurt to hear this, because to Ru Yan it felt like a ripoff. But the man had come at her request, he had indeed fixed the problem, and what's more, she didn't really know what the going rate was for such work. Although she felt ever so slightly discomfited, she managed a smile and said, "Very good. I'll go get it."

"*However*," Damo said when he saw her going into the bedroom, "today I forgot to give you an estimate, and it's not right to demand money when the price wasn't agreed in advance, no, that wouldn't be right at all. So this time, just forget about it."

She realized now that he had only been pulling her leg, and thought, "The scamp!" It was good that she hadn't made a face or started haggling with him. Coloring a little, she demanded, "How is that right?"

"We'll worry about it next time. Next time it crashes, you can pay me for both visits."

Suddenly she thought about some of the appliances in her home. Her husband had been gone three years, and they had been constantly breaking down. This is one of the biggest headaches that a woman living alone must deal with. At those times Ru Yan would get mad at herself and think, "I've got to marry someone, anyone who can fix these things."

When her husband had been around, Ru Yan had never troubled herself with all the tasks of replacement and repair and maintenance. She needed only to say, the pipe's leaking, or the fluorescent light burned out, or there's a smell of gas coming from the stove, and he would take over from there. When he was away on business, Ru Yan would just have to cope for a few days until he came home and could fix the problem. Her husband had enjoyed fixing things himself, and when he couldn't get them working it was up to him to find a repairman from downtown. Now that she was all alone in her incompetence, the appliances had ganged up on her, steadily developing ever more numerous and more serious problems over time. The light in the fridge had long since gone out; the vacuum leaked air; when the air-conditioner started up, it sounded like a tractor; only one side of her CD-player's earphones made any sound; the doors on a couple of her kitchen cabinets had broken hinges; her TV remote didn't work (it would either refuse to select a station or would skip channels); and the rice-cooker didn't know when to shut itself off anymore and was always burning the rice. The combined effect gave her home the feel of a civilization in terminal decline. She often found it depressing. She had thought of venturing into the street to ask someone, anyone, to help her, but she had heard tales of people who, once they'd gained entry to a home, had killed the residents and stolen their property. So she had never dared. She told Damo about these tribulations.

Damo accompanied her around the apartment to inspect, and said none of these problems posed too much of a challenge. The problem with the air-conditioner was that the compressor's mounting screws had worked loose; it would be OK once they were tightened over some shockproof washers. The wire on the CD-earphones was damaged but only needed to be soldered. The electrical contacts on the remote control had gotten dirty; he would take it apart and clean them with alcohol. All of this would be only a few minutes' work—he stopped, suddenly aware of the question posed by this household. "And your husband is, um . . . ?"

"He passed away," she said.

Damo seemed at a loss for words. "I'll come another day; it's too late now, and I don't have my tools."

Ru Yan felt bad. She had misjudged Damo when he played the prank about the money, and now, without meaning to, she had just given him a whole list of chores. "Don't give it any thought," she said, "Really, I don't know how to thank you for what you've done."

He went to the doorway and donned his helmet. "Well, you could write a nice essay for us all to enjoy online." And he was gone.

In a moment the *chucka-chucka* sound of a motorcycle wafted up from the street below, and then with a *vroom* receded into the distance.

At once she sat down to her computer and looked up his website. The forum he ran was called "Word and Thought," which sounded like "The Thread of Words" as well as "Fine Rain."[222] The page design was austere: faint brown lines on a yellow background gave it the flavor of old writing-paper, and the font was plain and formal and rather large. There was little in the way of decoration. Reading one magnificent, incisive essay after another, she had trouble making the connection with the short fellow who had just been in her living room. Had these elegant quick-witted paragraphs really been tapped out by those stubby, grease-stained fingers? If she hadn't heard with her own ears the casual brilliance with which he spoke, she would never have believed that this was the same Damo.

As she read, she began to feel vaguely uncomfortable that she had summoned a man of this stature for such an insignificant task, and had even wanted to make him come back to fix her air-conditioner and her headphones. After much thought, she picked up the phone and dialed his number. It rang only twice before he picked up. Ru Yan then realized she hadn't worked out what she wanted to say, and temporized awkwardly: "You made it home?"

Damo said, "Long time ago. Look at the clock!"

Unnecessarily, Ru Yan said thank you again.

"Didn't you already thank me?"

She started to laugh, and now she felt a little relaxed. "Isn't it all right for me to thank you again?"

"Sure," he said, "You can make it a daily routine. Haven't you gone to sleep yet?"

"I'm reading your essays," she said.

"That bad, huh? They cause insomnia?"

"They are truly powerful," she said.

"You really know how to build a person up," he said. "But really, there's a lot of powerfully good writing out there, you just haven't read much of it. Give me a couple of days and I'll send you some links."

"Is this work even better than yours?" she asked.

"You don't have a good perspective on this," he said. "Once you've read more, you'll know."

"You are a modest and magnanimous man."

"You wrong me, Madam; I am arrogant to the core. You have seen only one aspect of me, a misleading one."

She laughed again. "I don't know about that. I'd really like to see how you could be so arrogant."

The conversation ran on, and once again Ru Yan felt this Damo could not be the same as the other Damo, and in fact she had trouble remembering what the Damo who had come to her house looked like; there was only this voice on the phone . . . that was all there was to him.

"Make a note of my home phone number," he was saying. "I usually turn off the cell when I get home, tonight I just forgot. Sometimes they try to reach me at midnight 'cause something needs to be fixed in a hurry."

Ru Yan knew nothing of Damo's background, but her instinct told her he must have sprung from the common people of this city. Her own life circumstances had been rather sheltered. For forty years, she had moved in few circles. A military compound, then a government departmental compound, then a college campus, and finally the quiet office building that housed her research institute. In the course of all that, she had spent less than a year on the agricultural lands associated with her mother's System[223], and even then she had been surrounded by children from the same System. From childhood to maturity, her ears had grown accustomed to various forms of the language of northern China.[224] She had had little experience of genuine home-grown people like Damo. You could say that large swaths of this city, and most of the people who lived in it, were not much more familiar to her than a country in Africa.

Tonight Ru Yan was troubled by the discrepancy between Damo the writer and Damo the repairman. Everything she'd ever learned had led her to believe that a person of genius and nobility will be tall and handsome, a man of visible refinement. Even the Gadfly with his scarred face and lugubrious mien, hobbling on one leg, had once possessed the grace and elegance of Arthur Burton.[225] She thought that artists are too generous to the characters they create, and tend to endow their protagonist with every kind of excellence. But God is just, to the point of being cruel. When he gives someone a fine and lovely exterior, He often makes that person shallow and dull; and on those who are created to look mediocre and coarse, He may bestow uncommon genius and a noble heart.

Ru Yan was now beginning to have doubts about the divinatory way her mother appraised people's hands and feet.

33

Most of the social activity of the year was coming now, as they entered December. Amid the winter chill and a sense of time slipping away, people always strive to create a warm and cordial atmosphere. At the beginning of the month, electronic greeting cards began to appear on the forum and in e-mail as well as QQ, wishing a Merry Christmas and welcoming the New Year. Some of these cards had been composed by the senders themselves, while others had been scavenged off the Net or generated by a website which provided that service. Since the old birds of the Empty Nest mostly had children overseas, they participated, notwithstanding their age, in the outpouring of Christmas sentiments which grew stronger by the day. The forum got crowded with sleighs and reindeer and Santa Claus in his red cap, with Christmas music too. New Year's Day came soon after: ring out the old & ring in the new, for time is passing. The season always made people thoughtful and nostalgic, especially at this age. Once New Year's was past, the Spring Festival was not far behind. In any case the month would be full of merriment and, anywhere you turned, wishes for good luck. On this account the chat room organized several large-scale parties, one for Christmas Eve when parents and children would assemble, virtually, from the four corners of the world to hear and sing Western carols. On New Year's Eve they all gathered again to await the chimes of midnight. On the eve of the Spring Festival, they even chose to forego the CCTV Gala[226] in order to participate in their own folk-song competition. For these aging parents separated from their children, this made the loneliness and the longing easier to bear.

This year, for the first time in her life, Ru Yan would be alone for a holiday that can easily make a person weepy. On reflection, she was thankful for the Internet that made possible a party where the old would speak freely of youthful passions. Her son, too, would go online to get in touch, by voice and image, on that evening. And there would be the little dog who shared his name, and who was both lovable and needing to be cared for. And finally there was the one who had appeared out of nowhere in her life: Liang Jinsheng.

Ru Yan's father had been dead for many years. Her aged mother had moved in with Ru Yan's older sister down South. It was warm there, and for several years now if she wanted to get together with her mother it was up to Ru Yan to make the trip. That's what she had originally expected to do for Spring Festival this year, but then she had been unsure. The reason for her hesitation might not have been clear even to herself. A few days before New Year's, Liang Jinsheng had called to ask if she would spend the eve of Spring Festival with him. And only then did she realize that the reason she had not arranged a trip South was that she had been anticipating just this invitation.

"I've already worked out a couplet for the occasion," Liang Jinsheng had said. "The first line is,

Two human beings, bereft and alone

The second line is,

Celebrate the year in mutual support

and the *envoi* is

Let's have a party!"

Ru Yan laughed. She said, judiciously, "Well, the meter and construction are a little off—"[227]

He broke in, "Now don't expect too much of me! I never got any training for this."

"You didn't let me finish," she said. "I was going to say, '*but* the writing, though not flowery, has a certain grandeur of spirit.'"

"Thanks for the compliment," he was quick to say.

"Nevertheless," she continued, "there is a whiff of self-pity. *You*, 'bereft and alone'? How many banquets, pray tell, have you been invited to? Admit it, you could push open just about any door, at random, and announce 'I've come to crash your family dinner,' and wouldn't the TV station send a camera crew racing to the scene?"

"Would you like to join me for such a moment, for such festivities?"

"Me? What would I do there? I want to stay home and hear from my son. He promised he'd wish me a happy new year over the Internet."

Liang Jinsheng asked, "Can I join you for that?"

She phoned her mother. She didn't like to lie, but she said, "Train and plane tickets are sold out this year. I'm not sure I can manage to get one."

"I was just about to call you," her mother said. "Don't even think about coming down this year. We're in a tizzy here. They say there's a strange disease going around, a strange disease that no medicine can cure. You get it, you die. The stress at the hospital where your sister's husband works is incredible. All over town, the shops are completely sold out of Isatis root, and white vinegar has gone up to several hundred yuan a bottle.[228]"

Ru Yan asked, "How come we haven't heard even a whisper

of this up here?"

"They're not letting anyone talk about it," her mother said, "the news has spread via cell phones. Your sister gets many messages every day. You be careful up there. With all the people traveling home and passing through, it may spread to your part of the country."

Ru Yan looked it up online. A few forums had sketchy and fragmentary posts mentioning this strange disease, but there was no official information.

Some of her online friends in the South had invited her to stay with them when she passed through their part of the country, and they were now pressing her for an itinerary. When she told them she was canceling the trip and explained why, they too mentioned the strange disease and said in their region people were not allowed to talk about it. Oddly enough, these messages were only up for a few minutes before disappearing. Then someone reproached Ru Yan, `Why are you deleting posts???` Indignantly, she replied that when Lonely Goose had been moderator, she had taught Ru Yan how to delete posts, but she had never done it, and couldn't even remember how. Then someone else said, `Posts like this could cause turmoil in society; someone will be watching them very closely. Especially in a forum like ours, which is connected with people overseas.` A third person wrote, `Not sure how to say this, but they may be watching us right now and laughing at us.`

Ru Yan said, `Can't they give a reason?` Someone replied, `You think things like this need a reason? Moderator Such Is This World, you are an angel right out of a fairy-tale.` This post, too, disappeared after a few minutes.

Ru Yan couldn't believe it and tried posting again: `An unknown disease, highly contagious, has been discovered in the South. I hope all our Net friends will take precautions.` This time, the consequences were even more obvious: a window popped up on her screen:

SERVER ERROR
Your message is temporarily unable to be posted

Ru Yan now realized that in what she had thought was a little salon hosted by herself there was actually an old crone concealed and peering at everything from behind a curtain. Her mood changed in an instant: she was offended and discouraged. To pass a warning to everyone in a forum that had barely a hundred people in it, what was wrong with that? Her mother couldn't have been lying. Still less could her brother-in-law the doctor have made it all up. She clicked the mouse and turned off the computer. Then Ru Yan, who never used coarse language, muttered under her breath, *Screw you!* After further thought, she laughed. *Who am I mad at?*

34

One Sunday afternoon, Ruyan heard the noise of a motorcycle down in the street and had a feeling . . . sure enough, the bell rang and it was Damo.

He stood at her door in his blue overalls with a canvas bag slung over his shoulder and a motorcycle helmet in his hand. "Just finished a job in the neighborhood," he said cheerfully, "and seeing as it's still early I thought I'd drop by and take care of those things for you. It's been cool these last couple of days; I figured you must need the A/C."[229]

"You can't be serious," Ru Yan said. "I've gotten used to it. Please sit down and have some tea. I'm delighted you came."

"*You* may get used to it," Damo said, "not me. The thought of your A/C banging and rattling has felt like an itch I couldn't scratch."

She laughed. "When someone else itches, how does that bother you?"

"I guess you've never experienced it. It's called obsessive-compulsive disorder."

Standing on the threshold, he fished a pair of clean cloth shoes out of his bag and put them on, balancing on one foot at a time. Then he laid his leather shoes outside the door.

"You even bring your own cloth shoes?" she asked.

"People can be fussy these days, and sometimes it's a problem: if I don't change, I get their floor dirty; if I change into the cloth shoes the client provides, I get *them* dirty." He returned to his theme of obsessive behavior. "There was a woman tech at our factory who was a neat-freak. If you had a single hair on your shoulder, or a grain of rice on your front, she'd reach out and flick it off. Couldn't help herself. In stores, if the clothes on the mannequins were rumpled, she'd go over and smooth them out. Well, once she was on a bus and noticed the guy in front of her had his collar folded down on one side, like half of it was missing. This bugged her—I mean, the whole busride it gnawed at her. She didn't dare grab and straighten the collar, much though she wanted to do it; she thought of speaking to him but was afraid he might take it the wrong way. As the bus neared her stop, she screwed up her courage, took aim, and hit that collar with her elbow as she pushed past him. Looking back, she saw it had been straightened out. It was a good thing, because otherwise she couldn't have gone home with her mind at peace."

Ru Yan doubled over with laughter.

"Sometimes," he continued, "when I'm out on the streets and I pass stores or restaurants whose air conditioners or refrigerators are squealing and clanking, I want to walk in and turn the thing off and say, 'Just because it doesn't bother *you*, you think no one else minds this racket?'"

He had changed his shoes, and now he spread a plastic sheet on the living room floor and laid out all his tools. Then he took a safety belt from his bag, fastened it round his waist, and clipped it to the window frame. After testing his weight on it, he swung most of his body out the window and began to loosen the A/C casing. Ru Yan got nervous and grabbed the corner of his jacket.

"Hey, don't do that," he said, "It scares me."

"I'm just holding on to you, what are you afraid of?"

"I'm afraid you could get pulled right out the window."

So she let go. "Go away," he said. "If there's anything you need to take care of, now is a good time. I like to work alone."

Twenty minutes later, Damo clambered back into the room and Ru Yan breathed easier. He tried the A/C and confirmed that it no longer sounded like a tractor, but clear and crisp like some essay, originally verbose and confused, that he had deftly edited. Now he asked her for newspapers to spread over her tea-table, where he laid out her malfunctioning appliances. One by one he took them apart and fixed them. His motions were smooth, natural, and fluid. Ru Yan found an aesthetic pleasure in watching Damo work. Rapt in concentration, he didn't talk, didn't look around, didn't drink any tea and didn't smoke any cigarettes as he proceeded inexorably through his tasks. He didn't even look at the tools he had set within reach, but just reached out to where they were and nimbly grasped them; and when finished with one, he'd put it back with the same unerring accuracy. As he disassembled the items, tidy piles of screws, washers, and tiny parts came into being as if by magic; and when he put them back together, he was like a soldier reassembling his rifle, and all the little parts seemed to leap up and interlock as if of their own accord. To watch the orderly rhythm, one would think he gave the work neither a thought nor a glance. The stubby fingers fluttered between the parts and the tools like ten mute graceful elves dancing. A bit more than an hour passed, and her rice-cooker, remote control, vacuum cleaner, headphones, and even the refrigerator were all completely fixed. Then he whisked a couple of chairs over to the kitchen cupboard and fixed the top hinge on that, too. When all was done, he scooped up his tools and returned them to his bag, leaving everything clean and neat.

This was the first time Ru Yan had ever seen work done so beautifully. It was mesmerizing. "I never knew," she said with admiration, "that it could be so lovely to watch someone work."

Pleased, Damo said, "Is that so?"

"Yes, it's really a beautiful sight; I'm not just being polite."

"Well," Damo answered, "it's not everyone who could recognize the beauty in the way I work."

Ru Yan caught the undertone of arrogance and teased him, "And it's not everyone who would say that!"

"But it's a fact," Damo said, "that nothing is interesting unless it evokes a sensation of beauty."

He then shared some memories from when he had been sent to work in the countryside. The most skillful among the farmers had a beautiful way of working, he said; they were artists. When yoking an ox, for example, the experts would toss the yoke onto the beast's back and it would land just right, and then, like acrobats, they would leap up and tie a knot with a couple of quick pulls and the yoke would be tight and firm. It was exquisite, like watching a demonstration of the martial arts. When it was the turn of the "educated youth," the yoke would land askew and be either too loose or too tight, and the kids would get rope-burn on their hands and work up a sweat. Meanwhile the real farmers would have already taken their oxen half a mile into the fields. In their village, there was an old rich peasant [230] who was always much sought-after in planting season. When he went out to plant rice he'd sling a cotton bag over his shoulder filled with exactly the right amount of seed for the area he intended to plant. He'd start at one end of a seed-bed and walk backward, sowing. He never turned his head, until the last corner had been sown and the bag was empty. If you came along later you'd find the seedlings evenly distributed, with equal spaces between them, so that the field looked like the mesh of a wicker basket: and not a single seed would have fallen outside the boundary. His footprints would trace a narrow channel on either side of each seedbed, but his feet stayed out of the seeded areas, and the interval between rows looked to have been measured with a ruler, never an inch too wide or a degree out of line: as though some supernatural power had been at work. The seedlings cultivated in this way proved sturdy and uniform in height and girth. When they were transplanted, there was never a single one that didn't turn out well. Once the old fellow told Damo privately that before

Liberation, this skill of his had enabled him to buy more than an acre of farmland.[231]

Ru Yan's husband had also liked to fix things around the house, but he was always flustered and disorganized. Sometimes he'd take things apart that weren't supposed to be taken apart, and sometimes he'd put pieces together in the wrong sequence, and sometimes he'd forget where he'd put one of his tools, or some little nut or washer would go missing and he'd spend half an hour finding it. Sometimes he'd break one of the parts by prying at it and then have to go out for a replacement. When he finished, the house would look as though it had been ransacked, with messes everywhere. Consequently the repair of household appliances was an aspect of life that Ru Yan had always found discouraging and depressing.

Now that he had finished, Damo leaned back on the sofa with the look of one for whom life was good, and smoked a cigarette and drank some tea. His face, which had been a mask of concentration while he worked, now became animated.

"When you finish repairs like these, Ru Yan asked, "what do you usually charge people?"

"Want to settle accounts?" he chuckled.

"No, I'm just curious."

"Defining a standard scale of charges for the repair industry is actually a rather interesting question. I once wrote a paper on it and said I had long pondered the problem and come up with three factors that determine the value of a repair. First, the value of the time spent on the work itself; second, the value of having the use of the appliance; and third, the value that emerges from the negotiation itself. . . it's somewhat involved. The Price Board has a reference list of prices—I've got it in my bag—but I think it's a misleading guideline. You see, the average customer is like you: they don't really know what's broken, or how badly it's broken. If you had fallen into the hands of a crook he would have charged you four or five hundred for fixing these things. If he was really crooked, he would also have had you replace a few parts that didn't need to be replaced. The A/C, for example: he would have said, 'the compressor's shot,' and you'd expect to have to replace the part, just like when something goes wrong with a car engine. Replacing the compressor would have added a few hundred yuan, and there's no guarantee the new one would have been any better than the old. But after he took the old one out, he would have touched it up with paint and sold it to someone else as a replacement."

"Is that how *you* do things?" Ru Yan asked.

"What do *you* think?" Damo said.

"Well, if you don't, then where other people make a hundred yuan you must make only fifty."

"Maybe," Damo said, "but the guy who makes a hundred yuan may spend the next few days looking for work. I make fifty, but every day, all day long, people are chasing after me with jobs to do. And the other guy probably doesn't enjoy his work as much as I enjoy mine. That rich peasant I was telling you about, when the People's Communes came along[232], he got work points just like everyone else, except that because of his dodgy class status he was awarded fewer points than the average worker. Yet he still did his work conscientiously every day and seemed content with his lot. People from outside the commune would request his services, and to get them they'd have to wine and dine the Brigade leader and give him cigarettes. *He* never got anything out of these deals except extra work. A few of us sent-down youth asked him the same question you just asked me. 'When you know you'll get so few points, why do you work so hard?' He said, 'If I do bad work, the crops will suffer and I'll feel bad.' At that time we were studying Marx and it reminded us of what the old worthy had said about labor: that when Communism came, people would not just work to support themselves; work would become their life's primary need, for it would be the objective realm in which they'd find self-fulfillment. We thought it was funny that this old rich peasant had already attained the ideological plane of pure Communism."

Ru Yan smiled. "You, too, have attained the same level of Communist thought, perhaps with an even higher degree of awareness."

"That's why I say the people who talk Communism today

don't know the first thing about it. They're way behind that rich peasant."

Hearing this sally, and remembering some of his essays, Ru Yan wondered again what kind of man this was. What could have been his social background? How had he developed his ideas? According to the theory of classes in which she had been educated for years, *if the root is straight, the flower will be red*; if a person still had some feelings based on that upbringing, he could not adopt such a cutting and extremist tone. On the other hand, people from families that had been at odds with this regime tended to be obsequious out of fear, and would not speak so candidly (indeed recklessly) in front of a stranger. Besides, it had been so many years since Reform and Opening that the children of people tarred by association with the previous dynasty had long since come to enjoy changed circumstances. As citizens with relatives on Taiwan or overseas[233], they had become the new generation of capitalists or members of the intellectual establishment, even to the point of taking positions (whether low or high) in the Party. Anyway, they were living well, much better than the proletariat of yore, and they were quite content. In recent years Ru Yan had met many of the people on her mother's side of the family, and in every case their thought had undergone a considerable evolution. This evolution was not of a piece with the insincere professions of patriotism, denunciations of revisionism, etc., so familiar in an earlier era. It came from the heart. This was particularly evident in those who returned from overseas: as soon as they opened their mouths, you could tell they were even more gung-ho than Party members on the mainland. She had an uncle from Taiwan who'd been a KMT official and legislator, and he was more dead-set against Chen Shuibian than any 'angry youth' on the Internet.[234] To her surprise, his take on cross-strait relations was that blood is thicker than water.

Her curiosity got the better of her, therefore, and she asked Damo whether his parents were still alive. He said they had both passed away.

"And what did they use to do?" she pressed.

"My father was a shop clerk," Damo said. "He sold tea all his life. My mother was basically a housewife, though she worked for a while in a shoe factory."

"Then how is it," Ru Yan asked in perplexity (and unwittingly giving away what she was driving at), "that you take so much interest in the big questions?"

"What big questions are you talking about?"

She mentioned the essays by him which she had read.

Damo said, "Oh! Those are little questions, extremely practical and specific. You're talking about workers who've been laid off, medical care, housing, temporary residence permits, corruption and misconduct, an impartial judiciary, pollution, the siphoning-off of State property . . . Each of these topics is intertwined with us ordinary people. If we don't worry about these things, no one else is going to worry about them for us. Take the embezzlement of State property: to hear some academics, you'd think this was just an abstract theoretical matter; but to us, it means the difference between having food and clothing and not having them."

Ru Yan brought up the strange disease about which rumors were going around.

"They say a virus is no respecter of persons," Damo offered, "and both rich and poor will get sick: but when it comes to treatment, it's going to make a big difference whether you're rich or poor. Never mind the fact that, on account of the different conditions under which they live, the poor are more likely to get sick when an epidemic breaks out. A few years ago I wrote a post about environmental problems, and someone wrote to me, 'Ahh, you rich people have plenty to eat and drink, so you make up these things to worry about!' But who really bears the brunt of damage to the environment? The lowest stratum of the common people, that's who! Go into the slums, go into that no-man's land between the city and the countryside and look around, and you'll see.[235] Never mind the rights that are fundamental for people on the bottom: the right to reside in a place or move away, the right to vote or stand for office, and don't forget the right to know the facts. For many years, the right to know the facts has been the greatest privilege of V.I.P.s, of the elite. If we don't speak out, who will speak for us? Of the Three Years' Famine, all we knew was that there had been natural disasters for three years in a row, and that the Soviet revisionists—ingrates!—were forcing us to pay our debts. So as we starved, we still sang that He was the great liberator of our people. You see, we don't have a right to know the facts. We're like animals. We starved, then we were full, and we are oh-so-grateful—like *animals*."

What Ru Yan had read in Damo's essays was a fine standard Mandarin. What she heard in his speech was the dialect of the common people, and it fascinated her. She said, "The way you speak and the way you write articles are not the same."

"And this is when I'm talking to *you*!" he said with a wry laugh. "I'm still trying to choose my words and mind my p's and q's. If you could hear me talking with the guys from the factory, you'd find it pretty raw. Lots of foul language."

"I'll have to make an undercover investigation," she said.

He was clearly enjoying the conversation, but then he looked at his watch and said he had to go: his daughter was coming to supper that night. "She's about to give birth," he explained. "Today she settles in at our home and she's going to ask me to choose a name."

Ru Yan congratulated him and asked that he give her a call when he became a grandfather. "When is she due?"

"New Year's Eve," he said. "Didn't plan *that* right!"

35

At work, she ran into Jiang Xiaoli in a corridor. She beamed at Ru Yan as if she could tell something from Ru Yan's face. Ever since Maple Leaves Are Red had clued her in on Jiang Xiaoli's history, Ru Yan had thought she recognized a hint of sour distress in her smiles. It gave Ru Yan a bad feeling, as if she had stolen something.

"What are you looking at?" Ru Yan asked cheerfully.

"The glow of bliss on your face," came the reply.

"You can't help the innuendos, can you?"

"You're not going to see your mother?" Jiang Xiaoli asked.

"My mother said there's a strange disease going around down there. She told me not to come."

"Well, isn't that convenient! A city leader gets to spend New Year's with you, then."

"I knew you'd have a tart comment," Ru Yan said.

"If I need your help someday, I hope you won't deny you know me."

"When is a person like you ever going to need my help?"

"Just you wait," Jiang Xiaoli said, "someday crowds will gather outside your house for a chance to suck up to you. I'll be lucky to squeeze into the line."

Encountering her in this mood, Ru Yan had no choice but to play along. "OK, write me a list of requests. When the time comes, I promise I'll take care of everything."

"I'll take your word for that," Jiang Xiaoli said, "and now I know I didn't do all that work for nothing. But you know, a good man like him was not easy to catch, especially these days. From one end of the world to the other, all you find is sons-of-bitches. Today they're going to pay out the end-of-year bonuses, plus there's a science-and-technology award for your lab: everybody gets a share. I will collect this money for you."

Ru Yan was confused. "Why? Are you short of cash?"

Jiang Xiaoli snorted. "The pittance you're getting wouldn't do much for me. No, I'm going to take you shopping for some new outfits. Soon you'll be the mayor's wife. Look at what you're wearing; I'd like you to be a credit to me as a matchmaker."

"This is frightening," Ru Yan said. "I've got no idea what you're going to transform me into."

"Never mind," Jiang Xiaoli said. "Just report for duty and let me transform you."

Ru Yan thought about it and realized she hadn't bought any new clothes for years. Her few presentable suits had all been purchased when her husband was alive. For women today, clothes and accessories are like the parasol trees that line our streets: winter turns to spring, the wind shifts, and not a single leaf remains. And what has been blown down is nothing but a household nuisance. Pitch them, you say; but some are good, never been worn. If you don't pitch them, they'll just take up space until, a few years from now, you have to pitch them anyway. It used to be that you could trade in your old clothes for eggs, but not any more. It used to be that when calamity struck somewhere, there would be appeals to donate clothing; but now they just deduct your contribution from your pay. The rationale is that in the countryside they think city folk carry diseases, and the city folk say it's not right—and does not meet international standards—to give another person your castoffs. Ru Yan didn't have the problem of figuring out what to do with excess clothes, because she didn't have any; and although it made her feel a little old-fashioned, she stuck to her ways. Sometimes her clothes from ten years before came back into vogue, which made her look like a canny shopper indeed.

That afternoon, the money was handed out. Jiang Xiaoli then headed straight downtown with Ru Yan. Offices like theirs are not too strict about work attendance, and they were especially laid-back at the end of the year.

In recent years (Ru Yan wasn't sure exactly when), several luxury malls had sprung up, like the castles that rise overnight in Arab folktales. If you looked around from a main thoroughfare and saw a towering building with big entrances and glass façades, all bright and bustling, you could be sure it was a mall.[236]

Jiang Xiaoli took Ru Yan into a few stores she had never been to and had no idea what was inside them. She stuck close to her guide for fear of getting lost.

The various bonuses added up to a bit more than 3,000 yuan, which for Ru Yan was no small sum: but today it was at the disposal of Jiang Xiaoli, who had gone to this trouble for her, and Ru Yan decided to give her free rein. She was surprised to hear her say, "With so little money we'd better not go to any of the top stores; if we couldn't pay the bill they might lock us up to work off the debt."

It was clear that Jiang Xiaoli knew the ropes when it came to clothes and fashion. First she scurried through several stores without a word about buying anything, scanning the garments on the racks and taking stock of patterns and materials and prices, like a general inspecting the front on the eve of battle. Then she returned to certain stores and had Ru Yan try things on.

She chose well, for she understood Ru Yan; only the prices made Ru Yan wince. Ru Yan kept trying things on and taking them off; and gradually she got used to, and even began to like, the woman who was being transformed in the full-length mirror. It was exciting. Raiment can cast a spell over a woman. It doesn't merely change her looks; it can start the adrenaline flowing. Ru Yan finished buttoning a jacket and noted how it accentuated the curve of her waist. She felt suddenly light-headed as she tautened her belly and lifted her chest. Her complexion deepened, her eyes flashed, and her whole body came alive when the clothing, like some tutelary spirit, imparted a new discipline to the lines of her shoulders and back and legs: it all expressed femininity.

Jiang Xiaoli painstakingly assembled an outfit for her. Even the leather shoes and stockings struck the right note. She also bought a set of cosmetics. They spent Ru Yan's bonus down to the last penny. Pleased with her work, Jiang Xiaoli teased, "Well, that's the best we can do. You want better stuff, get the mayor to buy it for you later."

Ru Yan was overwhelmed, and muttered, "I'm too old for this!"

"Once you get used to the new look, you'll start to worry," Jiang Xiaoli said.

"About what?"

"About what to do with your old clothes. About what to wear when you have to change this outfit. You see, the things you're now wearing form a complete set. You'd be better off not wearing them at all than mixing them incorrectly—I'm afraid the effect would be comical."

"Then I'll only wear them at home. I can dress up by myself

and feel beautiful."

"Only problem is, he might not agree with that. I'm telling you, Liang Jinsheng likes pretty women."

When they finished buying clothes, their feet were tired. Ru Yan invited Jiang Xiaoli to a coffee shop on the revolving top level of the mall.

Men often cement their friendships and come to understand each other by discussing issues of historic importance; between women, however, intimacy usually arises from talking about the affairs of daily life. A hundred meters up in the air, Ru Yan and Jiang Xiaoli sat at a small table near a window, watching the cityscape shift slowly at their feet beneath a vast and open sky. It was a good place to talk.

"Ru Yan," Jiang Xiaoli said with a knowing smile, "Life without a man must be hard, no?"

Ru Yan wasn't sure what Jiang Xiaoli was getting at, and answered vaguely, "Yeah, lots of things are inconvenient."

Jiang Xiaoli grinned and pressed her point. "Only inconvenient? The conventional wisdom is that a woman in her forties has a drive like a wolf or a tiger."

She couldn't pretend any longer that she didn't understand, so Ru Yan said, "Actually, for me that hasn't been so important. My husband often said Plato had ruined me. When I found myself alone, the adjustment was not difficult."

"Yet people say you and your husband got along very well."

"We did. The passion of youth changes into a day-in, day-out affection, like pottery which glows hot in the kiln and then slowly cools down. Yet it is still a lovely pot. If you stayed on fire forever, wouldn't you get burned up?"

Until Jiang Xiaoli had raised the question, Ru Yan had never thought too closely about her relationship with her husband. It was like drawing a question from the jar[237]: she had to answer on the spot, and she herself wasn't clear how much of her answer had been the truth and how much had been invented to satisfy her inquisitor.

But Jiang Xiaoli brushed it off with derision. "Don't kid yourself, Ru Yan. If a woman feels no lust for her husband, the relationship has just gone cold—don't give me a song and dance about pottery."

This hurt, because it was true. For a few years before he died, Ru Yan's feelings for her husband had been tepid. There weren't any fights or squabbles—even when something bothered her, she wouldn't bring it up—but there was no passion, either. He was attentive to her in many ways, but it didn't mean that much to her. He never got angry but it would be going too far to call him kind; and yet to call him unfeeling would also be unjust. In a word, he took everything in stride, with a shrug and a smile, or perhaps without a word he would let it pass. All the same, when he was gone, the old fire began to burn again with a stubborn low flame, and it often gave her a dull ache in her heart. As a girl she had once jotted down a saying in her notebook: *Friendship is like health: you appreciate it only when you lose it.* That's what it had been like to remember her husband.

"After he passed away," Ru Yan said, "I started to think more and more about his good qualities. I've never forgotten him. If you hadn't undertaken your kind offices, maybe I would have stayed single. The last time Liang Jinsheng came to my house, my husband's picture was hanging on the wall. It's still there."

Jiang Xiaoli was suddenly quiet, and it dawned on Ru Yan that perhaps she had really been talking about herself, so she blurted, "I've heard you're single, now, too?"

Jiang Xiaoli shot her a probing look. "Did he tell you that?"

"No."

"Then who did?"

Ru Yan tried to pass it off lightly. "Hey, in today's information-rich society, could something like that stay hidden?"

Jiang Xiaoli said, "I think I know who it was."

Ru Yan now realized she shouldn't have disclosed what she knew. She tried to shift the direction of the conversation: "It's nothing out of the ordinary. Everywhere you look, people are breaking up. Society has moved forward." She was trying to mollify her.

But Jiang Xiaoli paid no attention. A shadow of gloom settled on her features. "So . . . you knew all along."

"Knew what?" Ru Yan asked.

"Don't put on an act."

Ru Yan knew she was not a good liar, so she kept silent.

Finally Jiang Xiaoli smiled and gave Ru Yan a thoughtful look before taking a deep draw on her cigarette and blowing out the smoke. "I'll be candid with you," she said slowly, "I really would have liked to marry him."

Feeling her way, Ru Yan said, "Seems to me it would have been a very good match."

"I wasn't that lucky. I am a person who has always worked hard and succeeded, and I never asked anyone for help. But in love, I have never been lucky."

"So you were already divorced?"

"Yes. When I got divorced, his wife hadn't died yet. So no one had any reason to suspect I was after him."

Ru Yan didn't know what to say.

"Back then," Jiang Xiaoli said, "I almost lost my mind."

Ru Yan stirred her coffee, slowly.

"We had always known each other," Jiang Xiaoli continued. "I watched him go up the ladder. He started as a low-ranking cadre in the Institute of Design. For a time he was even under my father's jurisdiction, a couple of levels down, and later he lived in the same compound with us. He'd often come to visit and was always good to us."

"Did that change, later?" Ru Yan asked.

"It would be better if it had," she said. "Then it wouldn't hurt so much, now. At worst, I could curse him as an ingrate. But because the relationship had always been good, one day on impulse I went to declare my feelings with girlish shyness, and no thought for my dignity."

"A momentary weakness, I guess? Just got carried away?"

"Yes and no. I'd say if people aren't made for each other it's not going to work out. Even if they're sleeping together, they'll break up. That's life. Like they say, the river flows east for thirty years, but then it's gonna turn around and flow west. Way back when, you know how many guys were after me? But I wouldn't give 'em the time of day. The only one who could take that treatment was my ex-husband: he didn't give up. I never guessed that later he'd treat me so bad."

"He beat you?" Ru Yan asked.

"That wouldn't have been a problem: I would have given as good as I got. No, he kept a mistress. Slimeball. The nerve! His dad served under my father, and for the sake of their darling boy his parents came to our house so many times, always ingratiating. Then he got promoted and my father retired. After that, he wasn't the same person anymore."

"Did he and Liang know each other?"

"No. He got transferred."

"What else could have held Liang Jinsheng back?"

"How would *I* know?" Jiang Xiaoli asked with a sardonic laugh. "Anyway, that wasn't the reason. In the closed world of Party officials, marriage can of course be a sensitive matter. Who can say what the problem might have been? Think about it. Personal connections build up over years and get pretty complicated. How can you be sure rumors won't start if So-and-so marries a daughter in a particular family?"

"Why have you played the matchmaker," Ru Yan asked, "for me?"

"I want him to have a really good life."

"You sure about that? That I'm going to give him a good life?"

Jiang Xiaoli gave another bitter laugh. "Didn't I tell you I have great judgment when it comes to *other* people's business? The way he thanked me! It killed me, but it made me happy."

"Does he know how you feel?" Ru Yan inquired.

"He's no fool. He may not let on that he knows. You could say he's a sly one, or you could say he understands people. Anyway, this boy has cost me more than a little heartache. I never was so crazy for love when I was young. To go through all this craziness at this stage in my life, and for nothing . . ."

The first time Ru Yan met Liang Jinsheng came back to her now, and she remembered the studied casualness with which Jiang Xiaoli had adorned herself. It was painful to think about. Women of any age still have a young girl's heart inside.

"I've got a mind," Ru Yan said half in jest and half in earnest, "to send him back to you."

Jiang Xiaoli raised her voice. "You will do no such thing! That would be awful! It would totally wreck the friendship I have with him. If you're good to him, that's the thing that will make me happiest."

"What if he's not good to me?" Ru Yan asked.

"How could that be? He couldn't conceal his bliss from me, even though he knew I'd tend to be jealous of you. But there's one thing of which I'd better warn you. As a top official, he's often not his own man. Some things may prove disappointing, but it won't be his choice."

"I have to laugh," Ru Yan said, "you're already acting like an in-law. I'm done for."

"See, the one who gets a good deal never has a kind word for the peddler! He'd be delighted to marry you tomorrow, but he tells me you're putting on airs and you've given him a six-month probationary period before he's inducted."

Having both revealed so much, they felt relieved now. On the spur of the moment, they veered into a Western-style restaurant where each ordered a few dishes out of which they made a supper. Colleagues for many years, all of a sudden these two women felt like intimate friends. They chatted as they ate. One laid plans for the happiness which awaited the other in a few months' time; and one brainstormed what the other might do with the second half of her life. They kept at it till the vast earth below them sparkled with a myriad points of light.

36

The five members of the *Qing Ma* eventually underwent that process which Maozi called dismemberment by five horses[238]: he meant that they were scattered to the four winds, and separated by large geographical distances. But there was another kind of distance, too, which Damo found more distressing.

One day Damo came across a volume by Maozi in a bookstore. It was tucked away in the Social Science section and looked as though it had been there for a long time. Picking it up, Damo found it was a Marxian interpretation of the Reform policy of a certain leader[239]. Skimming it quickly, he had a queasy feeling and bought the book in order to study it at home.

It had been published several years before. Maozi had brought out other books during this period, and in each case he had ceremoniously presented Damo with an inscribed copy, stamped with Maozi's seal, and humbly asked him for criticisms and corrections. He had also given copies to Teacher Wei and the far-flung members of the *Qing Ma*. But he had never even mentioned this book. During the gathering for Teacher Wei's eightieth birthday, the old man had made a point of asking Maozi about his books. Damo hadn't heard him mention this one. Damo felt Maozi's most trenchant, energetic, and innovative writings all dated from the Eighties, when Damo used to devour his articles as they came out, striking the table and exclaiming, "Damn, that's good! You keep getting better!" But it went downhill after that. Maozi's work became increasingly mediocre and perfunctory, though oddly enough this was precisely the time when his reputation started to spread and he received one promotion after another.

The dust jacket had wide flaps and included an official portrait of Maozi in a suit and necktie. The thrust of the brief bio was clear: N.N.N. (Maozi's formal name), Director and Research Fellow of the Philosophy department at the Social Science Institute. Member, Communist Party of China. Vice-Secretary-General of the Provincial Marxian Scholars' Association. And there was a string of other titles as well. There followed a list of his published works and a fulsome blurb.

Getting into the text itself, Damo began to feel nauseated. This was almost physically painful, and it took several evenings to finish the book. "Goddammit," he said, "Maozi, oh Maozi, how did you come to this?"

It's true, he thought, that systematizing the ideas of high officials is a service expected of intellectuals in the humanities[240], but it was ridiculous and required a lot of fakery, without any basis in fact or logic, to force an official's scattered impromptu remarks into a Marxian theoretical framework. Damo's intellectual development had begun with a serious study of Marx and Engels, and he had retained a proper and well-informed respect for them. He had no quarrel with those who gained their daily bread from Marx and Engels, but this kind of travesty was repugnant. It made him ill.

He snapped the book shut and dialed the number of Maozi's cell phone.

"Maozi," he said, "I just bought a book of yours."

"Which one? I haven't had any come out lately."

Damo named it. On the other end of the line, Maozi started to laugh. "What did you buy a book like that for? Even I was too embarrassed to show it to people."

"Yet you took the trouble to write it," Damo observed. "Well into the tens of thousands of characters."

"Well . . ." Maozi said, "It's what they wanted. Gotta do what you gotta do . . . It's how I chose to make a living. The assignment came down, you know? Plus there was a grant attached to it."

With Damo, Maozi had always been real, dispensing with academic pretensions. Their language might be vulgar or refined: there were no constraints. In the first place, they both knew there was no point in trying to impress each other. In the second place, whether Maozi chose low culture or high culture, he'd always carry it off with panache. But on this occasion, something didn't sound right: Damo could hear that he was distinctly uncomfortable.

"I guess money can make a person do anything," Damo said softly.

Maozi laughed. "Hey, I had just been allotted a new residence[241] and I needed money for other things, too."

Damo couldn't stand Maozi's frivolousness any longer. He said in a hard voice, "Even if you needed the money, how could you sell out the foundation of your life's work?"

"When you get too serious," Maozi shot back, "you're like Mr. Morality or something."

"And another thing, young man," Damo continued, "when did you sneak into the Party? And didn't breathe a word of it, as if you had joined a secret society."

"Well, you know," Maozi said, "It's kind of hard to pull off doing Marxism-Leninism without being a member of the Marxist-Leninist political party. It's basically an academic requirement."

"On Taiwan, in America, among the capitalist classes, there are many who study Marxism-Leninism."

"It's not the same there, it's not the same," Maozi objected. "The whole political environment is different."

"What year was it?" Damo asked.

"Oh, it was years ago . . . why do you ask? Is this an investigation?"[242]

"So you're keeping the date you joined the Party a secret?"

"Maybe it was the beginning of the Nineties. I don't remember exactly."

Damo was shaken. "The beginning of the Nineties? You turned that fast?"

Maozi noticed the change in Damo. "What exactly is going on, here? Are you doing a background check?"

"I . . . I don't even know where to begin."

"Well, if you've got something to say, you can just fucking say it. Enough with the tense pauses, already."

The two men's banter had begun half in jest, but had grown serious.

"How about this," Maozi proposed. "Why don't you come over when you have some time. I happen to have a favor to ask you."

"What's the favor?"

"My computer's been giving me trouble. I'd like you to wipe the drive and re-install everything. While you're at it, have a drink with me."

"I'll be there tomorrow morning," Damo said.

"No flies on you! What is this, 'Supreme directives must be promulgated the same day'?"[243]

"I sail while there's a fair wind," Damo said. "I'll have plenty to say to you."

"And I shall listen most respectfully, Sir. Name the hour, and I'll come pick you up."

"No need. I'll ride my motorcycle."

Not long after Maozi had been admitted to the Social Science Institute, Teacher Wei was restored to the Association of Social Science Scholars. It was the same 'System', though not the same work unit. They started to run into each other at functions, and some people became aware that they knew each other. The head of the Institute had been a subordinate of Teacher Wei's, and in keeping with the *mores* of that time he had been at the forefront of those who hounded Teacher Wei after his fall. By the time Teacher Wei was rehabilitated, decades later, this man had risen to be one level higher than he. Within a couple of years, although they never had any direct contact, the tenor of each man's writing showed the gulf which had opened up between them. At different times one or the other might get the better of an exchange, but only one of them had real power and it wasn't Teacher Wei. Consequently, Maozi suffered for years under this man's authority. The grief he took from his boss embittered him more than he could say. Damo recalled one time at Teacher Wei's house when Maozi talked about all the ways this man had managed to blight his career: how Maozi had been denied titles, housing, and foreign travel, and had been passed over for awards and distinctions.

"What a petty man," Teacher Wei said. "If he can't even free himself from his own spite, how is he going to emancipate mankind? But you just do your scholarly work well; the other things are mere worldly possessions, and you're in a much better position than I was, back in the day. Time will render judgment. The work you're doing now is not only what they have called for in their speeches, it's precisely the spot where they are vulnerable. Look how Zhou Yang, who was their left-wing counselor in the old days, came to his senses not long ago and wrote that humanitarian piece which was drawn, for sure, from the work of Marx himself—and it made them all go bananas. Someday, in the light of history, people will see how comical that was."

Maozi had been young and vigorous in those years, and since the general climate was relatively free and relaxed, he published good essays with notable frequency. As each one came out he would inform the members of the *Qing Ma*, and he would inform Teacher Wei. Then at the first opportunity there would be an energetic and raucous discussion of the points he had made.

Maozi's sudden change started with a public disturbance.[244]

One day in early June of that year, Maozi's wife Xiao Jin phoned Damo at the workers' college, out of the blue, and asked him to come over quickly. Damo had already been worried about Maozi, afraid that something might have happened to him. In those days neither of them had a telephone at home, and writing a letter could entail certain inconveniences, so he had been thinking of choosing a time when he wouldn't attract attention by going to see him. Xiao Jin's phone call was ominous and he asked, "What's wrong? Did something happen?"

"He hasn't seemed quite right these last two days," she said. "At night he can't sleep. At times he bursts out in sobs and sounds like a wild animal. You ask him whether he's in pain and he doesn't say a word. I want him to go to the hospital but he pays no attention to me. Please come see him. Just don't tell him I called you."

Damo didn't even ask for time off. He dashed over at once.

He had known since the start of spring that Maozi had been active in the unfolding events, signing petitions, marching, writing essays, speaking at colleges. He had made two trips to Beijing and been in the limelight. Maozi had even come to see Damo a couple of times, and the two had discussed the political situation at great length. They were in agreement on the major questions but had different views of where things were heading: Maozi was by far the more optimistic of the two.

"You're only looking at what goes on at the very top of the social pyramid," Damo said. "You should come spend a few days at my factory. You'd find out that the majority are quite pleased with their improved standard of living. The common people of

China have suffered for so long, they'd like to take it easy for a while. Plus, you expect too much from China's political culture: you forget it's been only eighty years since the queues were snipped off the back of our heads![245] Much of the change since then has been merely superficial. All over China it's still the same people in charge, both at a high level and farther down. Just like at our factory, where the same group has been in control since the Fifties and still runs the place today."

"You're at the grassroots," Maozi argued. "You can't be aware of the movement that's underway. At the bottom of the sea it seems perfectly still, but if you float to the top what will you find?"

"If the bottom of the sea is still, then whatever tumult and noise is taking place on the surface will subside after a few days. People's rice bowls are full; you think they're willing to risk all that?"

Maozi said, "I think the ideals we longed for in the old days are very close to being realized."

"I hope you're right," Damo smiled.

Well, that day Damo braved the summer heat and arrived at Maozi's home dripping with sweat. Xiao Jin opened the door.

"Where is he?" Damo asked.

She pointed to the bedroom. "He's in there, reading."

Damo went in and found Maozi leaning back on the bed calmly holding a book in his hands. Nothing looked amiss.

Damo smiled. "That's the ticket! The whole world's turned upside down, but you are at peace with your book."

Maozi paid no attention, remaining absorbed in his book.

Damo looked again and realized that Maozi was not actually reading. His vacant stare went right past the book. It was not clear what, if anything, he was looking at. Only now could Damo see that he was not all right. But in the same easygoing tone Damo continued, "Hey, somebody comes by and you don't even say hello?"

Like a statue, Maozi made no response. Damo pulled up a chair and sat down facing him. Maozi didn't appear to see him. But suddenly, just as Xiao Jin had described, he burst out in a loud sob like the howl of a wolf and then cut it short, making a long gagging noise as if his lungs were about to explode. He was like the old air-compressor at Damo's factory that used to let out a screeching hiss whenever the pressure rose too high and then would chug-chug-chug for a long time.

Damo tried the approach taken by Butcher Hu when Fan Jin passed the examination[246]: he pounded Maozi with his fist, just below the collar-bone, and roared, "What kind of fucking game are you playing? Can't you see you've scared the shit out of us?"

Maozi fell over on the bed and lay there for a while before he managed to whimper, "It's too frightening, it's just too fucking frightening. China is finished, finished . . . it's all over."

Damo let him cry and didn't try to comfort him. He agreed, "You're right, it's all over. Have a good cry and be done with it."

Maozi cried for a while and murmured for a while and then fell asleep.

Damo came back the next day. Maozi wept and mumbled some more. After a few more of these visits, he gradually calmed down but hardly spoke at all. He moved listlessly, as if he had contracted an enervating disease.

Maozi lived in the dormitory of his work unit, and a disturbance of this nature could not be concealed from his colleagues. The next day a rumor was making the rounds that Mao N.N. had gone mad at the sound of gunfire in Beijing, like Hua Ziliang in Zhazi Cave.[247] This rumor actually had the effect of shielding Maozi to a certain extent. The head of the Institute had long wanted to take disciplinary action against him but held off because the political situation was ambiguous. Now that it was clear which way the wind was blowing, he was set to move against Maozi when, unexpectedly, Maozi had this breakdown. Everyone had lived through the Cultural Revolution and was loath to act too hastily. What's more, by putting too much pressure on an unstable individual they risked bringing about an unfortunate incident that would be hard to explain to the higher-ups. So the Director held back. He kept holding back, in the belief that the situation did not require drastic action anyway, and the upshot was that the matter was left unresolved. Eventually the Director realized that a very large number of people in Beijing were basically just like Maozi. So he decided, sullenly, to let it go.

The Director was credited with a *bon mot* around then which others soon repeated to mock Maozi: 'These chickenshit democracy activists are all made of tofu and farts. It's only us Communist Party men who have the right stuff.' Ten years later he was busted for financial irregularities and his words came back, amid general hilarity, to haunt him.

Damo knew that Maozi's case was all about fear. And the fear in which it had begun was nothing to despise. But after the fear, he changed in a way that was painful to contemplate, and that was actually more terrifying than the fear. When Damo asked him about it later, Maozi said he couldn't remember anything. Something had gone 'bang' in his head and there was a blank stretch of time without even any recollection of Damo's visits to his home. He had seen a doctor, he said, and received a diagnosis of temporary insanity with amnesia. And there were some who said that he was faking it, that he really was a Hua Ziliang.

For years thereafter, Damo had been concerned only about Maozi's health and felt that it would not be wise, after such a shock, to raise any topic that could provoke a relapse. But now Damo had discovered that soon after his sickness, at the nadir of the Communist Party's prestige when its very legitimacy was being seriously challenged, this man who had been about to be severely punished became—of all things—a Party member. And Damo realized that Maozi had been very much in possession of his faculties, and the magnanimous Party officials very much knew what they were doing when they accepted him during that crisis.

It inspired another of Damo's essays: *The Power of Fear.* To terrify, he wrote, is more effective than to kill. Killing eliminates the dissident's body. Terror can transform his soul and turn an unruly rebel into a docile slave who will moreover serve as an example to the others. What is especially frightening is that the fear gets planted deep in your heart and grows there. No one can remove it for you.

More than a decade had thus passed. For all one could tell from the way they usually spoke on the phone and from their other contacts, Maozi seemed to have forgotten a great deal. Damo, too, had been willing to let the past fade away like smoke. That is why he was now so intent on going to Maozi's house. There were things he wanted to settle with him, once and for all.

37

The next morning, Damo switched off his cell so no one could reach him about work. He went to Maozi's place, driving his motorcycle very fast, as if he were on a mission to bring the old Maozi back and feared he might be too late.

Since the Eighties, Maozi had moved three times. Each new apartment was bigger than the last: Maozi had answered the call to do his part in quadrupling the national economy. The first one had been a bit more than 30 square meters, one bedroom with a living room and a private kitchen and bathroom.

Maozi had lived in the poor part of town for twenty or thirty years, with eight people (three generations) squeezed into an old two-room one-story house that wasn't even 20 square meters. It was ill-lit and musty and subject to annual flooding.[248] Within the poorer classes of this city, Maozi occupied a most unfortunate position, for his father was a policeman under the old regime just like the character in Lao She's *This Life of Mine*.[249] Such people had an extremely low status in the old society: both the rich and the poor despised them, giving rise to the children's ditty:

So-and-so's Pop,
Guy's a flop;
Couldn't make it:
He's a cop.

They were poorly paid, and unless they resorted to graft or extortion they had no hope of a decent living. This point is brought out clearly in Shi Hui's film of the same name. But when the new society came, Maozi's father was held up as an especially contemptible villain, the very dregs of villainy, utterly inferior to more reputable villains such as senior KMT officers, wealthy capitalists, and officials of the old regime who had studied abroad. These people all had something which ordinary people envied, whether money, or an imposing mansion, or cultural refinement. Some of them were placed in special work units after Liberation where they received a good salary and were even allowed to attend public meetings along with good people. But Maozi's father was not allowed to serve as a People's Policeman after Liberation, for he was stigmatized as a tool of the old regime[250]. He took a series of degrading jobs, driving a pedicab, selling jellied tofu, and carrying loads on a stick across his shoulders; he worked himself into an early grave. For the family he left behind, old and young, life was a lot harder than it had ever been for the proletariat. Maozi thus managed to experience the worst of both worlds. And so when after being inducted into the Social Science Institute at the conclusion of his studies, Maozi was assigned his first apartment, which was twice as big as the one his entire family had shared, and he no longer had to race into a stinking public outhouse first thing in the morning... well, he thought he had died and gone to Heaven. It was in this apartment that he had been married. His wife Xiao Jin was five years younger but only one year behind him academically, and later she was assigned to teach at the University. He moved to his second apartment in the early Nineties not long after joining the Party. It had three bedrooms and a living room totaling more than 70 square meters. At last he had his own little study where he could put his desk and feel at ease. At that time it was becoming fashionable to carry out renovations, and after moving up in the world, Maozi had sighed with a certain complacency, "Life is regrettably short, and it looks as though my life will finish here." His third apartment came in '99, when the practice of including housing in State workers' benefits was about to end. It was 180 square meters on the fourteenth floor, with four bedrooms, a living room, and a dining room. This high-rise had been rushed to completion on the grounds that it would house the province's eminent scholars in the social sciences. "Respect intellectuals, respect people of talent" was Central Government policy then, and this was the justification for exceeding the standard size of apartments. Only after the building was fully occupied did it come to light that almost half the apartments had been assigned to the administrative staff of the Party's Publicity Department. These apartments were a little smaller, but they happened to all be on good floors and have fine views. As some put it at the time, this was like hiding the meat under the rice. Some even made a formal protest, but it turned out that all these tenants held academic degrees and were listed in *Who's Who*. Since there was no agreed-upon definition of an eminent scholar, nothing came of the objections. What's more, the genuinely eminent academics who had already moved in had no objections, so after a few days of raised voices the matter was dropped.

Maozi had tenure by then. He was an expert in early middle age, enjoying a stipend from the government, and had won a few awards in his field. He also became an advisor to doctoral candidates, thanks to an arrangement with an affiliated university.

A fine position, a good income, a nice car and a beautiful home, a lovely wife and a promising son . . . he had it all. In candid moments he often said that Deng was The Man, and Maozi gave him unqualified support. Without old Mr. Deng, Maozi would never have had this good life.[251] A man must show gratitude to his benefactor. Not long after that public disturbance, when Maozi changed direction, this was a major reason why.

Marxism-Leninism holds the material stratum of life to be of primary importance. Indeed it is. As he held court in that spacious and luxurious apartment, Maozi's expression radiated a satisfaction that could not be hidden and that was of the first order. It was as if he himself had become part of this luxurious apartment: his every action was in harmony with his surroundings. You could sense from his bearing, as he stood in his foyer receiving visitors or pressed a button to slide open his automatic shoe-drawer, that he embodied the principle that the self-realization of man is his liberation.

He had been a scrawny child who didn't start really growing until he was sent down to the countryside. Then he took on the look of a tottering beansprout. His family's poverty meant that his clothes never kept up with his growth but were too short at every extremity. And the life of the countryside was hard on clothing, so it's no exaggeration to say he lived in rags. (When your clothes don't even fit, you are poor indeed.) Consequently, at that age he couldn't quite sit or stand properly: there was always something queer in his gait and manner. This was when Damo got to know him, and he sensed Maozi was little pleased with his life. His complexion was bad, too: he always had little white splotches on his cheeks and when Damo's mother saw him she said the boy had worms in his belly. Damo's parents had more children, who were all at ages that made them ravenous, eating a lot and quickly wearing out their clothes, but they were still a lot better off than Maozi's family. Whenever Maozi came over they tried to make him stay for supper and would cook something special for him. He was glad to stay for a meal and would eat it in a way that pained Damo's mother—it wasn't that she begrudged him the food, it was the way he ate that was so awful. When he got to know them, he came over often. When she had time, she'd have him take off some of his clothes so she could add cuffs to the trousers or a collar to the shirt. This was not hard, since they had a sewing machine. The only difficulty was that coupons for cloth were in scarce supply at that time, so she had to make do with scraps of old and tattered cloth. She improved the fit, even if the colors didn't match.

Decades later, Maozi had grown into a tall and sturdy man who looked good no matter what he was wearing. His complexion, too, had become healthy and fresh, and the head of hair which had once resembled a bird's nest of dried grass was now thick and glossy, and with a haircut he looked suave and handsome. Damo was a head shorter, and no match for him in physique or complexion, either. In recent years Maozi had put on a little weight, but that was in keeping with his domicile and his position in the world.

On arriving, Damo changed as was his wont into the cloth shoes he carried with him. Maozi was surprised and asked with good humor, "You even bring your own shoes?"

"With my own, I can be sure they'll fit."

Maozi invited him to sit down and remarked that it had been a long time. "First let's chat. No rush about the computer."

The parlor into which Maozi had led him was so large it had a cavernous feeling, and Damo said he wasn't used to holding conversations in such places. Maozi then brought him into the study.

The study was a room of the sort that has become fashionable among intellectuals. Against every wall stood floor-to-ceiling bookcases with shiny glass doors and packed with all kinds of books, neatly and handsomely lined up to display the owner's vast resources of knowledge. It was a contrast to Damo's house, where there were not so many books and they were of all different types and formats, crammed into a bookcase no bigger than a wardrobe, with the overflow scattered in piles on his desk, at the head of his bed, and even on the floor. In recent years many had been transferred to his hard drive, that little metallic box not much bigger than a book but able to contain half a library. And there was also the search engine called Gou-Gou, library to the world.[252]

Maozi's computer was practically a member of Damo's family. Damo had stayed intimately familiar with its innards ever since it was purchased. Whenever it developed a problem, Damo could usually diagnose it from Maozi's description and, if it wasn't too serious, walk him through the fix over the phone.

Damo went over to the computer at once and, after a quick inspection, started a format of the hard drive as he drew some software CDs from his pocket. He exclaimed with some irritation, "Maozi, this is such a waste! Fast broadband and a top-notch computer, and the thing is practically empty! Entire hard drives *are* empty. It's like you owned a big house and confined yourself to a room in the basement. I looked at your bookmarks, nothing but crap websites. Might as well spend your time reading *People's Daily*. You'd be better off with porn—that would at least do something for your sex life." (Damo spoke freely since Maozi's wife was out teaching that morning, and their child was in school.)

Fame, status, power, and wealth can take away a man's sound judgment, but they are likely to increase his psychological tolerance and equanimity. Maozi had not failed to notice the aggressive scorn with which Damo had spoken to him the evening before, but he wasn't going to overreact. Of course, if that criticism had come from a powerful official or a prominent academic, Maozi might have gone berserk a second time. To him, Damo was a friend from his youth, a friend to whom he was bound by a strong bond of loyalty. They had shared a furtive happiness during a long era of stress and darkness. Damo reminded him of a past he cherished, and that feeling of not wanting to forget a blood brother from a milieu he'd left behind often touched him. So he didn't want to squabble over the rudeness Damo had shown. He had plenty of theoretical ammunition with which he could have scathingly refuted his old friend, but he held back because he felt the moment called for forbearance.

Damo finished re-installing the operating system and showed Maozi it was working now. He also showed him a few websites he thought were worthwhile, and then shut down the machine.

Maozi had gathered some of his essays together and now gave them to Damo. "Here's some stuff I've written that I think you will find more interesting. I don't want you to think those puff pieces are all I can write."

Damo leafed through them and set them aside as he explained his indifference: "The only thing I want to talk about today is that book. Virtue after the fact doesn't help when a woman loses her virginity."

The veins stood out at Maozi's temples as he answered icily, "And if that was actually my conviction?"

Pointing to the printouts he'd just put on the desk, Damo shot back, "In that case, these here are worthless rubbish. A man can't have it both ways. Do you accept the consequences if that was actually your conviction? If I post that masterpiece of yours on the Internet, I hope you'll enjoy getting soaked in spittle."

"We learned dialectics a long time ago—"

Damo laughed. "'Policy and tactics are what we live by'[253] . . . Don't give me that kind of dialectics. It's a smokescreen for cynicism."

Maozi could not take this anymore, and sputtered, "Look, I know it hasn't been easy for you, being stuck at the bottom of society these last few years. As one of the era's losers, you are susceptible to a certain populism—"

"Hey, Mr. High-and-Mighty feeling sorry for the unfortunate, you can shove it. The powers that be use populism and elitism by turns, like a boxer's left hook and right hook. They alternate. What's in that book of yours is a whole lot of populism, pragmatism, and feudal autocracy coated in gooey Marxism and served on a platter." At that, he produced the copy of Maozi's book which he had brought with him and began reading passages aloud from dog-eared pages. Tucked away in different parts of the book, these passages had not stood out, but juxtaposed, they became jarring. Damo exploded, "For crying out loud! Is this Marx? I tell you, all along I have maintained a proper respect for Marx and Engels, and I am grateful to them. If nothing else, they taught me a way to look at the world and gave me a healthy skepticism during the period when we were blanketed in gibberish. After more than a century their work still ranks as a solid philosophy. You call what you've written Marxian philosophy? More like Douchebag Philosophy!"[254]

Maozi grabbed the book out of Damo's hands and flipped to the passages he had read. "I didn't catch this one," he muttered, "Damn, that grad student must have written it."

Damo laughed again. "Like a pig in shit. You exploit someone to do your work for you and if there's a problem, they're responsible. Sorry, pal. Yours is the only name on this book. You take full responsibility."

"No," Maozi said. "It's standard practice today. You ask around and tell me how many people are advising grad students and *not* letting them assist with their writing?"

"Do they get a share of the fees and royalties?" Damo asked pointedly.

"That's up to the individual. They usually wouldn't want it."

"Let's review," Damo said. "The first problem here involves the value system which ought to inform everything an intellectual does. The second difficulty arises from the ethics required of anyone worthy to be called a teacher. If one wanted to press the issue, there is also the matter of copyright. The third problem is the economic injustice. So even before addressing the principles contained in this book, we encounter a whole set of problems far more troubling than the question of academic correctness. How . . . did . . . *Marx's* name wind up on *this*?" And he guffawed.

The laugh disarmed Maozi, who had been about to get angry but now could only join in the laughter. Then he sighed, "You take things too seriously. You've blown this completely out of proportion."

Damo stopped laughing. "To disparage seriousness as blowing things out of proportion is another mark of cynicism. It's how one rationalizes a philosophy of expediency. The problem is that you had no qualms about filling your book with repugnant distortions—it was OK for *you* to blow things out of proportion. You know, you may die but this book is going to stick around. Ten years, twenty years, a hundred years . . . and what will people say when they lay eyes on it?"

"There's a ton of books like this," Maozi said, "and they all fade away the day after they're published. You think anyone will be reading this twenty years from now?"

"Then why did you write it? And why did you drag your graduate student into it?"

"I told you, we're only human, all of us; we want normal lives, we want to provide for the wife and child. We'd all like to be better off; we deploy our little bit of time and energy in any grubby business that will improve our standard of living, even if it lacks a higher meaning, just as the construction workers and rural vegetable-peddlers do. You have no right to demand that everyone suffer for the sake of your ideals."

Damo fixed him with a gimlet eye. "How dare you! That is the epitome of cynicism. Don't you hide behind the poor laborer or the man of the countryside. The way they earn their money is far more honorable than the way you earn yours. What you do is worse than peddling fake medicine."[255]

Maozi blanched and sat stupefied, glowering at Damo as if he wanted to kill him. It reminded Damo of the Maozi he had encountered on that summer day years before.

Maozi brought his face close to Damo and growled through clenched teeth: "You think I believe in this stuff? Since that summer day, I haven't believed in anything."

Damo was startled.

"They're using me," Maozi continued, "and I'm using them. Isn't this worthless theorizing just a kind of deconstruction?"[256]

"You think they believe in it?" Damo asked. "You think they've been taken in? You think they don't know what kind of merchandise you are? You think you're the Buddha, watching Sun the monkey hop around in your palm?[257] There is a director watching this scene, too, you know, and he's saying, 'Does this Buddha think he really is the Buddha?' And there's an audience that knows full well what's going on, and they're watching too."

Practically gnashing his teeth, Maozi snarled, "You won't be happy till you destroy me, is that it?"

"No, I want to save you, to help you. But ultimately you have to save yourself."

"Even if you could save me, can you save China?"

"A man isn't going to want to save China if he doesn't want to save himself."

Maozi's hands shook as he lit a cigarette without offering one to Damo, who therefore lit one of his own.

"To put it nicely," Maozi began with a sigh, as he stubbed out his half-smoked cigarette, "I understand your point of view. Our ways of thinking are just different. China today is a gravely ill old man. Anyone with eyes to see can see that. So, what'll it be? Major surgery and harsh medicine? Or 'support what is sound, strengthen the roots' for a slow cure?[258] The first way, you'll get quick results, but you risk an even quicker death. The second approach seems useless: you'll spend a lot of time spoon-feeding soup and water and carrying bedpans from the sickroom. It's a long haul; both the sick person and the caregiver must be patient and kind. But this way, you have a good chance of making it through and restoring the sick person's strength."

"And to put it not so nicely?" Damo asked, wry and alert.

"The truth is," Maozi offered, "neither of us amounts to anything. A couple of wispy clouds blown across the starry sky. Oh, when we were young we were full of fire. We thought we only needed to persevere in the good fight in order to achieve great things. We flattered ourselves with the name of *Qing Ma*, but to be honest we had the psychology of the young Mao, too: I mean, the Mao Zedong of way back. He was the child of Hunan peasants, with no connections and no money, but he shook the world. In those years we all loved those lines of his:

> *I believe a human life can last two hundred years;*
> *I'll smite the water for a thousand miles.*[259]

We kept reading his books, but we had no inkling how high heaven is, and how deep the earth."

He gave a queer laugh. Damo waited for him to continue.

"After June 4," Maozi said, "I finally realized that some things are fated. That is why they dared to do the most terrible thing in the world and risk completely losing legitimacy. To say they had become unhinged, or to call them despotic bloodsuckers who acted to safeguard their own interests—I'm afraid that's too simple. Especially Deng, who was at the height of popularity, a time when all the people looked up to him, and he knew he didn't have much longer to live . . . for him to take such a drastic step, it was absolutely not (as some say) because he was in his dotage. It was because he had no alternative. This inevitability arose from the clarity with which Deng saw that history was hanging in the balance. Radical surgery and strong medicine would have spelled doom for Court and Country. The proverbs have it that 'Going too far is as bad as not going far enough' and 'If you go too fast, you'll never get there.' So what use were all those empty ideals? If everybody would just work at scrounging a little profit and making it through these hard and mixed-up times, maybe the bad blood will be cleared up by the next generation. It will all work out when the time is right. Have I made myself clear?"

"Yes," Damo said. "The problem is, you didn't make yourself clear in your book. You could have said this in your book and I would admire you for it."

"You're muddling things," Maozi insisted. "Didn't I tell you that what I write is not what I think, and that this itself is a deconstruction, a kind of black humor for our time? Its significance lies precisely in the discrepancy."

"Then why don't you write a book making this point? How else will people know that what you write is not what you think? How will your deconstruction have any impact?"

Maozi said, "That, too, is up to the next generation."

"Life is easy when you can pass the buck to the next generation."

"I know," Maozi said, "It sounds bad. But that's how it's been for thousands of years. Those who come before leave much to be sorted out by those who come after, and they in turn leave much for those who come after them. As for the final outcome, whether things are resolved when the time is right, or just go on forever, we must leave that to Fate."

"I get it: 'Who cares if after me the floods rise?'[260] I see that you are not only a cynic," Damo remarked, "but with respect to history I must also call you a nihilist. How far back the cynicism goes! How hallowed by tradition! One who studies the greatest idealist in human history yet is himself an utter cynic . . . I've got to hand it to you, that's quite some deconstruction. I think this Institute of yours would best be named the Institute of Cynicism."

Maozi's savage look had faded, leaving only a bitter smile as he muttered, "You didn't understand what I meant."

"No, the problem is that you haven't carried this theory of yours to its logical conclusion, which would establish it as a school of thought in its own right. So you're worse than the old emperors and their eunuchs. One said, *We are the State.*[261] The other said, *Your most humble servant deserves to die.* They both played their parts naturally and didn't try to hide anything. And they certainly didn't need to scrounge up a theoretical justification for themselves from abroad.[262]"

Maozi finally stopped choosing his words for effect and blurted obstinately, "I don't care. I'm better off than I used to be. I am grateful for this era we are in."

Damo smiled coldly. "Well, well, the mask has slipped, hasn't it now? During the C.R. one of Chairman Mao's quotations was particularly famous, do you recall?"

Knowing Damo wasn't going to say anything nice, Maozi did not help him out. So Damo gave the answer himself: "Listen, I think I remember it exactly: 'Bah! Only a shameless person can say shameless things.'"

Still with the same strained smile, Maozi heaved an uncomfortable sigh. "Have you come to my place today to carry on a Great Cultural Revolution? I am fully aware that such a day will come to China, sooner or later."

Damo scoffed. "You used to be afraid of the officials; now you're afraid of the ordinary people. All the Marx and Engels you studied in the old days has gone by the board. How can you compare this to the C.R.? Let's take this book, along with the questions it has inspired, over to Teacher Wei's place—OK? Let's see what an old man who suffered the ravages of the C.R. has to say about it."

Maozi immediately became agitated, as if teetering on the edge of utter enmity, and snarled, "Don't mess with me like this."

Damo realized that until now their fierce back-and-forth had been only a private exchange of blows between two old friends who'd come to know each other thoroughly in the rough-and-tumble of life, but taking it to Teacher Wei would be a different matter.

At this tense moment, Maozi's wife Xiao Jin came home. She was now Professor Jin, mentor to a large group of graduate students. (As she put it, the guiding of grad students today was organized pretty much like raising hogs: there would be around twenty of them in a pen.)

The two men immediately dropped the subject they'd been discussing and smiled awkwardly. "What a rare honor!" Xiao Jin cried when she saw Damo. When Maozi had fallen ill, years before, Damo's use of Butcher Hu's therapy had saved him, and for this Xiao Jin had forever been grateful. She was always very cordial when he visited.

"He dropped his work in order to come fix that computer for us," Maozi explained.

Professor Jin poked her head into the kitchen and saw no evidence of usage. Lunchtime was practically over. "You should have let me know!" she scolded. "Well, let's go out to eat."

Damo smiled. "I have to be going. I've still got some work waiting for me. Thanks for the offer, but we've both had enough."

She was puzzled. "Had enough? What did you get to eat?"

He gestured to Maozi: "Ask him."

Just then her cell phone rang, and she stepped aside to take the call. Damo stuffed Maozi's essays into his bag of tools, changed into his shoes, donned his helmet, and waved a good-bye to Xiao Jin, who was standing out on their large balcony, talking on the phone.

Maozi, still fuming, accompanied him to the door. For years the members of the *Qing Ma* had often gotten into fierce quarrels, and (excepting Xiao Yong, the young woman) bad blood at one time or another had divided them all. But it had always happened that once the cursing, fighting, and raging were done, they still wanted to argue with each other.

"All the same," Damo said quietly, "I must thank you."

"For what?" Maozi asked.

"You have provided me with a living specimen of the contemporary intellectual. The average person couldn't bear to do it. Who would let his own stinking guts be opened up for people to look at?"

Maozi slapped the top of Damo's helmet so hard that the entranceway reverberated with the sound of the blow. It was half in jest, and half in hatred.

It was only when he got outside that Damo became aware of the ache in his heart, and as he sped off into the wind, there was wrung from his throat—just as there had once been from Maozi's—a long sob without tears. He remembered Maozi's idea of conducting a search for the missing persons in the history of thought. "Dammit, it's you who've gone missing," he grieved. "Lost without hope. They won't even find your body." His cell phone began to ring in his pocket. It's not a good idea to answer the phone when you're riding a motorcycle, so he just let it ring. But it kept ringing, relentlessly, until he pulled over to the side of the road and yanked the phone from his pocket and looked at it. It was Maozi. He yelled into the mouthpiece, "You trying to kill me? I'm on a motorcycle!"

"Are you free tomorrow?" Maozi asked.

"So what's broken now?" Damo said.

"It's my goddamned heart that's broken," Maozi answered, "I'll say more when you come. Xiao Jin raked me over the coals for not inviting you to lunch. Wants me to make amends."

At these words something happened to the ache in Damo's chest, and his eyes filled up. He knew that Maozi had not finished saying what was in his heart. Maozi was a competitive guy who combined arrogance with an inferiority complex. Today's lacerations had cut to the bone.

38

The next day, Damo came as promised. They were both calm this time. Yesterday had been too painful.

Maozi had already prepared some fine tea and had laid out good cigarettes. He had the look of a man prepared for a long and honest talk.

When he had got home the day before, Damo had studied the essays Maozi had given him. They made some excellent points. What is written thoughtfully is very different from what is produced in exchange for money and housing.

At the same time, Maozi had gone online to read Damo's

work. Friendship can reach a point where the friends stop noticing things because the desire for deep mutual understanding has faded. For years now, Maozi's view of Damo had been much as Damo had said: a man of the lower classes whom the new era had tragically left behind. Considering the manual labor he did, the place he lived, and the crowd he associated with, Maozi did indeed, as Damo had put it, 'feel sorry for the unfortunate' from his own superior vantage point. There had been times he'd wanted to give Damo a little money, but knowing the man's temper he hadn't dared. Only at the marriage of Damo's daughter had he seized the opportunity to make a substantial cash gift, knowing that Damo would let him because it was for the girl who had grown up calling him Uncle Mao.

Yet when he carefully read Damo's writing, it is no exaggeration to say Maozi was stunned. Even if it's unconventional and somewhat free-form, he thought, and it doesn't advertise to what system and academic coterie the author belongs, the work is vibrant and substantial and full of insight. It starts with emotion, is developed by thinking, and arrives at moral principles. Even from an academic perspective, his thoughts were of considerable value. But it is always the way these things go in China that one must have a platform in order to become known. Even with real expertise, until a person has mounted the stage he will not be recognized.

So Maozi got right to the point and said, "Yesterday I read your stuff online."

Damo expected Maozi to get even with him for the day before, and said with a faint smile, "I am prepared to hear your comments."

"Why didn't you tell me about these essays before?"

Damo understood. "Well, I told you my website, didn't I? And I gave you the addresses of a few other sites where I often post."

"You should have made it clearer. You mentioned the websites, but how could I have known there were such pieces on them?"

Damo pondered for a moment. Perhaps he had been too

proud to recommend his own writings to Maozi in so many words. There was more to it, though. Damo had assumed that at the province's top think tank for the humanities they must be overloaded with good things to read. He said as much now.

"You give the place too much credit," Maozi said. "You wouldn't believe how many are just putting in their time there, treating it as a sinecure, even worse than me. How else could I have become Director? It's bullshit, I tell you, it's all bullshit."

"You too?" Damo asked.

"Me too."

"So you have attained self-awareness? I'm just afraid that in a little while, once this conversation is over, you'll head into a conference room and then it will be a different story, know what I mean? There is a field of force, an extremely strong one, which leaves you powerless to control your own mouth. This happens even to the simplest, most honest people. On television, as soon as the camera is pointed at a person—any person—he starts spouting the conventional, grandiloquent declarations as if he'd been coached. Sometimes you see clips of people in the West excoriating the President and their government. I expect the message our TV means to get across is 'Look at that vaunted President and democratic government! People are cursing them.' But I think if a President and a government, no matter how flawed, allow ordinary people to curse them, they can't be all bad."

Maozi grinned.

Damo continued, "I've been thinking that back when they were going to punish you, that might have been the best thing that could have happened. There would then have been no turning back."

Maozi was silent.

"Remember what Teacher Wei said?" Damo added. "How if he had continued as the Chief of the Publicity Department and everything had gone his way for decades, we wouldn't recognize him today."

"I was too pessimistic about our future, then," Maozi said. "I thought that if they could go and kill people like this, a bleak century awaited us. China was too big, the population too large:

there was no one who could save the country. I compared it to the transition from the Ming to the Qing: all those loyal officials, all those celebrated writers, which way did they turn in the end? One by one, didn't they all switch their allegiance? None but a few courtesans gave up their lives for the Great Ming.[263] If the great dynasty of the Qing was destined to arise, then it would arise; and when fated to end, it would end of its own accord. Whatever Fate brings, events follow a process, as flowers bloom and fall."

Damo understood. He recalled the hollow stare, wolflike howl, and mousy timidity that Maozi had shown then.

"I was prepared for the worst," Maozi went on, "but the worst didn't come."

Damo agreed. "You dodged a bullet, which boded well for you. In the following years your fortunes improved, no?"

"But there was a problem, right then," Maozi explained. "The Institute got a new boss. I had had contacts with him in the early Eighties. In the Eighties, I was a rising star in Marxian Philosophy, with the wind at my back, and he took note of me. So after he came to the Institute he was very friendly to me."

"He didn't know about your more recent history?"

"How could he not?" Maozi shrugged. "The first task of an executive is to familiarize himself with the human resources."

Damo asked, "Was he still a liberal?"

"Yes and no," Maozi answered. "In the political arena, knowing which way the wind is blowing is more important than having ideas of your own. This man had a thin resumé and frankly was not all that capable, but the Institute was going downhill at that point; the well-connected and the talented no longer sought work there. Within the Institute, however, there were several people who had been interested in this position and when he took it, they were not happy. He needed to get some staff members on his side."

"Even if he needed to get some staff members on his team," Damo objected, "he shouldn't have picked you, a guy with shit all over his backside."

"You don't get it," Maozi said. "Somebody with shit all over his backside was exactly the kind of person he needed: someone he could control. *Starting to get uppity? I'll show everyone the shit on your backside.* There was another angle, too: the political situation had taken a sudden turn. Everyone had expected things would just keep moving farther to the extreme left, back to the Seventeen Years[264], back to the C.R.—but that wasn't happening. To make use of someone like me gave him flexibility, you see?"

"I don't see," Damo said.

"You're playing dumb," Maozi said, "but no need to belabor this. I'm going to tell you how I fell from grace. But this is for your ears only; don't let it get out."

"Well," Damo answered with a grin, "Maybe I need to hear the story to decide whether it's worth letting it get out."

Maozi knew Damo's character well enough to trust in his discretion. "It started," he began, "when I took the Director's hints and gave him a very large gift."

"A bribe?"

"You could call it a bribe. But it wasn't money. It was a scholarly article."

"You bribed him with an article?" Damo said.

"That's right. One day, he stopped by my desk with a few pages of draft paper and said, 'I recently wrote something about Deng's Southern Tour[265]. I'd like you to look it over and give me suggestions.' I had been following developments closely, but mindful of my shaky position I said, 'It's not for me to tell you anything. Of course I will be glad to read it with respect and learn from it.' He surprised me by saying, 'I've been swamped with work lately and I had to dash this off, but I think it has some valuable ideas. I want you to be quite bold with your suggestions: go right ahead and insert them into the document.' When I took it home I realized what he meant by being bold with my suggestions. That paper wasn't much more than a title and four or five sentences without any follow-through. He had basically assigned a topic for me to write on, except that he would be the author of record. I worked hard on that paper. In the first place, I actually did have something to say; and in the second place, I knew what general line the boss wanted to take. It took more than a month to finish my 'suggestions,' which transformed those two or three pages into an essay several dozen pages long. I gave it to him one morning and that afternoon he called me into his office. 'Xiao Mao, the revisions you made were excellent! I can see I picked the right man. I expect to grow the Philosophy Institute in the next few years: I'm going to need someone who can keep me informed about the situation on the ground. You and I used to know each other. In a work unit, that can sometimes make other people suspicious, so let's keep this just between the two of us, OK?'

"Of course I understood, and said, 'Don't worry, I won't talk.' That essay of mine first appeared in one of the province's academic journals, and then got reprinted in full by *People's Daily*. Even *Xinhua Digest* ran an abridgement of several thousand characters, and *Reference Materials for the People's Congress* used it too.[266] To be sure, his was the only name in the byline. This one coup cemented his position at the Institute, and overnight he became a bigshot in the province. He was invited to give speeches all over the place."

Damo burst out laughing. "That was a very classy bribe!"

"Later I realized that this is the best way to give a gift. Most officials today, you give them fifty grand, five hundred grand, you can't be sure it's going to mean that much to them, and besides, they run a risk if they accept it. But give 'em a good article, and as Du Fu said, a letter from home is worth ten thousand pieces of gold.[267] We're not living in wartime when it was enough to charge forward without fear of death. This isn't the Great Leap Forward either, when it was enough to exhaust yourself toiling shirtless in the sun. No, today you've got to show your educational record and prove some expertise. Money can buy the educational record. But talent—enough to get you into *People's Daily* and *Xinhua Digest*—that's a bit more difficult! When a cadre is up for promotion, sometimes it's an article of his that clinches it. That article I wrote was pure gold, wasn't it? Think about it. When I retire, I'll write a novel about the world of officialdom. The part about articles as bribes will be quite striking."

"By the time you retire," Damo said, "the phenomenon of

articles as bribes may be something everyone takes for granted."

Damo wasn't sure what had driven Maozi to this confession. Despite his lingering loyalty to an old friend, Maozi over the years had begun to put on the airs of a scholar, even to the point of being tiresome. What had got into him today, after the fashion of those exhortations in the C.R. to "Bare your selfish thoughts without concern for appearances," that had made him reveal something so embarrassing for himself and for others?

"Why are you telling me this?" Damo asked.

"I don't know. I just feel like it."

"Should I interpret that as 'I am a scoundrel and I fear no man'?" Damo asked drily.[268]

"It's not a good thing," Maozi reproached him, "for you to show no mercy when you're in the right."

Damo felt a little ashamed. "That you can say that tells me you're not wholly bad. You've still got a future as a scholar."

Maozi answered, "Since you took the friggin' trouble to come back here, can't you say a few kind words? I was planning to have a knock-down fight with you today, or at least try a few sophistries to defend myself, but I'm telling you, I read your essays yesterday, and—to say it with a flourish—the scales fell from my eyes. That's the truth: are you satisfied? I'm not sure whether I'm able to move forward. I need—how did Chairman Mao put it? I need someone to give me a sharp blow."

"Yeah," Damo remembered. "It was during the Anti-Rightist campaign. 'Those fogies who put out newspapers need a sharp blow to wake them up.'"[269]

"Yes, that's it exactly. Actually, the thought came to me later that I started out with barely the clothes on my back. What should I be afraid to lose?"

"You needn't frighten yourself," Damo said. "You may lose face, but what else are you going to lose now? Can they garnish your wages? Can they take back your housing? Even if you went as far as Teacher Wei, wouldn't you still find food and drink? The situation today is that we can't move forward, but we can't go backwards either. Turning backwards: how could they bear to give up the wealth that has come into their hands? *All ill-gotten gains to the peasants' association*?"[270]

"Actually," Maozi said, "I've bought my apartment." They both started laughing.

They spoke at length and agreed to go to Teacher Wei's place to talk things over frankly. He was sure to understand: the old man had made his eightieth birthday party a pitiless assessment of his own life and principles.

Maozi sighed. "This has been great. We need to keep having these fights for the rest of our lives."

Xiao Jin came home around noon, whereupon the two men went out for lunch to a small restaurant in the neighborhood. They ordered a bottle of Wuliangye[271] and two beer-mugs, and each of them poured half the bottle into his mug and sipped it until it was all gone.

39

Ru Yan was a Northerner. Liang Jinsheng, though his ancestral home lay south of the Yangtze, had been born in Beijing and raised in the North. So Ru Yan could think of no better way for them to celebrate New Year's Eve than to make dumplings according to the Northern custom.[272] When she suggested this over the phone, he agreed: "Sure. It's been years since I made dumplings; I may have lost the knack. I'll bring the wrappers and the filling. You don't have to do a thing."

"You know how to buy vegetables?" she asked skeptically.

"Don't worry about how I'm going to get them. Just have a pot of water ready."

Ru Yan had trouble imagining Liang Jinsheng's life as an official. She had never had a clear idea even of what her own father did after he walked out the door each morning. She still thought the life of an official must be the dullest and most meaningless way one could live. When a story bogged down in details of palace intrigue, she would invariably flip the pages or hit the fast-forward button. She remembered how her mother had once told her father, "You can park all that stuff from the office at the door, along with your hat and coat, and pick it up again in the morning on your way to work." This was hard for him; when he did it, he felt bereft and aimless. In consequence, her father had played for many years a non-speaking part in the drama of their family. If she and Liang Jinsheng were going to live together someday, she would say the same thing to him.

She went to the market to buy a few potted plants. She selected two chrysanthemums with tiny yellow buds (a breath of the countryside), and one hibiscus, fiery red, and a pot of ivy. When she placed them in her living room, the place came alive with intimations of spring. She liked flowers that were still drawing nourishment through their roots, still fresh and alive. As for cut flowers, she'd always had the feeling they were in pain. She had also bought some red candles because one could not have New Year's Eve without their quivering lights and shadows. She had acquired all these tastes from her mother. As far back as she could remember, except when the political environment was too harsh, these amenities had always graced their home during the days around New Year's.

When all was ready, she waited for nightfall. It had been years since she had felt such anticipation.

A few days before, Lonely Goose had reappeared in the forum with a bang: "`I'm back! I hurried home so I could wish you all Happy New Year a little early!`" Her message went on to explain that her son only celebrated Christmas, not the Chinese New Year, when he was overseas. Lonely Goose had come back to be where the action was.

A slew of responses followed, all friendly and solicitous.

Ru Yan was quick to post, "`Now that you're back, I'm off duty.`"

Although serving as Moderator hadn't been a real job, the need to be courteous to all and sundry—like A Qing, as Lonely Goose had said—had proved somewhat tiring.

Lonely Goose was online and responded immediately: "Lao Jiu can't go![273] During the time you've been at it, look how you've lit up this forum with beauty and warmth!"

"We want both you sisters!" the commenters cried. "Not one less! Collective Leadership!"[274] Some suggested, "You can take turns; that will give you both some free time."

In the midst of this slightly embarrassing acclamation, Ru Yan's QQ alarm sounded. She clicked to see who it was and didn't recognize the sender. The message read: I hesitated to bother you about this, but it would feel wrong not to say anything. She didn't actually go abroad. Her husband was placed under double regulations and these last few days she's been dealing with that.[275] Now that it's probably been resolved, she can venture out again.

Ru Yan quickly looked up the data on file for the QQ number that was the source of this message.

Phone number:	N/A.
Postal address:	N/A.
Location:	China.

The anonymous presence which had deleted her earlier post had made her angry, but this mysterious QQ informant had a different effect: it frightened her. She stared at the message for a while before it occurred to her to ask questions:

Who are you? Can you vouch for the accuracy of that statement?

A response came back: I'm just passing through. Who I am is not important. Of course what I said is accurate.

Even if this is true, Ru Yan typed, what does it have to do with her?

When she hit the Send button, QQ announced that the other party was no longer online.

She returned to the forum and refreshed the screen. Lonely

Goose had posted another comment: `Better to accept with respect than to decline with courtesy.`[276] `During the New Year's Season there will be a lot to do. Hey, I heard about a post that got deleted a few days ago: I hope it won't create any problems for the forum. If the responsibility is too much for Such Is This World alone, then let's do as the group asks and share the duties. When time allows, either one of us can go online and take care of things. Let's have a happy and auspicious New Year's.`

Lonely Goose's frank and equable attitude went a long way toward relieving the upsetting impact of that QQ message, but Ru Yan didn't post any more comments.

New Year's Eve is the high point of the Chinese year, and it is also the time when downtown streets are bare and desolate. Around 3:00 or 4:00 P.M., you start seeing fewer and fewer people outside. Some business districts look as though a plague has just swept them clean, with nothing in the big open spaces except dead leaves and dust-devils whipped up by the northwest wind. Streets that are usually bumper-to-bumper are empty. Every establishment along the shop-lined streets stands mute and shuttered. On sidewalks that are usually bustling, you're lucky if you see two figures scurrying away. In the past, before fireworks were banned, the booming of rockets and firecrackers would surge in waves across the city, setting the tone for New Year's; but today there isn't even this racket to be heard.[277] One could see in Western movies that Christmas was a holiday that brought people into the streets, into the public squares; but our great holiday drives people into their homes, and no matter how far they have traveled, they must get inside before dark. New Year's Eve has therefore become a night of deathly stillness. Ru Yan had been deeply affected by this ever since her husband passed away. She particularly regretted this desolate loneliness whenever her son hurried back from afar to spend New Year's with her: she wished there were parties for him to go to, parties packed with young people singing, laughing boisterously, drinking, and dancing: this would have pleased her as a mother. But all the youth who might have enlivened such scenes had disappeared, for now, behind the tight-shut doors of their parents' homes. One year she had suggested to him that they go for a walk. They encountered no one but themselves, and heard no sound but their own lonesome footsteps. Ordinarily she would have relished such tranquility, but that night it weighed heavy on her heart.

Ru Yan straightened up the apartment one more time, and then went into the bedroom to light two red candles beneath the photo of her husband. She was not usually one to set much store by folk ceremonies, but today for some reason she wanted to do this as an offering to him. It was her third New Year's without him, but it felt as though it had been many years, so long ago as to be getting a bit vague, and even the man in the photograph was not looking entirely familiar. In the swaying candlelight, her husband's features began to seem more lifelike. She looked at the picture for a long time, and then whispered, "Are you all right?"

He was smiling in a gentle, artless way.

Just before 6:00 Liang Jinsheng called to say that he was terribly sorry, but a party for which he was required to be present had been arranged at the last minute: he would come without fail in half an hour. After a while, the downstairs bell rang. Ru Yan thought that perhaps he had managed to avoid going to the party, but heard an unfamiliar voice on the intercom. "I am Mayor Liang's driver. He sent some things over for you."

The driver rapidly appeared upstairs, holding a big paper bag. It contained five or six boxes of delicacies, and each one was filled with some freshly-made dumplings, laid out daintily on a thin layer of flour. Ru Yan glanced at the name on the box and recognized one of the city's most famous dumpling shops. Each box contained dumplings with a different kind of filling.

The fact was, Ru Yan had already prepared everything, mixing the filling ingredients and kneading the dough. She felt these were a woman's—more precisely a housewife's—proper tasks. She had planned to wait for his arrival and then have him symbolically make a few dumplings and then drink some tea, watch her make the rest, and chat with her while she worked. That was how she remembered her mother doing this. But her father had often come home late—sometimes he hadn't made it home at all—and that's how it seemed to be playing out now. She thought for a while and then started wrapping dumplings by herself.

No matter how good the store-bought ones might be, New Year's Eve was a time for her own dumplings.

Liang Jinsheng arrived a bit later than he had promised. "If you're an official in China," he said with a rueful smile, "unless you've risen to the rank of, say, Emperor, you dare not utter the words, 'It's my time and I'll do what I want.'"

Seeing that Ru Yan was already making dumplings, he hastened to wash his hands and join her. He pinched the dough a little awkwardly to seal one dumpling after another. Ru Yan just let him do it, clumsy though he was.

Looking at herself she couldn't help thinking of her mother. But her father had lacked Liang Jinsheng's sense of humor and willingness to acknowledge his mistakes. When he had come home late, he had still wanted to hold forth on the great socialist truths of the hour.

As they made dumplings they talked about their pasts, as people who are in love must do. Early childhood and youth; parents, children, even their previous spouses. Every sorrow and every joy, with every interesting or embarrassing anecdote, flowed volubly. Sometimes they answered each other's questions rapid-fire; sometimes one of them would go on for a while in a monologue; and sometimes they would fall silent and hear the methodical whirring of the electric clock.

Making dumplings was a good occasion for such a conversation as this, that touched the heart. There was no pressure, but time did not drag: even during the intervals when they couldn't find anything to say, because their hands were busy the silence was not awkward. And since they did not yet have any food in their mouths, when they spoke they were able to express fine shades of meaning. This batch of dumplings took a long time to make.

When the time came to boil them, Ru Yan brought out a

plate of raw vegetables and a bottle of red wine and invited him to have a drink. He said he'd wait for her.

When she had finished cooking them, she pushed the sofa closer so as to sit facing him, just as she had done on his previous visit. He lifted his glass: "A new spring filled with joy."

"A new spring filled with joy," she echoed.

Then he added, "The moon represents my heart."

"What about the preceding line?" she chuckled.[278]

The phone rang. It was Ru Yan's mother. "It's New Year's, and you haven't called! Aren't you going to wish your old Mom a happy new year?"

"Hey," Ru Yan said, "It's not midnight yet!"

"You think I can stay up that late at my age? I was just talking with your sister, and we were saying it must be lonely for you this year. Are you watching the Gala?"

"Um, no . . . no, I'm not. I've got company."

"Please thank them for me," her mother said.

Ru Yan's older sister came on the line and offered the compliments of the season, which Ru Yan reciprocated with best wishes to her and her husband.

"He hasn't been home for days," her sister said. "I worry about him."

"I'm sure he'll at least make it home for New Year's," Ru Yan offered.

A little better at picking up cues than her mother, Elder Sister asked, "What friend is this who has time to be with you on New Year's Eve?"

"I'll tell you later."

Her sister said, "All the more reason to wish you a happy new year. You know this is Mom's biggest worry. She says until Ru Yan is settled, she cannot die in peace."

"Well, that's a good reason to procrastinate," Ru Yan said. "May she live to be a hundred. Hey, don't you blab."

"No deal, Ru Yan, but I'll tell you, this is the best New Year's present you could have given her." And she hung up. Ru Yan stood there with the phone still in her hand, not knowing whether to laugh or cry.

Naturally, Liang Jinsheng had been listening. "Why not go down and spend New Year's with your mother?" he suggested.

So Ru Yan told him about the strange disease in the South. He did not seem surprised, but only said, "It might be just as well if you don't go."

"You know about this?" she asked him.

"I know a little."

"Is this for real?" she asked.

"You could say so."

"Why aren't you telling everyone?"

"That's above my pay-grade," he said.

"Oh, well now I know why posts have been getting deleted on our forum."

"You posted about this?" he asked.

"I sure did," she answered. "If you people aren't going to talk about it, then we have to."

"For now," he said, "it would be a good idea for you to be cautious about posting that kind of information. This qualifies as a serious epidemic. There are rules for these situations and they're monitored closely. There are things I can't tell you now."

Ru Yan snorted.

"Well," he grinned, "I have to worry that you might put them online. For the time being, it would be wise to stay away from places where there are a lot of people. Take it easy at home for a while. I'll be able to visit you often in the days after New Year's."

"And you'll carry the disease to me?" she joked.

It was almost midnight. This was when her son had promised he'd reach her online to wish her a happy new year. Since Liang Jinsheng did not seem to have any intention of leaving, she told him her son would be expecting her online and went into the study to turn on the computer. Her son was waiting for her on MSN and when he saw she was online he sent a message in big red characters: HAPPY SPRING FESTIVAL, MOM! Then he opened up the two-way voice and video channel. The two video screens gradually came into focus: one showed her son's smiling face, and the other, Ru Yan's smiling face. They exchanged affectionate greetings. In the months since he'd gone abroad, her son had changed greatly. He was more sanguine now, more relaxed, there was even something . . . chivalrous about him. There's a proverb that with the passing of years, father and son become friends. Ru Yan discovered on this night that she and her son had become friends.

Suddenly he exclaimed, "Do I see someone in the living room?"

Ru Yan turned her head and saw Liang Jinsheng had crossed the room to pour himself some tea. Her son didn't miss a thing. All she could say was that she had company for New Year's Eve.

"How many?" he asked.

"You little rascal," she thought. Out loud she said, weakly, "One."

"Could it be that old alumnus of my alma mater?" he asked.

"Could be," she said.

"Why don't you introduce us to each other?" he prompted.

She had no choice but to call Liang Jinsheng into the room. Before he stepped in front of the webcam, she covered the microphone and murmured, "You did it on purpose!"

He only smiled, saw himself in the video window, and said to her son, "I wish you a happy New Year, young man."

"And I wish you the same. Thank you for keeping my mother company."

Liang Jinsheng said, "I should thank *her* for allowing me to."

As her eyes went back and forth between the two windows, one showing her son, and the other showing herself with Liang Jinsheng, Ru Yan discovered that she was wearing a goofy smile, like a girl who'd been caught out in her first love. She had Liang Jinsheng sit squarely in front of the camera as she withdrew to one side, out of view.

"Sir," her son was saying, "for someone who was more than 30 years ahead of me at school, you're younger than I expected."

"Thank you," Liang Jinsheng said. "But I never had your fine prospects. I didn't pursue my field of study, not at all."

"You didn't go into the career you had studied for?"

"No, I had to change direction. The result is that you're way ahead of me."

"What did you change direction to?" her son asked.

"I'm a common laborer."

"You mean there are college grads from the Sixties who are now common laborers?"

"Sure there are," Liang said, "and there are even some who are unemployed. But I still manage to earn a living."

"Over here, too," her son said, "there are grads from the Sixties who can't get suitable work. They've become night watchmen, they do tutoring, they're delivery men, they paint people's portraits in the street . . . you see it all."

Liang Jinsheng asked him, "You coming back when you finish school?"

"I'll see," her son said. "There will probably still be a demand for my profession back home."

"It's not merely in demand," Liang Jinsheng said, "It is sorely lacking. There is a tremendous need for good architects, especially ones who've seen the world and broadened their horizons. We've got so many good projects, and they've all been grabbed by those French architects you're hanging out with over there."

"Well, if there's work, of course I'll come back."

"Good," Liang Jinsheng said. "That's settled, then. Can you send me a few samples of your work to look over?"

"You can see them on our school's website. Mom has the address."

The two alumni chatted on as if they were old friends. Then Ru Yan heard cries from outside, as people all over the neighborhood shouted the countdown in unison with CCTV's New Year's Eve Gala, and she realized that the bell was about to sound.[279] She hurried to bring her face into the video frame just as the great booming bell began to reverberate.

"Mama misses you very much, Son."

"Same here. I wish you happiness. A healthy and merry new year!" He also said, "My old fellow-alumnus, I still don't know how to address you."

"Uncle Liang," Ru Yan put in.[280]

But Liang Jinsheng spoke up: "Liang Jinsheng: that's Liang as in *dongliang*, and Jinsheng, born in Shanxi."[281]

As the three continued speaking, a paragraph popped up in MSN's text-message box:

```
Droopy: Here's some information for you.
Liang Jinsheng: Deputy Mayor of City X; mem-
ber, Executive Board of Municipal Party Com-
mittee. Born 19__, graduated ___ University
in 196_ in Department of Architecture.
```

From the video frame, her son was watching their astonishment with a mischievous smile.

"Where did you get this?" Ru Yan asked.

"From Google; it only took a second to find it out. Try it. Input the keywords: 'Liang Jinsheng', 'City X, '___ University'—and you'll get a lot of data. Later you can check whether there's any dirt on this old alumnus. It's all there, on Google."

Her son had taught Ru Yan how to use Google and other search engines, but she had never used them to dig up information about private persons. She typed in the keywords he'd suggested, and sure enough, the search returned several thousand items about Liang Jinsheng, the first being the C.V. which her son had cut-and-pasted just a minute before. It included a serious-looking official portrait of him in front of a red backdrop. Then came a succession of congresses, inspection visits, ribbon-cutting ceremonies, receptions of visitors, and speeches he had given . . . you could see no end to them. Ru Yan kept talking to her son over the audio channel even as she scrolled down this list of references. "When I have time," she said, "I'll look up what this alumnus of your alma mater has contributed to the Revolution."

"You, too," her son said. "You can look yourself up, too."

She typed in a few keywords identifying herself and more than ten items were returned, including a few papers she'd written three or four years ago. Then she entered "Such Is This World" and was surprised to get more than a hundred items, starting with her most recent articles (including the one mentioning the strange disease down South). Some were on her forum, and some had been copied to other websites.

Hearing her gasp, her son said, "With the Internet today, nothing can be concealed."

He said he'd have to go now. A group of Chinese students over there was about to get together for a New Year's Eve dinner. He said that he had heard the bell ring in the New Year seven hours before the rest of them would. He asked Ru Yan to pick up Yang Yanping so he could wish the dog a happy Spring Festival.

Liang Jinsheng took the opportunity to say, "When you come back, we've got quite a few large-scale construction projects in the new part of town. But first I need to study some samples of your work."

After her son signed off, the room was suddenly quiet. "Happy Year of the Sheep," Liang Jinsheng said.

Ru Yan nodded. "A happy Year of the Sheep." At that moment she wanted to let him hug her and hold her tight. She didn't want what was in her heart to slip away, and if he left now, she'd be all alone. But she couldn't express any of this. There were times when she envied the modern girls with their free and easy ways, the girls who didn't care what people might think. In buses, on the sidewalk, she often saw them carrying on with their boyfriends, draped around his neck or sitting in his lap, caressing his hair or his cheek, gazing tenderly at him without embarrassment—and it always made her feel hopelessly old-fashioned. Occasionally she had imagined what would happen if she ever acted like that? Would the sky fall? No, but she just couldn't do it. A bird, by its nature, can chirp, but a fish will never make a sound its whole life long.

The silence made her anxious. Forcing a smile, she said rather stupidly, "Well, I guess you have a lot to do tomorrow."

He smiled, looked at her thoughtfully, and then said, "Yes. I must be going. Early in the morning I'll have to call on a bunch of foreign experts and wish them a happy New Year. Then I'll need to drop by the University and greet the students who haven't gone home for the holiday. At noon I lunch with staff from a foreign corporation. In the afternoon there's an important meeting to put together a document that may have a bearing on that contagious disease."

Liang Jinsheng said he'd come again when he had some personal time this week. She felt relieved to hear that.

When he left, she sat and stared at the computer.

Ru Yan had harbored a vague image of what this New Year's Eve would be like. She could scarcely admit to herself what she was imagining, but she had thought something important would happen, something she both longed for and feared. When her son's image faded from the screen she realized, more or less, that this anticipated moment had now arrived. But her fear proved greater than her longing. Thinking about it, she had to wonder whether a man and a woman who had barely spent three evenings with each other were psychologically ready for the openness and vulnerability that would have engulfed them had they entered into that moment. Human beings need to stay wrapped in their clothes for a long time in order to relate to one another in a relaxed way. A person is like a fine gift: you need to peel off the wrapping paper slowly, one layer after another, striking a balance between familiarity and expectation. This is what enables you to see the gift of the other and savor its beauty. Only exceptionally adaptable people can dispense with this process. And so Ru Yan, amid that delicate silence, had blurted those foolish words to Liang Jinsheng as if she had to escape some mortal danger.

It was late. She lay down on her bed.

Like many intellectual women of her generation, Ru Yan felt a natural taboo about sex. A *daimon* dwelt in her mind, always keeping watch over her. It was strong, noble, and relentless in its demands: so much so that it transmuted the instincts of her flesh into a kind of spiritual consolation, something spotless and pure. Spotless and pure she had lain alone in this bed for three years now, without so much as a fantasy.

But tonight, on the eve of a new year, she touched and stroked herself. Her arms, her chest, her belly, her legs. She was not trying to arouse herself. It was more as if she were carefully inspecting a gift she was about to give. Though Ru Yan's body retained most of its feminine beauty, she was not confident. Features of the female body, unlike the male, are oriented toward two different Others: the man and the child. Generally there is a natural sequence. The breasts, for instance: first the man sees, loves, and caresses a pair of fresh and tender breasts which have not grown flabby because they never suckled an infant. Only later, with pregnancy, do they grow big and dark, to be clutched and sucked by the child and so eventually to dwindle and sag. This was all part of Nature's design, like the flowers which bloom and fall. But when a second man arrives for a vivacious woman in midlife, the natural order is reversed. Ru Yan didn't know how other women dealt with this, but Ru Yan found the prospect even more unsettling than her sexual initiation had been.

Since she was a perfectionist, this made her feel very insecure. She preferred to see herself, and him, fully clothed. The invention of clothing, she had always felt, was one of mankind's great steps forward because it safeguarded human dignity. She felt quite uneasy about what lay ahead and might confront her at any time. After all, she was in her forties and lacked the natural, even heedless, confidence in her own body that today's young women feel. Actually, even in her youth Ru Yan had been skittish about her own body, not like the narcissistic girls of our time who have no qualms about displaying themselves for all and sundry to enjoy. They put everything on display: the pretty face, the shoulders, the back, the thighs, the waist, the cleavage, and even—something Ru Yan did not find in the least attractive—the navel. For those who grew up when Ru Yan did, even a girl's feet called for a certain modesty, and those who could afford them would be sure to wear socks and sandals even in the heat of summer. Ru Yan was particularly fond of plain cloth shoes, God's gift to girls, and wore them year-round unless it was bitter cold. When she had been sent into the fields to learn from the toil of the peasants, she had had to go barefoot, and since the moment of taking off her shoes was awkward for her, she would try to do it behind a crowd of girls, before jumping into the paddy where her feet would be safely hidden in the mud.

40

On New Year's Day, Ru Yan slept late.

When she got up, she quickly ate some leftover dumplings and switched on the TV, hoping to catch some of the New Year's Eve Gala she had missed the night before and so liven up a lonely New Year's. But she couldn't find a rebroadcast on any of the channels, which all seemed devoted to reports about the Spring Festival as it had been celebrated in various places, with scenes of feasting and merriment. She picked up the phone to wish her mother, sister, and brother-in-law a happy New Year. After a few sentences she could hear that her mother was not her usual chipper self and asked whether something was bothering her.

"*I'm* O.K.," her mother said, "but it seems like your brother-in-law has caught the disease. He didn't come home last night and we got a call that he was under observation in the isolation unit. . ."

Ru Yan knew that it must be very serious if her mother was worried. All these years, her mother had been the strong uncomplaining type. She had the manner of an easy-going lady, but for meeting a crisis not even Ru Yan's father had had her mettle. "Let me speak with Elder Sister," Ru Yan said.

When her sister came on the line, there was a long silence and then she began sobbing. Ru Yan anxiously tried to encourage her: "Don't do this, you're going to have Mom really worried."

Her sister stopped sobbing. "At the hospital, quite a few of the doctors and nurses have come down with this thing. They had no idea it was so virulent. Some of them caught it just by walking down a corridor outside a room. Word is, there's already been one death. They don't even know what medicines to try."

"How is Brother-in-Law?" Ru Yan asked.

"I wanted to be with him to take care of him, but they wouldn't let me. All his life he's worked with infectious diseases and never had a problem; but now, just when he was about to retire . . ." She started crying again, in a thin voice.

Ru Yan was badly shaken and tried, somewhat incoherently, to soothe her sister, who explained: "Your brother-in-law was very tense, those days when he was still coming home, but it wasn't himself he was worried about. You know what he's like: totally dedicated, been through all kinds of dangers. I asked him why he was looking so grim. He said, 'Let's try to make it through this year. Let's hope it doesn't spread.' He wanted us to be careful, said we shouldn't go out, we should stay away from places where there were lots of people."

All Ru Yan could think of was to urge her to try to comfort their mother. Of these two daughters, one was already widowed and it could only be hoped that nothing would happen to the other. By temperament the mother was inclined to keep mum about her troubles, and she could easily make herself sick this way.

Ru Yan hung up. Any air of festivity that might have attended this holiday was shattered, last night's warmth and gladness gone without a trace. She thought of the scenes she had just witnessed on television: the crowds having a good time together now that spring was in the air; millions of travelers hurrying from all corners of the land to return to their hometowns for these few days; the sightseeing which people were keen to do during this long holiday. The unknown disease was using all this jubilation to spread itself, soundlessly . . . it hurt to think about it. And she remembered how evasive Liang Jinsheng had been the previous night, and how any warnings about the disease were being blocked and deleted on the Internet. It all gave rise to a constricted feeling in her chest that made her want to scream.

She picked up the phone and called Liang Jinsheng. Voices buzzed in the background along with, more than once, merry challenges to drink another round.

"My best wishes for the New Year," Liang Jinsheng said.

"We're a year older now, aren't we?"

"My brother-in-law has fallen sick," Ru Yan said. "At his hospital, quite a few of the medical staff have been infected."

Liang Jinsheng was silent for a long time.

"Did you hear me?" Ru Yan said sharply. "The disease is continuing to spread!"

Liang Jinsheng said, "I know."

"If you know, why won't you talk about it? Why aren't you saying anything about it to us ordinary people?"

He lowered his voice. "This isn't a good time right now. I'll talk with you later, OK? The important thing is not to get anxious. Call your mother and try to reassure her. Comfort your sister, and please give them both my regards. I can't say any more. Let me know if there's any further trouble." Ru Yan heard a sigh on the other end of the line, and then he had hung up.

She put down the phone and began to cry. Yang Yanping had never seen its mistress look and sound like this. The dog stared uneasily and gently wagged its tail. Ru Yan scooped up the dog in her arms and as she stroked it she was reminded of her son. She understood perfectly well that he was far away in France, and there was no indication the disease had reached there yet, but she was still anxious for him with a nameless dread, though she was not sure whether she feared that she might lose him or that he might lose her. She didn't stop to figure what time it was over there but just gave him a call. The phone rang for a long time, beep-beeeep, beep-beeeep, without anyone answering, and this made her even more anxious. Just when she was about to hang up and try again, she heard a sleepy voice say something in what she took to be French, and she cried, "Ping'rzi, is that you?"

Groggily, her son said a single word: "Mom."

Ru Yan felt relieved. "Oh, Ping'rzi, a happy Spring Festival to you!"

He had now woken up a bit, and somewhere between laughing and crying remarked, "Mom, your zeal is admirable, but you know over here it's still the middle of the night."

With tears in her eyes, Ru Yan said in her own defense, "But it's broad daylight here! Are you all right?"

"I'm just fine," he said. "The party ran pretty late last night, I only just got to bed—"

Ru Yan felt a twinge of love and guilt and hurried to say, "Go back to sleep, I won't talk any more. Just be careful of your health. Stay away from parties and crowds..."

Her son was perplexed. "Mama, what's going on? Why did you have to tell me this in the middle of the night?"

"Oh, it's nothing," Ru Yan said. "There's some kind of disease going around, here, and I was worried for you over there. . ." She had been going to tell him about the trouble in his aunt's family but thought better of it. His aunt had always loved him as if he were her own child. If Ru Yan told him, he would not be able to sleep.

"Mother," he laughed, "You are something else! Whatever that thing is, I've got the entire Eurasian land mass between me and it. You're the one who needs to be careful. Stay away from parties and crowds."

The sound of her son's voice had been reassuring, like the far-off lights of home to a traveler at night. As long as he was there and was all right, Ru Yan wasn't afraid of anything.

Next she thought she ought to call Damo to wish him a happy New Year and tell him to be careful, what with all his running around town. No one answered his home phone, so she tried the cell.

When he answered, he beat her to the punch by crying, "A happy and auspicious New Year to you!"

"You're not at home?" she asked.

On the other end of the line he had to shout a little. "We're all here at the hospital. My daughter gave birth last night, a girl. Eight pounds, six ounces. Natural birth; mother and child resting comfortably."

Ru Yan had completely forgotten about this, and hurried to congratulate him, "Another year, another child: a double joy!"

"Thank you, thank you for your kind wishes," Damo said. "The little one couldn't wait for the year of the Sheep, too much of a hurry, slipped into this world at the tip of the Horse's tail.

This is what her other grandparents were hoping for: they say those born in the year of the Sheep have a hard life."

"You all need to be, umm, careful at the hospital," Ru Yan said. And she told Damo what had happened to her brother-in-law.

He thanked her and said this news was timely. He'd need to look around the hospital and if anything didn't seem right they'd beat it and stay at home.

"Above all," Ru Yan said, "Stay away from big parties and crowds. Just bring the baby home, keep it quiet."

"OK," Damo chuckled, "we won't tell anyone: we'll pretend it's an illegitimate child."

Ru Yan heard the voice of an outraged woman in the background: *What kind of a grandfather talks that way?*

"I'm going to announce this thing online," Ru Yan said.

"Good," Damo agreed.

"They'll delete it. They're watching our website very closely."

"Post it tonight at eight o'clock," Damo suggested. "As soon as you post it, I'll copy it to a bunch of other places."

She made a few more phone calls, brief New Year's greetings to which she added a warning to watch out for the unknown disease that was quietly spreading. A few laughed at her: "Ru Yan, it's the first day of the year; how can you talk about that kind of thing?" Jiang Xiaoli was the only one who was not surprised. "You mean Liang Jinsheng didn't tell you about this? At our place we've known about it for days! My mom and dad cleared out a long time ago to get safely home; they're staying in, now, and don't go out at all.

At 8 P.M., Ru Yan posted on the Empty Nest the message she had written. The subject line was camouflage, "`My brother-in-law. . .`", to make it look like some anecdote of daily life. This post about the unknown disease was specific about persons, times, places, and incidents: all the W's of news reporting were covered.[282]

Damo must have been waiting for it, because when she checked his website *Word and Thought* only seconds later, her post was already there, but with a new subject line: "Unknown disease! A physician has succumbed." He had appended to Ru Yan's article a brief commentary of his own, "Something more terrifying than the plague." In it he wrote:

Plagues are natural calamities. For ages they have dogged the footsteps of humankind and are simply part of life. But a man-made restraint on information which fatally delays both precautions and treatment and provokes a panic which is a plague of its own, far worse than the plague itself -- *this* calamity is not natural.

This post began to spread at once from one website to another, like that staple of horror films, the self-replicating monster. And in its wake, on each website, there followed a swirl of intense commentary. Hard on its heels followed a tidal wave of deletions. But as the post was deleted in each place, it was speedily re-posted. The wave crashed on the shore, obliterating the footsteps which the monster had left in the sand; but as soon as the wave receded, the invisible monster left another line of footprints. At some ISPs the managers had to come out and announce a ban on this topic, even threatening to permanently block the IPs of offenders.

A message came in from Lonely Goose on QQ. I received a warning from the authorities. You must not post anything like this again or they will shut down our forum. Such Is This World, we rent our webspace from a commercial provider and the agreement stipulates that we can't publish news articles of a political nature. Like it or not, this was the deal. So that our forum can survive, will you please consider calling a halt to this campaign of yours? Think about it.

Ru Yan replied: I understand. But this post was only talking about personal events that have occurred in my family; I don't know whether this can be counted as a news article of a po-

`litical nature? I'm not clear about the relevant regulations, where can I read up on them?`

Lonely Goose fired back: `Such Is This World, how can you be so naive? This kind of regulation is itself top-secret: no way are you going to read about it. When it comes to grave epidemics, our news has always been controlled like this.`

Ru Yan persisted: `But does my article count as news? It was about a misfortune in my family. You know, as if somebody had been in a traffic accident.`

Lonely Goose concluded, `They don't come any more stubborn than you, do they? There's no point. We'll see in a few days.`

Many of the repostings originated from Damo's *Word and Thought*, and some linked to it directly. So his website was, naturally, the first place the ax fell, especially since he already had a long record of misdemeanors. After a half-hour, when she pointed her browser to *Word and Thought*, it said only:

Page unable to be displayed

It had been done without cursing or abuse, without anything obviously terrifying, without bombs or daggers. No, very gently and quietly it had been done: the other websites, anyway, still had lovely layouts and played pleasant music. Nothing had changed in her home, around her. But Ru Yan began to be afraid.

She phoned Damo because that was the only thing that would allay the fear mounting inside her.

"I can't open your *Word and Thought*," she said.

But Damo was pretty calm about it. "This is normal. I'm used to getting temporarily shut down about six times a year, and kicked out maybe three times. Can't even count the times I've had 'technical difficulties.' The pity of it is that in the blink of an eye I'm now homeless and must look for a new server, either commercial or free, either domestic or foreign. I'm a world-class vagabond."

"I brought this upon you," Ru Yan said.

Damo laughed. "Why do you think that? You told everyone the truth. You deserve thanks."

"Why wouldn't they let it be posted?" she wondered.

"Because it was true," he said. "If you had made something up—that your dog had half eaten you, say, or that an entire family somewhere had suddenly gotten vaporized—I promise you, no one would have turned a hair. The fact they wouldn't let you speak proves that what you were saying is true. This is practically a law of the Universe. And when they are particularly swift and heavy-handed in silencing you, it proves that the situation they are covering up is extremely serious. This also is a law of the Universe. The only problem is, the virus isn't going to pay any attention. It has its own laws, as will soon become evident. I saw my little granddaughter today. She's pink and cute, faintly smiling with her eyes shut, doesn't know a thing about this world. Made my heart ache. It was good that we spoke out and said what needed to be said. We're trying to set an example for the kids, just as, once, the older generation tried to set an example for us. . . even though it's hard, and it's going to cost us."

Before they said goodbye, Ru Yan asked Damo if he'd be home the next day. She had been planning to go see his grandchild and New Year's offered an occasion to express a little of her gratitude. And deep down she was curious to see what kind of everyday life this peculiar fellow might have.

"Why?" he wondered. "Do you have something in mind?"

"Yes, Ru Yan said, "I'd like to come by and congratulate you."

"After ten tomorrow I'll be out."

She thought for a moment. "Then I'll visit a little before then."

41

Early in the Eighties the members of the *Qing Ma* developed the custom of paying their respects to Teacher Wei on the *second* day of the new year. After he had returned to society, more and more people wanted to visit him on New Year's Day. There were old friends, subordinates, admirers, and several groups of officials who would make formal calls. The scenes were noisy and awkward. Later, when those of the *Qing Ma* who would emigrate had emigrated, and those who would move away had moved away, only Damo and Maozi were left, and they kept up the custom of visiting on the second day of the year. Teacher Wei would do his best to keep other people from visiting that day so that the three of them could enjoy a leisurely discussion.

On the morning of the second, therefore, Ru Yan washed up and got dressed and took Yang Yanping for its walk. She expected to get home late and therefore left the dog plenty of food and water while warning it to be good and not make a mess anywhere. Then she phoned her older sister to ask about the health of her brother-in-law.

"They still won't let me see him," she said. "They say he's getting better, but how can I know without seeing him?"

Ru Yan tried to comfort her and promised to call every day. Then she headed out. She had put on the clothes Jiang Xiaoli had picked out for her, but at the last minute she decided to change and was now in her usual everyday garb.

A peaceful scene awaited her in the street outside. The people of the city were out with their families, bearing brightly-wrapped gifts as they hurried in all directions to pay New Year's calls. Buses and taxis were in great demand; she waited for twenty minutes without seeing an available cab. Ordinarily at this hour there would have been a surplus of empty cabs, turning the street red as far as the eye could see.[283] Eventually she flagged one down, but the driver asked "Where to?" and wouldn't let her in until she told him.

On the way there, she felt embarrassed that she hadn't bought a gift for the baby and had the driver stop for a minute at a vendor's stand, where she bought a red envelope embossed with the image of a fat baby as a symbol of good fortune. She stuffed 800 yuan into the envelope. Once in the neighborhood, she phoned Damo, who told her to turn left, then right, then straight ahead; and at last she reached the old dormitory district where Damo lived.[284] The cabbie stopped at the entrance to a lane, unwilling to go further because someone standing there wanted a cab.

So she called Damo again. He told her to wait—he'd come get her—but she wanted to find the way herself. So he told her which building, entrance, and apartment number to look for. This neighborhood had provided residences for the workforce of an old factory, and the architecture was strikingly disparate because the housing had been progressively added to over the course of fifty years. There were gray-brick houses from the Fifties and red-brick three-story tenements from the Sixties. The Seventies had contributed five-story apartment buildings in gray concrete. The housing from the Eighties consisted of eight-story buildings with shiny aluminum window frames. These were all crammed in together, but if you looked closely you could make out the patterns in which the buildings from different eras had been placed, how the later ones had been inserted into the spaces between the earlier ones. It was like archeological strata, but in a different dimension.

The people who lived under such crowded conditions here had managed to make the most of every bit of space. Those who lived on the top floor had built sheds on the flat roofs, while those who lived on the ground floor had added lean-tos. Anyone who had a balcony had enclosed it. Some had even built their own castles in the air, making extra rooms that jutted out from the third or fourth story into space, braced with steel girders and angle-irons, like the additions one sometimes sees constructed over the water's edge. There were chicken-coops and dovecotes too, and flower-boxes and fishtanks, putting every conceivable nook and surface to use. Many residents had hung salted fish or cured meat from the eaves outside their windows; a few had placed a small coal stove in front of their door and soup now simmered on it. The scene had the feel of a marketplace and the atmosphere of a merry festival. People came and went, calling out New Year's greetings as they passed with a bit of badinage or the loan of a cigarette or the exchange of friendly vulgarities. The development was home also to a population of little dogs—white ones, filthy ones, frolicking in pursuit of each other or just out for a stroll. They seemed a lot more free in their ways than Yang Yanping.

Ru Yan had never ventured into such an environment before. A milieu like this, hidden behind the skyscrapers and wide avenues and wealthy mansions of a modern metropolis, called to mind the underworld of beggars in *The Hunchback of Notre Dame*—the same earthy and up-beat boisterousness reigned here. The young women dressed fashionably and looked fresh and bright, the makeup a little gaudy perhaps, with their hair dyed in the latest style. The young men were robust and nattily attired. Were they to walk into the most upscale quarter of the city, no one would be able to tell they came from such a shabby and impoverished place. They were loud in their talk and their irreverent humor. For Ru Yan, their happiness was contagious, and she found herself smiling. Despite her best efforts, however, she lost her way and asked a passerby in his thirties for directions. "Where does Damo live?"

The young man looked baffled. "Damo? What Damo?"

Ru Yan remembered that Damo was only a screen name. "He, um, fixes appliances." And she recited the address he had given over the phone.

"Oh," the man said, "You must mean Teacher Chang. I'll take you there myself."

"Here in the neighborhood, you call him a teacher? What does he teach?"

"A better question," the man laughed, "would be what is there that he *can't* teach? Teacher Chang is a very versatile man. He's got more than enough talent to be Mayor."

As they walked, her cell phone rang: it was Damo. "Are you

lost again? Back where you started?" As she admitted that she had indeed got lost again, she saw Damo in the distance coming toward her, his phone to his ear, and she waved and grinned. But her guide, a very conscientious man, stayed with her till they came up to Damo, and then he wished Teacher Chang a happy New Year.

"This man has been singing your praises," she said.

"Ah, thanks for the kind words, young man," Damo winked at him, "I'll have a New Year's gift for you later." They chatted for a moment, and then the young man went away. Damo struck up conversation with Ru Yan as he led her toward his home.

Dozens of buildings of different sizes composed this labyrinthine housing project, and as he led the way she thought to herself that if she came to see him again, she would still be unable to find his home. He lived on the fifth floor in an apartment of two small bedrooms and a living room. She had trouble estimating the area, but sensed it was much, much smaller than her own apartment. The living room had only one wall against which a table could be placed; the others all had doorways. The apartment was spare and neat. Damo's wife came out of a room and said to Ru Yan, "It's very kind of you to come so far on New Year's Day." Then she led her into a bedroom, explaining there was more room to sit there. She was of above-average height (taller than Damo) and sturdily built; and she appeared capable, kind, and practical.

Damo introduced his wife as surnamed Zhang and working as a teacher in a local primary school. Ru Yan estimated she might be three or four years older than herself, and addressed her as Elder Sister Zhang. But Damo referred to his wife as Teacher Zhang, which Ru Yan found amusing.

It was a small bedroom with a pull-out sofabed as well as a regular bed, and between them stood a small tea-table on wheels. Fruit and melon seeds and other snacks were on the table, creating a bit of New Year's atmosphere. When Damo and Ru Yan sat down, Damo's wife brought tea in on a tray, explaining that the other room was usually for TV and Damo's online activities, but now with their daughter's temporary return it had been cleared out for her to stay in.

After a few sips of tea, Ru Yan mentioned that she would love to see the baby. They led her to the adjoining room, which had the scents of a nursery with a newborn. Mother and child were in bed. Damo's daughter looked tired and said softly, "Dad says the hospital isn't safe now, so we just came home. It's nice to be home, more comfortable, especially since it's New Year's."

Ru Yan inquired about the son-in-law. Sister Zhang said, "He's gone shopping for diapers—babies these days are so finicky! When we had kids, a bit of ragged dirty cloth, washed and dried in the sun, was good enough."

"What era do you think this is?" the daughter chided. "Women use pads, you know."[285]

Ru Yan asked the baby's name. "The child has the in-laws' last name," Damo said, "and we'll wait for the other grandparents to choose a name."

When she bent close to look, the child was sleeping with a slightly furrowed brow as if worried. It had been more than twenty years since Ru Yan had had such a close look at such a tiny baby, and the changes since when her son had been born made it seem as if a lifetime had passed. She was startled to realize that her son's generation had grown up to the point that they were having their own children now.

She worked up the courage to place the red envelope beside the baby's pillow, blushing as if she were doing something wrong: "Just a token for good luck . . . I meant to buy something, but I don't know what kids need these days."

Sister Zhang strode over and tried to force the red envelope back into Ru Yan's pocket. "The fact that you came to see the baby, that by itself will bring good luck."

Ru Yan flushed more deeply as she retreated out of the bedroom, whispering, "Don't wake the baby!" They pushed the money back and forth in a match that lasted for a few rounds, as Teacher Zhang called on Damo to intervene.

"Accept it," he said. "It's New Year's." This relieved Ru Yan's embarrassment, and they were quick to change the subject.

Maozi arrived as they were talking. He had come to drive Damo with him to Teacher Wei's. He came in to see the baby first, and he, too, gave the baby a red envelope. Damo introduced Maozi and Ru Yan to each other.

"You got to know each other over the Internet? You even do that? Man, you don't miss a trick."

Maozi was by no means insensible to the charms of pretty women, and when Damo described Ru Yan as a gifted woman who never made a show of her talents, Maozi became voluble. His cleverness, erudition, and humor all switched into high gear.

"At that Institute of yours," Damo suggested, "you ought to hire a few people like Ru Yan. It would raise the standards considerably. At least the nauseating articles, the ones that really stink, would be cut to a minimum."

Since Maozi apparently couldn't bring himself to stop talking, Damo said, "We've got to go. With a slight detour, you can drop this lady off at her home."

"Why don't we just bring her along to Teacher Wei's?" Maozi suggested. "Would you like to go?" he asked her.

Ru Yan realized she had no plans, but asked if she would be intruding.

"We're old friends. Such a meeting would be well worth it."

So the three of them got into Maozi's car and headed for Teacher Wei's home. Ru Yan reflected that as time went by, she was becoming increasingly impetuous. On the way, Damo told her about Teacher Wei, recounting the twists and turns of his path as well as the story of his tragic love.

42

Since Zhao Yi had come on the scene, Teacher Wei's household had undergone considerable aesthetic improvement. A few days before New Year's[286], she had dragged him to the flower market, where they had selected an enormous quantity of potted plants and flower arrangements and hired a man with a car to bring it all home. Then they went to a gift shop to load up on colored streamers, lanterns, and paper cutouts for their windows; and with all this they had decked out their living room to make it worthy of a festive gathering. The Christmas tree, twinkling with lights of different colors and festooned with delicate ornaments, was still standing in the corner. Trays of fruit and cookies were arrayed on their coffee table, and the stereo was playing classical music. It all gave the home of this elderly pair the tone one might expect from a newly-married couple celebrating the holidays.

On arriving, Damo first introduced Ru Yan.

Teacher Wei appraised her, beaming: "Do I have a new 'Net friend?"

Maozi chuckled that Teacher Wei never fell behind the times.

"Indeed," Teacher Wei said, "You take a look at my e-mail address book and you'll find a long list of names; the oldest are in their nineties and the youngest are in their teens. The electronic greeting cards go on and on, although I admit I still like the kind that comes through the mail."

When Damo's gang had visited at the Spring Festival in past years, Teacher Wei's apartment had stood out on account of all the cards of congratulation and good wishes which the old couple had strung across the room, line after line of them hung on colored ribbons in the study, and the cards bore inscriptions, long or short and often quite witty, so that you could have made a book of festive greetings out of them.

Once again, the old couple were wearing the flaming-red matching "sweethearts' suits" first revealed three years before, and their white hair had grown more dazzling. Ru Yan had never known white hair could be so beautiful. Perhaps on account of Teacher Wei's poignant and dramatic history, which Damo had shared with her, she liked him at once. She liked Zhao Yi, too, and felt that there was something uplifting about this old couple who were always together. They breathed a poetry ripened by time and a spirituality forged in suffering. Ru Yan could tell that

Damo and Maozi were at ease in Teacher Wei's apartment as if in their father's home, and that enabled her to relax also.

Teacher Wei asked her to tell him a little about herself. Damo soon remarked that she had a very good grounding in classical poetry and had a great feel for writing, a refined and old-fashioned style.

"Does it run in your family?" Teacher Wei asked.

"Couldn't possibly," Ru Yan said. "My father was a rough-and-ready soldier, and there hasn't been a scholar in the family for many generations. My mother, on the other hand, did go to college, though she didn't graduate but married my father instead."

Teacher Wei understood and grinned. "I, too, was once a rough-and-ready soldier. In fact, it was in that capacity that I first came to this part of the country. So in this respect I am like your father. And I, too, went to college but never finished, choosing instead to get married to the Revolution, so in this respect I am like your mother."

Ru Yan smiled and said that if you went farther back on her mother's side you would find a handful of scholars, and mentioned a few names from the Ming and the Qing Dynasties.

"There you go," Teacher Wei declared. "The gene of culture is unstoppable. Even when cut off by a revolution, it reveals itself in a throwback to an earlier generation."

As he spoke, Teacher Wei began to cough. Damo asked him what was wrong.

"His cough's been pretty bad at night," Zhao Yi said. He had insisted on taking a bath on New Year's Eve, said he wanted to be immaculate to welcome the New Year—and so he caught a cold.

Teacher Wei was still living in the three-room apartment that had been allotted to him in the early Eighties. The building had grown somewhat shabby, and the heat hadn't worked for years.[287] In view of his seniority in the Party, he ought to have been moved into a bigger and better apartment by now, but for some reason he had kept on living in the same place.

"You need to hurry and get him seen by a doctor," Ru Yan suggested. "At his age, respiratory diseases are not something to take lightly." And she told them about the strange disease which was afflicting the South and described what had happened to her brother-in-law.

"I read an article online that said the same thing," Teacher Wei remarked.

"It was probably the one Ms. Ru Yan wrote," Damo said.

"At the time, I didn't pay attention to who wrote it," Teacher Wei said, "but it made enough of an impression that I sent it on to a few of my old friends. I felt it had the ring of truth. You can tell when things are true, just as you can tell when they're bogus."

They all talked for a while about this strange disease. Teacher Wei said, "Actually, there are all kinds of pestilences in Nature; it's a perfectly normal phenomenon at every period of history and in every country. In the history of Europe, there were terrible plagues that wiped out half the population, but they're OK now. I don't know why these things become a political matter when they happen in our country. I remember at the very beginning of Liberation there was an internal regulation[288] warning that in the event of an outbreak of grave infectious disease no one should announce or discuss it in a disorderly way.[289] In those days, the common people were not well-informed, and if you didn't talk about something it might as well never have occurred; so this was an effective strategy. The people on the east side of town didn't know what had happened on the west side, never mind people thousands of miles apart. There was also a vague and constricting presumption that if you talked about something bad, it didn't matter whether it was true: you might be up to no good. There was a well-known saying, *You must behave yourself; it's forbidden to speak or act in a disorderly way.*[290] This is the origin of the concept of disorderly speech. Yet there was no problem with another kind of disorderly speech, the genuine article: you could fling that around without qualms. For example, they said when the attack of the American Imperialists reached the Yalu River, the Americans had begun infecting flies and rats with germs and then tossing them over into our country in bombs; when the bombs exploded the critters scurried out and made our people deathly ill. All this was said in a plausible way; it was even made into cartoons."

Damo and Maozi both laughed and said they remembered a children's song,

The American bandits are the bad guys,
Insanely they wage germ warfare.

Teacher Wei said, "And yet to this day no proof has been brought forward. Not long ago I read an article based on documents that surfaced from the archives of the former Soviet Union, saying that this was a fabrication."[291]

Then they all naturally took up the major topics of the day, both domestic and international: the problem of corruption, the prospects for amending the Constitution[292], the problems of education and public order; the issue of Korean nukes and the Israeli-Palestinian question as well as tensions between India and Pakistan . . . topics ranged widely, and they were knowledgeable about all of them.

When they had finished discussing the problems of the world, Damo mentioned that just a few days before, on New Year's Eve, he had acquired a granddaughter.

Teacher Wei, at first dumbstruck, finally roared with laughter. "You? You now have a granddaughter! How dare you have a granddaughter? How old are you, anyway?"

"Fifty-one," Damo said. "In the old days, they would have made much of my reaching the half-century mark."

Teacher Wei kept shaking his head. "Incredible, just incredible: time marches on. Forty years have passed in a flash since I met you in the Chamber of Enchantment. No wonder the ancients said man's life is like a dream."

They all pondered this, making their own calculations, and sighed in agreement.

"So what does it feel like to have a grandchild?" Teacher Wei asked.

"It's like having another kid," Damo shrugged. "I haven't figured out yet what it feels like to be a grandfather." They all laughed.

"I don't think I can manage to go see her, but of course I'll be giving her a gift," Teacher Wei said.

Zhao Yi added, "If there's anything you need, you can just say it; with us there's no need to stand on ceremony."

"If you're ever in the mood to write a few characters of calligraphy, that, from you, would be the best possible gift."

"This I will do," Teacher Wei said. "But I need to get something else for her, too. Don't worry, I'll take care of it."

Whenever they got together, Teacher Wei was like a young man sharing secrets with his peers. They liked to talk about trends and developments and rumors, and would swap recommendations of books and articles, chattering with enthusiasm.

These people and their conversation were utterly novel and refreshing to Ru Yan. But there was something vaguely familiar about them, too, and she had to think for a moment before she put her finger on it. They were reminiscent of far-off Russia: of Pushkin, Hertzen, Turgenev, Chernyshevsky, and the characters they created. In this air one could sense something sharp, passionate, rebellious, furtive, even dangerous. These people embodied an energy that could not be contained; you could feel it. Even apparently innocuous remarks proved to have more than one level of meaning. They kept you on your toes. Their ideas and wit made everything they said a challenge; their words never lacked a provocative edge.

Seeing that everyone's talk had got stuck in such grand topics, Zhao Yi teased them: "How come so much political consciousness for the Spring Festival this year? We get to see each other and it's nothing but world issues!" She offered everyone something to eat, explaining that she and Teacher Wei had made a special shopping trip just before the New Year.

For appearance's sake, Teacher Wei peeled a banana and nibbled on it. "Just came out with a new book. A copy for each of you: consider it your New Years' money.[293]" Then he asked Zhao Yi to fetch the books from the study.

Though he had embarked on a literary career before he was twenty years old, Teacher Wei hadn't published a book of his own till he was sixty. Ever since the 1980s, he had produced a book every few years and by the latter half of the Nineties they were coming out almost annually. As time went by, they became increasingly substantive and well-written. He mused in an informal style about a wide range of topics: the past, his friends, academic studies, music and the arts, political thought and culture. In recent years he had reworked into essays and commentaries the reflections on the political system which had preoccupied him many years before, and their hard-hitting insights had sent shockwaves through the Academy and the intellectual world. Each time he published a book, no matter how limited his supply of review copies might be, the members of the *Qing Ma* were sure to each receive a copy. One of his old friends had carved for him a couple of personal seals[294]. The first said, "At seventy I had no doubts," and the second said, "At eighty, I knew the will of Heaven."[295] He liked these very much and used them to stamp his books. On reaching his eightieth birthday, he had put away the former seal and begun using the second.

Zhao Yi brought out three copies and handed one to each of their three guests. The title was *A Dialogue Between an Old Man and a System*. Damo's and Maozi's copies had been inscribed. Seeing that the dedication page on her copy was blank, Ru Yan said, "You have to sign it for me!"

"I didn't know someone new was coming today," Teacher Wei said, as he took the book back from her. "What are the two characters in 'Ru Yan'?"[296]

Damo said, "'Ru' as in *ruguo* ['if'], 'Yan' as in *xinbuzaiyan* ['absent-minded']."[297]

Ru Yan said, "Write my real name, otherwise people will think you made a mistake." And she told Teacher Wei her real name.

"'Ru' as in *rumaoyinxue* ['to live a primitive life']? I suppose you're descended from northern barbarians, the nomadic tribes who fought on horseback."

"My mother used to say that," Ru Yan answered. "But those putative ancestors, busy riding their horses, weren't civilized enough to leave behind a book of genealogy, so one can only guess."

Teacher Wei smiled. "The descendants of those northern barbarians can be quite refined. I think Wang Anyi[298], the novelist, makes this point. On her mother's side, she too would be the progeny of northern barbarians . . . some Turkic people, as I recall."[299] He put on his spectacles and leaned closer. "Let's take a look . . . do you perhaps have a hint of the Turkic about you? I detect an exotic air, anyway."

Damo and Maozi joined in, declaring that they could indeed see something exotic in her. She blushed.

She picked up his book, indescribably pleased, for it was the first time an author had ever signed his book for her; an author, moreover, who inspired her love and respect.

"This book came out in Hong Kong," Teacher Wei said. "It would have been hard to get it published here."

Maozi leafed through the book and suddenly blurted out, pointing at Damo, "A few days ago I got into a big fight with him. We almost came to blows."

"You will observe," Damo remarked, "it is the party in the wrong who first files suit."

Teacher Wei teased them: "What were you quarreling for? Were you fighting over Ru Yan?" They all laughed.

"It was because of a book I wrote," Maozi said.

"That's right," Damo said, "Tell the truth and receive a lighter sentence."

"I'm really quite embarrassed to mention this book to you," Maozi continued, "but I thought about it and decided it was better to get it over with. As the Special Investigation Team said to me once: 'The faster you come clean, the faster you'll feel better.'"

As soon as Maozi named the book, Teacher Wei said, "I know about it."

Maozi had not expected this, and he was speechless.

Teacher Wei said, "When that book of yours came out, someone told me about it. I expected you would give it to me, I would read it, and then we would talk about it. But you never gave it to me. So I realized that you didn't want me to know about this book."

Maozi looked ill-at-ease.

Teacher Wei smiled. "This is a painful topic for you."

"Yes," Maozi said, "I never gave that book to anyone."

"However," Teacher Wei said, "someone later obtained a copy for me. I read it with considerable distress, and wanted to ask many questions. I don't know whether you gentlemen remember the time—I think it was when He Qiye and those others came back—I mentioned how young intellectuals can pass over from idealism to cynicism?"

They said they remembered.

"Well, I really wanted to bring up that book of yours and have it out with you, but for some reason I didn't have the courage. I could see how He Qiye and the others had changed when they returned from afar, and I think I just made a couple of veiled remarks and left it at that. I had spent half my life in the bleakest isolation, and in those hard times you were my only friends, and your friendship had been precious to me. In more recent years I had come back to society, but my genuine friends were still few and my old adversaries had not become any more kindly disposed toward me (on the contrary, they harbored new grudges). The most troubling thing was that kindred spirits with whom I went way back had gradually become estranged from me. I realized that we had actually been different in many ways, but misfortune had caused us to share what appeared to be the same fate. Most of all, the stance I took later—my way of thinking—was an embarrassment to them. For they could see in my personal choices the proof that we were different. Like Ali Baba and the Forty Thieves, they had hoped to mark every door with an X. But when some people were no longer willing to be marked with an X, it became awkward. I told you once, 'Many of the old ones have their problems.' Quite apart from their inability to entertain certain ideas, they have lost the courage to be creative and start over. They're just hoping for a somewhat better chapter in their life to make up for years of deprivation: they want good medical care so as not to suffer any more than necessary in the twilight of life, and they don't want to get their families in trouble again. This is why I was unwilling to hurt your feelings, you who have been my friends despite the difference in age. Perhaps it's an old man's weakness. On this point, I have gradually come to understand how Lu Xun found himself solitary and helpless in his declining years.[300]"

Maozi said, "I, too, thought long and hard before deciding to bring this up. I told Damo I didn't know whether it was still curable."

"A man can only cure himself," Teacher Wei said. "In problems with a spiritual dimension, there is no one who can cure you. There's no need for us to say anything more. The rest is up to you. I'll tell you this: the temptations you're up against, I too once faced. I even passed for an up-and-coming official, and I had a distinguished record, especially compared with today's crowd. I know the strength of these temptations, and to be quite honest with you, I have learned a great deal from Haigen."

"Who is Haigen?" Ru Yan asked softly.

Teacher Wei laughed. "You come to my house with someone and then ask me who he is?"

Ru Yan then realized this must be Damo's real name and remembered how a man had said "Teacher Chang" on the way to Damo's house. "So you must be Chang Haigen?"

Teacher Wei continued his train of thought. "Haigen's powers of concentration, his ability to see through the empty show of conventional reputation, his own origins from the grassroots of society, his aristocratic temper, and the warrior ethos that makes him indomitable: in today's world, these traits are extraordinary."

Damo grinned. "I already have a tendency to vainglory. You shouldn't praise me like this."

"I'm not praising you. I'm letting you know the value of what you do. It has turned out to be very difficult, in our era, for an individual to overcome the lure of fame, money, and power. And there seems to be unanimous agreement that a person who has these things, even if he's a complete bastard, deserves honor and respect. Of course, I also want to commend you, Maozi, because it wasn't easy for you to take the initiative in bringing up this matter. I know many people who resolve never to turn back once they start out on their way, because the cost of turning back is much greater than the cost of not doing so. We're all marked with an X, so what can they do to me? But the one who *does* turn back will be treated badly both by those who continue on their path and by those who stayed behind. I tell you, Maozi, when I learned about that book of yours I cursed you in my heart, but even more fiercely did I curse the environment that consumes a human being, devours him right down to the bones. China doesn't lack for experts in political thought. Her scholars don't lack for brains. It's just that some have been smothered, others have been intimidated, and still others have freely made themselves accomplices. If you want to talk about tragedies, *this* is the greatest tragedy that can befall a people."

Ru Yan had never heard such talk. She listened intently and strove to catch each word and remember it. Even an unvarnished transcript, she thought, would be a profoundly moving document. If the conversation could be broadcast for TV, it would make all those pretentious talk-show hosts fade away like ice-sculptures under the burning sun.

Ru Yan watched Zhao Yi listening on the sidelines and saw that she grasped everything they were saying. She probably had a lot to say, but she held her peace. She was a calm person of deep understanding. She left the room for a while and announced on her return, "I see we're still stuck in politics, on New Year's." She served a meal of steamed cornbread and soup.

The meal was utterly authentic. The cornbread was from coarse flour, with a golden crust, and when you took a bite a real corn aroma wafted out. The noodles were handmade and formed a chewy disc in the center of the soup bowl, where a few jade green leaves also floated, together with strands of egg-drop and a few pieces of fresh red tomato. There were four dishes of cold vegetables and a small plate of fermented tofu. A flair for presentation shone through the simplicity, and when Ru Yan saw it she let slip, "Ai! A hostess who puts such food on the table at New Year's is simply a master!"

Teacher Wei beamed. "Better not praise her like that. This wife of mine is like Haigen; she has a tendency to vainglory."

It was all fresh and crispy and so expertly laid out that no one wanted to stop eating. But when all had returned to their seats they chatted some more, and then Damo said Teacher Wei probably needed to get some rest.

After a pause, Teacher Wei announced, "There's one other thing . . . I don't know whether it's good news or bad news, but I want to tell you about it."

They all stared at him in silence, with no idea what this might be about. They looked at Zhao Yi, but her face gave nothing away.

"A few days ago I received a letter from my granddaughter."

They were all dumbfounded. Had he announced an invasion of space aliens he could not have astonished them more. They waited for him to continue.

"This person who calls herself my granddaughter," he said, "is named Fang Ya. She's in college in Beijing. Not long ago she called on a great-uncle of hers, the younger brother of her maternal grandmother. This great-uncle is a scholar from Taiwan who had come to the mainland to take part in some academic event. The old man told her that while he was abroad he had come across a book written by someone called "This Wei," whose real name was Wei Liwen. 'He's your grandfather,' he had told her. 'You should think about getting in touch with him.' So she looked me up on the Internet and contacted the publisher, learned my address, and decided to start off with a short note to find out whether it was possible to reach me. The note gave her address, phone number, and e-mail. When I received this note I almost had a heart attack."

He gestured to his wife. "She gave me medicine immediately, and added something to make me sleep, and I had a restful night. The next day I was able to be a little calmer about it. I judged that this granddaughter must be the daughter of my second child, who was born in 1953 and would be fifty now. My former wife and I were of the same age, and if she were still alive, she, too, would be in her eighties. I also had a son born in 1951. This short note, which almost killed me, made me start thinking about the past. I talked it over with my wife. She said, since it has come up, it were best to face it squarely. So I picked up the phone and called this granddaughter who had fallen from heaven, so to speak. The child was calmer than I, but sounded very affectionate on the phone and called me Grandpa. It was more than I could bear; the tears streamed down and for a long time I couldn't get any words out. 'What about your grandmother?' I asked. 'I never met her,' she said, 'she died before I was born.'

"'And your mother?' I asked. 'She lives in Urumqi,' the girl said, and explained that she herself had been born in Urumqi, leaving only after high school.[301] I asked about my son—'And your uncle . . . he would be your Mama's elder brother?' My granddaughter said she hadn't met him either, but had heard from her mother that he'd committed suicide during the Cultural Revolution. He was not yet twenty years old when he killed himself. She learned this only a couple of years ago. I had to wonder, what could have happened after my former wife took the two little children and left me? She said she wasn't clear about that, she'd have to ask her mother. 'Does your mother know you have found me?' I asked. 'Haven't told her yet,' the girl said, 'and I'm not sure how she'll react. But'—she added—'I'm really glad to have found you, especially after reading some of your articles... I'm proud to have such a grandfather.' She said she was looking for a chance to come see me. At the time we spoke, she was preparing to start her winter break and said she would first go back to Urumqi to see her mother. Then they would make a decision.

"The day before yesterday, on New Year's Eve, she phoned from Urumqi to say that she and her mother would like to visit in a few days. I said, 'Put your Mama on the line.' After some delay, she said, 'Mama's pretty emotional right now. She can't speak, but when we come to see you she'll have a good talk with you and explain about her mother.'

"Yesterday she called again to say when they're coming: they've already booked plane tickets for the eighth day of the new year. They'll stay with me for a few days, and from here my granddaughter will go directly back to school in Beijing."

Zhao Yi said, "I told him, 'You need to talk this over with Haigen and the others. We've grown old enough that there are things with which we'll need their help: ferrying the visitors, making arrangements, keeping everything calm. We're likely to get shook up when the old meet the young after half a century.'"

They all discussed what to do and decided Maozi would pick them up at the airport. Ru Yan wanted to go, too; it would be easier if a woman came along. Damo would remain with the old folks in the apartment. They noticed that when Teacher Wei was excited, as he was now, his voice quavered and he trembled a little, and it brought home to them that he had become a very old man.

43

Returning home, Ru Yan had barely set foot inside the door when the phone rang. It was Liang Jinsheng. "Your timing's perfect," she said, "I just got home and haven't even taken my shoes off."

"Is that so?" he said. "Must be telepathy. Where did you go?"

"A friend's house."

"I thought I was your only friend," he rumbled.

"*That* kind of friend? Yes, you're the only one—at present."

"Starting tomorrow," he said, "For three whole days, my time is completely my own."

"Three days!" she exclaimed. "What a luxury!"[302]

"Do you have any plans?" he asked.

"With your time so precious, I'll be glad to follow your lead."

"Wouldn't you like to take me to your mother for her to have a look at me?"

Ru Yan didn't immediately understand what she had just heard. "Take you? How's that?"

"I've booked two plane tickets to Guangzhou," Liang Jinsheng explained. "Tomorrow morning at eight. We'll be there by ten. On the fifth day of the New Year, we fly home."

Inwardly she was jubilant, and thought *this fellow is full of surprises.* But what she said was, "What did you do that for? You don't often get the chance to just rest for a few days."

"If we hurry down to offer the old lady the compliments of the season, that will give her a chance to express her approval."

"And if by some chance the old lady doesn't approve?"

"Then we'll have a few more months to work on her! Otherwise, she won't let you come to your wedding, which would be irksome."

Ru Yan couldn't help laughing. "If you've got time to impress an old lady, wouldn't it be better spent impressing the higher-ups? You'll get promoted to the Central Government!"

"A paltry reward," he said, "compared to the daughter of that old lady. Pack your things. I'll pick you up at six o'clock tomorrow morning. Don't tell your mother we're coming: let's give her a nice surprise that may comfort her after what's happened to your brother-in-law."

Ru Yan was moved. "Acting like that," she said, "you'll pass every test." But then she remembered the unknown disease. "Maybe it's not safe down there."

"It can't be that serious," he said. "Yesterday I was watching TV and the streets of Guangzhou were full of people, bustling with activity."

When her husband had been alive, Ru Yan had been prone to sleep late. But living by herself she had developed a better sense of her own time. Very early the next morning, while it was still dark, she awakened without an alarm clock, washed up, ate breakfast, and tidied up the apartment once more, closing what needed to be closed and locking what needed to be locked. Then she waited for Liang Jinsheng. Yang Yanping was already in the care of her downstairs neighbor, and this was the only aspect of her trip about which Ru Yan felt uneasy. It didn't seem right to make the creature spend this festive season alone under a stranger's roof.

Liang Jinsheng arrived in a taxi. He said he had canceled all his official engagements for the next three days. To be going on a long journey with him made Ru Yan feel as excited as a young girl. Once aboard the plane they looked around the spacious cabin and were struck by how sparsely it was occupied (there were but seven or eight other passengers). They chose window seats up front, with a view unobstructed by the wings. As long as you didn't turn around, you could imagine you were on a private plane. Soon they were above a sea of clouds.

As they had expected, Ru Yan's mother was overjoyed to hear her daughter's voice over the intercom. "Heavens! My little girl! I was just thinking of you!" Only when they went upstairs and she opened the door for them did she discover a man standing behind her little girl. Ru Yan gestured to him and said, "Mother, this is Liang Jinsheng."

She eyed him with the tiniest smile and said softly, "Have you brought me a present for New Year's?"

"I left in such a hurry, Ma'am, that there wasn't time to get you an appropriate gift."

Ru Yan hurried to explain, "The gift my mother means is the gift of yourself. Mom, I hadn't planned to come, but he said he wanted me to take him to you to have a good look at him."

"Come in and sit down," her mother said. "When you sit down I can take a good look."

Ru Yan's mother was in her seventies and spoke standard Chinese with the accent of the Lower Yangtze Delta, soft like sticky rice. Her hair was still basically black with a few white strands at the temples, and curled in a permanent that was reminiscent of American movies from the Thirties. Her complexion was fair and clear, her eyes unclouded, and her expression suggested a greater self-assurance than Ru Yan possessed, the kind that can come from a wealthy upbringing. One could tell she had been quite a beauty in her day. Her figure had remained trim. The winters of Guangzhou are not cold, so she was wearing a light-purple blouse under a rust-red knitted vest.

"How's my sister?" Ru Yan asked.

"She went to the hospital early this morning," her mother said.

When she left the room to pour some tea, Liang Jinsheng whispered into Ru Yan's ear, "She is beautiful. If your mother could go back twenty years, I might take a fancy to her."

"Good grief!" Ru Yan cried. "Mom, he says if you could go back—"

Her mother returned. "I heard him. You think I'm deaf? The smartest men have the sense to flatter their mothers-in-law from the very beginning. But no matter how smart she is, a mother-in-law can't resist such flattery." Ru Yan guffawed.

Surprisingly, Liang Jinsheng was embarrassed. "What I meant..." he stammered, "I mean, I meant what I said, I really did, even if I expressed myself poorly. Please don't be offended."

"Sit down," Ru Yan's mother said. "I am not offended. No matter how old they are, women love to hear this sort of thing. It's even better than buying them fine clothes."

Everyone sat down. "In the beginning," she explained to Ru Yan, "Your father was so attentive and nice to my mother that the fine old lady probably would have let him have all three of her daughters. What's the most vulnerable part of a woman's body? Her ear."

What she was saying, reinforced by her own graceful bearing and gestures, filled Liang Jinsheng with an admiration he tried not to show. He thought that compared to her mother, even Ru Yan seemed lackluster; the old lady was a striking combination of grace and intelligence. If in her time she had married someone a little more promising, there's no telling where she'd be today.

They chatted about the mysterious disease that was spreading, and about life in the South. Then Ru Yan's mother asked Liang Jinsheng what he had majored in as a student.

Ru Yan knew her mother had been itching to gain some personal information and would have been more direct in Liang Jinsheng's absence.

"He went to the same school as Yanping," Ru Yan said, "and had the same major."

"What a coincidence," her mother remarked.

"But it's been a long time since he did any work in that field," Ru Yan explained. "He's now a deputy mayor in our city."

Ru Yan's mother was startled and studied Liang Jinsheng

carefully. "That's quite something!" she smiled.

"What do you mean, 'It's quite something'?" Ru Yan asked.

"For an official to have reached that level and still be taken with a daughter from our family, that's quite something."

"Ru Yan is a remarkable woman," Liang Jinsheng said.

"I think so, too," the mother said with a faint smile, "and your fondness for her speaks well for your judgment: it's quite something. Most officials these days are like Ximen Qing and are interested only in young playmates—fresh, pretty, and coy. How can they have any real understanding of women?"[303]

Ru Yan noticed that the usual Liang Jinsheng, always calm and self-assured, was nowhere to be seen. All the man could do now was giggle somewhat foolishly. She couldn't help laughing, too. She remembered the first time she'd brought her late husband home, how he had found her mother utterly overpowering. He, too, had only been able to giggle nervously. On every subsequent visit to her family, he'd pause outside the door and say, "Let me get my trembling over with before we go in."

"This is just the way my mother talks," Ru Yan said. "You can imagine what my father endured when he lived with her."

"Your Dad was delighted, at least secretly. If I was ever listless and quiet, he'd get nervous and begin speaking disjointedly until I perked up." She then inquired about Liang Jinsheng's parents.

"I, too, have only my mother left," he answered. "She lives with my brother in Beijing. The Spring Festival has been so hectic this year that I didn't get to see her."

"How good of you to come see me and bring my daughter with you," Ru Yan's mother said.

He hastened to explain: "I went to see my mother not long ago."

"It's more important to me that you two are well than that you should come to see me every day." She asked how certain people in the city government were doing, saying that she had retired more than ten years ago and moved down South, and so had lost touch with many.

Liang Jinsheng answered her in detail about her old acquaintances. So-and-so had been retired for some time and was still in good health. This person had already passed on. That one had made some mistakes and been punished, while another had been sentenced to so many years in prison. Ru Yan's mother gave a little moan or sigh for each one.

"A deputy mayor," she mused, "that's pretty high up. Do you know who the mayor was back when we entered the city?"[304]

Liang Jinsheng uttered a name.

"Nope. He was the second one. In the period I'm talking about, the first generation of revolutionaries was in charge of the cities. Chen Yi, you know? and Li Xiannian. They were only mayors.[305]

"There's no comparing the mayors of today with the mayors of that era," Liang Jinsheng said. "Just counting up all the mayors now (in each city there are seven or eight, even ten, deputy mayors), you've got a whole regiment of them in a province."

When they had been talking for a while, Ru Yan's sister came home. Ru Yan ran to hug her, smiling with tears in her eyes and asking about her brother-in-law. Her sister took a look at Liang Jinsheng and said, "This must be the person who was with you on New Year's Eve?"

Ru Yan introduced him. Her mother added his title: Deputy Mayor of City X.

Her sister laughed: "Our little sister makes friends in high places!"

"It was I who pursued her," Liang Jinsheng said.

"You two were brave," her sister suddenly said, "to fly down here at a time like this."

Liang Jinsheng remarked, "On the drive into town, all the streets seemed full of people in a festive mood. How bad could it be?"

"That's Guangzhou'ers for you," Elder Sister said. "The world could be set to blow up tomorrow, but they still wouldn't miss their Evening Tea tonight.[306] Look, everybody says there's a connection between this disease and wild game, but the only impact that has had on the diet here is that people worry they're going to have trouble finding their favorite wild foods." In all the years Ru Yan's sister had lived in Guangzhou, she had never had a good word to say about the locals.

"He's in charge of public health," Ru Yan said, "so please tell him a little about the conditions here." Ru Yan's sister worked in the same hospital as her husband: as head of the administrative office, she was well informed about developments.

"I may already know a bit more than you think," Liang Jinsheng said. "I came to see Auntie, let's not talk about this. I don't know whether Auntie Ru feels up to it, but I'd like to take you sightseeing tomorrow, a spring day trip."[307]

"Since when does a guest who has come from far away ask to take his hosts out on a day trip?" the mother objected. "Are you very familiar with this part of the country?"

"Perhaps you've enlisted the help of people in the local government?" Ru Yan wondered.

"I didn't tell anyone about this trip," Liang Jinsheng answered, "except for an old classmate of mine. I phoned him and he's already arranged a nice place for us to go, about sixty miles outside town. Guaranteed to be virus-free."

Elder Sister and her husband were usually busy all the time, and the mother hadn't made any friends in Guangzhou. She didn't get out for recreation very often and was glad to accept his offer. Since it was time to eat, the mother suggested they go out to a restaurant.

"If it's no trouble," Liang Jinsheng, "it would be just as nice to stay home. Do what you ordinarily do. As the poor used to say, just bring out an extra pair of chopsticks and add a little water to the soup."

"This Mayor always strikes just the right note," the mother said.

Liang Jinsheng chuckled. "For cadres today, everything depends on saying the right things." And he sat down to chat with the mother while Ru Yan and her sister prepared lunch. (They did not think it would be quite appropriate, for a guest from so far away, merely to add a little water to the soup.) A peek into the refrigerator led the two women to discuss what dishes they could best manage.

Ru Yan's mother had a lot to discuss with such a fine son-in-law, for, perhaps surprisingly, her connections with the Party and the government went way back. She herself had been a cadre for decades.

Meanwhile the two sisters used their time in the kitchen to exchange confidences. Ru Yan's sister said, "You must have some pretty classy cadres up north. In our part of the country, it's hard to imagine a mayor so young being interested in an older woman who already had a child."

"Sis, how come you're sounding so mean?"

"After 30," she went on without acknowledging Ru Yan's protest, "nobody wants you. The desirable men who've got money and influence go in for . . . what's the current expression? That's right: 'opening a bud.'"

"What do you mean, 'opening a bud'?"

"Means a virgin," the sister explained. "They'll pay a couple thousand to do it to a virgin. Kind of nutty, huh?"

"I'm afraid that sort of thing is not unique to the South," Ru Yan said. "It's everywhere."

She inquired about her brother-in-law. Her sister said it looked as though he'd pull through, but he had been terribly debilitated by his sickness. When she had gone to see him, the hospital administrator had urged her to cheer him up. But when through the double-paned observation window of the isolation ward she glimpsed her husband lying in a bed at the far end of the room, her eyes had filled with tears. Fortunately, he could not see the tears, thanks to all the protective gear that gave her the appearance of an astronaut. She just held up a piece of paper with the words "REST WELL, GET BETTER, WE'RE LOOKING FORWARD TO YOUR COMING HOME," and, underneath, the names of everyone in the family. He had just lifted his hand toward her, she said; she couldn't clearly see his face because most of it was behind a big mask. Before going home, she had scrubbed herself for a long time in the shower at the hospital, crying all the while. She threw out the clothes she had been wearing and changed into a new set she'd brought with her. "In that environment," she explained, "you don't even dare take a step. Like a minefield."

After lunch, her mother wanted to take a nap and suggested that Ru Yan take Liang Jinsheng for a stroll in the botanical garden. "That will count toward our obligations as hosts." The mother thought the botanical garden was the nicest place in Guangzhou, and Ru Yan would be able to teach him to identify a few trees. In addition to its professional interest, she felt that the garden was an oasis of natural vitality in the middle of Guangzhou. Without it, there would have been nothing but the smoky aroma of stir-fried food and the sing-song of the street vendors. Finally, she pointed out that in all Guangzhou it was probably the best spot for courting.

The scene at the botanical garden was already one of early summer, and they wandered there for a long while, hand in hand, chatting like two young people. At times their fingers were lightly entwined like two swans necking; at other times they were tightly clasped; and sometimes Ru Yan gave him only one finger to squeeze gently in his big hand. As the people spoke, their fingers performed a separate drama in their own little world. Ru Yan forgot to teach him any botany.

For dinner, Liang Jinsheng took the family out for what was to all intents and purposes an engagement banquet. He formally asked her mother for Ru Yan's hand, proposing to marry her on May Day of that year, when he hoped her mother would show her approval by being present at the ceremony. Ru Yan couldn't understand how such a straightforward matter became so touching as a result of its formal and ceremonious expression. As she listened to him address her mother with such seriousness, she smiled and felt tears in her eyes.

After dinner, Liang Jinsheng drove Ru Yan's family home but said he had reserved a hotel room for himself. Ru Yan's mother was rather broadminded, however, and said it was fine with her if Ru Yan stayed at the hotel with him.

"Ru Yan doesn't get to see you very often," he replied. "It would be good for her to be with her mother tonight. I'm sure there's a lot to discuss." He appeared to be a past master at the art of winning over a mother-in-law. Ru Yan did have a long talk with her mother that night.

"It was your great good fortune, and mine too, that you met him," her mother said. "You know I've been worried these past few years about dying, but an even bigger concern has been what your life will be like after I'm gone. Tomorrow you may tell him that he has given me a beautiful gift for the Spring Festival."

Three days passed quickly. Liang Jinsheng drew Ru Yan aside and told her that his secretary, worried that something might have happened to him, had been phoning often enough to make his cell phone explode and had left a pile of text messages. Ru Yan asked whether there was a problem in the city.

"Yes, there's a problem."

"What is it?" she asked.

"That disease which has made your brother-in-law so sick? It has spread to our city."

On the day they were leaving, her mother brought out a small jewel box and put it in Ru Yan's hand. "I know this is an awfully conventional thing to do—trite, even," she said, "but just accept it as a token of love."

Ru Yan knew what was in the box: a ring of deep green jade that had been passed down from her great-grandmother. It had to be well over a hundred years old, and there were quite a few stories attached to it. She remembered watching her mother take it out to examine it, one day when Ru Yan had been little and had wanted to put it on her finger, but her mother had not allowed that. "Someday," she had said, "it will be yours."

One could not help feeling sad at the leave-taking; once more they would be far apart, and the visit had been brief. But at least they had seen each other, and she had brought a man whom her mother found satisfactory.

In that evening conversation, Ru Yan had asked her mother what she thought of him.

Her mother had said, "From what I can see, he should be just fine."

"Why do you qualify that with 'from what I can see'?"

"Well, he didn't go chasing after young beauties."

Somewhat impishly, Ru Yan pressed the question: "So *this*

time you approve?"

"It's not for me to approve," her mother said. "What's important is that you approve."

Later, she spoke up suddenly, with a sigh. "Actually, what people call 'approval' is not much more than a temporary mood. All those years married to your father, I was very, very unhappy. How many times I wept! And no one knew. I hated myself for not having resisted his entreaties. But you know in those days a revolutionary cadre was a sacred and heroic figure. I hated myself, also, for getting caught up in the competitive fashion of young women at that time: each strove to marry someone of greater prestige than her friends did. (It's a lot like young women today: *Your apartment is 140, I'd better get one that's 160.*) But as the years went by, I recognized that your father had many good points. This was the man Fate had given me; I said, 'If you don't love and cherish him, you've got nothing.'"

Ru Yan understood that these words were intended for her. She had thought of talking about her late husband with her mother, but feared the subject might make her uncomfortable. Her mother had felt guilty after he died, and (purposefully or not) had spoken about his strong points. She had never done so when he was alive.

Before getting into the car, Ru Yan asked her sister to give her husband some flowers on behalf of herself and Liang Jinsheng. "I really regret," she said, "that we didn't get to see him this time."

"Don't worry," her mother said, "your brother-in-law has a strong constitution and he's knowledgeable about medicine. He'll beat this thing." Then she turned to Liang Jinsheng. "This girl of mine, though in strict fact she's well into her forties, is nonetheless extremely innocent and inexperienced. Doesn't have a calculating bone in her body. She was pretty sheltered, growing up, and lacks the toughness to endure life's blows. In ancient times she would have done OK as a servant in a palace, but in the world of today, she's old-fashioned."[308]

"This," said Liang Jinsheng, "is precisely what I like about her."

44

On the eighth day of the first month[309], Ru Yan, Damo, and Maozi arranged to go to Teacher Wei's house.

Teacher Wei's cold had grown worse. When they arrived, he was still taking his afternoon nap. Zhao Yi said he had had a low fever the previous day; he had taken medicine and this morning the fever had abated, but he was very weak. She had tried to make him go to the hospital, but he had said not until he saw his daughter and granddaughter. Damo said it was better for the mother and her daughter to stay in a hotel, so Teacher Wei could rest. When the time came to meet the plane, Maozi and Ru Yan would go to the airport while Damo arranged accommodations nearby. The three sat there for a while and then left together.

It was the lull at the middle of the New Year's vacation, and the airport was unusually quiet. The plane arrived on time and when they heard the announcement, Maozi dialed Fang Ya's cell phone and reached her. They worked out how to find each other in the airport. A quarter of an hour later, they spotted a mother and her daughter in the distance dragging suitcases toward the exit. Sure enough, it was them. Teacher Wei's daughter did not have the surname Wei but introduced herself formally with the surname Fang and the given name Hongyi. She spoke Mandarin with a Xinjiang accent, and it reminded Ru Yan of Chen Peisi's skit of the kebab-seller.[310] Fang Hongyi looked older than her age, and her face seemed to have been bronzed by the sandstorms and the burning sun of the Northwest. In neither her appearance nor her expression could you see any trace of Teacher Wei. But in Fang Ya, although it was hard to pinpoint, there was some resemblance to her grandfather. Teacher Wei's daughter was taciturn and let Fang Ya do most of the talking.

In the car, Maozi said, "The old man caught cold a few days ago and is not fully recovered. When you meet, you definitely don't want to get him too stirred up; the old fellow couldn't handle that." Teacher Wei's daughter nodded and turned to look out the window. She seemed about to cry. Ru Yan had chosen to sit with the two women in the back seat, and she now hurried to strike up a conversation about Xinjiang, asking how things were out there. It was usually Fang Ya who answered.

As she thought about the impending encounter, after half a century, of a father with his daughter—a daughter who had brought a grown-up granddaughter along—Ru Yan almost wanted to cry herself. She realized she was afraid of what was coming and felt her heart pounding. As the car approached Teacher Wei's home, they all fell silent.

Maozi parked outside the building and helped the two women with their luggage. The four of them went through the entranceway together and walked upstairs without a sound. When Maozi rang the bell, Ru Yan was standing by Fang Hongyi and had gently taken her arm, which was rigid. Fang Ya, the granddaughter, took up the rear.

Damo opened the door for them with a smile. "Come in, we're waiting for you." Ru Yan watched Teacher Wei and his wife welcome the visitors. Teacher Wei said nothing but just looked at the two women, while they looked at him, and nobody knew who should be the first to speak. It was oddly quiet for a while. With a trembling hand, Teacher Wei drew the two photos from his pocket and handed them to his daughter. These were the pictures which, in his grave illness thirty years before, he had been ready to entrust to Damo. His daughter accepted the pictures with one hand, and with the other she drew a single photo from an inside pocket and handed it to Teacher Wei. In the car, Ru Yan had noticed Fang Hongyi repeatedly reaching inside her jacket to check something. The daughter's picture was one that Teacher Wei didn't have. It was a portrait of the whole family of four when she was one year old. He took a look at it and smiled, but then his face became distorted and he cried out, "Oh my babies!" and began to weep. He usually spoke in slightly accented Mandarin, but now, as he let forth this broken-hearted wail, he slipped for a moment into the dialect of Anhui, his voice strangely toneless. His daughter had begun to weep also, and threw herself upon him to embrace him. The rest shed tears in sympathy.

Damo and Maozi had known Teacher Wei for decades, but they had never seen him weep so openly. Even in the bleakest hours he had usually managed a smile. They feared such intense sorrow might be dangerous for his health, but they knew that keeping it locked up inside could also make him sick. In consternation they tugged at the father and daughter, trying to console them, but could not stop them. Sobbing like a child, Teacher Wei told them not to comfort him but to let him cry it out. He stood there for a long time with the mother and her child, weeping to his heart's content. Supporting him by the arms, his friends then led him over to the sofa.

Ru Yan, who was averse to shedding tears in front of people, had gone into the bathroom to weep silently. Then she wiped her eyes and gave her face a quick washing before coming back out to find them all seated.

Teacher Wei heaved a long sigh and murmured, "In all this wretched world, what could be worse? A single tragedy has wounded us twice, across half a hundred years."[311]

Having calmed down, they took out the photos again to study them. The picture Fang Hongyi had brought was a five-by-five bordered print mounted on cardboard, and prettily embossed at the lower right corner with the seal of a well-known local photographer's shop that was still in business. It was a black-and-white picture, slightly yellowed but very clear. In this family of four, the adults were radiant and the children were healthy. Teacher Wei was still wearing an Army uniform, though without insignia.[312] He looked astute and perceptive, in good spirits, perhaps even a little smug. His former wife was in a close-fitting Lenin suit, the kind with a double line of buttons and always worn with a belt. She was dignified, serene, and very beautiful, with a refinement that was not common among female cadres in those days. A boy about three years old, presumably Teacher Wei's son (with a mischievous look, and features that greatly resembled his), was leaning against his legs in a sailor suit, wearing a big navy hat with streamers. The wife was holding their daughter in her arms. The baby had a round face and big eyes, and gazed innocently at the camera.

Fang Hongyi said her mother had given her this picture two days before she died, and until then she hadn't even known she had such a father. Her stepfather was still alive, at that point, and Mama had said, don't let him know.

"When did your Mama die?" Teacher Wei asked.

"1968," his daughter said.

"How did she die?"

"Suicide."

The conversation had gradually entered the zone of a family's most private affairs. Damo stood up: "You know, the rest of us can step out now; we need to make dinner reservations. . ."

Teacher Wei understood and insisted, "You all may hear this. These are not family secrets. Anyway, why should I keep my troubles secret from *you*?"

Fang Hongyi told them what she knew. When she had been very young, they had lived in many different places of which she had no distinct recollection, because they had always kept moving. She had been three or four by the time they reached Xinjiang, and that was the first place she clearly remembered.

Teacher Wei said that on his release from prison he had inquired into their whereabouts. At his former wife's work unit they said she had been transferred to another part of the country. He asked where they had gone. They went to help build up the Northwest, he was told. When he asked where, exactly, he was told it might have been Lanzhou but the transfers had been done in large groups and there was no telling what specific work unit she might have ended up in. Then the man giving him this information had added, "You don't want to keep looking into this. You got divorced; you should leave her alone." Teacher Wei had protested that the children were still his children. But the man had said, "If you really care about your children, you won't try to find them."

His daughter recalled that her mother had been an instructor; she had trained teachers and then she had taught high school. On their arrival in Xinjiang, she and her brother acquired a father. When they got off the train a man was there to meet them at the station. Mama had told them, "This is your father. He's spent the last few years fighting the American Imperialists in Korea. He's a war hero, but now that the fighting's over, he's come back."

Her brother had been skeptical, and whispered to his mother, "Papa isn't like this. Papa doesn't have a scar on his face."

The mother had said, "Yes, it's your father. He got wounded when he was fighting the American Imperialists."

"How come he doesn't look like Papa?" the boy had asked. "Papa's voice was different."

Once, the stepfather for some reason gave her brother a thrashing, and her brother declared through his tears, "You're not our Papa. Our Papa doesn't beat people." And she had screamed, "You're not our Papa. You're mean." Mama found out when she came home, and she beat both of them as she wept, and said, "If you ever say anything like that again, I'll throw you into the desert and let the wolves eat you."

So they had never talked about this again.

Their stepfather was a veteran who had seen more than ten years of combat. At the time of Liberation he had come to Xinjiang with the Army and he stayed on as a civilian. He was an administrative section chief responsible for the motor pool and the food service in a large organization. He'd often take the kids out driving. During the years of hardship[313], he always brought home something to eat. At that time you couldn't get any rice in Xinjiang, but he always provided them with white rice to eat. When he wasn't drinking, he was good to Mama, and he was good to the children too. When he drank he liked to beat Mama. Later—before she killed herself—Mama told them that he had been wounded and couldn't have children, and that's why the black moods seized him sometimes: "You mustn't hate him." Fang Hongyi was fifteen: she was beginning to understand things a little, and felt sorry for her mother. It felt strange when Mama told her about this because Mama had never been one to discuss these things with the children, especially not her own private affairs. And then, a couple of days later, she died.

For years, the mother had never sat down to discuss anything with them. That night Fang Hongyi had already gone to sleep when her mother came and sat by her bedside. After a while, her mother called the brother in and spoke to them for a long time. That was when she gave Fang Hongyi the family portrait. The reason she didn't give it to her brother was that, as the boy had grown, his relationship with his mother had deteriorated and they were always at odds with each other. When Fang Hongyi had been very little, her brother had more than once told her secretly that he thought Mama was a spy. The stepfather was a spy too, he said. "Mama must be hiding something from us," he said. What frightened her most was the time her brother had blurted, "I wonder if Mama secretly murdered our Papa? And then she came to Xinjiang to make contact with this spy who is our stepfather." In any case, her brother had been given to fantasizing and as a child he was often in his own world. Later he recorded his thoughts furtively in journals he wouldn't let anyone read. He kept them in a hiding place. After he killed himself, she had managed to find them, but only after a long time.

Teacher Wei asked why the mother had killed herself.

His daughter said, "For a long time I didn't know why. I only heard the people on the Special Investigation Team say she had killed herself to escape punishment, cutting herself off from the Party and the People. My stepfather didn't say. To us her suicide came as a bolt from the blue. At school, my brother and I were conscious of being the children of revolutionary cadres, and when the C.R. began, we both were Red Guards. At her school, Mama was not subjected to many attacks because her revolutionary credentials were pretty good, and she wasn't with the faction that had been in power. Indeed, the Red Guards made her deputy director of the Revolutionary Committee. She was very dedicated, busy night and day, and it bothered our stepfather. I heard them quarreling a few times, and he'd say, "What's with these parades, these meetings, these struggle sessions? You can't eat them. When I was fighting the war, I still got to eat!" Mama wouldn't say anything; she'd just hurry to cook something. My stepfather never cooked—he *managed* the food service. But later, when things got chaotic, his mess hall stopped serving meals. Mama then taught me to cook. When she was out late, I would cook for the whole family.

"In '68 there came the push to 'cleanse the ranks of the Party'.[314] They found out that Mama had a younger brother who had been a military officer for the Kuomintang and had fled to Taiwan. She had never told anyone this, not even after she joined the Revolution."

Teacher Wei said, "Not even I ever heard about this."

"So the cleansers of the ranks went to the place she had been born," the daughter continued, "and they made inquiries and she was found out. At the start of the war against Japan, Mama's whole family had left their native place. Her parents wandered about in desperate straits and got sick and died, one after the other. The brothers and sisters all got scattered. In Jiangxi, Mama entered a training program for battlefield nurses, and later a Communist Party member she met there got her into the New Fourth Army[315]—"

"This I know," said Teacher Wei.

"Mama's little brother," his daughter continued, "was my uncle who would later go to Taiwan. He was the youngest in the family. He lived for a while with an acquaintance in Chengdu, and then he got into the military academy there, graduating after less than a year of study; and upon graduation, he went to the front. When they finished fighting the Japanese, they started fighting each other in the Civil War, and the losers went to Taiwan. Mama didn't learn of his whereabouts till just before Liberation, because she had lost touch with him, but she managed to meet with him once, somewhere. She never mentioned him after that. Even the rest of the family didn't know. But a few days before the Special Investigation Team went to her hometown to do a background check, it so happened that someone who had been my uncle's classmate at the military academy was also being investigated, and the two investigation teams ran into each other in Mama's home town and started comparing notes. If that team had come through just a couple of days later, or a couple of days earlier, she would have gotten away with it.

"When they called her in for questioning and mentioned my uncle's name, she knew she was finished. She agreed immediately to write an account of everything. Actually, by that time she had prepared herself to check out for the last time. You see, there was more: they said while she had been training to become a battlefield nurse, she had joined the *San Qing Tuan*.[316] This, too, she had concealed from the Party."

Teacher Wei heaved a sigh. "When she divorced me at the first sign of trouble and hurried away from this part of the country, leaving no traces . . . this must be why."

Fang Hongyi said, "And there was also your case, as the Special Investigation Team pointed out to her."

"Given your Mama's character, all this spelt certain death. She was so eager to shine, and yet too fragile."

And then, having a little trouble with the words, he asked how she had died.

"Under a train," Fang Hongyi said. "She left a note beside the tracks. It said that although even death could not expunge her guilt, her husband and children were not implicated, they didn't know anything about it. No, she said we loved Chairman Mao and we loved the Party. She had duped us."

Around them stood gorgeous potted flowers, elegant greeting cards, candy of all colors, and bright bunting, as well as the propitious figurine of a big white sheep which Ru Yan had brought as a gift.[317]

"Do you still remember the name you had when you were little?" Teacher Wei asked.

"No, I don't know what it was."

"You were called Wei Lan. Lan[318] like the azure sky, the azure sea. We both called you Lan-Lan. This name of yours summed up our frame of mind at that time."

"Lan-Lan," his daughter said, "I heard Mama call me that when I was young."

Teacher Wei said, "Your brother was named Ge. The Dove that defends peace. When your brother was born, the second round of the World Congress to Defend Peace had just been convened, and they had issued a set of postage stamps, with designs by Picasso of that famous dove of Peace.[319]"

Damo said he remembered those stamps. They were triangular, and the set consisted of three stamps. He had once made an album of cardboard and cellophane, and he remembered putting those particular stamps on the first page. They all had the same design, a sturdy dove with its wings outspread, but the three stamps were of different colors. Alas, the stamps had been lost along with the album, he didn't know when.

Teacher Wei finally asked about his son.

His daughter said, "Not long after Mama died, Elder Brother died too, also by suicide. He was very introverted. After he killed himself, he left behind quite a few diaries, and I brought them with me today. He was secretly very fond of a girl in the family of one of our neighbors, though he never breathed a word of it to her, expressing his feelings only in his diary. After what happened to Mama, he completely lost heart. I kept these diaries and never told anyone about them. I read them once, back then, but never looked at them again."

Such was the tale of woe and horror which this halting dialogue between father and daughter had brought to light after so many years.

"Within the space of a month," she said, "I lost the two people who were closest to me, and I had finally learned, from Mama herself, that the man who she had long insisted was my father was not, in fact, my biological father. I became like an imbecile, not knowing who I was or where I came from, living alone in a somber, clammy house with a man who had suddenly become a stranger. The thought came to me more than once that it would be better to die.

"But my stepfather started being very good to me. The day after Elder Brother died, he waited for me to fall asleep and felt his way into the dark room to my bed. I thought he was going to do something bad, and I shuddered under the blanket, but he just pulled up a chair and quietly sat beside my bed, and stayed till dawn. This happened for quite a few nights, every night. I realized he was afraid something might happen to me. Eventually there was one night when I couldn't stand it, I felt such pain in my heart and I didn't dare make a move, so I spoke to him. I said, 'Dad, go to bed. I'm all right.' I heard him sob in the darkness. 'Swear to me,' he said, 'You must swear. . .' I began crying, and said, 'I swear.'

"But if, later, I did not go down that path, I know there was another reason as well: there was something I really wanted. I wanted to locate my ancestral home and know who my father was. This thought only grew stronger as the years went by, especially after my stepfather died. . . But a fear also grew, for I didn't know whether I could bear this day if it should ever come. When my daughter came home for winter vacation this time, she said she had met her great-uncle in Beijing, and that he didn't have time to come to Xinjiang and was getting on in years. It's enough that *you* saw him, I said. And then she asked me whether she still had a grandfather on my side of the family, a biological grandfather? Now I had never discussed my family's history with the child. I thought this part of the past was buried in the hearts of my generation and we would take it with us to the grave. I never dreamed this kid would bring it up herself. The day she told me she had been in contact with her grandfather I was shaken, as if someone had whacked me over the head, and I hated her for meddling in this. . ."

Fang Ya said her great-uncle had been discharged from the Army after reaching Taiwan. He then enrolled in college and even went to grad school and earned a Ph.D. in America, and then came back to Taiwan to teach. "He used his contacts to track us down in '84 when things were pretty grim for Mama and me, and he's helped us financially ever since. He encouraged me to go abroad for further study once I finish college. This past December I went to see him at his hotel when he came to Beijing for some conference. Out of nowhere he said he'd picked up a book in Hong Kong written by somebody named 'This Wei.' When he read the dust jacket he saw the author's real name was Wei Liwen. 'It brought back to me,' he said, 'the last time I saw your maternal grandmother. She told me she had married a Communist Party cadre named Wei Liwen. She said he was a cultured man who had written articles under the pen-name "This Wen." And she said, "If the Nationalists and the Communists turn against each other, you and I won't be able to stay in touch; we'll have to pretend we don't know each other." That was in '47, the last time we met. In '84 I knew she had been divorced from your grandfather. I never imagined that a couple of decades later I'd be reading his book.'"

Seeing that Teacher Wei and the two women had regained their composure, Zhao Yi invited everyone to have something to eat and to drink some tea.

Teacher Wei asked his daughter what kind of work she did now.

"I didn't get a good education," she began. "After high school, since my stepfather was in the bureau supervising commercial enterprises, I got a job as a salesperson in a department store. The store folded in '87, years after my stepfather had passed away. Fang Ya was only three or four years old, and when my uncle learned of the situation he helped me with some money. Part of it I set aside for the child's education, and part of it I used to open a gift shop for tourists, as well as getting into the restaurant business. Sometimes these ventures worked out, and sometimes they didn't. My health isn't so good, now, and I can't manage the business very well. I'm barely getting by. Fang Ya, on the other hand, has done really well in her education, something I never dreamed would happen. I think Heaven has looked after us."

"And Fang Ya's father?" Teacher Wei inquired.

"He cut and ran when she was one year old. And once he left, he never took any interest in the child. Don't even know where he went."

"And you didn't remarry?" Teacher Wei remarked.

"Who would even have thought of it!" she said, "especially since I was saddled with a child."

Zhao Yi asked Fang Ya what she was majoring in.

"Philosophy," Fang Ya said.

Maozi was startled. "In this day and age, a girl who freely chooses to major in Philosophy is as rare as an extraterrestrial life-form."

"But look," Teacher Wei said, "you came here and you've run into two and a half people from the same discipline."

"What?" she asked. "Who are the two and a half?"

Teacher Wei pointed to Maozi. "There's one. A Fellow of the Philosophy Institute." Then he pointed to Damo. "And there's another: an expert in unofficial philosophy, yes, the genuine article." Finally he pointed to himself: "Here's the half. When I was in college, I too studied in the Philosophy Department. Did you ever guess that one day you'd run into your grandfather and he'd turn out to have followed the same branch of study?"

Fang Ya said, "When I first saw you, you looked familiar. Then I remembered: I've seen you many times—it's true!—in my dreams."

Fang Hongyi said "There's no telling what this kid will come out with. Even as a child, she always had an active imagination."

Fang Ya said, "No, it's true; in my last years in high school I had this dream."

Something had finally brought a smile to Teacher Wei's face. "So tell me, in your dream did I say I was your grandfather?"

"No," she said, "but I could feel that that's who you were."

This made him happy. "I would like to believe that. I'll tell you something: it must have been when I was thinking about you and your mother that I found my way into your dreams."

"She loved to read," Fang Hongyi said. "Any books at all. To tell you the truth, there wasn't anybody educated in the family and we didn't have any books, so she had to get them from outside."

"Maybe I came to her in her dreams in order to be her teacher," the old man said.

"When she was seven or eight," her mother continued, "she stole a book."

Fang Ya protested, "I swiped it only because they wouldn't lend it to me."

"In any case, I remember having to deal with the owner's mother. But you know," Fang Hongyi mused, "the child was not so studious when it came to schoolwork, yet somehow she always got good grades. I never had to worry about that, though at first I thought I'd have to."

The conversation had subsided into a calm and ordinary chat, even as evening fell. Damo spoke up, "We should head out to dinner, and we can keep talking while we eat."

With some diffidence, Fang Hongyi said, "We brought with us a little food in the Xinjiang style. Let me cook it for you. I started cooking when I was pretty young, and later when I opened a restaurant I was in the kitchen all day. When this occasion came along, I thought, I've got to fix something nice for you and Zhao Yi . . . a sign of filial respect—and to think it's the first time I've ever done it!"

"Mama," Fang Ya informed them, "is an excellent cook. It'll be better than anything we'd get in a restaurant."

"Very good," Teacher Wei agreed. "I'll finally get to eat something my daughter has cooked."

Zhao Yi said that would be fine. "I'll give you a hand, so you can let your Dad taste his daughter's cooking. More than eighty years old, and it's the first time he'll know that blessing." She led her into the kitchen to check whether she needed any utensils or seasonings.

It seemed that this long-delayed encounter had now got past its most difficult phase, and Damo and the others felt more at ease. There had been a catharsis in the telling of this harrowing tale. Teacher Wei breathed a few long sighs, as if he had finally spat out something that had been making him ill for half a century. It was the first time Ru Yan had ever heard such a tragedy, and it gave her tremors as if she had been watching a particularly bloody surgery.

In a little while Fang Hongyi was smartly serving the dishes.

On the broad highlands of the Northwest, the diet is a hearty one, and the first course was the pulled mutton that everyone has heard about. There were no large plates in Teacher Wei's house, so Fang Hongyi had piled up the meat in Zhao Yi's kneading bowl and brought it in as if on a tray. Of the company, only Maozi (who was familiar with Xinjiang cuisine from restaurants in Beijing) had ever seen this dish. The mutton was prepared with stark simplicity, white and clean on the bone with no flourishes, each piece about the size of an ice-cream stick. It looked unfinished, accompanied by only a couple of side dishes holding spiced salt and raw garlic. Next came the big-plate Shawan chicken, which by contrast was colorful and elaborately garnished: green with parsley, red with peppers, yellow with cumin, and strikingly pungent. Quickly the air of the room was filled with the untamed aromas of the tribes that wander the vast Northwest. Fang Hongyi said the mutton had been boiled the day before and only needed to be heated up; it was too bad she couldn't have brought the water it had been cooked in, which made for a flavorful broth.

Those two dishes would have been enough for the entire table. But now she brought in stuffed sausages, steamed bread, and golden crusty pancakes, big pancakes that had not been cut up, so Fang Hongyi told everyone to eat them with their hands. "That's enough!" Zhao Yi exclaimed, and urged Fang Hongyi to come and sit down.

While the others rose to wash their hands, Damo couldn't wait and helped himself to a kebab of the mutton, dipped it in the spiced salt, and started chewing. "Superb!" he cried, "Now *this* is mutton!" Inspired by Damo's enthusiasm, Ru Yan reached for a piece and tried it. As a rule, she did not eat this kind of gamey food, but she found that not only was it free from the unpleasant taste she expected, it even prompted a vision of our prehistoric ancestors who lived under the sky, stewing just such chunks of meat as they huddled round their campfires.

"I brought a bottle of premium Daqu from Xinjiang[320], if anyone's interested in drinking," Fang Hongyi said.

"Sure, let's drink!" said Maozi and the others. "How could we not, on such a special day?"

So she opened the bottle and poured each person a shot, but for herself she took a big cup and filled it to the brim. She stood before Teacher Wei and cried, "Dad, I salute you! On my way here, I remember thinking this was an occasion that called for getting drunk." And she drained the whole cup in a couple of drafts.

Although Teacher Wei was not a drinker, for this occasion he downed his shot glass in a single draft. They all scrambled to their feet and drank a toast to this reunion of three generations.

Teacher Wei said, "One tragedy, a half-century, three generations; and twice the rending of our hearts. Had you not come, I would have wrongly condemned your mother forever. At first, when she spirited you and your brother far away (he was three, you were one), and you all disappeared without a trace, I hated her for it; I felt sure this was the cruelest, most cold-blooded woman in the world. But now it's fairly clear she was terribly, terribly afraid. Disaster menaced her nest; she seized the two fledglings and ran, aiming to get as far away as possible so that they might live, no matter how bad it made her seem. She suffered as much as I. Alas, in the end she could not outrun death, a violent death. What can you say, oh, what can you say?"

Fang Hongyi spoke. "Mama was rehabilitated in '79. Only then did people learn that she had been one of the first revolutionaries, having joined the New Fourth Army as early as 1940. She had more standing than the top directors where she worked."

"I have to ask myself now," Teacher Wei said, "Whatever mistakes or wrongs your mother may have committed in her life, why did she have to pay such a price? You could say, one fault was the *San Qing Tuan*, and the other was staying mum about her brother. The first was just one of those choices a person makes, and you must see it against the background of the collaboration which, at that time, united the Nationalists and the Communists: just as, in America, you might vote for the Democrats today and side with the Republicans tomorrow. As for your uncle, remember that your mother went to the front line to succor wounded soldiers. She was not afraid of death. Why would she have run the risk of concealing this matter and endured such enormous psychological pressure if it weren't for that feudal policy of guilt by association?"

Fang Hongyi said, "When he first came back in '84, my uncle was already well-known in academic circles on Taiwan and had influence with the authorities there. Officials on our side, all up and down the line, received him as an honored guest. We turned into special people who had relatives on Taiwan, and received special treatment: they invited me each year to attend the meeting of the Association for Ties of Friendship with our Taiwan Compatriots. I thought, all those years Mama carried on the Revolution and I never received any honor for that! When my uncle came, he said, 'I had no idea your mother died on account of me. And now I'm a V.I.P. visiting the mainland, so many years after your mother was hounded to her death.'"

Teacher Wei poured himself another drink. "Let us raise this glass in honor of your mother and her memory."

Though she had drunk heavily of the strong liquor, Fang Hongyi was not in the least tipsy, just a bit more talkative, with more expansive gestures than before: she was, after all, a woman of the Northwest who had spent years in the restaurant business. So she poured herself a little more and drank the toast with her father.

Ru Yan was seated beside Fang Ya and they exchanged a few private remarks during the lulls in the conversation. "What led you to study philosophy?" Ru Yan asked her.

"Maybe it was the atmosphere in our family, something in the air that was conducive to philosophy . . ."

"What kind of atmosphere was that?"

"Even when I was very young," Fang Ya answered, "I could feel an air of secrecy in our family. As if there was something in the background, something hidden that I could not see. So many events whose cause and effect were mysterious, but you wanted to figure them out . . . doesn't this have something to do with philosophy?" She smiled and added, "The same curiosity that leads people to natural science can also lead to philosophy."

"What would you like to do after graduation?" Ru Yan asked.

"I'd like to study psychology," the young woman said, "I'd like to go to Harvard to study psychology. Then come back and do research into Chinese psychology. Just now, as I listened to them talk about those events of the past, I felt even more strongly drawn to that plan."

Damo asked Teacher Wei, "Before Fang Hongyi's mother

went away, did she leave a letter or a note for you?"

"There was nothing," Teacher Wei said. "Anything in the house that had any connection to me was gone, destroyed. But a number of things that were worth some money were still there. She hadn't taken them with her, nor had she tried to sell them. A camera, a wristwatch, clothes, some calligraphy I had collected, as well as some furniture that was quite good by the standards of the time: they were all still there. (Later, after I had been sentenced to labor in the countryside, someone else was assigned my apartment and I don't know what became of those things.) What I regretted most is that all my books were gone. Those two photographs, however, had been left in a pocket of my suit and when I got sent away I kept them with me. I think at that point she had become indifferent to money. All she had left was fear."

"Fear," he sighed, "fear. . . A people that is not afraid to suffer, that is not afraid of hardship, or famine, or freezing cold—yet some nameless fear grips every heart. This is the horror of it! Even now as they eat their fill, clad in soft garments, the fear at their very core has by no means left them. The poor man knows the poor man's fear, and the rich know the fear of the rich; those who count for nothing feel the fear that is proper to those who count for nothing, while the mighty suffer their own kind of fear; writers endure the fear that comes with writing, and those who read them taste the fear of being readers. Why else would so many go abroad? During the war of resistance against Japan, how many gave up lives of luxury in Malaysia, Europe, and America to rush back across the ocean to the aid of their country, to fight or to teach! You see, in *their* hearts there was no fear, only a hatred of the enemy and a noble exaltation."

Damo remembered how Maozi had once teetered on the edge of madness, and recalled the choking sobs that had made his friend sound like an animal.

It had all been too much for Teacher Wei, too much talk and excitement. He had drunk more than was good for him and looked abnormally pale except for his cheekbones and eyelids, which were flushed with an unnatural beauty as if he had suddenly become much younger.

Zhao Yi had been eyeing him quietly and when he became too voluble she had been gently changing the subject so he would pause and catch his breath. Seeing that everyone had now almost finished eating and drinking, she turned to Fang Hongyi and her daughter and said, "You had a long flight and you must be tired. I know there's a lot to talk about, but there will be time to discuss things in the next few days. Tonight you should turn in early and get some rest." Then she asked whether they wanted to stay in a hotel or remain at their house.

"We'd like to stay here, in your home," Fang Hongyi said. "After all these years, it's the first time I've been able to stay with my own family."

Maozi had been taking pictures of everyone and now he suggested that Teacher Wei should use the next couple of days to take the ladies out sightseeing.

Teacher Wei said, "I'd like to take them to see the old house where we used to live. Before it gets torn down."

When they left to go home, Damo and his friends rode in silence.

45

The next day, Maozi drove Teacher Wei's family of four to the building that had been his home in the 1950s.

His former home was in the old quarter of town, on a back street that was an oasis of calm amid the din of the city. Once, rich people had lived on this street; it had been what today we would call an upscale neighborhood. The houses were all in good taste, and over the lintels of some there was still carved the date of construction: 1904, for example, or 1923. Almost a century had passed and the street had gone to seed. Many a ground floor had been turned into a storefront and served as an eatery or a small shop or the office of some tiny company. They were haphazardly decorated, like an old woman who wears gaudy clothes that don't quite match.

Following Teacher Wei's directions, they parked in front of a little brownstone[321] that combined the Chinese and Western styles. Pointing to it, Teacher Wei told Fang Hongyi, "You were born here. Your brother was also born here. Originally, this building belonged to a member of the Kuomintang. When we took over the city, there were many empty houses like this; their owners had all fled, leaving behind lots of furniture, sometimes a piano. I married your mother in 1947 but we didn't spend much time together and it was only after the takeover that we had our own home. At first we lived upstairs, but when you two came along we were afraid you'd fall out a window and we moved downstairs. Then we worried that your brother might run out into the street, so we installed a half-height grille at the front door. A child could see outside but couldn't get out. In back, there's a little courtyard with two scholar trees that in spring brought forth great bunches of white blossoms. Beneath the trees there was a stone table with benches. You could eat there in summer and relax in the shade."

Fang Hongyi said she'd like to go in and look around. They pressed the buzzer at the tightly-shut security gate, and after a long wait the door was partially opened by a middle-aged lady who asked, suspiciously, "Who do you want?"

Teacher Wei stepped forward. "We used to live here once. Would you mind if we came in and looked around?"

"You lived here?" the lady said. "Why don't I know you?"

"We moved out in '55," he explained.

"Fifty-five?" she said. "Way back when, huh?"

"Yes," Teacher Wei said, "It was a long time ago."

The lady who lived there now took a good look at this group that included both old and young and decided they did not represent a threat. She relaxed a little and asked them what they wanted to see.

Fang Hongyi answered, "We just want to have a look at the rooms where we used to live."

After a pause the lady said reluctantly, "You want to look, OK, take a look." She stepped back to let them come in.

It was a two-story house and on entering they found themselves in what had once been a traditional Chinese reception hall. It had now been subdivided into several small rooms, each of which served as the kitchen for one of the tenant families, but it still had the original floor (insofar as you could make it out through a layer of grime), terrazzo inlaid with a copper floral design. Three families now lived on the ground floor, and another three upstairs. Teacher Wei pointed to one of the rooms and said, "This is where you and your brother were, and you had a live-in nursemaid." It happened to belong, now, to the middle-aged woman and she stood inside with no intention of inviting them in, so the best they could do was crane their necks a bit and get a view from the doorway. The doors and windows and walls of this apartment were all unchanged from the old days; only the floor had been worn uneven, and it had been repaired with a few extra planks. Pointing out two other rooms whose doors were closed, Teacher Wei said, "This room was the bedroom for your mother and me, and that room was my study."

He asked the lady whether the little courtyard was still behind the house.

"What little courtyard?" she asked. "In back, there's just another house."

Sure enough, the door that had opened onto the courtyard had long since been bricked up.

Maozi took a picture of Teacher Wei standing in front of the house with his family. Then he gave them a tour around the city, before taking them out to the suburbs to see a famous temple. Fang Hongyi said she wanted to light incense for her mother and say a prayer to Kuan-Yin that her mother might be granted a speedy return to her native place.[322]

Teacher Wei asked where her mother was buried.

"Because she had killed herself to evade punishment," Fang Hongyi said, "her ashes were quickly buried in undeveloped land on the outskirts of town and they dropped a few rocks to serve as a tombstone. One year I went back to visit and found the place had been developed into farmland. When my stepfather passed away, I bought a plot sized for a couple and in the grave for my mother I buried a few pebbles I had picked up at the place where she had been laid. I found someone to carve her name on the headstone."

In this wide-ranging conversation, a number of past events had gradually become clear.

Whenever they got out of the car to walk, Fang Ya stood beside Teacher Wei so that he could take her arm. He said, "When your Zhao Yi and I got married, I used to joke with her that we should have a child together, a daughter. Eventually, when I wasn't able to walk, I would be able to lean on her like a little walking stick. It came true, you see: my little walking stick."

Fang Hongyi and her daughter stayed with Teacher Wei for a week. Fang Ya would be resuming school, and Fang Hongyi also needed to get back. On the day they were to leave, Damo and the others came to help Teacher Wei see them off. Teacher Wei became very sad and his eyes filled with tears. "At my age," he said, "I can't help but think of death."

Damo tried to cheer him: "I started thinking of death when I turned fifty. And who knows whether I'll make it to your age?"[323]

"Yes," Teacher Wei nodded, "There are some things about which you can think clearly only when you are facing death. Those who do evil are invariably convinced they will live forever."

Fang Hongyi said, "Dad, I never foresaw that I'd have this chance to see you, and you know, you are still in very good health."

"To have seen you," he said, "and to have learned your mother's fate, fulfilled one of my deepest wishes. . . These last few nights I've been talking with your Zhao Yi; I wonder whether you two would be willing to come back for good?"

"That would be fantastic," Fang Ya said. "When I'm on vacation I'll chat with my grandfather every day and serve as his little walking stick."

Fang Hongyi smiled guardedly and said after a pause, "I've spent my whole life out West; I don't know if I could get used to things here. . . And my business, small though it may be, is back there. I have no other skills. To you, I am a daughter. Back there, everyone calls me 'Ma'am.'"

Fang Ya said, "You could open the same kind of business here, and it would be their first taste of authentic Xinjiang cuisine."

"Go back West and think about it," Teacher Wei said. "Any time you want it, you have a home here." He went into his bedroom and did not come out again.

Fang Hongyi turned toward his room and called in a loud voice, "Dad! We're going, but we'll come see you again!" Wiping her eyes, she walked out the front door.

Ru Yan and Maozi, who had picked them up at the airport, would now drive them there to see them off. After saying goodbye, Damo and Zhao Yi went back inside, opened the door to the bedroom, and saw Teacher Wei standing by the window and watching the car recede into the distance.

Fearing that the emotions of parting had been too much for him, Zhao Yi let Damo sit with him for a while. Damo said, "You've written so many articles that covered so much ground . . . did you ever think to write the story of your own life? What has happened to you is of no small moment."

"I wouldn't dare," Teacher Wei said. "Yes, I thought of it, but I knew if I tried I couldn't bear it; it would be tantamount to reliving it all. I am aware that China has many such stories, graven in the heart and etched in the bones, but the people who lived them have taken their stories with them to the grave. And those that are written down are written, for the most part, by people far removed from the experience." He pointed to his wife. "Your Zhao Yi, for instance: so gentle, so mild. Most would look at her and say, here's someone who knows how to live a peaceful, happy life. Yet she could tell you things about herself and her family that would grieve heaven and earth."

Zhao Yi smiled faintly to cover a flicker of pain.

"There's so much in China's past that no one can bear to remember," Teacher Wei continued. "The perpetrators don't speak of these things, for they have skeletons in their closet. The victims don't talk about them either, perhaps because it hurts too much, or because the perpetrators don't let them. The years pass, and history gets covered up until the next tragedy . . . down through the decades, the centuries, the millennia . . . over and over again."

He coughed more and more as he spoke.

"He's got to see a doctor," Damo said.

Zhao Yi said, "These last few days he's been caught up in the excitement of the visit and he was taking a cough-suppressant during the day. Now the children are gone, and the cough has returned."

The next day he went to the hospital and was seen immediately.

46

The unknown and increasingly terrifying disease eventually acquired a name whose obscurity reflected the peculiar genius of the Chinese language: *atypical pneumonia*, abbreviated as *feidian*, "the atyp."[324] Many of the common people felt relieved to hear this was its name. Even real pneumonia, they reasoned, was no longer an incurable disease, so how bad could an atypical form of it be? At that time, no one had an inkling that this ungainly term would become, for the better part of a year, one of the most frequently used words in the Chinese-speaking world, and that people would blanch when they heard it.[325]

Overseas, it was called SARS, rendered in Chinese as *sa-si* and meaning Severe Acute Respiratory Syndrome. But only after a long spell of evasion and secretiveness did the mainland media mention this name.

The odd thing was that both '*feidian*' and 'SARS', as soon as they came into use, became proscribed vocabulary on the forum. Any post containing them would be detected and automatically blocked by a software monitoring system. Users found ways to camouflage their messages. The disease came to be denoted as 'flying point' , 'boiling point', 'using a lot of electricity', 'worn-out mattress'; or as 'murder', 'scatter to death', 'incredibly stupid' . . . all that mattered was that people could figure it out.[326] The surveillance of the Internet has honed people's ability to decipher the intended meaning of muddled Chinese compounds. Unfortunately, this trick doesn't work against a human censor.

Many of the participants of the Empty Nest had access to news from abroad, in some cases because they were living there, so messages about SARS were constantly being posted, deleted, and re-posted. The atmosphere quickly became rather tense. Some reproached the moderators for deleting posts that concerned a matter of life and death. Others came to their defense, saying it wasn't the moderators' fault: *their* posts had been deleted, too. But then someone else chimed in, `So they deleted some of their own posts; you gonna fall for that trick?`

Another commenter said, `At a time like this, we ought to listen to the government and not make things more difficult for them.` The rejoinder: `All these years we've been listening to the government, and how many times have they told the truth? Haven't we common people suffered enough at the hands of the government?`

But a different view was: `If we go on like this, our forum may not survive. Those who are shooting their mouths off don't understand the real world.` Yet others replied: `It wasn't easy to set up a place where people can tell the truth. If we don't allow ourselves to use it that way, what good is it? Might as well go read` *`People's Daily`*`.`

As people worked themselves up, their language grew rough. Some of these disputes were carried on with real names, or the net names that were familiar to everyone; others with temporary pseudonyms. The smell of gunpowder grew strong. Ru Yan was never one to equivocate, and as the one who had touched off this whole argument she naturally left no doubt as to her own views. Lonely Goose never said anything directly but was always trying to defuse the tension and make peace. As she put it, she was the master bricklayer, doing her best to hold it all together.

Not long after, a Southern newspaper finally confirmed "rumors" about this disease, which greatly heartened one of the two factions in the forum, whose partisans redoubled their efforts to get to the bottom of this mystery, relaying news items and writing their own posts.[327] But a few days later, that newspaper was forbidden to cover the story any further, and it was even said that people were being arrested for starting or spreading rumors. A few days more, and senior figures in the government were coming out with the most solemn assurances. Experts even declared that this was a perfectly ordinary sickness, you didn't even have to go to the hospital. But the news from overseas was that the virus had not yet been isolated and in the absence of an effective cure, everything depended on the patient's immune system . . . which is to say, everything depended on your luck.

Since the medical facts were complicated and confusing and seemed to change from one day to the next, the climate of opinion on the forum was also quite mutable. But in the end, the problem took on an international character. Many who were scheduled to come weren't coming anymore, and many who needed to go were not allowed to go. Many events were canceled, and lots of business was lost. What had begun as a medical problem now became a global political problem. On countless internet forums, people made their voices heard in defiance of the deletion of their posts and threats to shut down their sites. Faced with any issue, Chinese have a tradition of dividing into factions; and in the first stage of SARS, when the government had not yet declared its position, every forum appeared split into hostile camps.

47

Liang Jinsheng practically disappeared after they returned from Guangzhou. Not a single phone call. Considering that they had taken a long trip together, that their relationship had been clarified, that he had been presented to her mother, that they had drunk the cup of betrothal and even fixed a date for the wedding . . . Ru Yan missed him now. She tried to phone him a few times but couldn't get through; of course he was busy, but she had a forsaken feeling all the same. But then at three or four in the afternoon on the day before the Lantern Festival[328], as the New Year's season was coming to an end, Liang Jinsheng suddenly showed up downstairs.

"Won't you come up?" Ru Yan asked happily. "You're not going to say you don't have time!"

"You come down," he said over the intercom.

"Why?" she asked.

"I have to take you out for a meal. Otherwise I'd be a moocher."

Ru Yan saw it was a little after four. "Is it time to eat?"

"It's the only time I've got."

Since he was insistent, there was nothing for it but to change and head down. She worked up her courage to finally wear the outfit Jiang Xiaoli had taken her to buy. *It cost me a few thousand yuan*, she thought, *I'd better wear it. Roll the dice.*

His face lit up at the sight of her. "A delight to the mind and a joy to the eye," he said archly.

"This," Ru Yan explained, "is Jiang Xiaoli's masterpiece."

"What a conscientious matchmaker!" he remarked. "She helps you onto a horse and then stays with you for the first mile."

Approaching the car, she discovered that his driver sat behind the wheel, the same man who had brought her the dumplings. She wondered if perhaps she was dressed a little provocatively. Evidently the Mayor was no longer trying to hide anything. All she could do was slide into the back seat beside him. "This is Master Luo," Liang Jinsheng said.[329]

"We've met," she said.

Liang Jinsheng wrote a phone number on a piece of paper and handed it to her. "From now on, if you can't reach me, call Master Luo. Sometimes I have to turn off my phone." He took her hand and held onto it. Nervously she glanced at the rear-view mirror and saw it had been flipped down.

As they rode through town, Liang Jinsheng didn't say anything; he just held her hand and looked very tired. With a third person present, Ru Yan, too, didn't know what to say. So she just let him hold her hand for the rest of the drive. After seven or eight turns, the car reached a quiet little street, one of the old lanes that had somehow been preserved in the big city. Many of the houses were in the European style and had been around for a hundred years. Though slightly the worse for wear, they retained a sumptuous and substantial quality, and the original decorations still graced the façade. Ru Yan had lived on just such a street with similar houses for part of her youth, and the sight stirred her like a sudden vision of her own childhood.

The car pulled to a stop in front of a three-story building of foreign design. There was a miniscule courtyard in front, which deserved the name only in that it had the same kind of wall that encloses a courtyard, but in truth it was no more than a strip to separate the building from the sidewalk. It ran the width of the building but was quite shallow: a few trees and a couple of parked bicycles were enough to fill it. Ru Yan wondered why he had brought her to someone else's home. "Here we are," he said. "The lady in charge here is a master chef of Shandong cuisine." And with that, they ascended a flight of steps and went in.

Hearing them enter, a gentleman in his sixties came out from a side room. "Mayor Liang!" he called warmly, and invited them upstairs. The old gent's suit and shoes were very fine, his thinning hair was meticulously combed, and he had a Shanghai accent. They climbed a wide wooden stairway to a bright and roomy hall whose large windows faced the street. There were a number of coffee tables. The old man led them into a room, seated them at a table, and poured tea. Classical music floated faintly in the air. The decor was that of a small parlor in someone's home, with bookcases, a pergola, a display case full of curios, a sofa, a tea-table, and a sideboard; each piece of furniture had with it the smaller items that suggested it was really in use, and not just there for decoration.

"Shall I serve now, Mayor Liang?" the old gentleman asked.

"Yes."

When he left the room, Ru Yan said, "But you haven't ordered anything."

Liang Jinsheng said, "Meals must be ordered in advance here. They buy the food after you order."

"What is this place?" she asked. "A friend's house?"

"No, it's a restaurant, or more accurately, a home-style restaurant. It doesn't have a name. In general, it doesn't serve outsiders."

As he was speaking, a woman of scholarly and refined appearance entered and hailed him in a genuine Beijing accent: "Mayor Liang! Only two today?"

"Only two," he said.

"I'm afraid we prepared too much," the woman said.

"I may have ordered extra," he said. "What we can't eat, I'll trouble you to wrap up for us to take home. I have brought a lady from Shandong. Where else could she eat such authentic food of that kind?"

"Very good," the woman said, "I feel better about it if you'll be taking it home. It will be out in a moment." And she left.

Ru Yan wondered what kind of people these were, the man and the woman. They did not have the eagerly attentive manner of restaurateurs. It was almost as if they were doing you a favor. They remained perfectly self-possessed in the presence of a mayor. "Our cook today is a college professor," Liang Jinsheng remarked.

"A professor opened this little restaurant?" Ru Yan was surprised.

"I wouldn't call it *little*," he said. "It's a place where foreign consuls, experts, and CEOs of multinationals want to eat but have to wait their turn. She prepares dinner for only two tables a day, and they're open only three days a week: Tuesday, Thursday, and Saturday. It's harder to make a reservation here than to get an appointment with a medical specialist."

He explained their background. For several generations the lady's ancestors had been chefs to the Imperial Court, and indeed the preferred entrées of the Qing Dynasty had been Shandong dishes. When it came to her generation, of course, no one still plied the trade of cooking for the Emperor, but she had learned a lot about the traditional chef's art from the conversation in her childhood home; you could say it was in her bones. In retirement she took up cooking the recipes of her ancestors, strictly adhering to the old practices, and the results, as you would expect, were remarkable. When friends came over, she would let them taste the very dishes that had graced the table of the Emperor and his mother.[330] This pastime developed a certain momentum, and eventually became what it was now: she charged anyone who wished to come, but if she didn't know you and you weren't introduced by someone she knew, she wouldn't take your order. She also made it a rule that no receipts would be given; if you wanted to eat here, you'd have to foot the bill yourself. Curiously, with all these restrictions, there was tremendous demand for her fare, and eating here became a badge of status and good taste. Customers joked that each scallion had been picked by someone with the highest academic credentials. The gentleman who had shown them to their seats was her husband, a retired professor of medicine. If you cared to know, he could advise you on what foods would be best for your health.

Ru Yan explained that though she had called herself a person from Shandong, she actually had little connection with that province, apart from half the ancestors on her father's side. She'd never even been to her ancestral home, never mind acquiring a familiarity with the cuisine. Her mother was from Jiangsu and they had often eaten food prepared in the style of Yangzhou.[331] The culture of her mother's side of the family had prevailed in her home.

Their hostess returned with the first course, cream of sea cucumber soup. It was a milky white, and the sea cucumbers were very dark, surrounded by emerald-green scallions and parsley scattered across the surface. Liang Jinsheng ladled out a small bowlful for Ru Yan. There were no waitresses here; once food and drink had been brought to the table, it was all in the hands of the diners, who then enjoyed a more relaxed atmosphere. Ru Yan brought a spoonful to her lips and found it warm and fresh, marveling that such a mild soup could pack such fine flavor. She nibbled a bit of the sea cucumber, which was soft but not mushy and had a gentle taste that was not at all fishy. The sea cucumber had lines of little bumps like seams and did remind her of Shandong. Whenever people from his old hometown had visited her father, they had brought gifts of seafood, including sea cucumbers that had dried out into thumb-sized black things resembling wooden pegs and bearing a whiff of the salt breeze. When Mother soaked them they would expand to several times their size.

When they had finished their soup, Liang Jinsheng poured them each a glass of red wine. "Red wine goes well with food from Shandong."

With a strange glint in his eye, he asked her what the date was.

"The fourteenth day of the first lunar month," she said. "The New Year's season is almost over."

"The date is significant for another reason."

She suddenly realized what it was, remembering the people she had seen selling roses in the streets, and she was moved in her heart, but what she said was: "Your birthday?"

"You could say that," he conceded. "Right, then, let's drink a toast to our birthday."

One after another, the hostess brought in the dishes: pan-fried oysters, sweet-and-sour Yellow River carp, steamed sea bream, razor clams with chive seedlings . . .

For some reason, Ru Yan was afraid to pursue this subject. Instead she said he'd ordered too much food and asked why he didn't invite Master Luo to come eat with them.

"He wouldn't come," Liang Jinsheng said. "Even if I asked

him, he wouldn't come."

"Why not?" she pressed.

"Drivers have their own code."

"So he just has to go hungry?" she asked.

"By no means. He will have found a little eatery in the neighborhood, and he'll be more comfortable there."

As he was speaking, his phone rang. As soon as he answered it, his face grew taut. "I understand," he said into the phone, "I understand." When he hung up he appeared disconcerted and didn't pick up the thread of their conversation.

"Do you need to do something?" Ru Yan asked.

"Don't worry about it," Liang Jinsheng shrugged. "It's the New Year's season. We have to eat."

They started eating again, distractedly.

Again the phone rang. When he finished the call, he said, "It seems they won't let us finish this meal."

Never one to have a big appetite, Ru Yan was feeling full anyway. "You go do what you have to do. I've had enough."

Liang Jinsheng called over their hostess with a sad smile, settled his bill, and had the food wrapped up. They left in a hurry and found Master Luo waiting at attention beside the car.

"I'm not treating you very well today," Liang Jinsheng apologized. "Ride with me to the place I have to go, and then Master Luo will drive you home."

The little car was speeding. They ran a red light, crossed the yellow line, passed illegally . . . they did everything you could do to incur a fine, make your insurance more expensive, or even lose your license. Ru Yan asked whether the police knew his car.

Liang Jinsheng twitched his mouth in Master Luo's direction. "Ask him."

Master Luo smiled. "Most of the time, I don't break the rules."

The car pulled up in front of a quiet guesthouse. Liang Jinsheng said a quick goodbye to Ru Yan, opened the car door, and strode quickly into the building.

On the drive back, Ru Yan asked Master Luo, "Another banquet?"

"What are you talking about?" he exclaimed. "You don't know what that place is? The guesthouse was requisitioned to serve as the city's command center during the SARS emergency. The physicians and experts who are working round the clock are lodged there. There are no other 'guests,' and getting in or out is about as easy as getting in or out of a prison. Didn't you see the Armed Policeman standing guard at the door?"

The abrupt and hasty end to what had been a delightful and comforting dinner left Ru Yan feeling somewhat melancholy. She placed a call to Jiang Xiaoli, who had phoned to wish her a happy New Year a few days previously and had inquired about Liang Jinsheng. At that time Ru Yan hadn't had any news. Now she ought to have a talk with her.

As soon as she knew it was Ru Yan, Jiang Xiaoli asked, "Where are you?"

Ru Yan said she had just eaten half a meal with him, and he had gone back to his official business. At the moment, she was riding home in his car.

"Tell Master Luo to stop at the entrance to our compound. I'll come along for the ride; I've got something to say to you." So Master Luo picked her up and drove the two of them to Ru Yan's house.

Once in the car, Jiang Xiaoli eyed Ru Yan's new clothes and asked knowingly, "So how did he like it?"

Ru Yan wasn't comfortable discussing this in the presence of an outsider. "That's a secret," she smiled.

Jiang Xiaoli scoffed. "Hm. Not married yet and you already have your secrets?"

At Ru Yan's apartment, before even sitting down, Jiang Xiaoli said: "Listen, Ru Yan, this is a time when you have to be very supportive to our Brother Liang. Whenever he's not too busy, you should have comforting conversations with him, lots of them."

"What's happened?" Ru Yan asked.

"You mean he hasn't poured out his troubles to you?" Jiang Xiaoli said.

"Um, what troubles does he have to pour out?"

"You . . . The men in your life must have spoiled you, that you can be so oblivious."

Ru Yan then told her the occasion for which Liang Jinsheng had taken her out to dinner.

"Couldn't have been easy for him," Jiang Xiaoli reflected, "to remember Valentine's Day just when everything is going down the tubes. He must be deeply, incurably, in love."

Ru Yan asked what she meant about everything going down the tubes.

Jiang Xiaoli didn't answer right away. "You two may have wined and dined on the Emperor's favorite Shandong dishes, but I haven't had a bite to eat."

"What do you know," Ru Yan said, "it just happens that we had some of it wrapped up to take home. Would you like a taste of royalty?"

"My lot in life," Jiang Xiaoli groused. "I get the leftovers."

"Actually," Ru Yan explained, "he purposely ordered extra so we'd have some to take away. Take a look: it's hardly been touched." And she heated some in the microwave and served it.

"You must join me," Jiang Xiaoli insisted. "Let's have some wine."

So they ate and drank together as they talked.

"Look at this," Jiang Xiaoli said. "They say a good deed earns a good reward. I must have done something right to get this dinner. Ah, men! When they're in deep trouble, that's when they are really affectionate. Think of the most touching love stories in the old dramas: invariably, they happen when the guy's in trouble. When things finally work out for him, you can cue the damsel's tears."

Ru Yan was getting impatient. "Stop beating around the bush. This is important!"

Jiang Xiaoli then explained why everything was going down the tubes for Liang Jinsheng. "Listen, our place has it now. I've heard a few people have already died."

"I didn't know things were so bad. Out on the streets, there's no sign of any emergency."

"Tense on the inside, relaxed on the outside—what's unusual

about that? With SARS here, you could say that things are now going badly in every single area under his jurisdiction. Never mind the huge economic losses: he's under a crushing political responsibility. Didn't he make the rounds of Europe and North America last year? That was to lay the groundwork for two major events scheduled for this May. The first was a science and technology conference, to which experts from dozens of countries have been invited; the second was a business convention to which a few hundred companies were invited. We've already spent several million on the preparations alone, both State and corporate funding, and both the government and the private investors were expecting to get that money back and even turn a profit. But now everything is up in the air. If they don't get this SARS thing under control *immediately*, nobody's gonna come. That's the first point. The second point is that for the last few years most of the government's funding has gone into boosting the science and technology sector. Medicine and hygiene, especially public health, disease prevention, basic health facilities—they're all in bad shape. Not only have they not gotten any increases, you'd have to say they've actually been cut back. So here comes SARS, and suddenly those priorities are looking kind of problematic. Now granted, he was not the only person involved in those decisions, but one person has to be the scapegoat: it's our tradition. Third point: he's responsible for the schools and colleges, and you know they're going to get hit hard by an epidemic. This is a very sensitive area. There's the risk the students will make trouble, plus the parents are likely to complain, especially at the new colleges which have been structured as joint ventures between the public and private sectors and which therefore charge high tuition. Instruction won't be able to continue on the normal schedule, you see, and the high tuition will become a sore point. The internal politics are also tricky. The climbers who would be more than happy to take advantage of his troubles, they're watching with secret glee, just waiting for a good position to become vacant early. So you tell me, to remember Valentine's Day at a time like this, is the guy or is he not a true love?"

Ru Yan's heart had begun to pound as Jiang Xiaoli went on. She would never have guessed that this mayor, who had discussed Palace cuisine with such relish, was facing an appalling crisis. But all she could find to say—for a silver lining—was that the worst that could happen would be an early retirement and more free time.

Jiang Xiaoli laughed. "So womanly. You don't think much of the world of work and power. But for someone who's spent more than half his life in the rough-and-tumble of officialdom, to have his career erased in one swoop would be unbearable; you shouldn't even mention the possibility. You should find encouraging things to say. Listen, I've known men who ended up like that. It didn't take them long to die of depression."

Ru Yan was silent.

"This mayor of yours," Jiang Xiaoli said, "he's too much of the old school."

Ru Yan asked what that meant.

"He keeps playing by the old rules, even at a time like this," she explained. "I'm afraid it's not good enough to treat the symptoms. You've got to go to the root of the problem, and a crisis like today's calls for fresh ways, new tricks, and risk-taking: nothing less will do."

"What do you mean by 'fresh ways, new tricks, and risk-taking'?" Ru Yan asked.

With a shrewd smile she answered, "That's something I could only teach him in person."

"Xiaoli," Ru Yan said, "I can see now how you were cut out to be an official."

"I think so, too. But my old man wouldn't let me go that route, said it was too hard on the mind and the body; an ordinary life was better. But there are times when, watching them go about their business, I worry for officials and get mad at them, too. The old saying had it right: the Emperor is not worried, but his lieutenants are."

Jiang Xiaoli had really been hungry and had gone on eating and drinking while she talked, polishing off several dishes till she sighed with satisfaction. "Ah, Mayor Liang, you only remembered Ru Yan, who's half of Shandong stock; you've forgotten someone else who's a genuine full-blooded woman of Shandong. He'd better invite me next time, or after the wedding I'll get even with you two!"

When the Army of Liberation had moved South in force, a single regiment had been left behind to take over the management of this city. People of Shandong dominated this regiment. As a result, in every department and every organization all the positions of importance had been filled by Shandong people, so much so that if somewhere in town you ran into a person with a Shandong accent and automatically addressed him as Director, or Chief, you'd be right a good 80% of the time. A few decades later the infirmaries for senior comrades were filled with the Shandong dialect, particularly the flavor that is spoken in Jiaodong, so that you could be excused for imagining you had wandered into a subsidiary of some Shandong hospital.[332]

Jiang Xiaoli left late, slightly tipsy. On her way out she said, "Oh, Ru Yan, this is not the time to act like a spoiled little girl. You should be more like a mother, giving him courage and wiping away his tears." Once she had left, Ru Yan phoned him but got the recording saying he had turned off his phone. She called Master Luo, but Master Luo told her that the Mayor was staying at the guesthouse tonight and had sent him home. She asked for the number of the guesthouse, but Master Luo didn't know it. This was the first time she had felt anxious and worried about Liang Jinsheng in all the months she had known him.

Whereupon Ru Yan used her cell phone to compose the first text message she had ever sent in her life:

Two human beings, bereft and alone
Celebrate the year in mutual support;
Happy Valentine's Day!

In a short time, Ru Yan had become extremely busy. Often she didn't even have time to miss her son or lavish affection on her dog. Her son left QQ messages for her, `Mom, what exactly is it that you're so busy with? Haven't seen` you online for a long time. Or again, Mom, I'm going to guess there's good news, is that right? Your life's not so empty anymore? This made Ru Yan feel guilty and embarrassed. In her mind she cussed out her son for the rascal he was, but she hurried to reply with a number of high-sounding reasons including his uncle's illness. Her son replied, They're talking a lot about this disease overseas. The Chinese government has come in for heavy criticism. For Chinese students here, it's been humiliating.

It was as if Ru Yan had finally broken the seal on a jug of liquor that had been fermenting for half a lifetime. With each draft, her life became more crowded with incidents and interests. Or as she put it when she chose to be hard on herself, life was getting crazier by the day.

'How soon the great forget,' it had been said in mockery, but there is truth in the words. As she moved in higher circles and busied herself with many affairs and contacts, her life, as her son had suggested, became more abundant, and she couldn't get too deeply involved with any one thing. How different from ancient times, when people lived simply, and a mere meeting of the eyes could prove an event which two people would remember for the rest of their lives.

48

That Teacher Wei was being kept in the hospital became known to Damo's circle within a few days. Teacher Wei had not wanted anyone to be told. He said he had already caused them enough trouble for this Spring Festival. But with a sudden change in his condition, Zhao Yi had no choice but to speak with Damo and Maozi. As soon as he'd been admitted, they'd done a routine examination and taken a chest X-ray. The X-ray showed shadowing on the right lung, and they said a respiratory infection had given rise to a pneumonia. The doctor said he'd be fine after a few days on antibiotics. Since Teacher Wei had a history of pulmonary TB, they added some additional treatment measures. Now Teacher Wei was not very good at following a regimen. After a few days in the hospital, once he'd finished his IVs and his pills, he felt better enough to go home in the evenings. But as the uproar over SARS mounted, the people at the cadres' infirmary became nervous about the way he was coughing, and when they heard he'd recently had visitors from another part of the country, they moved him into the isolation ward. The whole point of that ward was to watch for SARS, and they had several patients who'd already been diagnosed as "suspected SARS cases." Zhao Yi became extremely anxious. She was afraid he might have SARS, of course, but if he didn't have it already, he'd be likely to catch it in that place. Teacher Wei had been worn down by age; how could he endure such an ordeal? He was a free spirit, and Zhao Yi feared that after all those years of solitude if he were once again locked up this way it would make him sick, if he weren't sick already.

When Maozi and Damo hurried to the hospital, they weren't allowed to see him.

This hospital, the choice of which had been determined by Teacher Wei's work unit, was under the administration of the Province, and although it was triple-A rated it was not the best that could be found, especially in respiratory diseases (which were not its specialty). Damo talked it over with some friends and they agreed that Teacher Wei would be much safer if he could be transferred, even if he were still treated as a suspected SARS case. So they sought out the hospital administrator and asked for Teacher Wei's medical records to be photocopied so they could show them to another hospital and make arrangements for a transfer. The administrator did not agree. He said some of the tests were still being analyzed. Damo got irritated. "Look, we don't want him treated here anymore, got that? We're taking him out, OK?"

To their surprise, the administrator answered, "Ordinarily, if you said that, we'd discharge him for you right away. But at present, that's not possible."

"Why not?" Damo asked.

"Don't ask me why," the adminstrator said. "You can take this up with the relevant office. You can even take it up with the Ministry of Health." He walked out, leaving them there in the office.

"Well," Maozi said, "it looks as though we can't just push this one through. I'll try to reach someone at the Provincial Health Authority as soon as I can."

Ru Yan found out about Teacher Wei's condition that evening.

Immediately she called Liang Jinsheng, but his phone had been switched off. Then she tried Master Luo, who said that tonight Mayor Liang was still at the guesthouse and was going to be there for the forseeable future. This time, he told her the number of the phone in Mayor Liang's room. When she dialed it, no one was there. So she kept dialing, again and again, and finally reached him after midnight. She told him about Teacher Wei's circumstances and said she hoped he could help.

"Who is Wei Lao to you?" he asked after a pause.

His tone of voice suggested that he knew Teacher Wei. Ru Yan said she had no personal connection to him.

Liang Jinsheng tried again: "Does he have some connection to your family?"

"No," she said, puzzled.

"Well, um . . . how do you know him?"

"Why in the world are you so guarded about an old man in his eighties?"

"It's not that," he said, "but I'm going to tell you, Ru Yan, it would be better for you not to get involved with this, and it's not appropriate for me to get involved either."

"Why not?"

"The hospitals you're talking about," he explained, "none of them are under municipal administration. Besides the issue of jurisdiction, province vs. city, this man Wei Lao has had lots of problems lately. I can tell you all about it later."

"And is he supposed to wait for you to tell me all about it?

This is life and death. An old man has been locked in an isolation ward without any test results . . . it's not right."

"How can I make you understand that these are wartime conditions? A lot of the rules which ordinarily are fair and right can't be followed now."

Ru Yan got even more upset. "This is an old man who took part in the Revolution . . . years of meritorious service, more than my father. He's an old man who has had to suffer a great deal. To see that he enjoys proper medical care is not too much to ask!"

"I'm aware of everything you've mentioned, I know even more about those things than you do," Liang Jinsheng said. "And I know some things you may not know—"

She cut him off. "I don't care what you know. I just want you to help him. Treat him as you would treat my father."

Liang Jinsheng heard the strain in her voice, and some of what she had said had moved him. All he could say was, "Ai, I'll do the best I can, OK? You are . . . you are a kindhearted woman."

A few days later, there were no signs of progress with Teacher Wei's transfer. Reached by phone, Teacher Wei sounded angry. He wanted out, and said he was old enough that if he wanted to die then he should be allowed to die. He couldn't stand being locked up without a clear reason. Zhao Yi was distraught, as were Damo and Maozi. Ru Yan was almost out of her mind, and phoned Liang Jinsheng several times a day.

"Come on," he said. "You think I run the hospital? It's not that simple. I'm trying to find a way."

On the fifth day Teacher Wei was transferred to a university hospital. After a few days there he was categorized as a suspected SARS case. But whether this suspicion had been well-grounded all along or he had caught it in the isolation ward was a question that no one could answer. When Ru Yan brought this up to Liang Jinsheng, he said, "Don't dig too deep into this. The priority now is to get him the best possible care and save his life. You mustn't complicate matters. You're starting to scare me, you know. Above all, do *not* post anything about it on the Internet. Teacher Wei is a sensitive figure. You never know what kind of articles might try to exploit this."

But it got out of the bag. The news that Teacher Wei had been hospitalized for SARS appeared on websites both at home and abroad. Ru Yan didn't know who had made it public and she felt nervous about it, but there was no point trying to explain; that would be too much like "No 300 ounces of silver here."[333]

The relevant authorities were incensed and an order came down to investigate the leak. But of these developments Ru Yan knew nothing.

49

Spring that year was destined to be an eventful season.

Even as the disease called SARS was silently spreading like a fire in the underbrush, the Americans unsettled the world by igniting a war in Iraq.

CCTV did something it had never done before: it provided live coverage of the war, just like Western TV stations. They even invited military experts and specialists in international affairs to provide live commentary from their studios. Ordinary people all over China watched the unfolding of a distant war in real time. Squadrons of tanks and armored cars sped down highways, dust billowing behind them; buildings and palaces exploded and burned; anti-aircraft fire split the darkness like festive pyrotechnics; ambulances and fire-engines screamed down the avenues of Baghdad; all kinds of people stepped in front of the camera to recount, to rail, to curse. . . The military experts moved red and blue arrows around a big map, explaining developments, while the inset video frame showed the relevant activity. One frequently heard the rumble of high explosives as the precision-guided munitions of the British and American forces struck home. For Chinese, this was an utterly novel sight, and countless viewers stayed glued to the tube round the clock, enjoying this reality-TV series.

Half a century influenced by a political life which drew all things into its purview has made the Chinese a political animal. The stimulation of these world events had an effect like that of a firecracker tossed into a nest of songbirds. The modern Chinese tradition of airing one's views in open debate, now enhanced by the Internet, quickly turned every forum into a streetcorner or a city square.[334]

Ru Yan didn't know much about international affairs. For such questions she tended to rely on her feelings and intuition. She was convinced that a woman's intuition can often punch through the elaborate mental constructs, like so much papier-mâché, over which men expend such labor: it was a different way to get to the heart of the matter. When she saw one of those labored, circuitous essays, she would look to see what moved her; when she was moved in her heart, then she knew what to conclude. *You can explain the world in terms of correct and incorrect, but I'll judge it in terms of good and evil; you use your brain, I'll use my heart.* After she started going online and came across meandering, bombastic, hyperintellectualized discussions, she didn't even bother to read them. What she set store by was the details of an event, what happened to the people involved. A few years previously, an extremist regime had been overthrown. Ru Yan had not yet discovered the Internet and relied on heavily slanted news from newspapers and TV, but a few stories were enough for her to make up her mind: for example, how those men didn't let girls go to school, and didn't let women go to work, wouldn't even let them show their face, although the *men* were allowed to take four wives and could summarily execute any woman who'd had an affair. Plus they'd blown up the biggest Buddhas in the world, those beautiful, precious statues.[335] To strike at such bad men, and such a bad regime, was an action which Ru Yan agreed with on an emotional level. Some of her colleagues said it was a small, Third-World nation and this was just more bullying by the American Imperialists. She answered that she was OK with the bullying if, when it was over, their women wouldn't get bullied anymore. For them to have reformed of their own accord, without being attacked, would have been best; but since they were obstinate and would not change, a fight was the only solution.

While the fighting in Iraq was underway, an incident at home caused an uproar on the Internet. A young college graduate who had gone to work in the South was illegally detained and then beaten to death while in custody.[336]

Ru Yan wrote a piece with the title "A mother's pain in the darkness." She wrote that, when late one night she read about the death of this young man, she felt a stabbing pain in her heart, a physical pain, just as if her own son were enduring that savage beating and each blow shook his mother, till he died stretched out on a cold cement floor. It felt at that moment as if she were about to die too. A sudden terror overcame her and she feared the same fate could take away her son. Though she knew, objectively, that it had not been her son but rather a young man unknown to her, whenever the image of that man appeared in her mind, he always had her son's face. She had phoned her boy at once, for she had to hear his voice, and when it came to her across the wires from France, her eyes filled up with tears. Her son heard her sobs and asked her what was wrong. She said, "A young man about your age has died. He was beaten to death for no reason by an organ of the People's Government." And she wrote that as long as such unjust deaths continued to occur, no mother could be truly happy. "You must take care of yourself," she had told her son, "stay alive for your mother's sake, or else this world will have no meaning."

Her article attracted an outpouring of sympathy and support. But there were also a few insinuations, posted under pseudonyms, such as

```
So many ordinary workers have been beaten to
death or crippled with nary a peep out of
you! But a college boy dies, and then you
```

feel sorry?

and

You sent your son abroad, but weep for the son of a peasant family. Hypocrite!

and

Don't blame everything on the government. Your type is the kind that easily turns traitor to China.

She had been on the Internet long enough to know that this sort of follow-up post is as common a sight as creepers climbing a wall, but it was still hard to take, and it gave her a different kind of pain in her heart.

The people on this forum were all familiar to one another. But someone who two days ago was asking after your welfare and yesterday charmed you with some long yarn could change in an instant, just like the face-changing opera of Sichuan, and fix you with a cold and hostile glare.[337] Ru Yan felt like a traveler in the night who is surrounded by pairs of green eyes in the darkness and doesn't know what kind of creatures they belong to. It made her very uneasy.

In a long post, Damo concurred with her piece, whose emotions he thought insightful and whose moral judgment he found courageous. He refuted the bigoted mindset and muddled logic of the few hostile comments it had received. At the end, he mentioned that he had reproduced her article on his own forum. His writing style was gentle and kind, but his way of reasoning things out was trenchant. Ru Yan felt a lot better.

Ru Yan posted a response saying that she wrote from her emotions and could not enunciate big ideas: it had been no more than the feelings of a mother.

Those who frequented Damo's site, *Word and Thought*, were for the most part middle-aged people whose wide experience of the world had not dimmed their energetic spirits. They all wrote essays and critiqued each other's work. There were differences of opinion, but never any belligerence; the tone was unfailingly civil. Damo's forum was not one where anyone could post: only registered and approved users enjoyed that privilege. Consequently, there was never any hit-and-run arguing. As it said on the "About" page,

> We don't engage in spitting contests here. We don't welcome one-liners, much less personal attacks. There are many websites whose doors are open to all and sundry, and who aim for a high hit count. We do things differently. It's like a chess match between grandmasters: you may watch, but there is no kibitzing. If you have an itch to do so, then you may offer a contribution, but you must follow our rules.

Ru Yan thought this kind of website would tend to attract a lot of abuse, but since no abusive posts could appear there, it was remarkably tranquil. Ru Yan liked this kind of tranquility. It was like a small gathering of friends conversing equably, pausing from time to time to sip a cup of green tea. No chumminess, no teasing; everyone maintained a certain dignity.

On Damo's forum, too, there was talk of SARS, and the Iraq war, and that college kid who'd been beaten to death. They discussed these things from the point of view of the cultural context and the legal and systemic implications. Whatever indignation they might have felt was transmuted here into reflective insight. Every essay was moderate in tone, but serious and penetrating. The site expanded her horizons.

When she got there, she found her essay was already posted. Damo had added his own commentary:

While we explore the controversy surrounding the Sun case from the perspectives of the political system, culture, law, and public security, a mother gives anguished voice to her own indignation. And indeed, there are times when the highest logic stems from relationship, from the compassion one being feels for another's sorrows. She has something to teach us who are used to pondering and judging everything by means of our ready-made concepts, our neat systems of thought, our polarity of right and left. At a time when the media are once again shamefully silent, and when those in a position of responsibility remain callous, there is no stronger statement of outrage than this mother's pain. Until we feel the pain of sympathy for all who suffer, even the humblest, we won't be able to save our world—or ourselves.

Ru Yan wasn't convinced that what she had written on the spur of the moment actually had all this deep significance, but she was very happy to receive such an endorsement. Damo's words melted away the troubled feeling which the unpleasant comments at the Empty Nest had brought. She was like a child who hears a word of comfort from her teacher after being wrongly blamed.

50

Fear naturally grows in a warped and stressful atmosphere. It's like when you heard a ghost story as a child: the time when you were really afraid wasn't when the goblins and wolves were howling; it began later, when everybody was quiet and with strained faces tried to surround himself with other people. Then when the storytelling was over and each person went his separate way, walking home alone down dark alleys . . . that was when you knew the meaning of fear.

Soon after Spring Festival, rumors about the unknown disease died down, surprisingly. But out on the streets of the city, in stores and on buses, without any fanfare people began wearing masks. More and more of them.

For years, now, it had been unusual to see anyone but sanitation workers wearing a mask on the street. The fact that, at a time like this, more and more masks were appearing on the faces of strangers delivered a more frightening message than any rumor could do. Each hidden face—only the eyes showing—made you feel these people were hiding what they were thinking. As a result, the people who were *not* wearing masks felt they were now in greater danger. It was as if the others had donned suits of armor, but you were still walking around exposed to the deadly arrows—arrows which you could not see. (Something comparable happened in the first phase of the C.R.: when people started appearing on the streets with red armbands, those who were not wearing them began to feel uncomfortable and insecure. As time went on, and the number of armband-wearers kept increasing, those without armbands almost became a different species.) The upshot was that long lines, such as had not been seen in years, queued up at the doors to pharmacies, everybody waiting quietly and keeping a certain distance between himself and the next person. Waiting in line is such a civilized custom: finally it was catching on![338]

At Ru Yan's office, some were now wearing masks. Notably, the always nonchalant Jiang Xiaoli was wearing one. When Ru Yan noticed, she laughed, "On your way in, did you bump into someone named Fei Dian?"

"Aw, I'm not worried about it," Jiang Xiaoli said, "but my mother says, 'You're running around outside all day, don't bring that thing home with you. Let us live in peace.'"

Ru Yan had never liked masks. The way they stuck to your face after getting hot and damp was quite unpleasant. She liked to breathe free, sucking in the chill morning air and feeling it flow like spring water from her sinuses to her lungs.

"You ought to be careful," Jiang Xiaoli advised. "Wouldn't want to sacrifice your living happily ever after before it's even started."

Several of the sisterhood came around, and each had a mask. The ones who were particular about their appearance had masks of various colors and floral designs. Soon this kind of mask would become the newest fashion accessory.

That evening, Ru Yan got in touch with Damo via QQ, and she talked with him about this phenomenon of the masks.

"It's true," he said. "Hey, mask, haven't seen you for ages! But where you see a mask, I see panic." He also said that people weren't even getting their appliances fixed these days. "They're afraid if they let me in the door I'll bring the virus. The ones who've made appointments are all now saying, 'Some other time . . . I'll call you.'"

After they chatted for a while, Damo said this was an interesting subject and he was going to write an article about it. He logged off QQ and typed a title:

Hey, Mask—Haven't Seen You for Ages!
An Inquiry into the Roots of Panic

Then he lit a cigarette and tapped out the following piece:

In the last few decades there have been two or three large-scale campaigns promoting the wearing of masks. The one that made the deepest impression on me was in the Sixties. Meningitis was going around, then, or perhaps it was later called Encephalitis B.[339] But that time, it wasn't the common people who wanted masks; there were orders from above to wear them. Not like today, when the common people want masks but the officials & experts go on TV to declare that the situation is normal and there's no need to wear them. In some public places, the security guards are stopping people from wearing masks.

I have unhappy memories of masks. One year when I was still in primary school it was suddenly announced that you had to wear a mask if you were attending school. Without a mask, they wouldn't let you in the door but would send you home to get it. If you didn't get it and consequently weren't allowed into school, that would be counted as truancy. More than three days of truancy and you'd be expelled. This was the most draconian rule I can remember seeing imposed during my years of schooling. A mask cost 12 cents back then. That was about half a day's food for a poor family. The parents of some of my classmates went to the health office at their work unit and asked for a gauze bandage. They'd use it to make their own masks at home. Some of my classmates had just one mask, and when one side got dirty they'd turn it inside out and keep wearing it till both sides were dirty. In the evening, they'd wash it out and dry it on the coal stove so they could wear it again the next day. I knew kids who didn't wear the mask on their way to school but put it on when they reached the door, where there would be a team of students on duty, just like in the movies when the Japanese checked people's Good Citizenship Certificates.[340] They checked us one by one; there was no chance of sneaking past them.

One day I forgot my mask and remembered only when I was nearly at school. My parents had already left for work and our door at home was locked. Just as I was starting to panic I bumped into a classmate who agreed to toss his mask over the wall to me once he was safely inside. What I didn't foresee was that they would hold another inspection during the calisthenics that we did between classes, and this time there was no one to throw me a mask. The teacher sent me home and my parents received a summons. This was the first time my parents had ever been called into the school. My father chewed me out, big time. From that day I started putting my mask in my pocket each night before school.

During those months, the mask became oppressive, casting a shadow over my carefree childhood. Oh, and after our masks were inspected at the school door, we weren't finished. We also had to drink a broth of Chinese medicine. This was slightly sweet and many of the kids liked it. In those days there were no soft drinks and even candy was a rarity, so for many kids that broth was a treat. And after the broth, they would spray another kind of medicine into our throats, and this stuff was vile, completely ruining the nice taste left by the broth. Some kids suggested, first the spray, then the broth? But the school said no.

When I think back on it now I realize it must have been a horrific epidemic. How many were infected? How many died? How many are suffering the long-term effects? I haven't seen any statistics but the numbers can't have been small. Years later you'd still hear people saying, So-and-so got meningitis, his brain doesn't work right. Or a relative of So-and-so died of meningitis. You'd hear a lot of these remarks, enough to figure that the extent of infection then must have been a lot worse than it is with SARS now. Oddly, though, people didn't panic back then the way they're panicking now.

I think a large-scale panic in society depends on certain key conditions.

When the situation is grave but there is transparency of information and public institutions enjoy a high level of credibility, there's not going to be much panic. It's like what happens in wartime: if we know the size of the enemy forces and our own resources, and know that we have a good strategy, then there's going to be solidarity all up and down the chain of command, we'll be united in hatred of the foe. But when the troops don't know what's going on (and know they don't know), then a puff of wind or the cry of a bird will prove as terrifying as an armed host.

When the situation is very grave but information is completely cut off, most people will carry on in a simple-minded way, unconcerned, even if hundreds of thousands of people are catching the disease nationwide. For the average man sees only his immediate environment, and only a handful will be falling sick around him. In the nineteen-sixties, there were not many who had the opportunity to read a newspaper. Office-workers might occasionally hear the designated staffer read out the editorials and things like that.[341] But for an ordinary household to subscribe to a newspaper was very unusual. Even a cadre could manage access to, at best, two or three local and Central Party newspapers. The Cultural Revolution singled out for criticism cadres who had purportedly lost their revolutionary idealism, and it was said that a cup of tea and a perusal of the paper were the sum total of their workday. At that time, radios too were a rarity, and anyway they were just like the papers, apart from the beep to mark the hour. If the paper ran an editorial, the radio would broadcast it, and when the papers ran the Nine Criticisms, the radio went on and on about the Nine Criticisms.[342] For a long time no radio had a shortwave band. It's said that later, in order to enable the people of remote districts to listen to the voice of Party Central, a batch of shortwave sets was produced, but typically even a person who had one of them wouldn't dare touch the shortwave dial.[343] In consequence, that era actually did achieve unanimity of public opinion, or maybe I should say, unanimity of editorial opinion. People were like the pigs who get carted off to the slaughterhouse by the truckload. On each truck, none of the pigs know their destination; when they get there and see how they are about to die, they have no opportunity to send word back to the others.[344] And thus, even though the situation is very grave indeed, up until the moment of slaughter each pig is happy.

No, true panic arises when the situation is grave, the news is confused, the authorities are waffling, and the people have multiple ways to receive and relay information. Under these circumstances, imaginations run riot in tandem with the spreading fear. But the government sticks to its time-tested rule that it's better not to talk about anything that could cause trouble. This is based on years of experience: during the Three Years' Famine, if someone had gone around saying men were starving to death, the common people might have risen up and robbed the granaries. But the trick isn't working so well this time, because now it only takes a few dozen text messages for people to go nuts. It's as if there were a host of voices whispering in your ear, ZOMBIE INVASION! while meanwhile the people who actually know where the zombies are, and how many of them there are, blithely keep saying, "Zombies? What zombies? Everything's fine!"

From an instinct for self-preservation, people always tend to believe the warning of danger. The nice clean masks we see all around us are a signal. The Horror is upon us.

Damo's writing was vigorous and his illustrative anecdotes made it easy to read. The piece was immediately duplicated on a score of websites. Damo was that kind of online celebrity; anything by him was sure of many reprints and a high hit count, just as some actors' names are a draw at the box office. The difference was that Damo never made any money; his only reward was trouble, and lots of it.

51

SARS eventually proved impossible to keep under wraps. The virus had no respect for anyone; it couldn't be pressured, and it couldn't be bribed. It had its own agenda and pressed forward with that, regardless. In the three short months since this year had begun, it had invaded the North with massive power and the shaken residents of the capital were grabbing Isatis root off the shelves. The next items to sell out were cooking oil, rice, dried noodles, instant foods, and even mineral water. The merchants made a killing as warehouses were emptied of what it had taken years to accumulate. They didn't foresee that in a few weeks business would dry up for a long time during which even the biggest malls and superstores would stand deserted day after day, as if shuttered. Major international conventions here were canceled, and many visits abroad were canceled by the hosts (some consulates just stopped issuing visas). Online commenters cried that China was being sealed off by the rest of the world.

Finally some officials of the see-no-evil school were sacked and a new wave of apprehension swept over the people, now practically on a war footing. It was reminiscent of the years when the Japanese had ridden roughshod over Manchuria and there had been vacillation south of the Great Wall: would it be war or peace? Would we attack, or hang on to what we still held?

Resist foreign aggression, or secure peace in the interior?[345] The Japanese, as it turned out, showed no gratitude for our forbearance and in a single night launched their attack on the North China Plain. Only when brought to this desperate pass did the people rise up in a war of resistance.

Now Liang Jinsheng could tell Ru Yan more of the truth. As the deputy mayor responsible for public health, he had for some time borne the main responsibility on the front line against the disease. In the papers, Ru Yan started seeing pictures of him swathed in protective garb from head to foot like an astronaut. Without the caption, she couldn't have guessed who it was. In the midst of all his pressing duties he called her to say that for her own safety he wouldn't come see her during this time, since he couldn't be sure what germs he might be carrying and this thing was just too serious and still without a cure. He said that, if he should perish honorably in this fight, he hoped she would often come to his tomb and have talks with him, for their conversations had been one of his greatest pleasures. She said she saw him on TV and in the papers giving speeches and she felt for him, because it must be hard to have to give speeches like that all day.

"It's not likely to be over anytime soon," he said, "I'm not sure whether we'll be able to carry out our plan at the appointed time, unless we get married on the execution ground."[346]

Ru Yan chuckled. "For now, just keep yourself safe. There will be time to take care of other things later."

"I think about you a lot," he said.

"Me, too," she said.

Seeing that Mayor Liang was being run ragged on a dangerous and thankless mission, Jiang Xiaoli drew closer to Ru Yan and became remarkably understanding. She often dropped by to shoot the breeze and offer an encouraging word. She seemed to feel Liang Jinsheng was a soldier stationed afar and Ru Yan a woman bereft, like some songless oriole upon a bare branch. "Fortune and misfortune are not easily disentangled," Jiang Xiaoli said. "For an official these days to have such a disaster occur on his watch might seem like bad luck, but if you can muddle through—or, better still, handle it with flair—whoosh, you're on the up escalator. Presto, bad turns into good. Many experienced men would give their eye teeth for such a once-in-a-lifetime chance."

"We'd all be better off without it," Ru Yan said. "This is torture for him, and a catastrophe for the common people."

"It's the will of Heaven," Jiang Xiaoli shrugged. "Think about it. If a guy pushing sixty hasn't done anything that stands out, the rules will be applied without mercy. It was like that with my old man. And then, the following year, the floods were bad, and the fellow just behind my Dad in seniority distinguished himself in the flood-control efforts. On the verge of being kicked upstairs, he was assigned to the People's Congress instead and enjoyed five more years in harness."

"What's wrong with shifting to a quieter life five years sooner?" Ru Yan smiled. "Do you have to keep fighting for Communism to your dying breath?"

Jiang Xiaoli snorted. "You and your incurably female perspective on things. With such an understanding and helpful wife, Mayor Liang's going to have lots of rest, very soon. Some day you should ask him—insist that he tell you the truth—whether he'd like to stick around for five more years. If he says he doesn't want to, I'll treat you both to a dinner at Shangri-La.[347]

"Even if he wants to," Ru Yan said, "I don't want him to."

As soon as the words were out of her mouth she felt they had been presumptuous. In view of the relationship they currently had, who was she to say what he should do with his life? She hurried to change the subject.

After they had chatted a bit, Jiang Xiaoli suddenly lowered her voice and said darkly, "You should stop discussing sensitive matters on the Internet."

"What sensitive matters?" Ru Yan asked, somewhat startled.

"I don't have to spell this out for you," Jiang Xiaoli said, "but I've seen them and I've heard people talking about them. The online world has wheels within wheels, you know. There are people whose entire duty is to monitor and collect the articles that get posted. If you're by yourself it's no big deal as long as you don't stir up anything major. But if later on you're associated with him, there could be trouble. The world of officials can be pretty cutthroat, you know?"

"The author takes sole responsibility," Ru Yan sighed, "or are we still imputing guilt by association? What's more, hasn't everything I said turned out to be right?"

"Incredible," Jiang Xiaoli grumbled, "how can the daughter of an old cadre be so clueless about these things? At one time it can be right to say certain things, and at another time it can be wrong to say them. At the moment, it looks as though they were right, but you were wrong to say them when you did. If you don't believe me, you're going to learn the hard way."

Jiang Xiaoli's well-intentioned warning left Ru Yan feeling shaken for several days. As if in confirmation, the news came that some malicious individuals had been arrested for spreading rumors about the unknown disease or recklessly sending text messages about it. A few days later, the official media reported that these people had been dealt with according to law, pursuant to paragraph umpteen of section such-and-such. At first, Ru Yan thought this might be reasonable. To say that people had caught the disease at a certain shopping center would ensure that nobody would go shopping there, and to say someone had come down with the disease at a certain company would cause that company to lose a lot of business. But she couldn't help thinking that other motives were at play in examples like that. And if you wanted to talk about starting rumors, what about the people who, in the early stages, had denied there was a problem? Hadn't that been a big rumor, which had done harm extending far beyond the profit-and-loss of a shopping center or a company? She went to Damo's site and found a number of posts discussing exactly this question, approaching it from the perspectives of legality, news transmission, the credibility of public institutions, and so on. The diffidence and ambivalence Ru Yan always felt about these issues were dispelled as she read. Maybe it was the friendly feeling she had for Damo or the way he had praised her, but Ru Yan found that these writings, which at first had seemed so dull and dry, were becoming much more readable. She was drawn to this style of thought with an open mind, now, as a young woman would be. She had seen enough of the world to be able to make sense of these essays. But she only read them and never dared post her own comments on his site.

The war which the Americans had stirred up seemed almost to be moving in parallel to the disease: they were like two subplots which influence each other as they unfold. When many apartment buildings came under quarantine, the war broadcasts offered the best entertainment for those who were in effect stranded on a desert island. When the war entered an impasse with less and less to report, the daily SARS statistics took over as the news item that affected the mood of millions. The case of the college graduate also kept surging across the Internet in waves, for whenever it looked as though it was going to fade away, a few indomitable individuals forced it back to the top of the news pile. Many websites were set up to move posts to the bottom of the page after they had gone some time without a response or comment. As soon as anyone commented on them, they'd automatically move back to the top of the page. High-quality articles that held people's interest, or were controversial, could remain on top for a long time, in a process that could be considered the survival of the fittest. If some thought certain posts were important and wanted to help everyone read them, even if they had nothing more to say they would upload a comment consisting of the single character, 顶 *ding*, "top." This meant *move it to the top of the page*. Posts about the case of the college graduate kept being "topped," and many declared that until justice was done for the dead who'd been wronged, they would not cease "topping," not for a thousand years. So many incidents of the modern era, even the gravest, have vanished beneath the floodwaters of our history: if only this character "top" had been available, people could have kept those events afloat on the surface of time and oblivion. Historians of the future will take note of this magnificent ideogram.

In the forum of the Empty Nest, the aroma of gunpowder

kept growing stronger. As had happened in the C.R., three large factions eventually formed. The first approved of overthrowing Saddam; the second was anti-American; and the third was "My, isn't the weather today … hehehe."[348] Those in this last group, if they took a position at all, were both against Saddam and against America. The first faction pressed for an investigation into how the government was at fault in the matter of SARS; the second sympathized with the government's plight; and the third either mumbled about the weather or said that, yes, this SARS business needed looking into but one had to sympathize with the government, considering what they were up against. The same factions had set responses to the case of the dead graduate: the first called for justice to be done and the murderers to be punished; the second declared that public order was in a parlous state these days, and it was understandable if sometimes mistakes were made in an effort to keep the peace; the third kept mumbling about the weather, and if pressed, would say that yes, the matter needed looking into, but one had to keep the system going, and if there were no rules the nation would be plunged into chaos.

There was one extremely harsh post that attacked Ru Yan directly: "`An Open Letter to our Forum's Moderator.`" It ran:

> For some time now, the anti-China forces on the international scene have been exploiting a certain disaster that has taken place in our country. America has also used its hegemony to carry out an insane invasion of a sovereign state. Against this background of a temporary setback to the Communist cause, an unhealthy and corrupting spirit has even been introduced into this very forum—a political development against which we must be on guard. Here is what we find mystifying. A forum moderator, at a time like this, should be taking a firm stance and loyally upholding the interests of our nation, defending the great and glorious achievements attained by more

than twenty years of Reform and Opening, and preserving a high degree of unanimity with Party Central (or, at the very least, taking a fair and objective stance during this ideological struggle). But a certain moderator uses the little authority she possesses to spread treasonous speech far and wide, with the greatest zeal. The situation has become intolerable...

It then quoted from writings by Such Is This World and others, critiquing them point by point. It went on for several thousand characters, never at a loss for words. The pseudonym under which this post appeared was Love Our China. The style was recognizably that of one of the regulars on the forum.

Similar sentiments had appeared in brief posts earlier, most of which had likewise appeared under temporary pseudonyms. They had taken a swipe at "right-wing traitors" and then stayed out of the discussion. Some had been young college students. Incensed by what Ru Yan and her "gang" had said about the calamities of the past, they had challenged, "You say that X million people starved to death during the three years of natural disasters. Tell us, please, how many people in your family starved to death? Are you perhaps an agent for the Americans?" And there were exhortations: "Peoples of the world, unite! Defeat U.S. Imperialism and its Chinese running dogs!" and "I love Bin Laden!" Ru Yan could only shrug when she read this stuff, coming as it did from kids who had grown up in the world of their textbooks—you couldn't really blame *them*. But the long post was evidently not the work of a youth, and breathed a murderous spirit that hadn't been seen for many years. As some commented, "What do you know, it looks as though the Nine Criticisms are coming out again!" "Oh so familiar... the language of the C.R.!" But alas, this kind of post garnered many plaudits and endorsements in the follow-up comments. Some of those agreeing with it were familiar participants at the Empty Nest, using their customary screen names. Some of them didn't write any comment, but when they posted the icon of a warm handshake, words were unnecessary. One could sum it all up with a phrase that saw much use during the Cultural Revolution: *We've said where we stand: fight's on!*

A further embarrassment for Ru Yan was the intemperance of some of the comments posted in support of her. They not only didn't make much sense politically but overstepped the bounds of decency with coarse language. Ru Yan was a self-respecting person and she found it depressing to be involved in a spitting match. Since both sides transgressed at different times, both occasionally had posts deleted. When the other side suffered a deletion, they condemned the moderator as arbitrary and imperious and abusing her power. She preaches democracy, they said, but practices dictatorship: a typically hypocritical opportunist. When her own side was the target of deletion, some said that on a crucial moral question she had caved under the pressure of ultra-left forces instead of making a principled stand. And some read the posts but didn't add any comments in the forum; they would repair to the chatroom, where they could assume a new pseudonym and set about disparaging people. The sensitive topics inspired text-only sessions, since voices could be easily recognized, and the chatroom would fill up with densely-packed lines of characters as different viewpoints clashed with their pens. Ru Yan went to observe and found it dizzying, like a free-for-all among masked fighters. She thought, what if each nom-de-guerre were to be suddenly stripped away so that everyone had to appear as himself or herself? Reading along in the chatroom made her feel lonely and sad. It wasn't the way it used to be, when she'd be warmly hailed on arrival, with many an icon of a bouquet, or hot tea and refreshments, being electronically presented to her. These days, what usually awaited her was a confidential whisper, `the person using the name So-and-so was just talking about you`. If she replied, `And who are` *`you`*`?` the only response would be a smiley-face.

52

All kinds of reports were starting to circulate in the city where Ru Yan lived: that SARS had hit such-and-such a place; that people had died at this or that hospital. The specters which had occupied conversation for so many days now seemed to have stealthily drawn terribly close.

Early one morning Ru Yan was out walking Yang Yanping when she spotted that young married woman walking her frizzy-haired beagle. The two dogs greeted each other happily. Yang Yanping wasn't in heat anymore, so although she was as affectionate as before she no longer made those lascivious motions.

"There's an old couple in our building," the married woman said, "who came back from Beijing a few days ago. They seem to have caught that disease. Night after night you hear them coughing."

Ru Yan was shocked. "Haven't they gone to the hospital?"

"Word is that they *did* go, but the hospital wouldn't take them, said they needed to go somewhere else. I don't know exactly what happened but they came back home. They stay shut up in their apartment all day long and they've got the rest of us terrified. We don't even dare open our windows. Someone stuck a note on their door, begging them to have some consideration for the health and safety of their neighbors and *go to the hospital!* It's been reported to the property management, but all they will say is, 'We're not a hospital. As long as they stay inside their apartment, they can live or they can die, but what can we do about it?' So someone contacted the newspaper, but the newspaper asked whether there was a medical diagnosis. 'These kinds of things,' they said, 'when there's no proof, we can't make reckless statements and you'd better not either.' So now when I have to walk the dog I'm scared to even go outside. I just don't know what to do."

Ru Yan went home and called Liang Jinsheng to tell him about this. He listened, then said hurriedly that he'd send someone right away to check it out. The guy hung up before the end of his sentence.

Ru Yan finished breakfast and was about to go to work when she heard a siren. An ambulance was rushing into the housing estate, and a patrol car came fast behind. When their sirens stopped, the entire development fell eerily silent. From her window she watched the ambulance and the police car pull up to No. 8, and several medical personnel in full hazard suits sprang from the ambulance and made a beeline for the building entrance. In the past, whenever some incident had occurred in the development, a throng of busybodies had always swarmed around in order to gawk and comment. Such scenes added a little excitement to life in this place. But this time the entrance to No. 8 remained empty. No one came out. People from the other buildings on their way to work didn't even turn to look as they passed by. But many could be seen watching anxiously from behind their windows, as if in time of war the invading force had reached their doors.

Then everyone saw the elderly couple come out wearing masks and get into the ambulance. The spacemen then proceeded to spray a disinfectant everywhere, up and down, inside and outside.

The old couple never came back.

At once No. 8 was placed under quarantine. The main door was shut tight. Yellow tape was stretched around the building at a short distance from it. Two men in protective suits stood guard as if this were a crime scene. All residents of the housing development were notified that those without a pressing need should not go out, and that in case of need they would be issued a travel permit. Body temperatures would be checked on entering or leaving the building and the time, as well as the traveler's destination, would be noted. Those employed by a work unit should now report their status to the work unit.

When Ru Yan went to the office, the staff there told her to fill out a form for the SARS prevention group, at once. The people at the SARS prevention group said, "Until this all blows over, you should stay at home and rest. Any problems, just let us know; we'll help you work them out." Ru Yan was rather pleased; for years she had longed for just such a spell of ease and freedom.

But she sensed something amiss when she left the SARS prevention group and noticed that whenever someone in the hallway saw her coming, he or she would immediately duck into the nearest office. When she reached her own office, the few people present all left as if on cue. She didn't see them return. Feeling a chill, Ru Yan quickly straightened up her desk and left.

At the entrance to her housing estate, she had her temperature taken, filled out a form, and then observed a notice which the concierge had taped to the wall. Starting that very day, residents were strictly forbidden to keep any kind of pet. Violators would be fined 500 yuan, the relevant official personnel would dispose of the animals on the spot, and so on. Ru Yan's heart sank.

When she reached her apartment Yang Yanping was all over her—skipping, wagging, and nodding. The creature didn't know what had happened outside and, ecstatic that Ru Yan had come home so early, gave a great happy bark. Ru Yan grabbed the dog and crushed it to her breast, trying to prevent it from making any more sounds that could be heard outside. "You mustn't bark," she enjoined, "from now on, you can't just bark when you feel like it." This was the first time Yang Yanping had ever heard its mistress berate it so sternly, and it pouted at Ru Yan in ignorant mystification. "They're going to kill your kind out there. You need to be cagey now." The little dog didn't bark anymore.

Ru Yan had a premonition like that of the chaotic approach of war.

People who've spent time in prison all agree that the first day is the hardest. So it was for Ru Yan now. She stood alone in the middle of the room in a stunned aimlessness. From her window she could see Building No. 8. In many of the windows there were faces pressed against the glass, children's faces, women's, men's; even the faces of very old people framed in white hair. Pressed flat, unmoving, those faces reminded her of the made-up faces of Beijing Opera. But in the buildings *not* sealed under quarantine, all the windows were shut tight too. The experts said good ventilation was an important defense against SARS, but everyone insisted on keeping the windows firmly closed. The usually well-traveled walkways were empty. The occasional passer-by was always in a mask and swathed in a scarf or bandanna, hurrying past.

Without thinking, Ru Yan switched on her computer. When they had sent her home from the office she had looked forward to doing some good reading and writing, but that feeling had ebbed, and she opened and closed a series of web pages without really seeing them. Then she opened a new document, wanting to type something, but her mind was a blank.

At noon she fixed something for lunch. After that, she noticed Yang Yanping on its haunches by the door with its head turned to stare at Ru Yan, which was its way of announcing it needed to go out to relieve itself. Ru Yan picked the dog up and carried it into the bathroom, saying, "From now on, you do your business in here." She had already spread waste paper on the bathroom floor, and now she shut the dog up in the bathroom. She would keep it locked in there until it couldn't hold it anymore and would have to poop in the bathroom. This was a trick she had learned from a website devoted to the care of pets. Yang Yanping started a continuous whining and whimpering. Practicing tough love, Ru Yan paid no attention. Yang Yanping finally burst into loud barking. In all its time with her, the dog had never suffered such an indignity.

Ru Yan panicked when she heard the loud bark and rushed into the bathroom, grabbed the dog, and spanked it several times. This made Yang Yanping feel even worse, and it ran whimpering into her bedroom, where it hid under the bed and wouldn't come out for anything. Ru Yan was angry and anxious and guilty. She got down on the floor and spoke kindly to the animal, which only stared at her and wouldn't come out. Ru Yan had to give up, and walked out of the room.

She missed her son. Calculating that it was now morning for him, she went to drop him a line. She was about to write about the quarantine, but was hesitating, when her screen suddenly went black and the computer stopped humming. Her first thought was that the computer had burnt out the way a lightbulb does, and she felt weak and limp as if someone had taken out her backbone. Immediately she phoned Damo to tell him something had gone terribly wrong with her computer. "Is the lamp on in the main unit?" he asked.

"No," she said.

"Are the lights in the modem on?" he tried.

"No," she said.

"How about the lights in your apartment? Are they on?"

Ru Yan pressed the switch on her desk lamp a few times, and answered, "Nope."

Damo laughed. "Then I have to tell you, this problem is more than I can fix. It's a blackout."

Ru Yan remembered that for some time now the power outages had been growing more frequent. Hearing that it was a blackout came as a relief, somehow. For one thing, it had stopped her from telling her son about the quarantine, and she took this as a sign that it would be better not to tell him.

Then she phoned her mother. She had been doing that every day to make sure her mother was all right and to ask how her brother-in-law was doing. Every day her mother had answered that he was still in the hospital and no one knew how this was going to end. Her mother asked how she was doing, and she said she was OK.

Evening came, but the electricity did not come back on.

As it grew darker, she peered from her window and saw the streets in chaos as far as the eye could see. The only lights still shining were the orange streetlights, gauzy in the night mists. A few high-rises in the distance towered lonely in the blackness. It made her shiver to think of being stuck on one of the upper floors in pitch dark. Modern life is as fragile as a patient on life-support: yank out a tube or pull a plug, and it's curtains. For years, everyone had thought blackouts were quaint memories of the old days, and those of a romantic temper had taken to turning off the lights, lighting candles, and enjoying the atmosphere with red wine, soft music, and dancing cheek to cheek. But the phenomenon thus mimicked for effect had reappeared for real.

During one brief outage a few days before, Ru Yan had resolved to buy candles, but when the lights came back on she forgot. Actually, she wasn't sure where you could buy them. Then she remembered having seen a pair of candles somewhere recently. They were the candles that had graced her birthday cake for her fortieth birthday, one in the shape of a "4" and the other a "0", each about the size of a cigarette box, red, with sparkling little flames that had twinkled at the top of each numeral that day as they melted small holes in the wax. Her husband had not been a man for details; over the years he had usually forgotten her birthday. But this time he had made a point of hurrying back from a business trip and ordering a big cake from a well-known bakery, with the top colorfully decorated with flowers, hearts, books, birds, stars, and the moon, all sculpted in cream. It was as if he wanted to make up with this display of affection for all the birthdays he had missed over the years. To arts and letters, also, her husband paid little attention. Scholarship had been in his family for generations, but that all stopped abruptly with him. For Ru Yan, this had been particularly disappointing. She said, "After handing down the tradition of learning from generation to generation, how could your family fail to share it with you?[349] Her husband had smiled. "When I became old enough to start learning those things, who would have dared teach me? You'd do anything to avoid those things."

This had been the last birthday he'd spent with her. It was as if he were in a hurry to finish things, and one day not long afterward he was gone. It happened late at night. He had just finished negotiating a deal in a city a few hundred miles away and was driving home with a few colleagues. A tractor-trailer had stopped at the side of the road. Its driver had forgotten to leave his lights on, or maybe the taillights were broken. Her husband's driver was exhausted and he slammed into the underside of the big truck at ninety miles an hour. The whole upper half of the car, along with the upper half of everyone inside it, was neatly sheared off in a second.

Ru Yan stood up and, feeling her way in the dark, groped inside a few drawers until she found the candles. Then she realized she had no matches, and no lighter, so in the end she lit them from her stove.

Everything in her home looked strange in the flickering candlelight. Yang Yanping must have crawled out from under the bed at some point, for now it howled uneasily at the swaying light. Frightened again, Ru Yan rushed at the dog and kicked it, which had the desired effect of silencing it but the creature backed into a corner and eyed her with fear. Twice in a single day Ru Yan had resorted to violence against this little dog, and she felt horrible. She ran to it, spoke kindly, apologized, tried to explain. She picked it up and pressed it to her breast; the animal was still trembling in fear.

Ru Yan smelled a familiar smell. It came back to her now, the warm fragrance of the wax when she had bent down to blow out the candles on her birthday.

"Make a wish," she heard her husband say. He'd always been a man of few words, not one to gush; no, he preferred to say nice things in an offhand way. She remembered how she'd answered spontaneously, "May we have another forty years."

Well, he hadn't had another forty years, not even another four. Would she have forty more? It seemed like a long time, and if she should be granted it she wasn't sure what she'd do with it.

After his death, she'd often felt an unbearable loneliness. She feared the nights, especially. It's a quirk of human nature that when you are feeling very blue, a host of new anxieties will crowd your mind. When her son had not yet gone away and she still felt responsible for taking care of him, this had given her something to be busy with, but now she didn't even have that. Actually her son had been away from home most of the time for several years already, but it had felt as though he were a kite and the string were still in her hand. But now this kite had sailed a thousand miles away, beyond the clouds.

She'd always liked the poetry of Li Qingzhao, and when

some lines came into her head she felt that this woman who'd lived more than a thousand years ago had perfectly expressed Ru Yan's own state of mind.

Staying by the window,
How can one hold out, alone, till dark?
Fine rain patters on the parasol tree,
Dripping into dusk.
How can a word—Sorrow—
Encompass what's unfolding here?[350]

The two birthday candles gradually burned down. She put them on a bar of perfumed soap and the melting wax began to form a roseate layer over the cream-white soap. The last bit of wick glistened on that red film, dancing until it thinned out and was extinguished. The room returned to pitch black.

Solitude and darkness make for a nostalgic yearning which decants the intoxicating wine of sadness. In this desolate hour, Ru Yan picked up the little dog who was as sad as she, and let her thoughts wander far in time and space. Yang Yanping lay motionless on her lap, soft and warm. The creature had neither eaten nor drunk nor excreted anything all day, yet it seemed determined to stay exactly where it was, content. "How frail and powerless is Man," Ru Yan thought. "We can't assure even a little dog of safety and happiness." A wave of disconsolate bitterness rose in her heart.

Ru Yan had often been seized by this sudden feeling of emptiness after her husband died. She would just feel depressed for no reason, and life seemed without meaning. She had always taken for granted that the man who'd doted on her all his life would keep doing so forever, and she could always be childish when the mood was on her. It had come as a shock when he departed so casually, in his easy-going way, and had found that drastic means of revealing how much he meant to her. Her thoughts now turned to her father. When he'd been alive, she had often forgotten about him, too, assuming he'd always be there, scarcely noticed, like the furniture. She had not anticipated that one day he'd be gone. Then she thought of her mother, proud and aloof, dignified all her life . . . how had she suddenly come to be so old? Who knew when she, too, might disappear? And her son: from the day she'd given birth to him, his every step brought him closer to old age and death. How many setbacks and humiliations would be his lot, the pain of illness . . . and just such despair as Ru Yan was feeling now. She realized that most of his suffering would remain hidden from her, but just the idea of it gave her a tightness in the chest. It was some comfort, though, to know that her son would never learn of her grim thoughts; generation after generation, the hiding of burdens would always be honored.

Grief and pain are the steady undertone of human life; joy and pleasure are but way-stations, moments of respite on this harsh pilgrimage. God made man for suffering. Unlike the beasts of the field, God gave him a sensitive mind, that doing evil he might taste a twofold sorrow. Man flatters himself as the pinnacle of creation, the lord of the world who levels mountains and channels floods, mighty and proud and matchless: yet in truth he is like the grass or the insects that crumple at a blow. A taillight accidentally turned off, or a mild tremor in the earth's crust, or a few viruses invisible to the naked eye are enough to destroy people in an instant or blight the rest of their lives. The lofty towers, the highways that stretch thousands of miles, the ingenious tools, the exquisite finery of mankind . . . in the face of certain forces all these prove fragile and vanish at a breath.

Precisely because people have such illusions and such peculiarly human enjoyments, when disaster strikes it is all the more shattering psychologically, far beyond anything experienced by sheep and cattle whose necks are stretched out for the knife.

Whenever she got caught up in such thoughts, Ru Yan sank into despair. She sat thus dazed for a long time in the dark, and then she heard a mighty cheer outside. Looking out, she saw lights going on in windows all across the city. She hurried to turn on her own lights and in a moment the room was bright and cheery. Thanks to the electricity, thanks to these lights, she was able to extricate herself from the gloomy thoughts of a moment before. Turning on her computer, she began to put into words the melancholy she had just been feeling, under the title "The World Frets and Grieves Tonight." She wrote to discharge the anguish. She did not post the essay to the forum or add it to her online collection, but quietly saved it to her hard drive.

As she showered that night, Ru Yan suddenly burst into song. She sang "The Tibetan Plateau" again and again, full-throated:

Who was it brought this cry from out the distant past?
Who was it left this thousand-year-old prayer?
Is there a song without words,
A bond that can never be broken?[351]

She sang this resounding song of the high country with peculiar sadness. The shower of water splashed down like tears which one would need a thousand years to weep. It was the first time she'd ever sung this song, and the first time she'd ever sung anything so loud and free. With a song one expresses one's feelings; *to sing relieves the woeful heart.*

53

Her cell phone rang just as she was about to go to sleep. It was Liang Jinsheng.

"You all right?" he asked.

"Not really. How about you?"

"I'm not so good, either," he said. "Busy."

"You should get some rest," she said.

"You need to be careful, too," he said. "This is the time when it's spreading fastest. Do you have enough to eat and drink, and other necessities? Can I have someone pick anything up for you?"

"I can take care of it," she assured him. "It's just hard for Yang

Yanping. They're going to kill the dogs."

After a pause, Liang Jinsheng said, "I could have it sent to the next county where someone could take care of it until this blows over, and then you could bring it back home."

Ru Yan almost accepted his offer, but then said, "But I can't part with her. You know, to me she's not just a dog."

"I understand," he said, "but under the present circumstances . . ."

"Let's leave it this way for now," she said. "If things get bad, I'll ask for your help."

"I've seen them killing dogs in the streets," he said. "I feel bad about it, too."

"You've turned into a regular bleeding-heart," she joked.

"Come to your window," he said.

"What for?"

"So I can see you."

Startled, Ru Yan asked, "See me? What do you mean, see me?"

"I was passing your house," he explained. "I saw the light on in your window."

She ran to the window and saw him standing down there in the street beside his little car. He was holding the phone in one hand and waving to her with the other.

Angry, she cried, "You're that busy? Don't even have time to come upstairs?"

"This is the only way I can see you and hear your voice," he said. "All day long I'm running to hospitals and having contact with people on the front lines. I have become a very dangerous person. I'll leave right now."

"Don't move," she said. "I'm coming down."

She ran downstairs, practically flying.

"Don't come down," Liang Jinsheng shouted, "I'm leaving." But she didn't hear him because she had tossed her cell phone onto the couch, from which his voice kept talking to the empty room. He was just about to start his car when Ru Yan yanked open the car door, standing in her nightgown.

"So," she said sarcastically, "passing the door without going in: no manners at all."[352] She pulled Liang Jinsheng's hand off the steering wheel.

He shrank back. "Don't touch me. You have no idea how terrible this virus is—"

But she had seized his hand and was clinging to it.

He threw her off. "I came specifically to catch a glimpse of you, I wasn't 'passing the door without going in.'"

She grasped his hand again, holding very tight this time: "All the more reason to respect the wishes of your host." And saying that, she dragged him out of the car and led him, step by step, up the stairs of her building and into her apartment, as if she had caught some child who'd been up to no good. "So you want to play the part of a hero, is that it?"

"You, um . . ." Liang Jinsheng stammered, "if you actually catch it, I will have done something terribly wrong. Smell me. I reek of Lysol, Clorox, and disinfectants."

She laughed. "You're a lot cleaner than the rest of us, then." She hadn't seen him for more than a month. He had grown thinner and paler, but he seemed very well-groomed from head to toe, and had the same crisp energetic appearance as always. With that hospital smell, Ru Yan joked, if she were meeting him for the first time she'd suppose he was a doctor. "You'll never guess what I thought as I ran downstairs. I was thinking, by this time his Excellency the Mayor probably looks like an escaped convict."

He smiled. "I have never in my life been so careful about hygiene. Disinfectants, medicines, showers, vaccinations . . . but I might still be carrying the thing. You know, with a lot of the patients who are being treated for it, they can't actually find the pathogen. I can't even go home; been living in the guesthouse—"

Ru Yan covered his mouth. "Let's not talk about this anymore."

Liang Jinsheng impulsively drew Ru Yan to himself, holding her close, and said softly, "Sometimes I'm afraid, terribly afraid. Maybe we won't bring this thing under control . . . We don't know where it's going. We don't know where we stand."

Again she covered his mouth, but this time she did so with

her lips. The action was completely spontaneous, and afterward she couldn't explain why she had done it.

The mayor became like a lion awakening from anesthesia. He grasped her tight, as if about to devour this delicate woman, and there arose in his throat a strange sound, a roar mingled with a sob; Ru Yan could not see his face and sensed that right now his face must be terrifying, for the face of a man who could make such a sound was assuredly not his everyday countenance, which exuded tranquility and self-possession, even a certain arrogance. Yet it was this transformation in him which set her on fire. She and the mayor set about the same thing at almost the same time: madly tearing off the other's clothes and their own in clumsy excitement. They got entangled on the sofa, pushing and tossing, and they didn't even hear the little dog barking at them. They kept at it until they were both spent, like two wild animals that have been shot. They lay motionless, twisted into a curve upon the sofa.

After a long time Ru Yan opened her eyes ever so slightly. She felt extraordinarily calm. The scene looked like a battlefield where two warriors have fought it out to the end and now lie prostrate, covered in scars—and it all felt perfectly normal. This act which had once filled her with such dread and embarrassment had been consummated as something utterly natural. It was the first time she'd ever done it outside of bed. In the past, even when her husband had been in too much of a hurry to choose a place for their lovemaking, she had always remained in control, sometimes refusing, sometimes firmly leading him to the place where it was proper: she felt that this was a matter touching a woman's dignity. But tonight she hadn't had any time to think about that problem. And when it was over, she still didn't think about it. All she could feel was a sensation of sublimity.

Neither of them spoke any more. Liang Jinsheng only held her hand tight, the way her son had done when he was little and they were in the streets among crowds. Then he fell asleep. Ru Yan observed the disordered scene around them but didn't care. She who had always been fastidious (to the point of an obsession with cleanliness) now surveyed the articles of clothing and shoes and socks which had been littered across the floor, on the tea-table, and on the back of the sofa—not to mention the two rootless figures who found themselves naked and exposed—and nonetheless felt completely unselfconscious, like a wild animal. When she heard him start to snore, she glided into the bedroom and returned with a quilt which she tucked around him. Not even drowsy, but sensing that the night was cool, she also brought a blanket for herself, and sitting at the end of the sofa where his feet were, she crossed her legs and put his feet in her lap. Then she wrapped herself in the blanket, reached back and turned off the floor lamp, and kept her eyes open in the darkness.

The computer in her study had been left on, and its monitor cast a flickering light into the living room. The wrangling was continuing in the chat room, and Ru Yan's name appeared often as the page scrolled along. But now it all felt a million miles away. Ru Yan's mind was at peace, untroubled by the waves, like the waters of that moonlit lake.

Sometime after midnight Liang Jinsheng stirred and half sat up. Ru Yan asked him what he needed, and he said, "To pee-pee." He didn't say, "To use the bathroom," and he didn't say, "Excuse me for a minute," or even "I have to relieve myself"; no, like a drowsy child talking to his mother, he said "pee-pee."

Ru Yan led him to the bathroom and turned on the light for him. It was the first time the mayor had used the bathroom at her place. The mayor didn't close the door but just stood there on his bare legs in his unbuttoned wrinkled shirt, and soon an urgent tinkling rang out from the toilet. Equally disheveled, Ru Yan leaned in the doorway and watched the mayor finish peeing. Then she flushed the toilet for him and they both returned to the sofa.

"How long was I asleep?" he asked.

"It's almost daybreak," she said.

"That's a good long sleep," he said.

The mayor said he was thirsty, so Ru Yan steeped a cup of

hot tea for him. When he took a few sips he woke up completely. The second half of the night is imbued with a cold energy, and they both wrapped themselves tightly in their blankets, each leaning back cross-legged at one end of the sofa, like a couple of tramps on the street. Their funky posture and the bohemian intimacy they had shared gave her a feeling of warmth and closeness, a childlike delight. For some reason she found herself remembering a World War II movie, an American film she'd seen not long before.[353] There had been a scene in a ruined building near the front lines where everything was damp, dark, and filthy. The young sniper, together with a band of incredibly dirty Soviet soldiers, is sleeping in his clothes. A young female soldier is lying next to him. They make love, passionately, notwithstanding their coarse grimy uniforms and the comrades squeezed in on either side of them; as far as they are concerned, they could be in the Garden of Eden, oblivious in blissful seclusion. When Ru Yan had watched this provocative scene, it had shaken her in a way that was hard to explain. Could love, or rather sex, actually be like this?

She heard a metallic snap in the darkness and saw the flame of a lighter illuminate Liang Jinsheng's face and the cigarette in his mouth. "You smoke?" she asked. She had never seen him smoking, and when Jiang Xiaoli had first described him, one of the points in his favor had been that he didn't touch tobacco or liquor.

"I used to smoke," he said, "and then I quit. But," he explained with a smile, "I read somewhere that smokers don't catch SARS."

"You believed that?"

"I wanted it to be true," he said. "Anyway, I think I wanted to ease the tension. You've got no idea how I've been getting roasted, fried, and puréed in the blender." Slowly smoking his cigarette, Liang Jinsheng told Ru Yan many things she hadn't known. "That hospital administrator—the one who turned away the elderly couple from your neighborhood—was sacked on the spot."

"He deserved it," Ru Yan said.

"A deputy director of the Bureau of Public Health has been

suspended, and is writing a self-criticism."

"That's all? What was somebody at that level being paid to do?"

"It was for my edification," Liang Jinsheng continued, "that both these cases were handled the way they were. Who do you think will get the treatment next?"

"Would that be you?"

"That's about the size of it."

Liang Jinsheng said the sectors for which he was responsible, and which he called his "Western Front," could hardly be compared with others such as finance, urban development, telecommunications, industry, or politics and law.[354] These last two years, with the exception of science and technology (which had done a little better), education and public health had been the weakest points of municipal administration. The resources which had been invested in these areas of his had been very limited, and of that limited sum the lion's share had gone to science and technology. He said it was like when a whole family is poor and hungry and there's only one steamer of buns to go around: giving each person a bun wouldn't satisfy anyone. The only way is to give the strongest more to eat than the others, so that he can go out, get a job, and earn enough to feed the family. The choice was inescapable. Moreover, the higher-ups demand that you produce results for the sake of their GDP growth figures. That's why medical facilities and hygiene were so lacking, especially the public health infrastructure, which was basically a big zero. The resources which these departments had once enjoyed had almost all been taken away in recent years.

"As the saying goes, *It's the leaky roof that meets with a week of rain*, or *It's the toad who gets stepped on by the ox*. Nobody expected we'd all of a sudden become a disaster area. Our city has stayed somewhere in the top ten, nationwide, in the infection statistics. If you include the first phase, when the numbers were a little fuzzy, we're in the top five. Many of our hospitals don't even have respirators, and sometimes all they've been able to do is watch people choke to death.

"This year was going to be a make-or-break year for our city, and late spring to early summer was going to be the key season, with several big negotiations for investment, a batch of important construction projects, a business expo with global reach, a science & technology conference, even the tourist season . . . it looks like they've all gone up in smoke. A lot of manpower and money has already been invested in these projects, and I'm telling you, some of the higher-ups are biting their nails.

"You know," he continued, "it's been a funny thing. For decades, and I couldn't tell you why, it has somehow happened that my career has plodded along without any fireworks, but smoothly and steadily enough. Nothing earth-shaking, but no big screw-ups either. I passed for an honest if unremarkable official. Well into my fifties, I wasn't looking for much, just to finish out my last couple of years quietly and retire in comfort... and a little happiness. But now it looks as though Fate is going to destroy me."

"Is it really that bad?" Ru Yan asked. "I mean, what have you done?"

"It's not about what I've done or not done. As you should know, it's an unwritten rule in official circles that when something goes wrong, the person most nearly responsible will be singled out and made an example of. S.O.P. . . . this is the cheapest and least disruptive solution. For me, now, there's no way out. My back's to the wall, and I have to fight it through. We'll see whether I can dodge the bullet."

"It can't be as bad as you think," Ru Yan said. "You won't go to prison; you won't get your head chopped off. At the worst, you

> *Pick chrysanthemums by the east fence,*
> *And take a long look at South Mountain*[355]

and live the untrammeled life of an ordinary person. It would be good for your mental and physical health. Or if, by some freak misfortune, you do go to prison, remember there's a woman out there who's always thinking about you, and you won't kill yourself, OK?" There was mirth in her voice. "As long as you haven't taken bribes or perverted justice, you should be all right."

"That's why I wanted to talk with you," Liang Jinsheng said. "You're a breath of fresh air."

While they'd been speaking he had smoked several cigarettes, and Ru Yan, draped in her blanket, had stood up to refill his mug of tea more than once. Formerly, she hadn't liked the smell of her husband's cigarettes and he had stopped smoking in the house. Formerly, she had rarely refilled her husband's tea, but many were the times he had refilled hers.

"I see these patients," Liang Jinsheng said, "and the medical staff—in such danger, under such pressure . . . What strikes me is their loneliness. In a flash, they've been cut off from the world, treated like lepers . . . but then I decided to think about it differently, as if I, too, had already caught this disease: once it's over, if I'm still standing, I will be so grateful! Winning and losing, being in favor or disfavor—these things mean nothing if you're suspended between life and death."

Little by little the sky had brightened. Some things are very different by night and by day, and as the early morning light washed in through the gauzy curtains, each of them felt the situation was slightly absurd and awkward for both parties. Grinning, each set about gathering up the scattered clothes and dressed hurriedly. The mayor's inner garments were in more or less acceptable condition: there was still starch in his shirt-collar, enough of his tie was tucked under his sweater to pass muster, and as for his sweater, he had learned from his secretary the trick of smoothing down the front with a hot towel. But his expensive woolen suit was in no condition to wear to work. The garb of a peasant heading into town to sell his vegetables would have been more presentable. On this particular day, an inspection team from higher up would continue its fact-finding first thing in the morning, and if he were to chair the meeting dressed in that suit, it would probably inspire salacious speculation.

"When I pass a mall on my way in, I'll pick up something to get by."

Ru Yan snorted. "Obviously you don't know much about

malls. Where are you going to find one open before 8:00 A.M.? Even the independent small-business types tend to sleep late these days." Liang Jinsheng began to look worried. He took out his cell phone and said he'd have his driver bring over a suit.

Ru Yan stopped him. "Forget that idea! You really want to bring him here to have a look?" And with that she led him into the bedroom, where she opened a large wardrobe in which plenty of suits were hanging.

"These were his," she explained. "These two look as though they were never worn." Ru Yan's husband had managed the sales department in a joint venture and had often had to deal with senior executives, so he had several suits of extremely high quality. The only problem was that he had been a bit taller than Liang Jinsheng. When he tried on a suit her husband used to wear in late summer and early fall, it fit surprisingly well, though the beautiful color made him look more like an artist than an official.

"That's a lot nicer to look at than your bluish-black suit," Ru Yan commented. Liang Jinsheng struck a few poses, looked at himself from a few angles, and declared, "It's just right."

Her husband had often worn this suit. He'd really liked it, and that's why when autumn came that year he had taken it to the dry-cleaners . . . and soon afterward he was dead. It was spotless and freshly-pressed. Seeing this suit on Liang Jinsheng gave Ru Yan a strange feeling.

When the mayor said goodbye, he told Ru Yan (with a twinkle in his eye) not to walk him out. Naturally he was thinking that if anyone noticed a single woman seeing off a male visitor at this hour, it would become quite a story. Then he added, "You know what has really been getting me down lately?"

"Mm?" she murmured.

"That this damned plague was going to postpone our happy day. But what do you know, it made it happen sooner. Goes to show, good and evil fortune are intertwined, and life is full of surprises."

He had barely got into his car when he phoned her. "What are you doing now?" he wanted to know.

"Missing you," she said.

"Now that you're mine," he said, "this whole screwed-up mess sinks into insignificance. To hell with it."

"You have a flair for compliments," she said. "But what you say is true."

"You're quite a screamer."

"Me? Screaming?"

Liang Jinsheng laughed mischievously. "Last night. You made a lot of noise. So did the dog."

Ru Yan felt her face redden and sputtered, "What are you talking about?"

"I even thought, 'If the citizens' patrol hears us, I may spend the rest of the night squatting on the floor at the precinct house.'"

Ru Yan didn't remember crying out. For years she had always been as silent as a fish. Her husband had once said, "You, you're just too demure."

"I would never have guessed," Liang Jinsheng continued, "that such a refined woman could be so full of fire."

This was an occasion when offense was the best defense, and Ru Yan countered, "And I never would have guessed that a mayor could be as wild as a bandit in the movies."

"At such a moment, what's left of the 'mayor'?" he said.

In the background she heard the sound of car horns. "I'll come see you again," he said.

Ru Yan answered, "I'll be waiting for you."

When she hung up, she felt that some of what she had said had been awfully clichéd. She had always mocked the language in movies and TV dramas, where characters said certain words a little too often. It was a shock to hear herself doing the same.

For days afterward Ru Yan remained dazed and confused, as if she had had a pleasant but surreal dream that was awkward to recall. The odd thing was that she did not feel ashamed. On the contrary, she felt pleased and satisfied, like a child who has gotten away with a prank. But once Liang Jinsheng left, Ru Yan departed from her long-standing habits, whether from indolence or some other reason. She didn't straighten up the room for a whole day but left it untouched, like a crime scene. She also discovered that after holding out a long time her dog had at some point lost control of itself and pooped on the floor right next to the sofa. Once she would have punished it for this, but now she welcomed it in much the same spirit that a patient after surgery rejoices that the vital energies, cleansed, have begun to flow again. She just cleaned up the mess with toilet paper and put it down in a corner of the bathroom. People said that would teach a dog where it was supposed to go.

It was almost as if a shell which had long encrusted her body had suddenly cracked apart. The despondency she had felt in the blackout had vanished like mist. She went over in her mind all that had happened that evening, from beginning to end, and the way she had behaved now made her laugh. How had a respectable woman in her forties lost all her inhibitions and gone crazy in the blink of an eye? It came back to her from her childhood how that nursemaid from Shandong would lecture the girls: "To learn a good example takes a lifetime; to follow a bad example takes a single slip." To be a lady, or a loose woman? That was the question, as Hamlet might have said, and it was surprisingly easy to answer. She felt that she was of course still a lady, and at the same time she was a sincere and lovable loose woman. For inside every fine lady, is there not a loose woman? And cannot every loose woman be a fine lady, too? It's all right as long as there is love.

Looking back on the last few years of her life, she felt that a major factor in her quiet desperation had been the feeling that she could not accept a man, or give herself to a man, ever again. Whenever she had thought about the details of common life between a man and a woman, Ru Yan had felt she lacked the necessary courage. What she had lost sight of, she now realized, was that once the fire was kindled in her flesh, the process that had once terrified her would take its course, just as the rain brings forth the flowers, without hesitation or self-reproach or embarrassment.

Eating a kumquat as a child, she had naturally thought to

peel away the skin and eat the inside, but that turned out to be tasteless, even a little sour. Her mother watched and laughed: "With this kind of orange, you eat the skin, not the meat inside." Ru Yan felt that she had let decades of her life as a woman slip by without understanding, continuing to eat the insipid inside of the fruit simply because that was what you were supposed to do. She wasn't sure at what point in her life she had started down the wrong path. Was it that, as her husband liked to say, classical literature had damaged her, Plato had ruined her? As she found the courage to ponder this now, she realized that Anna Karenina and Yelena and Vera and all those beautiful noble women of the literature she had loved, they must all have known this experience, but the authors had not wanted to write about this precious joy for readers to share.[356]

54

This interval of time was like an action-packed play. Sorrows and joys, exultation and grief, started to pile up. Elder Sister called to say her husband had been released from the hospital in rather debilitated condition, and she was getting ready to take him into the mountains to rest for a while: it would be good for his lungs, which had sustained serious damage. Mama was going with them. She'd call again when they got there. Then her mother came on the line. "Is what you two have planned still going to happen on schedule?"

Ru Yan knew perfectly well what her mother was referring to, but pretended not to: "What plan are you talking about?"

"The plan which that Mayor Liang suggested to me on the third day of the New Year," her mother answered.

"Mom," Ru Yan laughed, "You're in more of a hurry than I am."

"You've still got many years ahead of you," her mother said. "I can't wait so long."

"In view of what's going on," Ru Yan answered, "it'll probably have to be postponed."

"We don't care the least bit about the reception and all that stuff," her mother insisted. "Just find a weekend like you did last time, fly on down here for a dinner. Let him address me as 'Mother.' That'll do it."

"If you really want to hear him call you 'Mother,' I'll have him phone you tonight so you can hear him say it."

Around the same time, the news about Teacher Wei started getting worse and worse. Zhao Yi said he had been in critical condition more than once. Damo and his friends were consumed with anxiety. It was like a city under siege; there are times when everyone thinks the city can't hold out, and there are other times when the enemy is beaten back, but no one knows how it will end.

A drizzling rain began to fall, day after day. Under gray skies with the constant sound of rain, the world seemed to have lost sunlight for good. The dank air put a damper on everyone's spirits. Opening a window would let such humidity seep in that even bright and clean places started to be seen through a faint fog, and running your finger along any surface left a wet trail.

At some other time Ru Yan would have enjoyed this atmosphere. She had always felt she was the kind of person who should pass her life in garrets redolent of lilacs and rainy alleys[357], enveloped in an aura of books, stringed instruments, and candlelight. As a girl, she had pored over an old edition of *Dream of the Red Chamber* innumerable times. It was in three volumes, with the text printed vertically. That world of morning breeze and evening rain, of falling blossoms and broken lotuses serenaded by cicadas in summer and the gnats of autumn—and at its center, Xiaoxiang House and Yihong Court—through countless rereadings it never staled, but moved her and filled her with a languorous sadness.[358] She often dreamt she was in one of those old buildings with a sky-well[359], with wooden window-frames carved in floral designs, paved with square gray bricks, and sporting varied shrubs planted up among the gables. Green grass grew between the paving stones and the little courtyard was always edged with moss. Once she told her mother about these dreams. Her mother said, "Why, your grandfather's house was just like that! Maybe you lived there in a previous life?"

If you said that the dreamy sadness she'd known as a girl had been only "forcing a funk to write a poem," what she experienced now was vivid and real.[360]

In her somewhat muddled state, she discovered that the potted plants she'd bought before New Year's had all died at some point. They'd had no sun for days, and she'd forgotten to water them. The withered daisies were still standing tall, but their bright yellow had changed to a dark brown.[361]

Building No. 8 remained sealed for a more than a week. There were no new cases of the illness. The rain finally came to an end and the sun shot lovely rays through the breaks in the clouds. Ru Yan's despondency began to lift. She was like a man in prison who after the first few days comes to terms with his fate and knows he must endure his full sentence, no matter how hard it may be—like the old saying, *Be at peace with what comes your way.*[362] Her wild behavior that night had made her feel of a sudden the joy of living and long for what was yet to come.

Rising early, she washed her face and cleaned up the mess left by Yang Yanping the previous night. The dog had finally learned to use the newspapers as its toilet, and this would save Ru Yan a lot of trouble: she'd no longer have to stop whatever she was doing to take it out for a walk three times a day. Now she only needed to roll up the newspapers, stuff them into a plastic bag and tie it tight, and toss it in the garbage. Yang Yanping had also learned to keep quiet. Even when, sometimes, it needed to bark, the sound was as subdued as a child's whisper: a short little truncated bark. There was something very sad about it.

Ru Yan ate a quick breakfast and went out shopping. She had a list of things she needed, the first item being five bags of dog-food. Since a bag lasted three days, that would take care of half a month, and with any luck the situation would be different by then. She also wanted to buy some feminine articles for herself as well as fruit and convenience foods.

There were very few people in the supermarket, which made for a better experience than usual. When she did catch sight of someone else at the far end of an aisle, that person ducked into a different aisle. It was like strolling through a museum, taking down from the shelves one by one the items on her list. She saw a pair of slippers very similar to the ones Liang Jinsheng had worn in his house. She picked them up, examined them, and dropped them in her cart.

When she got home she had a talk with Yang Yanping, gave her mother a call, and then went online—first to send her son an e-mail, and then to check the SARS stats from various localities and catch up with the war in Iraq. The authorities had done a 180-degree turn with regard to the college kid who'd been beaten to death: not only had the murderers been arrested but it was said that the relevant regulations were under review. The young life that had been snuffed out could not be brought back, however. She remembered the disputes that had earlier roiled the Empty Nest and felt vindicated, but the rancor had left a bad taste in her mouth that wouldn't go away. The ardor of first love which she had initially felt for the Empty Nest had cooled considerably. The online universe was enormous, there was no end to it; the Empty Nest was just one little point twinkling in that limitless sky.

Ru Yan had once read a piece by Damo called "The seven colors of the Internet." He argued that all the information on the Internet fell more or less into seven categories: red, orange, yellow, green, black, white, and gray. As for yellow and black, everyone knew what yellow meant[363]; and black, according to a longstanding terminology, referred to "reactionary illegal information." Damo's other colors had all become familiar to her since she started using the Internet. But she had no experience of the black and the yellow. Chatting with Damo once on QQ, she mentioned his seven colors of the Internet. He said, "The Internet is wide open; if you spent more time there, you'd take these things in stride as a natural feature of a multi-polar world of information. Of course, if you're interested in exploring them, there's nothing Google can't do. Just enter a few keywords and everything you're looking for will be laid out for you, better than the Encyclopedia Britannica."

As for the yellow and the black, Ru Yan wasn't interested in the least, so she had never gone searching for them. But the Internet has a way of bringing you even things that you don't want. There must be some very hard-working people somewhere who provide this service for free.

One day Ru Yan received an e-mail and opened it after running it past her anti-virus software. It contained the address of a website. Exchanging links to websites is a common practice among online friends and Ru Yan had discovered many worthwhile sites this way. The page opened with a swoosh and presented Ru Yan with a picture of a man's and a woman's body—certain body parts in particular—with nothing covered up; you could see the smallest hairs. Over the course of more than forty years Ru Yan had grown from a girl into a woman and had become a wife and mother, so nothing of this nature should have shocked her. But the sight of this image made her freeze as if struck by lightning. The people on screen were both Caucasian, the man strong and healthy, the woman gorgeous. In their demeanor there was no hint of obscenity, on the contrary, they seemed confident and at ease, as if they were doing exercises, as if they were engaged in a dance, as if they were exposing nothing but their arms or legs or faces. Though she had tasted that one round of trembling bliss with Liang Jinsheng, Ru Yan found this couple's exhibitionism hard to endure. It embarrassed her and made her nervous, and then she tried to make light of it: "Ah well, you see all kinds in this world." She recalled hearing the girls at the office speak suggestively about "adult films" and seeing peddlers force porn DVDs into the hands of passers-by.[364] Then she reflected that these things were just normal concomitants of human civilization and they'd always be there. Still, it was an eye-opener.

Ru Yan soon had a taste of what Damo called "black," also.

At the point when news about SARS was most confused and uncertain, an online acquaintance sent Ru Yan a software program which made it possible to view many overseas websites that you otherwise couldn't see.[365] Here, there were many alternative viewpoints on SARS in China. Browsing through them, Ru Yan suddenly saw an account of what had happened in her own little housing development. It said that the couple who'd been rejected by the hospital and gone into seclusion in their home had been the reason why the building was placed under quarantine. Scanning previous entries, she even found the article she had written about her brother-in-law two months before, the version with Damo's title, but signed "Such Is This World." Ru Yan's heart began to pound. She remembered that Jiang Xiaoli had told her more than once not to post unauthorized information on the Net, because there were people who were paying attention. Reading other articles on these sites, Ru Yan started to panic for real. It was the first time she'd ever seen writing that revealed and criticized people and events inside China so openly. By the standards instilled during her years of education, the posts were thoroughly reactionary.

She phoned Damo about it.

"Perfectly normal," he said. "What is abnormal is to be unable to read such material."

"The articles were pretty polemical," she said, "and there were some that revealed our country's internal affairs."

"Stand straight, and you need not fear your shadow will be crooked," Damo shrugged. "If the attacks are right, we'd better listen to them. If they're wrong, they can be refuted or ignored. Look at some of the websites we've got here: there isn't a day that goes by without attacks on the English, the Americans, the Germans, the French; we even caricature their President as a baboon . . . and don't the foreigners just go on about their business? As for 'our country's internal affairs', if we ourselves would only publish them first, nobody would bother going overseas to find out about them. Do some research: how many Americans read our *People's Daily* or surreptitiously tune in to our China National Radio? What kind of special software do you think they use to sneak a peek at our official websites?"

It was always like this with Damo: with a few casual sentences he made a big problem easy to understand.

Ru Yan said she'd seen her own article, and there had been the news about the quarantined building in her development.

"It's a good thing," Damo said.

"What's a good thing?" Ru Yan asked.

"The Internet. Think about it. Without the Internet, do you imagine the powers that be could change the habits of a lifetime? You think they'd be giving you a daily statistical report? If there were no Internet, do you think we'd know about that military doctor who told the world the facts as he knew them?[366] You might even wonder whether, without the Internet, that old military doctor would still be living in peace? In this light, we owe a great deal to the Internet."

Ru Yan also told him about the pornography she had stumbled upon. Damo just laughed. "*This* wasn't invented with the Internet! I'm telling you, when we were sent down to the countryside, every day the poor and lower-middle peasants told us dirty stories. You find this stuff wherever there are human beings, just like you find grass and flowers wherever there's soil."

Ru Yan couldn't help laughing at Damo's poetic take on the problem. "You ought to join the Publicity Department. Life would become a lot more interesting for people in the media."

"It's just that what you see every day," Damo said, "doesn't seem strange anymore. In ancient times, a woman's arms could never be exposed; now, walk through town and you see everyone's belly-button."

"Yes," she laughed, "when you look at something so much, you get used to it."

"During the C.R.," Damo said, "when anything even remotely associated with sex was taboo and everything had to be squeaky-clean, there was a Soviet film *Lenin in 1918*, black and white, shot in 16 mm and full of static."

"I saw it," Ru Yan said. "I still remember quite a few of the lines."

"It contained a scene of the ballet *Swan Lake*. It lasted just two minutes, but many who had paid fifteen cents for a ticket came only to watch that one scene. When the Soviets leaped onto the stage before the cygnets had finished their dance, you could hear the scraping of chairs in the movie theater as they all got up to leave. You think you could make anyone watch it again now? Not even if this time you paid *them* the fifteen cents. Maozi told me one year he went to Hong Kong and wanted to see what the X-rated movies were like, so he sneaked into a theater ever so discreetly and discovered there were barely ten people in the house! And most of them had fallen asleep. He explained that this theater held screenings one after another, and once you bought your ticket you could stay and watch 'em all, so it was popular with the homeless."

Ru Yan admired Damo's ability to express an insight in homespun language. Even though he could also make use of literary language and the latest intellectual jargon, as his essays showed, when he expressed himself orally it was always in the language of the streets. Once she'd heard him arguing with Maozi and letting slip an occasional profanity. 'And that's with me here,' she thought, 'I wonder how he talks when I'm not around.' It amused her that a man of such deep thoughts had such coarse language.

55

Teacher Wei was still in the hospital. More and more people were landing in such places, much as they had piled up in "cowsheds" during the C.R. The first ones still hadn't been released when further batches arrived to be locked away. They might be nearby, but for practical purposes they were very far away. It felt as if they had died.

Time seemed to have stopped. People counted the minutes and seconds, wondering when it would be over. At 4:00 each afternoon, CCTV announced the numbers and transfixed all listeners as if with the shifting fortunes of a daily war communiqué.

For a while, those watching the numbers rise each day felt that the whole city must soon succumb. A gloom settled over

Ru Yan's housing development. She found particularly unbearable the plight of dogs and cats, who in better days had been pampered as pets. You could often hear them wailing or howling as they were beaten to death by security guards or hurled down by their owners from apartments on the upper floors. Once Ru Yan heard an altercation break out between a man and woman who lived in the building across from her. The man then opened their sixth-floor window to fling down a spotlessly white puppy. The frightened animal tumbled through space, clawing the air with all four paws as though trying to clamber onto something, and then landed heavily on the concrete pavement in front of the building. It was the dog's rear end that had hit the ground first, and the creature appeared to have been compressed by the impact. It lay there for a long time without moving. Ru Yan felt she had died with it and shuddered. But after a while the dog began to wriggle, and raised its head with an effort, and gave what sounded like half a bark, because that was all it had strength for: half a bark. It then began to pull itself along (its hind legs were broken), using its forelegs to drag itself toward the front door to its home. The lady of the house rushed out that door emitting cries of anguish and scooped up the dog in her arms, heedless of the blood that stained her clothes, and left the compound by the main gate, weeping.

On another occasion, she suddenly heard a dog cry out in pain, and she thought that rending wail could be heard across town. She looked out and saw a few security guards, each wielding a long stick with a hook fastened at the end, pursuing and striking at a small dog.[367] Ru Yan wondered if these weren't just like the hooks mentioned in that line of Li He, "How can a man not wear a hook-shaped knife?"[368] The weapon with which the ancients pushed back the foe on bloody fields of battle has become in modern times a tool for burly men to slaughter puppies. Finally one of the struggling guards sank the curved end of his weapon into the dog's back, and the dog was impaled on it and could no longer jump around wildly. Then the other guards stuck their blades in too, like Spartan warriors. They dared not draw close to the animal, for they shared the widespread belief that every cat and dog, formerly prized as a delicacy for the hot pot, was now a carrier of SARS. So—much as Shang Yang had been dispatched of old[369]—each one pulled his hooked weapon in a different direction, tearing that little dog apart, till its small body stretched, and the white dog changed into a red dog, and finally a bloody mass of flesh.

In all her life Ru Yan had never witnessed such a brutal torture, and it was torture for her to watch. As the savagery proceeded, she had reached with trembling hands for the camera she used on field trips. It had a fairly long lens, and she snapped shot after shot of this sanguinary scene. Finally she couldn't take it anymore, and she pushed open the window and yelled at the executioners, "You Nazis!" She felt if she didn't shout these fiery words, she would burn up, her rage would consume her. The guards couldn't make out what she was saying, and they shouted up to her, "Is anything the matter?" She screamed again, "You're Nazis, that's what you are!" One of the security guards grinned and raised his hooked stick to make an obscene gesture at her.

From that point on, she could no longer bear to watch what happened to dogs and cats outside. But the sound of their cries could not be kept out, and each time she heard a dog howl, the day was ruined for her.

But *this* day, after witnessing that little dog's demise, Ru Yan went out to get the roll of film developed. Then she used her webcam to make digital images of the clearer photos. She uploaded a post to several websites under the title "A City's Disgrace," recounting the mortal tragedy she had witnessed and including a set of pictures. She concluded:

Now that SARS has come, many—including the denizens of what is considered a modern metropolis, as well as local law-enforcement organizations—are treating cats and dogs and other innocent living things in a way that reveals their own hypocrisy, selfishness, and cruelty. With great harshness they are taking mankind's woes out on weak and defenseless animals, even the cats and dogs which at other times have brought them much happiness and comfort: they've abandoned these creatures, tortured them to death, treated them as enemies, blamed them for our troubles... The days we are living through have laid bare things more dreadful than SARS.

This was a disgrace to the city, and a disgrace to the human race. Let us remember it, as we remember Auschwitz.

This post, together with its bloody photos, instantly spread through the Internet like wildfire. Everywhere it was reprinted, there were hundreds of comments. One little dog touched off an online tsunami of anger. Many of the comments repeated Ru Yan's line, "This was a disgrace to the city, and a disgrace to the human race." Many fulminated, This was a disgrace to City X. Boycott City X! I'll never set foot in City X again! Don't buy anything from City X! There were passionate calls to erect in memory of that dog a monument to ensure the crime of this city would never be forgotten. With this level of anger, all kinds of language were used, and some people poured out all the frustration and resentment that had been smoldering since SARS began. Some pointed fingers at the highest authorities. The overseas websites were quick to pick up the story and comment on it.

Ru Yan hadn't anticipated any of this.

During these days, Damo read all Ru Yan's posts as soon as they appeared. For his granddaughter's health and safety, he was going out as little as possible, and in consequence he had (to use his wife's phrase) become fused with his computer. He took pains to forward Ru Yan's articles to websites where they'd have wider influence, little suspecting the impact which this courtesy would soon have on the happy future she was on the verge of entering.

Many a time he clapped his hands and murmured, "How much potential lies hidden in this gentle woman!" He would phone Maozi and tell him to have a look at her latest article. Once Maozi said, "Damn, if she were ten years younger I'd take her on as a grad student and do a new course: Emotional Philosophy!"

Damo shot back, "You are such a blowhard. If you ever offer that course, you'll be the student and she'll be your teacher."

"Well," Maozi laughed, "we can learn from each other. But really, of the graduate students I have, there isn't one can write so well."

"It's not just the writing," Damo pointed out. "The thinking, the feeling, the morality, the personal integrity . . . where have you met her equal? The students who sign up for philosophy these days, except for the rare genius, they're all mediocrities and opportunists."

From Ru Yan's first piece, "A Son's Rite of Passage," to "A City's Disgrace," she had covered a broad range of topics and moods in just a few months. Damo remembered his first assessment: "Fine woman's literary grace; tender mother's hearfelt emotion." Truth be told, although he had liked her writing even then, his appraisal had not been without a hint of teasing. Taking stock today, he'd have to say those eight words didn't go far enough. From "A Mother's Pain in the Darkness" to the posts she'd written after the start of the Iraq War, along with a series of writings at the coming of SARS, Ru Yan had developed her own distinctive style, a special way of looking at things, a peculiar ability to make sense of world events. He was aware that she had little theoretical knowledge and had never relied on systems of thought to observe and explain the world. Her approach was introspective, intuitive, sensitive, aesthetic, perhaps one could even say religious, for though Ru Yan did not believe in any religion, her temperament was imbued with a religious spirit.

Had the Internet not existed, had there been no such free platform for personal expression, this marvelous potential within Ru Yan might have remained forever dormant, hidden beneath her lovely form until she took it with her to the grave. Damo decided that no one could know how many Ru Yans were in this world. Of those who have broken through to eminence and now pass for experts, scholars, and leading lights in their fields, most gained their renown thanks to some odd chain of events, to luck. If we look closely, we find these people make a great many mistakes but the mass of men don't notice—nor, often, do they themselves. More than once, Damo almost told Ru Yan his opinion of her but then thought better of it. If he had done so, it might have become a distraction and made her angle for fame, thus diminishing her authenticity. He had also come close to recommending she read certain works of theory but had thought better of that, too. Such things often prove more a hindrance than a help. When something missing from a person's natural disposition gets added, it will always be a foreign body. He thought he should let her find her own way and grow according to her own nature, as a man watches wildflowers grow without applying insecticides and fertilizers. What grows by itself will always be unique. What is produced in a factory, such as our colleges have become, will always bear the stamp of the assembly-line.

After Ru Yan's post went up on the Empty Nest, it attracted much sympathy and agreement. There was no shortage of voices denouncing the atrocity.

The next morning, when Ru Yan turned on her computer as usual, she was startled to see a murderous post with the title, "`I'm going to strip the mask off Such Is This World`"[370] and signed "`I Am a Fox Fairy`." The post began, somewhat self-righteously, by castigating Ru Yan and questioning her motives for writing a long article about the perfectly legal elimination of a dog at a time of national emergency, when the country needed to be of one heart and one mind in the struggle against SARS. It went on: `Ever since this individual began serving as Moderator, on many occasions she has disseminated reckless speech, catering to the international China-bashers who are slanderously attacking our government`. Then it adduced a number of quotes from Ru Yan's recent writings. These quotes, taken out of context and interspersed with critical comments, did indeed look rather shocking, and for a moment Ru Yan herself felt there might be a problem. But the killer came at the end, when the author launched into a new attack: `If the` above-cited remarks actually represented this individual's beliefs, we could file it away as one person's opinion. But in fact, this individual is a despicable hypocrite. On the one hand, this individual condemns our city for the sake of some little dog. On the other, this woman past her prime, who has lived for a number of years as a widow, has used all her wiles to seduce an important official of this city, none other, in fact, than the cadre who is leading the fight against SARS. So while in public she cultivates a fine reputation, in private she plays the whore. She knows no shame.

The timestamp and hit count showed this post had been up for more than ten hours and had been viewed more than a thousand times, a record. The author's tone was that of someone in the know and the post contained much confidential information, which increased its appeal. The forum had always taken a lively interest in such posts, which combined a forceful style with juicy personal secrets, especially in this case since it was about a woman, in fact, the forum's own moderator. Those who had supported her now fell silent, while those who had condemned her kept at it with mounting conviction. One sensed old grievances were being revived. Some of her detractors now cited posts she'd made long ago; it seemed they had filed them away in expectation of just such an opportunity. Most of them hid behind temporary pseudonyms but there were a few who used their familiar screen names, including some people with whom she'd been on friendly terms. She couldn't understand why they were in such a hurry to pile on. Was a post of this nature to be accepted unquestioningly? Some even said, *We always thought there was something fishy about this individual, a single woman on one salary who somehow managed to send her son to France.*

Having read this far, Ru Yan saw stars, as if she'd been whacked with a club, and she had a splitting headache. Her despair was like that of a dog who is drowning while a crowd of masked thugs, brandishing sticks and pitchforks, eye her balefully from the riverbank. For a moment she couldn't think at all, but stared dully at the screen, her mind a blank. After a long time she started to weep. It was the first time she had ever wept uncontrollably as an adult, and as she wept she set about deleting that horrid post and all the comments added to it. This was the first time she had deleted anything since she became moderator. Like a murderer, who having once broken his Buddhist vow of nonviolence finds it hard to stop, after deleting the posts she blocked the IP address of I Am a Fox Fairy. She thought if they ever met face-to-face she'd rip this person to shreds.

When she hit Refresh and saw the horrifying post wasn't there any more, she found herself trembling still. A bit later, she hit Refresh again, thinking to find some reaction from her Net friends, and was stunned to see that "I Am a Fox Fairy 2" had smugly posted, `So you thought you'd delete my post? Thought you'd block my IP? You've gotten a bit thin-skinned, huh? Have a guilty conscience, perhaps? Running scared, now? Where did all your arrogance go? What happened to the affected manners of that oh-so-refined aristocrat? To think you'd try to cover your misconduct with deletions and IP-blocks!` There followed the full text of the post which Ru Yan had just deleted.

By now Ru Yan had totally lost it. She deleted this post and blocked this IP, but first she ran a trace on the IP. What came back was: `Location Unknown.`

The next time she refreshed the screen she encountered "I Am a Fox Fairy 3."

`So . . . Hands and feet feeling cold? Blood-pressure rising? I'm telling you, you can delete all you like, you'll never lock me out. Kindly check your QQ.`

Ru Yan couldn't help starting QQ and sure enough the fox fairy had left a short message just for her: `Get me sufficiently annoyed and I'll block` *your* `IP. I can get into your computer, and sit there like a nice little doggie, watching your every move. I can send your son an e-mail, letting him see` `what an ass you've made of yourself. I can even print out a record of the disgusting web pages you've looked at, and the overseas reactionary websites you've visited . . .`

Each time it reappeared, that post from the Fox Fairy received hundreds of hits, which meant that many eyes were watching this bloody struggle. All those icons of warm handshakes which had greeted her when she first joined the forum were now nowhere to be seen.

By this time she felt utterly defeated. She recalled those demonic wraiths which never could be killed no matter how many times you struck them, or those robots which repair themselves after being smashed to pieces.

Finally, she just pressed the power switch.

Not much more than ten minutes, but it had seemed an interminable nightmare.

She stared mindlessly at the screen which she had just turned off, wondering when the demon who could not be killed would clamber out of the machine, sniggering at her.

The phone rang. She let it ring, but it persisted, and finally she had to answer. It was a man's voice, saying the appliance repairman was here. She was confused. "What repairman?"

"It's Damo," the voice said. "I'm at the main entrance, and they won't let me in. The guards need to check with you..."

Only now did she recognize Damo's voice. She recollected that for some time outsiders hadn't been allowed into the development.

Damo finished: ". . . please talk to them."

Over the phone, Ru Yan told the guard she had an appliance in need of repair. Damo went through a series of formalities that included having his temperature taken and filling out a form, and then they let him through.

He was in his blue overalls with a bag of tools slung over his shoulder, and he was wearing a mask. He stopped at her door to change into his own clean cloth shoes, as he always did. He smiled kindly and with understanding. He had been sent by Heaven, Ru Yan felt, for he was exactly the person she needed now, and her misery started to well up within her. When he first saw her she was still deathly pale and the life had gone out of her eyes. "I came posthaste, posthaste," he said cheerfully, "when I saw you'd got into a dust-up on your forum. First I thought I'd call, but then I realized it would be better to come over."

Ru Yan didn't say anything. She had surmised the motive for his visit when speaking with him on the phone. Damo took the liberty of pouring himself a cup of tea and sitting down. He was still smiling, with a hint of wry humor, the way a grown-up looks at a child who has flown into a panic about something.

"I had a hunch the rough-and-tumble might be too much for you. So . . . was I right?"

Ru Yan's misery swelled to a crescendo, with a stinging in her nose and a burning in her eyes, and it would have taken only the slightest push to release the tears pent-up like the spring melt behind a river.

"OK, let's begin," Damo said. "I'm going to do some ideological and political work with you."[371]

Ru Yan mastered the tears which had threatened more than once to pour forth, and said without emotion, "No need. I can get over it on my own. I just didn't realize the Internet could be so dangerous."

"What place isn't dangerous?" Damo asked. "Go walking through town and you may get run over by a car. First, you must be careful; second, you must not be afraid; third, you've got to take care of yourself, and the best way to take care of yourself is either to meet challenges head on and convince people by reasoning, or to ignore them, remembering that silence is golden."

"I find that kind of post revolting," Ru Yan said.

"You can write, so why would you need to delete a post? You think things on the Internet can be deleted in such a way that they don't come back? Even the government can't do that."

"This infringed on personal privacy."

"Anyone could see what this post was," Damo said. "It would have been written off as worthless. Any sensible person would have taken one look and seen through it. But when you reacted impulsively, you gave them the advantage and shifted the grounds of the dispute. Think about it: they were saying the wrong people were in charge, power was being abused for personal motives, someone was acting recklessly . . . and you played right into it."

Ru Yan listened but didn't say anything.

"When we were young," Damo said with a smile, "there was a saying . . . how did it go? *Don't be a hothouse flower; be an eagle in the storm.* But you, my friend, have seen too little of the world. A little trouble crops up and you fly off the handle. Consider: you can still say your piece, and so can the others who were involved in this. A post that was obviously in the wrong, even though it was already posted and people had already read it, why did you rush to delete it? Think about Teacher Wei, back then: only his adversaries had the right to speak. He didn't have the right, and no one spoke out on his behalf. He had to listen in silence to whatever they said to him. He had to take this treatment for decades . . . how could he endure it? But he did."

"The rules of the forum say you can delete something that involves a personal attack," Ru Yan pointed out. "And if they don't shape up after a warning, you can block their IP."

"That's right," Damo said. "You try to reason things out, you give a warning, and then you block them. That is right and proper. But you skipped a couple of steps in the process, no?" He smiled again. "For years we've been hearing how important it is to do things in the proper sequence. Look what grief you got yourself into this time."

The way he analyzed it and talked her through it helped Ru Yan calm down. She had known that a word from Damo would bring relief, a simple "It doesn't matter, let it go."

Finally she told him about the message which I Am a Fox Fairy had sent her via QQ.

Damo smiled. "Such talk could only scare a newbie. If this person is that skilled, why don't they turn themselves into a little dog sitting in their *bank's* computer and transfer a few million into their own account? It was just a shot in the dark. Even if they have a listing of sites you've browsed, what would that prove?"

Timidly, Ru Yan asked, "So, this person can't do these

things?"

"It would be very hard," Damo said, "and it would take a lot of time. To be that skilled, one would have to be a genius. It's just too bad this person came along to bother you. Listen, I know your computer inside and out and I fine-tuned it for you. As long as the software is working and remains properly configured, not even I could break in. You can be completely confident about this."

"I'm kind of sick of the Internet," Ru Yan said. "Some of what happens online I just don't like."

"I feel the same way," Damo said. "But you can't say you like or don't like the Internet, you can only say you like or don't like certain websites, certain forums. Oh, forget it; this is obvious and I'm sure you understand. You know, at first I thought I'd join you in the fight when it broke out online, but on reflection I realized you could solve this problem yourself."

"Yes," Ru Yan agreed, "that's the better way." She said she just couldn't understand how a post about a dog had provoked the other side to such rage. They hadn't scrupled to employ the most vicious tactics.

"I think it is for you to find the answer to this question, too," Damo said. "There seem to be personal feelings mixed up in this. Maybe resentment left over from a previous controversy. Or perhaps something outside the Internet."

What happened next made her troubles fade into insignificance. Damo got a call from Zhao Yi. As Damo listened, his face changed. Ru Yan knew at once that something must have happened.

He hung up. "Teacher Wei died."

Ru Yan asked, "When?"

"Eight o'clock this morning."

Eight o'clock, she thought, that was the very moment when she was so distraught over that post.

"No visiting," he said. "No farewells to the remains. Until the cremation, the relevant department will handle the whole process behind closed doors."

Although Damo had anticipated this eventuality more than thirty years ago and lately had had reason to think of it often, especially since Teacher Wei went into the isolation ward (after which his death was almost a foregone conclusion)—all the same, now that it had actually happened, the grief cut to the bone.

Something passed over Damo's face, whose keen and lively glance, gleaming with kindness and wit, had given way to a ferocity that under any other circumstances would have been repellent.

Ru Yan pondered the extreme brutality of letting a man die this way. It had been brutal not only to Teacher Wei himself, but to Zhao Yi and to Damo and the other friends. She wondered what his last days had been like. Dying like this on the white sheets of a hospital bed had been no better than dying in an unlit dungeon.[372]

After a long silence, Damo said grimly, "To certain people, this is the best way it could have ended."

"I'm going," he added.

"Where?" she asked.

"I must go see him." His tone of voice now was purely one of grief.

"Will they let you in?" she wondered.

"I don't care," he said.

Ru Yan said, "I'll come too."

56

The hospital into which Teacher Wei had gone was now entirely dedicated to the treatment of SARS. Armed Police stood guard, and the area around the main gate had been cordoned off with yellow tape, leaving only a passage wide enough for cars to enter; pedestrians couldn't even get close. No one even walked on that side of the street. This hospital, which had once been as bustling as a country fair, now had the bleak air of a prison.

Damo and Ru Yan both carried a bouquet of white chrysanthemums and each had stuck a blossom into a lapel. They stood quietly across the street from the hospital, gazing at the large building in silence.

They soon drew the attention of passers-by. Some just stopped, not too close, to look at them and at the ominous hospital with its haunted air. Vehicles in the street slowed down and glided by.

Zhao Yi arrived with Maozi. Emerging from his car, Zhao Yi was wearing the flaming red sweethearts' outfit. Damo and Ru Yan gave them chrysanthemums, and Zhao Yi pinned one to the front of her fiery dress. These four who stood thus in mourning attracted a crowd that grew steadily. Everyone wore a mask and stood in silence. Someone was taking pictures.

Soon friends from the academic world and from the press, as well as other acquaintances, found out and hurried to the scene from far and wide. Some carried bouquets, and those who had none would accept a flower from one of those who did. In this crowd some knew each other and some didn't; there were aged contemporaries of Teacher Wei, but there were also some very young people. Those who knew Zhao Yi and Maozi drew near to offer a brief greeting. No one shook hands today but kept an appropriate distance, and the eyes above the masks were all forlorn.

The day was overcast like the faces and the mood. At this extraordinary time and place, a crowd of people who knew Teacher Wei, alongside others who did not know him, found this remarkable way to bid him farewell. It had been a long while since such a large number of people had gathered on the street here.

At the sight of this crowd in mourning, a few passers-by asked quietly who it was that had died.

The staff in the hospital initially thought the crowd had gathered to express respect and appreciation for the medical personnel on the front lines of the epidemic. Demonstrations of that sort had in fact been organized in recent days, and TV crews had recorded the moving scenes. But eventually they realized that something else was going on, and some staff members came out to demand that everyone leave.

Damo spoke up. "A friend of ours has died. We've come to say goodbye."

A few Armed Policemen came over.

Zhao Yi said, "We are the family of the deceased, and this is our last opportunity to bid him farewell."

An Armed Policeman answered, "You won't be able to see anything here. The vehicle will be all sealed. No windows."

"You may not be able to see," Zhao Yi said, "but we will be able to see."

Just as they were arguing, a middle-aged woman hurried out from the building. Zhao Yi recognized her as a deputy director with whom she had spoken a number of times about Teacher Wei's condition and treatment. The director now said, "I didn't know you were coming! I planned to notify you once we took care of everything."

Zhao Yi said, "I needed to say my goodbyes."

"These are not normal circumstances," the director said, "and at your advanced age, Ma'am—"

"My age is irrelevant."

As they were speaking, Damo saw a hearse equipped with a siren emerge from the hospital compound. There was a placard in the windshield, "RESERVED FOR THE SARS TASK FORCE," and the driver was in a hazmat suit. A hush passed over the crowd until Damo cried out at the top of his lungs, "Teacher Wei, we came to say goodbye, Sir." Then he squatted down on the sidewalk and began to sob. Ru Yan was struck by the sight of this man, who had always been debonair and sharp as the sword of Damocles, now weeping like a woman. "Forty years," he murmured, "it was all of forty years."

Zhao Yi remained sober and calm, and called him back. "I must go to the mortuary.[373] I must be there to receive his ashes."

The four of them hurried into Maozi's car and followed the hearse. All told, the city had four mortuaries, and the direction they were going led to the newest one, just built.

As for the others in the crowd, some dispersed but others also started driving (or grabbed taxis) to follow along.

This mortuary stood at the foot of a mountain on the outskirts of town, where it was ringed by a patch of woodland as well as agricultural land that now lay waste. The road there had not even finished being paved, and there was still scaffolding whose gaps were shielded with yellow tape. Peering into the yard from the main gate, one could see a line of granite pavilions designed for rites of mourning. Outside were piles of construction debris. This place had been requisitioned by the Bureau of Civil Affairs for the cremation of the bodies of people who had died, or were suspected to have died, of SARS. Forbidding, without movement or sound, it utterly lacked the bustling atmosphere of the typical mortuary, where pipe and drum can always be heard.

A car from the hospital pulled up. The first to emerge was the deputy director. She came over to Zhao Yi and said, "We did everything we could. Wei Lao was a very strong man."

"He always was," Zhao Yi agreed. "I'd like to know a little about his condition at the end."

"There's a group that's wrapping things up," the director said. "We'll be in touch with you. Wei Lao had some personal effects which are being disinfected."

Then a few cars from the Provincial Social Science Scholars' Association arrived. One of those gentlemen approached Zhao Yi to say, "Teacher Zhao, restrain your grief.[374] At the present time, we cannot conduct the customary funeral, so we are considering another way to express our sorrow." He then invited her to his car, saying there were matters he wished to discuss with her.[375]

The minutes went by. Suddenly they heard the blowers of the crematorium start up. Ru Yan visualized flames jetting out inside the furnace with a roar and engulfing the form of Teacher Wei. In a little while the filter-equipped chimney emitted a wisp of faint gray smoke. Ru Yan imagined Teacher Wei in the curling smoke, ascending to the sky.

After more than ten minutes, Zhao Yi emerged from the officials' car. Her face gave nothing away. Ru Yan drew near to give her her arm. Zhao Yi had aged much in a few weeks, becoming wan and thin, and her gait was unsteady. Damo asked her what that had been about. With scorn she answered, "We'll pay them no mind."

Under a dismal sky amid the fields gone to waste, this throng of friends and strangers stood quietly on the bumpy slope facing the courtyard of the crematorium. After more than an hour, a man in a hazmat suit emerged and walked the long path to the gate. He carried in his hands a dark brown cinerary casket. Zhao Yi stepped forward, with Damo, Maozi, and Ru Yan behind her. She met the man at the gate, and he placed the casket of ashes in her hands. It was hot to the touch, almost hot enough to burn you.

Zhao Yi turned and addressed the assembled crowd. "I want to thank everyone who came to bid farewell to Wei Liwen. He died the loneliest of deaths: I was not with him. His children were not with him. Nor were his friends. This is the most miserable way a man can leave this world. I do not know what he was thinking in his last hours, for by that time he no longer had the strength to use the phone. He must be happy now, that so many have come at short notice to see him off. At least his journey hence shall not be lonely. Thank you. Once again, Wei Liwen and I would like to express our thanks to you all."

Tears were running down Maozi's face as he stepped before Zhao Yi and bowed deeply to the casket. Then he turned and spoke to the still motionless crowd.

"Of those who have come today, some are my teachers, old friends of Wei Lao; others, of my generation, were Wei Lao's students; and there are some here with whom neither I nor Wei Lao's wife are acquainted. It was as a young man in the turbulence of the Cultural Revolution that I came to know Wei Lao and we remained friends ever after. To all of you I offer my thanks. Wei Lao was always a model to me and a mentor, not only during those years of darkness but in the era of social transformation.

From him I have received enlightenment and inspiration and intellectual nourishment which will help me all my days. I did not live up to his standards, however. We scholars of the new generation have more to answer for than those of his era, and this will trouble me for the rest of my life."

Others came forward to speak, one after another. Their remarks were short and crisp, saluting Teacher Wei. They wished him a peaceful journey. They hoped his spirit would live on. Some looked back to the time when they had been associated with him, and some said that particular writings of his had changed their lives. One old man tottered up to the casket, placed his hand upon it, and in a choking voice said, "Rest now, my friend . . . after a lonely life, such a lonely death."

Reacting to the tone that was being set, one of the officials from the Provincial Social Science Scholars' Association also made a speech. He said, "We'd like to thank everyone for coming at this special time to say farewell to our Wei Lao. We are planning to hold a memorial service for him at an appropriate time, and you all will be invited when the time comes."

Another figure slid beside Zhao Yi and whispered, "It would be best for you to go home, now. Some matters remain to be settled."[376]

Zhao Yi understood. She asked Ru Yan to take from her bag the matching red sweetheart's shirt that Teacher Wei had worn, and she wrapped it tenderly round the casket of his ashes. "Finally," she said to it, "we can go home."

57

A few days later, the hospital notified Zhao Yi that she should come collect Teacher Wei's personal effects.

The return of his effects and the recounting of the course of his treatment took place in a small conference room at the

Public Health Bureau. The summons came suddenly, so Maozi drove her there. Two officials from the Retired Cadres' Office of the Social Science Association were also present for the meeting.

When Teacher Wei had been transferred from his previous hospital, all his personal belongings had been hurriedly sent along with him. These things were sealed in a plastic bag. A member of the hospital staff presented Zhao Yi with this bag, together with an itemized list, and said, "These have all been thoroughly disinfected, so there's no problem with them. Wei Lao had some clothes and toiletries which we burned, for safety reasons. We hope you can understand."

When she accepted the plastic bag, the staff member said she could check it.

"No need," Zhao Yi replied. "He had nothing that was worth any money."

A person from the Administrative Office gave a presentation on Wei Lao's course of treatment in the hospital. He went on and on, but the gist was that Wei Lao had been transferred from another hospital as a suspected SARS case, but since the patient's condition had many complications there had never been a definitive diagnosis, and therefore he had never been labeled.[377] He thought for a moment and smiled, but then suppressed the smile and continued: "It's actually better for the family members this way. There's a stigma attached to this disease, and even the relatives of the sick person can suffer discrimination. Therefore we have concluded that in his case, it was chronic acute pneumonia that caused heart failure. The specialists on our staff have signed off unanimously on this diagnosis."

The man from the Social Science Association said, "Wei Lao was an influential and senior figure. His unfortunate death is a great loss to our province's community of theoreticians. We are all very saddened. We hope that, together with members of his family, at a time when the whole country is united with one heart and one mind in the struggle against SARS, we can contribute to stability and the larger interests of the nation."[378]

Finally the Head Nurse spoke of Teacher Wei's time in the hospital. She said he had a positive attitude and a strong will. In his last days, though his breathing was extremely labored, he often hummed a song. Once she bent down close to listen and was able to make out the tune: "In Unity There is Strength." She noticed a tear rolling from the corner of his eye.

The person from Administration said, "How touching! Why didn't you ever make a report about this? When you get back to your office, I want you to write it up and give your account to the Administrator."

When Zhao Yi went home, Damo invited Ru Yan to come over and see her. The plastic bag was still sitting on a sideboard in the living room, unopened. One got the feeling Teacher Wei was hiding inside as a practical joke.

Zhao Yi said she had called his daughter, who had immediately burst into tears and declared she'd come right away for Dad's funeral. Zhao Yi had explained that because of the peculiar situation, everything was over already, and on account of the SARS epidemic regions were being kept isolated from one another. "If you come, you'll be locked up for ten days, maybe two weeks, before you can see anybody." Only after a long conversation did she persuade the daughter to come later, for the interment.

Damo said he wanted to look at Teacher Wei's personal effects.

"Go ahead," Zhao Yi said, and her voice cracked and she began sobbing. It was the first time since his death that they'd seen her cry. Relieved, they sat quietly and let her cry.

Ru Yan had felt ever since he died that something was not right with Zhao Yi. She seemed to have gone numb, and it had been painful to see her this way. When Ru Yan's husband had been killed, she had been just like that for four or five days, until one evening, after all the funeral affairs had been concluded and her son had taken all their guests out to a restaurant to give her a break, she had come back home by herself. As she took off her shoes at the door, one of her husband's leather shoes tumbled from the shoe rack, and it gave her the odd sense that he was still wearing that shoe and had nudged her foot mischievously. She picked up that shoe, which had molded itself to the shape of his foot and still smelled like him, and staring at it she suddenly recalled a host of incidents in which this shoe had played some part: how he had worn it walking, squatting, standing . . . lightly pressing down the computer's packing case with his foot while he sealed it with tape . . . it all came back to her. She hugged that shoe to her heart and wept.

As Zhao Yi now wept, Damo cut open the bag and began removing Teacher Wei's items one by one and laying them on the tea table. There were a few books, a notebook, a pair of reading glasses, a portable CD-player, a few packs of batteries which he'd never got to use, an electric razor, and a small amount of cash. The books were all signed copies that had been presented to him by friends who had written messages to him on the flyleaf. The CD-player was one Zhao Yi had bought for him when he went into the hospital, and it still had the disc of Shostakovich inside. A number of snapshots had been pressed between the pages of the notebook, all taken during the visit from his daughter and granddaughter. One was a group portrait at their dinner showing Damo, Maozi, and Ru Yan too, everyone smiling broadly around the platter of pulled mutton and raising their glasses in a toast.

The first part of the notebook recorded Teacher Wei's thoughts on various questions, along with notes he'd jotted down while reading. There were also outlines of a couple of essays he must have thought of writing. The latter part of the notebook contained fragments he'd penned after being hospitalized, notes on the progress of his disease and the course of treatment, notes from phone conversations, and reflections on death. Some of these writings appeared to be in the nature of a last will and testament. He said, for example, that if his daughter and granddaughter were willing, he would like them to come live with Zhao Yi; three generations of women would then be together, none of whom had any other surviving kin.

Seeing that Zhao Yi had gradually grown calm, Damo told

her she should come look at what Teacher Wei had written. Then he turned to the last page, where the handwriting had become almost indecipherable with the characters askew and irregularly spaced and not all of the same size, rather like a child's scribble. One would naturally guess he'd written this near the end, and sure enough, the page was dated two days before his death. They put their heads together and studied it closely, trying to guess at the words as one might piece out an inscription on oracle bones.[379] Finally they made out this sentence:

> *When it is not, they say it is;*
> *When it is, they will say it is not.*

None of them could figure out the meaning of this utterance, which had the tone of a prophecy. Then Zhao Yi said, "Just insert the word SARS, and then you will understand. When he was still able to use the phone, he expressed this thought to me."

A few days later, a brief obituary appeared in the official newspaper of the province. It was about 150 characters long, which was standard for a person of Teacher Wei's rank. It read:

> A retired cadre of our Province's Social Science Association, the renowned theoretician Comrade Wei Liwen, passed away on --/--/-- at the age of 83 after a long illness. Comrade Wei Liwen joined the Revolution in 1937, and in the course of his long struggle on behalf of the Revolution he achieved much that was of benefit to the Party and the People, and here in our Province he made a significant contribution to our academic field. Owing to the extraordinary situation at present, and in deference to wishes which Comrade Wei Liwen expressed while living, funeral arrangements will be simplified.

58

As she kept it hid like one of the wounded left behind by the Eighth-Route Army, Ru Yan suffered anxiety every day on account of the dog who shared her son's name.[380] Outside, the cries of animals being beaten to death were no longer to be heard, nor was there any further sign of the strays that had been running like fugitives through the streets. It was as if there had never existed in this world such a thing as a dog.

Her dog seemed to know what was going on out there. Since that incident with the security guards, Yang Yanping had never barked again. Ru Yan judged that the appalling cries of that dog must have made a deep impression on Yang Yanping, like a stark warning of the end of the world. Yang Yanping was like a Jew who lives quietly in fear of the pogrom. The dog had a wretched look in its eyes and was eager to please. When from time to time it wanted to express itself, it would emit a series of groans in a constricted voice, sounds it wasn't easy to hear even from the next room. It moved back and forth between rooms like a mouse, scurrying along the wall, but most of the time it lay prone on the little rug in Ru Yan's bedroom. From there it could eye a little patch of sky and catch two or three hours of sun. But at the slightest stir, even Ru Yan's footsteps or cough, it would instantly prick up its ears and look round warily. Only if it found there was no danger would it put its head back down to resume its nap. At times, the sound of voices or footfalls in the corridor would make the dog forget and it would rush forward as had once been its wont, but just as it was about to howl at the door, it would suddenly restrain itself and from its gaping jaws would come only a tiny snoring sound. Vexed and disheartened it would then stare at the door for a very long time. It wrung Ru Yan's heart to see the dog carry on this way, and she would hurry to pick it up, holding it to her breast and murmuring words of comfort and praise. Through the soft fur she felt the warm little body trembling in her arms.

In the larger world, too, it had grown eerily quiet. On the

streets it seemed as though the city had lost more than half its population. All day long, in the development where she lived, not a sound was to be heard. There were no longer old folks exercising in the early morning, nor workers streaming home at the end of the day. The children no longer made a racket after school. At night it was deathly still. But there was nothing peaceful about this quiet. You could feel the edginess, the apprehension.

Ever since the post from I Am a Fox Fairy, Ru Yan had felt disgusted with the Empty Nest. After Damo had had a talk with her that day, she had thought of writing a riposte and in fact had it half written, when she suddenly felt there was no point and closed the document without saving it. For days now she hadn't returned to that place where her heart had been broken. In the evenings she went online but now it was only for her son, to exchange e-mails and QQ messages and sometimes to meet face-to-face on MSN. She never mentioned to him the things that had been happening here; she didn't want these squalls to spoil the sunshine of his youth. Her son sent her many pictures, as beautiful as postcards, showing his happiness and the beauty of that land. She was quick to copy them and take them out to get large prints made, for which she bought floral picture frames that seemed suitably French in style. She covered half the wall of her study with these pictures, and they brought into her home the brightness of youthful joy.

Often she found herself anxious and grieved for no reason; often she wanted to cry. These fluctuations in her mood made her suspect she might be entering menopause. She tried to busy herself with work around the house, washing the dishes and cookware, cleaning out bureau drawers, and neatening up that room of her son's where nothing had been touched for years.

During one such bout of housework she raced to answer the phone. It was the telecom bureau reminding her to pay her phone bill. When she hung up, she realized she had been hoping it would be Liang Jinsheng. This made her thoughtful. There had been no word from him for more than ten days.

After that night, he had called every day to talk with her,

even if only briefly. She tried to reassure herself by considering everything he was dealing with, how overloaded he must be. But surely there were bathroom breaks, there were the moments before he fell asleep, and in the course of his frantic running around there must be times when he had a couple of minutes to call. This line of reasoning made her somewhat uneasy. Then after long hesitation, for she realized this was not a good time to call, she tried to reach him on his cell phone and got the recording saying the phone had been switched off. She tried again, and got the same message. Then she called his room at the guesthouse, but no one answered. Finally she decided she might as well try Master Luo's cell phone, but to her surprise she found that *his* phone had been switched off. Now she started to feel real anxiety. For a living person to suddenly disappear like this was surreal, actually frightening. We live under the impression that we can contact anyone at any time, but it's also true that we can lose contact with a person at any time.

Many years ago a girlfriend had talked with her about what men are really after and had warned her to be careful and never to give in easily, no matter how much desire she felt. For men and women act differently, after that happens. To the man, it's as if he's tucked you into his briefcase; the pressure's off, and he doesn't worry about you anymore. But for the woman it's as if she has swallowed a fishhook, and the line now holds you tight, tight as flesh and blood, and no matter how much you struggle you'll never break free.

These trite warnings about sex used to make her smile. She assumed they mostly came from women who had been unsuccessful in love and were bitter. But now she realized she had gotten herself into just such a bind.

Then she thought of Jiang Xiaoli and realized that Jiang Xiaoli hadn't called her for quite a while, which was a striking change, since previously Jiang Xiaoli had been constantly in touch and warmly looking out for her. Ru Yan thought that perhaps she had missed Jiang Xiaoli's calls because she'd often gone out in recent days. She scrolled back through the caller-

ID records on her phone's LCD, covering more than ten days, but there had been no calls from Jiang Xiaoli. She thought for a moment and then dialed Jiang Xiaoli's office. No one answered. Then she tried her cell phone. It took a while to connect and then rang for a long time before Jiang Xiaoli answered. There was a lot of background conversation, as if she were in a conference room.

"Hello, who is this?" Jiang Xiaoli responded in a whisper.

"You don't recognize my voice? You have to ask who it is?"

"Very sorry," Jiang Xiaoli said, "there's quite a racket here—"

Ru Yan heard the background noise recede, presumably because Jiang Xiaoli was walking to a quieter place. "I just called your office," she said, "and no one was there."

Jiang Xiaoli now realized who it was. "What's up?"

"Nothing in particular," Ru Yan said, "I'm shut in alone at home and, hey, I miss you!"

Only half in jest, Jiang Xiaoli answered, "You actually still miss me?"

Ru Yan was feeling a little guilty, for she knew that as she'd grown closer to Liang Jinsheng she hadn't thought about Jiang Xiaoli that much and had seldom taken the initiative to call. "Now don't give me a hard time, matchmaker! I've been locked away so long, won't you come cheer me up?"

"I'm in a meeting right now," Jiang Xiaoli said. "If there's something going on, tell me quick."

"No, nothing like that, but I thought we might go for a ride in the country tomorrow."

"Look, I'm not feeling free and easy right now," Jiang Xiaoli said. "I'm in Beijing."

Ru Yan was astounded. "Why did you run off to Beijing at a time like this?"

"Institute business," she said. "Let's wrap this up, OK? The meeting's still going on. When I come back, I'll be in touch." Then she hung up without even saying "Bye."

Ru Yan sensed Jiang Xiaoli had been strange and cold. She felt uncomfortable about the conversation and slightly listless.

59

What Ru Yan didn't realize was that during this time she had made a series of terrible mistakes, one after another. As Jiang Xiaoli expressed it to some of her trusted friends, that woman had lost her mind; a man was crazy about her and good to her, and she repaid him by pushing him step after step to the edge of the fiery pit.

The trouble had begun on the Internet.

Ru Yan's first post after her brother-in-law became sick had attracted attention. It was one of the first posts to reveal the spread of SARS in the South, and because it had names and dates and locations, it was cited both at home and abroad as evidence of an official cover-up. Luckily, the incident did not involve her own city, so they let it pass. Liang Jinsheng had given her some hints around that time, but she hadn't taken them seriously. Then when a building in her residential development was quarantined, her post about that was quoted everywhere, and this got some people very angry indeed.

May was to be a golden season for the city, an occasion when the saying *an inch of time is an inch of gold* would be no exaggeration. In addition to a holiday week promoting domestic travel, there were the two major events that had been planned the year before, one an international scientific conference and the other an expo to attract investment to the new part of town, and both had been scheduled in the same month. At the end of the previous year, Liang Jinsheng had led two enormous delegations across Europe and America and spent a huge amount of money. The preparations had all been finished and as soon as the May Day holiday was over, the grand openings would occur one after the other. The city's top leadership announced, "This spring is brimming with hope: we shall celebrate our city's second founding!"

But the counsels of Heaven are higher than Man's, and the

advent of SARS cast a pall over the sunny Maytime. Foreign organizations and individuals slated to participate were eyeing the progress of the epidemic nationwide and in this city in particular. Some had already hinted they might cancel their plans; some had decided to defer their decision to the last possible moment. Consequently, the city government had handed down the strictest orders to give the two conferences every possible boost, and they let it be known that anyone who screwed up would be fired. Moreover, the media were placed under tight restrictions: unless authorized, no one was to report anything having to do with the epidemic in the city.

These were days of acute stress and tension. It felt like a movie in which a time-bomb is ticking: will they find it in time to disarm it? Or will it blow up in the middle of some crowded festival? About ten days before the conferences were to start, of those invited more than 60 percent were either planning to attend or at least were still considering it. In China today, to pull off an international event on that scale is not merely an economic success but a political feat of a high order. Just then, when so much hung in the balance, the first batch of suspected SARS cases cropped up. The city government formulated a strategy: *Treat it vigorously, prevent it from spreading, keep a close watch, be cautious about diagnosing.* Without approval from the Publicity Department of the Municipal Party Committee, the media could not inquire into or report about the epidemic.

At this juncture appeared Ru Yan's post about the old couple that was turned away from the hospital, the post which ultimately led to the imposition of quarantine in her residential development. Within a few days it had spread to many websites around the globe. For those who had signed up to attend the two conferences and who were anxiously monitoring local conditions, the post was a deal-breaker. It was soon followed by the post about the dog getting beaten to death, and although that was not really adding any new information, the revelation of the savage abuse of animals—specifically, of dogs, which Westerners are accustomed to treat as their own flesh and blood—was profoundly repugnant to them. Someone even contacted the conferences' planning committee to say, "We'll never come to your city until you do something about the horrible way animals are treated there." Now, this was a city many of whose restaurants specialized in Dogmeat in a Hot-Pot, and where the eating of dogmeat and the drinking of *baijiu* were just part of life, so the foreigners' reaction seemed bizarre. But it was those people, so strangely fond of dogs, who held tight in their hands the money for plane tickets.

The reaction at City Hall can be easily imagined. They were going to come down hard on the author of those posts, but then there occurred at the highest level of the national government a sudden 180-degree change in policy. Two top officials were fired from the Beijing municipal government and the Ministry of Health; a group of doctors and nurses combating the disease was selected for a public encomium; even that old military doctor, who had disclosed to the international media the true facts of the epidemic in Beijing, was treated with kid gloves this time. Amid these bewildering changes in fortune, the city government became flustered and didn't know what to do. A week before the grand opening of the conferences, owing to the situation both nationwide and locally, fewer than ten percent of invitees would still confirm their participation, and most of these were coming from within China. Consequently it was announced that these two conferences, in which so much had been invested and for which such elaborate preparations had been made, were being postponed indefinitely.

A mood of dismal disappointment must needs find an outlet, and Liang Jinsheng was the most obvious target, especially since the Central Government had already set a precedent for scapegoating. Ru Yan's posts, in fact, yielded some clues as to how Liang Jinsheng was at fault. The more they looked into it, the more they found to blame him for. The New Year's holiday had been a crucial time for SARS prophylaxis. What had he done? Taken this woman sightseeing through the epicenter of the plague zone! The quarantine measures in that housing development seemed to have been lax and slipshod, and one could not rule out the possibility that this had happened because that woman lived there. There had been terrible consequences.

By the time Liang Jinsheng became aware of all this, it was too late. He murmured to himself with a rueful smile, "Ah, Ru Yan, Ru Yan, you're forcing me into the role of a man who loves a beautiful woman more than he loves his country." As a Party cadre, he was resolved to do whatever he could, manning his post to the bitter end, in order to atone for his mistakes. A few times he thought to call her and have a talk with this headstrong girl about the trouble she'd caused, but he knew that what's done can't be undone. He'd have to take his medicine alone. Someday, when he'd taken off his helmet and gone back to his fields to plant beans in the shadow of the southern mountains, it would make a good tale for Ru Yan to hear.[381]

Jiang Xiaoli's father had also been responsible in his time for the public health sector and had excellent contacts at all the major hospitals. Ru Yan's request for help getting Teacher Wei transferred had put Liang Jinsheng in a predicament. In the first place, he didn't have much expertise about medicine, having taken over these duties only with the most recent batch of appointments. In the second place, he understood that Wei Lao's condition was precarious, and if his treatment were mishandled the consequences would not be good. Third, if he (as an official in power) were to intervene on behalf of a man who had once been extremely controversial, this would obviously give his political rivals something they could use against him. He thought of Jiang Xiaoli's father, therefore, reasoning that a retired cadre with (as far as he knew) no connection to Wei Lao would have more latitude in this matter.

So he sounded out Jiang Xiaoli about what could be done.

Over the years, Jiang Xiaoli's family had assisted countless people who needed medical advice, drugs, or surgery. She readily agreed to help. Now although it had been with sincere goodwill that she had brought Liang Jinsheng and Ru Yan together, Jiang Xiaoli had never lost her love for him. She was the kind of spirited woman, capable of real sacrifice, who would go to great lengths to ensure a good life for the man she loved even if she couldn't have him for herself.

But to her surprise, her father reacted badly when she brought up this request. "Why in the world are you trying to help this Wei fellow? Who's having you do this?"

She was confused. "What's the matter? What did he do to you?"

But her father would only say, coldly, "Don't get involved in this."

"Why?" Jiang Xiaoli pressed him.

"He's a bad man."

"Don't they say he's an old cadre?" Jiang Xiaoli asked.

"He's a degenerate," her father said.

When she kept asking him to explain, her father recounted Teacher Wei's history, in a form, of course, that was shaped by his own ideas. Jiang Xiaoli's father was an extremely orthodox man, orthodox to the point of bigotry.

Three forces were involved when the Communists took control of this city. The first was the regular army, sweeping powerfully south: specifically, a certain corps which had made the Long March to Yan'an, had seen action against the Japanese in the north, and then had fought for Liberation in the northeast. These were the crack troops of the Chinese Revolution. The second force had come from staging areas in the South, as well as the periphery of the city, in order to harass the enemy's rear. These troops had originally belonged to a certain brigade of the New Fourth Army, but the old soldiers of the corps, who had fought so many bloody battles, considered this group second-rate. Finally there was a third force consisting of the underground Party which had been active in the city. After they came to power, there were constant turf battles among these groups. The regular army had access to considerable resources; the old New Fourth Army men were highly educated; and the underground Party stalwarts were most familiar with the city. For a long time after the founding of the People's Republic, one faction and then another would rise to preeminence. The wrangling never ceased, with much uniting and splitting.[382] For the officialdom of the province and the city this became a grave and long-standing source of difficulties. Each mass campaign furnished a pretext for these factions to hold a trial of strength and inflict deep wounds on one another. The conflicts had ebbed only in the last ten years as the old guard of each faction retired and died out, to be replaced by a new generation that had donned the Red Scarf only after Liberation. Yet even these had family backgrounds and pedigrees, so even among them the tensions of the old days were not wholly resolved.

It was the *Corps*, the *New*, and the *Underground*, therefore: and of these, the first to get into trouble was the Underground. They had held most of the power in the early days of the new regime because they were so familiar with the citizens and the structures of the city. Most were in the top rank of finance and industry. They became natural targets when the Three Antis and the Five Antis came along. The veterans of the epic campaigns put aside their differences with the troopers from the liberated areas to team up against their common foe. His intellectual background had given Teacher Wei an instinctive distaste for people and enterprises tainted by the stink of money, so when the cry rang out to "Nail the Crooks!", he didn't stop to ask himself whether this campaign might have ulterior motives. Although he didn't involve himself with specific cases, he wrote fiery articles. Teacher Wei belonged to the "New" and, enjoying a position of power and prestige, he was somewhat arrogant in his youth: it was widely understood that his prospects were bright. Two or three years later, he was quickly chosen as the next symbol to be struck down, and in succeeding years the "New" group was badly mauled. But then the men of the "Corps," who had long headed the administration, bore the brunt of the Cultural Revolution and suffered no less opprobrium than had been heaped on the New and the Underground.

Looking back on the internecine struggles that had riven the Party in the second half of the twentieth century, Teacher Wei wrote a short but famous essay, "Each Day, Break Off Half: How Long Will This Go On?" It cited Zhuangzi's chapter on the Earth: *Take a stick ten inches long, break off half of it each day;*

you will not come to the end of it, even after ten thousand generations.[383]

This saying was once quoted by the Great Leader as an important philosophical insight into the principle of divisibility.[384] Thinking of all the internal strife that has occurred in the Party since our nation's founding, I can't help feeling that this quotation has another meaning as well. At the start of the People's Republic, I was full of enthusiasm, and when the higher-ups gave the order to criticize *The Life of Wu Xun*, I didn't know the ulterior meaning of this, but began writing lots of fluent essays, glad to serve as the point of the spear, and I harmed many innocent people. I was on this half of the stick, you see, and it was right and proper to break off and throw away the other half. It took me years to understand that in making such a fuss over a trifling film and launching the first wave of criticism to roil the intellectual world of China, their real target was the intellectuals of the democratic parties which in concert with the Communist Party had done much to establish the new order. These included the noted educator Tao Xingzhi.[385] The insensate attacks on Hu Feng broke out soon afterward, and this time I was identified as on the other half of the stick. Many old friends and Party associates, both senior and junior, now played the part I had played before, and they did not go easy on me but cut deep. Immediately thereafter came the Anti-Rightist campaign, and those who had been so forceful in cutting me down now found it was their turn to be cut down by others. After that came the Pull up the White Flag campaign[386], the Oppose Rightist Deviation cam-

> paign[387], the Four Cleanups, and the Great Cultural Revolution . . . During the C.R., this kind of cutting-down became even more frequent. Today you cut off the half I'm on, tomorrow he cuts off the half you're on: it's true, the process can go on forever! But after enough cutting here and cutting there, all that's left of your fine ten-inch stick is a few splinters. And even then, the exhausting task of cutting away another half must continue, day after day. I wonder when this self-inflicted tragedy will end?

In recent years Teacher Wei had written many retrospective essays of reassessment which, layer by layer, revealed the political misgivings he had developed over more than fifty years. The number of individuals and undertakings which these articles addressed grew to be quite large, and many people became increasingly uncomfortable. Now to be fair, in matters of historical fact and interpretation one should allow for the way various individuals will have different perspectives, but these people, either because they couldn't speak out or because they had no good rejoinder, never criticized Teacher Wei openly or engaged him in debate, but disparaged him behind his back as if their consciences were not entirely clear. In fact, the overall political situation was still very much in their favor, and all the important media were under their control. Jiang Xiaoli's father had once worked briefly as Teacher Wei's subordinate, and in the campaign to destroy Teacher Wei he had been active and forceful. Consequently her father had always looked sourly on him as well as the others who made a comeback after being rehabilitated. Teacher Wei's outspoken positions in recent years had added immeasurably to this man's surly resentment and he'd often said to people, "Look, we were quite right to knock him down; he's always been at cross purposes with the Party, and he's still going strong, even more rabid now than he was back then."

When certain individuals (not involved in the conflicts just mentioned) did things that wouldn't bear scrutiny, Teacher Wei had sent accounts of their misconduct to the Central Government and so provided the impetus for them to be charged with corruption and dereliction of duty. What he wrote found its way onto the Internet and was very damaging to a group of people. Some were punished while others got off lightly in the end, but the incident engendered strong ill-feeling toward him. They called him the old nut job.

Jiang Xiaoli's father and the circle around him had mixed feelings about Teacher Wei's stand against corruption. On the one hand, they too detested the amoral perversion of justice. But on the other, they couldn't help feeling that a Party heretic like Teacher Wei must be up to no good when he stepped forward to talk about these problems. As Jiang Xiaoli's father put it, "We're trying to help, but he's trying to undermine." So it often happened that after Teacher Wei took a position on an issue, they were reluctant to speak out on the same side.

Jiang Xiaoli didn't bear the grudges of the last generation, but she did feel the anxieties of the next. For years there had been a stream of exposés, historical revelations that sometimes appeared on the Internet, and these had both angered and frightened the younger generation of people like her. She knew that once one of these things made it into an online database it would be around forever, and anyone could download the file at any time. The sages of old had said so much you could scarcely get to the end of it all, yet a USB drive the size of your finger was enough to hold that entire body of literature, and with that you could make unlimited copies and transmit them anywhere in a flash. Many people who didn't know how to use the Internet had nevertheless learned how to enter their own name, or a relative's name, into a search engine and find out whether there was anything bad on record. For many years people had known that once a campaign was over, all the records of what had been done would vanish like mist. This had been a comfort, but it was no longer the case. She hated this insane desire to dig up the past and mete out punishment, and she hated the Internet. She didn't want this kind of harassment to shatter the peace of her father's declining years, and she shuddered to think of the ways children of people like her father might be humiliated. She was starting to transfer this hatred to Ru Yan.

From her earliest years growing up in the compound for the families of the Municipal Party Committee, Jiang Xiaoli had a highly-developed instinct for politics. Because she stayed out of politics herself, she often had a better insight into what was happening than the people in office did. She only lacked the opportunity to put her gifts to work—as had long been the case for Ru Yan with her talent for writing.

After her father's angry reaction, she didn't bring up the business of Teacher Wei's transfer again. But Liang Jinsheng was counting on her, and she didn't want to let him down if she could help it. There was another angle, an important one: the treatment Teacher Wei received (and whether he lived or died) would undoubtedly be talked about. And the fact was, his initial treatment had been mishandled, and this could spell trouble for Liang Jinsheng and indeed the larger political situation. Not long before, a similar personage had passed away in Beijing and the incident had led to all kinds of speculation and adverse reactions. The authorities had been cast in a bad light, for these days people are easily swayed by rumors.

Jiang Xiaoli decided to take care of it herself.

There was a university hospital where she was known as Director No. 5. This hospital had one director and three deputy directors, but people liked to say in jest that she was the fifth director of the hospital. She couldn't count the people whom she had been glad to help over the years, thanks to her father's connections, whether it was to get into the hospital, or to obtain medications, or to arrange surgery. What's more, she had persuaded many an eminent specialist to take on the care of an old cadre or some celebrity or tycoon—even to make house calls. For the hospital, too, she had often served as a troubleshooter. Successive administrators and Party Secretaries at the hospital, as well as prominent physicians, were all on a first-name basis with her. When she walked into the building, it was like walking into her own office.

Through urgent negotiations, she succeeded single-handedly in getting Teacher Wei transferred to this hospital. But she didn't tell anyone about it.

60

One evening, Jiang Xiaoli went unbidden to Liang Jinsheng's guesthouse.

She told the guard at the door that she was from the Botanical Institute and had an important report to make to Mayor Liang about developments in the SARS program. The guard phoned Liang Jinsheng, who hurried out and seemed somewhat surprised that it was Jiang Xiaoli. His first thought was that something had happened to Ru Yan, and he asked quickly, "Is Ru Yan OK?"

Jiang Xiaoli smiled. "Why ask me? She's yours, now."

Realizing he'd been a bit rude, Liang Jinsheng tried to smooth over the awkwardness: "I figured you, being the guardian, would know better than I."

"Forget it," Jiang Xiaoli said. "Neither of you can spare a thought for me anymore." Then she tugged at him to go back inside. "Tonight you must give me all your time."

Liang Jinsheng was startled, but then he smiled. "All right, what do you want to do?"

"Let's go to your room, and then I'll tell you."

Now he was even more startled, but he knew her stubborn temperament and thought it best to go along with her to his room. Before entering, Jiang Xiaoli casually hung the Do Not Disturb sign on his door. It was a luxurious suite, and she stretched out on the long sofa and sighed, "Work is killing me."

Liang Jinsheng wasn't sure what she had on her mind. There was nothing unusual in her expression and she was plainly dressed, just a little more wan and thin than usual. Her manner was not that of a woman who'd come with some personal agenda. He made tea and washed some fruit.

When he brought the tea on a tray and peeled the fruit, she sat up. She leaned forward, sipped the tea, and stated with unusual gravity, "I have come to report to you on my work."

Liang Jinsheng broke into a grin. "You're making me nervous."

She didn't miss a beat. "For years the pharmacology group at our Institute has been researching substances with antiviral properties. With the coming of SARS, that research has been accelerated. Now, a breakthrough: we've found that certain animals which are carriers (in particular, the masked civet) have elements in their diet which are none other than the substances our group has been studying. The experts have offered a striking hypothesis: the fact that these civets can carry the virus without getting infected may have something to do with the presence of these substances in their diet. If we can isolate a medicine that effectively controls or treats the SARS virus, this would have global significance."

Liang Jinsheng had sat up very straight and his eyes shone. "Please continue."

"We immediately got in touch with the Viral Research Institute," Jiang Xiaoli said, "and had a meeting to discuss the question. Everyone agreed this is important. They, too, had just made some discoveries. They've got specimens of the virus, now. We put together all the data on SARS that's available here and abroad, and made preparations for the next step, which is experimental research."

"Uh-huh, keep going."

"That's where you come in. I think you should launch this research project as soon as possible. If there's a victory in this war, you'll be a national hero."

Liang Jinsheng's background was in applied technology and he knew that it's a long, slow process to take a new medicine from experimental research to actually using it. It's not like pulling buns out of the steamer! "It's a great idea," he said, "but I'm afraid it won't become usable soon enough."

"What's the matter with you?" Jiang Xiaoli said. "All these

years an official, and you still don't understand this country?"

"What does that mean?" he demanded.

"You think what we really need now is medicine? Consider: since the start of SARS, how many have died? A hundred? A thousand? Worst case, ten thousand? With all the hundreds of millions of people in China, can you name a cause of death that *doesn't* kill more people than SARS? Hepatitis, cancer, heart disease, poisonings, suicides, car accidents, occupational injuries, fires, mine disasters . . . the papers are full of 'em. The common cold kills more people than SARS. No, what we really need now is not medicine. We need calm and stability among the general population, we need to stop the panic: this is much more important. You want to talk about medicine, then you can call this a medicine: a tranquilizer for society. You need it, and the higher-ups need it even more!"

Jiang Xiaoli's words hit Liang Jinsheng with the force of a revelation.

"How far along are you?" he asked.

"The laboratory work will soon be finished," she said. "What I want to tell you is we can't treat this as a conventional project and do everything by the book. No, we have to play our strongest card right away."

"What do you mean?"

"It is necessary to go to Beijing as soon as possible and hold a press conference."

"Too risky," Liang Jinsheng shot back. "If something goes wrong now or proves to be a problem later, won't it be a case of losing the lady and one's soldiers, too?"[388]

Jiang Xiaoli was growing irritated at the anxious way he kept raising objections. "Why so wishy-washy?" she said sternly. "You think I'm going to let you lose the lady and your soldiers, too? Am I that kind of an idiot? All you have to do is sit there and listen thoughtfully, and then make a few wise and safely general remarks (I'll have drafted your speech for you). Basically, if it succeeds, you get the credit; if it fails, our particular office will take the blame."

Everything she'd said this evening was the fruit of a brainstorm that had come to her a couple of weeks before. She had the talent of methodically turning a moment's inspiration into something big. What had happened was that she had seen how the SARS outbreak and then Ru Yan's behavior were putting Liang Jinsheng in a terrible position, one that worsened by the day; and though her romantic interest in him had gradually cooled, a motherly protective feeling now joined itself to what remained of her old passion, and she was once again on fire for him. She would stop at nothing to save him and racked her brains to find some miraculous way to extricate him from his troubles.

One day she had been chatting with the staff of the Pharmacology Group and asked whether there were any Chinese herbal medicines that could help treat SARS. Liu Yan, a member of the group, answered, "Sure, take some of those berries the masked civet likes to eat, boil 'em, and drink the water. I can almost guarantee that would have some effect. Everyone says the masked civet is a carrier but on our field trips all these years we've never seen one that had died of disease, and of those that we trapped and kept, not one ever died of disease. I'll bet you, there's something prophylactic against SARS in the vegetation they eat."

Sometimes a word uttered casually is heard with great seriousness. Jiang Xiaoli asked whether in all their years of developing antiviral drugs from botanical sources they had found any that might be useful against SARS. "Hard to say," Liu Yan answered. "We don't have a sample of the SARS virus. Can't test any medicines on it."

Jiang Xiaoli said, "Look into this for me right now: do you happen to have done research on any of those plants? Liu Yan discovered that several of the items they had researched were indeed found in the diet of the masked civet.

Jiang Xiaoli told them to carry on, full speed ahead, and said she would speak to the Director immediately about making this a special project. She turned on her heel and went upstairs to find the Director, whom she told about her idea.

The Director was doubtful. "Rushing a project now that

there's a crisis . . . too risky. And you know, there's no money in the budget for anything like this."

"Nothing ventured, nothing gained," Jiang Xiaoli answered. "As for the funding problem, I'll work that out."

The Director knew that Jiang Xiaoli was a bit of a magician in these matters, but the vaporous nature of the project made him uneasy.

"At a time like this," Jiang Xiaoli pressed, "if you want what the Nation wants, and worry about what the Nation is worried about, then even if something goes wrong you'll be in the clear. Science tolerates failure. On occasion, science needs time, yes, but what's the worst that could happen? Hasn't our institute, like others, had a fair number of inconclusive projects? Isn't that perfectly normal? If someone must be blamed, it will be the researchers; as long as you're not corrupt," she smiled, "as long as you're not siphoning off funds and depositing them in overseas accounts, you'll still pass for a good cadre."

That very afternoon she had Liu Yan draw up a quick proposal, and together with the Director she walked it over to the Institute of Virology.

The Institute of Virology had made a recent breakthrough toward isolating and culturing the virus and was looking to take it further. The staff were excited by the botanists' idea. They couldn't see much downside in providing viral samples and conducting joint experiments; at the worst, they'd establish that the substances which the botanists had isolated were not in fact effective against SARS. When they heard Jiang Xiaoli was applying for a grant to fund the research, they cheerfully agreed to the collaboration. On the spot, the heads of the two institutes worked it out and initialed a letter of intent. The project was formally underway.

For the next week, Jiang Xiaoli shuttled back and forth between the institutes all day, every day, looking for signs of progress on which she could base a request for funds.

When she came to see Liang Jinsheng, that was the start of Phase II. She handed him the letter of intent and the first progress report. He took a long time to read both documents carefully. Then he looked up. "What should come next?"

"What's next is for you to take the limelight. First make an inspection visit to both institutes so they can make a report to you. You will respond on the level of generalities; don't ask any substantive questions; that's not your forte, and you have full confidence in the specialists. Tell them to move ahead right away, for in the race against SARS time is of the essence. When they ask you about funding for the research, you can agree in principle. Then take it to the Executive Committee and present it to them. Basically, you want to get them involved, tie it to them. If the thing succeeds, the one who proposed it will be seen as a wise leader; and if it doesn't succeed, they can't blame it on you alone."

"What if they say there's no money," he asked, "and turn it down?"

"At a time like this," she laughed, "with SARS the biggest political problem, they won't dare."

So Liang Jinsheng carried out the plan exactly as she had laid it out for him. He brought an entourage with him on inspection visits to the Institutes of Botany and Virology. The media ran suggestive reports with headlines like "Has SARS met its match?" and captions identifying Mayor Liang on his inspection visits, encouraging the specialists to make a speedy breakthrough in the fight against SARS.

It so happened that the city had just received a grant earmarked for SARS prevention, and since the mood of the moment was to try anything, the first installment of RMB 800,000 was allocated to the two institutes in order to fund the R&D budget for this project. The spread of the disease had reached crisis proportions here as elsewhere, and after that series of news items about the city had appeared on the Internet, all hope was gone for the two conferences that had been supposed to make May a golden season. Jiang Xiaoli persuaded Liang Jinsheng to stake everything on one last gambit of going to Beijing to hold two new meetings: a symposium on the development of a SARS vaccine and a news conference announcing the latest research into drugs that could treat SARS. The latter would confidently proclaim that an effective cure was already being developed from certain botanical extracts, and that since the laboratory phase of the work was complete, it was expected that after testing and clinical trials the new drug would very soon go into large-scale production. "Atypical pneumonia" was about to become as easy to cure as normal pneumonia. In addition, a vaccine was in accelerated development and had already achieved a certain stage of success.

These two meetings went smoothly and were extraordinarily well-received. A few former top-level leaders of the Central Government were in attendance, as well as eminent figures from the world of medicine and pharmacology. They showered the new initiatives with praise, though their reactions were based more on hope than on science. The media at once gave top billing to these developments and the newsstands were filled with headlines like "They'll Make SARS Just a Normal Sickness" and "We're Going to Be as Healthy as the Masked Civet" and "A Cure for the Fear of SARS." In no time at all, the scientists of City X had brought the light of spring to people all over the country.

Jiang Xiaoli's political judgment had been sound. No one was just then in a position to prove or disprove the science on which these brand-new lab results were based, but the reassurance which the announcement gave to the population was immediately effective. This had been exactly what higher authorities needed so badly. There was no question now about the continuation of support: the research would go on, and no one was demanding a timetable of results. As Jiang Xiaoli put it, this problem wasn't going to be around forever. Someone would solve it eventually. "The key is that we are leading the way. We can hire the people, purchase the technology, even buy the drugs if someone else invents them. We have established a brand. And anyway, every epidemic runs its course. This one will come to an end. At that point, when Chinese will have forgotten about it, we'll have time to clean up any messes we've made."

Liang Jinsheng now could see Jiang Xiaoli for who she really was. All those years as her father's subordinate, colleague, and successor, he had been under the impression that she was just a girl, a bit spoiled and headstrong, a little reckless. Now he could see that, compared to her, he was just a useless figurehead.

After this bravura performance, those in the City government who had been maneuvering to make him a scapegoat, force him into early retirement, and step into his shoes, realized that this was not a smart move. Moreover, in the campaign against SARS Liang Jinsheng had truly thrown himself into the front lines, heedless whether he lived or died, and the incident of his taking a woman down South after New Year's now appeared in a different light: he was entitled to a holiday, he was a widower, she was a widow . . . what was there to reproach? But the clincher was that not long after Liang had chaired the two meetings in the capital, a major figure in the Central Government made an inspection visit to City X and expressed high praise for City X's work on SARS. He even met one-on-one with Liang Jinsheng for more than two hours. This, plus Liang Jinsheng's political pedigree and the rest of what was known of his background, made people stop and reevaluate him.

61

When she got off the phone with Jiang Xiaoli, Ru Yan felt a bit glum. Something wasn't right, and her unease did not dissipate with time.

The next day, all the local media reported how Liang Jinsheng had gone to Beijing with experts from the Botanical Institute and the Institute of Virology, and had chaired two successful meetings there. A string of upbeat accounts appeared online. Ru Yan was about to celebrate when it occurred to her that Liang

Jinsheng must have been present at the meeting from which Jiang Xiaoli had spoken to her on the phone the day before. In other words, Jiang Xiaoli had been present at Liang Jinsheng's two meetings. When a woman finds herself in this position, her intuition becomes acute. Ru Yan finally realized that something was amiss between herself and Liang Jinsheng. Under normal circumstances, the first words out of Jiang Xiaoli's mouth would have been about Liang Jinsheng. And once the meeting was wrapped up, Liang Jinsheng would have phoned to tell her the good news, especially since she was, after all, on the staff of the Botanical Institute. Ru Yan became aware that the ground had shifted underneath her. Things had changed.

She wondered what might have caused a problem and mentally reviewed all that had happened since that night of bliss. She hadn't seen him since then, but all their phone conversations had been affectionate, sometimes boldly intimate. The only time she'd got on his nerves had been when she was trying to get Teacher Wei transferred, but that was over, now, the man was dead; and Liang Jinsheng hadn't complained. She thought more carefully and considered some of the posts she'd written... about the quarantine imposed where she lived, for example, and the killing of the dog. He knew those things were going on; she only wrote about them, and he may have been too busy to read anything. If he did read them, he must have understood where she was coming from. She could not stop telling the truth for the sake of their personal relationship: this was one of the things he especially liked about her.

The next day, the news was full of Liang Jinsheng's return and the formal visits swiftly paid by important local leaders to praise and encourage the staff of the two Institutes. Faster, they said, you're almost there: you have a great contribution to make in the nation's fight against SARS.

A few times she thought about calling him, for the occasion merited a word of congratulation. But she held back, and made up her mind to wait and see if he would call her first. The days went by and there was no call from him—or from anyone else, for that matter. The excruciating stillness made her fidgety.

A couple of times she even wondered if there was something wrong with her phone and used her cell to call her home phone and vice versa. She hoped to find that one or both of them had stopped working. But the call went through each time, and she stood there with a phone in each hand, saying "Hello, hello" and hearing her own voice clearly. Now Ru Yan experienced the torment of one who is in love.

She knew that, after that night, another Ru Yan had awakened inside her, a woman named Ru Yan who'd been fast asleep for ever so many years, but was now awake. She had discovered how powerful an experience sex could be. It was amazing that what had long been furtive and secret could turn out to be so wild and free. More than once the thought crossed her mind that she could have died that night with no regrets. Whenever her mother plied her with questions about when the ceremony would take place, she answered with cheerful vagueness. The truth was that, even more than her mother, she couldn't wait for that day to come. Again and again she used that night as a blueprint for imagining the life together she would soon begin with Liang Jinsheng. These thoughts made her deliriously happy. Even the household objects that were somehow connected with that night—the rather narrow sofa, the toilet he'd used, the rumpled suit he'd left behind, even the slippers she'd bought for him which he'd not yet worn—any one of these could launch her into daydreams.

For many years Ru Yan had felt detached from her own body, treating it gingerly, with a somewhat distant courtesy as if it were someone else's. Now she started to pay particular attention to it and became quite fond of it. She took stock of it, caressed it, caused it to produce delicate sensations . . . and often, without any clear intention, she would imagine these little movements of her own as part of a game for two, as if that were not her glance, but his; not her hand, but his. She gazed at herself for long spells in the mirror, smiling at herself or pouting her lips and raising her eyebrows: she wanted to see what she looked like to him. After this went on for a while, she would laugh and scold herself. On her loneliest and most troubled nights she masturbated, which she hadn't felt an urge to do in a long time. Though she knew many single women did it, and modern medicine and psychology viewed the behavior in a positive light, she had not tried it before now. And she knew that these days it was with the help of a fantasy that she brought these sexual caresses to a sense of completion. But now she dimly sensed the crisis that threatened what she longed for and hoped for.

Bored one day, Ru Yan turned on the computer and browsed one website after another. She hadn't been to the Empty Nest for a long time, and she noticed that where she and Lonely Goose had used to be listed in the upper-left corner of the screen as Moderators, only Lonely Goose's name remained. The forum's content, too, had reverted to the kitsch that had characterized it in the beginning. With the coming of spring, some had posted photos of flowers and told of spring outings they had made in the past. There were also articles about the kind of diet which is salubrious in spring and summer, and that sort of thing. The clashing controversies of recent memory had given way to a pleasant dullness. The familiar names still cropped up; it was only Ru Yan who wasn't there anymore, as if a clean wind had swept through a little garden and left no trace of her. Scrolling down, she found that even the posts from I Am a Fox Fairy and their many comments and replies were no longer to be seen. It was like the Arabian fairy-tales she'd read in her childhood: on waking, you'd find the castle of the previous night had been changed into a desert. Then she looked for the anthology of her writings and to her surprise found it still online, proof that she had once existed here. This, too, was like the fairy-tales, where after the castle vanished one would still find in the sand a single palace lamp, proving that what you'd seen the night before had not been merely a dream.

As she skimmed those first essays of hers, ingenuous and so full of enthusiasm, it felt like watching a young woman who knew nothing of life carry on in some cute but naive fashion. With a wry smile she clicked the Close button and left the browser. Then she started QQ. There were messages from her son, sent every few days to report that all was well and to recount his recent experiences and ask after Mom's health, warning her to be careful about SARS. These trifling, carefree notes from her son had often disappointed Ru Yan with their insipidity, but now she saw it was better this way. If misfortune and anxiety were to befall him, how would she bear it?

She sent him an answer and turned to the other QQ messages that awaited her with little bouncing icons. They all dated from many days before. Spring River Flows said,

`Haven't seen any posts from you for a long time. I know you're unhappy. I wanted to offer a word of comfort, but I think you are wiser about life than I am, and I'm afraid I wouldn't say things right. Most of the people on this forum represent the vested interests, some even come from families tainted by corruption. Those posts of yours, your whole way of thinking, could never be to their liking. Don't take them seriously. Birds of a feather, you know. I don't often come here anymore either. If there's anything I can do for you, please drop me a line.`

Another message, from even farther back, was from the anonymous person who had informed her that Lonely Goose's husband was under double regulations: `Be on your guard against those who are closest to you!`

This kind of message was disturbing: at the sight of it, her heart began to pound. She hurriedly closed QQ. She now regretted yielding to the temptation to revisit the Empty Nest and check her QQ messages: if before she had been anxious, now she was depressed. She kept thinking about it, though, and pondered how much of this world's suffering is forged in our own minds. Consider the peasant women who had paid no heed to the ravages of SARS as they set up their stands at the vegetable market, glad to make a little extra money thanks to the rise in prices during the crisis; or consider the shopkeepers who didn't care how bad business was but opened their shutters each day, standing ready, and when finally a customer came along they strode forward to welcome him with a big smile; and all this time she had been wallowing in her own unhappiness.

She ate a quick lunch and was about to take a nap when she heard a blare of gongs and drums outside. Leaning out the window, she saw a line of vehicles driving into the residential development and stopping at the front door to Building No. 8. All kinds of people poured out of the cars as the marching music rattled on, and they formed a line in front of the yellow security tape that blocked the entrance. A few TV reporters had already threaded their way past to find good locations for their cameras inside the cordon. An anchorman took up a position in front of the cameras and began saying something. Next a woman with the look of a top official started making a speech directed at No. 8:

Residents of _____ Estates! Residents of Building No. 8! In the name of the neighborhood, district, and municipal government, in the name of the SARS prevention office of the District Health Bureau, I announce that the quarantine of Building No. 8 is officially lifted!

The people who lived in No. 8 had all opened their windows by now and they cheered as they banged basins, woks, and ice-buckets. The impatient ones had already run downstairs and come outside. Then the line of men and women stepped forward, as if at the ribbon-cutting ceremony for a construction project, and they cut that yellow tape which had sealed off the residents of No. 8 for more than three weeks.

The woman cadre continued her speech.

The residents of _____ Estates and Building No. 8, together with all the people of our city, have passed through the grim trial of SARS and have won a significant victory, though not the final one: in the twenty-odd days since the quarantine was imposed, there hasn't been a single new case of SARS in this neighborhood.

It was as if she'd given the signal for a riot. There were more than ten buildings in this development, and the people from all of them streamed in from all directions, converging on the open ground in front of No. 8. Ordinarily these were acquaintances who played cards, or danced for exercise, or shared an interest in plants or goldfish (if they knew each other at all), but in that moment they were like long-separated kinsmen. The men clapped each other on the back, the women embraced in tears... the moment was very touching. Several cameras were busy recording it.

Ru Yan hadn't been to the office since the start of the quarantine. Her first thought was to go there and report the good news. She imagined that when a person who'd been confined as she had been, for no short time and not without hardship, walked in the door of the office, she would get a sympathetic reception. Oddly, though, there weren't many people at the office and those she encountered either went off in another direction, pretending not to have seen her coming along the path, or brushed past her with a forced smile and a quick "How's it going?" Then they were gone so quickly that Ru Yan didn't have time to tell them that she was now free.

She went to her own office first. Only the elderly Zhang Yan was there, who had always been the person with the best attendance record in the Institute. "Things are OK, now?" Zhang Yan asked.

"They just ended the quarantine," Ru Yan said. "It was a stifling experience."

"But your building wasn't under quarantine, was it?" Zhang Yan asked.

"No, but they told me here not to come in, and considered me a possible carrier." Then she asked, "Isn't anybody else here?"

"You didn't know?" Zhang Yan answered. "Every single group had staff transferred to the Task Force for that SARS medicine."

Ru Yan then went to Jiang Xiaoli's office. The door was closed and no one answered her knock. This was her real reason for coming to the Institute, and her heart sank. She turned and made her way to the Resource Room, usually a lively place, but today Xiao Li was typing away by herself. However, she greeted Ru Yan warmly and kept saying how she'd missed her. "I've been going crazy, they give me so much to type—a huge pile of documents every day!"

They talked about SARS for a while. Then Ru Yan inquired about Jiang Xiaoli.

"She's a bigshot now," Xiao Li said.

"How did that happen?" Ru Yan asked.

"You don't know about the project we're doing with the Institute of Virology?"

"I've read about it in the papers," Ru Yan said.

"It's a joint effort and she's the top coordinator. The Directors on both sides take orders from her. She's moved her office to the Command Center."

Ru Yan had intended to see the Director to ask whether she should resume her normal duties, but she suddenly felt somewhat drained and left in a hurry. She hailed a cab and only when the driver asked "Where to?" did she realize she didn't know where she was going. When she found her voice, what came out was the name of the guesthouse where Liang Jinsheng was staying.

Arriving at the guesthouse, she realized she was being presumptuous, but the cab had stopped and the driver had switched on his *For Hire* lamp. She paid the fare, braced herself, and walked in. She told the guard she was from the Botanical Institute. "You here for the meeting?" he asked.

"Yes." Then she filled out a form. The guard tore off the acknowledgment on the bottom half and handed it to her, saying, "Have the person you're seeing sign this. Turn it in on your way out. The meeting's in 801."

Ru Yan found the conference room. The door was closed, but you could hear voices inside. Without really thinking, she tapped lightly, twice, on the door. Someone came and opened it a crack. She could see him sitting at one end of the long table, only a few meters away. At the same time, she saw Jiang Xiaoli sitting at the first place next to him. Her head was down and she was taking notes. The person at the door asked quietly, "Who are you looking for?"

"Deputy Mayor Liang Jinsheng," Ru Yan said.

"Can I help you?" the person asked.

"It's an urgent matter," Ru Yan said.

"He's chairing a meeting right now," the person said. "Can you come back at 5:00?"

"Just tell him that someone from ______ Estates has come to see him. He knows me."

The person appeared unconvinced. "Do you have an appointment?"

"Yes," Ru Yan said.

The electric clock in the corridor ticked off the seconds one after another, and Ru Yan wasn't sure she could hold out. She decided that when the second hand reached the top of the dial she would flee.

Liang Jinsheng came out. Even though he had an inkling it would be Ru Yan, he still looked surprised when he saw her, and quickly smiled. "You sure know how to track a fellow down!" he said very quietly.

"I miss you," Ru Yan said.

"Me, too," he said. "I've just been so busy."

"You haven't had a second to make a phone call?"

The tears began to flow. She could feel she was making a fool of herself.

Liang Jinsheng became flustered and quickly pushed open the door of the adjacent room, leading Ru Yan in and smoothly flipping the lock once they were inside. He produced a tissue with which he wiped away her tears. "Ai, ai, ai . . . nothing scares me more than a woman crying. Tell me: what should we do?"

Ru Yan abruptly stopped crying, took the tissue from him, and wiped her eyes. "I'm sorry. I don't even know why I came here. I'll leave now. You should go back to your meeting."

He seemed to waver. "Well, you could rest in my room. I'll come by once the meeting is over."

"No need," she said. "When you've got a moment, give me a call."

She pulled open the door and left. As she walked briskly

away, she expected him to catch up with her and escort her to the main entrance with a few words of reassurance. But there was no sound behind her.

When the guard asked her for the paper, she said, "Mayor Liang was making a speech and had no time." She stuffed the unsigned pass into his hand and strode away.

62

Teacher Wei had died in an extraordinary way at an extraordinary time.

Initially, the news did not make much of a stir. History was painting the global scene with vivid prodigality, like a director who fills his stage with hair-raising subplots that unfold simultaneously. SARS was still wreaking havoc round the world. Baghdad had fallen. The masses who had endured so many years of Saddam's ruthless dictatorship now slapped his cheeks with the soles of their shoes.[389] As the debate over the war continued to seethe, Iraqi insurgents started setting off car bombs. At the cost of his own life, that college graduate brought about the repeal of an evil law, as his killers were identified and arrested with unprecedented energy. There was another murder at this time, of a beautiful young schoolteacher, and once again a tide of rage surged on the Internet.[390] These incidents touched off a new round of debate on the subject of constitutional government, a debate that raised fundamental questions about the system. There were also poisonings, mine disasters, fires, and the ineradicable problem of corruption . . .

The memorial service which the Social Science Association had promised for Teacher Wei never came to pass. His friends and students said they had never believed it would be permitted to say anything meaningful at such a service anyway. An effort began to take shape online, beginning with a few culture-and-philosophy sites that published memorial essays and set up a page with writings from his last years. More and more pieces of various lengths were written overseas about Teacher Wei, and they contained statements which it would not have been convenient to make inside China. By various paths, copies of these essays made their way back home. Suddenly a lot of attention was being paid to this old man, and there was a growing recognition of the significance of his ideas. Some proposed a conference dedicated to "This Wei." Since Maozi was well-placed within the system and, living in the same city, had known Teacher Wei for many years, friends from all over called on him to lead this project. Honored with this trust by so many senior academics as well as his own colleagues, and relying on the fact that the Social Science Association had already broached the idea, Maozi agreed. But when he then contacted the relevant department, he met with a clear refusal; in fact, they said they hoped he would not involve himself in this matter. Maozi therefore found himself in a difficult position.

He approached Damo to talk it over.

"Something like this ought to be extremely simple," Damo said. "A bunch of people come together from all over. They talk. They discuss things. Everybody brings a paper to read, and we collect these papers. Why do we need anyone's permission?"

"Well," Maozi said, "right now this kind of an unofficial activity, drawing people from several provinces and focused on a sensitive figure like Teacher Wei, if it doesn't enjoy official approval or at least tacit consent, first, it will never make it into the mainstream media, and second, there might even be trouble."

"The trouble starts in your own mind," Damo answered. "If *you*, at the very outset, think this is something disreputable, how can we possibly carry it off in an open and proper fashion? You talk about high ideals, but you show no confidence, like you were doing something crooked."

"To you, it's always a matter of principle," Maozi sighed. "We've said for a long time that the democracy movement must learn to compromise."

"It takes two to compromise," Damo said. "Only when there's some dialogue can there be real compromise."

Maozi lapsed into an awkward silence.

"Let's keep things simple, OK?" Damo said. "We'll send letters to the people who will most likely want to participate. We'll present it as a tea party. Everybody says his piece, exchanges papers, and goes home. It's just relatives and friends of an old man, sitting down in a tea house so they can talk about a guy who was a thinker, a progressive cultural figure, an old Party member, an old cadre who was incorruptible and never took an extra dime from his country. What's the problem?"

Actually, Damo had realized from the beginning that this project was going to put Maozi in a difficult position. He was an indecisive man, the kind who needs clear guarantees and feels he has more to lose than to gain, for terror still haunted his mind; at a time like this you couldn't expect too much from him. Damo felt bad about the terrible quarrel they'd had. He was unwilling to give up on the close friendship they had forged over the years. This was a part of his life that included things which went beyond issues of right and wrong. And he couldn't change him; still less could he change himself. Often he'd felt that his intellectual relationship with Maozi was past its shelf life; each ought to go his own way. Let the pair live on forever in that enchanted era of the *Qing Ma*, in the Eighties, that decade of enthusiasm. Erase the present.[391] It was because of Teacher Wei that these two had kept exchanging ideas and been forced to face the difference in their outlooks. Damo reflected that these days there were an awful lot of people like Maozi. What good did it do to quarrel with someone who'd been such a close friend? It would be kinder and more humane to treat the Maozi of today as a stranger met upon the road, while holding fast to the Maozi of the old days. Now that Teacher Wei was gone, once this memorial conference was finished, it would be time for these two intellectuals to part, lest they tear even the thread of cordiality that still bound them from long ago. Maozi was not a wicked man. He wasn't even a mean-spirited man. But over the course of an era he had been molded, slowly, into who he was. Maybe someday he would come to understand himself and draw a valuable lesson. But that was up to him; as Teacher Wei had said, a man can only save himself.

"Look, I'll set everything up," Damo said. "If all goes well, you can still chair the event. If there's trouble, for instance if it has to be called off or if we have to keep things extremely vague, well, we can still do it: not necessarily with a lot of people or a long session, but we'll be able to say that it was done, and there won't be anything else but what each person wrote."

Maozi looked somewhat guilty, but he was touched. "Dammit," he murmured, "it's a pain to wear the constricting crown."[392] Then he took out five thousand yuan. "You'll need some money to make the arrangements. Take this to start with."

Damo grinned. "Think you can buy an easy conscience?"

"You've always got to say something mean, blast you. Just consider it money I'm spending for Teacher Wei."

"Everybody will pitch in on this one," Damo said. "We'll spread the expenses evenly among the participants. But you can leave this money with me for now, and we'll settle accounts later."

"I'll do whatever I can," Maozi said.

"It's OK if you can't be there," Damo said.

Just when Ru Yan was engulfed in the sorrows of love, Damo was struggling to arrange the conference in honor of Teacher Wei. He was making calls and sending out letters each day and receiving essays that had to be edited and printed for the conference. As the date approached, he also had to arrange a place for the gathering. The city was still in the throes of SARS, and other places though not so hard hit were still on high alert. These districts had an indiscriminate policy of isolating all new arrivals for about two weeks in what was basically a form of administrative detention. Damo put out feelers to a new resort in the hill country more than sixty miles away. Business had not been too great for them and since SARS came they had been positively languishing. So when they heard of an activity being planned for 110 people, they were thrilled. "There isn't a single SARS virus at our place, no Sir! You folks come here and you'll be cleaning out your lungs with every breath! Where else could you still find such clean air? Plus, meals and accommodations are very reasonable."

When Ru Yan walked out of Liang Jinsheng's guesthouse that day, she realized she wasn't far from Damo's home and hailed a cab to go to that neighborhood. But she couldn't remember exactly where he lived and didn't have his address with her. After she had gone in circles for a while in his labyrinthine old dormitory compound, she had to call him. Damo came out and led her into his house.

"Now that they've set me free, I've come out for fresh air," she explained.

Damo was delighted to hear this, and he apologized for being so busy and not calling on her earlier. His wife had not yet come home from work. His daughter was still nursing the baby, who had grown considerably and was plump with a nice pale complexion and spirited, shining black eyes. The room held the scents of urine and milk, the atmosphere of a nursery.

Ru Yan noticed that the computer was on and printed documents were piled across the desk of the tiny room which doubled as bedroom and study. Damo told her about the memorial service for Teacher Wei.

"I've gone through two ink cartridges, it's like a copy-shop here. I wanted to take it to a print shop, but they were too expensive."

"You should have told me," Ru Yan said. "I would have given you a hand. Lately I've had nothing to do."

Damo mentioned he'd be making a trip the following week to take a look at the location he'd reserved for the conference and attend to a few details. Ru Yan said she was practically bored to death and would like to go with him.

"That's fine," Damo said. "If the two of us go, I'll have someone to bounce ideas off."

They chatted for a while and then he remarked with a sudden smile, "It seems something is going on in your life."

"What have you noticed?" Ru Yan asked, taken aback.

"Your eyes are telling a different story than your words."

"So you can read the story in my eyes?" she said with a melancholy smile.

"Naturally."

Ru Yan realized that she had come here wanting to talk about herself. But seeing how busy he was, she said she'd tell him about it when they were on the road together the next week. She insisted he give her some tasks she could do for him at home, and then took her leave. She was thinking that Liang Jinsheng might call.

63

It was almost six o'clock when the meeting finally broke up. Liang Jinsheng then had some of the participants to dinner at the guesthouse. After dinner, he returned to his room to wash his face and comb his hair and was about to get dressed to go out when Jiang Xiaoli knocked on his door. She had the minutes of the meeting. "If you look these over, I'll have someone type them up tonight."

Throughout this period, Jiang Xiaoli had radiated intelligence and indefatigable commitment. She had taken care of everything methodically and with good judgment. In a break with the past, she had stopped using makeup and her clothes and jewelry were now simple and plain. She kept working late into the night and rushed about in all directions, with an extraordinary taste for hard work, though she had grown wan and thin. Liang Jinsheng's early impressions of a delicate, privileged young lady were hard to reconcile with the person she had now become. When they traveled together on official business, she looked after him with thoughtful propriety, and whenever small problems cropped up she either took care of them herself or made sure no one bothered him about them. Her presence eased the tension of his work. She even prevailed on him to make time for a visit to his aged mother. Liang Jinsheng had gone on many business trips, but none had ever been as free from worry as this one. Most importantly, once the events in Beijing were over, she accompanied him on courtesy calls to some of her father's former superiors and comrades-in-arms. Although they had retired, they still had some say in decisions at the capital, and some of their children had attained high office.

Liang Jinsheng accepted the minutes but only skimmed them. "If you think they're OK, they're OK. You have executive authority now." Then he made as if to go.

"You're going out?" she asked.

"Yes, I have things to do."

"I think it would be better if you didn't go."

He stopped and asked with a smile, "You know where I'm going?"

That afternoon when Ru Yan had knocked at the door, even without looking up Jiang Xiaoli had known who it was. When Liang Jinsheng had returned to the meeting room, she had noticed that he was in a trance and seemed no longer to be really listening.

All through this period, Jiang Xiaoli and Liang Jinsheng had avoided mentioning Ru Yan as if this person, whom they had needed to discuss at every previous encounter, had never existed. They had likewise avoided all other topics of a personal nature, as if they were two officials of different rank who never let their personal relationship interfere with the performance of their duties. They had even started addressing each other as Mayor Liang and Director Jiang. Years before, she had called him Xiao Liang as her father did, and after they got to know each other she had called him Brother Liang or Jinsheng, but she had never used his official title. When she'd fallen in love with him a couple of years ago, she just didn't call him anything at all. For his part, he had always called her Xiaoli. Jiang Xiaoli had never declared what she felt for him, or anything she did say was vague enough that no one could ever corner her about it. She knew that Liang Jinsheng was aware of her feelings, but he pretended not to be and that spared them both considerable awkwardness. Not even her parents knew. There had been just one time, when she was out with two or three close friends and drank too much and babbled tearfully. On sobering up, she phoned her friends and hinted that it would be good for them to keep mum about this. Each of those close friends had played dumb and said they had no idea what she was talking about. "Very good, then," she had said with a smile.

So when Ru Yan had one day suddenly steered the conversation toward this subject, it had surprised and embarrassed her, just as if some well-dressed, attractive woman had come along and noticed that her stockings were ragged. She had hidden her feelings on that occasion and remained very calm, but a knot of discomfort had been planted in her mind. It couldn't be dislodged, and as time went by it only grew.

As she gathered up her notes, Jiang Xiaoli said matter-of-factly, "You shouldn't go. Not anymore."

Liang Jinsheng sat down. She poured them each a cup of tea and added, slowly, "I blame myself for this. When I first set you up with her, I didn't know her that well."

Liang Jinsheng said nothing, but just cradled his teacup and took little sips.

"Later I realized," she continued, "that you two are not well-suited to each other."

"Why?" he asked.

"She is too willful," Jiang Xiaoli said. "Her willfulness is bred in the bone. And she's proud with the kind of pride that is so deeply ingrained you may not even notice it. What's more, she's selfish, and prone to whining and wheedling, and she gives herself airs."

Mumbling a bit, Liang Jinsheng said, "But I rather like these traits in her . . . and I've never found her selfish."

Jiang Xiaoli said, "With some people, selfishness is about money; with others, it's about fame . . . If you two were still young, and if you weren't now in this job, or if you wanted to start living the life of an ordinary citizen a little early, I wouldn't say these things."

"But what if I *am* planning on that?" he asked.

"I don't believe it," she declared. "Can you state that firmly and clearly, please?"

He thought for a while, and didn't say anything.

"It's clear to me," Jiang Xiaoli went on, "that of all those in the city government at this time, you are the one who most deserves promotion. You may not even be aware of what you've got going for you. You've got the best educational background, having graduated from a high-quality school before the C.R.[393], and you've also got political advantages. You're not identified with any faction and appear to lack any power base, but that's exactly what the higher-ups are looking for. Financially, I can say you are the cleanest of the lot, plus you've got a good image, you conduct yourself well, and you're in good health. These are traits which officials need more than anything else today, but when they try to acquire them it's too late."

Liang Jinsheng chuckled. "If only you were the head of the Central Organization Department!"[394]

But she insisted in all seriousness, "I am regarding you precisely from the point of view of the Central Organization Department."

Only now was Liang Jinsheng beginning to lose heart. He said candidly, "Aw. . . It seemed fine. You've got me all confused."

She knew now that she had touched his vulnerable spot, and pressed on. "I've only been talking about some flaws in her personality. If you choose to like them, that's normal. When men are in love, they like women who are self-centered, temperamental, affectedly sweet, and liable to burst into tears at the drop of a hat. They are erratic, and that can make a man solicitous and forbearing, especially if he's on in years; he wants a woman's impetuousness to remind him of his own youth."

"How come you've given this so much thought?" Liang Jinsheng asked.

She ignored this sally, intent on what she had to say. "These questions of character and temperament may not matter so much, but I have come to realize that on the really big issues, she's not with us."

Starting to get serious, he asked, "What does that mean?"

"At first I thought we were both the children of cadres and so should basically be alike, but you take a look at those articles of hers on the Internet, take a look at the kind of people she associates with. And think about this: at the time when you were in the greatest difficulties, what was she doing? These are things I simply cannot tolerate, though I have held my tongue for a long time."

He asked her to give some concrete examples.

She recounted the contents of Ru Yan's posts, one by one, and talked about Ru Yan's contacts with Damo, Teacher Wei, and other dissidents.

"At first," she said, "I thought she was just naive and attracted by the novelty of these people. But later I found out that these were actually her convictions. I was astonished. The daughter of an old cadre, how could she have changed so much? I decided it must have been her mother's influence. Ideologically, the mother had more than a whiff of feudalism, capitalism, and revisionism[395] about her, and the way of the fallen class.[396] Plus there was the influence of Western literature. She'd like to be a rebel; that's fashionable now. In the more than ten years since the Soviet Union fell apart and the huge changes occurred in Eastern Europe, some people, especially opportunists inside the Party, have been itching to make trouble. Then there's the so-called Children of the Revolution[397] who want to curry favor in the right places so that if the wind shifts they won't be left out . . . But individuals like her are exactly what certain people need. A fortress is most easily breached from within. That's why those hostile websites, those overseas anti-communist websites, would so quickly reprint her essays. Birds of a feather . . ."

"If you want to talk about rebels," Liang Jinsheng objected, "then how many of our proletarian revolutionaries were once rebels—"

"No!" she cut him off, agitated. "Rebellion was OK only once, the first time: then it was loyal officials contending for control of the State. The next time, it's just unfilial sons plotting rebellion."[398]

"Oh, Xiaoli," he said with a smile, "I'd say your way of thinking is stuck in the time of our youth. These days, don't we accept anything that makes sense, even if it came from the American Imperialists or the Soviet Revisionists? Aren't we gradually integrating into the international order? Even assimilating aspects of Western political culture that could be useful to us?"

"I'm not stuck in the era of leftist extremism, not at all," Jiang Xiaoli retorted. "I've never been more realistic in my life. I know we've got lots of problems right now and have made ourselves look bad. The contradictions between us and the people keep getting worse, and the misconduct of officials keeps getting more common and more odious, almost beyond retrieval. But all these things are for *us* to work out; we can't let outsiders take care of them. If we ever do that, they will screw up not only what we've done but everything our fathers' generation built. Read those articles by Ru Yan's friends and you'll understand what I mean. This is not about right and wrong; it's about winning and losing. I'll tell you something else: if they ever came to power I don't believe for a moment they'd be any better than the group we've got now. You can't tell me that they wouldn't become corrupt in their turn and start pushing people around. We saw a lot of that during the C.R., didn't we?"

"You were saying," Liang Jinsheng prompted, "that Ru Yan is not the same kind of person we are?"

"At first I thought she was," Jiang Xiaoli answered. "But now I can say with certainty that she isn't. As I recall, you once said, 'The writing is like its author, and the author is like her writing.' That stuff she wrote, nobody made her write it. I just can't believe she could call our Communist city a city of disgrace. I can't believe she could look at some temporary difficulties in the midst of SARS and say we were telling lies. Take a close look at her choice of words: she never said 'we,' but only 'they'!"

"I think when she said 'they,' she didn't mean us."

"It included us."

Liang Jinsheng seemed to be struggling to understand what Jiang Xiaoli had said, and spoke only after a long silence. "I think she was right about many things," he said, "and her sense of justice deserves respect. She is able to rise above the viewpoint and interests of a narrow group. This ought to be how a true Communist thinks."

Jiang Xiaoli smiled coldly. "You're a kind-hearted man, Mr. Mayor. A person who bad-mouths our cause and puts it in the worst possible light . . . right, a true and generous Communist."

"Xiaoli," he said, "I will tell you frankly, on this point she and I have much in common. Many of the people on the scene today make me sick with what they're doing. They're a lot worse than she is."

"That's why the Communist Party needs people like you, and no other kind. No party likes rotten people; no party likes grafters and incompetents. The common people don't believe the old line anymore; not even we do. But only we can fix it. Maybe reversing direction will give us a black eye, but that's OK. The vital thing is not to let anyone dig up our ancestral grave or cut off our resources.[399] If somebody wants to do that, no matter how many good reasons they give, we must never agree. Let me tell you something very seriously, Mayor Liang: if you are genuinely in agreement with her, then I will respect your choice. But if you are at odds with her on this fundamental level, I advise you to stop right now. Not only for the sake of your future career, but for your personal happiness. If your life with a woman is a case of 'same bed, different dreams', what do you think that will be like?"

Liang Jinsheng had been educated as an engineer and after graduation he had gone directly into work of a technical nature. Though he later served many years as a leading cadre, that was after Reform and Opening, and even then he had been in charge of concrete projects and had never had to think too hard about the big issues of the Party-State. So Jiang Xiaoli's powerful and visionary speech left him a bit overwhelmed and he couldn't say anything right away.

She took from her briefcase a sheaf of printouts and handed them to him. "These were downloaded from overseas websites. Each is an article she wrote, followed by a stream of enthusiastic comments and responses. The anti-communists used to be subtle, trying to disguise what they were up to and only insinuating their attacks. Not anymore; you can see it's all in the open, now. When you finish reading these, you'll still have time to keep your appointment if you want to. These documents have been seen by a number of people in the city government. They didn't get them from me. They are not unaware of your relationship with her."

Liang Jinsheng said heatedly, "I can't believe that in the twenty-first century there are people who want to get me in trouble for a reason like this!"

"This isn't the reason they want to get you in trouble, but it might do as a pretext. If reasons are needed, reasons can always be found. The SARS business alone could be enough to bring you down. Actually, that wouldn't be too bad, because with that, the worst they can pin on you is not handling it well. If they start looking into finances, I'm afraid there could be more of a problem."

Pausing between each word, Liang Jinsheng asked, "Looking into *my* finances? In *this* city of ours, they're going to pick *me* to investigate for *that*?"

"You don't believe me?" she laughed. "You think they can't find anything?"

Liang Jinsheng seemed discomfited by this line of questioning, and asked uncertainly, "They're going to make something up?"

She laughed again. "Why would they need to make anything up?"

He stared at her with fury, but speechless, as if he were trying to remember whether he actually had done anything that could be used against him.

Barely holding back laughter, Jiang Xiaoli finally exclaimed, "Look at you! A man like you, even though you didn't do anything, you'll incriminate yourself if you're falsely accused! Think back. Did you receive any gifts? Buy some shares?[400] When you were traveling abroad, you had some expenses? You attracted foreign investors? Authorized construction? Let's suppose that you are in fact squeaky-clean: can you guarantee that all your subordinates are? Can you guarantee that all the projects to which you gave approval are clean? If people start getting arrested, can you guarantee they won't incriminate you when they're being grilled? Even if with all their digging they can't find any dirt on you, the rumors will have traveled everywhere, and dealing with this will consume all your time. Just that beach of yours, you spent more than a million on the sand . . . you think nobody's wondering about that?"

Liang Jinsheng, who showed signs that this was beginning to get to him, said slowly as he stared at her, "How come I never heard about this?"

"When you hear about it, maybe it will be too late. A little while ago you didn't have a clear idea of the trouble you were in. Now you've gotten a break, and you have a chance with all your affairs to put them in a better light." Jiang Xiaoli was gathering up her things and preparing to take her leave. She allowed herself a self-deprecating laugh. "You see, I got into this with the best of motives, just wanting to be kind; but now I have to play the heavy. If you don't want to hear this, let it blow past you like the wind. I won't mention it to anyone else, and I won't bring it up to you again. You know, it hasn't been easy for me, either, to say what I've said: this has concerned a girlfriend of many years, and the man for whom I have most respect in the world."

Liang Jinsheng looked exhausted. "Couldn't we talk about this another time?" he muttered. "You think I don't have enough problems already?"

"If I put it off, you might someday say, 'Why didn't you tell me sooner?'"

Just before she headed out the door, she seemed to remember something and asked, "Last time ___ [401] came through, did they drop by to talk with you?"

"Yes," he said.

"What did they want to talk about?"

"They wanted to clear up some questions about the effort against SARS."

With a knowing smile, Jiang Xiaoli asked, "But that wasn't all, was it?"

"The other things," he said, "I can't talk about."

"Then I'll talk about them," she said. "They're investigating a corruption case. I know because they also looked up some old retired guys and talked with them about the current state of the city government. A couple of times they just happened to mention your name."

Liang Jinsheng was suddenly very tense. "They mentioned *me*?"

Jiang Xiaoli laughed as she looked into his face. "Yes, but not like that. And anyway the old guys put in a good word for you. Oh well, I've spoiled your evening, haven't I? These next few days I'll work extra hard to atone for it."

Just before going out, Jiang Xiaoli got choked up and fixed him with a penetrating gaze. "You know, some people in my family died for this country. Two of my uncles, and one of my father's cousins. Some in your family, too. Let's hope they didn't die in vain."

64

When Ru Yan got home it was not yet dark and she was thinking that Liang Jinsheng's meeting must be over, and she settled herself quite deliberately to await his phone call. It even occurred to her that he might just show up downstairs, as had happened sometimes in the past. The sky gradually darkened. She thought, he's probably eating dinner. When another hour went by, she thought, maybe he had to take a bath. As still more time went by, she wondered if someone had sought him out on business and was delaying him further. There had been a few times, she remembered, when he hadn't called until it was very late. Only when midnight came and went did Ru Yan realize she had spent the whole evening making up explanations with which to console herself.

For Ru Yan, this was a time of waiting for Liang Jinsheng.

It was the kind of waiting where each minute, each second is filled with expectation, the kind of waiting from which you cannot turn away because it is inseparable from you.

The days passed one after another, and they were hard. She made a point of paying the bills for her landline and cell phone on time and often checked to make sure the handset had not been left off the hook. When she had to take the garbage downstairs, she always took her cell phone with her, in her pocket . . .

It was an interminable time of waiting, excruciatingly uncomfortable.

More than once her fingers stole over the keypad of her cell phone, or she put on nice clothes and vacillated about going out, but she always managed to restrain herself. She had already barged in once and banged on the door in search of him and forced herself to look upon a scene which she was most unwilling to see. She couldn't make a fool of herself like that again. She had never humiliated herself that way before and she now despised herself for it. The longer this silence dragged on, the lower she felt. There were a few times she thought to screw up her courage and (after the fashion of those love-crazed women you hear about) just go and harass him, stalk him, give him hell, plead with him, even threaten him . . . Others had cast their dignity to the winds, why couldn't she? At least she would get the satisfaction of closure, whatever the outcome.

With her heart thus in turmoil, Ru Yan engaged in some serious introspection. Times of disappointment always furnish the best opportunities for introspection, even if the latter is then tinged by masochism.

Had she been too reserved toward Liang Jinsheng? Had she assumed an air of aloofness with him? She had never seized the initiative and expressed her love to him, and had always made him, the Mayor, think up things for them to do. Even her way of speaking to him had often verged on disrespect; when she seemed to make fun of him, hadn't she really been asserting her superiority?

But she couldn't find an explanation for his behavior. Was he just another heartless philanderer? In today's moral climate, it was hard to believe anyone would expend so much time and effort to have a brief fling with a woman well into her forties. Besides, that one time—the only time—it had been on her initiative. Perhaps he had wanted to play with her feelings? But again, to devote so much time to some weird emotional game just when he was under tremendous pressure in his work would have required a seriously abnormal psychology.

Ru Yan considered many hypotheses; the one thing she did not consider was how the writing which had come from her heart might have harmed the standing of a man in the world of officialdom. She continued to think that, since he had said at the beginning that the writing was like the person who wrote it and the person was like the writing, he must have liked those pieces.

Then she thought of Jiang Xiaoli. Mixed in with a warm and gentle understanding, had there not also been a certain arrogance in her own recent attitude toward Jiang Xiaoli? Hadn't there been something satisfying about the discovery that, before choosing her, Liang Jinsheng had rejected Jiang Xiaoli?—Followed, to be sure, by a hint of pity for her. And as she had grown close to Liang Jinsheng, seldom had she made any effort to keep in touch with Jiang Xiaoli, even though she knew what a deep interest (doubtless mingled with complex feelings) the latter took in their relationship. Ru Yan had felt little sympathy and had taken her support for granted.

After many such thoughts, Ru Yan felt rather insecure and guilty and had no idea how she could make up for these faults. Should she invite them both to her home and offer a *mea culpa*, only half in jest? Or write them each a letter and, after the normal chitchat, slip in an expression of regret? Or just go straight to Jiang Xiaoli's home and try to make the great matchmaker think well of her again; once she had *her* full support, she wouldn't need to say too much to Liang Jinsheng. But after mulling all this over, Ru Yan rebuked herself with sudden revulsion: "How could you do such a thing? You think you can fix this kind of problem that way?" Ru Yan was a proud woman, to the point that she'd prefer a jade that was broken to a tile that was whole. There had been a few occasions in her life when a single quarrel with a good friend (or even a single misunderstanding) had made her feel that something precious had cracked; after that, she preferred to shatter it and consign it to the past rather than let it linger on with its scars. She had seen too much of that on the Internet, where people would have fierce ugly quarrels online that left both parties lacerated, and then, a few days or a few weeks later, they'd come back with perky smiles and rejoin the gossip sessions as if nothing had happened. Ru Yan couldn't do that. Once she felt the magic had gone out of a relationship, it was finished: there would be no goodbyes and no turning back.

So she decided to do nothing at all, lest she have reason to despise herself for the rest of her life. Better to live in tears and on tenterhooks, in loneliness and self-reproach, and to wait it out.

65

When the day came, Ru Yan took care of all Yang Yanping's needs early in the morning and joined Damo, as arranged, at the long-distance bus station. They took their seats in a luxurious big coach heading out of town. It was practically empty.

"If all goes well," Damo said, "we should be able to come back tonight. You know, Maozi was going to drive us, but just a couple of days ago he received notice of an important meeting at the provincial level. That's why he had to bail." Ru Yan said it was OK, she liked these big buses; you rode so high above the ground you had a great view.

As they passed outside the city she realized that spring had come to an end, though between SARS and her own private miseries she hadn't even noticed. The fields had long been full of lush vegetation, the garb of early summer. She opened her window a crack and found the breeze warm and fragrant. As a young woman she hadn't liked this early summer wind: its touch on her body gave her a sad and restless feeling, with mixed-up impulses to weep and to skip and to sing in a loud voice, and to fall in love with someone from her daydreams.

They rolled across the broad earth under the big sky, watching green hills and bright lakes wind past in the sunlight. Beyond the guardrail at distant intervals among the fields, from time to time she saw a farmer toiling peacefully with his draft animals, as silent as a painted landscape. The only sound was the occasional vehicle passing on the highway with a cheerful whoosh like an arrow in flight.

The wide flat land gradually turned into undulating hill country, and the soft carpet of the rice paddies gave way to patches of forest. The bus stopped at the county town where they changed to a mid-sized bus that would take them into the mountains. As it wound its way up the switchbacks, the greens grew deeper and the air more bracing: it felt purer than in the lowlands.

Ru Yan and Damo made small talk along the way, but most of the time she looked out the window, enchanted by the scenery. Damo had put his seat back and occasionally snored. "I've been a little tired, lately," he said once, and then went back to sleep. He woke up only when they had entered into the mountains. Suddenly he prompted, "You mentioned that day there was something you wanted to talk about."

She smiled faintly. "Having seen this road, I don't need to talk about it anymore."

"You let it go?"

"It seems so," she said. "At least for now."

"Some things are like that," he mused. "One moment they seem terribly important. Step back from them for a bit, and they turn out to be less serious."

The place they were going had a stately old name: Purple Rock Mountain Stronghold. It was a converted logging camp with, as you would expect, stunning views. Apart from a few lodges at the foot of the mountain, there was nothing manmade to be seen, only nature in its pristine form. The mountain woods and rivulets and rocks were stark with authenticity, and even the flowers were all wildflowers growing naturally at random. But business appeared to be very slow at the Mountain Stronghold. There weren't many staff on hand, and the place had the depopulated feel of a mountain village. A few dogs ambled around and when they saw the two visitors they barked a couple of times for effect and then gave it up. One poked its nose at Ru Yan's trouser legs and wouldn't stop sniffing. "It smells your dog," Damo said.

Two employees emerged from a building to greet them and show them the lodging offered by newly-built log cabins that had four or five rooms, each of which could sleep two or three. The place could accommodate seventy or eighty guests—maybe more, in a pinch, by adding cots or making beds on the floor. The staff called attention to the wood plank floors and the way every cabin was built on stilts for protection against the damp. If it gets cold at night, they said, you can light a fire in the brazier. It all looked good to Ru Yan and even though the cost had not been mentioned she blurted, "It's great! Such an interesting place. I can sleep on the floor."

"We've got quite a spot, here," the staff person said proudly. "It appeals to people with good taste. We've got electricity but prefer not to use A/C. This is a place for drinking spring water, eating wild herbs, burning firewood . . . Green Tourism! That's what we're about."

After coming to an agreement about the cost of room and board, Damo paid a thousand-yuan deposit and considered the matter settled. It was a couple of hours until the next bus back, so they had a quick meal in the staff cafeteria and went out to the parking lot and sat on a boulder at the side of the pass to wait for the bus. They contemplated the blue sky and, far-off, a sea of clouds beneath the peaks, and they breathed the fine mountain air. Damo sat in stillness as if he were one of the rocks himself. He could have been thinking about something, or not thinking about anything at all.

Ru Yan felt at peace with him. Damo was like a dependable older brother whom you could safely take for granted, although he was half a head shorter than herself. There was nothing about him to make an impression at the first encounter, but when you had known him for a while you sensed he could put you at ease in any situation, for he was pleasant in an indefinable way, like the mountain breeze. In him there were no nagging anxieties, nor the egotism that leads to inappropriate responses; there was only the thorough understanding of a person who has experienced life and its troubles. What you did not say, he knew anyway; and what you said he accepted, neither adding to your upset nor burdening you with advice that missed your point; without apparent effort, he would take the thoughts that had got you down and make them melt away. He was like a good masseur who chats with you amiably as he frees up the knots in your muscles where the *qi* is blocked. It put Ru Yan in mind of the saying (coined from a man's point of view) about the *rosy face who understands you*. Couldn't a woman speak of the *blue gown who understands you*?[402] Ru Yan decided that no matter how much heartache and bitterness the Internet had brought her, getting to know such a person had made it all worthwhile.

Arrangements continued busily for the conference to honor the life and work of Teacher Wei. Ru Yan relieved Damo of a few tasks which she dispatched at home, sending and reading mail, editing drafts of papers, and typing handwritten submissions. She copied the work onto a CD and took it to a shop to be printed. As she read the materials, she was struck by what a marvelous man Teacher Wei had been. The papers came from the young as well as from Teacher Wei's contemporaries, and some of these, too, were marvelous people of dazzling insight. They were sharing ideas that in many cases had never occurred to her, in language that was trenchant and beautiful; the topics under discussion were ones she had always found very difficult. She discovered there were in this world two kinds of poetry: a poetry of the emotions and a poetry of the intellect. If the former was like the sea and the clouds, the latter was like lightning and thunder.

66

A week before the conference was to be held, Damo said he wanted to get a memorial card printed and would need a picture of Teacher Wei. He asked Ru Yan to go see Zhao Yi and ask for one.

Zhao Yi produced a few photo albums and let Ru Yan make her choice. Right away, Ru Yan liked a candid shot taken on Teacher Wei's eightieth birthday. It showed him together with Zhao Yi; for some reason they were both laughing, and their merriment shone with candor and serenity. There was a hint of the shy mischievousness of youth, though the light that came from the window beside them brought out the fine lines of age in their faces. Their white hair above their fiery red clothes was dazzling like sunlight. "This one," Ru Yan said. "It's perfect."

"Don't you want to find a picture that's just of him?" Zhao Yi suggested.

"Come on, is there anything better than this?"

"Well, you can crop me out. It's OK. I'll know I was beside him."

Ru Yan took the picture and asked Zhao Yi, respectfully, how old she had been when she married Teacher Wei. The answer was, "Almost sixty."

"And how old was he?"

"He's a cycle older than me."

Isn't that a coincidence, Ru Yan thought. *A twelve-year difference between* them, *too.* She recalled that when she had read *Jane Eyre* in her youth she had thought it bizarre for such an old maid to fall in love with a man more than twenty years her senior. Now she realized that Jane Eyre had been not much over thirty.

"I admire your courage," Ru Yan said with a smile.

"Love is ageless," Zhao Yi said, "though I didn't always understand that."

"Before meeting him," Ru Yan asked, "had you always been single?"

"Yes," Zhao Yi said.

"You just never fell in love?" Ru Yan asked.

"Did you come here," Zhao Yi asked with mock indignation, "to investigate my love life?"

Ru Yan hurried to explain, flushing, "I was wondering how a woman so vibrant and full of life could remain single for so long, and during an era that was so perilous . . ."

"Whether a person is happy," Zhao Yi said, "isn't determined by whether she gets a lot of things, but by whether she gets the thing she wants most."

"Did you get what you wanted most?"

"Yes," Zhao Yi said.

"Did you ever feel sorry it came to you so late?"

"Why would I feel that way?" Zhao Yi exclaimed. "No, the fact that I found what I really wanted near the twilight of my life has been a source of nothing but joy and gratitude. A person's happiness is not about how long you have something, but just that you found it and will never lose it." She seemed to have been moved by Ru Yan's questions, for now Zhao Yi reminisced about the circumstances of her meeting Teacher Wei. It had been at a conference, and she sounded like a young woman as she fondly recalled the chain of events. It must have been the will of Heaven, she said, that she met him at all: Fate wouldn't give up. At first there had been countless reasons why their paths should never have crossed, but Fate, which had dealt each of them so many blows for half their lifetimes, finally smiled on them. First, her invitation to the conference was mislaid by the department secretary. Then, two days before the conference was scheduled to begin, a phone call came, but her lectures could not be rescheduled. The night before she was to take the train, she came down with a fever. Oddly enough, she still went . . . Because she was arriving two days late, she was assigned to a floor where men were housed, across the hall from Teacher Wei. His roommate was an acquaintance of hers, and this acquaintance, owing to some other engagement, had to leave early and would be gone the next day. That evening—a brief window of opportunity amid a throng of strangers—she was introduced to Teacher Wei.

When the week-long conference concluded, she told him, "I'm going home to take care of some things, and then I will come to live with you."

He laughed. "I was waiting for you to say that. If you hadn't said it, I would have had to."

And during that whole time, the two had never been closer to each other than a meter apart.

Ru Yan was moved by this account and urged Zhao Yi to write about it. "The love stories of today are shallow in comparison."

"Some things belong only to the two people," Zhao Yi said. "You can write whatever you like when I'm gone." She fixed Ru Yan with a thoughtful gaze and asked, suddenly, "Are you in love?"

Flustered, Ru Yan stammered, "How can you tell?"

Zhao Yi smiled. "The tradesman can't help crying his wares; the patient can't help talking about sickness."

Without knowing why, Ru Yan then poured out to her the whole story of herself and Liang Jinsheng.

Zhao Yi listened intently, occasionally asking a question, until Ru Yan was finished. Then she thought for a while and said slowly, "I'm afraid it's over now."

These words caused Ru Yan great pain, for she had dreaded hearing them; yet she had really wanted to hear them, too, for she knew that she couldn't face squarely what had befallen her until these words were spoken. In the silence that hung in the air, her tears began to flow. Haltingly, she asked, "What makes you think that?"

"There was one aspect of your story that you yourself may not have noticed, but it is very important."

Ru Yan asked what it was.

"Of two people, one seeks the overarching values in life, its ultimate meaning.[403] The other seems unable to detach himself from worldly fame and power."

"He's not that kind of man," Ru Yan was quick to say.

"Yes, he is," Zhao Yi said. "Even if he doesn't know it himself. It often turns out this way."

Ru Yan found the courage to tell Zhao Yi about that night, and the change it had wrought in her.

"Yes," Zhao Yi sighed, "we women *are* profoundly affected by this experience, especially those who had a traditional upbringing. It's as if a woman signed herself over as a piece of property and was delighted to do so. But I tell you, without the love that binds kindred souls, the future would have brought you even greater pain."

They talked until late into the evening, and Zhao Yi recalled some of the most mundane aspects of her life with Teacher Wei. Illness, cooking, the winter cold, water cutoffs in summer,[404] the din of the construction sites near their home, the time a month's wages were filched by a pickpocket . . . and then Zhao Yi mentioned something which startled Ru Yan. She said when they were married she had already passed through menopause; and as for Teacher Wei, he had been single for many years and had suffered many illnesses: they could no longer live as a normal married couple and therefore, in one sense, she was still a virgin. All the same, she thought Teacher Wei had been a real man.

After a shaken pause, Ru Yan asked gingerly, "So . . . you lived as brother and sister, then?"

Zhao Yi laughed. "I wouldn't say that! Think about it: two lovers with relaxed and spontaneous temperaments; we had ways to enjoy each other. After he died, I often found myself remembering all that we did together. In that sense you could also say that I am a real woman.

The old woman was so frank and open in her innocence that Ru Yan felt, of the two of them, *she* was more like an old woman.

Ru Yan inquired about Teacher Wei's burial.

"It can wait," Zhao Yi said. "We agreed that my ashes would be buried along with his. In that way, we will be united for good."

She brought Ru Yan into the bedroom, where the small brown wooden box was still resting on the bureau next to the rusty canister of tea. "He also said that this container of tea, which had stayed with him for half a century, should be poured in together with our ashes. I wish I could see what this woman looked like. I've always felt she was an earlier incarnation of myself. I wonder who might still have a photo of her?"

A mere two days before the conference about Teacher Wei was scheduled to begin, Damo received a call from Purple Rock Mountain Stronghold. They said they'd been notified that they could not host any large gatherings for the duration of the SARS emergency. They were extremely apologetic about this change, which was beyond their control. If Damo would give them his postal address, they would mail back his 1000 yuan deposit.

Damo hardly ever lost his decorum with strangers, but now he yelled: "Why didn't you tell me sooner, asshole! It's not like SARS broke out yesterday."

Chaos ensued. There were phone calls to be made, letters to be mailed, notices to be posted on various websites. But there were still about a dozen people, en route from various directions, to whom it was not possible to get word in time. Damo had to enlist Maozi and Ru Yan to go to the pre-arranged staging point where, since many of the participants were not personally known to them, they had to carry little signs referring to the meeting at Purple Rock. Every time an enthusiastic traveler approached them for directions, they told him of the cancellation and the reason for it. And even with all this, there were a few who slipped through and made their way all the way to Purple Rock Mountain Stronghold, which they found deserted. When these poor souls came home, they humorously let it be known that they would count the trip as a vacation at their own expense: the scenery had been pretty good.

This outcome was a relief to Maozi. At one stroke it removed two weights from his shoulders: one was conscience, and the other was fear.[405] He cursed a blue streak and said, "Wait a bit, when the political situation improves, this conference will take place." He said he would cover the losses they had incurred in preparing it.

"We didn't spend much," Damo answered. "If in time we do hold the conference, we can talk about the money then." And he gave Maozi back the 5000 yuan.

The memorial card had cost some money, but Zhao Yi insisted on paying for it herself. It had been very nicely printed and was visually striking. It was folded into four pages a little larger than a 3 x 5 card, on yellowish-brown linen paper. The first page had that picture of Teacher Wei with Zhao Yi cropped out so that he seemed to be smiling at the person holding the card. Beneath the photo they had reproduced the sentence from Teacher Wei's notebook, with a caption explaining that these were his last words: *When it is not, they say it is; when it is, they will say it is not.* The handwriting was strange, almost illegible, and the convoluted language added to the mystery. It was like some ancient inscription found on a rock face. The reaction of many was to stare at it in perplexity, taking guesses; with sudden recognition, they were amused . . . but then they became very grave.

The two inside pages offered a brief chronology of Teacher Wei's life and writings. The last page quoted from tributes written by his friends.

They had had only a hundred copies printed. As a memento of the aborted conference, this card was much treasured by his friends. Many wrote in to ask for copies, but there were no more to be had.

Damo wrote a piece: "A conference devoted to one man's life and work, convened in the mind." At the conclusion of the essay he quoted from the song which Teacher Wei had sung as he lay dying:

In unity there is strength. In unity there is strength,
A strength like that of iron and steel.
Open fire on the fascists, let the whole undemocratic system
be wiped out!
Facing the sun, moving toward freedom and a New China,
Glory to the ends of the earth!

Damo had this piece serve as a preface to the dozens of essays he'd received as tributes to be shared at the conference, and he posted them all to his website, *Word and Thought.* Two days later, the site was shut down and deleted. Damo was prepared:

he had already made a zipfile suitable for download, for he knew that these voices would be propagated, even as the light from a star continues to spread out through the universe for thousands of years. Other websites were quick to pick this up, for they saw it as a kind of intellectual torch relay as well as an act of love and reverence for the old man.

67

Ru Yan had read all kinds of romantic novels. Some dripped with sentiment; some were taut with suspense; they might have happy endings or tragic endings, *but they always had an ending.* The story in which she now found herself dragged on ambiguously with no end in sight. Ever since the day she had gone to the guesthouse, she had stuck firm to her resolution not to try to contact Liang Jinsheng. And he seemed to have made the same decision, for he did not communicate with her in any way. Even Ru Yan's mother, after the month of May had come and gone, never brought up her daughter's marriage again. They talked about all kinds of things in their phone conversations; the only thing they never mentioned was that man.

This was a horrible ending, worse than any heart-rending and dramatic scenario. It was the death by a thousand cuts, one little slice after another, slowly; one drop of blood after another, with no idea when it would stop . . .

Ru Yan threw herself into a variety of activities. She meticulously cleaned her entire apartment and washed and dried her clothes and bedding, even things she hadn't touched for years. She went into a frenzy of shopping—food, clothing, utensils—and in a few weeks she gained almost ten pounds. In the evenings she read, listened to music, went online, and wrote until she was exhausted. Then she would hurriedly wash up and fall asleep as soon as her head hit the pillow.

68

Jiang Xiaoli had been right when she predicted that SARS would eventually pass and her compatriots would forget. When we look back over the past century, there were many things that seemed at the time as if they would never pass away, yet they did—events that inspired hatred and shame and that seemed etched indelibly on the mind, yet they were forgotten. As Teacher Wei had once said, time takes its toll. [406]

The epidemic had surged like a flood from the last week of April, but by June it was starting to subside. The common people had no way to know (and didn't really care) how many people worldwide were sick with SARS. The preceding panic had been, rather, a kind of psychological entertainment that added a bit of drama to the banality of their lives. That's why when the nation's infection statistics, as broken down by region on CCTV every day at 4:00 PM, began to be a few here, a few there, adding up to a number smaller than the size of the National People's Congress[407], people soon lost interest: and those who still paid attention were tracking the numbers in much the same way they would note how many goals were scored by the German or Italian teams in the European championship. It had nothing to do with their daily life.

At the end of June, the W.H.O. rescinded its travel advisory for Beijing and took that city off the list of epidemic sites. If truth be told, Chinese gave more credence to what foreigners said, and this announcement was considered to mark the end of SARS. Traffic now jammed streets that had been empty for miles. The people of Guangdong, after denying themselves their favorite delicacies for months, started munching their gamy food again. Life returned to malls, internet cafés, and dance halls.

Ru Yan's life went on as usual. She went to the office with steady regularity. The only difference from her past routine was that she never ran into Jiang Xiaoli, which was a relief, actually. At the special project team formed by the alliance of the two institutes, work continued to be exciting: they were constantly announcing good news and expected to have a deliverable medicine by year-end. The Institute was commended and everyone got a bonus, and it was anticipated that once the medicine came to market, the Institute would be living off the fat of the land. The many who reported these developments always gave credit to Jiang Xiaoli in the most glowing terms.

There commenced a series of meetings devoted to summarizing the achievements of the campaign against SARS and issuing commendations at every level, and reporting teams[408] were organized at every level and made the rounds giving speeches. The calamity, panic, rage, desolation, and suffering of a few months before—not to mention the discord, the enforced isolation, the confrontational defensiveness, the back-stabbing and buck-passing—were now transformed in retrospect into an inspiring narrative, a thing of beauty. The TV was filled with scenes of people talking about it and moving both themselves and their listeners to tears. It was very affecting.

Liang Jinsheng, along with the city's top leadership, led a delegation to the capital where they took part in a number of functions. Every time, he kept a low profile and did his best to avoid the cameras. Unless you looked closely, you wouldn't know he was there. He always sat to one side or in the corner and let the top leadership make the important speeches. Soon after, he was summoned to a training seminar for mayors at the Central Party School. At the conclusion of the training, he was appointed Mayor of a midsized city in the Yangtze River Delta.[409] At first glance, this might have seemed a sideways career move, for the city had only one-fifth the population of the city where he had been in office, but it had more than twice the GDP and the real financial resources were even greater than that. In the world of officials today, everyone knows it isn't the size of your jurisdiction that matters, but the weight of the moneybag in your hand and your position on the chessboard of the Central Government. Taking note of his personal and academic background, some observers figured this posting would prove only a stepping-stone, and there were many predictions as to where he would end up. During the few days that he returned to town, many were those who called on him to pay their respects. When he arrived at the new city with a minimum of pomp and fuss, he suddenly remembered that his father had started out as a farmer on the outskirts of this town more than 60 years before . . . and now he was returning as a county magistrate to the place where his family had its humble roots. The realization moved him deeply, but he said nothing to anyone.

Six months later, Jiang Xiaoli was transferred to this city and brought a few pharmaceutical projects with her. She established a drug factory jointly with the city. Soon she and Liang Jinsheng were living together, having begun a new chapter in their lives. As she liked to say, it was a second spring, both personally and professionally. But that's another story.

69

One day when Ru Yan was watching the TV news there was a report on an economic development conference in the Yangtze River Delta, and there he was, sitting in the back row on the rostrum, studiously leafing through some printouts. In that quiet moment he exuded the serene confidence which was familiar to Ru Yan. He was wearing a fine tailored dark suit; his hair was neatly combed, and on TV you couldn't see the white hair at his temples, no, under the Klieg lights his hair appeared black and glossy.

Studying him closely, she found that this man had become a stranger. She wouldn't even have made a connection between him and the Liang Jinsheng with whom she had gazed at the moon, or the Liang Jinsheng with whom she had dined on Shandong cuisine. There'd also been the Liang Jinsheng who'd brought back a box of hot dogs from America, and the Liang Jinsheng who'd performed that wild real-life scene with her on the sofa, and the Liang Jinsheng who'd had amorous conversations with her over the phone, and the drowsy, casual Liang Jinsheng who hadn't bothered to close the door when he peed into the toilet in her bathroom. This man wasn't any of them.

The next morning she overslept. She became dimly aware of a nearby sound of breathing and opened her eyes to see Yang Yanping staring anxiously at her, its furry front paws up on the edge of her bed.

A shaft of sunlight reached into the dark room through the crack in the curtains and cut a sharp-edged path of light upon the wall.[410] Deeply moved, she reached out from under her blanket and caressed the dog's head. "I'm OK now," she said. Then she sprang out of bed and dressed nimbly. "Today we're going to make a fresh start, you and me," she announced. "Let's go out and get energy from walking on the ground[411]!"

One day, having found her composure again, Ru Yan resumed browsing the Internet. First she went to the Empty Nest, which she hadn't visited in ages. Some familiar faces were still there, and some she did not see. On the very first page was a message from a new user who sounded just the way Ru Yan had once sounded, timidly announcing, "I'm new here; I like this place, I hope you'll bear with me." And just as had happened with Ru Yan, there followed a heap of cordial welcoming messages, as hands were offered in friendship. Lonely Goose still maintained the persona of a salon hostess, showering this newcomer with enthusiastic encouragement.

As she kept reading, Ru Yan came across a brief message that Night Owl had posted weeks ago: `Haven't seen Such Is This World for ages and I kind of miss her. Is anybody still in touch with her? Please give her my regards.` Beneath Night Owl's message there were several replies. One said, `Yeah, it's been a long time since I read any of her lovely prose.` Another said, `Around here there are still people stuck in the C.R., it's a damn shame!`

Ru Yan was touched, yet again, and almost typed out a few characters in acknowledgment; but after reflecting, she dropped the idea, saying to herself, "Best to keep these friendly feelings. Let the acrimony fade into the past."

That evening she saw her son on MSN and he said, "Mom, guess what day it is today?"

"What day is it?" she asked.

Her son grinned. "Your first anniversary! It was one year ago that you ventured onto the Internet. I called to congratulate you."

And with that, he began displaying on the screen a series of pictures of himself in France. There was one photo in particular that made her eyes light up. It showed him with a young woman. Her son was sitting on a lawn and the young woman was kneeling behind him, leaning on him with her long arms draped around his neck. Her long light-brown hair was blowing in the wind, and with her blue eyes, small mouth, and straight nose she was remarkably beautiful; and you could tell from the innocent sweetness of her smile that she was a wonderful girl.

"And who might this be?" Ru Yan teased.

"A classmate of mine."

"A Parisian girl?"

"She's Russian," her son said, "her name is Lyushenka."

"What more can you tell me?" Ru Yan probed.

"It's a work in progress," her son said.

"Bring her home for me to meet her," Ru Yan said.

"*Her* mother wants the same thing," he said.

"Take good care of her, Son," Ru Yan said.

"I'm trying," he said.

She kept thinking about this for the rest of the evening and it filled her with a sweet elation. "A Russian girl," she thought, "Wow. A Russian girl." She went over many Russian woman's names in her mind, Anna, Liubov, Vera, Zoya, Masha, Tanya, Yelena, Tatiana: in her youth these had been her intimate friends. Her imagination even extended to a very little girl, Russian but of mixed race, who would be partly like this young woman and partly like her son, and would be known by an odd name such as Yelena Yang.

After saying goodbye to her son reluctantly, she was not the least bit sleepy, so she browsed the Internet at random and came upon a post about a very little girl, a little Chinese girl whose mother was sent for compulsory detox. The little girl was left locked in the apartment alone, but the police seem to have forgotten this point. Seventeen days later she was found starved to death, her small corpse in an advanced state of decay. She had rotted just inside the locked door to her home, and the door bore scratches from her hands.[412]

Once again, a violent pain wracked Ru Yan. There was no detox by which this pain could be forced out of her system.

70

One day, when Ru Yan heard the cry of the junkman down in the street outside her building, she opened the window and shouted, "Hey! You take old clothes?"

The man waved his hand from side to side in refusal.

"Don't want any money for them," Ru Yan explained, "I'll *give* 'em to you."

He stopped and peered up at her.

From a corner of the wardrobe she hurriedly scooped up that wrinkled suit and threw it down from her window. "Give it a washing," she said, "and it'll do for rough work." Then she remembered the slippers and pitched them out the window, too, yelling, "These are new, never been worn."

The man picked up the two articles of clothing and looked them over, bringing them to his nose for a careful sniff. Puzzled, he stared for a moment at her high window, then turned to the plastic barrel on the back of his three-wheeler and tossed them in.

December 17, 2003—March 16, 2004
Wuhan[413]

Translator's Notes

1. *two politically daring works were banned…in 2004* Namely *The Past is Not Like Smoke*, by Zhang Yihe, and *An Investigation of China's Farmers*, by Chen Guidi and Wu Chuntao.
2. *The Beijing edition bowdlerized most of the politically sensitive passages* In early 2009, there appeared on the Internet a list of the censored passages compiled by a blogger with the screen name 食砚无田 (*shi yan wu tian*, a phrase from a Su Dongpo poem meaning 'a fellow who owns no farmland and lives by his pen'). Not all the excisions seem politically motivated, but a great many of them obviously are. A copy of this document is available at the Ragged Banner website. The present edition is based on the author's manuscript.
3. *Ru Yan@sars.come* The Chinese title, 如焉*@sars.come*, involves an untranslatable pun on a phrase and a name, both pronounced Ru Yan, as will be explained in note 14. The spelling ".come", though emended by many a journalist, is not a typographical error but rather a punning reference to the coming of the SARS epidemic which shapes Ru Yan's experience both on the Internet and off.
4. *a planned American translation had been abandoned.* This was disclosed by Perry Link in an interview with Paul Mooney. The article ("Want Access? Go Easy on China") was originally published on June 21, 2008 in *The National* (of Abu Dhabi) and is available online at http://www.pjmooney.com.
5. *Self-censorship does the rest.* The denial of visas to academics of whose research the Chinese government disapproves, as well as the impact of such denials on Western scholarship, has been reported a number of times. "The Blacklist Academic Leaders Ignore," by Elizabeth Redden, http://www.insidehighered.com/news/2008/07/14/china. "Censors Without Borders," by Emily Parker, http://www.nytimes.com/2010/05/16/books/review/Parker-t.html. The classic statement, however, remains Perry Link's 2002 essay "The Anaconda in the Chandelier." Though available only by subscription at its original home of *The New York Review of Books*, it has been reprinted at several other websites.
6. The author wrote this book while his wife Li Hong (李虹) was being treated for cancer. She liked the manuscript but didn't think he'd ever get it published. She died in December 2004.

7. *cadre* This standard translation of the Chinese 干部 *ganbu* is slightly confusing. In French and English, as well as Russian (кадр), the word 'cadre' is reserved for *a group* of dedicated individuals qualified for a particular kind of work. Bolsheviks used the term for the dedicated Communists who were in the vanguard of the Revolution. Initially the Chinese Communists used it this way too, but at some point they began using the word for the *individual* member of that vanguard group. The sense today would be roughly "Communist civil servant in a leadership position." See Franz Schurmann, *Ideology and Organization in Communist China*, pp. 162-6, University of California Press, Berkeley, 1973.
8. *the martial Yang clan of the Northern Song* A tenth-century family whose valor has been honored in several made-for-TV dramas.
9. *zaijian* 再见, the proper Chinese word for "goodbye."
10. *Tale of the Red Lantern* One of the 'eight model works', a limited repertory of edifying dramas which were widely performed during the Cultural Revolution.
11. *work unit* 单位 *danwei*, literally "unit," the organizational form by which not only work but also housing and many other aspects of urban Chinese life were managed under Mao. It still functions, less comprehensively than before, in sectors of the economy directly administered by the State, but sometimes the word means simply "the office."
12. *QQ* The most popular instant-messaging service in China
13. *I am a scoundrel and I fear no man* A line from the 1989 short story "An Attitude" by Wang Shuo.
14. Ru Yan's name is written with the characters 茹嫣. She wants a screen name that sounds like her real name, and given the Chinese language's abundance of homonyms, this should not be difficult. Her first choice, 如烟, means "like smoke," i.e., evanescent, but this name turns out to be unavailable. Her second choice, 如焉, is a classical expression meaning "Such is reality" or "Things are like that." The reader should bear in mind something the translator has not been able to show in English: *Such Is This World* (her online identity) is a pun on her real name. As for her real name, the surname 茹 is a fairly uncommon one that might bring to mind the Communist author Ru Zhijuan, greatly respected in the author's generation,

and the given name 嫣 means approximately "womanly smile" and conveys a hint of beauty and elegance.

15. These names all have political significance. *Jianguo*: Establish the Nation. *Xinhua*: New China. *Kangmei*: Resist America. *Yuanchao*: Help Korea. *Jianshe*: Build (the economy, socialism, national defense, etc). *Xiansheng*: Birth of the Constitution (the first constitution was promulgated in 1954). *Yuejin*: Leap Forward (an allusion to Mao's disastrous attempt at rapid economic modernization between 1958 and 1961). *Siqing*: Four Cleanups (a political campaign conducted in the three years before the Cultural Revolution). *Weidong*: Defend the East (or, possibly, Defend Mao Zedong). *Weiqing*: Defend Jiang Qing, Mao's wife and a leading figure of the Cultural Revolution. *Weibiao*: Defend Lin Biao (a military leader who gained political power in the 1960s but would perish after possibly attempting a coup in 1971). *Jiuda*: "Great Ninth", referring to the ninth session of the National Party Congress, convened in April 1969.
16. *Droopy, an intelligent cartoon dog* Droopy was created in the 1940s for MGM by Fred Avery, the animator who also created Daffy Duck and Bugs Bunny.
17. *88888888888888* In Chinese, "eight" is *ba*. A string of eights is often used in text-messaging to mean "bye-bye" even though that is more formally written with different characters that are pronounced "bai-bai."
18. *Smart Pinyin* One of many software applications that facilitated writing Chinese with a keyboard. This functionality has since been subsumed into the operating environment, whether Windows or Linux or OS X.
19. *it looked like a Chinese Checkers piece* "Chinese Checkers" is the English name of a game that originated in America and developed into its classic form in Germany, where it is known as Stern-Halma. Only in the last century did the game make its way to Asia. In America the pieces are usually marbles; in China, where the game is called *tiaoqi*, "jumping chess," they are often peglike figures that resemble chess pawns.
20. *Forty and Bewildered* Alluding to a stage in the outline offered by Confucius of his life's milestones: "At forty, I had no perplexities" (*Analects* II.4)
21. *Our Years in the Countryside* A reference to the "sending

down" of "educated youth" for rural work during the Cultural Revolution.

22. A playful allusion to the Maoist slogan, "Wherever the Party points, that's where we fight."
23. *The Way gives rise to One . . .* from the *Tao Te Ching*, Chap. 42.
24. *watch their silhouettes recede into the distance* The choice of words probably alludes to a celebrated 1928 essay by Zhu Ziqing, "Receding Figure" (背影), in which a son bound for college watches his father walk away from the train.
25. *and poker* 斗地主 *dou dizhu*, a popular card game resembling poker. Wikipedia has a detailed explanation of the rules under "Dou Di Zhu." The name means "fight the landlords," evoking a campaign of expropriation and humiliation conducted in the 1950s.
26. *residential compound* The 大杂院, *dazayuan*, built around a common courtyard and shared by several households, defines a somewhat inbred social milieu.
27. *Xiao Li* In informal conversation, people of long acquaintance will often address each other using the family name preceded by one of the adjectives 小 (*xiao*, 'small' or 'young') or 老 (*lao*, 'old'). The choice of one or the other reflects seniority.
28. *a sheet of draft paper* a handwritten draft on ruled paper.
29. *the 'cat'* 猫 *mao*, the informal Chinese term for a modem.
30. *Spring River Flows* Alluding to a poem by Li Yu, the last ruler of the Southern Tang kingdom, who was deposed by the Song Dynasty in the tenth century C.E. The relevant lines are "How many sorrows can befall a man? / Like a river bearing the waters of Spring to the east." The phrase served as the title of a classic 1947 film.
31. *an older man? An older woman? . . .* The original uses pinyin abbreviations (GG, JJ, etc.) for "older brother," "older sister," etc. This is typical of the telegraphic style of much Chinese internet discourse.
32. *give concrete particulars* the original is a slogan associated with Deng Xiaoping, "seek truth from facts."
33. *inserted into the work teams* The text uses the terminology of the Cultural Revolution which Mao launched in 1966 and which lasted for almost ten years. "Educated youth"—that is, high-school or college students in towns and cities—were dispatched en masse to the countryside in order to live with the

peasants and learn from them. Higher education was basically shut down for a decade. The terms "insert" and "sent down" regularly refer to this episode.

34. *her mother's System* The bureaucratic structure of Maoist China was supplemented by "systems" defined to provide functional coordination among offices that needed to cooperate in certain economic domains. Teiwes lists as examples of these functional systems "agriculture and forestry, industry and communications, finance and trade, culture and education, political and legal affairs, and foreign affairs." (Frederick C. Teiwes, "The Chinese State During the Maoist Era", p. 118 in *The Modern Chinese State*, ed. David L. Shambaugh (2000) New York, Cambridge University Press)
35. *No Regrets About Youth* A novel published in 1991 by Wang Shuo.
36. *it was signed 'Damo'* Damo is the Chinese name of Bodhidharma, the fifth-century C.E. founder of Chan (Zen) Buddhism who sat for ten years facing a wall. As a screen name it therefore suggests detachment, concentration, and spiritual lucidity.
37. The Chinese word 思想 *sixiang*, literally "thought," can denote a specific school of opinion or a broad range of intellectual endeavor devoted to understanding society, history, and politics. In official contexts it has a dogmatic sense, implying a set of approved answers to questions, and is often translated as "ideology."
38. *keeping up with the times* This phrase spoofs the tone of official exhortations to adapt to the latest policy change.
39. *the Reference News* One of several digests of foreign news articles that used to be prepared exclusively for senior officials. At about the time the story is referring to (early 1980s) its circulation became unrestricted—and concomitantly its content became more restricted, i.e., indistinguishable from that of other official media. Damo is presumably referring to the earlier era, without explaining how he would have had access to the periodical then.
40. Qian Xuesen (a.k.a. H.S. Tsien) was a pioneering aerospace engineer at the California Institute of Technology in the 1940s. In the following decade, he was accused of Communist sympathies and interned for several years. Embittered by this experience, on his release he returned to the land of his birth,

where he led the development of ballistic missile technology and exercised a formative influence on scientific education in the PRC. He died in 2009. That he was the architect of China's atomic bomb is a popular misconception which was fostered by the secrecy surrounding him during his most productive years. His life and work were recounted by Iris Chang in *Thread of the Silkworm*, Basic Books, New York 1996. A different assessment was given by two arms-control experts, Gregory Kulacki and Jeffrey G. Lewis, in a 2009 paper available online from the American Academy of Arts and Sciences, "A Place for One's Mat: China's Space Program, 1953-2003." (esp. p. 30)

41. *thirty and well-established* A Confucian ideal, *Analects* II.4
42. *he had been an educated youth* i.e., rusticated during the Cultural Revolution.
43. *'yellow books' and 'black books.'* 'Yellow' books were translations of foreign literary works of limited circulation ; 'gray' books were translations, with even more restricted circulation, of foreign writings about social science and politics; 'black' books were proscribed for purveying bourgeois or counter-revolutionary poison. The 'yellow' and the 'gray' designations described the cover styles which distinguished these books.
44. *a Class 3 electrician* Tradesmen are ranked in eight levels of experience and proficiency, of which Class 8 is the highest.
45. *Academy of Social Sciences* Not the national institution of this name in Beijing, but a provincial-level institute of higher learning devoted to the social, and especially political, sciences. Most (if not all) of the provinces have such schools.
46. *Quick turnaround* Literally, "sell as soon as you buy," a figure of speech for teaching what you've just learned.
47. *When the exam was reinstated* In 1977, after the Cultural Revolution ended.
48. *all the people became businessmen* Alluding to a phrase of Mao's much used during a time of tension with the Soviet Union in the 1960s: "All the people are soldiers!"
49. *information* Probably in the sense of "stock-market tips."
50. *What does the last player have?* The words for "last player" and "next player" (上家， 下家) are terms from mahjong, where it is vital to guess from the tiles each player discards what groups of tiles he is trying to complete.

51. *the only 386* Intel introduced the 80386 processor in 1985.
52. *Liberation* The Communist victory that ended the Civil War in 1949.
53. *the Three Years' Famine* Estimates of the toll from the famine which began in late 1958 and in some districts lingered into 1962, and which was caused by counterproductive policies of the Great Leap Forward, run as high as 35 million lives. Yang Jisheng, a retired journalist, painstakingly explored the history using primary sources for his monumental 2008 work *Tombstone*. An English translation by Stacy Mosher and Guo Jian is being published by FSG and Penguin UK. Until Yang's work, the most thorough account was Jasper Becker's *Hungry Ghosts: China's Secret Famine* of 1996 (U.S. title: *Hungry Ghosts: Mao's Secret Famine*).
54. *a page of 16mo could wrap two ounces* The paper sizes are as in the West. In the original, however, the "pound" and the "ounce" are the 斤 *jin* and the 两 *liang*, each somewhat heavier than the corresponding English measure.
55. *national language . . . language arts* The old and new terms are respectively 国语 *guoyu* and 语文 *yuwen*.
56. The unit of money used here is the yuan, which is divided into 100 *fen* here rendered as 'cents'. "In the early 1960s, the average monthly income per capita for Wuhan residents was about 18 yuan." footnote 40, p. 87, Kam-yee Law, *The Chinese Cultural Revolution Reconsidered*, 2003, Palgrave Macmillan.
57. *The New Class* An influential critique written in 1957 by the Yugoslav Milovan Djilas and first published in the United States.
58. *this Hayek* Friedrich von Hayek wrote *The Road to Serfdom* in 1944 and won the Nobel Prize in Economics in 1974.
59. *My only close friend . . .* From "琴茶" *Qin Cha* ("Music and Tea"). The qin is a classical stringed instrument. The name of the river Clearwater 渌水 could suggest the appearance of brewed green tea.
60. *the Qing* China's last imperial dynasty, 1644—1912 C.E.
61. *Daoguang* A title of the sixth Qing emperor, who reigned from 1821 to 1850.
62. *at the start of the Cultural Revolution* Summer 1966.
63. *Four oceans surge . . .* Mao Zedong, "Reply to Guo Moruo, to the tune of Man Jiang Hong". From its first appearance in

1963, this hortatory poem was widely reproduced in Mao's distinctive calligraphy and it adorns his mausoleum today.

64. *the new era of Reform and Opening* Commenced in 1978 under Deng Xiaoping.

65. *Wang Hongwen . . . gang of four, gang of five* Wang Hongwen was one of the four people who amassed power during the Cultural Revolution, but as Damo noted, they had nothing to do with its beginning. When China repudiated the Cultural Revolution it was convenient to blame the Gang of Four for it. But in private conversations, "Gang of Five" became a veiled way to suggest that Mao himself shared the blame.

66. *Two years before the Cultural Revolution* i.e., in 1964.

67. *they called him Teacher Wei* The use of a profession as a title of address is common in China. On account of the tradition of reverence for those who impart knowledge, however, the title of Teacher, 老师 *laoshi*, can convey deep respect as well as serving as an occupational identifier.

68. *wasn't called No. 1 or No. 2* In China, institutions such as schools, hospitals, and prisons are usually numbered.

69. *a very bad family background* This would be a matter of *class* in a Marxian sense. A child whose parents had been landlords, for example, would have a very bad background.

70. *the Republican era* The Republic of China was declared in 1912 and lasted, on the mainland, until 1949. From information that will be provided later in the story, we can infer that Damo's issue of *High-Schoolers* was printed around 1936.

71. *Xin and Ye Shengtao* Bing Xin was the pen name of Xie Wanying (1900 - 1999), a widely traveled writer known for her lucid style. In the 1920s she earned an M.A. at Wellesley College. Ye Shengtao was the pen name of Ye Shaojun (1894 - 1988), a writer, journalist, and educator at the forefront of the May 4th Movement.

72. *Feng Zikai* An artist, music teacher, and essayist known particularly for his work as an illustrator of children's literature. See Geremie R. Barmé, *An Artistic Exile: A Life of Feng Zikai (1898 - 1975)*, University of California Press, 2002.

73. *home but four walls* One of the thousands of idiomatic four-character phrases, 成语 *chengyu*, found in the Chinese language. Children learn them in primary and early middle school. This expression means "to live in miserable poverty."

74. *Red Flag*, a magazine covering Marxist theory and other topics of interest to Party cadres, was started in 1958 and remained in publication for thirty years.
75. *quotations* Presumably from Chairman Mao.
76. *C. C. Spy* a spy for Taiwan; in the 1920s the KMT's first intelligence bureau, the Zhong Tong, effectively monitored the radio transmissions of northern warlords. The bureau was led by two officials both named Chen (Chen Lifu and Chen Guofu), and was known as the Chen-Chen or C.C. faction. Its attempts to monitor Communist activities proved ineffectual, however, because by 1928 it had itself been infiltrated by moles under the direction of a Moscow-trained Communist ironically named Chen: Chen Geng. (Maochun Yu, *OSS in China: prelude to Cold War* p. 33-34, Yale University Press 1996) Nevertheless, the sinister figure of the C.C. Spy was still being conjured up on the mainland as late as the 1970s.
77. *the Yiguandao* Also rendered "I Kuan Tao": a religious sect with syncretistic beliefs and a decentralized organization, banned in the PRC in 1951. To this day it claims many adherents on Taiwan.
78. Hu Feng (1903–1980) was a left-wing literary figure associated with Lu Xun. He resisted the subordination of art to politics and became a target of persecution in the 1950s. See Kirk Denton, "The Hu Feng Group: The Genealogy of a Literary School," a paper presented during a symposium at Ohio State University in 2002 and available at http://mclc.osu.edu. In 2009 Peng Xiaolian and S. Louisa Wei released *Storm Under the Sun*, a documentary film about the persecution of Hu Feng. The script is available in English from Blue Queen Cultural Communication, Ltd.
79. *a dogskin plaster* A traditional remedy for ailments of the joints and muscles. It would be spread on dogskin and so applied to the afflicted area.
80. *Henry Norman Bethune* Canadian surgeon who assisted the Communists at Yan'an in the 1930s. After his death in 1939, Mao wrote an essay praising him as an example of selflessness, and he consequently became (and remains) extremely well-known in China.
81. *Zhang Side* A soldier who died in a fluke accident and because he was eulogized by Mao ("To die for the people is weightier

than Mt. Tai") became a by-word for heroic selflessness.

82. *Old Man Yu Gong* The hero of a children's fable: by his diligence, he moves two mountains. Like the historical figures mentioned previously, Old Man Yu Gong was prominently featured in the motivational literature of the 1960s.
83. *Li Diming* Mao's physician during the Long March.
84. John Leighton Stuart was a Presbyterian minister, the president of Yenching University, and US Ambassador to China. He was imprisoned for three years by the Japanese. In 1949 he was expelled and vilified by Mao. In 2008, forty-six years after his death, his ashes were interred at his birthplace of Hangzhou.
85. *Liu Qingshan and Zhang Zishan* The Party Secretary and Regional Administration Officer, respectively, of Tianjin. They were arrested in 1951 for large-scale corruption and sentenced to death the following year.
86. *Zhang Bojun*, at one time an English professor in Guangzhou, was appointed to high office in the 1950s but like many others made the mistake of speaking up during the "Hundred Flowers" episode of 1956-57. He was singled out for scathing denunciation in the ensuing Anti-Rightist campaign and withdrew from public life. His daughter Zhang Yihe is a writer whose history of Peking Opera stars (伶人往事) was censured in early 2007 by the General Administration of Press and Publication along with the present work and several others. *Luo Longji*, a Western-educated political scientist who wrote an influential essay on human rights in 1929, was associated with Zhang Bojun and suffered along with him in 1957. It is notable that neither Zhang nor Luo has ever been "rehabilitated."
87. *Peng Dehuai* A foundational figure in the PLA from its beginnings through the Korean War, in which he was the supreme commander on the Chinese side. He was disgraced for criticizing the Great Leap Forward in 1959 and tortured by Red Guards in 1966.
88. Yan'an, a city in the northern province of Shaanxi, served as a Communist center for the decade following the Long March in the mid-1930s. "Going South" probably refers to the final victorious campaign of the Civil War, when the Red Army crossed the Yangtze in April of 1949.
89. *labor under supervision* A person sentenced to 监督劳动 *jiandu laodong* would serve his time in a factory or a farming

village, not a labor camp, and this was a less severe penalty than 're-education through labor' and much less severe than 'reform through labor'. Nevertheless, it entailed unusually long hours at wearying or demeaning tasks, with no freedom of movement and no days off. Persons so penalized were to be watched closely and encouraged to "give up their reactionary thoughts and the viewpoint of the exploiting classes." Harro von Senger, "Strafrechtliche Begriffe in der Sicht einer internen Cihai-Ausgabe aus dem Jahre 1961", in Schwind, Wegmann, and Legarth (ed.s) *Studien zum Chinesischen Recht*, vol. 1, p. 268, Freiburg 1979

90. *cut himself off from the people and the Party* A reproachful formula, here used with irony, that was standard in reporting the suicides of persons who had been the targets of mass campaigns.

91. *a criticism session* "Criticism sessions were planned out in advance, and a propaganda team selected three or four people to criticize the target's work in detail. These criticism sessions, called *Pi Dou Hui* (Criticism and Denunciation Meetings) were most often directed at the most senior members of a *danwei*." Gregory Eliyu Guldin, *The saga of anthropology in China* p. 193 M.E. Sharpe, Armonk 1994

92. *Huang Shiren* The evil landlord in the 1945 musical ballet *The White-haired Girl*, later made into a film and strongly promoted during the Cultural Revolution.

93. *a neighborhood garment factory* Neighborhood factories (街道厂 *jiedao chang*) often made simple items such as matches under the supervision of the residents' committee. People assigned to them as workers would be frequently harangued and kept under surveillance by the members of the committee.

94. *the Arts & Letters Militants* The Red Guards were organized into units reflecting the branches of the economy from which their members were drawn.

95. *Walking beside the stream . . .* 'Asking Heaven' (天问 *tian wen*) is a mythological poem ascribed to Qu Yuan, an exiled scholar and statesman of the 3rd century BCE who became an archetype of the man too honest to succeed in government. He drowned himself in a river. 'The Song of Guangling' (广陵散 *guangling san*) is the melody which Ji Kang, a poet and musician of the 3rd century CE who had offended the sensibilities

of the tyrant Sima Zhao, is said to have played on the way to his own execution.

96. *National Day* October 1, a major holiday always accompanied by official observances. Subsequent events make it clear that the year is 2002.
97. *the old society* i.e., pre-1949.
98. *The ladies all want to marry a man like Putin* The song, whose original title is Такого как Путин, was first heard on Russian radio stations in the summer of 2002. Its obscure origins prompted speculation that the music had been produced by the Kremlin.

    My boyfriend is in trouble yet again,
    He drinks vile stuff, is constantly in fights,
    Enough! I said, and told him to get lost.
    What I want now's a man like Putin:

    A man like Putin, full of strength;
    A man like Putin, who won't drink;
    A man like Putin, who won't insult me;
    A man like Putin, who'll never run off.

    The Russian Wikipedia credits Alexander Yelin with the words and music.
99. *disks* For many years, the most common format for recorded video in China was the Video CD (VCD). It is now giving way to the DVD.
100. *double eyelids* A natural crease in the upper eyelid, less common in Asiatics than in other races, has in modern times come to be considered attractive. Putties, tapes, and cosmetic surgery are widely used in East Asia to give eyes a "double-fold" appearance.
101. *Imperialism runs away with its tail between its legs* From "Socialism is Good" (社会主义好 *shehuizhuyi hao*), music by Li Huanzhi, lyrics by Xi Yang, written in the 1950s and ubiquitous during the Cultural Revolution. The song has by no means faded into history. Prisoners are still required to sing it regularly, and as recently as 2005 the teacher and activist Zhao Changqing, while incarcerated in Shaanxi's Weinan Prison, was

sentenced to 40 days' solitary confinement for refusing to sing this song during a flag-raising ceremony. ("News Roundup", *China Rights Forum*, No. 1, 2006, p. 11) "Socialism is Good" was performed at the 2008 Olympics in Beijing.

102. *curly-haired beagle* In a personal communication, the author explained that there are few purebred beagles on the mainland and the name is applied to mixed breeds with a variety of traits.
103. *The Past that is Like Smoke* A pun. "The past which is like smoke" sounds in Chinese like "Ru Yan's past" and alludes to the proverb, "The past is like smoke."
104. *A fox fairy* A seductive and dangerous figure from Chinese folklore.
105. *Catholic University* Furen (in the Wade-Giles transliteration, Fu Jen) University was founded in Beijing in 1925 by American Benedictines. Control later passed to the German Society of the Divine Word, another Catholic order; yet for most of its history on the mainland, the school's president was a Chinese Protestant. It was ordered closed in 1952 and its resources were absorbed into Beijing Normal University. In 1960 it was reestablished on Taiwan as Fu Jen Catholic University.
106. *one cycle* Of twelve years, according to the arrangement of the Chinese calendar into the Year of the Rat, the Year of the Ox, and so on.
107. *open a direct line and go underground* Alluding to a genre of stories and films about Communist agents working against the KMT before 1949.
108. *see the true face of Mt. Lu* A phrase of the Song Dynasty poet Su Dongpo. In its original context, it referred to the difficulty of objectively perceiving anything that is close and familiar.
109. *a person from the Peach-Blossom Spring* Alluding to a celebrated work by Tao Qian (365-427 C.E.) imagining a blissful community that has been cut off from the outside world for hundreds of years.
110. *touch the flowers and vex the grass* An expression meaning to womanize, to behave promiscuously.
111. *summon the bees and attract butterflies* An expression meaning to flirt.
112. *the Four Cleanups* (四清 *si qing*) was a political campaign targeting corrupt rural cadres and promoting loyalty to Mao. It commenced at the end of 1962 and gathered steam in different

parts of China over the following three years. In some ways, such as its emphasis on public denunciation meetings and the sending of college youth to the countryside, it foreshadowed the Cultural Revolution.

113. *the grass top and the woman lateral* The 'grass' and 'woman' pictographic components differentiate the characters of Ru Yan's real name 茹嫣 from those of her screen name 如焉.
114. *You ask the date of my return . . .* This is the full text of 夜雨寄北 ("A letter sent north during night rain"), a suggestive and concise Tang Dynasty work that defies translation, though many have tried.
115. *But soon afterward the teacher stopped. . .* The story places Ru Yan's birth around 1957. The change in her teacher's standards reflects the onset of the Cultural Revolution in 1966.
116. *Fanyi* The wife and stepmother in Cao Yu's 1934 drama *Thunderstorm*. Bored, lustful, and cruel, Fanyi goes insane at the tragic dénouement.
117. *Yan my dear* In the original, "Older Sister Yan". Friends can be informally addressed as siblings using their given name. "Yan" is written with the "Yan" character of Ru Yan's screen name.
118. *Battle of Wits* (智斗 *zhidou*) is a scene from *Sha Jia Bang*, one of the Eight Model Operas of the Cultural Revolution. Madame A Qing, who runs a teahouse, outwits the Japanese and their corrupt KMT stooges in order to protect some wounded Communist soldiers.
119. *You unna-stand?* A familiar line from Chinese war movies in which the imperious Japanese invaders frequently punctuate their orders to the locals with 你的明白？ (*ni di mingbai*, ungrammatical Mandarin for "You understand?") The phrase now carries a humorously mocking tone and has lost its original connection to the War.
120. *Mid-Autumn Festival* 中秋节 *zhongqiujie*, a harvest festival when friends and family gather to view the full moon and eat mooncakes. In 2002, the holiday fell on September 21.
121. A line from 声声慢 *sheng sheng man* ("To the Tune of 'Let each note be slow'") by a woman poet of the Song Dynasty, Li Qingzhao.
122. *the Lin Biao affair* Lin Biao distinguished himself as a brilliant military commander against the Japanese and during the Civil War. He accompanied Mao on the Long March and in 1949

led the PLA into Beijing. During the 1950s he kept a lower profile than might have been expected from his earlier achievements. Upholding Mao's disastrous policies during the Great Leap Forward, however, he supplanted Peng Dehuai as Defense Minister and by dint of unwavering, even sycophantic support of the Great Helmsman (he was credited with compilation of the *Quotations from Chairman Mao*) he positioned himself as Mao's designated successor in 1969 after the fall of Liu Shaoqi. But Mao turned on him in the fall of 1971 and Lin died when his plane crashed in Mongolia during an apparent attempt to escape to the Soviet Union. He remains an enigmatic figure; according to some accounts, he was not entirely of sound mind. The circumstances surrounding his death—in particular, whether Lin had been plotting a coup or was merely trying to avoid becoming Mao's next scapegoat, and even whether he was actually aboard the plane that crashed in Mongolia—are still disputed. He was vilified after his death and anyone associated with him paid a high price.

123. *neither jade rabbit nor Chang'e nor sweet-scented osmanthus* Instead of "the man in the moon," Chinese learn from childhood to perceive these three figures in the dark patches on the surface of the full moon. *Jade rabbit*: see the Wikipedia entry for "Moon rabbit," which helpfully superimposes the silhouette from folklore over a photograph of the moon. *Chang' e*: a mythological woman who floated up to the moon after overdosing on the elixir of immortality. *sweet-scented osmanthus*: The *osmanthus fragrans* blooms around the time of the Mid-Autumn Festival and is therefore associated with the moon legends. "To the Chinese the object visible in the moon is an osmanthus bush. It seems that an immortal, Wu Gang, was banished to the moon for infidelity and spends his time there continuously trying to chop it down. However, it possesses the power to heal its wounds immediately, so is unaffected by his efforts. Another ancient legend describes how osmanthus seeds fall from the moon on bright moonlit nights." Peter Valder, *The Garden Plants of China* p. 313, Timber Press 1999.

124. *the classic documents down through the years* He is referring to the documents that make up the canon of Chinese Communist doctrine and policy, for example Mao's "On the Ten Major Relationships" or Deng Xiaoping's "One Country, Two Systems"

(both these examples were speeches).

125. *Taiwan campus song* With the "opening-up" of China in the late 1970s, popular culture from Taiwan rushed in to fill the vacuum created by years of regimentation in the arts. Pop songs that were current among youth on Taiwan (then under the authoritarian regime of the KMT but vastly freer, with respect to cultural expression, than the PRC) were known as Taiwan campus songs.
126. *Sunshine, sand, the ocean waves . . .* From a 1979 hit single by Pan An-Pang (潘安邦) titled "Grandmother's Penghu Bay." Penghu is an archipelago in the Taiwan Strait. The singer recalls idyllic scenes from his childhood on the beach.
127. *Beidaihe* A beach resort on Bohai Gulf (in Hebei Province) to which the senior leadership of the Communist Party of China repairs each summer.
128. *May flowers bloom and the moon be full* 花好月圆 *hua hao yue yuan*: a complimentary formula for the newly married.
129. *Even playing mahjong?* In many circles mahjong is looked down on as a pastime of the uneducated.
130. *The moon sweeps through cottony clouds . . .* From the children's song "Hearing Mama tell about the past" (听妈妈讲那过去的事情) which recounts the hardships which landlords inflicted on the poor.
131. *The Lantern Festival* 元宵节 *yuanxiaojie* Celebrated on the fifteenth day of the first month of the traditional calendar, i.e., in late winter.
132. *The Dragon-boat Festival* 端午节 *duanwujie* Celebrated on the fifth day of the fifth month of the traditional calendar, i.e., in late spring.
133. *How long have you been here, bright moon?* The opening lines of a *ci* or lyric poem "To the tune of *Shui diao ge tou*" by the Song Dynasty poet Su Dongpo (a.k.a. Su Shi).
134. *Somewhere in the northwest* From "Gazing at the Moon from the *Pen* Pavilion on the fifteenth night of the eighth month", by the Tang Dynasty poet Bai Juyi.
135. *This life, as brief and lovely as this night* From Su Dongpo's lyric *ci* "To the tune of 'The Sunlit Pass.'"
136. *The bright moon rises o'er the sea* From "Gazing at the moon and missing one far away" (望月怀远) by the Tang Dynasty poet Zhang Jiuling.

137. *Qiu Jin* An advocate for a Chinese Republic and for the rights of women. She was tortured and executed in 1907 after a failed uprising against the last Imperial dynasty.
138. From the end of 1966 to the middle of 1968, the Cultural Revolution was marked by intense fighting between factions of Red Guards that in some places used automatic weapons and artillery against each other. The role of the PLA during this time was ambiguous and inconsistent.
139. *the Three Highs* High blood pressure, high cholesterol, and high blood sugar.
140. *May we live long . . .* The closing lines of the lyric by Su Dongpo of which Ru Yan earlier quoted the opening lines, "How long have you been here, bright moon?" (see note 133)
141. *the fine rain moistens all things* From "Pleased by the rain on a spring night," by the Tang Dynasty poet Du Fu.
142. *Economic-Philosophic Manuscripts of 1844* A collection of essays which Marx wrote at age 26 while exiled in France and never published. In comparison to his later and more influential work, they are notable for what has been called a "humanist" perspective. They were first published in 1932 by an institute in the Soviet Union.
143. *a pinyin abbreviation* Pinyin, or Hanyu Pinyin, is the system adopted in the PRC during the 1950s (and eventually accepted as an international standard) to represent Mandarin with the Latin alphabet. It aids phonetic instruction in primary school as well as providing transliteration for foreigners. With the rise of the personal computer it became the basis of most methods of entering Chinese text by means of a keyboard. Pinyin's assignment of letters to sounds does not fully correspond to that of any Western language: the unsuspecting English speaker may be perplexed by the use of 'x', 'q', and 'zh' to represent sounds that roughly resemble 'sh', 'ch', and 'j' respectively.
144. *Qing Ma* An abbreviation of the phrase *qingnian makesi* "the young Marx."
145. *The early Seventies* The Chinese phrase 七十年代之后 could be construed as referring to the latter part of the Seventies, or even later. But in a personal communication, the author explained it with reference to several events which occurred in the years 1970-75.
146. *Triple Tasty Noodles* 三鲜面 *san xian mian* In a personal com-

munication, the author identified this dish as noodles heaped with meatballs, sausage, and a fried egg.

147. *a cowshed* The term for a detention house established by the Red Guards to hold broadly-defined classes of domestic enemies, called 牛鬼蛇神 *niugui sheshen*, 'monsters and demons,' literally 'ox-ghosts and snake-spirits'. This designation was used by Mao during the Anti-Rightist campaign of 1957-58, but it received the widest application during the Cultural Revolution. Wang Youqin cites a song composed by a middle-school student, "I am an ox-ghost and a snake-demon," which teachers were compelled to sing as they were beaten or paraded. See her informative article, "Student Attacks Against Teachers: The Revolution of 1966" at http://humanities.uchicago.edu/faculty/ywang/history/1966teacher.htm

148. *the three men and one woman* The Gang of Four was closely identified with the extremism of the Cultural Revolution and wielded enormous power during Mao Zedong's declining years. Their chief was Jiang Qing, Mao's wife. On October 6, 1976 (less than a month after Mao died), the other three members of the Gang were seized at a Politburo meeting which had been set as a trap, and minutes later Jiang Qing was arrested at her residence by an elite military unit. The move was carried out on the orders of Hua Guofeng, who shortly thereafter was proclaimed Chairman of the CPC.

149. *The Sagacious Leader* An epithet for Hua Guofeng, who led China from the fall of the Gang of Four until he was pushed aside by Deng Xiaoping early in the 1980s.

150. *even before the head of that alleged clique* Hu Feng would be rehabilitated in September 1980.

151. *a full cycle of the zodiac* The Chinese calendar assigns every year not only to one of twelve "branches" (which are named after animals) but also (in two-year blocks) to one of the five elements. 1980 was the year of the Metal Monkey; 1992 was the year of the Water Monkey. This system defines a cycle of 60 years' duration, and it accounts for the solemnity of 60th birthday celebrations among Chinese.

152. *like the sun at eight or nine in the morning* "You young people, full of vigor and vitality, are in the bloom of life, like the sun at eight or nine in the morning." Mao Zedong, from a speech delivered to Chinese students in Moscow in November 1957.

153. *Spiritual Pollution . . . Anti-Liberalization* The campaign against Spiritual Pollution, announced by Deng Xiaoping in October 1983, sprang from the hostile reaction of staff at the Central Party School to a speech given by Zhou Yang in March of that year (the centennial of Marx's death) in which Zhou highlighted the humanistic doctrines of the early Marx (specifically alienation), rejected "the orthodox view that alienation existed only in capitalist societies," and "pointed out that because of the lack of democracy and a legal system, 'the people's servants would sometimes abuse the power vested in them by the people to become, instead, the masters of the people. This means alienation in the political field, or power alienation.'" (Merle Goldman, *Sowing the seeds of democracy in China: political reform in the Deng Xiaoping era*, Harvard University Press 1994, p. 119) The ideas of the fictional *Qing Ma* and Wei Liwen were historically in the air at the start of the 1980s, if not earlier.

    The Anti-Liberalization campaign followed the ouster of General Secretary Hu Yaobang at the start of 1987 and aborted his reforms. The desire of many students to publicly mourn Hu Yaobang after he died on April 15, 1989 would snowball into the massive protest at Tiananmen Square.
154. *Notes of the Fatherland* In the nineteenth century there were two Russian periodicals by this name (Отечественные записки), the first published annually from 1818 to 1830 and the second published monthly, with interruptions, from 1839 to 1884. Liu Su probably hoped to imitate the second of these, which published works by Turgenev and Dostoyevsky and was eventually shut down by the Tsarist government on account of its support for liberalization and democracy.
155. *Our Sofia*: an allusion to Sofia Perovskaya (1853-81) a Russian revolutionary whose energy and iron will became legendary, and who was responsible for the assassination of Tsar Alexander II.
156. *when the American economy was hitting bottom* In a personal communication, the author confirmed that "the last year of the twentieth century" denotes 1999. With respect to both the stock market and employment, however, the U.S. economy was near its peak that year. The Nasdaq fell in 2000; employment and the S&P 500 did not turn down till 2001. (The European

markets followed a similar path.) It is possible that the text echoes reporting in the Chinese media, which have consistently painted a dark picture of conditions in the United States. It is also relevant that the 1997 Asian financial crisis which began in Thailand (and almost brought South Korea to its knees) inflicted no currency shock on the PRC and only a mild and temporary deceleration of growth there. China's immunity to that crisis prompted widespread feelings of satisfaction and is probably the historical kernel behind this detail of the story.

157. *A Beijinger in New York* A prime-time serial produced in 1993 for China Central Television from the novel by Glen Cao. The story follows a fictional Chinese musician named Wang Qiming who moves to New York with his wife, starts a business, and discovers that life in the capitalist West is a seductive nightmare.

158. *the female Rakhmetov* Rakhmetov is a heroic character in the novel *What is to be Done?*, written from prison in 1863 by the Russian utopian socialist Nikolai Chernyshevsky. In order to strengthen himself for revolutionary activities, Rakhmetov sleeps on a bed of nails.

159. *somebody had already written about that* In 1999, Zhu Xueqin published a book of political essays called 思想史上的失踪者 (*Missing persons in the history of political thought*). Professor Zhu recalls a group of young people, slightly older than himself, who held themselves aloof from the frenzy at the outbreak of the Cultural Revolution and continued to meet and discuss ideas. As the Cultural Revolution progressed, he lost contact and now, thirty years later, wonders what happened to them. The title seems to have inspired Maozi to undertake a study closer to the present: what has become of individuals who once articulated an independent viewpoint but fell silent in the 1990s, intimidated by the crackdown of 1989 or mollified by subsequent prosperity?

160. *Afanti* The Chinese rendering of the Uyghur name of the thirteenth-century Turkish storyteller Nasreddin. The sly and pithy tales attributed to him have long been popular in China.

161. *the Model Works* The eight 样板戏 *yangban xi* were plays, operas, or ballets with revolutionary themes that had been approved by Jiang Qing, who had been a stage and film actress in her youth and as Mao's wife exercised considerable influ-

ence over cultural affairs even before she led the Gang of Four. Practically no other theatrical works were performed during the Cultural Revolution.

162. In his 1818 poem "To Chaadaev," Alexsandr Pushkin openly expressed the longing for freedom felt by one "under the yoke of autocracy." In "*Exegi Monumentum*" (1836), he anticipated posthumous fame because "I sang the praise of freedom in a cruel age."
163. The original Russian song is По диким степям Забайкалья, sometimes entitled Бродяга ("The Vagabond"). It has been traced as far back as the 1880s, when it was popular among convicts in Siberia. Although the lyrics were later attributed to I. K. Kondratieff, the authorship is unknown, and the song's large number of variants is typical of true folk music. The Chinese sung by Teacher Wei is a faithful translation of the Russian lyrics listed as Variant #3 in the *Songbook of Anarchists and the Underground*, a compendium from which the information in this note has been drawn. See ://www.a-pesni.golosa.info/popular20/podikim.htm.
164. *Song at Midnight* The opening song from a 1937 movie of the same name, Ma-Xu Weibang's adaptation of *The Phantom of the Opera*. It begins:

    In the empty yard fireflies are dancing,
    On the rafters mice are scampering.
    A lonely figure with a lantern
    Strikes the third watch.
    The wind blows cold, the rain patters on wet leaves.
    In this long dark night, who will wait up with me till dawn?
165. *Song of Meiniang* Words by Tian Han, music by Nie Er, composed in 1934 for the opera *Song of the Returning Spring*.
166. *Ode to the Yellow River* This was one section, adapted as a popular song, from the *Yellow River Cantata* composed by Xian Xinghai to words by Guang Weiran in 1939.
167. *You are the Beacon* (你是灯塔) Composed in 1940 by Wang Jiuming to words by Sha Hong; performed at the 1949 ceremony of the founding of the new nation. The song is said to have irritated Soviet cultural authorities, either because its tune sounded suspiciously like that of the Russian anthem Вы жертвою пали, a paean to Russian revolutionary martyrs, or because some of its lyrics suggested that the Communist Party

of China stood in the vanguard of world revolution (a place of honor claimed by Moscow). As a result, the song was in disfavor for many years until it was rehabilitated after Mao's death with the new title *Following the Communist Party* (跟着共产党走). This curious history is recounted in a July 10, 2009 article in the Shenyang Evening News, "《你是灯塔》的曲折故事".

168. *May 4* A movement named after a student protest that occurred in Beijing on May 4, 1919, sparked by the Chinese government's acquiescence in an unfavorable territorial settlement after the First World War. A broad-based wave of labor strikes followed the initial protests. The movement represented a turning point in nationalist awareness and radicalized many intellectuals.
169. *they sought to save the nation* The quest to "save the nation" was a reaction to the widespread (and well-founded) perception after 1919 that China was a 亡国 *wangguo*, a doomed and humiliated country whose backwardness had put it at the mercy of hostile foreign powers. It would be hard to overstate the role which this sentiment and its compensations have played in the national psychology of modern China.
170. *Visitor on Ice Mountain* A 1963 spy movie directed by Zhao Xinshui.
171. Gulandanmu is the heroine of the film; another character impersonates her on behalf of the KMT. Hence the care to specify "the real Gulandanmu."
172. The reform of land ownership (土改) was carried out from 1949 to 1950; the suppression of counterrevolutionaries (镇反) was a campaign that ran from 1951 to 1952.
173. *The Five Antis and the Three Antis* Campaigns launched in 1951 and 1952, initially targeting corruption. They evolved into persecutions of businessmen.
174. From 1941 to 1944 in the Communists' base at Yan'an, Mao launched a campaign called the Rectification of Styles which in some respects presaged the Hundred Flowers program of 1956-57. An invitation to discussion and debate paved the way for purges that assured Mao's supremacy.
175. *the Anti-Bolshevik League* In 1930 in the Jiangxi Soviet, the Party directed a purge of thousands of Red Army officers and troops suspected of belonging to a secret "AB League." Origi-

nally, the letters may have denoted two classes of members, but the name was soon interpreted as "Anti-Bolshevik." During the purge, torture elicited both confessions and accusations. Though Mao does not seem to have initiated this campaign, he joined it and guided it. In December of that year, an entire battalion was methodically massacred at Futian. While it must be acknowledged that the Communists were under the pressure of a brutal civil war (and the KMT *was* attempting, with little success, to infiltrate their ranks), one must also be struck by the paranoia and callous use of terror that foreshadow so much of the subsequent history. See Chapter 8 of Philip Short's 1999 biography *Mao: A Life* for an account of this episode and a reflection on its significance.

176. *The Life of Wu Xun* A 1950 film about a revered beggar who lived in 19th-century Shandong and used the money he collected to build schools. It was heavily criticized on ideological grounds (starting with a 1951 editorial in *People's Daily*) and provoked intense hostility during the Cultural Revolution, when many involved in the making of the film were persecuted. In August 1966, Red Guards exhumed the corpse of Wu Xun and after a public "trial" dismembered it and burned it.

177. *Franz von Sickingen* A German military adventurer of the early sixteenth century whose support for Luther and other Reformers was idealized in popular memory. Ferdinand Lassalle, a socialist contemporary of Karl Marx, wrote a play about the Reformation knight which caught Marx's attention and led both him and Engels to comment on the artistic representation of revolutionary movements and figures. Their letters to Lassalle are reprinted in the volume *Karl Marx and Friedrich Engels on Literature and Art* which has been transcribed for the Web at http://www.marx.org/archive/marx/works/subject/art/index.htm

178. *Zhou Yang* A Marxist literary theorist who was associated with Lu Xun in the 1930s and was appointed Vice-Minister of Culture after the founding of the People's Republic. During the 1950s he was responsible for the ideologically-motivated persecution of many artists; with the coming of the Cultural Revolution, however, he was deemed insufficiently radical and endured nine years of imprisonment. Rehabilitated at the end of the 1970s, Zhou Yang advocated a "humanistic" interpretation

of Marxism which placed a higher value on artistic freedom—a position which, under pressure of the campaign against "Spiritual Pollution," he recanted in 1983. He died in July 1989.

179. *and flog their corpse* Alluding to the revenge taken in 506 B.C.E when Wu Zixu, returning in victory to the state of Chu where his family had been persecuted, exhumed the king's body and gave it 300 lashes.

180. *thrice-daily self-examination* A Confucian practice: *Analects* 1.4

181. The crew of the cruiser *Aurora* sparked the October Revolution in 1917. It is permanently moored as a museum in the River Neva at St. Petersburg.

182. *The Little Road*, 1941, words by N. Ivanov, music by C. Podelkov, original title Дальняя дороженька; *Lamplight*, 1942, words by Mikhail Isakovsky, composer unknown, original title Огонек; *The Lenin Hills*, 1949, words by Evgeniy Dolmatovsky, music by Yuri Miliutin, original title Ленинские горы. The first two are ballads about love in the shadow of war; the third is a cheerful paean to the part of the capital where Moscow State University was being constructed.

183. *enemy radio stations* Such was the tension with and antipathy toward the USSR after 1962 that Radio Moscow could indeed have been numbered among the "enemy radio stations" (敌台).

184. *a few bars from a famous song* The melody which Radio Moscow used for decades to introduce its news programs was "Wide is my homeland" (Широка страна моя родная), words by V. Lebedev-Kumach, music by I. Dunayevsky, written for the 1936 film *Tsirk*. These words come from the first verse.

185. *a little more than ten years ago when the Army was engaged in a large-scale operation* Teacher Wei is referring to the massacre of civilians carried out in 1989 by martial-law troops in Beijing during the June 4th Incident.

186. *In Unity There Is Strength* Composed in 1943 by Lu Su, words by Mu Hong.

187. *Liu Shaoqi* President of the PRC from 1959 to 1968 (Mao Zedong, who ceded this position to him, remained Chairman of the Communist Party and seems to have distrusted Liu as a potential rival). The cause of Liu Shaoqi's death in 1969 is unknown, as his body was taken from prison in secrecy and cremated under a false name.

188. *Three Hundred Tang Poems* is an eighteenth-century compila-

tion of classic works from the Tang Dynasty. It has long been a staple of both elementary school and home reading. *Selected Lyrics of the Song*, on the other hand, is a relatively new anthology of Song Dynasty lyric poetry compiled in 1962 by Hu Yunyi.

189. *in living memory* This anecdote's historical context is the great famine of 1959-61. Because it was largely if not entirely man-made, that disaster remains among the historical events which are "neglected, buried, or repackaged" in the history of the PRC.
190. The taxonomic name for Lao gong yin is *Cicuta virosa*, whose North American and European varieties are known as Cowbane and Water-hemlock, respectively.
191. *Black Flag . . . Bad Bug* In the original, the first name is "666," which is the brand name of a popular Chinese insectide and roach-killer whose TV commercials dramatized the product's elimination of animated "Bad Bugs."
192. *holidays that mark the turn of the year* The Double-Ninth Festival falls on the ninth day of the ninth month in the traditional calendar, which in 2002 corresponded to October 14 in the Gregorian calendar. Mao's Birthday is December 26. The Spring Festival is the Chinese name for what in the West is called the Chinese or Lunar New Year. In 2003, it fell on February 1.
193. *near the fire on a kang* Homes in northern China traditionally have a 炕 *kang*, a brick platform built over some kind of heat source, and covered with quilts or mattresses where the family sleeps.
194. *calls for the Colon* In a "crosstalk" TV comedy routine that became very popular, a moronic official read aloud the punctuation in the text of his speech. As a result of this skit, "colon" (冒号 *maohao*) became a slang term for an unimpressive official. Applied to Ru Yan at this point in the story, the humor is doubtless good-natured.
195. *A Little Gift* Words and music by Horacio Guarany, 1958, original title "*Regalito.*"
196. *Think about what time of year this is. Up and down the line, everybody's under pressure* The time is the late autumn of 2002. The Sixteenth Party Congress had been postponed from September to November. Rumors suggested that Jiang Zemin was maneuvering to hold on to as much power as he could,

notwithstanding his long-scheduled handover to Hu Jintao. The new administration would not be fully in place until the National People's Congress in March 2003.

The relevance of this historical background goes beyond the "pressure" the fictional characters are said to be feeling. During a sensitive transition of power, the instinct of the Party would be to strive even more than usual for an appearance of harmony and successful efficiency. Bad news would tend, even more than usual, to be suppressed. The initial cover-up and denial of the SARS epidemic were probably motivated by the domestic political environment. See John Wong and Yongnian Zheng, *The SARS Epidemic: Challenges to China's Crisis Management*, pp. 49-50, Singapore, World Scientific, 2004.

197. *When Westerners receive a present* One Chinese offered the translator the following explanation of contrasting customs: "Chinese feel that if you open a gift immediately, you are rudely checking its value. Implicitly, the Chinese giver does not feel much confidence in his gift. The Western giver feels more confident that the recipient will enjoy the gift and wants to see the impression it makes."
198. *Xin Qiji* A patriotic poet of the Southern Song Dynasty.
199. *Next year the flowers will bloom* The song is from Wang Jiayi's 1959 film *Wu duo Jinhua*, which combined a romantic comedy with propaganda for the Great Leap Forward.
200. *warm up the hot dogs and cook some oatmeal* This seems to have been Ru Yan's idea of an American supper.
201. *zhacai* 榨菜, is a dish of pickled mustard tubers, often served with rice soup and traditionally popular in Hubei.
202. *the rain and the dew water the seedlings and make them strong* From the 1964 song "To sail the ocean, one must depend on the Helmsman" (大海航行靠舵手), words by Li Yuwen, music by Wang Shuangyin. It was sung with great frequency during the Cultural Revolution.
203. *The challenge ... and the response* This use of passwords is a playful allusion to the cloak-and-dagger atmosphere in many mainland films about the struggle of Communist agents against the KMT before 1949.
204. *asked in an odd tone* Perhaps in humorous imitation of a challenge-and-response scene from *Taking Tiger Mountain by Guile* (智取威虎山), one of the Eight Model Plays that was

made into a popular movie in 1970.

205. *At the head of the table* (上席) Pre-Communist China adhered to a detailed protocol for the arrangement of seats at a banquet. The most important person would sit facing the door and assign places to the other participants according to well-understood criteria of seniority. This practice disappeared under Mao but has since made a comeback.
206. *got killed in a bombing* It is almost impossible for a civilian to obtain firearms in China, but it is not difficult to procure explosives, and bombs are instrumental in a surprising proportion of reported violent crimes.
207. *The President? The General Secretary?* From November 2002 to March 2003, these two offices were held by different people (Jiang Zemin and Hu Jintao, respectively).
208. *Rebecca* In Hitchcock's first U.S. film, issued in 1940 and based on the novel by Daphne du Maurier, the heroine marries a widower who lives in an eerie mansion with troubling secrets.
209. *CDI.* In the original, 中纪委 (*zhongjiwei*), an abbreviation for the Communist Party of China's Central Commission for Discipline Inspection, the nation's highest anti-corruption bureau.
210. *She came from an Air Force family* Lin Biao's son, Lin Liguo, had been deputy director of the Air Force since 1969 and there seems to be a consensus among historians that *he* was plotting against Mao, whatever his father's stance may have been.
211. *a factory on the Third Line* In 1964, concerned about the possibility that China might be vulnerable to nuclear attack either from the U.S., whose involvement in the Vietnam conflict was in its early stages, or from the U.S.S.R., with whom the CPC had had a falling out, Mao ordered a massive relocation of military-related industry to the western and southwestern regions. At great difficulty and expense, factories and bases were moved to caves and remote mountainous areas in Sichuan, Guizhou, and Yunnan before there was an adequate transportation system to support them. The military-industrial resources so placed were called the "Third Line of Defense"—the first two lines being the coastal and central regions of China.
212. *a broadcaster in the factory.* In Mao's time, every factory and school would have multiple loudspeakers from which exhortations and political instruction would blare throughout the day.
213. *I've never liked people who put down one woman . . .* American

readers may be struck by the backhandedness of this compliment. The translator has been told it reflects Chinese dating protocol, according to which it is unseemly for a woman to praise a potential mate directly.

214. *Five Wants and Five Rejects* The original phrase (五要五不要) would remind a Chinese reader of the Three Do's and Three Don'ts （三要三不要）, a formula coined by Mao in 1971 as tension with Lin Biao was building to a crisis.

215. *I know the names . . . but I'm not telling* Echoing the heroic defiance of a Communist prisoner being tortured by the KMT under American guidance in a scene from the 1961 novel Red Crag (红岩) by Luo Guangbin and Yang Yiyan. For a careful inquiry into the narrative imbibed by generations of Chinese that the United States operated a concentration camp at Chongqing—an assertion which has only recently, and very quietly, been corrected in official statements—see Xujun Eberlein's "Another kind of American History in Chongqing," *The Atlantic*, January 31, 2011.

216. *treat them to some candy* a term for announcing a wedding, alluding to a traditional gesture made by the engaged or newly-married couple.

217. *associates in the Youth League* The Communist Youth League took members from Middle School age into their twenties. The Red Scarf Society was a similar organization for elementary school students. Both had a path to full membership that involved a probationary stage of being an associate (literally, an 'activist' 积极分子). Both were, of course, at the disposal of the Party.

218. *the 721 directive* The number reflects the Chinese style of abbreviating a date. On July 21, 1968, Mao Zedong called for a new kind of school for adults where workers and peasants would learn technical skills for 1 - 3 years. The school would neither award a degree nor administer an entrance exam. Colleges established along these lines were dissolved after the Cultural Revolution.

219. *a spiritual pilgrim* the term 修行者 can be applied to a Buddhist monk or to one of the itinerant eccentrics who adorn the Taoist tradition, and whose genius is discerned only by the perceptive.

220. *add four letters* In the original, "three more characters," turn-

ing Da-mo into Da-mo-ke-li-si (the Chinese transliteration of Damocles).

221. *bat-wing blouses* Bat-wing sleeves—billowing wide sleeves that would hang down like wings when the arms were stretched wide—were a feature of Victorian fashion that was revived in the late 1970s and early 1980s. The style then caught on in several Asian countries as a daring import from the West.
222. *Word and Thought . . . the Thread of Words . . . Fine Rain*: Homonyms. The second phrase was the title of a journal co-founded by Lu Xun in the 1920s.
223. *her mother's System* See note 34.
224. *the language of northern China* By this the author means not only Mandarin, but the flavor of Mandarin spoken north of the Yellow River. Although the text scrupulously avoids identifying the city in which the story is set, Damo's oral style seems to place him in Hubei, a central-eastern province, which Chinese consider part of "the South."
225. *Arthur Burton* Ru Yan is remembering *The Gadfly*, a novel written in 1897 by the Irish-born Ethel Lillian Voynich. The tale opens in Northern Italy in the 1830s, where a delicate young Englishman, Arthur Burton, has become involved with the radical circles that will unify Italy in defiance of the Papacy and the Austrian Empire. Betrayed by a priest and arrested by the police, he learns that he is the illegitimate son of another priest, Father Montanelli. Believed to have committed suicide, Arthur flees to South America, whence he returns years later as Felice Rivarez, 'the Gadfly', to lead the revolution in Italy. He perishes, after many edifying words, during a protracted execution witnessed by his father (now a Cardinal). The work had little impact at the time of publication and is now almost unknown in the West, but its anti-religious tone and revolutionary melodrama recommended it to the Commissars, and in translation it became part of the curriculum for millions of schoolchildren first in the Soviet Union and then also in China.
226. *the CCTV Gala* Each year on the eve of the Spring Festival, China Central Television broadcasts a variety show featuring song and dance and comedy routines. In prestige, glitz, and audience size it is the premiere mass entertainment event of modern China.
227. *the meter and construction are a little off* The form in which

Liang Jinsheng had jocularly composed his thoughts is the 春联 (*chunlian*), a classical couplet (*duilian*) written specifically for the Spring Festival (lunar new year). The *envoi* is the 横批 *hengpi*, always four characters long, summarizing the meaning of the two lines. The *chunlian* would typically be written on red paper and affixed for the holiday at the doorway of a house: first line on the right side, second on the left, and the *hengpi* across the top. The stylistic conventions governing classical couplets are subtle and elaborate, and such writing is generally considered to be a lost art.

228. *Isatis root . . . white vinegar* Isatis root or *banlan'gen* is considered a cold remedy.
229. *you might need the A/C* In the south of China, central heating is rare and during the cold months residents rely for heat on a unit mounted in or under a window, called air-conditioning (空调 *kongtiao*) but equally capable of cooling or heating the room.
230. *rich peasant* This was a formal category. All rural families were classified as either landlords, rich peasants, middle peasants, or poor peasants. The criteria by which a family would be assigned, fatefully, to one group or another were not always clear. In 1933, Mao laid down a complicated definition of 'rich peasant' which caused much confusion. It was subsequently altered to mean a peasant who gained more than 15 percent of his income from exploitation, defined as the hiring of long-term laborers or the collection of rents. (Fairbank et al. *Republican China, 1912-1949* [Vol. 13 of *The Cambridge History of China*], Cambridge University Press, p. 195) The classification that had the most lasting impact, however, was the one applied during the redistribution of land immediately after the Communist victory in the Civil War. The concept of exploitation remained key but its operational definition could be arbitrary.
231. *more than an acre of farmland* In the original, "seven or eight *mu*." The *mu* was a traditional measure of area equal to 0.1647 acres.
232. *when the People's Communes came along* The People's Communes were officially instituted in 1958 as part of the Great Leap Forward. All resources and tools of agricultural production, as well as many activities traditionally reserved for the family (such as meal preparation), were vested in communes

each of which comprised several thousand rural households. Labor was recompensed with "work points" which functioned as money in the commune, and the scale of compensation applied to an individual's work could be, and was, adjusted to reflect many factors.

233. *as citizens with relatives on Taiwan or overseas* There was a widely-held perception that, starting in the late 1970s, mainlanders with relatives abroad, especially on Taiwan, received preferential treatment from the government. (This contrasted with the suspicion and discrimination which had been their lot in Mao's time.) The popular understanding was that for strategic reasons, the regime wished to make a good impression on overseas Chinese and therefore took pains to ensure that their relatives on the mainland would paint a favorable picture of life under Communism.
234. *more dead-set against Chen Shuibian than any 'angry youth' on the Internet.* Chen Shuibian, President of the Republic of China (Taiwan) 2000-2008, was the first person *not* from the KMT to hold that office. He was sympathetic to *de jure* Taiwanese independence and made a few gestures in that direction. The term 'angry youth' (*fenqing* 愤青) denotes the nationalistic young men who used to pepper Chinese discussion forums with indignant commentary, especially about foreigners. While they remain an important presence, they have been eclipsed by the *wumaodang*, the 'fifty-cent party,' a mercenary claque for the Government.
235. *that no-man's land between the city and the countryside* Many large cities are ringed by a lightly-administered zone whose inhabitants lack legal residency. These belts came into being after the collapse of State-owned enterprises and are marked by relatively high unemployment and crime, poor educational facilities, and environmental degradation.
236. *you could be sure it was a mall* In 2003, high-end shopping malls were still something of a novelty in second-tier cities.
237. *drawing a question from the jar* A common practice both in schools and on TV game shows.
238. *dismemberment by five horses* A penalty of ancient times, comparable to drawing and quartering. A different horse would pull in a different direction on each of five ropes which were attached to the victim's head and four limbs.

239. *the Reform policy of a certain leader* Presumably Deng Xiaoping, who ruled China for more than a decade as Paramount Leader without the formalities of high office. He brought a far-reaching pragmatism to a society exhausted by Maoism. His signature phrases during the 1980s were "Reform and Opening" and "The Four Modernizations." In June 1989, he gave orders for the army to crush the Tiananmen demonstrations.
240. *the humanities* For many purposes, the world of scholarship is viewed through a simple dichotomy between science (科学 *kexue*) and humanities (人文 *renwen*). Social Science is classified among the humanities.
241. *I had just been allotted a new residence* The practice of *fen fang* (分房) continued into the 1980s. State employees would be allotted an apartment for which they would need to make a partial contribution (though still less than the market rent).
242. *is this an investigation?* Maozi uses a specific term, *waidiao* (外调), which described background checks carried out during the Cultural Revolution.
243. *Supreme directives must be promulgated the same day.* Utterances of Mao Zedong, especially those that hinted at a new direction or focus, were exalted as "supreme directives" by Lin Biao in a speech delivered on August 18, 1965. (Li, Kwok-sing, *A Glossary of Political Terms of the People's Republic of China*, p. 603, Chinese University Press, Hong Kong 1995) During the early years of the Cultural Revolution, throngs commonly took to the streets with placards in order to help disseminate each such 'directive' as soon as it was issued.
244. *a public disturbance* The author's vagueness here and in the following paragraph, where he refers to "a day in the first part of June that year" was probably an effort to slip this passage past the scissors of the censor. Public discussion of the Tiananmen incident of 1989 is still strictly repressed.
245. *the queues were snipped off the back of our heads* Under the Qing dynasty, the Manchu custom of wearing a queue, or plaited ponytail, was imposed on all Chinese males. This practice was of course abandoned with the overthrow of the Qing in 1911, a turning point which for most Chinese represented the transition to modernity.
246. *when Fan Jin passed the examination* In Chapter 3 of Wu Jingzi's eighteenth-century satire *The Scholars*, Fan Jin goes berserk

when he learns he has passed the Imperial examinations after many years of unsuccessful attempts. His father-in-law, Butcher Hu, slaps him to bring him to his senses.

247. *like Hua Ziliang in Zhazi Cave* Another allusion to the 1961 novel *Red Crag* by Luo Guangbin and Yang Yiyan, set during the Civil War in 1949, and adapted for the 1965 film *Forever Alive in the Flames of Revolution*. The story of Hua Ziliang does not seem to parallel Maozi's experience very closely, except that both are under political stress and develop (or feign) insanity.

248. *subject to annual flooding* Areas of southeastern China without good drainage are prone to mild flooding during the monsoon season.

249. *Lao She's This Life of Mine*. A 1937 novel which in 1950 was made into a film and has more recently been adapted for TV and the stage.

250. *a tool of the old regime* In the original, 旧警察伪警察 : an old policeman, a collaborationist policeman. It is striking that after their victory in the Civil War, the Communists applied to those who had served in office under the Nationalist government the same term (*wei*: puppet, illegitimate, collaborator) that they used for those who collaborated with the Japanese invaders.

251. *Deng was The Man . . . old Mr. Deng* The original expression in both cases is 邓大人. I have been advised that the usage is jocular and affectionately respectful.

252. *Gou-Gou, library to the world.* At the time when the story is set, Google had no local operation in China and since it had not yet chosen the Chinese name Gu-ge (谷歌, 'Harvest Song') by which it would later be known, it was subject to transliterations like this one (Gou-Gou,狗狗, means 'Doggie'). In 2003, Baidu, the local firm which would rapidly come to dominate the market, still had less than a 50% share of Chinese internet searches.

253. *Policy and tactics are our life* Echoing a remark Mao made on March 20, 1948 in an internal Party document called *A Circular on the Situation*: "Only when all the policies and tactics of the Party are on the correct path will it be possible for the Chinese revolution to win victory. Policy and tactics are the life of the Party." [from the Foreign Languages Press translation of the *Selected Works*] These words achieved wide circulation later when they were included in the first chapter of the Little Red

Book.

254. *More like Douchebag Philosophy* The original term 流氓 *liumang*, traditionally rendered "hooligan," has a range of meanings, but (except when claimed ironically by social rebels) always conveys contempt for people judged to be unproductive and unethical.
255. *fake medicine* i.e., counterfeit drugs. See Peter S. Goodman, "China's Killer Headache: Fake Pharmaceuticals," *The Washington Post*, August 30, 2002, p. A01.
256. *deconstruction* This appears to be a loose invocation of Derrida's philosophy to denote an effort to undermine a mental construct by overanalyzing it.
257. *watching Sun the monkey hop around in your palm* In the classic *Journey to the West*, the Buddha wagers Sun Wukong, the Monkey King, that the latter cannot escape from his hand. Leaping away, the monkey climbs one of five mountains. He returns, confident he has won the bet, only to discover that the five mountains were the Buddha's five fingers.
258. *support what is sound, strengthen the roots* (扶正固本, *fuzheng guben*) Summing up a principle of traditional Chinese medicine: Instead of attacking the illness, fortify the body's healthy systems (so that they can overcome the illness).
259. *I believe a human life can last two hundred years...* A fragment of a poem in the classical style which Mao Zedong wrote around age 23. The line about smiting the water is an allusion to a mythical bird of prodigious energy mentioned in the first chapter of the *Zhuangzi*; it also expresses Mao's passion for swimming, which appealed to him as a metaphor for living.
260. *who cares if after me the floods rise?* This interpretative rendering of *Après moi, le déluge!* is conventional in Chinese.
261. *We are the State.* Although this looks like a reference to another one of Louis XIV's apocryphal remarks ("L'état, c'est moi"), in a personal communication the author has said he did not intend any reference to foreign history.
262. *to scrounge up a theoretical justification from abroad* Damo is most likely referring to Maozi's invocation of Deconstructionism, but there could also be a veiled reference to the CCP's reliance on Marxism, another European philosophy.
263. *None but a few courtesans gave up their lives for the Great Ming* When the Ming Dynasty fell in 1644 to Manchu invaders who

would found the Qing, it took time for Chinese society to reconcile itself (not without bitterness and soul-searching; but the Manchus also adapted). Maozi is alluding to the fact that many courtesans of the Ming Court committed suicide to express their fidelity, while most of their male partners and patrons proved willing to serve their new masters.

264. *the Seventeen Years* 1949-1966, from the founding of the People's Republic to the Cultural Revolution. The sequence in this sentence is ordered according to degrees of extremism.

265. *Deng's Southern Tour* In 1992, when he was 87 years old and had ostensibly relinquished power, Deng Xiaoping traveled through Shanghai, Guangzhou, and the Special Economic Zone which he had established in Shenzhen more than ten years before, giving speeches about the benefits of economic liberalization. His actions at first went unreported in the media and seem to have met opposition within the Politburo, but eventually they won the support of Jiang Zemin and confirmed China on the path of tolerance for entrepreneurship and reliance on market forces.

266. *...used it too.* The three publications mentioned are all authoritative State-run outlets. The latter two cater especially to officials of the Central Government. *Reference Materials of the People's Congress* is a monthly: the Chinese name is 人大的复印资料.

267. *as Du Fu said* Referring to the Tang Dynasty poem 春望, "The View in Spring."

268. *Should I interpret that as 'I am a scoundrel and I fear no man'?* As mentioned when this phrase was first quoted during Ru Yan's introduction to the world of Internet screen names, it comes from a 1989 story by Wang Shuo. Geremie R. Barmé translates part of the story when he analyzes the cultural figure of the *liumang* in his book *In the Red: On Contemporary Chinese Culture* (Columbia University Press, 2000; pp. 77-78). In Wang Shuo's satire, a speaker being heckled by a student audience responds with a doctrinaire righteousness reminiscent of Deng Xiaoping's public speeches. When the audience continues to give him a hard time, however, he snaps: "Don't any of you try pulling any shit on me—I'm a *liumang*, and I'm not scared of anyone." [Barmé's translation]

269. *those fogies who put out newspapers* The Anti-Rightist cam-

paign of 1957-59 numbered many journalists among its targets. Mao used the term 死人 (literally, 'dead man', here translated 'fogy') for anyone he felt was stuck in the past and sympathetic to the pre-Communist order.

270. *All ill-gotten gains to the peasants' association* In the 1920s, in those areas where it held sway, the Communist Party organized Peasants' Associations with the slogan "All power to the Peasants' Association." This line appears in the 1964 musical production of *The East is Red*, which can be viewed among the materials supplementing the documentary *Morning Sun* at http://www.morningsun.org/east/index.html. Damo has substituted the word for graft or ill-gotten gains, 贪污 *tanwu*, for the original 权力 *quanli*.

271. *Wuliangye* is a clear liquor made from five grains: sorghum, rice, wheat, corn, and sticky rice. There is more than one grade of it: alcohol content ranges from 108 proof to 136 proof.

272. *New Year's Eve . . . dumplings according to the Northern custom* The holiday is the Chinese New Year, which in 2003 fell on February 1 in the Gregorian calendar. In the South, the custom is to eat sticky rice cakes.

273. *Lao Jiu can't go!* In the 1970 film *Taking Tiger Mountain by Guile* (which was based on one of the eight model operas of the Cultural Revolution), the hero impersonates a bandit named Lao Jiu in order to infiltrate a bandits' lair during the Chinese Civil War. At a tense meeting of the bandits, he falls under suspicion; hoping to escape, he pretends to be offended and starts to leave. The chief of the bandits stops him by growling "Lao Jiu can't go!"

Because the name Lao Jiu means "Old Nine," this line also gave rise to a celebrated pun at a late stage in the Cultural Revolution. Eight classes had been enumerated by the highest authorities as worthy of loathing: 1) landlords 2) rich peasants 3) counter-revolutionaries 4) moral degenerates 5) rightists 6) renegades 7) enemy agents and 8) capitalist-roaders. Around the same time, some local cadres impatient with unreconstructed intellectuals derided them as "Stinking Intellectuals." In consequence, some intellectuals identified themselves humorously as the ninth detested class category: Stinking Old Ninth. This designation became popular—so widespread in informal speech, in fact, that some works of historical reference mistakenly list intellectuals as the ninth of the official categories. Then an address to the Politburo on May 3, 1975, Mao Zedong sought to distance himself from the attitude summed up in this phrase by quoting the line from the film, "Old Ninth can't go," to suggest that intellectuals played an indispensable role in society. (I am grateful to Han-ping Chin for adding precision to the facts provided in Li, Kwok-sing, *A Glossary of Political Terms of the People's Republic of China*, Chinese University Press, Hong Kong 1995, p. 225)

274. *Not one less! Collective leadership!* The first phrase evokes a film by Zhang Yimou. The second is the name for a policy introduced by Deng Xiaoping as a corrective to Mao's personality cult. Before that, the concept had enjoyed a fraught history starting with Khrushchev's posthumous criticisms of Stalin and fiercely resisted by Lin Biao's unqualified exaltation of Mao.

275. *Her husband was placed under double regulations* "Double regulations" (双规 *shuanggui*) is the house arrest of a Party member under investigation for corruption. This practice, which is regularly and openly imposed by the CCDI, the Central Commission for Disciplinary Inspection, is not authorized by the Constitution or by any statute. For a detailed discussion, see Florence Sapio, "Shuanggui and Extralegal Detention in China," *China Information* 2008 (22), pp. 7-37.

276. *Better to accept with respect than to decline with courtesy* A proverb whose original application was to gifts offered by one's superiors, but which has a wider application enjoining obedience.

277. *before fireworks were banned* In 1994, fireworks were banned in about 200 Chinese cities. The cities started revoking the bans in 2005. ("Chinese fireworks blast kills 36", news.bbc.co.uk, 30 January 2006)

278. *What about the preceding line?* Liang Jinsheng quoted from the 1973 song 月亮代表我的心 *Yueliang daibiao wode xin* ("The Moon Represents My Heart"), a favorite of crooners throughout the Chinese-speaking world. The preceding lines are: "You ask how deep, and how great, is my love for you; my affection is real, my love is real." On his blog Sinosplice.com, John Pasden offers the full text with a translation and videos of the song being performed in a variety of styles (search for "The Moon Represents My Heart"). Music by Tan Ni, lyrics by Sun Yi;

popularized by the Taiwanese singer Teresa Teng (Deng Lijun).

279. *the bell was about to sound* The Great Bell Temple in Beijing houses a 46.5 ton bronze bell commissioned by the fifteenth-century Emperor Yongle. The only time it is rung is at midnight on the eve of the Chinese New Year, an event which is always televised.

280. *Uncle Liang* "Uncle" and "Aunt" are used with the surname to address people of one's parents' generation in informal situations. Ru Yan is *not* hinting that Liang Jinsheng will soon have a familial relationship to her son; she is trying to avoid identifying him.

281. *Jinsheng, born in Shanxi* The character jin (晋) is an abbreviation for Shanxi Province. The mayor's given name does in fact mean "born in Shanxi", just as the common name Jingsheng means "born in Beijing."

282. *the W's of news reporting* The original uses the English letter W, in a reference to Who, What, When, and Where.

283. *cabs, turning the street red* The paint color which distinguishes taxis varies from one city to another and can change over time, but in many cases it has been red. In Wuhan in 2003 it was red.

284. *the old dormitory district* This would have been built to house the workers of a State-owned enterprise. Many would continue to live there even after the demise of their employer.

285. *Women use pads* Sanitary napkins came into use only in the 1990s. The daughter is arguing that the kinds of amenities which are now recognized as proper for adults should be recognized as proper for children.

286. *a few days before New Year's* The holiday referred to throughout this chapter is the Chinese New Year, which in modern times has been known on the mainland as the Spring Festival. In the novel's historical context, the holiday fell on February 1, 2003.

287. *the heat hadn't worked for years* The central heating, that is. It can be presumed that the apartments had "air-conditioners" which provided some heat in winter. But this detail nevertheless signals striking neglect.

288. *an internal regulation* (内部规定, *neibu guiding*) A directive to officials which was not to be made public.

289. *no one should announce or discuss it in a disorderly way* The following note provides some background to the jargon "not permitted to speak in a disorderly way" (不许乱说). It would

be understood to mean, "not permitted to speak without authorization."

290. *You must behave yourself; it's forbidden to speak or act in a disorderly way* This saying originated in a speech delivered by Mao in June 1949, before the Communists had established the new government in Beijing. The meaning was clear in the original context, and the blustering tone (the word for 'behave yourself', *laolaoshishi,* befits a finger-wagging admonition) was appropriate there. But when in later years it became a slogan removed from that context, frequently intoned over loudspeakers (as one of my consultants vividly remembers), it took on a new meaning, and the now weirdly inappropriate tone passed unnoticed amid the general debasement of language for the purpose of totalitarian control.

 The original context was Mao's explanation of democratic dictatorship, a concept which avoided absurdity by defining two different groups as targets of policy. The working class and their allies would enjoy democracy; the remnants of the capitalist class and others hostile to the Revolution would be tightly controlled by dictatorship. "The combination of these two aspects, democracy for the people and dictatorship over the reactionaries, is the people's democratic dictatorship," Mao said, and his words about what was allowed and what was forbidden were directed solely at the reactionaries. But over time, with ahistorical repetition, workers and peasants and even junior-level cadres would hear those words directed at *them*: and the term *laolaoshishi* therefore became a term of art with a simple meaning: "Do as you're told."

291. *this was a fabrication* A disinformation campaign conducted in 1952 with the assistance of Soviet Intelligence, and largely successful in its impact on world opinion. Contrary to Teacher Wei's recollection, evidence *was* presented to prove American use of germ warfare, evidence that had been elaborately fabricated, even to the extent of killing a small number of North Korean convicts with a plague bacillus furnished by China so that their bodies could be shown to international investigators. For the disclosures from Soviet archives, see Kathryn Weathersby, "Deceiving the Deceivers: Moscow, Beijing, Pyongyang, and the Allegations of Bacteriological Weapons Use in Korea", in *Cold War International History Project Bulletin*, Winter 1998,

from the Woodrow Wilson International Center for Scholars, p. 176-184, and Milton Leitenberg, "New Russian Evidence on the Korean War Biological Warfare Allegations: Background and Analysis", *ibid.* p. 185-199.

292. *amending the Constitution* Proposals to amend the Constitution of the PRC in order to effectively establish civil rights were much discussed in the 1990s and for a few years into the new millennium. This was largely due to the efforts (begun in 1981) of Cao Siyuan, an expert in business law who had been an adviser to Party Secretary Zhao Ziyang until the latter was ousted from power and placed under house arrest after the 1989 Beijing crisis. Some of Cao's economic ideas were adopted by the National People's Congress when it made Constitutional adjustments in 1999, but he was subjected to intense official harassment in 2004, and public interest in his work has since waned.
293. *Consider it your New Year's money* At New Year's, seniors traditionally make a small gift of money to each of the children in their family.
294. *personal seals* Distinguished from the formal seals which supply the legal equivalent of a signature, personal seals (闲章, literally, leisure seals) are engraved with a quotation or a witticism.
295. *At seventy, I had no doubts . . . At eighty, I knew the will of Heaven* These phrases from the second chapter of the Analects of Confucius are familiar to every Chinese; but here the ages associated with milestones of spiritual development have been increased by thirty years.
296. *What are the two characters in 'Ru Yan'?* Because of the abundance of homonyms in Chinese, this is a perfectly natural question even from a highly literate person. The manner in which it is answered, "'Ru' as in . . ." is also normal.
297. *'Ru' as in 'ruguo'* Damo spells her Internet screen name, "Such Is This World."
298. *Wang Anyi, the novelist* Author of the acclaimed 1995 work *Song of Everlasting Sorrow*, which is available in an English translation by Michael Berry and Susan Chan Egan. Wang Anyi's mother was Ru Zhijuan, the 'Ru' being the same character that appears in Ru Yan's real name.
299. *some Turkic people* Beginning with the Göktürks who flour-

ished from the sixth through the eighth centuries C.E., Turkic peoples dominated Central Asia and made forays farther east. An even earlier nomadic race that may have been Turkic is the Xiongnu whose depredations inspired the Qin Dynasty to begin construction of the Great Wall. Repeated episodes of migration and conquest, combined with the paucity of written records, make the reconstruction of this history speculative.

300. *Lu Xun . . . in his declining years* Lu Xun (1881-1936), who led the League of Left-Wing Writers but never joined the Communist Party, acted in old age as a literary godfather to many younger writers whose friendship he valued, but with whom he had frequent and intense disagreements, usually of a political nature.
301. *she lives in Urumqi* The capital of the Xinjiang Uyghur Autonomous Region, in the far northwest of the PRC, lies about 1700 miles from such central-eastern cities as Wuhan.
302. *Three days! What a luxury!* Most people are granted a full week's holiday for the Chinese New Year. Either she is being ironic, or she is making allowances for the almost total absence of leisure in the life of an official of his rank.
303. *like Ximen Qing* Alluding to a remarkable novel of the Ming Dynasty, of uncertain date and pseudonymous authorship: *Jin Ping Mei*, which has been translated both as *The Plum in the Golden Vase* and as *The Golden Lotus*. In this sexually graphic tale, Ximen Qing acquires a number of wives and concubines.
304. *when we entered the city* 'We' means the Communists. This formula refers to the gaining of local power during the Civil War. What year it was would depend on the city.
305. *Chen Yi . . . and Li Xiannian* Chen Yi (1901-72) was a commander of the New Fourth Army, won key victories during the Civil War, and became the first Mayor of Shanghai after the establishment of the People's Republic. In 1958 he became Foreign Minister. Li Xiannian (1909-92) was also a captain in the Civil War who became Mayor of Wuhan after Liberation, as well as holding high positions in Hubei's provincial government and Party structure. In the 1950s he served as Minister of Finance and in the 1980s held the office of President of the PRC (at that time a largely symbolic position).
306. *wouldn't miss their Evening Tea tonight* 'Evening Tea' (晚茶, Mandarin *wancha*, Cantonese *mancha*) is a term used by the

people of Guangdong for *dim sum* eaten in the evening.

307. *Auntie Ru* (茹阿姨 *Ru Ayi*) Mayor Liang thus designates Ru Yan's mother with affectionate courtesy. The Western reader is puzzled, however, because in China married women do not take their husband's surnames. The Mayor can therefore be presumed to be using the wrong name (Ru) for his fiancée's mother, which ill accords with his tactful and meticulous personality, especially at so important a meeting. At least one Chinese reader found this detail plausible, however. It would feel awkward, that reader explained, to ask your fiancée her mother's name, and since all parties would know that, his ignorance of her name would not be offensive. At some point, of course, the mother will tell him her name.
308. *This girl of mine . . . inexperienced . . . old-fashioned* More than one Chinese reader has assured me that this speech from a person of the older generation must be understood as highlighting Ru Yan's qualifications for matrimony, though in suitably modest language.
309. *the eighth day of the New Year* As counted on the traditional lunisolar calendar. In the Gregorian calendar, this was Saturday, February 8, 2003.
310. *skit of the kebab-seller* For the nationally-televised New Year's Gala in 1986, the comedian Chen Peisi impersonated a Uyghur vendor of shish kebab. For any Han Chinese whose path had seldom crossed that of a real-life Uyghur, this performance would have furnished a vivid image of the "typical" person from Xinjiang.
311. *a single tragedy has wounded us twice* Ostensibly, Teacher Wei's words refer to the agonies of the family's separation and reunion. But there may be a veiled reference to the thought of Hu Ping, who has written that the Communist Party robbed the Chinese people twice: first through violent expropriation and then, in the era of marketization, through the abandonment of all socialist ideals in a manner that left people nothing to believe in. Other signature themes of Hu Ping, such as the corrosive effect of cynicism among Chinese intellectuals, also appear in the discourses of Teacher Wei. The interested reader is referred to his influential 1998 article, "Sick with Cynicism: the Spiritual Crisis of Contemporary China" (犬儒病--当代中国的精神危机) which was first published in *Beijing Spring* and

is widely available on the Internet.

312. *without insignia* The insignia referred to would not necessarily have been those of rank. Until 1955 (and this photograph would have been taken no later than that), the PLA eschewed a formalized system of rank in favor of an egalitarian style to which it would return during the Cultural Revolution. Nevertheless, insignia to identify the unit or attest to the soldier's campaign experience seem to have been part of an active-duty uniform, as evidenced by the image at http://www.globalsecurity.org/military/world/china/images/uniform-1955.jpg

313. *the years of hardship* An allusion to the famine of 1959-61. "As elsewhere, the Great Leap policies produced famine in Xinjiang. . . . nevertheless, Xinjiang was undoubtedly better off than other Chinese provinces, from which over a million rusticated youth and refugees migrated to Xinjiang during the famine years." James A. Millward & Nabijan Tursun, "Political History and Strategies of Control, 1884-1978", in S. Frederick Starr (ed.), *Xinjiang: China's Muslim borderland*, p. 93, M.E. Sharpe 2004. This article mentions the role played by the Xinjiang Production and Construction Corps, the *bingtuan*, in the transformation of Xinjiang during the 1950s, and the large number of former soldiers who found employment with it. The "organization" for which the stepfather worked sounds a lot like the *bingtuan*.

314. *the push to cleanse the ranks of the Party* Of this campaign, called 清队 (*qingdui*), Roderick MacFarquhar offers the following summary: "From late 1967 through 1969, an organized Campaign to Purify Class Ranks was implemented, focusing on CCP party members whose backgrounds were 'suspect' (containing some link to the West, to 'bourgeois thought,' or to the Nationalist Party defeated in 1949)." [from the timeline at http://athome.harvard.edu/programs/macfarquhar/macfarquhar_timelineset.html]

315. *the New Fourth Army* A Communist-led division of the army of the Republic of China which opposed the Japanese after 1937, when the CCP and the KMT declared an uneasy truce in order to fight the invader together. This collaboration broke down at the end of 1940 when the two parts of the Army began fighting each other.

316. *the San Qing Tuan* The "Three Principles Youth League,"

founded in the late 1930s, was the youth group of the Kuomintang. The "Three Principles" after which the group was named were those set forth by Sun Yat-sen: civic nationalism, democracy, and social welfare. It was not uncommon for a youth to join this organization for reasons of expediency when the KMT were in power and subsequently be branded as a counter-revolutionary for that decision: see *China Witness: Voices from a Silent Generation*, p. 140, by Xinran, Pantheon 2009

317. *propitious figurine of a big white sheep* The new year which had begun the previous week was the Year of the Sheep.
318. *Lan like the azure sky* Lan (蓝) means 'blue.'
319. *Dove of Peace* Ge (鸽) means 'dove'. The stamp set referred to was issued by the PRC in August of 1951, and is listed as No. 108-110 in the Scott philatelic catalogue. Picasso created many dove images after the second World War, some expressly for the use of Communist organizations.
320. *a bottle of premium Daqu from Xinjiang* Daqu is a Chinese white liquor, whose process of distillation in moldy cellars was invented at least three hundred years ago in Sichuan. The term *tequ*, used in the original, is reserved for batches of *daqu* that pass a taste test with highest marks and so command the highest price. Although weaker versions are produced for export, the typical domestic *tequ* is 120 proof.
321. *brownstone* The Chinese term is 青砖 (*qingzhuan*), "gray brick." Large gray bricks became a preferred building material for houses of the wealthy during the Qing Dynasty and into the Republican period. The bricks were gray because doused with water while still hot in the kiln. (Patricia R.S. Batto, "Les Diaolous de Kaiping (1842-1937)", Note 21, *Perspectives Chinoises* May/June 2006.
322. *and say a prayer to Kuan-Yin that her mother might be granted a speedy return to her native place* The religious sentiment here is not easily preserved in translation. The "prayer" is more precisely an "expression of desire, a wish"; Kuan-Yin is not named, but referred to only by the generic term *pusa*, literally, Bodhisattva, but that is how Kuan-Yin is commonly referred to in popular religion. Devotion to Kuan-Yin (sometimes glossed as the Goddess of Mercy; in Japanese, *Kwannon*) is complex and its roots are fraught with historical uncertainty. For the Western reader, an analogy to the Virgin Mary may be help-

ful: Kuan-Yin is a compassionate, motherly figure whose name (originally *Guan-shi-yin*) means "Who hears the cries of the world." That the spirit of the deceased may find its way back to the place where that person was born, and so be at home with the spirits of the ancestors, is a traditional and still heartfelt concern of Chinese mourners.

323. *and who knows whether I'll make it to your age?* This exchange illustrates a characteristically Chinese style of commiseration. The proper response to another's distress, according to the translator's informants, is to complain about one's own similar problems.
324. *atypical pneumonia, abbreviated as "the atyp."* The Chinese term is *feidianxing feiyan* (非典型肺炎) and the abbreviation is *feidian* (非典). Although the text explains the English acronym SARS and its Chinese transliteration *sasi*, almost all subsequent references to the disease use *feidian*. For the sake of familiarity I have usually translated it "SARS."
325. *people would blanch when they heard it* 谈非色变: playing on the proverb 谈虎色变, 'when a tiger is mentioned, the complexion changes'.
326. *The disease came to be denoted . . . all that mattered was that people could figure it out.* Ever since keyword-filtering software began being used to monitor and censor the Internet, users have employed an ever-expanding repertory of puns and homonyms, in which the Chinese language is naturally rich, to avoid triggering a block. *'Flying point'* . . . These phrases (飞点, 沸点, 费电, 废垫) are all pronounced 'feidian.' *or 'murder,' 'scatter to death. . .* These phrases (杀死, 撒死, 傻死) all sound roughly like the Chinese transliteration for SARS.
327. *a Southern newspaper finally confirmed* This was Southern Metropolitan News (南方都市报), which also took the lead in publicizing the Sun Zhigang case that will be mentioned in Chapter 49. Exposure of the Sun case ruined the career of at least one high-level police official, which was widely assumed to be a factor in the arrest of two senior editors and the general manager less than a year later, purportedly for financial crimes.
328. *the day before the Lantern Festival* The Lantern Festival is the fifteenth day of the New Year. In 2003, the day before it would have been February 14.
329. *This is Master Luo* Master, *shifu* 师傅, is a polite term of ad-

dress for an artisan.

330. *the Emperor and his mother* The original could refer generically to the Imperial Household, or specifically to Guangxu and Cixi. The Empress Dowager Cixi, the last person to hold absolute power in the Qing Dynasty, died in 1908.
331. *in the style of Yangzhou* Yangzhou cuisine, also called Huaiyang cuisine, is not spicy. It is particularly known for a kind of fried rice. Yangzhou is a city in the lower reaches of the Yangtze, about 50 miles northeast of Nanjing.
332. *Jiaodong* The peninsula that forms the eastern part of Shandong Province.
333. *No 300 ounces of silver here* With this placard, a character in a folktale tried to conceal his buried treasure. The next morning it had been replaced with a new sign: "Your neighbor Wang did not steal."
334. *The modern Chinese tradition of airing one's views in open debate* The author is referring to the intensity of political discussion among the population through much of the Maoist era. The fact that the range of permissible opinions was rather narrow does not mean that all discourse was scripted or that a uniformity of views reigned. During the Cultural Revolution, for example, policy pronouncements were often formulaic, not to say Delphic, and citizens engaged in spirited debate as to their proper application.
335. *they'd blown up the biggest Buddhas in the world* The Buddhas of Bamyan were dynamited by the Taliban in March 2001.
336. *beaten to death while in custody* On March 20, 2003 (the same day the invasion of Iraq began) a 27-year-old graphic designer from Wuhan died in a detention center in Guangzhou. Sun Zhigang had been arrested at an internet bar for failing to have on his person the identity papers required by a set of regulations called 收容遣送, variously translated "custody and repatriation" or "detention and transfer." The PRC had used these regulations for more than twenty years to control vagrants. When his death became public more than a month later, it ignited a firestorm of online criticism which led to the repeal of the custody and repatriation rules that autumn. The Sun case was hailed as showing the power of the Internet to bring change to China. It should be noted, however, that the larger legal framework which conditions citizens' rights on their local

residency status remains in effect.

337. *the face-changing opera of Sichuan* This performing art has been made known to Western audiences through the 1996 film directed by Wu Tianming, *The King of Masks.*

338. *Waiting in line is such a civilized custom!* An ironic reference to recurrent campaigns to instill "civilized" habits in the residents of Chinese cities. Cutting in line and spitting have been two of the practices which officials have often sought to curb by means of educational materials and fines.

339. *Encephalitis B* Also called Japanese Encephalitis. A mosquito-borne viral illness found in the Far East and Southeast Asia, it causes inflammation of the brain. China suffered major outbreaks in the 1960s and 1970s before the disease was brought under control by vaccination.

340. *Good Citizenship Certificates* 良民证, *liangminzheng*, the term for identity papers under the Japanese occupation.

341. *hear the designated staffer read out the editorials* In the Mao era, the 读报员 *dubaoyuan* was the employee picked to read portions of the newspaper aloud for the edification of a work unit. This practice was widespread during the Cultural Revolution but started earlier.

342. *the Nine Criticisms* From September 1963 to July 1964 , *People's Daily* published nine lengthy statements attacking the policies of the Communist Party of the Soviet Union and Khrushchev specifically. (Li Kwok-sing pp. 208-209). Forty years later, a newspaper associated with Falun Gong issued a polemic against the CCP under the same title (although the text was rendered as "Nine Commentaries" in English).

343. *wouldn't dare touch the shortwave dial* During the Mao era, listening to foreign radio broadcasts was a serious crime.

344. *they have no opportunity to send word back to the others* Damo's fable of farm animals kept in the dark about their fate invites comparison with the 1952 short story by James Agee, *A Mother's Tale*, in which an animal escapes from the slaughterhouse with ghastly wounds and returns to the farm to warn his fellow cattle—who do not believe him.

345. *Resist foreign aggression, or secure peace in the interior?* The author is recalling the strategic dilemma which a weak and divided China faced after Japan invaded the three northeastern provinces of Heilongjiang, Jilin, and Liaoning and established

the puppet state of Manchukuo in 1931-32. Chiang Kai-shek gave priority to "securing peace in the interior," by which he meant consolidating KMT rule at the expense of domestic rivals, particularly the CCP.

346. *married on the execution ground* An allusion to the 1928 wedding of Zhou Wenyong and Chen Tiejun, undercover Communists who had helped engineer the unsuccessful Guangzhou Uprising. Arrested and sentenced to death, they undertook to marry each other shortly before being executed.

347. *a dinner at Shangri-La* Shangri-La is an upscale hotel chain known for its fine restaurants.

348. *isn't the weather today . . . hehehe.* This representation of an attempt to say nothing, but to say it diplomatically, alludes to an extremely short 1925 essay by Lu Xun, 立论 *Giving One's Opinion*. What should one say when shown a baby? One can predict a fortunate and wealthy life, a comment which will be well-received but is probably a lie; or one can predict that the baby will die, which is certainly true but is likely to provoke a hostile reaction. The only alternative is to say: "Gosh, take a look at this kid! So . . . Wow! Ha ha! Hehehehe!"

349. *the tradition of learning* The original phrase is 诗书, a reference to two works attributed to Confucius, the Book of Odes and the Book of History—or, generically, classical learning.

350. *Staying by the window. . .* The close of the lyric poem "To the Tune of Sheng Sheng Man," by the Song Dynasty woman poet Li Qingzhao. Liang Jinsheng alluded to this poem in Chapter 20. For a complete translation and a meticulous analysis, see pp. 47-57 of an essay by Stephen Owen, "Meaning the Words: The Genuine as a Value in the Tradition of the Song Lyric," appearing in a volume edited by Pauline Yu, *Voices of the Song Lyric in China*, Berkeley, University of California Press, 1994.

351. *Who was it brought this cry...* The opening words of "Tibetan Plateau," a song by Han Hong (*née* Ingdzin Droma).

352. *Passing the door without going in* This is a proverbial allusion to the legendary Yu the Great, an official at the dawn of history whose devotion to the consuming task of flood control led him to go for many years without seeing his own family. When his duties required him to pass through his own neighborhood, he would never take the time to stop at his house.

353. *a World War II movie, an American film* In a personal com-

munication, the author identified it as *Enemy at the Gates*, a 2001 film directed by Jean-Jacques Annaud and inspired by an incident that occurred during the battle of Stalingrad.

354. *and which he called his Western Front* An allusion to the relatively undeveloped western part of the PRC, which over the years has been the target of numerous campaigns of economic development.

355. *Pick chrysanthemums by the east fence* From "Drinking Wine," by Tao Qian (a.k.a. Tao Yuanming), 365-427 C.E.

356. *Anna Karenina and Elena and Vera* Three heroines of Russian literature. Elena Nikolaevna is the central character of Turgenev's 1859 novel *On the Eve*. Vera Pavlovna is the central female character of the revolutionary novel *What is to be Done?* which N. G. Chernyshevsky wrote from prison in 1863.

357. *lilacs and rainy alleys* An allusion to Dai Wangshu's celebrated poem 雨巷 *yuxiang*, a dreamy and melancholy incantation that owes something to Dai's study of French poetry.

358. *Xiaoxiang House and Yihong Court* These are the family residences of Lin Daiyu and Jia Baoyu, whose relationship provides a major subplot in the *Dream of the Red Chamber*. The mention of "broken lotuses" evokes a scene in Chapter 40 of that work, where a boating party has ventured out onto a pond: Jia Baoyu calls for the broken lotuses to be cleared away but Lin Daiyu quotes a Tang Dynasty poet, Li Shangyin: "Leave the withered lotuses, to better hear the rain."

359. *a sky-well* 天井, a colorful term for a very small, sunken courtyard surrounded by high walls, popular in southern China.

360. *forcing a funk to write a poem* A lyric poem by Xin Qiji of the Song Dynasty ran:

> In youth, not knowing the taste of grief,
> I loved to go into an upper room,
> And force myself into a funk
> So I could write avant-garde lyrics.
>
> How well I know it now, the taste of grief.
> I want to speak but don't . . . no words
> Unless to say of the cool weather,
> 'Tis a fine autumn.

361. *daisies* The flower mentioned (小山菊) resembles a daisy but is the *dendranthema oreastrum*, which grows in summer on the grasslands of China and the Russian Far East.
362. *Be at peace with what comes your way.* (既来之，则安之。) From Book 16 of the Analects of Confucius, where it means, "Since they have come, make them content." Once the ruler, by means of his virtuous conduct, has persuaded even distant people to accept his sovereignty, as a matter of good government he must strive to keep them content by treating them justly. The extreme concision of the classical language has allowed it to be reinterpreted beyond recognition in modern Chinese usage, where it means "Since this is the situation in which we find ourselves, there's no point complaining."
363. *Everyone knew what yellow meant* In Chinese, it means 'pornographic'.
364. *force porn DVDs into the hands of passers-by* In this marketing technique, an associate of the peddler will accost the "customer" for payment a few steps later.
365. *made it possible to view many overseas websites that you otherwise couldn't see* In 2002, building on work that had begun a couple of years earlier, Chinese engineers living in the U.S. founded Dynamic Internet Technology and UltraReach, whose software (respectively, FreeGate and UltraSurf) would have been the most effective censorship circumvention tools available to Ru Yan at the time of the SARS epidemic.
366. *that military doctor who told the world* In April 2003, concerned that SARS cases in Beijing were being seriously underreported, Dr. Jiang Yanyong wrote to Chinese Central Television. Official media took no action, but four days later two American journalists contacted him after hearing rumors about his letter. He spoke freely to them, and the resulting publicity led to the sacking of the Mayor of Beijing and the Minister of Health as well as the adoption of a much more open official policy. Less than a year later, Dr. Jiang wrote to the Politburo to urge an official reassessment of the massacre of June 1989, many of whose victims he had treated at the PLA General Hospital in Beijing. Word of this letter also leaked out, and Dr. Jiang was arrested and kept in custody for more than a month. There was no reassessment.
367. *security guards holding long sticks* To understand the repercus-

sions of this scene, it is helpful to know that in China, private security firms have a close relationship with official law enforcement. Susan Trevaskes reports that of the four million private security guards working in China in 2006, almost a quarter were employed by companies *owned* by the Public Security Bureau, and almost all the rest were "monitored and managed" by the PSB. To a great extent, private security services function as low-wage subcontractors for official law enforcement. (Susan Trevaskes, "The Private/Public Security Nexus in China," *Social Justice*, Vol. 34, Nos. 3-4, 2007-2008)

368. *that line of Li He, "How can a man..."* The line comes from a brief verse that is part of "Thirteen South Garden Poems" by the 9th century C.E. poet.

369. *much as Shang Yang had been dispatched of old* Shang Yang was a Legalist reformer during the Warring States period (4th century BCE). On the accession of a king who bore him a grudge, he was tied to several chariots which then drove off in different directions, tearing him to pieces.

370. *strip the mask off* The original is "flay," but this was a term used for attacking someone during the Cultural Revolution. It means, "I'll lay bare So-and-so's real motives and character."

371. *I'm going to do some ideological and political work with you.* The language of the Cultural Revolution, used here with irony.

372. *extreme brutality . . . no better than dying in an unlit dungeon.* These sentences refer to Teacher Wei's dying "this way" but do not make explicit the characteristic of his death which inspired Ru Yan with such horror. It can be presumed to be the enforced isolation, even after death. The comparison to treatment in a dungeon is not merely rhetorical. Owing to the family's shame, it is highly unusual for a person who has died in prison to receive a funeral.

373. *the mortuary* The 殡仪馆 (*binyiguan*) is an institution closely managed by the State and run with an efficiency which accounts for the small number of establishments to be found even in a large city. It is not usually the scene of funerals, but does provide ancillary services such as preparing the body for viewing. Typically, mourners wait till their number is called, and then view the body briefly for one last time immediately before it is cremated.

374. *restrain your grief* 您节哀 *nin jie ai* A formula of condolence.

The sense is, "You must take care of yourself and not let your sorrow endanger your health."

375. *we cannot conduct the customary funeral . . . there were matters he wished to discuss* By convention, the employer of the deceased bears primary responsibility for funeral arrangements. This is especially true if the deceased was employed in a "work unit" of a government office or State-owned enterprise.
376. *Some matters remain to be settled.* The word translated "matters" refers specifically to the affairs that need to be settled after a death. Prominent among them would be the determination of the pension to be paid to the family of the deceased. The speaker is probably to be understood as another official from the provincial Scholars' Association.
377. *he had never been labeled* The Chinese reader would readily understand the awkwardness that results from this choice of words. Throughout the Mao era, to be "labeled," literally "to be made to wear the cap," referred to the classification of an individual as a particular kind of public enemy. Teacher Wei had, of course, been labeled in this sense more than once in his life.
378. *at a time when the whole country is united with one heart and one mind in the struggle against SARS* The official from the Scholars' Association uses the same trite phrase with which the Fox Fairy launched her vitriolic attack on Ru Yan. On a realistic level, this reflects the tendency for official talking-points to be widely reproduced in a society marked by strong central control. On a symbolic level, it is one of several details suggesting a parallel between the stories of Ru Yan and Teacher Wei.
379. *the inscription on oracle bones* The "oracle bone script" is the earliest form of Chinese writing to have survived in much quantity. Notes for divination scratched onto bones and shells of tortoises around the thirteenth century B.C.E. are written with the ancestors of modern Chinese characters, but the forms are sufficiently different to puzzle anyone who has not studied the script.
380. *like one of the wounded left behind by the Eighth-Route Army* In the war against the Japanese, the Eighth-Route Army, organized in 1937, was one of two large Chinese units controlled by the CCP. Popular history includes accounts of wounded Communist soldiers left behind in the flux of war and sheltered by sympathetic locals.

381. *taken off his helmet and gone back to the fields to plant beans...* Colorful expressions for retirement.
382. *uniting and splitting* Echoing a phrase in the first sentence of the *Romance of the Three Kingdoms*: 分久必合，合久必分 (After long being split, it must unite; after long being united, it must split).
383. *Zhuangzi's chapter on the Earth* In older English texts, the name of this fourth-century BCE philosopher (and the sole book that has come down from him) is often rendered "Chuang Tzu." This saying about the never-ending reduction of the stick occurs in Chapter 33 in a list of apothegms, mostly paradoxical, which the sophist Hui Shi liked to debate with his friends. It differs from the celebrated paradox of Zeno because Zhuangzi's reduction of the stick proceeds at an ever-decreasing rate; Zeno considers motion at a constant rate, but measured at ever-decreasing intervals.
384. *once quoted by the Great Leader* Mao applied this saying to atomic fission in a "Talk on Questions of Philosophy" dated August 18, 1964.
385. *real target . . . the noted educator Tao Xingzhi* Since Tao had died in 1946, a few years before the movie which was the occasion for this campaign, Teacher Wei presumably means that the Party sought to discredit that reformer's ideas and intellectual heirs. Wu Xun, the subject of the film, had been honored for promoting education during the nineteenth century; Mao condemned Wu Xun (and the film extolling him) for failing to challenge the feudal system.
386. *the Pull up the White Flag campaign* "...the Party also carried out an education movement in 1958, in which Chinese people were asked to 'pull up the white flag and hoist the red flag' (ba baiqi, cha hongqi)—and Communist thinking was praised as the 'red flag', while individualism and various so-called 'unhealthy ideas' were criticized as the 'white flag' or the 'grey flag'." (He, Henry Yuhuai, *Dictionary of the political thought of the People's Republic of China*, p. 58. M.E. Sharpe, Armonk, 2000.
387. *the Oppose Rightist Deviation campaign* Mao launched this campaign in 1960, in reaction to skepticism expressed about the Great Leap Forward by senior Communists including Marshall Peng Dehuai at the Lushan conference in August 1959. A

purge ensued.

388. *losing the lady and one's soldiers, too* The jeer directed at Zhou Yu, a counselor of the Eastern Wu, in Chapter 55 of the *Romance of the Three Kingdoms*, after the miscarriage of his scheme to render Liu Bei harmless by inviting him to marry a sister of the Emperor of Wu and then keeping him on a short leash. As it turned out, the bride fled with her husband and the pursuit which Zhou ordered incurred heavy losses. Mayor Liang means that the political costs of an unsuccessful project would be greatly compounded by premature and triumphalist publicity.
389. *now slapped his cheeks with the soles of their shoes* Members of a crowd made this gesture of contempt to the massive statue of Saddam in Firdos Square, after it was pulled down by U.S. Marines on the evening of April 9, 2003.
390. *another murder at this time, of a beautiful young schoolteacher* Huang Jing was found naked and dead in her school dorm in Hunan in February 2003 after a visit from her boyfriend, who was a local official. Authorities initially ruled out homicide. Huang's family disagreed, and an online memorial established in April attracted many visitors and prompted a nationwide discussion of date rape.
391. *Erase the present* Damo's thought inverts the "politics of forgetting" implicit in exhortations, by no means uncommon on the mainland, to forget dark chapters of the past on account of current progress.
392. *the constricting crown* the 紧箍咒 *jinguzhou* was a magical headband which the monk Tripitaka placed on the brow of the Monkey King in Chapter 14 of *Journey to the West*. Whenever the Monkey King resisted his commands, Tripitaka would intone a chant that made the crown tighten, causing the Monkey King excruciating pain until he obeyed.
393. *a high-quality school before the C.R.* There was a widespread sense that institutions of higher learning never fully recovered after the Cultural Revolution, so that a degree earned before that time was a more solid credential than one earned after.
394. *the Central Organization Department* A powerful and secretive office of the Communist Party which supervises senior-level appointments in government, the press, academia, and State-owned enterprises. See Chapter 3, "The Keeper of the Files," in

Richard McGregor, *The Party: the Secret World of China's Communist Rulers*, HarperCollins, 2010

395. *feudalism, capitalism, and revisionism* Expressed with a three-character abbreviation, this list brings together three mutually exclusive objects of the CCP's wrath. (Revisionism was the deviant form of Communism imputed to Soviet Russia during the estrangement of the early 1960s.) The phrase should probably be understood to mean "bad stuff."
396. *the fallen class* 没落阶级 *moluo jieji* After the revolution of 1911, this phrase was applied to families which had been prominent under the Qing. After 1949, it was applied to families that had been prominent under the Republic of China.
397. *so-called Children of the Revolution* whose parents had been revolutionaries before 1949.
398. *rebellion was OK only once* Two things stand out in this striking passage. First, Jiang Xiaoli's defense of the status quo does not base the legitimacy of the current regime on any objective characteristic such as the consent of the governed, a founding compact, or even superior performance. It would seem that power is its own justification (as per the proverb, "胜者为王，败者为寇" *The winner becomes a king; the loser becomes a bandit.*). But second, she refuses to apply that principle consistently. Only *our* power is its own justification.
399. *dig up our ancestral grave or cut off our resources* According to traditional Chinese beliefs, to dig up the grave of someone's ancestors cuts off an important source of energy and good fortune for that person. The symbolism is probably being applied here to the debunking of reverential historiography about the Mao era and the beneficence of the Party.
400. *Buy some shares?* The impropriety that might have marked an official's purchase of stock is not specified; perhaps the implication is *at a special price*. Some of the other actions in this list are likewise not criminal *per se*.
401. *Last time ___ came through* It is not clear whether the placeholder in the original refers to an individual or to a team visiting from a government agency.
402. *rosy face who understands you . . . blue gown who understands you* The blue gown was the scholar's robe. These are stylized classical expressions for a woman and a man, respectively.
403. *overarching values* The original is 普世的价值, "universal

values." The choice of words has political implications, though I am not sure if they were as prominent at the time of writing in 2004 as they became after a 2008 *Southern Weekend* editorial touched off an intense debate which continues to this day. For a summary of the first stage of the controversy, see the article written by Sean Ding and Jingjing Wu for *China Elections and Governance* and available online at http://en.chinaelections.org/newsinfo.asp?newsid=18222.

404. *water cutoffs in summer* Temporary interuptions in the water supply, like temporary outages of electric power, are not uncommon in second-tier cities.
405. *two weights from his shoulders* The image is of the pole on which a Chinese porter carries a weight suspended from each end. Each weight would tend to pull the man in an opposite direction.
406. *When we look back over the past century, there were many things* In this passage, the allusion to "events that inspired hatred and shame" uses language that is often associated with the wartime acts of the Japanese and, earlier, the humiliations inflicted upon China by other foreign powers. Teacher Wei's aphorism about the power of time is recalled from Chapter 25.
407. *smaller than the National People's Congress* This legislative body has about 3,000 delegates.
408. *reporting teams* The 报告团 *baogaotuan* will give numerous presentations to different audiences in order to report an achievement, relate lessons learned, and give credit to relevant officials, some of whom may accompany the team and sit on the stage during the presentation.
409. *the Yangtze River Delta* This would be the region around Shanghai, a place of high social status.
410. *A shaft of sunlight . . . upon the wall.* This image combines the Metaphor of the Sun (Book VI) and the Allegory of the Cave (Book VII) from Plato's *Republic.*
411. *get energy from walking on the ground* Reflecting the belief that artificial floors do not transmit the energy of *qi* from the earth.
412. *a very little girl, a very little Chinese girl* Li Siyi was three years old when she starved in Chengdu after her mother, a heroin addict, was detained for shoplifting on June 4, 2003 and referred to a compulsory detox program. After her arrest, the mother repeatedly told police that her daughter had been left

alone in the apartment, but the police took no action. The story was first broken by a reporter for *Chengdu Business* and gained traction on the Internet, where an outpouring of revulsion led to criminal charges against two of the police officers. Yu, Haiqing. *Media and Cultural Transformation in China* pp. 99-105, Routledge, London 2009.

413. *Wuhan* In the original, the dateline for the first draft reads "Guandong, Wuchang." The modern city of Wuhan was formed in 1926 from the three cities of Wuchang, Hankou, and Hanyang. Wuchang is on the south bank of the Yangtze. Guandong is a neighborhood within it.

LITTERA SCRIPTA MANET, LECTA VIVIT, DISSERTA MOVET

Ragged Banner Press depends on word-of-mouth advertising by satisfied readers. If you found this book of value, please tell your friends—and your librarian.

For orders, corrections, and further information, visit

http://www.raggedbanner.com